Praise for *The Other Side of the Story*

"A hilarious and wonderfully woven tale . . . you will be enchanted" *Ireland on Sunday*

"There's a laugh in almost every line and Keyes' dialogue is as sparky and sparkly as ever" *The Irish Times*

"Marian Keyes pulls it off with her usual style and wit . . . but it is Keyes' characters that make her one of the best novelists" *Sunday Tribune*

"Keyes brilliantly intertwines the lives of these three women and tells their individual stories in a clever, unique and heart-warming way" *RTÉ Guide*

"If we could have given this gem of a book more stars, we would have *****" *Heat*

"A delectable treat for Keyes' many fans" *Sunday Times*

"Another chart-topping blockbuster from publishing goddess Marian Keyes . . . packed with sound writing, wit and common sense" *The Guardian*

"Quick and witty, this is Keyes at her best. Don't go on holiday without it" *Company*

"Another stunner . . . funny, fallible female characters are like new best friends" Kathy Lette, *InStyle*

Praise for *Marian Keyes*

"Keyes is a rare writer in the popular fiction genre in that most of her characters are as strong as her plot lines and the dialogue sparkles and rings true" *The Irish Times*

About the author

Marian Keyes began her career writing short stories in 1993. Her previous novels, *Watermelon, Lucy Sullivan is Getting Married, Rachel's Holiday, Last Chance Saloon, Sushi for Beginners* and *Angels* have all become bestsellers worldwide and have been translated into a variety of languages including Greek, Hebrew and Japanese. Marian Keyes lives in Dun Laoghaire with her husband. *The Other Side of the Story* is her seventh novel.

marian keyes

The Other Side of the Story

POOLBEG

Published by
Poolbeg Press Ltd
123 Grange Hill, Baldoyle
Dublin 13, Ireland
E-mail: poolbeg@poolbeg.com

First published 2004

1 3 5 7 9 10 8 6 4 2

ISBN 1-84223-193-6

Printed by
Litografia Roses, Spain

www.poolbeg.com

For Niall, Ljiljana, Ema and Luka Keyes

*'Times are bad. Children no longer obey their parents,
and everyone is writing a book.'*

Marcus Tullius Cicero, statesman,
orator and writer (106–43 BC)

*'There are three sides to every story.
Your side, their side, and the truth.'*

Anon

Acknowledgements

Thanks to all at Penguin, especially Louise Moore, everyone at Poolbeg and all at Curtis Brown, especially Jonathan Lloyd.

I required a lot of expert advice while writing this book and everyone I asked gave generously of their time and knowledge – any mistakes are entirely mine.

Thanks to the New York Fire Department, with special gratitude to Chris O'Brien and the firefighters at 1215 Intervale Ave. (Sometimes I just *love* my job.) Thanks to the officers Anthony Torres, Daniel Hui, Charlie Perry and Kevin Perry of the NYPD; to Kathleen, Natalie, Clare and Shane Perry; to Viv Gaine of Visible Gaine Event Management; to Orlaith McCarthy, Michelle Ní Longain and Eileen Prendergast of BCM Hanby Wallace; to John and Shirley Baines; and to Tom and Ann Heritage of Church Farm, Oxhill.

Thanks to the 'Able ladies': Orlaith Brennan, Maria Creed, Gwen Hollingsworth, Celia Houlihan, Sinead O'Sullivan and Aideen Kenny.

For encouragement, reading half-written chapters and general hand-holding, thank you Suzanne Benson, Jenny Boland, Susie Burgin, Ailish Connolly, Gai Griffin, Jonathan 'Jojo' Harvey, Suzanne Power, Anne-Marie Scanlon, Kate Thompson, Louise Voss and the entire

Keyes family. Because this book took a long time to write, I've a horrible feeling that I've forgotten to thank someone who helped me in its early days. If that person is you, I can only apologize and point the finger at my gammy memory.

Finally, as always, there aren't words to thank Tony enough for his phenomenal generosity, patience, insight, kindness, hard work, resourcefulness and all-round fabulousness. I'm not messing when I say this book wouldn't have happened without him.

PART ONE

GEMMA

I

TO: Susan_inseattle@yahoo.com
FROM: Gemma 343@hotmail.com
SUBJECT: runaway dad

Susan, you wanted news. Well, I've got news. Although you might be sorry you asked for it. It looks like my dad has left my mam. I'm not sure how serious it is. More as and when.

Gemma xxx

When I first got the call, I thought he'd died. Two reasons. One: I've been to a worrying number of funerals over the past while – friends of my parents and worse again, parents of my friends. Two: Mam had called me on my mobile; the first time she'd ever done that because she'd always persisted in the belief that you can only call a mobile *from* a mobile, like they're CB radios or something. So when I put my phone to my ear and heard her choke, 'He's gone,' who could blame me for thinking that Dad had kicked the bucket and that now it was only her and me.

'He just packed a bag and left.'

'He packed a . . . ?' It was then that I realized that Dad mightn't actually be dead.

'Come home,' she said.

'Right . . .' But I was at work. And not just in the office, but in a hotel ballroom overseeing the finishing touches to a medical conference (*Seeing the Back of Backache*). It was an enormous deal which had taken weeks to pull together; I'd been there until twelve-thirty the previous night coordinating the arrival of hundreds of delegates and sorting out their problems. (Relocating those in non-smoking rooms who had slipped and gone back on the fags in between booking their room and showing up for it, that sort of thing.) Today was finally Day Zero and in less than an hour's time, two hundred chiropractors would be flooding in, each expecting

a) a name-badge and chair
b) coffee and two biscuits (one plain, one fancy) at 11 a.m.
c) lunch, three courses (including vegetarian option) at 12.45 p.m.
d) coffee and two biscuits (both plain) at 3.30 p.m.
e) evening cocktails followed by a gala dinner, with party favours, dancing and snogging (optional).

In fact when I'd answered the mobile I thought it was the screen hire guy, reassuring me he was on his way. With – this is the important bit – the screens.

'Tell me what happened,' I asked Mam, torn as I was between conflicting duties. *I can't leave here . . .*

'I'll tell you when you get home. Hurry. I'm in an awful state, God only knows what I'll do.'

That did it. I snapped my phone closed and looked at Andrea, who'd obviously figured out something was up.

'Everything OK?' she murmured.

'It's my dad.'

I could see on her face that she too thought that my father had bucked the kickit (as he himself used to say). (There I am talking like he actually is dead.)

'Oh, my God . . . is it . . . is he . . . ?'

'Oh no,' I corrected, 'he's still alive.'

'Go, go, get going!' She pushed me towards the exit, clearly visualizing a deathbed farewell.

'I can't. What about all of this?' I indicated the ballroom.

'Me and Moses'll do it and I'll call the office and get Ruth over to help. Look, you've done so much work on this, what can go wrong?'

The correct answer is, of course: Just About Anything. I've been Organizing Events for seven years and in that time I've seen everything from over-refreshed speakers toppling off the stage to professors fighting over the fancy biscuits.

'Yes, but . . .' I'd threatened Andrea and Moses that even if they were dead they were to show up this morning. And here I was proposing to abandon the scene – for *what* exactly?

What a day. It had barely started and so many things had already gone wrong. Beginning with my hair. I hadn't had time to get it cut in ages and, in a mad fit, I'd cut the front of it myself. I'd only meant to trim it, but once I started I couldn't stop, and ended up with a ridiculously short fringe.

People sometimes said I looked a little like Liza Minnelli in *Cabaret* but when I arrived at the hotel this morning, Moses had greeted me with, 'Live long and prosper,' and given me the Vulcan split-fingered salute. Then, when I told him to ring the screen guy again he said solemnly, 'That would be illogical, Captain.' No longer Liza Minnelli in *Cabaret* but Spock from *Star Trek*, it seemed. (Quick note: Moses is not a beardy biblical pensioner in a dusty dress and child-molester sandals but a hip, sharp-suited blade of Nigerian origin.)

'Go!' Andrea gave me another little push door-wards. 'Take care and let us know if we can do anything.'

Those are the kinds of words that people use when someone has died. And so I found myself out in the car park. The bone-cold January fog wound itself around me, serving as a reminder that I'd left my coat behind in the hotel. I didn't bother to go back for it, it didn't seem important.

When I got into my car a man whistled – at the car, not me. It's a Toyota MR2, a sporty little (very little, lucky I'm only five foot two) number. Not my choice – F&F Dignan had insisted. It would look good, they said, a woman in my position. Oh yes, and their son was selling it cheap. Ish.

Men have a very conflicted response to it. In the daytime they're all whistles and winks. But *at night time*, when they're coming home pissed from the pub, it's a different story; they take a penknife to my soft-top or hurl a brick through the window. They never actually try to steal the car, just to mortally wound it and it's spent more time at the dentist than on the road. In the hope of currying sympathy with these bitter mystery men, my back window sticker says, 'My other car's a banjaxed '89 Cortina.' (Anton made it specially for me; maybe I should have taken it down when he left, but now wasn't the time to think about that.)

The road to my parents' house was almost car-free; all the heavy traffic was going in the opposite direction, into the centre of Dublin. Moving through the fog that swirled like dry-ice, the empty road had me feeling like I was dreaming.

Five minutes ago it had been a normal Tuesday morning. I'd been in First Day of Conference mode. Anxious, naturally – there's always a last-minute hitch – but nothing had prepared me for this.

I'd no idea what to expect when I got to my parents' house. Obviously, something was wrong, even if it was just Mam going loola. I didn't think she was the type, but who can ever tell with these things? '*He just packed a bag . . .*' That in itself was as unlikely as pigs flying. Mam always packs Dad's bag for him, whether he's off to a sales conference or only on a golf outing. There and then I knew Mam was wrong. Which meant that either she *had* gone loola or Dad really *was* dead. A surge of panic had me pressing my foot even harder on the accelerator.

I parked, very badly, outside the house. (Modest sixties semi-d.) Dad's car was gone. Dead men don't drive cars.

But my rush of relief kept on going until it had circled back and become dread once more. Dad never drove to work, he always got the bus; the missing car gave me a very bad feeling.

Mam had opened the front door before I was even out of

the car. She was in a peach candlewick dressing-gown and wore an orange curler in her fringe.

'He's gone!'

I hurried in and made for the kitchen. I felt the need to sit down. Mad though it was, I was nursing a wish that Dad would be sitting there, saying in bemusement, 'I keep telling her I haven't left, but she won't listen.' But there was nothing but cold toast, buttery knives and other breakfast-style paraphernalia.

'Did something happen? Did you have a fight?'

'No, nothing. He ate his breakfast as normal. Porridge. That I made. See.' She pointed to a bowl which displayed the remnants of porridge. Not much remained. He should have had the decency to have his gullet choked with shame.

'Then he said he wanted to talk to me. I thought he was going to tell me I could have my conservatory. But he said he wasn't happy, that things weren't working out and that he was leaving.'

'"That things weren't working out"? But you've been married thirty-five years! Maybe ... maybe he's having a mid-life crisis.'

'The man is nearly sixty, he's too *old* for a mid-life crisis.'

She was right. Dad had had his chance for a mid-life crisis a good fifteen years ago, when no one would have minded, when we'd been quite looking forward to it, actually, but instead he'd just carried on losing his hair and being vague and kindly.

'Then he got a suitcase and put stuff into it.'

'I don't believe you. Like, what did he pack? How did he know how to?'

Mam was starting to look a little uncertain, so to prove it to me – and probably to herself – we went upstairs and she pointed out the space in the spare room cupboard where a suitcase used to be. (One of a set they'd got with tokens from buying petrol.) Then she took me into their room and demonstrated the gaps in his wardrobe. He'd taken his top coat, his anorak and his good suit. And left behind a staggering quantity of colouredy, knitted jumpers and trousers that could only ever be described as 'slacks'. Fawn of colour and nasty of shape, cut and fabric. I'd have left them behind too.

'He'll have to come back for his clothes,' she said.

I wouldn't have counted on it.

'I thought he'd been a bit distracted for the last while,' Mam said. 'I said it to you.'

And between us we'd wondered if maybe he had the beginnings of Alzheimer's. All at once, I understood. He *did* have Alzheimer's. He wasn't in his right mind. He was driving around somewhere, stone mad, convinced he was Princess Anastasia of Russia. We had to alert the police.

'What's his car reg?'

Mam looked surprised. 'I don't know.'

'Why not?'

'Why should I? I only sit in the thing, I don't drive it.'

'We'll have to look it up, because I don't know it either.'

'Why do we need it?'

'We can't just tell the peelers to look for a blue Nissan Sunny bearing a fifty-nine-year-old man, who might think he's the last of the Romanovs. Where do you keep the documents and stuff ?'

'On the shelves in the dining room.'

But after a quick scout in Dad's 'office' I couldn't find any car info and Mam was no help.

'It's a company car, isn't it?'

'Er, I think so.'

'I'll ring his work and someone there, his secretary or someone, should be able to help.'

Even as I rang Dad's direct line I knew he wouldn't answer, that wherever he was, it wasn't at work. Hand over the speaker, I instructed Mam to look up the number for the Kilmacud peelers. But before she'd even got off her chair, someone answered Dad's phone. Dad.

'Da-ad? Is that you?'

'Gemma?' he said warily. This in itself was nothing unusual; he always answered the phone to me warily. With good reason – because I only ever rang him

a) to say that my telly was broken and would he come with his toolbox
b) to say that my grass needed cutting and could he come with his lawnmower
c) to say that my front room needed painting and would he come with his dust sheets, rollers, brushes, masking tape and a large bag of assorted chocolate bars.

'Dad, you're at work.' Indisputable.
'Yes, I –'
'What's going on?'
'Look, I was going to ring you later, but things went a bit mad here.' He was breathing hard. 'The prototype plans must've been leaked, the oppo are going to issue a press release – new product, nearly identical, industrial espio –'
'Dad!'
Before we go any further, I have to tell you that my father works in the sales department of a big confectionery company. (I'm not going to say their name because under the circumstances I don't want to give them any free publicity.) He's worked for them my entire life and one of the perks of the job was that he could have as much of the produce as he wanted – free. Which meant that our house was always littered with bars of chocolate and I was more popular with the kids on the road than I might otherwise have been. Of course Mam and I were strictly forbidden from buying anything from the rival companies, so as not 'to give them the edge'. Even though I resented his diktat (which wasn't really a diktat at all, Dad was far too mild for diktats) I couldn't find it in myself to go against it and although it's ridiculous, the first time I ate a Ferrero Rocher, I actually felt guilty. (I know they're a joke, all that

'ambassador, you are spoiling us' stuff, but I was impressed, especially by their roundyness. But when I casually put it to Dad that his crowd should start playing around with circular chocolates, he gazed at me sadly and said, 'Is there something you'd like to tell me?')

'Dad, I'm here with Mam and she's very upset. What's going on, please?' Instead of my father, I was treating him like a bold child, who was doing something idiotic but would knock it on the head as soon as I told him to.

'I was going to ring to talk to you later.'

'Well, you're talking to me now.'

'Now doesn't suit me.'

'Now had better suit you.' But alarm was building in me. He wasn't crumbling like something crumbly, as I'd expected he would the moment I spoke sternly.

'Dad, me and Mam, we're worried about you. We think you might be a little . . .' How could I say this? 'A little mentally ill.'

'I'm not.'

'You think you're not. Mentally ill people often don't know they're mentally ill.'

'Gemma, I know I've been a bit distant for the past while, I'm well aware of it. But it's not from senility.'

This wasn't going the way I'd expected *at all*. He didn't sound bonkers. Or chastened. He sounded like he knew something that I didn't.

'What's going on?' My voice was little.

'I can't talk now, there's a problem here needs dealing with.'

Snippily I said, 'I think the state of your marriage is more important than a tiramisu-flavoured bar of –'

'SSSSHHHH!' he hissed down the phone. 'Do you want the whole world to know about it? I'm sorry I ever told you now.'

Fright deprived me of speech. He's never cross with me.

'I will call you when I can talk.' He sounded very firm. A little like . . . funnily enough, a little like a father.

'Well?' Mam asked avidly when I hung up.

'He's going to call back.'

'When?'

'As soon as he can.'

Chewing my knuckles, I was uncertain of what to do next. He didn't sound mad, but he wasn't acting normal.

I simply couldn't think what I should do. I'd never been in a situation like this before and there was no precedent or set of instructions. All we could do was wait, for news that I instinctively knew wouldn't be good. And Mam kept saying, 'What do you think? Gemma, what do you think?' Like I was the adult and had the answers.

The only saving grace is that I didn't get all cheerful and say, 'How about a nice cup of tea?' Or even worse, 'Let's get a brew on.' I don't think tea ever fixes anything and I vowed that, no matter what, this crisis would not turn me into a tea-drinker.

I considered driving over and confronting him at work, but if he was in the middle of a tiramisu-flavoured crisis, perhaps I wouldn't even get to see him.

'But where would he stay?' Mam blurted plaintively. 'None of our friends would let him move in with them.'

She wasn't wrong. The way it worked with their circle of friends was that the men held the purse strings and the car keys but the women were the power-brokers in the home. They had the final say over who came and went, so that even if one of the men had promised Dad he could kip down in their spare room, his wife wouldn't let him over the threshold, out of loyalty to Mam. But if not one of his friends' houses, then where?

I couldn't imagine him in a mildewed bedsit with a gas ring and a rusty kettle that didn't click off automatically when it boiled.

But if he had taken some mad notion he'd last no length away from Mam and his home comforts. He'd spend three days playing with his golf ball machine and come home when he needed clean socks.

'When's he going to ring back?' Mam asked again.

'I don't know. Let's watch telly.'

While Mam pretended to watch *Sunset Beach*, I wrote the first email to Susan. Susan – known as 'my lovely Susan' to distinguish her from any other Susans who mightn't be quite as lovely as she was – had been one-third of the triumvirate, with me and Lily the other two, and after the great debacle she'd taken my side.

Only eight short days ago, on January the first, she'd moved to Seattle on a two-year contract as PR for some huge bank. While she was there she'd hoped to bag herself a Microserf but it had taken no time to discover that they all work twenty-seven hours a day, so they don't have much time left over for a social life and romancing Susan. Drinking multiple-choice coffees can only fill the gap so far, so she was lonely and looking for news.

I kept the details brief, then pressed 'send' on my Communicator Plus, a huge brick of a thing with so many functions it could nearly read your thoughts. Work had given it to me, in the guise of a present. Yeah, right! In reality it just made me more of a slave than I already was – they could contact me in any way they wanted, whenever they wanted. *And* the weight of it tore the silky lining of my second-best handbag.

When *Sunset Beach* ended and Dad still hadn't rung back, I said, 'This isn't right. I'm going to ring him again.'

2

TO: Susan_inseattle@yahoo.com
FROM: Gemma 343@hotmail.com
SUBJECT: runaway dad, still at large

OK, more news. You're going to need a Valium when you hear, so don't read any further until you've got it. Go on, go.

Back? Ready? Right. My father, Noel Hogan, has a girlfriend. It gets worse. She's thirty-six. *Only four years older than me.*

Where did he meet her? Where do you think? Work, of course. She's his — God, the tedious predictability of it — his PA. Colette's her name and she has two children, a girl of nine and a boy of seven, from another relationship. She wasn't married to the other man and when I told Mam she said, 'Small wonder. Why buy the cow when you're getting the milk for free?'

The story goes that they'd spent a lot of time working on the new tiramisu bar, and become very close.

Yes, I'd already told Susan about the tiramisu bar. I know it was a secret and I'd promised Dad I wouldn't tell anyone, but Susan had such enthusiasm for the topic that I couldn't keep my mouth shut. She'd love to do a thesis on the subject 'From Curly Wurly to Chunky KitKat – whither bars of chocolate in the twenty-first century'. 'Think of the research I'd have to do,' she says.

I had to leg it home from work (leaving two hundred frisky chiropractors in the hands of Andrea) and weasel the info out of Dad like it was a game of twenty questions. 'Do you owe money?'

'Are you sick?' Then finally I hit bedrock with, 'Are you having an affair?'

It's only been going on three months – or so he says. What's he doing walking out on a thirty-five-year-old marriage for a three-month fling? And when was he planning on telling us? Did he really think he could just pack a suitcase one Tuesday morning and leave for good without ever having to explain himself?

And the yellow-bellied cowardice of the man. He fesses up to me, on the phone, then leaves me to break the news to Mam. He-llo? I'm his daughter. She's his wife. But when I reminded him of this he sez, 'Ah no, you tell her, women are better at that sort of thing.'

He didn't even have the kindness to let me go and tell Mam immediately; he had to Share The Joy about Colette, while Mam watched like a wounded animal.

'She makes me feel young,' he declared, like I should be happy for him. Then he said – and before he even said it, I knew he was going to – he said, 'I feel like a teenager.' So I said, 'I'm sure we can find you one. Male or female?' And he didn't get it at all. Ridiculous old fool.

Telling Mam that her husband had left her for his secretary was literally the hardest thing I've ever had to do in my entire life. It would have been easier to tell her he'd died.

But she took it well – too well. She just said, 'I see.' Sounding very reasonable. 'A girlfriend, you say? Stick on *Buffy* there.'

So, mad as it sounds, we sat in front of *Buffy*, not seeing a thing, well I didn't anyway, then, without warning, she switched off the telly, and said, 'You know, I think I'd like to speak to him.'

Back out to the phone and this time she rang him and got him at his desk, and they had what sounded like a calm conversation – very: 'Yes, Gemma did tell me, but I thought she might have got it wrong. Uh-huh, she didn't. Uh-huh, yes . . . Colette . . . you're in love with her . . . I see . . . I see. Yes, of course you deserve to be happy . . . nice apartment . . . well that's nice. A nice apartment can be nice . . . solicitor's letter . . . I see, yes, I'll look out for it, well, bye for now.'

And when she hung up she said, 'He has a girlfriend.' Like it was news.

Back she went into the kitchen, me following. 'A girlfriend. Noel Hogan has a girlfriend. He's going to live with her in her nice apartment.'

Then she opens a press, takes out a plate, says, 'My husband of thirty-five years has a girlfriend,' and casually frisbeed the plate at the wall, where it smashed into smithereens. Then another, then one more. She was picking up speed, the plates were twirling faster and the gaps between me having to duck to avoid the explosion of splinters were getting shorter.

While she was just flinging the ordinary blue and white kitchen crockery, I wasn't too bothered. I thought she was only doing what was expected of her. But when she went into the sitting room, picked up one of her bone-china ballerinas – you know them, *awful*-looking yokes, but she loves them – and, after only the tiniest hesitation, fecked it at the window, *then* I was bothered.

'I'm going to drive over there and kill him,' she growled, sounding like she was possessed. And only that

- a) she can't drive,
- b) Dad had taken the car and
- c) she wouldn't be seen dead in my car because it's too 'showy'

I'm certain she'd have done it.

When she realized she couldn't go anywhere, she began pulling at her clothes – 'renting' them, perhaps? I kept trying to grab her hands and stop her, but she was much, much too strong for me. By then I was very scared. She was way out of control and I hadn't a clue what to do. Who could I ring? Ironically enough my first thought was of Dad, especially as it was his fault. In the end I rang Cody. Naturally I didn't expect any sympathy, but I hoped for some practical advice. He answered in non-work mode, i.e. as camp as a row of cerise tents with marabou feather trimming. 'A shock? Do tell.'

'My dad's left her. What should I do?'

'Oh dear. Is that her I hear?'

'What? The shrieking? Yes.'

'Is she . . . ? Is that the sound of Aynsley shepherdesses breaking?'

I took a quick look. 'Belleek creamers. Close enough. What should I do?'

'Hide the good china.' When it became clear that I wouldn't play ball, he said – kindly for him, 'Call the medics, dear.'

Round here it's harder to get a doctor to make a house call than it is to eat only one cashew nut. (Absolutely impossible, as we both well know.) I rang and got Mrs Foy, Dr Bailey's foul-tempered receptionist – did I ever tell you about her? She's worked for him since before the flood and always acts like a request for an appointment is a gross imposition on his time. But I managed to convince the old sourball that this was an emergency; the sounds of Mam in hysterics in the background may have helped, of course.

So half an hour later Dr Bailey shows up in his golf clothes and – get this – gives Mam a shot. I thought it was only people who lived in bodice-ripper-land who got given shots by doctors when they became a bit overwrought. Whatever they put in them must be good gear because before our eyes Mam stopped gasping and sagged feebly onto her bed.

'Any more of them?' I asked and the doc goes, 'Ahaha! So what happened?'

'My father has left us for his secretary.'

I expected the good doctor to act shocked, but you know what? Something like guilt skipped across his face and I'm not joking, I could have sworn the word 'Viagra' crackled in the air, like a blue lightning flash. Dad's been to see him recently, I'd put money on it.

He couldn't get away fast enough. 'Put her to bed,' he sez.

'Don't leave her on her own. If she wakes up . . .' He shook two pills onto his hand and handed them over. 'Give her the two. Emergency only.' Then he scribbled a prescription for tranks and hot-footed it back to the thirteenth hole. His spiky shoes left little clumps of grass on the hall carpet.

I helped Mam into bed – she hadn't got dressed, so there was no undressing to be done – pulled the curtains then lay beside her, on top of the eiderdown. I was in my Nicole Farhi suit and even though I hadn't got it in the sale and even though I knew I was going to get feathers all over it, I didn't care. That's how freaked out I was.

It was all way too weird. You know what it's like round here, *no* one leaves their wives. People get married and stay married for a hundred and seventy years. Even if they hate each other. Not that Mam and Dad ever seemed to hate each other, not at all. They were just . . . you know . . . married.

I paused and deleted that last paragraph. Susan's mother had died when Susan was two and her dad got married again when Susan was twenty. The marriage had broken up about three years ago and even though Carol wasn't her mother and Susan hadn't been living at home when it all started to go wrong, she was still upset about it.

Anyway, so I'm thrun on the bed in my good suit and then the church bells start ringing the midday Angelus: I was lying in a darkened room with a sedated parent by my side and it wasn't even lunchtime yet. This gave me a bad bout of the fear so I rang work, just to feel I wasn't the only person in the world. Andrea let it slip that the screens had never turned up for the chiropractors' conference, but insisted it was fine. Of course it wasn't fine – how could the chiropractors look at their pictures of gammy spines without screens?

But who cares, I felt. In fairness, something always goes wrong at a conference, no matter how much preparation I do, and at

19

least the flowers for the gala dinner centrepieces had arrived. (We were wrapping wire around hollyhocks and other lanky ones and kind of bending them to make them look like spines. Andrea's idea – she's really come on a lot.)

Poor Andrea was *dying* to know what was up with Dad, if he'd had a heart attack or a stroke or what but, you know yourself, etiquette dictates that you can't ask outright. I just said he was OK, but she wouldn't let it go.

'Stable?' she asks.

'Stable? He's certainly not acting it.'

I got off the phone fast, but I've a problem here. Everyone at work thinks Dad's at death's door, but how on earth can I tell them the truth – that all that was wrong was that he'd got himself a girlfriend?

Not only is it exceptionally embarrassing, but loads of them have met Dad, so they're just not going to believe me. In fact, even though Dad *himself* has told me that he has a girlfriend, I've stopped believing it too. He just isn't the type. Even his name is wrong, don't you think? Ladies and gentlemen, look into your hearts and ask yourselves, is Noel Hogan the name of a man who leaves his wife for a woman young enough to be his daughter? Should not his name be Johnny Chancer or Steve Gleam? Instead I give it to you, esteemed ladies and gentlemen of the jury, that Noel Hogan is the name of a man who reads John Grishams, who does up a family tree going back four generations, a man whose hero is not Arnie or Rambo, but Inspector Morse; in other words, ladies and gentlemen, a man who would never give his wife and daughter a moment's worry.

Anyway . . . After ages more of lying on the bed, I decided I'd better clean up the broken china and I swear to God, you'd want to have seen the kitchen; the smashed plates had gone everywhere – into the butter, floating in the milk jug. There was a four-inch long piece sticking out of a Busy Lizzie pot, it looked like modern arse.

And as for the sitting room where it was ornaments which'd

bitten the dust . . . Obviously some of them were so horrible it was a good thing, but I felt really sorry for the poor little ballerina – her dancing days were over.

Then I went back and lay on the bed beside Mam who was doing these cute little whistley snores, but I stayed on top of the covers. There were some crappy magazines on the floor on her side, and I stayed there for the rest of the day, reading them.

Now, Susan, from here on in, I'm a bit worried about my behaviour – the heating clicked off at eleven and the room got cold but I wouldn't get under the covers. I think I felt that as long as I wasn't actually *in* bed, I was only keeping her company, but the minute I got in it meant that Dad wasn't coming home. Anyway I dozed off and when I woke up I was so cold I couldn't feel my skin; like when I poked my arm with my finger, I could see the indent but felt nothing. It was quite entertaining, actually, a bit like being dead. I did it a good few times then put on Mam's coat – no point getting hypothermia just cos Dad had gone a bit loola – but I still wouldn't get into the bed. The next time I awoke the bloody sun had come up and I was annoyed with myself. While it was still night-time, there was hope that Dad would come home, and if I'd stayed awake and on guard, morning would never have come. Mad, I know, but that's how I felt.

The first words Mam said were, 'He never came home.'

The second were, 'What are you doing in my good coat?'

So that's you up to date. More news as and when.

Love
Gemma xxx

PS I blame you for all of this. If you hadn't got the job in Seattle, where you know no one, you wouldn't have been lonely and in need of news from home and my life wouldn't have self-destructed just to oblige.

PPS I was only joking about that last bit.

3

My mobile rang. It was Cody. Cody isn't his real name, of course. His real name is Aloysius, but when he started school none of his young chums could pronounce it. The best they could manage was, 'Wishy'.

'I need a nickname,' Cody told his parents. 'Something people can say.'

Mr Cooper (Aonghas) gave Mrs Cooper (Mary) a look. He'd been against calling the boy Aloysius right from the start. He knew all about the misery of being saddled with an unpronounceable name, but his more religious wife had insisted. Aloysius was a top-notch saint – at the age of nine he'd taken a vow of chastity, then died aged twenty-three while nursing plague victims and contracting the disease himself – it was an honour to be named after him.

'Right, pick a nickname. Anything you like, son,' Mr Cooper said magnanimously.

'The name I pick iiiiiisssss . . . Cody!'

A pause. 'Cody?'

'Cody.'

'Cody's a funny name, son. Would you not think of another? Paddy's a nice one. Or Butch, maybe.'

Cody/Aloysius shook his five-year-old head haughtily. 'Thrash me if you must, but my name is Cody.'

'Thrash you?' Mr Cooper said, aghast. He turned to Mrs Cooper. 'What stories have you been reading to the lad?'

Mrs Cooper coloured. *The Lives of the Saints* was good and educational. Was it her fault that they all met their ends being boiled in oil, or pierced with a quiverful of arrows or stoned to death?

Cody is the only person I ever met who thought they had a 'vocation'. He spent two years in a seminary, learning the rudiments of priesthood (especially how to thrash people) before, as he puts it, 'coming to my senses and realizing that I wasn't holy, I was just gay'.

'OK, Gemma,' Cody says to me, 'You're going to have to be brave.'

'Oh God,' I said, because if Cody tells you you're going to have to be brave, it means the news he has for you is really horrible.

Cody is a funny one. He's very honest, almost gratuitously so. If you say to Cody, 'Now tell me, and be honest, be really honest, I can take it, does my cellulite show through this dress?' he will give you an answer.

Now, obviously, no one asks that question if they expect the answer to be yes. People only ask because they're smugly convinced that after a month of body brushing, thrice-daily use of some French 'minceur' gear, and the wearing of anti-cellulite tights and an expensive, industrial-strength lycra skirt, the answer will be a big, fat NO.

But Cody would be the one person to tell you that he can see a hint of orange peel skin. I don't think he does it out of cruelty; instead he plays Devil's Advocate to protect his nearest and dearest from ridicule. It's almost as if he disapproves of hope and feels that erring on the side of optimism makes fools of us and hands the rest of the world the advantage.

'It's Lily,' he said. 'Lily Wright,' he repeated, when I said nothing. 'Her book. It's out. It's called *Mimi's Remedies*. The *Irish Times* are reviewing it on Saturday.'

'How do you know?'

'Met someone last night.' Cody knows all sorts of people. Journalists, politicians, nightclub owners. He works in the Department of Foreign Affairs and has a kind of Clark Kent thing going on: serious, ambitious and 'straight' in the daytime, until quitting time rolls around, when he whips out his poppers and minces for Ireland. He straddles many camps and he's privy to all kinds of advance info.

'Is it a nice review?' My lips weren't responding properly to my need to speak.

'I believe so.'

I'd heard ages ago that she'd bagged herself a publishing deal; I'd nearly gawked at the injustice. *I* was the one who was supposed to write a book; I'd talked about doing it often enough. And so what if my writing career thus far had consisted of me reading other people's books, firing them at the wall and declaring, 'Such shite! I could do better in my sleep.'

For a while, every time I passed a bookshop I went in and looked for Lily's book but I never saw it and so much time had elapsed – over a year – that I'd concluded it wasn't going to happen.

'Thanks for telling me.'

'Has Noel come home?'

'Not yet.'

Cody clicked. 'When God closes one door, he slams another in your face. Well . . . you know . . . call me if you need me.' As far as Cody went, this counted as deep concern and I was touched.

I closed my mobile and looked at Mam. Her eyes were bulging with anxiety. 'Was it your father?'

'No, Mam. Sorry, Mam.' We were halfway through Wednesday morning and the mood was very, very low. She'd been so pitiful when she'd woken up, then on our way down for breakfast as we passed the front door, she gave a huge gasp and said, 'Jesus, Mary and Joseph, the chain wasn't on.' She took a closer look. 'And neither was the mortice lock.'

She hurried into the kitchen and examined the back door. 'The back door wasn't double-locked, and the alarm wasn't on. And don't tell me the windows weren't secured!' Dad obviously had some sort of nocturnal routine when he sewed the house up tighter than Fort Knox.

'Why didn't you do it?' Mam asked. She wasn't accusatory; more puzzled.

'Because I didn't know about it.'

This gave rise to more puzzlement and after a pause she said, 'Well, you know now.'

I'd been all set to go to work but Mam was so lost and child-like that I rang Andrea to see how things were; she surprised me by saying that the gala dinner had been 'great fun', and the chiropractors had been wild crack, bending the hollyhock centrepieces in two and saying 'slipped disc' and suchlike. I think she got off with one of them.

She said I needn't come in, which was very decent of her because the post-conference mop-up is a big job – ferrying the delegates to the airport, returning the chairs, the lighting and the screens to the hire companies – although as the screens had never arrived, that was one less job – arguing with the hotel over the bill, etc.

In return for her decency I told her, briefly, what had really happened with Dad. 'Mid-life crisis,' she promised me. 'What car does he drive?'

'Nissan Sunny.'

'Right. Any minute now he'll trade it in for a red Mazda MX5, then soon after he'll come to his senses.'

I went back and relayed the good news to Mam but all she said was, 'Insurance is higher on red cars, I read it somewhere. I want him to come home.'

She had her elbows on the table, which was still spread with the previous day's breakfast debris: bowls, buttery knives, teacups (Aaaaagh!). I hadn't bothered doing it when I'd been clearing up the broken crockery, probably because I thought it was Mam's area. She's very houseproud – at least under normal circumstances – but right now she didn't even seem to see the mess. I made a start on it, clattering side-plates on top of each other, but when I picked up Dad's porridge bowl, Mam cried, 'No,' took it from me and placed it on her lap.

Then, once again, she dialled Dad's work number. She'd been ringing him approximately every five minutes since eight-thirty, and it kept going to his voicemail. It was now ten-thirty.

'Can we go over to his work, Gemma? Please. I have to see him.'

Her naked desperation was un*bear*able. 'Let's wait until we can talk to him.' Because what if we turned up at his office and we were turned away? I couldn't risk that.

'Mam, would you mind if I popped out for ten minutes?'

'Where are you going?' Her voice thickened with tears. 'Don't leave me.'

'Just down to the shops. I promise I'll come right back. Can I get you anything? A pint of milk?'

'Why would we need milk? Doesn't the milkman bring the milk?'

A milkman. Another world.

I was looking for my coat until I remembered I'd left it with the chiropractors. I had to go as I was – yesterday's suit creased and covered in little sticky feathers.

'You'll come right back?' Mam called after me.

'Right back.'

I burned to the local shopping centre and was nearly out of the car before I'd finished parking. My heart was pounding. For the time being the drama with Dad had been relegated to second place. Lily's book was the cause of my dry mouth. I ran across the concourse, hoping that I wouldn't bump into anyone from work, and entered the bookshop on full alert, adrenalined to the max, feeling like an SAS man breaking into an enemy embassy. I flicked my eyes from left to right, expecting to be ambushed by big displays of Lily's book, then twirled around very fast to see if there was anything behind me. Nothing, so far. With my Super-Anxious Vision, I spotted the New Titles wall and in under a second I'd scanned every cover – the Six Million Dollar Man couldn't have done it faster – but there were none by Lily.

What if they didn't stock the book here? After all, this was just a small, local store. Already I knew I would have to go into town to a bigger bookshop and keep searching. I couldn't give up until I had a copy of Lily's book in my hand.

Next, the alphabetical listing. The Ws were on the lower shelves, near the floor. Down I sprang. Waters, Werther, Wogan . . . oh Christ, there it was. There was her name. Lily Wright. Done kind of curly and wacky. Like this: Lily Wright. And the title was the same: Mimi's Remedies.

My heart was banging and my hands were so sweaty they left a smear on the cover. I turned pages but my fingers would only fumble. I was looking for the little bit that tells about the author. And then I found it.

Lily Wright lives in London with her partner Anton and their baby girl Ema.

Sweet Jesus. Seeing it in this book made it more true than it had ever been before. It was *in print*.

Everyone – her publishers, her readers, the bookshop staff and the people who worked in the printworks – they all thought it was true. Anton was Lily's partner and they had a little girl. I felt out in the cold and excluded from the loop because I was the only person in the whole world who still thought Anton was rightfully mine. Everyone else *everywhere* thought Lily's claim to him was legitimate. The bitter injustice. She'd stolen him, but instead of treating her like the common criminal she was, everyone was slapping her on the back congratulating her, 'Well done, that's a lovely partner you've got there. Good girl yourself.' No mention of the fact that she was thinning on top, of course. Not even a hint that she'd look a damn sight better if she got herself a Burt Reynolds-style hair-follicle transplant – and that's not just me being bitchy, she often said it herself. But no, projecting only a positive spin, everything was lovely and hirsute. On the back cover there was a small black and white photo. I gazed at it, my mouth in a bitter-sweet twist. Look at her, all delicate and wide-eyed and blondey and tendrilly, like a long-limbed, slender angel. And they say the camera never lies . . .

I almost felt that I shouldn't have to pay for the book – not only had the author stolen the man I'd loved the most, but she'd written a book about me. I got one of those well-nigh irresistible urges to croak at the assistant, 'This is all about me, you know,' but I managed not to.

Somehow I'd paid and I was outside the shop where I stood in the cold, skimming the pages for my name. At first glance I couldn't see it. I kept looking, then understood that she'd have had to change my name, in case I sued or something. I was probably 'Mimi'. I got as far as page seven before I came out of the trance I was in and saw that I could just as well be in Mam's in the warm, as standing here reading it.

As soon as I let myself back into the house, Mam stood framed in the kitchen doorway and choked, 'He has a girlfriend.'

While I'd been out, she'd finally managed to track Dad down and she was experiencing the news afresh.

'This has never happened to anyone I know. What did I do wrong?'

She walked into my arms, sagged against me and something hard banged off my hipbone – the porridge bowl, she had it in her dressing-gown pocket. She cried like a child, proper wa-wa-waaaas, with gulping, coughing and hiccups; my heart nearly broke. She was in such a terrible state I gave her the two emergency tablets and put her back to bed again. As soon as she was breathing peacefully I closed my fist around the tranquillizer prescription Dr Bailey had left – the first chance I got, I'd go to the chemist.

Then, in a riptide of fury, I rang Dad, who sounded surprised – *surprised*, no less – to hear from me.

'You come home tonight and explain yourself,' I said angrily.

'There's nothing to explain,' he tried. 'Colette says –'

'Fuck Colette, I don't give a fuck WHAT Colette says. You get over here and have some respect.'

'Language,' he said sulkily. 'All right. I'll be round at seven.'

I hung up the phone and the ground actually rocked beneath my feet. My father was having an affair. *My father had left my mother.*

I settled myself on the bed beside Mam and began to read the book that was all about me.

Mid-afternoon, Mam opened one eye. 'What are you reading?' she mumbled.

'A book.'

'Ah.'

4

TO: Susan_inseattle@yahoo.com
FROM: Gemma 343@hotmail.com
SUBJECT: What kind of woman steals the love of her life from her best friend, then writes a book and doesn't mention it?

Another day, another *douleur*.

More shocking news just in. Lily's book is out. Yes, Lily 'Every man for myself' Wright. Lily 'Bald Patch' Wright. It's the maddest thing I've ever read, sort of like a children's book, except there's no pictures and the words are too big. It's about a witch called Mimi (yes, you heard me, a witch) who comes to a village, which might be in Ireland or might be in England or might be on the planet Mars, and she starts interfering in everyone's lives. Making up spells with instructions like, 'Include a handful of compassion, a sprinkling of intelligence and a generous helping of love.' Gag-making. And I'm not in it, you're not in it, even Anton doesn't seem to be in it. The only person I recognize is a spiteful girl with ringlets, who has got to be Cody.

It took me only four hours to read but I suppose millions of people will buy it and she'll be a millionaire and a big celebrity. Life is such a bastard.

As soon as I'd finished, I had to get Mam up because Dad was coming. She refused to get dressed – she's getting way too fond of that dressing-gown. And as for Dad's porridge bowl, she's holding on to it like she's waiting for the Forensics people to bag and label it as Exhibit A.

Then in comes Dad – using his own key which I thought was well out of order – and I got a real fright. Less than two days and already he looks different. Sharper, more defined around the edges, less blurry, and it struck me how very serious this whole business is when I saw that he was wearing new clothes. Well, I'd certainly never seen them before. A brown suede jacket – Christ in the marketplace! Rudimentary sideburns, much comb-over action going on with his hair, and, worst of all, trainers. Oh, mother of God, the trainers. Blinding white, and so chunky that it looked like they were wearing him, rather than the other way round.

'So what's going on?' I asked.

And without even sitting down, he announces that he's very sorry, but he's in love with Colette and she's in love with him.

It was the weirdest, most awful thing. What's wrong with this picture? Absolutely fecking everything.

'But what about us?' I said. 'What about Mam?' I thought I had him there because all my life he's been devoted to us. But do you know what he said? He said, 'I'm sorry.'

Which of course meant he wasn't. He just didn't care, which I didn't understand, because he'd always been so gentle and kind. It took a while to get what was happening, because this was my DAD, you know? Then – with another terrible fright – I saw that he was in that loved-up cocoon where all you can feel is your own happiness and you can't imagine that everyone else doesn't feel it too. I never knew it happened to old people, to *parents*.

Then Mam says in this tiny voice, 'Will you stay for dinner?' I *mean*! I am so sure. So I go, all narky, 'He can't, there aren't enough plates.' Then I tell him, all accusing, 'She broke most of them yesterday because she was so upset.'

But not a bother on him. He just said, 'I can't stay anyway.' Then he gives the front door a furtive look and something clicked into place and I yelled, 'She's outside! You've brought her with you.'

'Gemma,' he shouts, but I was already at the front door and yes, there was a woman sitting outside in the Nissan Sunny. I thought I was going to gawk. There really was another woman and Dad *wasn't* in an overworked state of delusion.

You know how in books they always say that women who steal other people's men look 'hard', just so we'll have no sympathy with them. Well, Colette did, she really did look hard. She spotted me and gave a kind of don't-mess-with-me stare. Like a complete looper I ran over, pressed my face against the window on her side, pulled my bottom lip over my top one and bulged my eyes at her, then I called her the C word and, all credit to her, she didn't retreat even an inch, she just gazed coolly at me with roundy blue eyes.

Dad shows up behind me and goes, 'Gemma, let her alone, it's not her fault.' Then he murmurs, 'Sorry, love,' and it wasn't me he was talking to. Deflated to fuck, I went back inside, and Susan, do you know what I was thinking? I was thinking, She has highlights, her hair is nicer than mine.

Dad stayed only about five more minutes, then just as he was leaving, he produced four of the prototype tiramisu bars from the pocket of his (I can hardly type this) brown suede jacket. For a minute I was almost touched – at least he was planning to keep us in chocolate – then he says, 'Let me know your impressions, especially if you think the coffee flavour is too strong.'

I threw a bar at him, which caught him on the sideburn and said, 'Do your own fucking market research,' but Mam held on to hers with a death-grip.

And next thing you know it's just me and Mam again, sitting in silence, our mouths agape.

It was then that shock really got a grip of me; none of it seemed real. I couldn't get anything hardwired into my system.

How had it all happened? But do you know what? In amongst all the other feelings I've still enough room to feel embarrassed. That's bad, isn't it? But, Christ, the thought of my father cavorting, *cavorting* with a woman my age. It's bad enough to think of your parents having sex with each other. But with different people . . .

Remember when your dad married Carol? And how the thought of them 'doing it' was too horrific so we decided they were just together for the companionship? If only I could convince myself that this is the case here!

And what's in it for hard-faced, highlighted Colette? My dad wears a vest. A *vest*, for God's sake.

Aaargh! Just had an image there of them 'at it'.

'After all I did for him,' Mam said. 'And to leave me in my twilight years. What did I do wrong?'

You know what, I've always worried about having children because I felt I couldn't watch them endure their teenage heartbreaks. Not in my worst nightmares did I think I'd have to do it for my *mother*.

You know what she's like – the perfect wife, always cooking wonderful meals, keeping the house perfect, never braining Dad when he was narky about bars of chocolate not selling as well as they should have. She kept her figure right into the menopause. Even her menopause was carried off with aplomb; not once was she stopped leaving a supermarket with an unpaid-for can of sardines in her handbag. (Why is it always cans of sardines?)

I'll tell you something, this has made me very bitter about men. What's the point? You give them your life, cook yourself blue in the face, starve yourself into osteoporosis and for what? For them to leave you just when you're commencing your final descent into old age, for a vest-loving woman who has highlights.

'He didn't deserve you,' I said.

But she looked annoyed and said, 'That's your *fa*ther you're talking about.'

But what was I meant to say? Plenty more fish in the sea? You'll meet someone else? Like, Mam is sixty-two; she's soft and comfy and looks like someone's granny.

If you get a chance, call me at Mam's. She's terrified of being on her own, so I'm going to stay here for a little while, just until he comes to his senses and returns home.

Love
Gemma

PS No, I don't mind about you not having a Valium and yes, a rum and Coke was a good substitute. You did the right thing.

Mam let me out to collect clean clothes from my flat, a fifteen-minute drive away. 'If you're not back in forty minutes, I'll be afraid,' she promised.

At times like this I hate being an only child. Mam had had two miscarriages – one before having me and one after – and no amount of rocking horses and pink tricycles made up for not having brothers or sisters.

As I drove my mind was on Colette and her highlights. The greatest shock was that she was almost the same age as me; did this mean Dad had been eyeing up my friends? He had no history of affairs or flirtations – until yesterday the thought would have been thigh-slappingly funny – but all of a sudden I was looking with fresh eyes. Thinking back, he'd always been nice to my friends, giving them chocolate whenever they called round, but that was almost the same as inviting them to partake of the fresh air in the house. And when I was in my late teens and early twenties he was the dad who used to come out at two in the morning with his coat on over his PJs to collect me and nine or ten others from a club in town. We were usually a bit the worse for wear and the highwater mark was the time Susan opened her window and gawked half a bottle of peach Schnapps down the outside of the car door. Dad didn't notice until the next morning when, jingling his car keys, he was leaving for golf only to find one of his doors caked in gunge. But instead of going on a mad rant like Mr Byers did the time Susan gawked into his flower bed ('You tell that little brat to get round here and clear it up! She shouldn't be drinking, she's under age and she can't hold it!' etc., etc.), all Dad said was, 'Ah, sugar! That Susan,' and tramped back inside to get a basin of water and a J-cloth. At the time I thought Dad was simply being kind but now I was wondering if it implied something far more lecherous.

A revolting thought.

I got caught on several red lights, which ate into my time, but at least the code on the electronic gate was working. My flat is in a complex which aspires to be swinging and 'modrin' and among its many facilities are a (laughably poor) gym and an electronic gate which is meant to provide 'security'. Except that, on a regular basis, the code on the gate doesn't work and people either can't get out for work, or can't get back in for their dinner, depending on what time of the day it happens.

I flicked through my post – six or seven leaflets advertising power yoga, a flyer for colonic irrigation – and checked my answering machine: nothing urgent; everyone finished their messages by saying, 'I'll try you on the mobile.' (Mobile indeed. My life would be easier if they just put wheels on it.) Then I flung toiletries, underwear and my mobile charger into a bag and tried to track down clean clothes for work. I found one crisply ironed shirt hanging on the wardrobe door, but I needed two. A rummage through the hangers produced another, then I saw that the reason it was unworn was because it had funny yellow stains under the arms that washing couldn't shift, so I never wore it any more. Well, it would have to do; I just wouldn't take my jacket off. Finally, I packed my pinstriped suit and four-inch heels. (I *never* wear flats. My shoes are so high that sometimes when I step out of them, people look around in confusion and ask, 'Where'd she go?' and I have to say, 'I'm down here.')

Before I left I gave my bed a wistful look; I'd be sleeping in my parents' spare room tonight and it just wouldn't be the same. I love my bed. Let me tell you about it . . .

A few of my favourite things
Favourite thing No. 1
My Bed: A love story

My bed is a lovely bed. It is not just any old bed. It is a bed I assembled myself and by that I don't mean it came in a flat pack from Ikea. I bought an expensive mattress, in other words, not the cheapest one in the shop. I think it was only the third cheapest. Extravagance indeed!

Then the bedding. I have not one, but two duvets. One to cover me – obviously. But – you're going to like this – the second one goes *under* my sheet, so I lie on top of it. It's a trick my mother taught me and it's hard to convey the bliss of climbing in and being received by the fluffy, feathery envelope. The duvets seem to stroke me, murmuring, *You're OK now, we've got you, we've got you, let it go, it's all OK, you're safe now* – like the hero does to the girl at the end of the movie, after she's been on the run from rogue elements of the FBI, and she's finally managed to expose them without getting shot.

Sheets, duvet covers and pillow cases: cotton, of course, and they are white, white, white (apart from the coffee stains).

Unique feature: the headboard. Aka: the best bit. Cody's friend Claud made it for me (I paid him for it, it wasn't a present) and it's a headboard fit for a fifties movie star: big, padded and all curves and curlicues, upholstered in faded bronze silk with a scattering of tea-roses, it's a bit fairy tale, a bit Art Nouveau, in other words, a bit fabulous. People always remark on it. Indeed the first time Anton saw it he exclaimed, 'Look at your girlie bed!' then roared laughing, before rolling me onto it. Ah, happy days . . .

I gave my bed a final regretful look, wishing I didn't have to leave it. I consulted my ghost sisters. 'You go on over to Mam,' I said to the first one. 'You're the eldest.' But nothing doing, so I went myself.

When I got out of the car and came into the house, carrying my clean suit and shirts, Mam said, 'What do you need them for?'

'Work.'

'*Work?*' Like she'd never heard of such a thing.

'Yes, Mam, work.'

'When?'

'Tomorrow.'

'Don't go.'

'Mam, I have to go. I'll lose my job if I don't.'

'Take compassionate leave.'

'They only give it when someone dies.'

'I wish he had died.'

'Mam!'

'But I do. We'd get a ton of sympathy. And respect. And the neighbours would bring food.'

'Quiches,' I said. (Because they do.)

'And apple tarts. Marguerite Kelly makes a lovely funeral apple tart.' (Said with a certain amount of bitterness, you'll see why in a minute.) 'But instead of having the decency to die he's got a girlfriend and left me. And now you're talking about going to work. Take some of your holidays.'

'I've none left.'

'Sick leave, then. Dr Bailey will give you a note. I'll pay.'

'Mam, I *can't*.' I was starting to panic.

'What could be so important?'

'Davinia Westport's wedding next Thursday.'

'Big deal,' she said.

One of the society weddings of the year, to be precise. The most important, complex, costly, terrifying job I'd ever worked on and the logistics had occupied me for months, both in my waking hours and in my dreams.

The flowers alone involved five thousand refrigerated tulips arriving from Holland and a flower specialist and his six assistants flying in from New York. The cake was to be a twelve-foot-high replica of the Statue of Liberty, but was to be made of ice cream so couldn't be prepared until the last minute. A marquee, big enough to hold five hundred guests, was to be set up in a field in Kildare on Monday night and transformed into an Arabian Nights Wonderland by Thursday morning. Because Davinia – in every other respect an obliging, sensible girl – had elected to get married in a tent in January, I was still trying to track down enough heaters to ensure we didn't freeze.

Among other things . . . Many, *many* other things. It was a real stamp of approval that Davinia had picked me to pull together her dream wedding. But the *stress*, I can't *tell* you – chefs could get food poisoning, florists could develop sudden pollen allergy, hairdressers could break their wrists, the marquee could be vandalized and, at the end of the day, the problem was mine.

But I couldn't tell Mam any of the details because they were strictly confidential and she was even worse than me at keeping secrets – half the locality already knew about the tiramisu bar.

'But if you go to work, what about me?'

'Maybe we could get one of the neighbours in to sit with you.'

Silence.

'Is that OK? Because, you see, it's my job, they pay me to be there, and I've been away for two days already.'

'What neighbours?'

'Ehhmm . . .'

A recent shake-down had seen a change in the fabric of the local community. One minute it seemed that all the neighbours were women of Mam's age and older, and were called Mary, Maura, May, Maria, Moira, Mary, Maree, Mary, Mary and Mary. Except for Mrs Prior who was called Lotte but that was only because she was Dutch. They always seemed to be dropping in, distributing envelopes for a church collection or looking to borrow a jumper de-baller or . . . or . . . you know, that sort of thing.

But recently three or four of the Marys had moved; Mary and Mr Webb had sold up and moved to a retirement apartment by the sea 'now that the children have grown'; Mr Sparrow had died and Mary Sparrow, a great friend of Mam's, had gone to live with her sister in Wales. And the other two Marys? I can't remember because I must admit I didn't always pay as much attention as I should have to Mam's recounting of local events. Oh yeah, Mary and Mr Griffin had gone to Spain because of Mary Griffin's arthritis. And the other Mary? It'll come to me.

'Mrs Parsons,' I suggested, 'she's nice. Or Mrs Kelly.'

Not a great idea, I realized. Relations had been strained – polite, of course, but strained – since Mrs Parsons had asked Mrs Kelly to make the cake for Celia Parsons's twenty-first, instead of asking Mam, who the whole cul-de-sac knew made the cakes for everyone's twenty-firsts; she did them in the shape of a key. (This took place a good eight years ago. Grudge-holding is one of the hobbies around here.)

'Mrs Kelly,' I repeated. 'It wasn't her fault Mrs Parsons asked her to make the cake.'

'But she didn't have to make it, she could have said no.'

I sighed. We'd been through this a thousand times. 'Celia Parsons didn't want a key, she wanted a champagne bottle.'

'Dodie Parsons could at least have asked me if I could do it.'

'Yes, but she knew that Mrs Kelly had the decoration book.'

'I don't need a book. I can just make up designs out of my head.'

'Exactly! You're the better one.'

'And everyone said that the sponge was as dry as sand.'

'They did.'

'She should just stick to what she's good at – apple tarts for funerals.'

'Exactly and really, Mam, it wasn't Mrs Kelly's fault.'

It was important to broker closer links with Mrs Kelly because I couldn't take any more time off. Francis and Frances – yes, *the* F&F of F&F Dignan – had been pleased when I'd won the Davinia account and said if I got it right I might get to do all of her weddings. But if I messed it up, well . . . The thing was, I was terrified of Frances and Francis – we all were. Frances had an iron-grey bob, all the better to highlight her boxer's jaw. Although she didn't actually smoke cigars, wear men's trousers and sit with her legs apart, that's what I saw whenever I closed my eyes and thought of her – something that didn't happen often, at least not voluntarily. Francis, her partner in evil, was like an egg on legs: all his weight was piled on his stomach, but his pins were Kate Moss-skinny. He had a roundy face and was bald except for two tufts of hair which stuck out over his ears, so he looked like Yoda. People who didn't know him well thought he was a hoot. They said of Frances, 'She wears the trousers.' But they were wrong, they both wore the trousers. They each had a pair.

If I got this wedding wrong, they'd take me into the RWNW (the Room With No Windows, their version of room 101) and say that I'd disappointed them. And then, almost as an afterthought, sack me. Because they're a married couple they often boast that their company is more like a family. Certainly they know how to make me feel like a guilty schoolgirl and they encourage account managers (I'm one) to compete with their colleagues in an echo of – I'm told by those who know – sibling rivalry.

Anyway.

'So will I ask Mrs Kelly to come in?'

Mam had relapsed into silence.

She opened her mouth. For a while nothing emerged, but I knew something was on its way. Then from somewhere far inside her came a long, thin keen of pain. Almost like white noise but with a slight, ragged human undertone. It was chilling. Give me plate-breaking over it any day of the week.

She stopped, gathered breath and began again. I shook her arm and said, 'Ma-am. Please, Mam!'

'Noel's gone. Noel's gone.' At that, the white noise stopped and she was yelping uncontrollably, the way she had that morning, when I'd had to calm her down with Dr Bailey's emergency tablets. But we were out of pills; I should have gone to the chemist when I'd had a chance. Perhaps there was a late-night one somewhere?

'Mam, I'm just going to get someone to stay with you while I go out and get the tablets.'

She paid me no attention and I pelted up the road to Mrs

Kelly and when she saw the state of me at the door, it was clear she thought it was time to start making pastry and peeling cooking apples.

I explained my plight and she knew of a chemist. 'They close at ten.'

It was now ten to ten. Time to break the law.

I drove like the clappers and got to the chemist at a minute past. But there was still someone inside. I pounded on the glass door and a man calmly walked over and opened it for me.

'Thank you. Oh, thank God.' I fell in.

'It's nice to be wanted,' he said.

I thrust the crumpled prescription at him. 'Please tell me you have them. It's an emergency.'

He smoothed it out and said, 'Don't worry, we have them. Take a seat there.'

He disappeared behind the white partition bit to where they keep the drugs and I sank onto the chair, trying to catch my breath.

'That's right,' his disembodied voice came from behind the melamine divider. 'Nice deep breaths. In, hold, out.'

He reappeared with the tranks and said kindly, 'Mind yourself now. And remember, no driving or operating machinery when you've taken them.'

'Fine. Thanks. Thanks very much.' It wasn't until I was back behind the wheel that I realized he thought they were for me.

5

Normally, I never read book reviews so it took me a while to find them in Saturday's paper. As I skimmed critiques of biographies of obscure English generals and a book about the Boer war, I began to suspect that Cody might have been wrong for once. But then, my heart gave one big bang that hurt my chest. Bloody Cody was right. There *was* a review. He knows everything.

CHARMING DEBUT

Mimi's Remedies *by Lily Wright. Dalkin Emery. £6.99*

This debut from Lily Wright is less of a novel and more of an extended fable – and none the worse for that. A white witch, the eponymous Mimi, mysteriously arrives in a small village – location unspecified – and sets about working her own particular brand of sorcery. Rocky marriages are cemented and sundered lovers are reunited. Sounds too sweet to be wholesome? Suspend your cynicism and go with the flow. Shot through with magic, *Mimi's Remedies* manages to be a charming comedy of manners and a wry social commentary. As comforting as hot buttered toast on a cold evening, and just as addictive.

Shaking, I put the paper down. I think they liked it. Deep breath in, hold, deep breath out, deep breath in, hold, deep breath out. Oh God, I was jealous. I was so jealous, it was hot and green in my veins.

I could see it all now: Lily Wright was going to turn into a major celebrity. She'd be in all the papers and everyone would love her. Despite her bald patch she'd be in the pages of *Hello!*. She'd get on *Parkinson*. Even on *David Letterman* or *Oprah*. She'd be loaded and finally able to afford a Burt Reynolds-style hairweave and everyone would love her even more. She'd do charity work and get an award. She'd have a limo. And a huge big house. And a stalker. Every bloody thing!

I picked up the paper and read the review again, looking for something – anything – negative. There had to be *something*. But no matter how I read it, I really couldn't see that this review was anything but a rave.

I threw the paper from me with a sharp rustle. Why is life such a bastard? Why do some people get every fucking thing? Lily Wright has a gorgeous man – mine, a lovely little girl – half mine, and now a glorious career. It wasn't fair.

My mobile rang and I grabbed it. Cody. 'Have you seen it?' he asked.

'I have. You?'

'Yes.' Pause. 'Fair play to her.'

Cody walks a very narrow line between Lily and me. He refused to take sides when the great falling out occurred and he won't bitch with me about her, even though under normal circumstances he could bitch for Ireland. (If only it was an Olympic sport.) One time he even had the cheek to suggest that Lily stealing Anton from me might have caused her as much pain as it did me. I mean! In theory I can understand his position – Lily had done nothing to him – but sometimes, like today, it gives me a right pain in the arse.

It was Saturday morning, five days since Dad had gone – *five days* – and he still hadn't returned. I'd been certain he would have by now. It was what had kept me going, thinking that the situation was very, very temporary; that he'd had a rush of blood to the head, coupled with the stress of the tiramisu situation, but that he'd come to his senses in no time.

I'd been waiting, waiting, waiting. Waiting to hear his key in the lock, waiting for him to rush into the hall, yelping about what a dreadful mistake he'd made, waiting for this hell to be over.

On Thursday I rang four times to ask him to come home and each time he said the same thing – that he was sorry but he wouldn't be returning. Then I thought that I'd rung him enough and perhaps a few days' silence from me and Mam might jolt him to his senses.

A week. I'd give it a week. He'd be back by then. He'd have to be because the alternative was unthinkable.

I didn't go to work on Thursday and Friday. I couldn't – I was too worried about Mam. But I worked from Mam's, spending Thursday making calls, sending faxes and emails, as I chased up Davinia's arrangements. I even managed to zip off a couple of emails to Seattle where I vented big time and agreed with Susan that yes, Dad's jacket could have been worse, it could have had fringes.

On Friday morning Andrea came to Mam's with the files and we worked our way through the lists. Davinia Westport's wedding arrangements consisted of list after list after list; lists of the guests' arrival times; lists of the drivers who'd be collecting them; lists of where everyone was staying and lists of their specific requirements.

(I love lists and sometimes at the start of a job, I'll put things on the list that I've already done, just so I can draw a nice 'done' line through them.)

Then there were the timetables. Hour by hour breakdowns of when the marquee was being erected, when the acres of satin would arrive, when the floor would be laid and the lighting and heating should be set up. We were making good progress until Davinia rang on Friday afternoon to say that her friends Blue and Sienna had broken up and could no longer be seated at the same table as each other. All other work had to be shelved for the next two hours as we constructed a new seating plan – this one tiny sundering had set off shock waves which rippled through the entire wedding party, because they all seemed to have slept with each other. Every proposed move impacted negatively: Sienna couldn't sit at Table 4 because

Blue's new girl, August, was there. She couldn't sit at Table 5 because her ex, Charlie, was there. Table 6, Blue's ex, Lia, whom he'd dumped for Sienna. Table 7 . . . etc. And if we tried moving the obstacles – August to a new table, for example – *she'd* end up face-to-face with someone she'd shafted or slept with. It was like trying to solve a Rubik's cube.

What made things worse was that I didn't have Andrea's full attention. She kept eyeing the bars of chocolate thrown casually along the window sill, in the bread bin, and on top of the fridge. 'It's like,' she exclaimed, 'being let loose in a sweet shop.'

Because chocolate had been so freely available to me all my life, I could pretty much take it or leave it, but it had come in very handy since Tuesday: more alarming even than Mam losing the will to live, she'd lost the will to cook. And as I had no clue how to, it was just as easy when mealtimes rolled around to have biscuits and chocolate.

I loaded Andrea up with a selection of stuff in the hope that she might concentrate on the job in hand.

'Focus,' I entreated. 'Do it for Davinia if you won't do it for me.'

You see, Davinia Westport was a bit of a rarity. Even though she was posh, rich and good-looking, she was nice. (Apart from, like I said, insisting on getting married in a tent in the coldest month of the year.) More often than not the client is the worst thing about my job – worse than hotel ballrooms burning down two days before the event or the guests at a fund-raiser being fed salmonella chicken and having to be ferried off, puking their guts up, during the raffle. But Davinia was different. She didn't ring me at home in the middle of the night shrieking that her polo neck was the wrong shade of black or that she'd got a cold sore, and that I'd better fix it.

Andrea and I finished up at about eight o'clock on Friday night. No sooner was she gone, gratefully clutching an armful of confectionery, than Mam presented me with a list and dispatched me to the supermarket for the weekly shop. She didn't come with me because whenever I suggested she get dressed, she hugged her (increasingly grubby) peach dressing-gown tighter around her and whimpered, 'Don't make me.' But as I unpacked the groceries when I got back, Mam complained that I'd got all the wrong things. 'What did you get this butter for?' she asked, puzzled the way she'd been puzzled when I hadn't locked up the house the first night. 'This isn't the bread we get. And we don't get proper cornflakes, we get the own-brand stuff. Throwing money away . . .' she muttered.

Before I went to bed, the locking up had to commence; checking the windows, shooting bolts and putting chains on all the doors as I secured the house to Mam's high standards. I was exhausted by the time I trudged up to bed – and I couldn't help feeling a little sorry for myself. It was Friday night, I should have been out on the razz instead of babysitting my mam. How I wished that Dad would come home.

I was too upset to sleep so I took refuge in a fantasy. Conjuring up imaginary story-lines where runaway boyfriends return and enemies are vanquished is my party trick. I've gained quite a reputation, especially among Cody's gang and sometimes people I've just been introduced to ask me to do it for them.

How it works is, they give me a thumbnail sketch of the disaster: for example, their boyfriend had been spotted in Brown Thomas getting a Burberry bag giftwrapped. Naturally the aggrieved party thought it was for her and did what any sensible woman would do – went directly out and bought matching sandals. But the next time they meet, the fella breaks it off . . . without cushioning the blow with the bag. Obviously he's met someone else!

I take a bit more information, like length of relationship, cost of the bag etc., give it a little think and come back with something like, 'OK, picture the scene. It's three months from now and you bump into him and as luck would have it, you're looking great . . .' Pause to plan the hair and wardrobe – yes, they could have the candy-striped trews they saw in *Vogue* and yes, they would go with those scoop-necked tops. OK, high-necked if they preferred. And the new season's boots, well, *obviously* – then I continue. 'The Burberry bags have been marked down and you've bought yourself *two*. No, no wait, you haven't bought yourself *any* because who wants a bag that no one else wants? No, you got a bonus at work and you bought yourself an Orla Kiely that there was a waiting list for and you're just back from a sun holiday where you caught jaundice so not only are you rake-skinny, but you've a lovely colour. His car has just been clamped, it's pelting rain and one of his shoes has been stolen by a vicious inner-city fox.' Etc., etc. It's my attention to detail which people rate me for, I'm told, and when Anton ran off with Lily, it was a case of fantasist heal thyself.

The scenario I'd comforted myself with involved escaping to some remote rural Mills & Boon community. Beside the sea, naturally; some fantastically wild sea with big waves and surf and spray and the whole lot. I'd go for long, mad walks along the sea or the cliffs and while I was out tramping along gloomily, some hunky farmer would spot me and, even though I hadn't had my roots done for ages, he'd take a shine to me. Of course, he wasn't just a farmer, he was also a film director or a former entrepreneur who'd sold his innovative company for millions. I'd have an ethereal fragile quality about me, but because I was so wounded I'd be rude to him in the village shop when he tried to be nice to me. However, instead of calling me a stupid bitch, like he would in real life, and recommencing his fling with the village floozie, he'd take to leaving two fresh eggs on my doorstep in the morning. I'd get back from my four-mile stomp along the cliff to find the eggs – still warm from the hens, of course – waiting for my breakfast. (And never mind that my breakfast would normally consist of a mini-Magnum and three bowls of sugarpuffs.) I'd make a delicious omelette, with some wild parsley snipped from the garden that came with the house. Or else he'd leave a freshly picked, hand-gathered bouquet of wild flowers, and the next time I met him I wouldn't sneer, 'Do Interflora not deliver out here, then?' Instead, I'd thank him and say that buttercups were my favourite flowers. (As if.) At some stage I'd end up in his kitchen where I'd see him tenderly feeding a tiny lamb from a baby's bottle and my heart would begin its long overdue thaw. Until one morning, when I was out on my hike, a piece of the cliff would dislodge itself, taking me with it. There had been warnings about the unstable cliff edges, but in my death-wish state I'd discounted them. Somehow the hunky farmer would have seen me toppling over into the briny and he'd come with his tractor and ropes and rescue me from the little ledge I'd fortuitously landed on. Bosh. Happy Ever After land.

6

TO: Susan_inseattle@yahoo.com
FROM: Gemma 343@hotmail.com
SUBJECT: non-stop drama

Wait till you hear. Last night I was in bed, comforting myself with the film director-farmer fantasy when I heard a noise coming from Mam's room. Some sort of bump, then she was calling piteously, 'Gemma, Gemma.' Like this – Ddgemmmmaaah ... ddgemmmaaah ... so I pelted into her and she was turned on her side, writhing like a dying haddock and said, 'My heart!' (So people really *do* say that in the real world.) 'I'm having a heart attack.'

I believed her – she was grey, her chest was heaving and her eyes bulged. I grabbed the bedside phone so hard it fell on the floor.

It's the weirdest thing, making a 999 call – I'd only ever done it once before: Anton had had badly bad hiccups and I'd been very drunk. (Actually, so had he, it was the reason for his hiccups.) We'd tried everything to stop them: cold key down his back; drinking from the wrong side of the glass; looking at his bank statement to see just how overdrawn he was. It had seemed like an emergency at the time, but the 999 operator had given me short shrift.

This was a different story. I was taken very seriously, told to put Mam in the recovery position (whatever that is) and promised that an ambulance was on its way. While we waited, I held Mam's hand and begged her not to die.

'I've a good mind to,' she gasped. 'That'd teach your father.'

The awful thing was I didn't even have a phone number for Dad.

I should have insisted on getting hard-faced Colette's number, in case of emergency, but I'd been too proud to ask.

Mam was wheezing and fighting for breath – it was absolutely terrifying, I can't tell you – and I couldn't get over my bad luck. Imagine! Losing two parents in one week. It had never said that in last Sunday's horoscope.

This was the time that I wished that the autumnal evening classes you and I used to sign up for (but never go to after week three) had been in first aid, instead of yoga or Spanish conversation. I might have learned something that made the difference between my mother living and dying.

I half-remembered something about aspirin – weren't you meant to do something with that for heart-attack victims? Either you were definitely supposed to give it to them, or you were definitely *not* supposed to . . .

In the distance came the sound of sirens, getting closer, then through the bedroom curtains the blue light flashed. I ran down to open the front door and ten minutes later when I'd undone all the chains and locks, two fine hefty young men (you'd have liked them) burst in, pounded up the stairs with a stretcher, strapped Mam on, then pounded back down again, me scampering to keep up. They slid her into the ambulance, I hopped in after her, then they were attaching Mam to all kinds of monitors.

We wee-wah'ed through the streets as the men checked Mam's readings and I can't say how I knew but very shortly the atmosphere changed from efficiency to something less pleasant. The two men were giving each other funny looks and the knot in my stomach got worse.

'Will she die?' I asked.

'Nope.'

'Um . . . ?'

Then one of the lads said, 'There's nothing wrong with her. No heart attack. No stroke. All her vital signs are fine.'

'But she was gasping,' I said. 'And she'd gone grey.'

'Probably a panic attack. See your GP about it, get some Valium.'

Can you imagine! The siren switched off. The ambulance was doing a u-turn and, at a much slower speed, Mam and I were returned home and deposited outside our front gate. Mortified. The lads were quite nice about it. When I clambered out I apologized for wasting their time and they just said, 'No bother.'

I went back to bed and I swear to God I was burning with shame, in *flames* from it. Every time I was just drifting off I'd remember again and go Aaaagh! and have to sit up. It took hours to get to sleep and when I woke up it was Saturday morning and time to read the rave review of Lily's book in the *Irish Times*. (Copy attached from the *Irish Times* website.)

I hate my life.

Although I'm glad it's cheering you up – but soon you'll make friends and you won't be lonely any more.

I have to go now because Dr Bailey is here (again). Please write and tell me nice things about Seattle.

Love
Gemma

PS I shouldn't even humour you on this, but if you really need to know, I thought the coffee flavour was too concentrated and I'd much prefer it with milk chocolate instead of dark.

I was allowed out to collect Mam's prescription from the chemist. Dr Bailey had prescribed stronger tranquillizers. Then he'd scribbled on his pad and said, 'Perhaps some anti-depressants too.'

Mam said, 'The only anti-depressant I want is for my husband to come home.'

'That's not on the market yet,' Dr Bailey said, already edging down the stairs and back to the golf course.

I went to the same chemist I'd gone to the other night. Not only had they been nice to me, but it was the nearest.

The door pinged and someone said, 'Hello again.'

It was the same man who'd saved my life on Wednesday night.

'Hello.' I handed over the prescription. He scanned it and clucked sympathetically. 'Take a seat.'

While he ducked behind the melamine divider to get Mam's happy pills I noticed they'd all kinds of nice things that I'd missed on my mercy dash on Wednesday night.

Not just the usual chemist paraphernalia of painkillers and cough mixtures but mid-range face creams and, most distracting of all, nail polishes. This is how I feel about nail polish . . .

A few of my favourite things
Favourite thing No. 2
My nails: A testimonial

All my life I've hated my hands. I'm prone to short limbs anyway and nowhere is it more pronounced than my fingers. But about six months ago, at the behest of Susan, I started getting my nails 'done'. Which means getting them lengthened and strengthened with all sorts of fake jiggery-pokery. But the best bit of all is they don't look fake. They just look like nice nails, a nice length, painted a nice colour. (No horrible witchy femme fatale red talons for me.)

I am different when my nails are done. I am more dynamic, I gesticulate more, I am better at scaring my staff. I can indicate impatience by drumming on table tops and I can wrap up a meeting with a few choice clatters.

I am now utterly dependent on my long nails. Without them I'm like Samson without his hair, I feel naked and devoid of power. And I no longer laugh when people make fun of girls who regard breaking a nail as a disaster, because a broken nail has the same effect on me as kryptonite on Superman.

For the first time in my life I've started buying nail varnishes. I'd always felt sort of left out in that department but I've made up for lost time and now I have lots of them. Opaques and clears and metallics and glitterys and opalescents.

The only problem is what to do when things go wrong at work, now that I can't bite my nails any more. I might have to get false ones to bite, the way people get fake fags once they've given up smoking. Or indeed, I could take up smoking.

When the man re-emerged with the happy tabs, I'd selected a nail polish: a milky beige colour, the same colour as the January sky, which is absolutely horrible on the January sky but, interestingly enough, quite chic as a nail varnish.

'That's a nice cheerful shade,' he said.

I thought that was a funny remark for a man to make. Especially because it wasn't true.

But then when he started reeling off instructions – 'Take the anti-depressants once a day, if you miss a day, don't double up the dose the next day, just carry on as normal. Only take the tranquillizers as an emergency, they're highly addictive' – I remembered that on Wednesday night he'd thought the tranquillizers were mine. Evidently, he also thought these pills were for me and I wasn't sure quite how to go about telling him they were for my mother.

'Um, thanks.'

'Take care,' he called after me.

Back at Mam's, anxiety began growing inside me. I needed to go home.

I had to

a) do my laundry
b) put out my wheely bin
c) pay bills
d) set the video to record *I love 1988*.

Also, in the outside world, I had to

53

e) get a birthday present for Cody

f) get fancy tights for Davinia's wedding (I had to masquerade as a guest even though I'd be working at it.) (I really should get a clothing allowance because I have to buy so many gussy clothes for work. Hats and cocktail dresses and whatnot.)

g) get my nails done.

The second I stood up, I must have conveyed my purposeful air to Mam because she said anxiously, 'Where are you going?'

'I have to get home, Mam. I've my laundry to do and –'

'How long will that take you?'

'A few hours, so –'

'So you'll be back here by three. Or why don't you bring your laundry here and I'll do it for you?'

'There's no need.'

'I do it much nicer.'

'Yes, but I've other things to do too.'

'What about me? Are you going to leave me here on my own?'

I drove away, fear sitting in my stomach like a bag of stones. There *had* to be other people who could help, but I scrolled through the options and found thin pickings.

1) Siblings of mine? None.
2) Caring and supportive spouse of mine? None.
3) Siblings of Mam's? Also none. Like me, Mam was an only child – obviously it runs in the family.
4) Siblings of Dad's? Check! Two sisters – but one lived in Rhode Island and the other in Inverness – and one brother, Uncle Leo, who had died nearly seven months ago of a massive heart attack while buying a new bit for his drill in Woodys. The shock was appalling, and made far worse when his wife, Margot, who was one of Mam's best friends, died only five weeks later. Of a

broken heart, you're probably thinking. Of taking a corner too fast on a wet night and coming into collision with a pebbledashed wall, actually. It was horrific, especially so soon after Uncle Leo – Margot was a hoot and although I'd only seen her at weddings, Christmas and other family beanos, even I missed her.

5) Neighbours? The best I'd come up with was poor maligned Mrs Kelly. This I struggled to comprehend because when I was growing up the cul-de-sac felt like a community; all the families seemed to be roughly the same age. Now, without me having noticed, it had switched over to much younger families. When did it all change? When did everyone start dying or settling in those easy-to-manage apartments which are the final port of call before the great three-bed, semi-d in the sky?

6) Friends? Mam and Dad weren't exactly part of a large, glittering set and any of Mam's friends were also Dad's friends – they were a 'couple', they went out with other 'couples', they talked about people being 'a lovely couple'. There were 'the Bakers' – Dad played golf with Mr Baker. And 'the Tyndals'.

7) Mam's spiritual adviser? Father something or other – worth a try.

You picked a fine time to leave us, Noel Hogan, you prick. Didn't scan but I liked it all the same. I couldn't help thinking, What if he never comes home? What if it's always like this? How will I cope if Mam starts to hyperventilate every time I leave her house? How will I hold down my job? How will I have a life?

7

I *had* to go to work on Monday morning. I really, *really* had to. Davinia had requested a face-to-facer, plus I needed to go to Kildare to check on the site and ensure that the marquee was being erected in the correct field. I know this seems like a total no-brainer, but it had actually happened to Wayne Diffney, from the boyband Laddz (you know him, he's the 'wacky' one with the extra-stupid hair). His wedding marquee was put up in the wrong field and there wasn't time to take it down and reassemble it, so an extortionate sum had to be paid to the farmer who owned the land. It wasn't our agency, thank God, but nevertheless it shook the foundations of Irish Event Organizing.

So on Sunday night, feeling guilty and defensive, I pressed 'mute' on the telly and said, 'Now, Mam, I absolutely *must* go to work tomorrow.'

She didn't answer, just sat staring at the silent images, like she hadn't heard me.

It had been a terrible day – Mam hadn't gone to Mass, and it's impossible to convey how serious this is to someone unfamiliar with the Irish Catholic Mammy. The ICM won't miss Sunday Mass even if she's got rabies and is foaming at the mouth – she'll simply bring a box of tissues and brazen it out. If her leg falls off, she'll hop. If her other leg falls off, she'll walk on her hands while still managing to wave graciously at neighbours passing by in cars.

At ten o'clock on Sunday morning, I interrupted Mam who was sitting passively in front of the telly watching a weekly round-up of the stock market. 'Mam, shouldn't you be getting ready for Mass?'

(At that point I suddenly remembered who the fourth Mary who'd moved was. It wasn't a Mary at all. It was Mrs Prior – *Lotte*. No wonder I hadn't been able to remember. The incipient Mass must have prompted it because Mam had once said, 'I'm very fond of Lotte, even if she is a Lutheran.' But the previous summer Lotte had gone to that great clog-dancing competition in the sky and Mr Prior had sold the house and gone into sheltered housing.)

Mam didn't seem to hear me so I said, 'Mam! It's time to get ready for Mass. I'll drive you.'

'I'm not going.'

My stomach plunged. 'OK, I'll come with you.'

'Didn't I just say I'm not going? They'll all be looking at me.'

I employed the line that she'd fed me throughout my life every time I'd been self-conscious. 'Don't be silly,' I said. 'They're far more interested in themselves. Who'd be bothered looking at you?'

'All of them,' she said woefully, and actually, she was right.

Under regular conditions, eleven o'clock Mass counted as a 'promenade'. For Mam and her cronies it counted as 'going out'. If someone in the cul-de-sac got a new winter coat, the first time it was unveiled to the public was at eleven o'clock Mass.

But now that Mam was a deserted wife, she'd knock any new winter coats off today's agenda – and there was bound to be one or two, it was January, it was Sales time. All mutterings and sly glances would be directed at Mam and her aban-donedness, completely bypassing, say, the maroon wool/poly-ester mix topcoat that Mrs Parsons might have bought at a whopping seventy-five per cent off.

So Mam didn't go to Mass, she spent yet another day in her dressing-gown and now she was refusing to hear me.

'Mam, please look at me. I've really *got* to go to work tomorrow.'

I turned the telly off altogether and she turned to me, wounded, 'I was watching that.'

'You weren't.'

'Take tomorrow off.'

'Mam, I have to go to work in the morning because over the next four days every second counts.'

'That's just bad planning, leaving everything until the last minute.'

'It's not. The marquee costs twenty thousand euros a day to rent so we have to cram everything into the few days we have it for.'

'Can't Andrea do it?'

'No, it's my responsibility.'

'So what time will you be home at?'

Panic rose in me. Normally I'd live on site for a job like this, so that every moment that wasn't spent working was devoted to catching up on precious sleep. But it looked like I'd be doing the hour-and-twenty-minute drive from Dublin to Kildare and back, every day. Two hours and forty minutes of lost sleep. A day. Aaagh!

On Monday morning when the clock went off at 6 a.m., I was crying. Not just because it was 6 a.m. on a Monday morning but because I missed my dad.

It had been the strangest week of my life – I'd been so shocked and trying so hard to mind Mam. Now all the other stuff had gone and sad was all I felt.

Tears spilled onto my pillow. With child-like unreasonableness, I wanted Dad to never have left and for everything to be the way it had always been.

He was my dad and home was where he should be. He was a quiet man who'd left most of the talking to my mother but still, his absence in the house was almost tangible.

This had to be my fault. I'd neglected him. I'd neglected the pair of them. All because I had thought they were very happy together. In fact, I *hadn't* thought about it, that's how happy they seemed. They'd never given me a moment's worry, just jogged along nicely, seeming extremely fond of each other. OK, Dad worked and played golf and Mam was at home all day but they had plenty of shared hobbies – crosswords, drives to Wicklow to look at the scenery and they were very keen on gentle murder-in-the-community programmes, *Morse*, *Midsomer Murders* etc. Once they even went away for a Murder Mystery weekend although I don't think it was quite what they'd hoped for: they'd been looking forward to a serious murder investigation-style thing, with a 'crime', and a series of clues which would lead them to the villain. Instead they were plied with drink, bundled into wardrobes and groped by giggling co-sleuths.

Had Dad been unhappy for a long time? He'd always been such a nice mild-mannered person but had this been a cloak for something darker, like depression? Had he spent years secretly yearning for another life? Until now I'd never thought of him as a *person*, just as a husband, father and golf-lover. But there was much, much more to him and the extent of the unknown territory confused and shamed me.

I dragged myself from the bed and dressed for work.

By 10 a.m. the site in Kildare looked like a film set – lorries and people everywhere.

I was wearing a microphone headset so I looked like Madonna on the *Blonde Ambition* tour, except my bra wasn't as pointy.

The marquee had arrived from England and seventeen of the twenty staff contracted for had shown up to erect it. I had signed for four portaloos, a team of carpenters were hard at work laying a temporary walkway, and over the phone I had convinced a custom's officer to let the refrigerated lorry full of tulips into the country.

When the ovens for the catering tent were delivered – two days early, but at least they'd come – I sat in my car, turned the heater on and rang Dad at work to ask him, once again, to come home.

Gently but firmly he said no, then I had to voice a concern which had grown over the weekend. 'Dad, how will Mam manage for money?'

'Didn't you get the letter?'

'What letter?'

'There's a letter, it'll explain everything.'

Straight away I rang Mam and she answered by gasping, 'Noel?'

My heart hit bottom. 'No, Mam, it's me. Did we get a letter from Dad? Could you go and look?'

She went off and came back. 'Yes, there's an official-looking thing addressed to me.'

'Where was it?'

'On the window sill, with all the other letters.'

'But . . . why didn't you open it?'

'Oh, I always leave those official things for your father to deal with.'

'But this is *from* Dad. From Dad to you. Could you open it?'

'No. I'll wait till you come home. Oh, and Dr Bailey came, he gave me a prescription for sleeping tablets. How will I get them?'

'Pop down to the chemist,' I cajoled.

'No,' her voice shook. 'I couldn't leave the house. Will you go? The chemist stays open until ten, surely you'll be home by then.'

'I'll do what I can.' I hung up and mashed my face into my hands. (Hitting the redial button and hearing my mother gasp, 'Noel?' again, with *Groundhog Day* repetition.)

Leaving the wedding site at 8.30 p.m. was almost like taking a half day. I drove as fast as I could without getting stopped by the peelers, got to Mam's, grabbed the prescription and gunned to the chemist. The nice man wasn't there, thank God. I handed the piece of paper over to a bored-looking girl, but then the nice man popped out from behind the drugs bit and gave me a jaunty, 'Hello there.' Did he actually live in the chemist shop, I found myself wondering. Surviving on barley sugar sticks and cough sweets and resting his head at night on a bundle of springy corn plasters?

He took the prescription and murmured sympathetically, 'Not sleeping?' He surveyed my face and what he saw there had him shaking his head regretfully. 'Yes, the anti-depressants can often have that effect in the beginning.'

His sympathy – though entirely misplaced – was comforting. With a small smile of gratitude, I went home to Mam, where we sat down and opened the scary letter from Dad.

It was from his solicitor. Jesus, how serious was this? Although tiredness was making the letters dance before my eyes, I gleaned the gist.

Dad was proposing what he called 'an interim financial settlement'. This had an ominous ring because it promised a more permanent financial settlement to come. The letter said he would give Mam a certain sum a month, out of which she'd have to pay all housekeeping bills including the mortgage.

'OK, we have to take stock. How much is the mortgage?'

Mam stared as if I'd asked her to explain the theory of relativity.

'Well, how about utilities? Roughly how much is the electricity bill?'

'I . . . I don't know. Your dad writes all the cheques. I'm sorry,' she said, so humbly I felt I couldn't go on.

With anything.

Hard to believe that Mam had once had a job – she'd worked in a typing pool, which is where she'd met Dad. But she gave up work when she got pregnant with me; after the previous miscarriage she wasn't taking any chances. Maybe she would have given up her job anyway, after I'd been born, because that was what Irish women did in those days. But when other mothers returned to work when all their children were at school, Mam didn't. I was too precious, she said. More prosaically we didn't need the money; even though Dad never got promoted to fat-cat, Merc-driving, executive status, we always had enough.

'I think we've taken enough stock,' I sighed. 'Let's go to bed.'

'There's just one thing,' she said. 'I've a rash.' She extended a leg and parted her dressing-gown. Sure enough, her thigh was covered in raised red bumps.

'You'll have to go to the doctor.' My mouth twitched. Hysteria.

She actually laughed too. 'I can't ring Dr Bailey and ask him to make another house call.'

And I can't go to the chemist again. The nice man must think I'm a total nutter.

Tuesday morning saw ructions in Kildare. The interior designer and his eight-strong team swanned in to effect the transformation of a tent smelling of damp grass to a glittering Arabian Nights Wonderland. But the marquee wasn't fully hoisted, so both crews were trying to work around each other, and from the moment one of the marquee men marched along a length of gold satin in his muddy boots, battle lines were drawn.

The interior designer, a bouffed Muscle Mary, called the marquee man 'a cack-handed brute'.

However the marquee man thought being called 'a cack-handed brute' was the funniest thing he'd ever heard and kept saying it. 'Listen, lads, I'm a cack-handed brute. A *brute*!'

Then he called Mary 'a big fat ponce', which was nothing but the truth, but not exactly conducive to a harmonious working environment and I had to use my considerable negoti-ating skills to prevent the interiors team from flouncing (what other way?) out.

Once calm was restored, I stood in the freezing field, hoping for privacy and rang Auntie Gwen in Inverness.

With a mini-shriek, she began marvelling at how lovely it was to hear from me and what age was I now, which I short-circuited rudely – I couldn't help it, time was in scant supply. Succinctly I outlined the situation re Dad and finished by saying, 'I was thinking that maybe you could have a word with him.'

Instantly Auntie Gwen became Dithery Old Lady. 'Well, I don't know . . . I couldn't . . . it wouldn't be my place . . . a girl, you say . . . but what would I say to him . . .'

My attention was caught by something: in the clearing between the portaloos and the pathway the interior designers and marquee men had spilled out of the tent. To my horror they seemed to be squaring up to each other. Several marquee boys were rolling up their sleeves and one of the interior lads was swinging his Evian bottle menacingly. Time to go. 'Yeah, thanks, Auntie Gwen,' and with her still wittering her luke-warm excuses, I snapped my phone away and strode across the frozen ground.

Later that same day I tried Auntie Eilish in Rhode Island. But she had fallen in with a bad crowd, a highly therapied lot, who couldn't commit to an opinion if there was a gun to their head. Her response was, 'We're all grown-ups. Your father is responsible for how he lives his life just as your mother is responsible for how she lives hers.'

'I'll take that as a no then, will I?'

'No. "No" is just a different type of opportunity. I don't believe in the word "no".'

'But you just said it.'

'No, I didn't.'

Later I tried Gerry Baker, Dad's golf partner, who did a big, fake, mortified laugh. 'I thought I might be hearing from you. Well, from your mother, actually. I suppose you want me to have a word in his ear.'

'Yes!' *Thank Christ, someone who was prepared to help.* 'Would you?'

'Go on outathat. He'll come to his senses in his own good time.'

Disconsolate, I rang Mrs Tyndal, in the hope that she might take Mam under her wing. No chance. She was noticeably cool then pretended someone was at the front door, just to get rid of me.

I'd heard abandoned women complaining that their 'friends' would no longer play with them in case they tried to nick their husbands. I'd put it down to paranoia, but it was true.

I didn't get home that night until almost 1 a.m. Mam was still awake, but to my surprise she seemed a bit better. The dead, draggy look in her eyes had lessened and she had a lighter air around her. Then I found out why.

'I read that book,' she said, almost jauntily.

'What book?'

'That *Mimi's Remedies*. It was the nicest thing.'

'It was?' I was suddenly very frightened. I didn't want anyone to like it.

'It cheered me right up. And you never said it was by Lily! It was only when I saw her photo at the back that I realized. What a great achievement, to write a book.' Then she said wistfully, 'I was very fond of Lily, she was always so *kind*.'

'Excuse me, he-llo! She stole my boyfriend, remember?'

'Er, yes. So has she written any more books?'

'One,' I said shortly. 'But it hasn't been published.'

'Why not?' Mam sounded indignant.

'Because ... because nobody liked it.' I was being cruel. Some literary agents had sort of liked it. They'd *nearly* liked it. If only she'd take out this character or change the setting to Maine or write it in the present tense ...

For years Lily had written and rewritten the book – what was it called? Something to do with water? Oh, *Crystal Clear*, that was it. But even when she'd made the requested changes, still no one wanted it. Nevertheless she'd succeeded in getting rejected by not just one, not even two, but *three* agents and I'd been highly impressed by that.

64

'I'm going to lend this *Mimi's Remedies* to Mrs Kelly,' Mam said. 'She likes a good read.'

Mam liking Lily's book retriggered the anxiety that my horrible week had managed to obscure; the first chance I got the following day, I rang Cody. He wasn't in the office so I got him on his mobile. He was breathing heavily and I deduced he was on the treadmill. Either that or having sex. 'How's Lily's book doing?'

'Not setting the world on fire.'

'Thank God.'

'Now, now.'

'Ah, fuck off.'

Then, almost hesitantly, he asked, 'Have you read it?'

'Course! The maddest yoke ever. Have you read it?'

'Yes.'

'And?'

He paused. 'I thought . . . actually, it was beautiful.'

I thought he was being sarcastic, I mean this was *Cody*.

Then I realized he wasn't and the fear nearly killed me. If Cody, the biggest cynic on the planet, thought it was beautiful, then it must be.

8

TO: Susan_inseattle@yahoo.com
FROM: Gemma 343@hotmail.com
SUBJECT: The demon drink

Saturday night was Cody's birthday – need I say any more? He had a knees-up in Marmoset, Dublin's newest restaurant, with twenty of his closest friends and he was raging that I didn't bring my full organizational skills to bear on it. In fact, it's only because I'm more afraid of him than I am of Mam that I was there at all. Anyway, the long and the short of it is that the relief of Davinia's wedding going off without too many hitches coupled with the strain of my home life, meant I went pure mental.

Clearly I was worried from the off because I constructed a foolproof plan to keep me on the straight and narrow: I wouldn't drink wine because with the constant refills, you can't control the quantities. Instead I'd drink vodkas and tonic and – here's the foolproof bit – after each one I'd move the slice of lemon to the fresh glass. Thereby keeping a tally on the number of drinks I'd had and when the glass was so full of lemon slices that no more drink could fit in, then it was time to go home. Ingenious, no?

No.

I was one of the last to arrive, not just because Mam kept constructing excuses to stop me from leaving but because Marmoset is one of those pitiful establishments that doesn't advertise its existence – no name, no street number, no windows. Just like all the cool places did in New York and London five years ago. Anyway, in I go and there's Princess Cody at the head of the table, receiving his presents. I was in trouble because that afternoon was the first time Mam had let me go shopping since this business with Dad began, and the excitement kind of went to my head and I couldn't decide where to start or what to buy. So instead of buying Cody a birthday present, I ended up buying – of all things – a coal scuttle. Don't ask me why, but something about it appealed to me; I was cutting through the homeware department in Dunne's when I saw it and suddenly I really wanted it. Then – and you're to keep this to yourself – I went to the toy department and bought myself a fairy wand. It's a glittery silver star, backed with lilac fluff. I'm puzzled and ashamed by how much I wanted it and I've decided it's because with Dad doing a runner I've been robbed of my childhood and this was an attempt to recapture it.

Anyway, what I'm trying to say is that there was only time left to buy Cody a bottle of champagne and stick a rosette on it, which went on crooked because I seem to have a permanent dose of the shakes, and when I gave it to him, he did his haughty displeased face and sez acidly, 'I can tell you put a lot of thought into that.'

I was about to turn on my heel and go home to watch *Winning Streak* with Mam. 'I don't have to stay here to be insulted,' I said. 'There's loads of other places I can go.'

So he – roll out the flags! – apologized and made Trevor get up so I could sit at his right hand.

It was the usual Cody crowd: screechy, good-looking and great fun. The men had had manicures and the women were all super-groomed and no stranger to Burberry. Sylvie was there and Jennifer and some other ones whose names I can't remember at the moment.

I launched myself with gusto into the V&Ts and all in all I was having a great old time. Then I mentioned to Cody how much I was enjoying the novelty of eating my dinner off a dinner plate because we've been making do with side-plates at Mam's since the day she smashed them all and I haven't found time to buy new ones.

So Cody jing-jinged his knife on his glass (knocking a lump of parsnip into his champagne and not even noticing), called for a hush and made me tell the story about Dad leaving. As I was on my sixth vodka, it didn't seem terrible any more but strangely funny. I had the attention of the entire table as they creased and choked in convulsions at my description of Dad's new look, of the trip in the ambulance and the many visits to the chemist. Then I told them about the week I'd had, my 5 a.m. starts, then getting home from Kildare at 1 a.m. How, on the morning of the wedding, the main consignment of portaloos turned up in an awful state, and no one would clean them because it wasn't their job, so I had to roll up the sleeves of my wedding suit, don Marigolds and wield a toilet brush. And as I scrubbed I had to leave on my dramatic peacock-feathered hair ornament because there was nowhere clean to put it down.

At the time it had been *repulsive* but as I regaled the party, I suddenly saw the funny side. It was HILARIOUS. So hilarious that at some stage I found myself roaring-crying. Sylvie and Raymond took me to the ladies' to tidy me up, then I ordered another vodka and tonic and I was back on track.

I told everyone about the tiramisu bar, even the waiters and people at other tables.

After that things get a bit hazy. I remember that the bill was horrific and everyone blamed me because the V&Ts were a tenner a pop, and I'd had at least eleven of them. Hazier still is a paper-thin memory of me refusing to leave Marmoset because I still had room for three or four more bits of lemon in my glass. Followed by an image which may or may not be a dream of me getting into a taxi with Cody and Sylvie and somehow managing to close the door on my ear – although my ear is like purple sprouting broccoli today so perhaps it really did happen. Then I knew no more . . .

I paused. If I didn't condense what happened next this email would be as long as *War and Peace*. Because the morning after Cody's party I woke up in my own bed in my own flat and even before I discovered I was *inside* the duvet cover, I was full

68

of foreboding. I had a strange *unarranged* feeling about me and further investigation revealed that I was fully dressed but my bra was open under my dress and my knickers were pulled down to the top of my thighs, but my tights were still fully on. As soon as I was aware of it, it became so uncomfortable I couldn't bear it.

While I was wriggling around trying to fix myself I – as you do – glanced over the side of the bed and there, thrown on the floor like a police outline of a corpse, was a man. Dark hair, wearing a suit. I had *no* idea who he was. None. He opened one eye and squinted up at me and said, 'Morning.'

'Morning,' I replied.

He opened his second eye and then I *thought* I knew him. I recognized the face, I was pretty sure of it.

'Owen,' he supplied. 'You met me last night in Hamman.'

Hamman was a hot new bar – I had no idea I'd been there.

'Why are you lying on the floor?' I asked.

'Because you pushed me out.'

'Why?'

'I've no idea.'

'Aren't you cold?'

'Freezing.'

'You look very young.'

'Twenty-eight.'

'I'm more than that.' Looking around the room, I said, 'What's my coal scuttle doing in here?'

'You brought it in to show me. You told a lot of people about it last night, you seemed very proud of it. Quite right too,' he added. 'It's a beauty.'

He was taking the piss and I wanted him to go away and for me to go back to sleep and find I'd imagined it all.

'You're in the horrors,' he said, which was pretty observant. 'I'll make you a cup of tea and then I'll be off.'

I cried, 'No tea!'

'Coffee?'

'OK.'

And the next thing I knew was I'd jerked awake, my mouth was lined with sheepskin, and I was wondering if I'd dreamt it all. But there was the cup of coffee beside me – stone cold – I'd lapsed back into my coma before managing to drink it. And the coal scuttle was still on top of my dressing table and all kinds of lovely things – nail varnishes, toner, my Origins powder – were spilled and scattered around the floor looking to my morning-after-the-night-before eyes like rag-doll victims of a car crash.

It was horrific and when I got out of bed my legs nearly gave way on my first attempt to stand. In the front room the cushions had been knocked off the couch, like someone (me and Owen?) had had a wrestling match on it. Sticky red rings patterned my lovely wooden floor, courtesy of an open bottle of red wine and there was a horrible blood-like stain on my eighty per cent wool silver-grey rug. From the broken glass around the stain it looked like we'd landed on a wine glass during the wrestling bout.

Then I was really in the horrors when I thought the wooden floor had come out in strange silver bubbles but a closer look showed that it was just loads of CDs scattered around the room and catching the sun. Out in the hall, an extremely angry note had been shoved under the door: Gary and Gaye upstairs, complaining about the noise. They were RAGING and I wished I was dead. I would have to apologize and I didn't think I'd ever be able to speak again.

Obviously this sort of scene was once par for the course every Saturday and Sunday morning, but it was literally years – well, *a* year, anyway – since I'd gone this mad.

Mind you, something must have changed since the last time I brought home a man I couldn't even remember meeting, because the smart-arse youth had left me a note. I thought those sort of blokes normally scarpered at 4 a.m. with their underpants in the pockets, never to be seen again. The note –

scribbled with my eyeliner on a colonic irrigation flyer (I'd been sent *millions* of them) – said:

Coal Scuttle Angel, I find you strangely alluring. Let's do it again sometime. I'll call you, just as soon as my bruises have healed. Owen

PS Live long and prosper.

I'll call you.

With those words something made its way through my aching eye-sockets, my bruised hair, into my swollen brain and I knew that the horrible ominous feeling weighing me down wasn't just the hangover horrors, but Mam! My eyes went to the phone – I was almost afraid to look. The answering machine light was hopping; it looked like it was going at triple speed, like it was *furious*. (Could that actually happen? Does it speed up if you've got a lot of unlistened-to messages on it?)

Oh the dread. The horrible, awful, dreadful, dready dread. Like my alarm clock didn't go off and I missed my best friend's wedding, a free flight on Concorde to Barbados, life-saving surgery . . .

I wasn't supposed to be in *my* flat. I should have gone back to Mam's last night. I'd promised, it was the only way I was able to persuade her to let me out at all. But how could I have forgotten? How could I have gone back to sleep this morning? How could I not have remembered about her until now?

I pressed 'play' and when the flat Margaret Thatcher voice intoned, 'You – have – ten – new – messages,' I wanted to die. The first four were from Gary and Gaye upstairs. They were very, very angry. Then the messages from Mam began. The first one was at five in the morning. 'Where are you? Why haven't you come home? Why aren't you answering your mobile? I haven't been able to get to sleep at all.' Another call at six-fifteen, then at eight-thirty and twenty past nine. She sounded more and more frantic and on the ten-thirty call she

71

was wheezing, 'I don't feel well. It's my heart. It really is this time. Where are you?'

The next message was not from Mam but from Mrs Kelly. 'Your poor mother's gone to hospital in a terrible state,' she said coldly. 'If you could find time to contact home we'd all appreciate it.'

9

TO: Susan_inseattle@yahoo.com
FROM: Gemma_343@hotmail.com
SUBJECT: It took three days for the horrors to lift

It's only today that I'm back on solids.

Mam – thanks be to Christ – didn't have a heart attack, just another panic attack. The nurses gave her a little talking-to, along the lines of 'It's an offence to waste police time.' But when she explained to them about Dad leaving and me not coming home, they redirected their annoyance to me and I felt so guilty I took it on the chin.

Dad still hasn't come back. All last week when I was working like a machine, I didn't have time to think about it, really. But now that my routine is back to normal, I've realized it's over two weeks since he went. It's like I've been in a trance – how on earth did it get to be two weeks? It's a shockingly long time but I'll give it a month and he'll probably be back by then.

Cody and Mrs Kelly and everyone at work keep tut-tutting and saying what a stupid old bastard he is, but as soon as I try to agree I go wobbly and weepy and they look at me funny and I can see what they're thinking – it's not like it's *my* husband who has left. Wives are allowed to go wobbly and weepy but daughters are supposed to join in with the insults. I tried calling him 'a mad old gobshite' and Mrs Kelly said, 'Good girl.' But then I started to cry and she was visibly irritated.

This thing has layers. I keep thinking I understand that Dad has left and has ruined everything, then I perk up and think he'll have to come home soon. But then the fact that he hasn't come back yet kicks in again, deeper and much more painful than the

73

previous time. But like I say we'll give it a month, that's a nice round sum.

And yes, about the wand, thank you for reminding me that I was always partial to cheesy kitsch. Although what's cheesy about my 'Kitty goes to New York' shower cap? It's beautiful, not to mention functional.

I'm back in the office all this week. It's such a relief to be working only ten-hour days – and to be near the shops. I am buying things. Odd things. Yesterday at lunchtime I bought a keyring in the shape of a sparkly glass stiletto with a blue flower on the toe. Then I painted my nails ten different colours, each one more sugary pastel than the previous. Thank God for middle-youth.

Anawah, on we trudge. Send me a joke.

Lots of love
Gemma xxx

On the way home from work that evening – like most evenings – I popped into the chemist to get something for Mam. This time it was athlete's foot ointment – I had no idea how she caught that, considering that the most athletic thing she ever did was open a packet of biscuits. But before I even got to ask for it, the nice man behind the counter said, '*You* were in good form on Saturday night.'

All the blood that had been milling around in my face began a sudden and speedy exodus and my legs and hands started their shaking lark again, which was very annoying because I'd only just got them to stop.

'Where did I meet you?' I asked through bloodfree lips.

He paused, looked surprised, then uncomfortable and said, 'In Hamman.'

'In *Hamman*?' Jesus Christ, who *else* had I met in Hamman on Saturday night?

'This comes as a . . . surprise?'

Too right it did. All of it. That I'd met the man from the chemist in Hamman and remembered nothing about it. *And* that he'd been allowed out from behind the counter. What had he been wearing? I couldn't imagine him in anything except his white coat. And was he with a gang of other chemists, all in their white coats?

'I was scuttered,' I whispered.

'It was Saturday night,' he said, but then he went just a little bit stern and said, 'Didn't your doctor tell you that you shouldn't drink while you're taking anti-depressants?'

Now was the time. 'No, he didn't,' I said, 'because you see, the thing is, the prescriptions that I've been picking up from you, they're not for me, they're for my mother. I'm sorry I haven't told you before now, the time just never seemed right.'

He stepped back, did a long stare and tiny head-nods while he absorbed the info, and eventually spoke. 'Was any of the stuff for you?'

I thought back over the long list of medication I had got for Mam; not just the anti-depressants, the tranks, the sleeping tablets but the antihistamine stuff for her rash, the antacids for her stomach, the painkillers for her sinuses . . .

'The nail varnish was mine.'

'You know what?' he mused. 'I feel like a right fool.'

'Don't,' I said. 'It was my fault, I should have told you straight away and I enjoyed someone being nice to me even though there was nothing wrong with me.'

'OK.' He still looked uncomfortable.

'Just out of curiosity,' I asked, 'what's Hamman like?'

'Ah, it's alright. The crowd was a bit too young.'

Straight away I wondered how old he was – up till now I'd never thought of him having an age. In fact I'd never really thought of him as human, just a benign presence who dispensed tablets that kept my mammy from going totally doolally.

'It's the white coat,' he said, reading my mind. 'Very dehumanizing. I'm probably not that much older than you,

Maureen, and I've just realized that that's probably not your name.'

'No, it's Gemma.'

'I've a name too,' he said. 'It's Johnny.'

TO: Susan_inseattle@yahoo.com
FROM: Gemma 343@hotmail.com
SUBJECT: Wonders never cease

Guess what? The youth rang me. The youth I met the night of Cody's birthday. Owen or whatever he's called. He wants us to go out. 'For what,' I asked. 'A drink,' he sez. 'It took you nearly two weeks to call,' I said. 'I was playing hard to get,' he replied.

Anyway I told him I couldn't and he said, 'I understand. You want to spend more time with your coal scuttle.'

Obviously it's not that, it's because there's no way I'll get a pass from Mam at the moment. She only lets me out to go to work and collect her prescriptions from the chemist and I don't have the energy to resist, especially after I disgraced myself so badly on the night of Cody's birthday . . .

Anyway, let me know how you are. Any fellas yet?

Love
Gemma

Speaking of prescriptions, Mam was out of sleeping tablets – she was eating them like Smarties – so I hopped into the car and as always the nice man in the white coat was standing behind the counter.

'Hi, Gemma,' he said. 'Not Maureen. Gemma. It'll seem natural after a bit of practice. Look at how they changed Jif to Cif – for a while everyone felt like a bit of a thick saying it, but now it's second nature.'

'And Oil of Ulay to Oil of Olay,' I agreed. 'Are you ever not here?'

He thought about it for a moment. 'No.'

'But why? Can't you get another pharmacist to help you?'

'I have someone – my brother. But he was in a motorbike accident.'

Pause where I made a sympathetic noise even though I didn't know the brother. 'When was that?'

'October.'

'God, ages ago.'

'And it'll be ages still before he's better. He wrecked his leg.'

More sympathetic noises.

'And it's impossible to get a locum.'

'But do you have to do such long hours? Couldn't you just shut up shop early?'

'Everyone knows we stay open till ten. Remember that first night when you came here? What if we'd been closed?'

I shut my eyes at the thought. One mad mammy on my hands and no way of defusing her. He had a point.

'I don't get out much either.' I didn't want him to feel he was the only one. 'Coming here counts as a social event.'

'How so?' He was very curious and who'd blame him, I'd have been bored out of my skull too, sitting in that shop, reading the back of Anadin boxes. So I told him the whole story – like the *whole* story – the phone call, Colette's highlights, Dad's sideburns, Mam's 'heart attack' and the amount of television I now watched.

Then someone came in looking for eye-drops and I left him to it.

I O

Because I'm an only child it was inevitable that I'd end up taking care of an aged parent. But I wasn't ready, not yet. I'd thought it was a long fuzzy way off in the future and the hazy picture always included a man to share the burden with me. Furthermore, I thought the absent parent would have the decency to be dead, not shacked up with their secretary. Well, the best laid plans and all that.

In a shockingly short time my old life was flat-lining. Although I admired it from afar – my flat, my friends, my independence – it was easier to just give in to Mam. And, to be honest, without Dad I felt the need to cling to the one parent I had.

Totally without my meaning to, me and Mam got into a routine, which mostly consisted of us being stuck in the house, like two oddballs. I was allowed out to go to work – or the chemist for her prescriptions – then I came home, sat on the couch with her and every night we watched the same sequence of programmes: a double bill of *The Simpsons*, an hour of *Buffy*, then the nine o'clock news.

If I had to work late she watched the programmes on her own, then related the events to me when I returned. At weekends we watched *Midsomer Murders* or *Morse*, the kind of things she used to watch with Dad and the weird thing was that even though I was never alone, I was terribly lonely.

Mam and I had little to say to each other. Sometimes she would say, 'Why do you think he went?'

'Probably because of Uncle Leo and Auntie Margot dying so close together.'

'My heart is broken over Leo and Margot too,' she said. 'And you don't see me having an affair.'

'Well, maybe it's because he's going to be sixty in August. People often go mad when it's a birthday with a nought on the end of it.'

'I was sixty two years ago and who did I have an affair with?'

We were holding out for Dad to return and life had become a vigil, although we never acknowledged it as such. Mum no longer cooked, so we subsisted on crackers, pâté and Baileys. If I got up off the couch to make my wees she looked alarmed and I felt guilty.

No one could believe it when I couldn't get Dad to come home. 'But you can fix anything,' Cody said.

'Apart from my own love life.' I wasn't being self-deprecatory, merely saving him from saying it.

Things weren't going great at work either. While I hadn't actually lost any accounts (Aaargh! What a thought, a definite Room With No Windows offence.) I hadn't brought in any new business either and Frances and Francis weren't best pleased because, as they reminded me almost daily, I had to grow my turnover every year by fifteen per cent. (It was only ten per cent until last year but they've their eye on a holiday home in Spain.)

'New business isn't going to come to you,' Frances growled. 'You've got to hunt it down, Gemma. Hunt it down like a dog.'

The thing was I'd lost my spark. My whole business depends on me being up and 'on'. When I take human resources people of big companies to lunch they have to be dazzled by my energy and be certain that their next conference would be a special, glittering, fun affair that couldn't help but reflect well on them.

People worried about me, Cody in particular. 'You never come out any more. It's not like you to just give up.'

'I haven't. It's only till Dad comes home. In my head I've given him two months to cop on, and it's only been six weeks.'

'What if he doesn't come back?'

'He will.' I was hanging my hopes on several things, especially that there had been no more solicitor's letters about the 'permanent financial settlement'.

'If your mother won't go out, you'll have to leave her on her own.'

'I *can't*. She starts crying and hyperventilating. It's easier to just stay in. She won't even go to Mass. She says that religion is all nonsense.'

Cody was appalled. 'I mean, she's right of course, but I didn't know things were that bad. I'm coming over.'

He called around, sat with Mam and said, 'Now listen, Maureen, sitting here isn't going to bring him back.'

'Neither is going to ballroom dancing, or playing bridge.'

'Maureen, life goes on.'

'It doesn't for me.'

He gave up after a while and out in the hall he said with a certain degree of admiration, 'She can really dig her heels in, can't she?'

'I told you. Stubborn as a bloody mule.'

'I see now where you get it from. Any new chocolate? Whoops.' Theatrically he clapped a hand over his mouth. 'No, I suppose there isn't. And by the looks of your mammy she's eaten the slush pile.'

'Oi –' I started to object but he interrupted firmly and placed his palm on his chest.

'Cody Cooper, keeping it real. Telling it like it is because someone has to. She was an attractive woman, your mother, in a kind of fifties, Debbie Reynolds way. And what's happened to her hair?'

'Roots, that's all it is, roots. She won't go to the hairdresser.' I'd been measuring Dad's absence by their length. They were far too long.

'She's gone to hell.' Cody paused for impact. 'And you might too. Think on.'

Then, like the caped crusader, he was gone, and I didn't

want to think about what he'd said about me so I thought about my mother instead.

You don't look at your parents the way you look at other people, but I supposed Mam had been kind of cute, in a roundy sort of way. Curvy calves, smooth upper arms, a neat little waist and small soft hands and feet. (I take after her, which is a shame because that sort of body is currently very unfashionable.) For a long time she'd looked younger than Dad and I couldn't really pinpoint when the changeover happened but she didn't any more. Until the current crisis, she'd got her hair done regularly – obviously not in a feather shag or the like, the only way I knew she'd been was that it was more shiny and rigid than usual, but the point is she tried. And she loved clothes – I need hardly point out it was stuff I wouldn't wear if my life depended on it: appliquéd cardigans or blouses with sparkly buttons. But she loved them and got an especial kick out of bagging a bargain. At Sales time, she'd set off into town on her own on the bus and always came home triumphant. 'It was like the end of the world in there – old hags pushing and digging their elbows into me – but I gave them a run for their money.'

Gleefully she'd display the spoils of her trip; she'd spread stuff out on her bed and invite me to guess how much it cost.

'God, I dunno.'

'Go on, guess!'

'Before or after the sale?'

'Before.'

'Seventy-five.'

'Seventy-five? It's wool!'

'A hundred.'

'More.'

'One-fifty.'

'Less.'

'One-thirty.'

'Yes! And now guess how much I got it for.'

'Forty?'

'Ah come on now, Gemma, that's not playing the game.'

'A hundred.'

'Less, less!'

'Ninety?'

'Less.'

'Seventy?'

'You're getting warm.'

'Sixty?'

'More.'

'Sixty-five?'

'Yes! Half price. And it's wool!'

This had to be done with each item she'd bought and Dad always shared in her delight. 'That's very nice, love.' And he often said to me, in all sincerity, 'Gemma, your mother is an elegant woman.'

Is it any wonder I was so surprised when he left her?

Mind you, she'd make *him* go through the whole price-guessing thing too, so maybe it wasn't that much of a surprise.

TO: Susan_inseattle@yahoo.com
FROM: Gemma 343@hotmail.com
SUBJECT: Disloyal cow

Do you know what? Andrea comes running up to me at work and goes, all shiny-eyed, 'I read that book Lily Wright wrote!' Like she should get a medal or something for reading it. She said she loved it, that it put her in great form. Then she must have seen my face because she shut up. God, people are thick.

Neither Mam nor I have clapped eyes on Dad since the day I threw the tiramisu bar at him. He hasn't rung either of us – not once. Can you credit it? The only times I get to talk to him is when I ring his work and Colette isn't there to lie and say he's at the dentist. He never comes to the house to get his clothes, his post, nothing. He asked me to forward his letters and I refused because I wanted to use it as leverage to get him round here and see us.

But he still wouldn't come. He said, 'Ah, sure, it's only bills and stuff, not that important.'

I paused before writing the next bit. The bit where I told Susan how, every morning for the past fortnight, I've been waking at 5 a.m. Wondering what was going to happen – while the panic nearly choked me. I was thirty-two and my life looked finished. When would things get back to normal? I had no relationship – no escape route. And with the life I was living, I was never likely to. Either Dad came back, or . . . or what?

Something *had* to change.

But nothing worked with Dad. Not apologies or promises, not anger or appealing to his sense of responsibility. 'Dad,' I'd said, 'please help me, I can't cope. It's Mam, she's just not equipped for . . . life without you.'

'It's bound to be tough, but she'll get used to it.' His tone was still gentle but alarmingly uninvolved. He didn't care.

The innocence was all gone, it had turned dirty and corrupted. When I was young I thought my dad could fix *anything*. Auntie Eilish used to tell a joke – at the time, daringly blasphemous: 'What's the difference between God and Noel Hogan? Gemma doesn't think God is Noel Hogan.'

But it was a different world now. No magic solutions. I couldn't bear it. Especially because I used to be a right daddy's girl. Every day until I was about four, he'd come home from work and hand-in-hand we'd walk to the shops with my pram and Tiny Tears to get his cigarettes.

Now all that closeness was gone for ever and I'd never be his little girl again. He'd found someone else and though I knew it was stupid and irrational, I felt rejected. What was so wrong with me that he had to take up with someone only four years older?

Mam was right – it was like he was dead, only worse.

My greatest fear of all was that Colette would get pregnant. That would really copperfasten this whole sorry mess and we'd *never* be able to go back to the way things used to be.

The sad thing is that all my life I'd wanted a sibling. Be careful what you wish for.

Each time I spoke to Dad I felt like gawking with fear in case he said, 'You're going to have a little sister or brother.' Was it on the cards? I was afraid to ask because it might put ideas in his head but I was never much good at endurance so I rang and said, 'Dad, there's something I want you to do for me.'

'Is it your grass?' he replied. 'Because it won't need to be cut until April, and the mower is in the shed.'

'If Colette gets pregnant . . .' I deliberately left a pause for him to jump in and bluster that nothing of the sort would happen. But he didn't. I forced myself through the dread. 'If she gets up the pole, I want you to ring me. You hear me? Do you think you could possibly manage that?'

'Ah, Gemma, don't be like that.'

I sighed, regretting my spite. 'Sorry. But you'll tell me?'

'I will.'

So even though it hurt that he never rang me, it was also kind of a relief.

Back to Susan.

I have also become fixated with the idea of owning a Hello Kitty toaster. It's so cute, and – get this – it puts the Hello Kitty face on the slices of toast.

I've managed to get Internet access software onto Dad's crappy old PC. Multi-talented and all as my ball and chain (communicator brick) is, it can't give me colour pictures of Hello Kitty toasters.

Wish me luck.

Love
Gemma

PS it is now six weeks since Dad left and Mam is doing great. She's lost three stone, got blonde highlights, a discreet face-lift and a thirty-five-year-old boyfriend. They are going on holiday together to Cap Ferrat. She's still refusing to learn to drive but it doesn't matter because her new man (Helmut, he's Swiss) always sends a car for her or else picks her up in his red Aston Martin with gull-wing doors.

I pressed 'send' then turned on Dad's old computer. I would track down a Hello Kitty toaster on the Internet, or die in the attempt.

'What are you doing?' Mam came into the room and stood looking over my shoulder as I clicked and typed.

'Looking for a Hello Kitty toaster.'

'Why?'

'Just . . .' I was scrolling down the merchandise with fierce concentration, 'I read that Reese Witherspoon has one.'

Mam paused, then said, 'If Reese Witherspoon jumped off a cliff, would you do it too?'

TO: Susan_inseattle@yahoo.com
FROM: Gemma 343@hotmail.com
SUBJECT: A black day

The last of Dad's free confectionery is gone. Perhaps this will shake Mam out of the rut she's in. Not so much stuck in a rut, as lying down in it, almost buried by chocolate.

Yes, of course I was joking about her transformation! God Almighty. I don't think she's got out of her candlewick dressing-gown since the morning Dad left and she still hasn't surrendered his porridge bowl. And as for losing three stone, I'd say it's three stone the other way. She won't stop eating chocolate, she says she 'feels closer' to Dad by consuming what his company makes.

Love
Gemma

PS I've ordered the toaster and now I want a Barbie rucksack.

PPS Helmut has bouffant blondish hair (very similar to Mam's), a permanent tan and a tall lithe body which I find curiously repellent. He uses La Prairie products, the really, really expensive skin-caviar stuff. He left a jar in the bathroom, so of course I used some and the following day he confronted me about what he called 'the stealing'. Naturally I denied it, but he said he knew it was me, that I'd left the shape of my finger in the jar and that no one but a savage just sticks their hand in and gouges out a lump of La Prairie skin caviar.

I objected to being called a savage, so I told on him to Mam. She was sitting up in bed wearing a silk, oyster-coloured negligee and eating breakfast – one slice of wholemeal toast with an invisible scraping of honey. Her hair and make-up were already done. I made my complaint.

'Oh darling,' she sighed. She never used to call me 'darling'. 'I do wish you two would stop fighting over me and try to get along.'

'I don't know what you see in him!'

'Well, darling.' She quirked a plucked eyebrow at me – when did Mam begin getting her eyebrows plucked? And then quirking them? 'Let's just say he's . . . veeerrry gooood between the sheets.'

'Too much information! I am your daughter.'

She got out of bed. Her negligee barely covered her bottom. She has very good legs for a sixty-two-year-old woman. Although she's begun telling people that she's only forty-nine and saying that she'll be celebrating the big five-oh next year.

I pointed out that if she's only forty-nine, then she was sixteen when she had me. 'I was a child bride, darling.'

'It means Dad was only thirteen.'

'Who?' She smiled absently.

'Dad. My father. The man you married.'

'Oh,' she gave a little wave of her hand, which managed to be dismissive and pitying of Dad.

TO: Susan_inseattle@yahoo.com
FROM: Gemma 343@hotmail.com
SUBJECT: I'm living in a fantasy world

I've written a little story. I thought you might like to read it.

Noel Hogan was quietly watching the golf when another almighty crash in the room overhead made the fake chandelier sway. Geri and Robbie were wrecking the place above but he was too tired to go up and give out to them. Not that it would make any difference, they'd only laugh at him. He turned his attention back to the golf and told himself it was normal for children to hurl television sets off their bunkbeds.

Colette had left him babysitting while she went into town. She'd said it was a good opportunity for him to build bridges with the psychotic little bastards (his words, not hers), but he couldn't shake a suspicion that she just wanted to go round the shops without having children hanging out of her.

After a while he noticed that the crashing noises had stopped. Feck it. Now what? His heart sank as the door opened and Robbie and Geri slid into the room, each as evil-looking as the other. Funny how they were both the image of their mother and she wasn't evil-looking at all. Was she . . . ?

Geri picked up the remote and idly changed the station.

'I was watching that,' Noel said.

'Tough bananas. It's not your flat.'

Geri flicked through the channels, discarding anything of interest until she found what seemed to be a state funeral of a cardinal; slow moving and dirgy.

They sat in silence, listening to the tuneless chanting, until Robbie remarked, 'We hate you.'

'Yeah, you're not our dad.'

'More like our grandad. Except older.'

More silence. Noel couldn't tell them that he hated them too. He was still trying to win them over.

'She's out there spending your money,' Geri said. 'It's the only reason she's with you. She's going to buy lovely things for her and me and Robbie and our dad, then when she's spent it all, she's going to break it off with you. If you're still alive.'

Geri's spiteful remarks struck a chord. Colette *was* going through the greenbacks at a ferocious rate.

'Have some chocolate.' Children loved chocolate.

'Nah, that stuff's shit. We only like Ferrero Rochers.'

Eventually he heard Colette's key in the door. Thank God. She came in and threw what looked like dozens of Marks and Spencer carrier bags on the table.

'Hello, love.' She kissed Noel on the nose. 'I,' she teased, 'have a little present for you.'

Pork pies! Noel thought. Marks and Spencer full-fat ones, the nicest you could get. What a woman! He'd been right to leave his lovely, loyal wife of thirty-five years for her.

Colette reached into the bag and slowly pulled out something. It crackled like the wrapping on a packet of pork pies – but it wasn't pork pies. It was a bra. Black and turquoise nylon. Fancy. Then the hand went in again and out came matching knickers.

'Nice pants,' he said gamely.

'Not pants.' Playfully Colette threw the scrap of lace at him and it draped itself on his head, disturbing his comb-over and making his wispy hairs all staticy. 'A *thong*!'

A thong. Noel knew what a thong meant. It meant she'd be looking for the ride tonight. Again. But first they'd have to have the fashion show, her parading up and down in her fancy pants, shoving her bottom at him, doing the dance she did around the trouser press, in the absence of a pole. Every bloody night.

She was insatiable and he was exhausted.

'Anything else in the bag?' he asked, still hoping for the pork pies.

'There certainly is!' She slid out a matching suspender belt.

Noel nodded miserably. He was mad to have thought she'd get him pork pies. She'd never allow him to have one ever again. She said he was old and clapped out and his arteries were mink-lined.

But this healthy low-fat diet she had him on was killing him.

THE END

What'cha think? Could it really be like that? Wouldn't it be great? I'd give anything for him to come home.

It was time for my visit to Johnny the Scrip. He was in conversation with a woman who was buying something for a chesty cough.

'Here's Gemma, she'll know.'

'Know what?'

'How much money should you bring with you for a weekend in Paris?'

'Plenty,' I said. 'Tons.'

'He thinks four hundred,' Mrs Chesty Cough nodded at Johnny.

'Oh, at *least*. They've lovely shoes in Paris. And jewellery. And clothes. And think of the meals out.' Dear God! 'I'd *love* to go to Paris.'

'So would I,' Johnny said.

Our eyes met. 'I'll take you,' he said. 'For a couple of weeks.'

'How about a month?' With that we both creased over with uncontrollable laughing.

Smiling, Chesty Cough watched us. But when Johnny and I looked up from our mirth, saw each other and doubled over again with renewed vigour, her smile wilted. 'What's so funny?'

'Nothing,' Johnny gasped. 'Nothing at all.' That was the whole point.

TO: Susan_inseattle@yahoo.com
FROM: Gemma_343@hotmail.com
SUBJECT: Hit me, baby, one more time

Guess what? The Owen youth rang again. He said he was looking at his leg and felt that something was missing, which he then realized was the huge bruise I'd given him when I pushed him out of bed that time. He wondered if there was any chance of a repeat performance and he must have got me at a vulnerable time because I said yes. Details to be finalized. I don't know how I'm going to get it past Mam, but I'll think of something. And I plan to enjoy myself . . .

Love
Gemma

It was good that I was going out. The hours at home with Mam were having a detrimental effect on my grasp of reality. I couldn't stop speculating on everything going wrong for Dad and Colette, and then writing little essays about it. It was the only thing that gave me comfort. I constructed a vivid imaginary world where, amongst other things, Colette refused to do any work now that she was living with Dad, Dad gets into trouble with his higher-ups and gradually begins to come to his senses.

I so badly wanted Mam and Dad to get back together. It was horrible being from a broken home, even though I was thirty-two.

Instead of the film director-farmer fantasy, I spent my sleepless early mornings imagining scenarios plucked from various romances, where Mam and Dad ended up being thrown back together. I was very fond of the one where on some pretext – say, a mutual old friend's birthday – they have to go on a long journey together but the car breaks down and they end up in a cottage in the middle of nowhere and there's a big storm and the electricity fails and they hear a funny noise and have to sleep in the same bed for safety.

But my favourite was the one where Dad dropped in to Mam, ostensibly to collect his post. Her hair was done, her make-up was discreet and flattering and she was wearing a sarong and bathing suit. She looked great.

'Noel,' she said, with a warmth that confused him. 'How nice to see you. I was just about to have lunch. Would you like to join me?'

'Aah, depends. What are you having?'

'Toasted cheese and ham sandwiches and a bottle of wonderfully dry chardonnay.'

'Colette won't let me have cheese.'

'And Helmut thinks I'm a vegetarian,' she said dryly.

'That stymies that then.'

'Really?' A slow wicked grin spread across Mam's face. 'Let's be naughty. I won't tell if you won't.'

'Right, so.'

'As it's such a beautiful day let's take it out to the patio.'

They sat at the little table and the sun smiled down. Bees buzzed fatly in and out of the swaying magenta foxgloves. Mam wore Chanel sunglasses and her lipstick didn't come off when she ate her sandwich. Dad gazed at the lovely mature garden that had once been his pride and joy before he got lured away by thongs. 'I'd forgotten what a suntrap this is.'

'I haven't.' Mam extended a toned tanned leg. 'The Kilmacud Riviera, my dear. So tell me everything. How's life with Claudette?'

'Colette.'

'Oh I *am* sorry. Colette. Going well, is it?'

'Fine.' Said dolefully. 'How's life with Helmut?'

'Peachy. More sex than I know what to do with.'

'Er . . . aye.'

'Sex,' Mam said dismissively, sucking cheese from her fingers. 'It's all they think about, young people. You'd think they'd just invented it. It's rather pathetic.'

'Aye. They'd have you worn out.' Suddenly the words began to pour out of Dad. 'What's wrong with just a snuggle? Why does it always have to be the full business? Why can't I go to bed and for once just GO TO SLEEP?'

'Quite. A dreadful bore.'

They sat in silence. (Companionable, of course.)

'And Claudette's two little ones? How are they? Lots of energy at that stage, haven't they?'

'Aye.' Said grimly.

'Little shits, actually.'

'Aye.' He looked at her in surprise. She hadn't always been that salty, had she?

'And it only gets worse. Wait until that young madam hits adolescence! Then she'll really keep you on your toes!'

Noel couldn't be more on his toes if he was a prima ballerina and suddenly the thought of returning Chez Colette plunged him into darkest despair.

'I'd better go. I've to collect Geri from hip-hop.'

Out in the hall, he nearly left without his post, until Mam reminded him.

'You'd forget your own head if it wasn't attached,' she said affectionately. In the shade of the hall and the splashy blues and greens of her bathing suit, she looked like the girl he'd married.

'Lovely to see you,' she said, kissing him on the cheek. 'Do give my best to Claudette. And remember,' she said with a roguish smile. 'About the cheese – I won't tell if you won't. It'll be our little secret.'

JOJO

12

Manoj stuck his head around the door. 'Jojo, Keith Stein is here.'

'Who's Keith Stein?'

'Photographer from *Book News*. To accompany the piece on you.'

'Oh right. Two minutes,' Jojo said. She swung her feet off the desk and tossed aside the crossword which was making her crazy. From her hair she slid out the ballpoint which had been holding it in a makeshift up-do. The auburn waves tumbled to her shoulders.

'Why, Miss Harvey, you're beautiful,' Manoj said. 'Except your mascara's gone flaky.'

He passed her her handbag. 'Put your best face forward.'

Jojo needed no encouragement. Every one in publishing read the questionnaire in *Book News*; it was the first thing they went to.

She snapped open her compact and reapplied her trademark vamp-red lipstick. She wished it wasn't her trademark; she'd love to wear pale pink lipgloss and great neutral taupes. But the one time she'd come to work in 'Crushed sorbet', people looked at her oddly. Mark Avery told her she was looking 'a little peaky' and Richie Gant had accused her of having a hangover.

Same with the hair; it just didn't suit her any other way. Too long and she looked like an unkempt ceramicist, and too short, well . . . In her early twenties, shortly after she'd arrived in London, she'd got what she'd thought was a gamine crop and the next time she went into a pub, the barman looked at her suspiciously and demanded, 'What age are you, sonny?'

That had been it for the short-hair experiment – and the fresh-faced look.

'More mascara,' Manoj suggested.

'You're so gay,' Jojo said, indulgently.

'And you're so politically incorrect. I mean it about the mascara. Two words: Richie Gant. Let's sicken him.'

Jojo found she was applying her mascara with renewed vigour.

After a speedy colour-by-numbers circuit through the rest of her face – blush, concealer, glow – Jojo pulled the brush through her hair a final time and was good to go.

'Very sexy, boss. Very noir.'

'Send him in.'

Laden with equipment, Keith came into the office, stopped and laughed out loud. 'You look like Jessica Rabbit!' he said in admiration. 'Or that red-head from the fifties movies. What's her name?' He stamped his foot a few times. 'Katharine Hepburn? No.'

'Spencer Tracy?'

'Wasn't he a bloke?'

Jojo gave in. 'Rita Hayworth.'

'Yes! Anyone ever say that to you before?'

'No,' she smiled. 'No one.' He was so bright-eyed it was hard to be mean.

Keith unloaded his camera equipment, surveyed the tiny book-lined room, considered Jojo, then looked around again. 'Let's do something a bit different,' he suggested. 'Instead of the usual shot of the desk and you sat behind it like Winston Churchill, let's sex it up a bit.'

Jojo stared stonily at Manoj. 'What have you been saying to him? For the last time, read my lips. I am NOT taking my top off.'

Keith lit up. 'Would you be prepared to do that? It would be very discreet. Two carefully placed thumbs and –'

A look from Jojo silenced him abruptly and when he spoke again he was a little less buoyant. 'This is a great desk you have here, Jojo. What about lying on it, on your side, giving a big wink?'

'I'm a literary agent. Have a little respect!' And she was too tall; she'd spill over the ends.

'I've an idea,' Manoj said. 'How about we copy that famous shot of Christine Keeler? You know it?'

'Where she's sat backwards on a kitchen chair?' Keith said. 'Classic pose. Nice one.'

'She was naked.'

'You don't have to be.'

'OK.' Jojo guessed it was better than sprawling full-length on her desk, resting her elbow on empty air. Let's get this done; she had tons of work and she'd already wasted half an hour on the crossword.

Manoj went racing off and returned with a kitchen chair, which Jojo straddled, feeling like a dumbass.

'Fantastic.' Keith knelt before her to start snapping. 'Big smile, now.' But before he pressed the shutter, he lowered the camera from his face and got to his feet again. 'You don't look very comfortable,' he said. 'It's your suit. Could you take off your jacket? Only your jacket,' he added quickly.

Jojo didn't want to, not at work. Her pinstriped suit held her like a safety harness and, without it, she felt way too busty. Released from the confines of the jacket her body's behaviour made her think of a spilt mug of coffee – so much comes out it was impossible to believe that once upon a time, it had all fitted in. But her boobs would be hidden by the chairback so she slipped the jacket off and restraddled the chair, pulling its back to her chest.

'One other thing,' Keith said, 'could you roll up the sleeves of your shirt? And open just one more button at the neck. Just one, that's all I'm asking for. And, you know, shake your hair about, loosen up a little.'

'Think sultry,' Manoj urged.

'Think dole queue, you.'

'Let's get going,' Keith interrupted. 'Jojo, eyes to me.' SNAP! 'They were saying back in the office that you used to be a cop in New York before you got into this game. Is that right?'

SNAP!

'What is *with* you guys?' They all loved that she'd been a cop. Even Mark Avery admitted to sexy imaginings of Jojo kicking down doors, snapping on the cuffs and murmuring, 'I'm taking you in.' 'Like, don't you have any women police of your own?'

'It's not the same here, they have flat shoes and minger hair. So you really were one?'

'For a couple of years.'

SNAP!

'Cool.'

Not cool. It was a shitty job and she blamed TV for making it look glamorous.

'Ever kick any doors down?'

'Hundreds.'

SNAP!

'Ever go undercover?'

'Oh, always. I had to seduce Mafia bosses. Sleep with them and get all their secrets.'

'REALLY?'

SNAP!

'No.' She laughed.

'Hold that look. Ever get shot at?'

SNAP!

'Always.'

'Tilt the head slightly. Ever shoot someone?'

SNAP!

'Yeah.'

'Big smile now. Ever kill someone?'

SNAP! SNAP! SNAP!

Later Monday afternoon
Keith left, Jojo fastened herself back into her jacket and was about to start work when Manoj buzzed her.

'Eamonn Farrell on the line.'

'What now?'

'Apparently Larson Koza got a blinding review in today's *Independent* and why didn't he? Shall I jerk him off and get rid of him?'

'You love saying that. I should never have taught it to you. No, put him through.'

With a click, Eamonn's rage streamed down the phone line and into the room. 'Jojo, I've had it with this Koza fucker.'

He let it all out as Jojo 'Uh-huh'd sympathetically and scanned her emails. One from Mark; she'd save it until she was off the phone.

'. . . plagiarism . . . I was the first . . .' Eamonn was saying. '. . . owes everything to me . . . thinks it's all about image . . . good-looking prick . . .' Jojo held her receiver away from her head for a second, just to see if it was foaming. On he went. 'And d'you know what they called him? "A Young Turk." *I'm* the Young fucking Turk around here.'

Poor guy, Jojo thought. She'd been here before with other authors. After their first flush of joy at being published, the craven gratitude dissipated to make room for jealousy. Suddenly they noticed they weren't the only new writers in the world – there were others! Who got good reviews and high advances! It was hard to take on board, especially for someone like Eamonn who had enjoyed a lot of early success. He'd been described as a 'Young Turk', a wunderkind. Now it was cuckoo-in-the-nest Larson Koza who was getting the plaudits.

Eamonn drew his rant to a close.

'So what are you going to do about it? Let's not forget you're walking around with twenty-five thousand pounds of my money in commission.'

I wish.

She had got Eamonn an advance of a quarter of a million pounds for his book. One of her biggest deals and pretty impressive by most standards – especially as Young Turks got great reviews but didn't tend to sell in commercial quantities.

'That ten per cent you're skimming off me is paying your salary.'

That's where you're wrong, buddy. Jojo didn't get any of it. You had to be a partner before you pocketed a percentage of any deal; even so it was never more than five.

But she kept it zipped. He was angry and insecure and she didn't take it personally. Anyway, a few more insults later, he stopped abruptly and said, 'Aw, Jojo, I'm sorry, I'm as sorry as anything. I'm a stupid bastard, doing this to you. It's just the competition is so fierce in this business, worse than any other, it really gets to me.'

He'd want to try being an agent, she thought. Then he'd really know about competition. But all she said was, 'I know, I totally understand. Don't even think about it.'

'You're a gem, Jojo Harvey. The best. Can you forget all that shite I said?'

'It's forgotten.'

TO: Jojo.harvey@LIPMAN HAIGH.co
FROM: Mark.avery@LIPMAN HAIGH.co
SUBJECT: Miss

Miss *(v.)* 1. Feel the want of. 2. Not have. 3. Notice esp with regret the absence of ~ e.g. I miss you.
M xx

TO: Mark.avery@LIPMAN HAIGH.co
FROM: Jojo.harvey@LIPMAN HAIGH.co
SUBJECT: Tough

Tough *(adj.)* 1. Hard, severe, unpleasant ~ e.g. tough luck, you
shouldn't have gone away for whole week to book fair. (Joke *(n.)*
1. Thing said or done to excite laughter.)
JJ xx

PS I notice esp with regret the absence of you too.

Ten minutes later
Manoj buzzed again. 'On the line we have your cousin Becky,
who looks like you, only not so fabulous, if the photo on your
desk is anything to go by. I think she wants to hook up with
you tonight, she was muttering brokenly about Pizza Express.
And if you ladies are requirous of male company, I'd be happy
to cancel your order with the male escort agency and volunteer
myself. Do you accept or decline this call?'

'Put her through.'

'No, you have to say, "I accept".'

Jojo sighed. 'I accept.'

14

Most people had already gone home when Jojo started to fill in the *Book News* questionnaire.

Name
Jojo Harvey

Age
32

Career path?
Three years in the NYPD (no, really). A few months barmaiding when I first came to London, six months as reader in Clarice Inc. before being promoted to assistant, then junior agent. Made full agent four years ago and moved to Lipman Haigh Agents a year and a half later.

What's your favourite smell?
Mark Avery

Jojo scribbled, wishing she could inhale him right then.

No, wait; she could *not* write that. Quickly she scored so many lines through it the page almost tore. What had others put? A quick flick through previous editions showed that some bow-tied old guy had written 'the agèd must of a rare first edition'. Another, his tie even bigger and floppier, 'the fresh ink of a new author's first novel'.

Richie Gant (no tie at all because who wears ties with a T-shirt) had written 'Money' and his crassness had had all of publishing buzzing. But, Jojo thought reluctantly, she had to admire the guy's honesty . . .

Next question.

What makes you depressed?
Richie Gant

A pause, then more heavy pen scoring.

What's your motto?
Richie Gant must die!

Nope, couldn't put that either.

Jesus. She'd wanted, really badly, to be asked to do this questionnaire, but it was way harder than she had expected.

Which living person do you most admire?
Mark Avery

Which living person do you most despise?
Mark Avery's wife? No, no, no. It's got to be me – see next question.

What traits do you dislike most in others?
Women who hit on married men.

What would you change about yourself?
Apart from my boyfriend having a wife and two children?

How about her perfectionism, she wondered. Her tenacity? No, she thought: it had to be her calves. They were too hefty and leather knee-boots were a no-no for Jo-jo. Even stretchy sock boots were a bit of a struggle. A common enough complaint perhaps, but on Jojo, the zip wouldn't go all the way up even on ankle boots. Worst still, she insisted her calves had the mottled consistency of corned beef. As a result she nearly always wore tailored trouser suits to work. They had become her trademark. (Another goddam one.)

How do you unwind?
Sex with Mark Avery. Or, if he's not around, a bottle of Merlot and a wildlife programme, especially the ones about baby seals.

What makes you cry?
A bottle of Merlot and a wildlife programme, especially the ones about baby seals.

Do you believe in monogamy?
Yes. Yeah, I know, how can I? I'm a hypocrite. But I never meant for this thing with Mark to happen. I'm not that kind of person.

Which book do you wish you had agented?

Easy, she thought, not that she'd ever fess up, even under torture. It was *Fast Cars*, the current talk of the town. A great novel except that Richie Gant was the agent – not Jojo – and he'd secured a £1.1 million advance at auction. Jojo had had similar coups but nothing as high and she had been disgustingly envious even before Richie Gant made a special trip down the hall to her office to wave the contract at her and crow, 'Read it and weep, Yank.'

Where do you see yourself in five years' time?
As a partner in Lipman Haigh Agents. And hopefully a lot sooner than five years. Like, as soon as someone retires.

At Lipman Haigh there were seven partners – five based in London and two in the Edinburgh satellite. Then there were a further eight agents who weren't partners, and while there was no way of knowing who the board would pick to replace the next retiree, Jojo had hopes that it might be her. Although there were three agents who'd been there longer than she had, she brought in a lot of income to the agency – for the last two years she'd generated more than any of the other agents.

What's your favourite phrase?
What doesn't kill us makes us funnier.

What are your distinguishing qualities?
I can whistle for a taxi and swear in Italian. I do a great Donald Duck impression and I can fix bikes.

What five things could you not live without?
Cigarettes, coffee, vodkatinis, the Simpsons . . . What else? A regular heartbeat? . . . More cigarettes.

What achievement are you proudest of?
Quitting smoking. I think. It hasn't happened yet . . .

What's the most important lesson life has taught you?
Bad hair happens to good people.

She paused. This is total crap, she thought, sticking her pen back in her hair where it was more useful. Manoj would have to do it. It was time to meet Becky.

15

8.45 Monday evening

Out on Wardour Street, it was still busy even on an iron-cold night in late January. Jojo clipped along so quickly she caused a homeless man to mutter, 'Where's the fire, love?'

Jojo hurried on, she didn't want to be late for Becky.

Jojo and Becky were very close, as close as sisters. When she first arrived from New York and was earning a pittance, first as a barmaid, then as an agent's reader, Jojo had bunked down in Becky's bedroom. Squashed together in such close quarters, it could have been a bloodbath. Instead they had bonded in a million different ways, thrilled and enchanted by their similarities, despite having been brought up thousands of miles apart. They discovered that their mothers (who were sisters) both kept the plastic coverings on new upholstery for up to a year. And when their daughters were out of line, both mothers said, 'I'm not angry with you, I'm disappointed,' then cuffed them upside the head in a way that looked much more like anger than disappointment.

Becky and Jojo even looked alike. But Jojo, taller and curvier, was like a '25% extra free!' version of Becky. (Although both of them had naturally auburn hair Becky's was short and highlighted to bits and as a result she was almost never accused of looking like Jessica Rabbit.)

After months of living on top of each other, they had eventually moved into a flat where they had a bedroom each and cohabited in harmony for several years, until Jojo bought her own place and Becky met Andy.

Even though Becky was eight months older, Jojo seemed

like the big sister. Somehow she attracted a lot more attention than Becky, who was at heart a gentle soul.

In Pizza Express, Becky was drinking red wine and picking at garlic bread. She waved and beckoned Jojo over.

They hugged, then Becky pulled back and bared her teeth at Jojo in a silent snarl. 'Are my teeth black?'

'No.' Jojo was alarmed. 'Why, are mine?'

'No, but I'm on the red wine. Keep an eye on me.'

'OK, but I will be too, so you'd better keep an eye on me also.'

They scanned the menu and Becky said, 'If I get the Veneziana will you tell me if I get spinach caught in my teeth? Can you *believe* that Mick Jagger once got an emerald set into his teeth? What was he thinking of? Bad enough to have real food trapped in there, but to put something fake . . .'

After they ordered, Jojo said, 'So what's up?'

Becky was an administrator in private health care, responsible for the schemes of large companies, and was going through hell.

'You're not going to *believe* this – she gave me four new clients today.' 'She' was Elise, Becky's boss and tormentor. 'Four! And each of them has dozens of employees, all of them needing health plans. I've more than I can handle already. I've started making stupid mistakes and they're going to get worse because I don't have the time to check my stuff properly.'

'Becky, you've got to tell her it's too much.'

'You can't do that. It makes you look like you can't cope.'

'You've got to.'

'I *can't.*'

'If she's giving you more clients, she must think you're good.'

'No way! She's overloading me so that I'll crack and leave. She's a bitch and I hate her.'

Caught up in the stress of Becky's tale, Jojo produced a box of cigarettes from her bag. 'Back on them.'

'What happened with your acupuncture?'

'Every time I twiddled the pin in my ear, I got a craving for mashed potatoes. Like, *really* bad. But I'm going to be hypnotized on Friday night. One of the partners, Jim Sweetman, gave me the number. He was a forty-a-day man and now he's on his third cig-free week.'

'We all need a vice,' Becky said virtuously.

'I know, but they make it so hard for smokers. If I want to smoke at work I have to stand on the street and sometimes men mistake me for a prostitute.'

Becky swigged some wine, then checked her teeth in her spoon. Upside down but not black. Good. 'I feel better,' she said. 'You can't beat a good vent. Now, your go, Jojo. Share the joy.'

'We...ll, OK, I haven't sold anything in a while. Nothing good has come my way. Like, *nothing* and Skanky Boy Gant has done two big deals in the past two months and it scares the pants off me.'

Becky wagged a finger. 'Now, now, didn't you just do a deal last week? The reason you bought the celebratory Marc Jacobs wallet?'

'Which? Oh that was just for Eamonn Farrell. I'm not talking about my existing authors. I need to keep adding to my client list. If things don't pick up soon I won't make this year's bonus.'

'And then how will you keep yourself in Marc Jacobs wallets? Bonus, my bum. You should get some of the percentage you negotiate. Become a partner!'

'I'm working on it.'

'Are you still talking to the wallet?'

'Not as much.'

'So how's your new guy working out?'

'Manoj? Young, keen, smart as a whip, but . . . well, he's not Louisa. Why did she have to get pregnant and leave me?'

'She'll be back in four months.'

'You think? You don't think she'll love her baby too much to leave it?'

'Louisa? Not bloody likely.'

Louisa was a heel-wearing, vodkatini-drinking, razor-brained babe. She'd knocked off the vodkatinis when she'd got pregnant but not much else had changed.

'I really miss her,' Jojo sighed. 'I've no one to talk to now.' Louisa was the only person at work who knew about her and Mark.

'What does Manoj look like?'

'Oh no, Becky. Oh, no, no, no. Seventy-five pounds, soaking wet. A bit of a fussy britches. Likes me to look great, thinks it's his job to keep me that way.'

'Gay?'

'No.'

'JGE?'

'Huh?'

'Just Gay Enough.'

'Right! And like I say, he's smart. After two weeks, he already knows about me and Richie Gant.'

'Does he know about Mark?'

'No! Are you insane?'

'When's Mark back from the book fair? Where is it this time?'

'Friday. Jerusalem.'

'Why didn't you just go with him?' Becky asked.

'And miss a whole week of work hanging around in a hotel room waiting for him to come back from meetings?' Jojo tried to look indignant but couldn't sustain it. 'Ohmigod, *think* of it. Five whole days in bed. Room service, movies, fresh sheets every day, there's something about hotel sheets . . . But there were too many others from Lipman Haigh going and staying in the same hotel. Someone would have seen us.' Jojo looked at her pizza a little sadly.

Becky offered solidarity by squeezing her hand but there was nothing new to say. Since it had started, about four months ago, they'd analysed the situation so much that sometimes soft-hearted Becky began to regret ever getting involved.

Received wisdom has it that something must have already been lacking in the marriage for Mark to have strayed. But it was different when you were actually *having* an affair, Jojo thought. You can't help but feel ashamed. Well, she couldn't anyway.

But she hadn't liked a man so much in the longest time. Her last boyfriend ('Poor Craig') had become rather needy, then went a tad stalkery when she broke up with him. The relationship before that had started well until the bloke ('Richard the Dick') discovered that Jojo earned more than he did, then the criticism began; the speed she walked at; the fact she wore heels even though she was already five nine; the way she never wore skirts.

'What's the rest of your week like?' Becky asked.

'Tomorrow night, launch party for Miranda England's fourth novel.'

'Oh, will you get me a copy, I love her. And what are you up to on Wednesday night?'

'Ohhh.' Jojo put her face in her hands. 'A dinner. Biography of Churchill launch. Old guys talking Second World War stuff and me face down in my soup, passed out with boredom.'

'Why are you going? That's not one of your books.'

'Dan Swann asked me along.'

'But he's not your boss. Tell him to shove it.'

Jojo laughed at the idea of telling intellectual old Dan to shove anything. 'He's a senior partner *and* he's been real good to me. It's an honour to be asked. Thursday night I'll go to yoga.' A pause. 'Maybe. Friday night I'm going to be hypnotized and Saturday I'll see Mark.'

'So come round on Sunday. Andy says he hasn't seen you in ages.'

'Less than two weeks. Hey, Becky, am I spending too much

time being third wheel with you and Andy? It's just because you're family and you know about Mark so I can talk for as long as I like and you won't tell me to shut up. Well, only sometimes.'

'No way, we love it. Come over and we'll read the papers, eat ice cream and complain.'

'About what?'

'Whatever you like,' she said magnanimously. 'The weather. Your job. The way Creme Eggs have got smaller. The choice is yours.'

An hour later, as they kissed goodnight, Becky asked, 'Are my teeth black?'

'No. Are mine?'

'No.'

'We didn't drink enough. Too bad. See you Sunday.'

16

Tuesday afternoon

TO: Jojo.harvey@LIPMAN HAIGH.co
FROM: Mark.avery@LIPMAN HAIGH.co
SUBJECT: Miss

To pine, yearn, long, wish, want to remove clothing from and sleep with.
M xx

TO: Mark.avery@LIPMAN HAIGH.co
FROM: Jojo.harvey@LIPMAN HAIGH.co
SUBJECT: Tough

Hard, harsh, severe, stringent, unpleasant, but has to be endured as result of great stupidity involved in going away to book fair for an entire week.
JJ xx

Wednesday afternoon

TO: Mark.avery@LIPMAN HAIGH.co
FROM: Jojo.harvey@LIPMAN HAIGH.co
SUBJECT: Crossword

I'm stuck.
Attractive affirmative back around ten? Four letters.
JJ xx

TO: Jojo.harvey@LIPMAN HAIGH.co
FROM: Mark.avery@LIPMAN HAIGH.co
SUBJECT: Sexy!

(ten = x in Roman numerals. Affirmative is yes. Yes back is sey. Attractive = sexy.) Please confirm soonest: When will I see you again? When will we share precious moments?
M xx

TO: Mark.avery@LIPMAN HAIGH.co
FROM: Jojo.harvey@LIPMAN HAIGH.co
SUBJECT: When will I see you again?

Saturday, Saturday, Saaaturday, Saturday, Saturday, Saaaturday, Saturday, Saturday, Saturday night's all right. (So is the daytime.)
JJ xx

TO: Jojo.harvey@LIPMAN HAIGH.co
FROM: Mark.avery@LIPMAN HAIGH.co
SUBJECT: Saturday

Good. The bed's too big without you.
M xx

17

Jojo heard them before she saw them – the assistants and readers gathered around the latest *Book News* and exclaiming like a flock of sparrows.

Pam was the first to spot her.

'Your questionnaire is in!'

'You look great!'

A copy was thrust into her line of vision and Jojo jumped back. The photo! She looked like a fifties B-movie siren – wavy auburn hair swept over one eye, dark pouting lips – and she was winking. Keith had used the winking photo! It had only been a joke and he had promised not to run it.

'Your answers are great. So funny!'

'Thank you,' Manoj said. 'Er . . . on behalf of Jojo.'

What's your favourite smell?
Success

Which living person do you most admire?
Myself

What would you most change about yourself?
My lack of modesty

Which living person do you most despise?
Myself – for my lack of modesty

How do you unwind?
In bed. I like seven hours a night.

What traits do you dislike most in others?
Their filthy minds

What makes you cry?
Chopping onions

What makes you depressed?
My lack of psychic ability

Where do you see yourself in five years' time?
See previous answer

Which book do you wish you had agented?
The Bible

Do you believe in monogamy?
It's a board game, right?

What are your distinguishing qualities?
I can whistle for a taxi and swear in Italian. I do a great Donald Duck impression and I can fix bikes.

The only one of the original answers that Manoj had permitted to remain – not that she'd shared the more personal ones with him.

What five things could you not live without?
Fresh air, sleep, food, a circulatory system – and books

What's your favourite phrase?
Do you take Visa?

What makes you happy?
When the answer is yes.

What's the most important lesson life has taught you?
Nice girls finish last.

It was a good note to end on. Jojo exchanged a wink with Manoj, and Pam watched carefully. She had once tried to copy Jojo's sexy wink – drink had been taken – but she had simply succeeded in dislodging her contact lens which had made her eyelid flutter like a trapped butterfly. By the time she'd managed to calm the spasms the man she'd been trying to hook had bought someone else a Slippery Nipple.

But not everyone was happy for Jojo. On the walk back to her office, she passed Lobelia French and Aurora Hall, who'd been Golden Girls One and Two until Jojo joined. Both of them ignored her. As did Tarquin Wentworth, a so-so agent who'd thought the 'Hon' in front of his name would guarantee automatic partnership – until Jojo's arrival.

Eleven minutes later

Jojo hadn't even started getting her emails when Jocelyn Forsyth, one of the senior partners, rapped on her door and said, 'Permission to enter.'

English as Beefeater gin, he was hitting his palm with his rolled up copy of *Book News*, which he unfurled to display Jojo's picture. 'My dear girl, you're literary Viagra. May I?' He indicated a chair.

Ohmigod. 'Sure.'

He pulled up the knees of his hand-tailored suit and sat down. 'You're quite the comer, aren't you?'

Just then Manoj stuck his head around the door and nodded at Jocelyn. 'Wotcha, Jock. Sorry, Jojo, Eamonn Farrell is on, going mental. He was in Waterstones and they had twelve copies of Larson Koza's book and only three of his. He's talking about changing publishers. Shall I jerk him off and get rid of him?'

'Shall you what?' Jocelyn asked.

'Jerk him off –'

Jojo interrupted. 'It means, like, to humour him and send him away happy. Tell him that there are twelve copies of

Larson Koza's because no one bought any. You know the drill.'

'And what is the provenance of this pithy adage?' Jocelyn asked. 'Your law enforcement days?'

'Um, yeah.'

'Please explain.'

Feeling like a performing seal, Jojo obliged. 'Let's see. Well, people sometimes came by the precinct, kvetching that there weren't enough cops on their street. And they were totally right, there weren't enough to go round. But we'd say, "Don't worry, we've got lots of plain-clothes and undercover. You can't see them but take it from me, they're there." And they went away happy.'

'An exercise in psychology.'

'You got it.'

'Another example please.'

Jojo itched to get to her emails but he was a nice old guy. And a partner.

'Let me think. OK, a woman came into the precinct and said the CIA were spying on her through her plug sockets.'

'Something similar happened to an aunt of mine,' Jocelyn murmured. 'MI5 instead of the CIA, but not a million miles away.'

'That's gotta hurt.'

'I must admit, my dear – and it's not something I'm proud of – I found it terribly funny.'

'OK. Well, my poor woman was a crazy and should have been in the hospital. When we took her home, she lived opposite a dress shop that had, like, mannequins in the window, so we told her that one of the mannequins was a plain-clothes policewoman and she'd look out for her.'

'And she believed this?'

'Sure.'

'I see. "Jerk them off and get rid of them,"' Jocelyn said, rolling the phrase around on his tongue. 'Quite marvellous. I shall use it in future. Well, I must get on, my dear. Needs must, but perhaps you'll join me for lunch some day soon.'

'Sure.'

'I think he likes you,' Manoj said quietly, once he'd left.

'Um.'

'It's good for the senior partners to like you.'

'Um.'

'I bet he wears his vest when he's on the job.'

'You're gross.'

Two minutes later

'Louisa's husband rang,' Manoj said. 'Her waters have broken.'

'What, already? She's not due –'

'Two weeks early,' Manoj confirmed.

Good, Jojo thought. The sooner Louisa had her baby, the sooner she'd be back at her desk, no?

'She'll still take her full maternity leave.' Manoj read her mind. 'They always do. Now, we ought to send flowers.'

'Who's "we", Paleface?'

'You, I mean. Shall I organize it?'

Lunchtime

Manoj had gone out to buy a hot-water bottle and the whole floor was quiet. Jojo was eating an apple and reading Eamonn Farrell's 'difficult second novel'.

She didn't hear anyone come in, but somehow she sensed she was being watched and she jerked her head up from the manuscript.

It was Mark.

'You're back!'

She sat up straight. Happiness, she thought. A positive emotion triggered by seeing Mark Avery.

Which was kind of nuts because, on paper, Mark Avery wasn't so much of a catch. He didn't have the tall, dark and handsome specifications usually required for the role of romantic hero. He was maybe five ten, but seemed shorter because he was bulky. Though his hair was darkish, there was no exotic olive colouring, just ordinary English skin and eyes. But it didn't matter . . .

He was smiling his head off. 'I saw your questionnaire. You're a class act, Jojo.' He softened his voice. 'And seven full hours, eh? Well, I'll do what I can.'

But before she got a chance to reply, there was the sound of chattering – some of the others back from lunch – and Mark was gone. They were so paranoid about being seen together that she was often left talking to his slipstream, the words dying in her mouth.

18

Four seconds later

Jojo felt like jumping up and running after him, bruising her thighs against her desk in her haste – Jesus, she hadn't seen him in a week – but she couldn't.

She tried to resume work, but Eamonn Farrell's difficult second novel suddenly held no charm at all. Not that it had held much to begin with.

Now how am I going to get any work done?

But help was unexpectedly at hand.

Thirteen and a half minutes later

Pam burst in, closed the door and leant against it as though a pack of wild dogs was after her. She was hugging a manuscript tightly to her chest. She jabbed it with her finger and said hoarsely, 'We've got a live one here.'

Pam was Jojo's reader. Each agent had one – it was how Jojo had started in agenting herself. The readers worked their way through the hefty pile of manuscripts that arrived every day at Lipman Haigh Agents. Occasionally they came across a winner but for the most part they had to discard them and write to the authors urging them not to give up their day job.

It made Jojo think of a documentary she'd seen about Rio or Caracas – some Latin American city, anyway – where armies of poverty-stricken people made their living on the city garbage dump. Their days were spent picking through the piles of reeking trash, looking for anything of value to sell or barter with.

'The first three chapters of something called *Love and the Veil*,' Pam said. 'It's great.'

'By who?'

'Nathan Frey.'

'Never heard of him. Gimme.'

Two pages in Jojo was hooked. All her dials were up to ten and she was so psyched she almost forgot to breathe. How lucky was it that it had been Pam and not any of the other readers who had picked it up.

When she finished the three chapters, she leapt up. 'Manoj, call this guy. Tell him we've got to see the rest. Send a bike.'

There was no point offering to represent Nathan Frey until she'd seen the entire book. It wouldn't be the first time that a promising first three chapters had given way to talk of twelve-foot lizards ruling the world, in chapters four and further.

TO: Jojo.harvey@LIPMAN HAIGH.co
FROM: Mark.avery@LIPMAN HAIGH.co
SUBJECT: You

What Jojo gives – a horn blowing around 500.(4–2)
M xx

Jojo doodled with it. Some people have affairs, she thought, and learn Tantric sex. Me, I get tutored in cryptic crosswords.

While she waited for Nathan Frey's book, she scribbled on her pad. 'What Jojo gives – a horn blowing around 500.' Four letters, then two. Linked words. In Roman numerals, 500 was D. 'Blowing around' could indicate an anagram? A horn d? Daho-rn? Horn-ad? Then she got it and laughed. Hard-on.

One (record-breaking) hour and fifty-five minutes later
Manoj placed the entire manuscript in her hands, with as much care as if it were a baby.

'Great. Oh *great*. Thank you.'

'Hold all calls?'

'You're way ahead of me.'

Jojo swung her feet up on her desk and disappeared into the book. It was a beautifully written love story about an Afghani woman and a secret service Brit. *Bravo Two Zero* meets *Captain Corelli*. One of those rare books that had suspense, pathos, humanity and lots of sex.

A long time later

Manoj stuck his head around the door. 'Any lizards?'

'Not yet. Looking good.'

'We're going to the pub now.'

'You shiftless brat.'

'It's Friday night. Come to the pub. I've been here nearly three weeks and you haven't bought me a drink yet. They say you got trousered with Louisa all the time.'

'As if! She's been pregnant for the last nine months. I've got to finish these pages, I'm too far in now to be able to stop.' Especially because she had a great feeling there was going to be a tragic ending – which was likely to guarantee good reviews, possibly even a literary award.

But Manoj was right, she used to go out more with the people from work. Rowdy Friday night vodkatini piss-ups which often ended with the available women going clubbing, scoping for men. But Jojo had met her man . . .

She'd barely started reading again when someone else asked, 'Coming for a drink?'

Jim Sweetman, head of media and the youngest partner.

'Nope.'

'You don't come out any more.'

'Did Manoj send you in here?'

Jim frowned. 'Have I offended you? Did I try to snog you one drunken night?'

'No. And you know how you can tell? Because you still have all your teeth.' She laughed. 'I'm finishing this great, great book then at nine, I'm seeing your hypnotist. To stop smoking, remember?'

'Ah. Good luck.'

'Nice weekend. Bye.'

On she read, for twenty, maybe twenty-five minutes, and then she heard someone say, 'What'cha doing?'

Who now? But it was Mark. Flooded with well-being she smiled her widest smile. 'Reading.'

'When did you learn to do that?'

She tipped back her chair, one foot on her desk and swivelled slightly. It was great to be able to look at him for as long as she wanted. Most times at work she could only allow herself short side-long glances – she probably looked at Mark less than she looked at any of her other co-workers. And even then she feared that someone would pounce. 'Aha! Busted! You were *staring* at Mark Avery. What's going on with you and the Managing Partner?'

'I thought you'd be gone home by now,' she said.

'Stuff to catch up on.'

'How was your book fair?'

'You should have come with me.'

'Oh, should I have?'

A smile spread slowly up to his eyes. 'Don't I get a kiss?'

'I don't know.' She used her foot to swing herself in her chair. 'Do you?'

He came behind her desk and she got to her feet. Arms around his neck, she rested her face against his and took a moment to absorb the sheer relief of his presence; his heat, the hard back-rest of his arms, his smell – not aftershave or cologne, just something unnamed and male. The knot of tension in her gut unwound, and floated free.

Then she moved her head, letting the prickle of his stubble drag gently on her cheek, to find his mouth.

'Jojo,' Mark whispered, his face in her neck. They kissed again while he tried to slide his hand up under her jacket. In her ear his breath was hot and loud and the edge of her desk dug into her hip. Then he had opened her jacket buttons, his hand was on the pillowy softness of her breast and she was jelly-legged with longing.

His erection was pressed against her and his hand was hard on her shoulders, trying to persuade her to the ground. He was strong and determined but Jojo resisted.

'Everyone's gone,' he said, his fingers finding her nipple. 'It's OK.'

'No.' She slid away from him. 'I'll see you tomorrow.'

No matter how badly she wanted him she would not have sex on her office floor. What did he think she was?

19

Even later on Friday evening

Jojo, tell me about your father.
.................................Um.................................... You're kidding, right? ....

Tell me about your father.
.... What are we, in a Woody Allen movie? .... Excuse me, are you hearing me OK? ....

I can hear you perfectly.
So why aren't you talking to me?

We're here for you to talk, not me.
No, wait a minute, what's going on here, I've come to get hypnotized to stop smoking.

I need to know you before I can help you.
No, no you don't. I've seen hypnotists on TV, making people think they were chickens who'd lost their butts. And they'd never met them before in their lives, they knew nothing about them.

I'm a hypnotherapist, not a hypnotist.
There's a difference?

A big one. They are entertainers, possibly even charlatans. I'm a professional.

....
.... Oh ...... my ...... God. You're a shrink.

Do you have a problem with that?
No. Well, yes! I wanted to come here, look deep into your eyes, feel sleepy, then leave and never smoke again.

Smoking is a deep-seated addiction. There are no magic solutions.
....
..........Yeah, well I want a magic solution....................................
So when I leave here tonight I'll still be a smoker?.....................

Correct.
I'll have to come here again next week?

Correct.
And tell you about my pop?

Correct.
Please stop saying correct. How many weeks will I have to come for?

How long is a piece of string?
Not as short as my temper. How many weeks?

Between six and nine is the average.
Thank you.

You seem to have a problem with trust.
I don't have a problem with trust. I have a problem with time.

You can walk out the door right now.
I could, but I've missed *Friends*, I may as well stay. So let's get going! The sooner we start the sooner I'll be a non-smoker. You want to know about Pops. Hey, can I smoke in here? No?....................It was worth a try. OK. Name's Charlie, half Irish, quarter Italian, quarter Jewish. About six three, weighs two-twenty, maybe two-thirty. First he was a cop, then a firefighter. What else is there to say?

What kind of person was he when you were growing up?
Um .... you know, he was just...............Pops.

You're his youngest child and his only daughter. Did he treat you differently to your three brothers?
No way, I was always one of the guys, a fourth son. I didn't find out I was a girl until I was about fifteen!

Why is that funny?
Excuse me?

Why are you laughing? Why is being confused about your gender a matter for humour?
Hey, I give up, I was joking. I just meant I wasn't one of those pretty pretty girls who wore party frocks and never got their hands dirty. Can I chew gum in here? No? *No?*

So what did you wear?
The cigarettes I can understand, but *gum*. And it's not even regular gum, it's Nicorette. Medicinal! I'm not going to stick it under my seat when I leave, you know. What do you say?

So what did you wear?
I'll take that as a no, then, yeah? *Damn.* So what did I wear? Regular stuff – jeans, sneakers. Ski-goggles. Fake tails. Feather boas...
....I'm sorry. Just jeans and sneakers.

Your own?
Some.

Who else's?
My brothers'. Hey, there wasn't so much money and me and my mom didn't care what I wore.

What do your brothers do now?
They're cops.

All three of them?
Um . . . yeah . . .

Your home environment sounds quite a macho one.
Excuse me, I don't think my mom would appreciate hearing that! She's a real lady. If we so much as said 'damn' she smacked us upside the head.

She smacked you upside your head?
.....................................Ahhh.....................................I see what you mean...........................But she didn't want her children cussing. She was trying to teach us values.

Tell me more about your mother.
She's English, her name is Diane, she's a nurse. She met Pops when he was bringing a shooting victim into the hospital.

Having a mother as a nurse must have been nice when you were ill.
Are you kidding me? She said she had to take care of sick people all day at work and she didn't want to do it on her down time. Like, if I fell and cut my knees, she'd say she had a little girl on her ward who had third degree burns on seventy per cent of her body. Or if Pops had a headache, she'd say he should try having his skull bust open with a baseball bat – then she'd offer to do it for him.

So your parents' marriage was an unhappy one?
No! They were crazy about each other. When she said that thing about the baseball bat, she was only kidding.

What happened when you were fifteen? When you found out you were a girl?
Look, I always knew I was a girl, it was just, you know, I was one of the guys....................But when I was fifteen I beat a guy at pool........... D'you want me to say more?........... OK, we had a pool table in our basement at home and I used to play with Pops and my brothers, and they used to *destroy* me. But I guess with all the practice I got good. Then I met this guy and I liked him.

Liked him how?
Liked him, *liked* him. Fancied him.

Was this your first crush?
Noooh, I was *fifteen*, I'd been having crushes since I was about eight – but not on real guys, mostly on movie stars. Like, I loved Tom Cruise and I had a big thing for Tom Selleck . . . maybe it was just men called Tom. You know, now I think about it, I really liked Tom Hanks in *Big*.

What was your crush called?
Melvin. Not Tom. Maybe that was a sign it wasn't going to work out.

What happened?
It was my first proper date. He came by the house and Pops told him that if he laid a finger on me, he'd kill him. Then, after he'd put the frighteners on him good he said, 'En*joy* yourselves, kids,' like we were in *Happy Days*. So me and Melvin went out and played pool and I beat him. He didn't like it and afterwards he didn't want to know.

How did you feel about that?
I thought he was a dumbass. I didn't want a guy who had to be better than me.

Now we're getting someplace.
We are?

But the time is up. See you same time next week.

20

9.07 Saturday morning

The phone rang: Mark.

Bad news. She'd been half expecting it. He'd been away for a week and if she were his wife, she'd expect him to stick around for his first day back – garbage to take out, kids to yell at, all that stuff.

'Jojo?' he whispered. 'I'm very sorry. I can't make it today.'

She said nothing. Too disappointed to make it easy for him.

'Sam's in a bit of trouble.' Sam was his son. 'We got a call last night. He went drinking with his mates – told us he was watching videos – and got so bad he ended up in hospital.'

'Is he OK?'

'He is now. But we've all had a bit of a fright and I ought to stay close.'

What could she say? Sam was a thirteen-year-old boy. This was serious stuff. 'Where are you?'

'In the shed.'

In the shed. Surrounded by weed killer, slug repellent and spiders' webs. She nearly laughed – the glamour of an affair.

'Well, take care of yourself, and him and er, the others.' *Your wife, your daughter.*

'I'm sorry, Jojo, you know I am. But there's a chance that tomorrow I could –'

'Tomorrow, I've got plans. I hope Sam will be OK. See you Monday.'

She disconnected and pulled her comforter up to her chin, having a moment. She wasn't going to kvetch. Right from the get-go she'd known what she was getting herself into and that was the deal she'd made with herself.

But she'd been so excited, it was more than a week since she'd spent any time with him . . .

She looked at her bedside table, where she put her new wallet every night so it would be the first thing she saw when she woke up, and said to it, 'Ah, *fuck*.'

Now she was sorry she hadn't had sex with him on the office floor last night. When you're seeing a married man, you take your chances where you can.

How did this happen? Where having sex on a floor covered with man-made fibre looked like a prize? How did she and Mark Avery end up this way?

She had always *liked* him; she respected the down-to-earth way he motivated his staff without scaring the shit out of them. And it was clear that he liked her. Theatrically he used to flatten himself against the wall as she strode through the corridors of Lipman Haigh. 'Watch out,' he'd say as she passed. 'She's moving at speed.'

He called her 'Red' and she called him 'Boss'. They dead-panned conversations out of the sides of their mouths, as if they were in a noir movie.

He was a good boss, the type you could go to for advice. She had tried not to bother him; she liked to figure out stuff on her own – unless she was snarled up in something that no amount of juggling could get her out of. Like the Miranda England time, a messy, solution-free situation that nearly drove her crazy.

She dropped in to Mark, sat down and said, 'You're going to *love* this one, Boss.'

'It was a slow day,' he drawled, in his deadpan voice. 'In a slow week. In a slow life. Then *she* shows up. What is it, Red?'

She explained it all. Miranda England was a great author but her career had been badly mishandled. She wanted to sack her agent, Len McFadden, and become Jojo's client. She also wanted to switch publishers. But Len had in his possession a contract with the old publishers for two more books. Miranda had signed the contract; if he returned it to her she'd be free to move to the new publishers, but if he gave it back to the old publishers she'd be stuck there for two more books. And in a fit of sour grapes when he heard that Miranda wanted to sack him that's exactly what he was talking about doing.

'And you'll get no income from it? Not until the next contract is up for negotiation?'

'Right. If Miranda's career hasn't been totally wiped out by then.'

Mark considered the ceiling, then swung down to face her. 'First question. Is it worth the trouble?'

'Yes, for *sure*. Miranda England is great, really great. She's going to have a long career writing great books but she needs the right publisher. Pelham didn't stump up any marketing money but Dalkin Emery would. Her career could get on track right away with Dalkin Emery, we could even try to buy back the first two books and reissue 'em, treat 'em as new publications, this time do it right, it could be totally *great* . . .'

'OK. So the problem is Len McFadden. What does he stand to lose?'

'His ten per cent on the new two-book deal.'

'Can you negotiate a better deal with Dalkin Emery? Enough to cover McFadden's ten per cent without leaving Miranda with any less money?'

Jojo thought about it. About how badly Dalkin Emery wanted Miranda. 'You know, I guess I could.'

'Well, there we are then.'

'God, you're good.'

She'd gone into his office trapped in a Catch-22 – whichever way she jumped she'd lose something. But he'd unravelled a win-win.

'You are the knees of a bee,' she told him.

'The pyjamas of a cat?'

'That too. Thanks.'

That was about eighteen months ago and it shot her regard for him so high, it rang the bell. There was suddenly a lot more warmth between them. When she pitched proposals at the Friday morning board meetings he had a way of listening to her but looking away and smiling that she found affecting; he admired how she worked and she liked that.

But not once did she think of him as a potential boyfriend – he was married and that automatically meant he was off-limits. Also, if she'd thought consciously about it, she'd have decided that, at forty-six, he was a little too old for her.

However, things had changed the afternoon he appeared in her office, looking for someone to represent the agency at a dinner that night. He was meant to be going, but his wife had a migraine and he had to attend a parent–teacher meeting in her place.

'I know it's very last minute,' he said, 'but are you free this evening?'

Jojo squinted at him. 'I dunno. How much did I charge you last night?'

She expected him to laugh but the look on his face let her know that something had gone wrong. He wasn't smiling; instead he looked sort of frozen. Her light-hearted mood plummeted – *and* she was surprised; previous to this he'd always been up for a bit of banter but she'd presumed too much. No matter how friendly he was, he was still her boss.

'Sorry,' she said, soberly. 'Of course I'm free.'

After that she thought things had got back to normal, but a few days later it became clear they hadn't.

There had been a publishing awards ceremony, a long, rowdy affair at the Park Lane Hilton. At the end of the night Jojo was outside the hotel, queuing for a taxi and swinging her slingbacks from her fingers, when Mark appeared. She hadn't seen him all evening.

'Red.' He hurtled up to her. 'I've been looking for you.'

'Here I am.'

Someone further back in the line yelled, 'Mark Avery, what do you think you're doing?'

'Jumping the queue!'

'At least he's honest,' Jojo heard the person mutter.

'How was tonight?' she asked.

'Blah, blah, blah, books,' Mark laughed, a little drunkenly. 'Blah, blah, blah, sales.' Then he noticed her shoes in her hands and, in surprise, looked down at her feet, bare on the night-cold pavement.

Jojo shrugged. 'They were hurting.'

He shook his head in what could have been admiration, then passed the rest of the wait singing quietly to himself. '. . . hates California, it's cold and it's mank . . . that's why the lady is a tramp . . . she likes the cool clean wind in her hair . . . life without air . . .'

'Care,' Jojo corrected. 'Here's my cab. Night. See you tomorrow.'

The door was open and she was climbing in when Mark tugged her hair. She turned back in inquiry and he asked, 'Can I come home with you?'

'You want me to drop you off?'

'No, I want to come home with you.'

She thought she was hearing things. 'No,' she said, in surprise.

'Why not?'

'You're married. You're my boss. You're drunk. You want me to keep going?'

'In the morning I'll be sober.'

'And you'll still be married. And my boss.'

'Please?'

'*No.*' She laughed and moved away from his touch and into the cab. Before she shut the door, she said, 'I'll forget this ever happened.'

'I won't.'

The following day she expected a sheepish jokey apology –

eye-rolling talk of, 'Christ, I was in some state last night,' then perhaps a peace offering of an Alka Seltzer. But there was no apology, no Alka Seltzer, nothing.

She didn't even see him until the afternoon and that was only by accident, when they passed in the hall.

As soon as he saw her his eyes altered visibly. She'd heard about pupils dilating – she got enough romantic fiction sent to her – but she'd never before seen it happen in real life. Now, as if by special request, they dilated until they were almost black. He didn't say one word to her and after that everything was different.

21

11.12 Saturday morning

Jojo had just drifted back to sleep when the buzzer went. Flowers. Since she'd begun this thing with Mark she'd never got so many flowers in her life and she'd kind of gone off them; they represented broken dates, bikini lines which had been waxed for no reason, punnets of strawberries which she had to eat all on her own, so many that they gave her hives.

In her long T-shirt, she stood at the door, waiting for the flower man to come up the stairs. She lived in a fifth-floor flat in Maida Vale, in one of the redbrick apartment blocks which had originally served for married men to house their mistresses in. Although when she'd moved in she hadn't known she was going to end up as a mistress. She would have laughed, not just at the idea, but at the very word.

A huge bunch of stargazer lilies climbed the stairs. At the top, they bent over and wheezed, trying to catch their breath, then a young man appeared from behind them.

'You again,' he accused Jojo, and with a crackle of cellophane, the handover was transacted. 'Oh wait, the card.' He felt in his pocket and found the little envelope. 'He says he's sorry, he'll make it up to you.'

'Whatever happened to privacy?'

'I had to write the thing. How private can it be? Must be a bad one this time, he told them to go all out.'

'OK. Thanks.' Jojo moved inside.

'Could you stop having bust-ups? These stairs are killing me.'

Jojo closed the door, dumped the flowers in the kitchen sink and rang Becky. 'What's up?'

'Thought you were spending the day with Mark.' Becky sounded concerned.

'Change of plans. So what's up?' Her tone was cheery; she didn't want sympathy.

'Dentist,' Becky said. 'One of my fillings fell out last night, then I'm going shopping with Shayna. Want to come?'

Jojo hesitated. She had a bust, a waist and hips, the kind of body that was last fashionable in 1959. Shopping with Slinky Shayna was a bit gnarly because she frequented stores which only seemed to cater for malnourished thirteen-year-olds.

'I know,' Becky picked up on her hesitation. 'She'll make us go to Morgan. But come anyway. We'll have a laugh.'

'Sweets, I'll skip it. But I'll see you later.'

12.10 Saturday afternoon

'Shayna, your dinner party tonight? I know I blew you off but can I change my mind? Sorry about screwing your placements but I'd be glad to eat chicken nuggets at the card table with the kids.'

'Again,' Shayna said.

'Yeah, again.'

One of the side-effects of seeing a married man was having to force yourself on people at the last minute and not always being a comfortable fit.

'You shouldn't take this shit from him,' said Shayna, who took shit from no one.

'Do you hear me complaining?'

Shayna kissed her teeth. 'Chah! Anyway, no kids tonight, so you get to sit at the big table.'

'Yay.'

Shayna was Becky's childhood chum and when Jojo came to live in England, she became Jojo's pal also. She was off-the-scale fabulous. She was the first black – and female – partner at the management consultancy firm where she worked and she earned more than Brandon, her barrister husband who did *everything* she told him to. Though she'd had two children her stomach was flat and hard and her bum showed no sign of slipping off her back and towards the floor. Home was a big three-storey house in Stoke Newington which they'd bought for seven pounds fifty or some such negligible sum. They'd fixed the dry rot, the wet rot, the damp and the dodgy plumbing and restored the crumbling house to beauty – just in time for property values to start rising in that area.

And Shayna gave sophisticated dinner parties. At least they were sophisticated to begin with but she plied her guests with so much drink that by the end of the evening they were dishevelled and a lot closer to the table than they had been at the start.

2.10 *Saturday afternoon, Kensington High Street*

Jojo liked to shop alone – it meant she could change her mind whenever she liked without anyone getting snippy with her. See, her plan for the afternoon had been to trawl for household stuff, like nice bed linen and exotic bath oils, something she'd done *all the time* when she'd first bought her apartment twenty months ago – she'd lavished love and money on it; she'd swapped reading normal magazines for interiors ones; out of nowhere she was more interested in paint colours than nail colours; she spent more on picture frames than shoes; she'd bought a huge comfy sofa and repro Indian furniture and considered a Laz-E-Boy recliner with built-in ashtray and beer cooler until Becky advised her not to. In short, she'd experienced New Flat Madness.

Then it all settled down, she started buying *Harpers&Queen* again – until she started seeing Mark. As they never really went out, her flat had become love-nest central and buying things like scented candles and Egyptian cotton sheets made her feel more in control.

But this afternoon suddenly she saw no point buying another pair of sheets – his wife and family were not going to disappear

– and she had enough scratchy 'sexy' underwear to open her own shop, so she exercised the prerogative of the lone shopper and Changed her Mind. Bed linen was toast and clothes were the thing. Ten minutes in Barkers and she'd found a pair of trousers, so pricey that she yelped at the tag.

'Something wrong, madam?' An assistant shimmered from nowhere.

Jojo laughed in embarrassment. 'No wonder you say Americans are loud. This is the price, right? Like, not the style number?'

'They're beautiful on. Why don't you try them?'

Jojo looked at the assistant's namebadge, 'But Wendy, that's just what they'll be expecting.'

She should have walked away quickly, sprinting down the escalator and out into the safety of the street. Instead she followed Wendy to a changing room and with the whizz of a zip became taller, flat-stomached, long-legged and curvy-hipped.

'They're perfect,' Wendy observed.

Jojo sighed, did a quick survey of her finances, knew she shouldn't, and said, 'What the hell? You take your chances where you find them.'

She changed back into her own clothes and handed over the trousers. 'Do they come in any other colours? No? OK, now I'm really going to scare you – do you have any more of the same?'

'Perhaps, but wouldn't you like to try something different?'

Jojo shook her head. 'I do this a lot. They laugh at me, but the thing is, with my shape, when you find something that fits well, you go for it, you know? Once I bought five identical bras. They were five different colours but like my friend Shayna said they were still the same bra.'

Still talking, Jojo followed Wendy to the till.

'My cousin Becky does the same as me, could be it's a family thing. Except sometimes Becky is so embarrassed that she pretends to the assistant that the extra ones are for her sisters. And she hasn't got any sisters.'

Wendy studied the screen, checking the stock list for an extra pair.

'But could be I'm embarrassed too,' Jojo admitted. 'Else why am I telling you all this?'

Wendy continued clicking and said nothing. She was a shop girl, not a psycho-bloody-analyst. She wasn't paid enough for this.

8.15 Saturday evening

When Jojo arrived, Shayna was flitting around in a tight white ensemble that displayed three inches of shining mahogany stomach and plying people with a killer rum-based concoction. 'My own recipe. I call it Life Support Machine.'

The guests were a mix of opinionated know-alls from Brandon's work, go-getters from Shayna's and a couple of right-on neighbours. Then there were old friends like Becky and Andy.

Jojo accepted a drink, said hi to the others and realized – with a little shock – that she was already just the teensiest bit bored.

The dining room was lit by the flickering of fat wax candles, casting shadows on the distempered white walls. On the gleaming cabinets stood fashionable flower arrangements – twigs and stuff. Nothing so gauche as petals.

'When I grow up,' Becky said, 'I want to be Shayna.'

'Mmm,' said Jojo. *Not exactly bored. But I'd prefer to be with Mark.*

Her world had shrunk – no matter who she was with, she'd prefer to be with Mark. That's what happened when you fell in love – you only want to see *them*.

And it had taken her all of five seconds to notice that everyone else was two-by-two: Shayna had obedient Brandon, Becky had Andy – it was like the Ark. But because Mark was married she was in a twilight zone where she was neither single nor paired off.

Yikes. This is not a good way to think.

Suddenly Becky was toe-to-toe in front of Jojo. She leant even closer and exhaled a big 'Hah!' right into her face. 'Does my breath smell OK?'

Earlier in the day her dentist had told her that her gums were slightly receding, that an electric toothbrush would take care of the problem, but Becky – who was anxious about the state of her teeth at the best of times – was afraid she was in the grip of full-blown gingivitis.

'Smells fine. What does Andy think?'

'He's so used to me that he wouldn't notice if I swallowed a skunk.'

Another pang. Would she and Mark ever have the chance to get so used to each other that he wouldn't notice if she swallowed a skunk?

Then she noticed the long darkwood dining table: it was set with twelve antique Weeping Willow plates, twelve handmade silver cutlery sets, twelve Murano wine glasses – and one plastic Teletubbies bowl, a Bob the Builder beaker and a Peter Rabbit knife and fork. Jojo's place. Shayna was making a point.

When they sat down to eat Shayna, point made, took the Teletubbies bowl for herself and passed Jojo a Weeping Willow plate piled high with down-home food: jerk chicken, rice'n'peas, Johnny cakes. Jojo took a deep breath, then tucked in.

'Good Christ,' said the man beside her. Ambrose was his name – some guy from Brandon's work. 'You can really put it away.'

'It's food,' Jojo said. 'What am I supposed to do with it? Weave baskets?'

The man watched another mouthful of food disappear into Jojo's mouth and breathed, 'Blimey,' loud enough for everyone to hear.

Jojo hunched lower over her plate. What a prince. Some men just took exception to her – her appetite? her height? – something, anyway. But knowing they were assholes didn't mean it didn't get to her.

'Jojo never diets,' Shayna said proudly.

Well, she'd tried it once when she was seventeen and didn't even last a day.

'That's obvious.'

'Ambrose, apologize, for God's sake!' exclaimed the woman opposite. She was so thin she was almost transparent and Jojo deduced she was Ambrose's girl.

'For what? I simply endorsed a fact.'

'Fucking barristers.' Shayna closed her eyes.

Unabashed, Ambrose nodded at Skeletor. 'Look at Cecily. She eats nothing and she's well fit.'

One way of putting it, Jojo thought, wondering when Skeletor had last had a period.

'I'm really sorry,' Cecily apologized across the table. 'He's not normally so rude.'

'Hey, no need for *you* to apologize.' Jojo smiled through her upset. This moron wasn't worth causing a scene over.

'He's an idiot. Please ignore him.' Cecily was very taken with Jojo; she'd been watching her since she'd arrived. Jojo was a big girl – bigger than Cecily could imagine being in her worst Maltesers-filled nightmares – but she was gorgeous. Luscious and ripe in those fabulous black trousers and clingy burgundy top, her decolletage and shoulders satin-smooth and luminous. (Actually thanks to pearlescent body lotion, Jojo would have happily told her if she'd asked.)

But it was the way Jojo seemed so comfortable in her own skin that most entranced Cecily. To the point where she'd wondered tentatively about cancelling her gym membership. Even – dammit! – eating whatever she wanted. If it worked for this Jojo, couldn't it work for her?

Occasionally this happened to women around Jojo. While

they were with her, they saw through the advertising industry's lies and believed that size didn't matter, that it was intangibles like *joie de vivre* and confidence that counted. But then they went home and discovered, to their great disappointment, that they weren't Jojo Harvey and couldn't understand why they'd felt what they'd felt at the time.

11.45 Saturday evening

When the first of the noisy drunken discussions about politics began, Jojo thought, Right! That's enough. Suddenly she couldn't bear being with people who weren't Mark and just wanted out. She always seemed to be the first to leave things these days.

Shayna and Brandon tried to make her wait while they rang a taxi, warning her that the area hadn't upped and come so much that she'd be safe wandering through it on a Saturday night, but she wanted to be gone. A trapped panicky feeling grew until amid a flurry of hugs and kisses she was finally permitted to leave. Out on the silent road, she gulped in lungfuls of lovely, cold night air, then saw the yellow light of an approaching cab. Yay!

Half an hour later she arrived in her silent flat, poured herself a glass of merlot, switched on the TV at the foot of her bed and got under the duvet to watch her video about meerkats in the Kalahari. Olga Fisher had lent it to her. Olga Fisher was one of Lipman Haigh's seven partners – the only woman – and she and Jojo shared a mutual fondness for wildlife programmes. Everyone else laughed at them about it, so they swapped their David Attenborough videos as furtively as if they were pornography.

Olga was in her late forties, single, wore pearls and elegantly draped scarves and because she negotiated good terms for her authors she was known as a ballbreaker. If she were a man, Jojo thought scornfully, they'd simply call her 'a great agent'. She wondered if they called her a ballbreaker too. Probably. Assholes.

She settled into bed and chuckled as a macho meerkat, keeping lookout high in a tree – paws on hips, eyes on the middle distance – lost his balance and tumbled to the ground, where he picked himself up and dusted himself off, looking dreadfully embarrassed. He glared at the camera, like Robbie Williams facing down the paparazzi.

Suddenly Jojo stopped laughing and thought, I'm a woman in my prime. I shouldn't be spending Saturday night in bed alone, watching videos about meerkats falling out of trees.

She turned to her wallet, which was lying beside her on the pillow. 'This is not right,' she said. But she already knew that.

22

I should never have started this thing with him, Jojo thought. I could be in love with someone else right now, someone who wasn't married. Well, shoulda woulda coulda . . .

If only it was just about sex, she thought regretfully. If only it was about thrillingly dangerous bonks. Relationship gurus always said that an attraction based on friendship and mutual respect was far more likely to stay the course – and the bastards were right.

Even before Jojo had come to work at Lipman Haigh, she'd respected Mark; he was well known in the industry as a visionary. Five years previously, when he had come in as Managing Partner, Lipman Haigh had been a sleepy little agency and some of the partners were so old they made Jocelyn Forsyth look like a surly adolescent. Mark's first act had been to headhunt several young snappy agents and make three of them partners as soon as the three most doddery incumbents could be persuaded to retire. Then he'd added a foreign rights department and a vibrant media arm and within eighteen months Lipman Haigh had gone from being a bunch that no one bothered much with to being the hot 'new' London agency.

He was tough – he had to be – but he wore it with grace. In negotiations with publishers he could become as unmovable as cellulite, but he did it decently. Nothing personal, his manner said, but this just won't do. I won't be caving, so you'd better. Not stern, not slimy, just straight.

And he had a sense of humour. Not a laugh-a-minute like his chosen one, Jim Sweetman, who certainly knew how to win friends and influence people, but there was plenty of mirth just beneath the surface.

But what Jojo had admired most about Mark Avery was his incredible trouble-shooting abilities. His instincts were sure, nothing unnerved him and he was a man with all the answers: Don Corleone without the voice, the entourage and the paunch.

But she hadn't, like, *fancied* him. Then came the night outside the Hilton followed by the pupil-dilating stuff in the corridor and it all went weird. When Jojo did her Friday morning round-up, Mark listened to her while doing his thing of looking away and smiling – but without the smiling. He no longer flattened himself theatrically against the wall while she strode at high speed through the halls of Lipman Haigh. He addressed her only as 'Jojo' and there was no more cat's-pyjamas-style banter.

She didn't like it but she could wait it out. She was good at waiting – a lot of practice with publishers – and could tune out the voices of fear and doubt in her head.

But Mark hadn't become Managing Partner of a literary agency without also having nerves of steel, so the stand-off endured.

I can outwait anyone, Jojo thought, but with all that tension flying about, could she help it if she found herself wondering about him? Once she focused on him as a man rather than a boss, her imagination took flight and her resolve began to buckle. The meaningful look in the corridor was the start of a slide into a violent attraction to him and it really pissed her off. Eventually she admitted to Becky, 'I keep thinking about what it would be like to sleep with Mark Avery.'

'Crap. Bound to be. Old guy like him?'

'He's forty-six, not eighty-six.'

Becky was concerned – could any good come of this? 'It's only because you haven't had sex for nine months. Since Poor Craig. Maybe you should sleep with someone else.'

'Who?'

'Now you're asking. Anyone.'

'But I don't want to go out looking for someone just to sleep with. That's not who I am. I want to sleep with Mark. And not anyone else.'

'Jojo, snap out of it. *Please.*'

'And considering I already like, admire and respect him, I'm doomed,' she continued disconsolately.

More prosaically, she had her career to consider. She hoped to be made partner some day soonish and how would that ever happen if her boss had decided to behave as if she didn't exist?

After five weeks she caved in and made an appointment to see him. She came into his office, shut the door firmly behind her and sat before him.

'Jojo?'

'Mark. Ah . . . I don't know how to say this, but things have been, like, *tense* with us. Is it my work? Do you have a problem with it?'

She knew it wasn't that, but she wanted it clear.

'No, no problems with your work.'

'Riiight. So can we drop the weird stuff? Can we go back to the way we were?'

He considered it. 'No.'

'Why not?'

'Because . . . because . . . how can I put this?' he said. 'Because – please don't laugh – because I'm in love with you.'

'Please! How can you be?'

'I've worked with you for two years. If I don't know you by now . . .'

After a period of silence Jojo looked up from her lap and said, 'You're married. I would never be with a married man.'

'I know. It's one of the reasons I feel how I feel about you.'

'Well,' she sighed, 'ain't that a kick in the head.'

23

It was only meant to be a one-off – to get it out of their systems so they could get back to being colleagues at ease with each other. This was a total lie, of course; Jojo knew it and Mark knew it. Neither of them was interested in getting anything out of their systems, but dressing it up as A Good Thing made it a little less appalling.

After Mark had made the dramatic announcement that he was in love with Jojo, Jojo rang Becky and hissed the whole story down the phone.

'Don't worry,' Becky reassured. 'It's just a ploy to get you into bed.'

'You think?' Relieved and disappointed.

'I'm sure.'

TO: Jojo.harvey@LIPMAN HAIGH.co
FROM: Mark.avery@LIPMAN HAIGH.co
SUBJECT: I meant what I said

Not just a ploy to get you into bed.
M xx

'He used those exact words?' Becky said. 'My God, he's clever.'

'Yes. I keep telling you he is.'

Becky looked surprised at Jojo's evident irritation. 'Easy, girl.'

For the next nine days, Jojo and Mark tiptoed around each other, blushing and dropping things whenever they came into contact. Jojo reported every little encounter to Becky, who remained concerned but reluctantly fascinated. She'd never slept with a Managing Partner – a Head of Sales had been her most senior post.

On day ten Mark asked Jojo out for dinner; he wanted to 'have a talk'.

'A talk about getting into your knickers,' Becky sighed.

Good, Jojo thought.

'Here's how it is,' Mark said, between the starter and the main course. 'I'm not going to tell you that my wife doesn't understand me. I won't tell you that we never have sex because, very occasionally, we still do. And I love my two children, I don't want to do anything to hurt them.'

'Like leave?'

'Yes. So now it's up to you. You deserve a hell of a lot more than I'm offering, but what I can say is that I've never felt about anyone else the way I feel about you.'

'And you don't make a habit of this sort of thing?'

He looked shocked. 'Absolutely not.'

As soon as Jojo got home she rang Becky and relayed the conversation.

'He's moving fast,' Becky observed. 'You don't want him to leave his kids. You just want to sleep with him.'

'Do I? That's OK then.'

At work the next morning an email was waiting.

TO: Jojo.harvey@LIPMAN HAIGH.co
FROM: Mark.avery@LIPMAN HAIGH.co
SUBJECT: Please

Please. (Interrogative form of) to beg, beseech, plead, implore, supplicate or entreat.

M xx

149

To her surprise, her eyes were suddenly swimming with tears. It was too much, all of it – his wife and children, his tender humility. *We have to do something.*

It was Becky who came up with the idea of them Getting it Out of Their Systems. 'He might be atrocious in bed,' she said hopefully. 'He might turn your stomach.'

Jojo doubted it but, in jokey embarrassment, ran it by Mark. 'And with a bit of luck you'll go right off me.'

The look he gave signalled how unlikely that was. 'Well, if you're sure . . .'

She nodded.

'So where shall we . . . ? I mean, I could . . .'

'Come to my place. I'll make dinner. No,' she amended. 'I won't. If I cook for you, I'll never get rid of you.'

He approached sex with her like he approached everything else: with determination, confidence, attention to detail, and he removed her clothes as if he was unwrapping a gift.

Afterwards she asked, 'How was it for you?'

'Disastrous.' He stared at the ceiling. 'I haven't gone off you at all. You?'

'Even worse than I expected.'

'Well? Was he fabulous?' Becky asked the following day. 'Or a bit crap? Sometimes those old guys can be terrible.' Becky had once slept with a drunken thirty-seven-year-old and regarded herself as an authority.

'It's not like that,' Jojo said irritably. 'It's much more than sex, Mark's my favourite person.'

'Sorry,' Becky said, shocked.

'No, I'm sorry.' Jojo was also shocked.

'So what happens now? Now that you've got it all out of your systems?'

'Only a fool would start a relationship with a married man.'

'And you, Jojo, are no fool.'

'No.'

'So when do you see him again?'

'Tonight.'

That night Mark asked Jojo about her first boyfriend and she laughed and said, 'I can't tell you, the jealousy will kill you.'

'I can handle it.'

'OK, he was a proby from my pop's firehouse.'

'Proby?'

'New guy. Rookie.'

'You mean he was a firefighter? Oh fuck, how sorry am I, I asked. But keep talking, I have to know now. Huge, was he?'

'Huge. Six four, arms like tree trunks, he worked out with weights. He had, like, this *chest* that he used to crush me against and I couldn't break free until he said so.'

'Aaaagh.'

Jojo laughed. 'You did ask. But you know what? Anyone can be a gorilla with a big chest. Takes more'n that to keep me interested.'

The funny thing was that after she'd fallen for Mark, she discovered that everyone else fancied him – Louisa, Pam etc.

She was surprised that she hadn't realized. 'I thought Jim was the man?' she asked Louisa. 'No?'

'Don't get me wrong, Jim is beautiful, but Mark . . . Mark is pure sex. I would give . . . let me see . . . OK! This is how bad it is – I would never buy shoes again if I could have just one hour in bed with Mark Avery.' She shivered dramatically. 'I bet he's an ABSOLUTE *animal*.'

Sunday morning

Jojo woke up and reached for a P.G. Wodehouse from the pile of comfort reads beside her bed. She loved him and Agatha Christie, all the stuff she used to read growing up in New York and fantasizing about the British part of her heritage. Even now she knew the books were nothing like the real world, she still derived great pleasure from them.

Then she got up and did her ironing while she waited for it to be late enough to ring her parents in Queens; she called them every Sunday and they had pretty much the same conversation every week.

'Hey, Pops!'

'When're you coming home?'

'You just saw me! Remember Christmas? Like, a month ago?'

'Nah, when're you coming back for good? Your mother worries about you. You know the precinct would have you back in a heartbeat.' Noises in the background. 'Waidaminnit, I'm talking to her! She's my daughter too. Aw, here, your mother wants to talk to you.'

A staticy rustle as Charlie relinquished the phone.

'Hello, my darling girl, how are you?'

'Fine, Mom, great. Everyone OK?'

'Fine. Don't listen to that old fool. It's just that he worries about you. Is there any chance –'

'I'll try to come in the summer, yeah?'

When she hung up ten minutes later, she felt vaguely guilty but as she explained to her wallet, 'I live here now, see? This is home.' She loved her wallet. It was great company and much more convenient than having a dog.

Then she left to get the bus to Becky and Andy's cosy West Hampstead flat. The tube would have been faster but she preferred the bus because you got to see things; after living there for ten years, she still loved London, even though it had a lot of catching up on New York to do, especially in the area of nail-care.

'Oh good,' Andy said, when he opened the door to her. 'We're going to Sainsbury's. You can help carry the bags.'

After the weekly shop was done, she traipsed after them to the garden centre.

'Do you mind me always playing third wheel?'

'No,' Andy said. 'Livens things up a bit, gives me and Becks something to talk about.'

Andy and Becky had been together for eighteen months and they liked to make it sound as if they never had sex and were bored rigid with each other, a sure sign, Jojo knew, that they were crazy about each other. No one made those kinds of jokes unless they felt very secure. As a result Becky wanted everyone to be settled down and happy, especially Jojo.

'The Wyatt girls are having a party,' Becky announced, back at home, when they'd lugged the shopping bags into the kitchen.

The Wyatt sisters, Magda, Marina, and Mazie, were friends of Becky's since they'd shared a house for a six-month period before Becky moved in with Andy. They were blonde, posh, beautiful, rich and astonishingly kind and warm. They moved in more high-octane circles than Becky's but were so nice that they stayed in touch and always invited her and Jojo to their parties.

Becky had a crush on all three of them, all three had a crush on Jojo, and even Jojo had a slight pash for Magda, the eldest, the one with the best organizational skills. 'But NOT in a sexual way,' she kept telling Andy.

'Whatever,' he said. 'I'm terrified of them. They're so . . . fabulous.'

'It's Mazie's thirtieth. She's having a bash in the parents' Hampstead mansion. Not until June but they want to make sure you're available.'

'June?' Jojo exclaimed.

'Is that a posh thing?' Andy wondered. 'Giving several months' notice?'

'How would I know? Just one thing. It's fancy dress.'

'Fancy dress,' Jojo moaned softly. 'Why does it have to be fancy dress?'

She hated fancy dress – normal dress was difficult enough – and she always went as a red devil: neck-to-toe tight-fitting black with red horns in her hair and a red tail on her butt.

'But it'll be a great party and you might meet someone. Like –' Becky stopped, embarrassed – 'available.'

'Not everyone is as lucky as you,' Jojo said.

'No, there's only one of me to go round,' Andy said.

'No one else would have you,' Becky said.

'Yeah,' Jojo agreed, although she figured Andy was quite good-looking for a faithful man.

'Work tomorrow,' Becky said sadly, looking up from a sea of newspaper. 'Last night I dreamt I gave the wrong figures to British Airways and over-refunded hundreds of people, and they're not even my client. Although they will be soon,' she added gloomily, 'the way things are going. Every bloody company in the whole bloody world will be my client. It was a nightmare, I woke up shaking.'

'This is turning into an obsession,' Andy said. 'You've got to confront Elise.'

'How?'

'Calmly. Just say what you say to me.'

'What if it turns nasty?'

'Nasty? It's just business, stop being so emotional about it. Be like Jojo. If someone was messing her about at work, she'd tell it to them straight.' Andy stopped. 'Mind you, she's sleeping with her boss, which could turn *extremely* nasty.'

'Enough already,' Jojo said.

'How *is* your adulterous liaison?' Andy asked. 'What's going to happen?'

Jojo squirmed. 'Ask Becky. She's director of emotional affairs.'

'Well?'

Becky considered. 'There are several possible outcomes. I'll make a list.' She scribbled for a few minutes on the 'Style' section of the *Sunday Times* then announced, 'OK. Possibilities.'

a) Mark leaves his wife
b) His wife is also having an affair with, let's say, their son's teacher and she leaves Mark
c) Jojo and Mark gradually go off each other and end up being friends
d) The wife dies tragically from — what do people die of? Scarlet fever. Jojo enters Mark's household as governess to his children and after a respectable time has elapsed, he can go public that he's fallen for her

'Which one do you like the most?'

'None. I don't want him and his wife to break up.'

'So you just want to carry on being a sidecar in the motorbike of his life?' Andy asked.

'No, but . . .' She didn't want to break up anyone's marriage. Part of the moral code she'd been brought up with was that family was paramount. If ever any of the firefighters in her father's firehouse was fooling around with a woman who wasn't his wife, the other guys on the rig got involved. They urged and counselled the renegade husband to return to the wife: he usually did. And on the rare occasions when he didn't, ranks closed around the wife and the man found himself out in the cold.

'And what about his kids? They'll hate me.'

'They'll live with their mother.'

'But they'll come to us and ruin our weekends. Sorry,' she said a mite defensively. 'I'm just being honest.'

'But you're so good with kids,' Becky said. 'Shayna's two love you.'

'I want kids but I want them to be babies first. Not a teenager who's already showing signs of delinquency and a goofy girl who falls off ponies. I'd spend all my down time at the Emergency Room.'

'Isn't George Clooney a hunk of a man?' This came from Andy.

'I prefer Mark.'

'Bloody hell. So what *do* you want?'

'I want him never to have been married and for there to be no children.'

Becky consulted her list. 'Sorry. That option isn't on it.'

'What a bummer,' Jojo sighed.

'How bad actually is it?' Becky asked. 'How strongly do you feel about him? On a scale of one to Dominic?'

'Who's Dominic?' Andy asked.

'Before your time,' Becky explained. 'The Big One.'

'See, when I first came to Britain ten years ago, I didn't realize that some of the guys I met were assholes,' Jojo said. 'I just thought they were being British. And even when I knew they were assholes, they were British assholes, so it didn't seem so bad. It took a little time before I became discriminating in my choices.'

'The idiots she went out with . . .'

'Then I met Dominic.'

'And he wasn't an idiot. He was a six-foot-three hunk, a journalist. He deserved her. She nearly married him, they got engaged, a ring and everything. But he got cold feet. Well, not exactly cold feet, he thought he *might* have cold feet . . .'

'He decided he "wasn't sure",' Jojo said. 'The week before we were supposed to move in together. I could keep the ring but we were no longer engaged. We weren't ruling out getting married but not at any definite time. Then he thought we should take a break from each other –'

'– but he kept showing up pissed, keen to play hide the sausage –'

'– salami –'

'Sorry, I forgot he was The Big One in more ways than one.'

'He broke my heart,' Jojo said simply. 'But luckily I'm one of the world's stronger women and I wouldn't take that kind of crap from him. From any man.'

'Ah, you did a bit,' Becky said. 'Remember the time you lied to me and swore he just needed a bed for the night and then I walked in and caught you at it –'

'OK, OK, I might have succumbed once or twice –'

'– or twenty times.'

'But I finished it. And I got over it.'

'If it was me, I'd still be hanging on, hoping he'd finally make his mind up,' Becky said. 'I'd be a wreck. Five and a half stone, nails bitten to the knuckle and my hobby would be sucking the ends of my hair. I'd be on Prozac and Valium and I'd sleep on the floor by the phone. I'd eat baby food out of the jar and –'

'How long ago was this?' Andy interrupted.

Jojo had to think. 'Six years?' She consulted Becky who looked as though she'd just come out of a trance. 'Six and a half?'

'What's he doing now?' Andy asked. 'Did he meet someone else?'

'I haven't a clue. And I couldn't care less.'

'Do you still have the ring?'

'Nah. I sold it and me and Becky went to Thailand for two weeks.'

'Do you love Mark as much as you loved Dominic?' Becky asked.

Jojo thought about it for a long time and concluded, 'Probably more. But he's married.'

The thing was, though, that lately Mark had begun half hinting at the possibility of leaving Cassie. *Unprompted* half hinting. Jojo would never instigate it. Perhaps eventually all the cloak and dagger stuff would become unbearable, instead of being merely irritating, and maybe then she'd press for more. But at the moment the speculation about their happy future – such as it was – was all coming from him.

24

8.30 Monday morning
On her way into Lipman Haigh Jojo passed a man loitering in the street outside. He was combing his hair in someone's wing mirror and his face was the colour of keylime pie. She was almost certain that it was Nathan Frey, horribly, nervously early for his nine o'clock appointment.

9.00 and ten seconds, Monday morning
Manoj announced Nathan and it was indeed the same man, keylime-pie face all present and correct.

He was a wreck. He'd spent three years writing the book; he'd taken out a second mortgage on his house, left his wife and family for six months and, disguised as a woman, lived in Afghanistan. He'd already been turned down by a couple of agents – 'More fool them,' said Jojo – and now that he was this close to a real live agent, a person who had the power to realize his dream of getting published, he fell to pieces a little.

But when Jojo congratulated him on his wonderful book and explained how she thought it could be sold worldwide, his keylime pallor receded and gradually he took on a healthier colour, more like a Bailey's cheesecake.

'Is the manuscript with anyone else at the moment? Any other agents?' Jojo asked. It wouldn't be the first time that an author had done a mass mailing and ended up with several agents claiming the author as their own.

'No, I've been doing them one at a time.'

Good. At least she wouldn't have to pitch against any other agents.

'I couldn't believe it when you rang. I want an agent like you wouldn't believe . . .'

'Well, you've got one,' Jojo said and immediately two bright spots of raspberry coulis burst onto his cheeks.

'Wow,' he said quietly, and clenched his fists. 'Christ.' He wiped his forehead with the back of his hand. 'I can't believe this.' His entire face had pinkened into a pretty strawberry mousse glow. 'So what happens now?'

'I get you a deal.'

'Really?' He seemed startled. 'Just like that?'

'It's a great book. Lots of publishers will want to buy it.'

'I hate to ask . . . I know this sounds a bit funny . . . but . . .'

'Yes, you should make plenty of money. I'll get you the best advance I can.'

'I don't want much,' he said hastily. 'Just to be published is reward enough. But we've had nothing coming in and it's hard for my wife and kids . . .'

'Don't worry. I've the feeling lots of people will want this book and will be happy to pay for it. Give me about ten days and as soon as I have news I'll be in touch.'

Nathan backed out repeating, 'Thank you, thank you, thank you.'

Manoj watched him go and when the 'thank yous' from the corridor had faded from earshot, he remarked, 'The honeymoon period. But how long before the abuse starts and he's calling you up when he can't find his tube pass?'

Jojo smiled.

'So, is he ours?' he asked.

'He's ours.'

'Tell me about him. Anything interesting?'

'You bet.' Jojo related the Afghanistan story. 'He's what's known in the trade as a "highly promotable" author.' She thrust the manuscript at him. 'Get copying. I need six perfect copies and I need them half an hour ago.'

'You're going for an auction?'

Jojo nodded. *Love and the Veil* was so wonderful, she was confident that several editors would step up to the plate and engage in a bidding war.

While Manoj inhaled photocopier fumes and groused about having a 2.1 in English and doing work that a monkey could be trained to do, Jojo drew up a shortlist of editors in her head.

First, though, she had to check in with Mark about how Sam was doing. Pretending she cared about his domestic crises was difficult. Because they were way important to Mark, she tried – but the bottom line was that every time there was a drama, Jojo lost Mark to his family. And they really were the most accident-prone bunch. His wife, Cassie, a primary school teacher, got debilitating migraines whenever she ate cheese, a fact that did nothing to deter her from tucking into a ploughman's whenever she felt like it. Sophie, the ten-year-old daughter, was a danger to herself: in the time Jojo had been seeing Mark, she'd fallen off a pony and got a protractor stuck in her arm.

Nor was the drinking incident Sam's first offence – he'd been caught stealing a packet of fruit Mintoes from the newsagent's, an event that necessitated a visit to the school psychologist. Even Hector, the Avery family dog, conspired to keep them apart. The night Jojo cooked an entire Indian meal from scratch, Hector got hit by a car and was badly concussed; Mark had to go home before he'd touched his first poppadom. Then, a week later, Hector swallowed one of Mark's squash socks and Sam attempted the Heimlich Manoeuvre on him, succeeding only in breaking one of Hector's ribs. Once again Mark had to rush home.

TO: Jojo.harvey@LIPMAN HAIGH.co
FROM: Mark.avery@LIPMAN HAIGH.co
SUBJECT: Sam

He's OK now. I'm very sorry. How about Tuesday night?
M

TO: Mark.avery@LIPMAN HAIGH.co
FROM: Jojo.harvey@LIPMAN HAIGH.co
SUBJECT: Tuesday

Tuesday it is.
JJ xx

TO: Jojo.harvey@LIPMAN HAIGH.co
FROM: Mark.avery@LIPMAN HAIGH.co
SUBJECT: You

Veliyoou

Veliyoou? Jojo wondered. What the hell did that mean? Veliyoou? An anagram of some sort. She puzzled over it for a few moments, then it clicked. She laughed and, after playing with the letters a little, sent a reply.

TO: Mark.avery@LIPMAN HAIGH.co
FROM: Jojo.harvey@LIPMAN HAIGH.co
SUBJECT: Veliyoou?

Well, Oiyvoule more!
JJ xx

Then Jojo phoned six of the best editors in London, told them that they'd been hand-picked and promised that a gem was being biked over. A date was set for the auction, a week hence – enough time for the editors to authorize with their higher-ups the big money she was hoping for.

And could this day get any better? When Jojo spoke to Tania Teal at Dalkin Emery about *Love and the Veil*, Tania said, 'Good timing. I was going to call you today anyway, about Lily Wright.'

Lily Wright was one of Jojo's authors, a gentle, intelligent and intuitive woman, and Jojo felt instinctively that she was one of life's 'good' people. When Jojo first took Lily on, she came with her partner, Anton, to see her; they both sat nervously in front of Jojo, finishing each other's sentences and generally being adorable. Lily had written *Mimi's Remedies*, a magical little book about a white witch. Jojo had loved it and really felt it had something very special. But because it was so esoteric, she'd been unable to persuade any publisher to go big on it.

Tania had bought it for the small advance of four grand. At the time she'd said, 'Personally *I* adore it, it's better than Prozac. I have to admit that in my heart of hearts I can't see it going mainstream, but what the hell, I'm going to try anyway.'

But although Tania had tried her best to persuade her colleagues that this book could surprise everyone, no one bought the idea. As a result, Dalkin Emery had done a small print run, almost no publicity and – surprise, surprise – so far *Mimi's Remedies* had resolutely not set the world on fire.

'What about Lily?' Jojo asked.

'Lovely news, actually.' Jojo could hear her glee. 'There's a rave review of *Mimi's Remedies* in this week's *Flash!. And* we're reprinting. The reports from the reps are good. Would you believe we've almost sold out.'

'You have? Fantastic! And that's on almost *no* publicity.'

'Well, in light of the reprint I've persuaded marketing to run a few ads.'

'Great! And what kind of reprint are we talking? Another five k?'

'No, we thought ten.'

Ten? Double the original print run? The reps' reports must be spectacular.

'Look at what the readers are saying about her on Amazon,' Tania said. 'This book seems to be tapping into something special. Looks like we were right about this, Jojo!'

Jojo agreed, thanked her and hung up, high on excitement. It was always good news when, against the odds, a book started to take off, even slightly. But in this case, because the author was such a sweetie, she was overjoyed. She connected to Amazon and found *Mimi's Remedies*'s site – Tania was right. Seventeen readers' reviews and they all adored the book. 'Enchanting . . . comforting . . . magical . . . I've already reread it . . .'

Right away Jojo rang Lily, who sounded stunned and grateful, then she sat back, at a sudden happy loss. What now? Lunch, dammit! She'd done enough for one morning.

She picked up the phone and punched an internal extension. 'Dan? Free for lunch?'

'Lunch?'

'Where we eat food together in the same room?'

'Oh yes. Seeing as it's you.'

'See you in a few.'

Dan Swann was the way Jojo imagined English men were, before she ever came to live in England. He was slight and fair and although he was almost sixty, he still looked like a boy. Best of all he wore a funny porridge-coloured tweed jacket with patches on the elbows. It looked like a family heirloom and when it got wet it smelt weird – of dog or perhaps decaying vegetation. Jojo thought it simply added to his charm.

It was he who had persuaded Jojo to join Lipman Haigh. They first met at a launch party for a Young Turk. (Yes, another one.) Dan hurtled in out of the rain, in his smelly jacket, and paused before the bustling scene. 'Oh, Lord,' he said wearily. 'What fresh hell is this?'

Jojo, who was by the door, taking a moment to dry off before launching herself into the ruck, noticed the patches, the attitude, the smell. Great, she thought. A proper English Eccentric.

In dismay, Dan surveyed the room. 'More wretched Young Turks than there are stars in the firmament.'

'Yeah,' Jojo laughed. 'The place is lousy with them.'

'Lousy,' Dan repeated. 'The perfect word.' He extended his hand to Jojo. 'Dan Swann.'

'Jojo Harvey.'

'Miss Harvey, you remind me of my fourth wife.'

But there was no Mrs Swann, not even one. Dan's gate swung the other way. It was why he kept agenting war biographies, he later admitted to Jojo. He couldn't resist a man in uniform, even if he was eighty and gaga.

On the way to Dan's office, Jojo passed Jim Sweetman's.

'Hey, you.' She stopped at his door and called in. 'You swizzed me. The smoking woman's not a hypnotist, she's a SHRINK.'

Jim laughed, displaying gorgeous white teeth. Jojo shielded her eyes. 'Jeez, I'm dazzled. Do you have to do that?'

Jim laughed even more. 'Look at my sign.' On the wall behind his desk was an A4 piece of paper, which said in black marker

Currently enjoying

25

smoke-free days

'Who cares how it works,' he said. 'So long as it does?'

'Humph.' That was the trouble with Jim Sweetman. He was such an accomplished charmer it was hard to stay pissed off with him. 'But I don't want to go to a shrink.'

'Why not? Jojo Harvey isn't the type of woman to have deep dark secrets. Nothing to be scared of.'

He was doing his smile again; the picture of innocent good fun. But Jojo wasn't so sure. He and Mark were very close and sometimes she wondered how much Jim knew.

She turned away and, 'Wah!' went slap bang into Richie Gant. Skinny, with oiled black hair, he looked like a mean young shark, who would mug other young sharks for their mobile phones. She got away as fast as she could. *Eww, I touched him.*

Round in Dan's office, Dan seemed startled to see Jojo even though it was ninety seconds since he'd spoken to her on the phone. 'Oh yes,' he said vaguely. 'Eating. I suppose one must.'

From his coat-stand he removed an ancient shapeless felt hat that looked almost alive, as if it were made of moss. He pulled it tightly onto his head; suddenly he looked like he had a green beehive. Then he extended his elbow to Jojo. 'Shall we?'

25

10.15 Tuesday morning

The first call came. 'Monkey boy here,' Manoj said. 'I've Patricia Evans on the line. Accept or decline?'

'Accept, accept!' First out of the gate!

A click, then, 'Jojo, I've read *Love and the Veil*.'

Jojo's heart banged as the adrenalin kicked in. This was going to be good.

'I love it,' Patricia said. 'We all love it here and I want to make a pre-emptive offer.'

'It would have to be a very high offer to take the book off the table right now.'

'I think you're going to be happy. We're offering £1 million.'

Suddenly her hands were hot and adrenalin was racing through her like an invading army. Jojo was thinking fastfastfast. A million pounds was crazy money, especially for a debut novel. But if Pelham were prepared to go so high, wouldn't some of the other houses also? Maybe in an auction she could get the money higher. Higher than the £1.1 million that Richie Gant had got for *Fast Cars*? . . .

But what if she'd read this all wrong and Pelham were the only ones who were hot for *Love and the Veil*? What if no one else bid, or came in with a super-low offer? There was no way of knowing, but she was reminded that two agents had already turned Nathan down – clearly they hadn't seen any potential . . .

Think calmcalmcalm. Sound calmcalmcalm. No shallow breathing.

'That's a very generous offer,' Jojo said. Calmcalmcalm. 'I'll talk to Nathan and get back to you.'

'The offer is on the table for the next twenty-four hours,' Patricia said. Not so calmcalmcalm. Sounding quite pissed-offpissedoffpissedoff that Jojo hadn't shrieked an immediate, 'YES!' 'After that, it's withdrawn.'

'Gotcha. Thanks, Patsy. Talk soon.'

She hung up.

When she had this adrenalin thing going, her thoughts were cut-glass clear. Twenty-four hours to accept the Pelham pre-empt. If rejected, Pelham were still free to bid in the auction. *But* she knew from past experience that if they chose to do so it would be a much, much lower offer – kind of sour grapes. And there was always the chance that they may not bid at all. They were in first-love frenzy at the moment but by this time next week all that initial knee-jerk desperation to buy might have drained away and they could decide the book wasn't as good as they'd initially thought, or as commercial, or whatever. Meanwhile all the other publishing houses might pass, and Jojo would be left with no deal at all for Nathan Frey. This exact situation had happened, not to her, but it had happened. A disastrous debacle; everyone with egg on their face and no one with any money.

Anyway, she could advise but ultimately it was Nathan's call. She picked up the phone, 'Nathan, it's Jojo. We've had an offer from Pelham Press. A high one.'

'How much?'

'A million.'

There was a clatter – the phone might have fallen – then she heard retching sounds. Patiently she waited until he returned and asked faintly, 'Can I call you back?'

Half an hour later Nathan rang. 'Sorry about that. I felt a little dizzy. I've been thinking.'

I betcha.

'If they've offered that much, someone else might too.'

'There's no guarantee, but we're on the same page.'

'What do you think? What are Pelham Press like?'

'Very commercial, very aggressive, they have a lot of best-sellers.'

'Eww. They sound dreadful.'

'They're very good at what they do.' Which was piling them high and selling them cheap.

'You see, I have no clue. Jojo, don't make me do this, *you* have to decide.' He sounded on the brink of tears.

'Nathan, I want you to listen very carefully to me. This is a gamble. If we turn this down, we might not get as high in the auction.'

Still tearful, he demanded, 'Do you know how much I got paid last year? Nine grand. *Nine grand.* Anything you get me will be beyond my wildest dreams.'

He'd turn down £1 million? What a weirdo. But he *had* dressed and lived in Afghanistan as a woman for six months. Go figure.

'Don't decide now. Wait until tomorrow.'

'I have decided. What do I know about any of this? You're the agent, the expert. I trust you.'

'Nathan, a book auction is not an exact science. There's a chance it could all fall apart and I get you nothing.'

'I trust you,' he repeated.

So Jojo was on her own, the decision was hers.

11.50 Tuesday morning

She'd carried on working – quite a productive couple of hours actually; she'd reviewed the cover for Kathleen Perry's new novel and knocked it back for being too drippy; she'd rung Eamonn Farrell's editor and told her they'd need to change publication date if Eamonn's new book wasn't to clash with Larson Koza's; she'd read a horrible review of Iggy Gibson's latest and rang to commiserate.

But all the while, just beneath the skin of her thoughts, she was playing *Love and the Veil*'s two opposing scenarios off against each other. Accept or reject? Accept or reject?

Pelham weren't her publishers of choice, they were so crassly commercial that she wasn't sure they were right for this book. But a million smackers was a million smackers. Accept or reject? Accept or reject?

Accept, she decided. Then Manoj buzzed her. 'Monkey boy here. Any bananas you want eaten? Ungainly dancing you'd like done?'

'What do you want?'

'I have Alice Bagshawe for you.' Another of the chosen editors.

'Accept or –'

'Accept.' Click. 'Hey, Alice.'

'Jojo. *Love and the Veil*,' Alice said breathlessly.

'Didn't I tell you it was great?'

'It is. Completely. So much so that we at Knoxton House want to make a pre-emptive offer.'

Jojo couldn't help smiling.

'We want to offer a cool . . .' Alice drew the words out for dramatic effect, 'two . . .'

Two, Jojo thought. Two *million*. Thank *God* she hadn't accepted the Pelham pre-empt – a full million less.

'. . . hundred and twenty thousand pounds,' Alice finished.

It took a moment.

'Two *hundred* and twenty thousand?' Jojo asked.

'That's right,' Alice confirmed, mistaking Jojo's shock for happy incredulity.

'Oh. Oh, Alice, I'm really sorry, we have a much larger pre-empt on the table right now.'

'How much larger?'

'Like, a lot.'

'Jojo, we went to the wire on this. We can't go any higher.'

So Knoxton House were out. Well, there were still five in the game.

'To be honest, Jojo, I don't think it's worth any more than our bid. You really ought to accept the other offer now.'

'Yeah, thanks, Alice.'

Jojo swung in her chair, deep in thought. Alice's call had shaken her faith badly.

The four publishers who hadn't come back to her yet, which way would they jump?

Olive Liddy at Southern Cross had had a run of flops and was desperate for a hit. She could step up to the plate with a big sum – or she could have lost her nerve.

Franz Wilder at B&B Calder was in the zone: he was Editor of the Year and had edited one of the Booker shortlist. He was all set for another hit but it could be that his huge success had blunted him and he just wasn't hungry enough.

Tony O'Hare at Thor was a great editor, but Thor had recently had a major shake-down – firings and resignations – and was a house in disarray. They could badly use a hit but their chain of command was currently so confused that they might not get it together to authorize the money for Tony.

And Tania Teal at Dalkin Emery? Another smartie – Miranda England's editor. No reason why she shouldn't make the numbers.

But there was no way of knowing, not until they called her. It was out of the question for her to call them; that would trigger a major loss of confidence.

I've got to hold my nerve, she thought. I've got to keep it steady.

It wasn't the first time she'd been in a situation like this – although never for such high stakes – but there were no precedents. Just because it had worked the other times was no guarantee that it couldn't go horribly wrong this time.

And the damage would be incalculable, not just to poor penniless Nathan Frey but to her. To orchestrate a flop, before the book had even been sold . . .

Word always got around, everyone's faith in her would be shaken, and the gossamer-fine relationships she'd built up with editors over the years would take a long, long time to repair.

26

Tuesday evening, Jojo's bed (post-coital)

'So what are you going to do?' Mark asked.

'What would you do?'

'Accept the £1 million pre-empt.'

'I see . . .'

'It's an astonishing sum, especially for a debut.'

'I seeeeee . . .'

'Like that, is it?'

'What?'

'You're not going to take it, are you?'

'Yes. No. I don't know.'

'You want to beat the £1.1 million that Richie Gant got for *Fast Cars*, don't you?' Mark wound his fingers in her hair. 'It's not a good way to make decisions. If you're trying to get one over on Richie, it'll cloud your judgement.'

'I didn't ask for your advice,' she said haughtily.

'Yes, you did,' he laughed, kissing her knuckles, one by one. 'And that's the thing about asking for advice, Red, sometimes you don't get the answer you want.'

She lifted her head, disentangling his hand from her hair, then flopped back against her pillow and sighed.

'Wish you were back in the precinct?' Mark prompted. He had a little boy's interest in her police life and was always trying to get her to talk about it.

'It wasn't all *Charlie's Angels*, you know.' She was slightly testy. 'How would you like checking out a body so ripe you can smell it four floors away and having to keep watch until the bus showed up?'

'Bus?'

'Ambulance. We were supposed to wait in the apartment but sometimes the smell was so bad we couldn't. We'd haveta stand in the hallway, trying not to puke.' She turned to look at him and burst out laughing. 'Oh Mark, you should see your face. That's the thing about asking for gory details,' she deadpanned, 'sometimes you don't get the answer you want.'

He pinched her. Somewhere interesting.

'Don't do that unless you mean it.'

'*I* mean it but –'

'But?'

'– but the optic needs refilling.'

'Beautifully put.'

'While we're waiting, tell me what this terrible smell is like.'

'The worst there is, once you experience it you'll never forget it.'

'Would it make you ill?'

'Would it make you ill! The first whiff makes you gag, and you keep on gagging. And the smell gets on you – sticks like glue to your clothes and hair so everyone else gets it from you. Then *they* all start heaving. But,' she said cheerfully, 'you could get lucky and get a nice fresh one, who'd been dead only a few hours. They might have a nice apartment so you could watch TV for a coupla hours while you waited. Even get some beers in. That'd be a good day.'

'You're joking about the beers?'

'No.'

After a thoughtful silence Mark asked, 'Did it ever get to you?'

'The beers or the dead people?'

'The dead people.'

'Sure.'

'Like when?'

After another thoughtful silence Jojo replied, 'A four-year-old girl, a victim of a car crash, died in my arms. I couldn't eat dinner that night.'

'That night? Just that night?'

'Maybe for a few days. Hey, don't look at me like that.'

'Like what?'

'Like I'm a monster. I *had* to be tough, that's how we coped. You can't go out with a bleeding heart, you won't last a lick of time. Can we talk about something else?'

'Alright. How's Manoj working out?'

'He's OK. He'll do until Louisa comes back.'

'If Louisa comes back.'

'Don't.'

'And even if she does,' he teased, 'it'll all be different. She'll often be late and distracted and smelling of baby sick. Falling asleep and leaving early to bring her child to the doctor and she'll have lost the killer instinct.'

Jojo pinched him. Somewhere interesting.

'Don't do that unless you mean it.'

'Oh, I mean it.'

Afterwards they dozed off and when Jojo awoke with a jump, she saw that it was 1.15 a.m.

'Mark, get up. Time to go home.'

He sat up, his skin wafting a sweet heat to her. He was sleepy but it was clear he'd been giving this some thought. 'Why don't I stay?'

'Just not go home?'

'Yes.'

'You want to get caught?'

'Would it be so bad?'

'Yes. No matter what happens this isn't the way to do it.' She threw a sock at him. 'Get dressed. Go home.'

27

10.00 Wednesday morning
The clock ticked closer and closer to Pelham's deadline and Jojo was still no nearer to fixing on a decision.

Take the million and lose the chance of getting more? Or turn down the million and run the risk of getting far less?

There was no way of knowing: it was just a guess. Although it felt better to call it a gamble.

It was no different to the poker she used to play with Pops and her brothers. Pops used to sing,

> *You've got to know when to hold them,*
> *know when to fold them,*
> *know when to walk away . . .*

'Jojo, Patricia Evans is on the line. Do you accept or decline?'

> *. . . know when to run.*

'Decline. I'll call her back in ten.'

Jojo whooshed by Manoj's desk. 'I'm going to see Dan.'

'Your mentor,' Manoj said. 'Ment*lor*,' he amended when she was gone. Manoj feared Dan Swann and his funny green hat.

Dan was in his office doing something with a cloth to one of his pieces of war memorabilia. He was wearing his green hat – he must have forgotten to take it off when he'd come in – and underneath it his face was small and imp-like.

'Hello, Jojo, you've caught me polishing my helmet.'

Jojo was never sure how many of Dan's *double entendres* were intentional. All, she suspected, but now wasn't the time . . .

'You're looking a little hot under the collar.'

'I bet I am. I need to say this out loud: I've been offered a £1 million pre-empt from Patricia Evans. Should I accept it and lose the chance of going a lot higher? Or turn it down and run the risk of getting nothing at all? You're an experienced agent, what do you usually do?'

Dan rummaged in the pocket of his cords and emerged with a coin. 'Heads or tails?'

'Oh come *on*.'

'Sometimes I go to Olga Fisher –'

'Why Olga? Should I go see her?'

'– and we play paper scissors stone.'

Jojo looked displeased and Dan said vaguely, 'I can't give you any answers. It's a game of chance and I suspect what you should do is look at what those crass young men call the worst case scenario.'

Jojo considered it. 'Worst case scenario? I could lose £1 million. I could destroy an author's career.'

'Quite.'

'Yes,' Jojo said thoughtfully. 'Thanks, Dan. This has really helped.'

'You'll accept it?'

Jojo looked surprised. 'No.'

'Excuse me, my dear, but you've just said you could lose £1 million and destroy an author's career. You did say that, didn't you, because if you didn't I fear I may be going the way of Jocelyn Forsyth's barking auntie.'

'I said it was the worst that could happen. It's not a matter of life or death. Like, no matter what happens no one gets hurt. No, I'm going all the way. Thanks.'

A one-hundred-and-eighty swivel on her high heels and she was gone. Dan spoke to the air. 'That woman would eat her young,' he observed, with warm admiration.

Later

It was a hard call to make. Patricia wasn't pleased. Not one bit, and abruptly she withdrew the warmth she usually reserved for Jojo.

'You can still bid on Monday,' Jojo said, gently.

'I've made the only bid I'm going to make.'

'I'm sorry, I really am. If you change your mind . . . I'm going nowhere and you have my number.'

Afterwards Manoj asked, 'How did she take it?'

'She hates me.'

'I'm sure she doesn't.'

'Oh no, she does. But hey, it's not like she was my best friend. And the next time I have a good book, she'll want to know. Now tonight,' she said, changing the subject entirely, 'which yoga class should I do? I could go to the hard one and stand on one leg like a heron, sweating like a pig, or I could go to the class where I lie on the floor and breathe deeply. Which shall I do? Tell me, Manoj.'

'Lie down, breathe deeply.'

'Correct answer. You're a good boy.'

'A man, Jojo, a man. When will you see it?'

Later still

She decided to skip yoga. It had gotten too late and she could lie on the floor and breathe deeply just as easily at home in front of the TV.

She gathered up her stuff and on the way out saw that the light in Jim Sweetman's office was still on. On impulse she stopped for a quick chat, but when she rapped on the open door, then pushed it, she saw that Richie Gant was in there with Jim. They looked up at her blankly, then turned their attention back to a speaker from which a disembodied and very deep voice boomed, 'Hey, there's always residuals.'

'Sorry,' Jojo whispered, moving away.

It was seven-thirty and Jim Sweetman and Richie Gant were

on a conference call. What the hell were they up to? Who could they be talking to at this time of night? No one on Greenwich Mean Time, that was for sure. Which meant they were talking to *somewhere else.*

28

'Jojo?' Mark asked. 'Anything to report?'

'Sure have. My author Miranda England is number seven in this week's *Sunday Times* best-sellers.'

Murmurs of 'Well done' and 'Good stuff' came from around the table. Only Richie Gant said nothing at all. She knew because she looked hard at him, trying to catch his eye to have a good gloat.

Mark moved on. 'Richie?'

Both Jim Sweetman and Richie shuffled and sat up straighter. They exchanged some kind of look and Richie got the nod. *You tell them.*

Ah fuck, Jojo thought. Scooped again.

'The blinding Mr Sweetman,' Richie sounded like a disreputable used-car salesman, 'and his media department have sold the movie rights of *Fast Cars* for $1.5 million to a major Hollywood studio. We've been talking to the West Coast all week –'

Talking to the West Coast. He *loved* saying that. So that's what they'd been doing on Wednesday night.

'– and we wrapped it up late last night.'

Then Richie met her look. A full-on smirk right across the table and into her face.

3.15 Friday afternoon

Manoj buzzed her. 'I have Tony O'Hare from Thor. Accept or –'

'Accept.'

Jojo's adrenalin was in sudden full spate. This could be good.

Another pre-emptive offer, perhaps. A funny time to do it, on Friday afternoon, but . . .

'Jojo? It's Tony. It's about *Love and the Veil*.'

'Yes?' Breathless.

'I'm very sorry but I'm going to have to pass on it.'

Shit.

'Personally speaking, I loved it, but we're pulling in our horns a little here. Not such a great year, not too much spare cash, only temporary, but that's how it is. I'm sure you understand.'

'OK.' She had to clear her throat. 'OK,' she said again in a more normal voice. 'Don't worry, Tony. Thanks for letting me know.'

'No, thank *you* for sending it to me. I really am sorry, Jojo, but it's a great book and I'm sure you'll have no trouble selling it.'

Jojo was no longer sure of any such thing.

'Well?' Manoj came in.

'He's not interested.'

'Why not?'

'Says they're short of cash. Can you open the window?'

'Why? Are you going to jump?'

'I'd like some air.'

'It's painted shut. Don't you believe him?'

'It's hard to know because they'll never say outright if they don't like a book. Just in case it's a huge hit and everyone knows they passed. I'm going out to have a cigarette.'

Jojo stood on the street, inhaling and exhaling thoughtfully. There were still three publishers in the running. There was still everything to play for.

But there was very little point in going to tonight's hypnosis session. She needed to keep smoking to get her through this weekend.

29

Jojo looked up from the Sunday paper and asked, with sudden curiosity, 'Doesn't Cassie ever wonder where you are?'

Mark had shown up shortly after ten. They'd gone to bed, gone for breakfast, then back to bed and now they were making their way through a pile of magazines and newsprint. He seemed in no hurry to go home.

Mark put down Jojo's *Harpers*. 'I don't just disappear. I always tell her something.'

'Like what?'

'That I'm working, or playing golf or . . .'

'And she believes you?'

'If she doesn't, she doesn't say.'

'Maybe she's up to something herself.'

'You think she might be?'

'Would it bother you?'

After a long pause Mark said, 'It would be a relief.'

Jojo couldn't really imagine Cassie having a torrid affair. Mind you, affairs didn't have to be torrid, not all the time. Cassie might go for walks by the canal and do crosswords with her man also.

She'd seen her once, but that was long before she was interested in Mark, so she hadn't paid her much attention. She remembered her as looking like the primary school teacher she was: Suzy Hausfrau smiley and cosy with a frosted bob. She was in her early forties but Jojo only knew that because Mark had told her.

She and Mark had been married about fifteen years. Jojo

knew the story. Mark was friends with her brother – still was – and he'd met Cassie when they'd all shared a flat.

Jojo often wondered if he still loved her; she could have asked him, but she was scared he might say he did and scared he might say he didn't.

'Yikes,' Jojo said. 'I'm sorry I mentioned Cassie, now I feel, like, really guilty.'

'But –'

'Tell me something. Entertain me.'

Mark sighed, then rallied. 'OK. Look at her.' He pointed out a tennis player in the magazine. 'She gets ten million a year in sponsorship, think of the commission. We're in the wrong business, Red.'

'We could *try* getting Coke to sponsor authors. Nah, you're right, books aren't sexy enough.' She laughed at his downcast face. 'Oh, alright then, what about product placement?'

'What?'

'Well, you know – hand pick a few hot authors, match them to a product and they write about it in glowing terms in their novel.'

'I can see the industry loving that.'

'OK, *initially* it would cause uproar, but money talks.'

'So give me an example of this product placement.'

Jojo put her hands behind her head and stared thoughtfully at the ceiling. 'Take . . . say . . . let's see. Right, take Miranda England – she's good for quarter of a million copies of her current paperback, and her readers are almost entirely women aged between twenty and forty.'

'And what product would you place?'

'Ah . . .' Jojo bit her lip as she thought. 'Well, cosmetics is the obvious one. The protagonist could wear a certain brand every time she goes out. Say, Clinique.' Jojo was a Clinique girl and had been since she took herself into Macy's, aged sixteen, and had her chart done. 'You don't have to hit readers over the head with it, but you could make your point. More subtle than advertising and much more targeted.'

'God, you're good.' Mark shook his head in admiration.

'I'm only joking,' Jojo said, suddenly anxious.

'I know, but I'm enjoying it. Go on.'

'OK.' She warmed to her theme. 'Men and cars. Pick any of those guy books and have the hero driving a Ferrari. No, scrap the Ferrari, too expensive, regular people couldn't afford that. Maybe a Merc, or a Beemer.'

Then her imagination really kicked in. 'No, no, I know! Something like a Mazda. A medium-price car that's maybe trying to sex up its image. As well as putting it in the book the author would have to drive that car for a year. And the book's anti-hero could drive one of their rival's cars, it could break down at a vital moment, that sort of stuff. The possibilities are endless . . . And another thing! We could name books after the products. Not just new publications but back-list titles could also be auctioned off. *The Horse Whisperer* could become *Coca-Cola's Horse Whisperer*. Or *Bridget Jones's Diary* – "brought to you by Clinique". They do it with sport, so why not books?'

Mark was doing his thing of smiling but not looking at her. 'And how would we persuade our authors to agree to this? They're a precious lot, you know.'

'If the money was right . . .' Jojo said archly.

'You're brilliant,' Mark said. 'Brilliant. So,' he teased, 'first thing tomorrow I should set up meetings with car manufacturers and soft-drink companies.'

'Hey, it was my idea!'

'Tough. The world of business is a savage one.'

Jojo lapsed into thought. 'Wouldn't it be horrible?'

'Disgusting.'

30

Monday morning

Big day. Big, big day. The day the first-round bids for *Love and the Veil* came in. If it was a good auction, and Jojo hoped it would be, it could last all week, with bids and counter-bids, phone calls to and from editors, breath-holding gaps as they went to their publishers to get more money approved, plateaux when it looked like it was all over, until someone rode in with a last-minute bid and the entire process sparked into life again, the money spiralling up and up into the clouds . . .

10.45 a.m.

Tania Teal from Dalkin Emery was the first to throw her hat in the ring. Jojo held her breath and into the silence Tania lobbed, 'Four hundred and fifty thousand.'

Jojo exhaled. Not a bad place to start. If all three came in around this level, there was a chance they would bid against each other until they got to over a million.

'Thanks, Tania. Let me come back to you when I've heard from the others.'

She hung up. She felt great.

11.05 a.m.

Olive Liddy from Southern Cross was next.

'Hit me,' Jojo said.

'Fifty thousand.'

Jojo froze and when she unfroze the first thing she did was laugh although, of course, it was no laughing matter.

'Am I way out?' Olive asked, in a small voice.

'Not even in the same zip code.'

'I'll see what I can do.'

'Mmmm.' Jojo knew she wouldn't be hearing from her again. Her initial reading of Olive had been the correct one: her string of flops meant she'd lost her nerve.

11.15 a.m.

And then came Franz Wilder, Editor of the Year.

'I'd like to offer three-fifty.'

'Three hundred and fifty thousand?' *And not three pounds fifty? Probably as well to check, considering the way things were going.*

'Three hundred and fifty thousand.'

Thank Christ. There were still two players.

'That's a very healthy bid, Franz. Not the highest I've had but close. If you'd like to come back to me later with a higher –'

'No.'

'Excuse me?'

'That's my final bid.'

'But –'

'I could really knock this book into shape . . .' Franz trailed off, his point made.

Her heart sank and sank and kept on sinking, through her body, through the soles of her shoes and into the graphic designers on the floor below. That was the trouble with those intellectual, black-poloneck-wearing, chin-stroking editors. Give them a couple of prizes and they start thinking they're all that.

'Thing is, Franz,' she forced an uplift into her voice, 'Nathan is very hot right now and everyone wants a piece of him.'

'This is a great book, I could really do a lot with it.'

'Oh, for sure,' she agreed earnestly. 'But –'

'That's my final offer, Jojo.'

'Yes, but –' If she could only get him up to Tania's bid, then she could push it higher.

'No, Jojo, that's it.'

'OK. Thanks, Franz.' What else could she say? 'We'll consider what you said. And if Nathan decides that he'd prefer less money in exchange for your expertise, you'll certainly be hearing from us.'

Like fuck, she thought, hanging up and feeling the life force drain from her. The full horrible truth kicked in and suddenly she was flailing in empty space. There was only one editor in play: Tania Teal. *How can I have a bidding war with only one bidder?*

How could this have happened?

Short of lying to Tania and telling her there were other parties bidding their heads off, there was no way of leveraging the money any higher. Not only was lying disgustingly unethical but there was a big chance it could backfire: Tania might be near her limit and decide not to go any higher – and Jojo would be left with nothing at all.

So, was this it? Going once, going twice, going three times – sold to Tania Teal for four hundred and fifty thousand? A mere five hundred and fifty thousand less than Patricia Evans had offered. Not even half. *Oh my God.*

Jojo couldn't make the call to Tania; not yet. It was only eleven-thirty on Monday morning – this *couldn't* be over already. Something *had* to be retrievable. There must be something she could do.

She swallowed, pushing down nausea. I screwed up, she admitted. I got it so wrong. I should have taken Patricia Evans's offer.

Patricia Evans! she thought, like a light bulb going on over her head. I could try her again. She mightn't come in as high as before, she mightn't come in at all, but she might bid something. *Anything* to kick this back into life.

Suddenly she felt insanely hopeful but it took three fumbly attempts to open her address book. As the number rang she rehearsed the call; she'd be casual and friendly. 'Hey, Patsy,' she'd say. 'Just to remind you that today's the day for the bids for *Love and the Veil.*' No need to mention the £1 million pre-empt and Patricia's anger when it had been turned down.

Over the years she'd learned that if you act like things are a certain way, sometimes people are confused enough to play along.

But Patricia wasn't available. She could have been any number of legitimate places – in a meeting, at the dentist, in the loo, but Jojo was so paranoid, she was convinced that Patricia was mouthing elaborately at her assistant, 'Tell her I'm dead.'

Jojo hung up and tried hard to get things in proportion. Four hundred and fifty thousand pounds was a phenomenal sum of money; it would change Nathan Frey's life for ever.

But she could have got him so much more – and the higher the advance, the higher the marketing and publicity budgets as the publishers sought to ensure they recouped their advance.

And this terrible feeling of loss wasn't just to do with the money. It was because she'd fucked up. She'd been so sure of this book, so certain it would break records, she would have staked her career on it. A horrible thought – perhaps she had. Without realizing it, maybe this had been the biggest chance she'd ever get, and she'd blown it. A million quid was so much money, and she'd turned it down. What had she been *thinking*?

What if this ruined her chances of being made partner? What if Richie Gant beat her to it? He'd only joined Lipman Haigh eight months ago and Jojo had been there for two and a half years – but he was doing so well. And Jojo wasn't . . .

The panic was closing about her and threatening to choke her and she made herself think reasonable thoughts. No one died, no one got hurt. We'll all be dead some day and it'll all be irrelevant. And the old favourite of losers: you win some, you lose some.

But it wasn't nice to lose some and even less nice when people heard about it . . . She'd have to try to contain this – if Richie Gant found out, she'd never hear the end of it.

Manoj came in and took one look at her face. 'Oh no.'

'Oh yes.'

'Tell me.'
'Not now. I'm going out to buy something.'
'What?'
'Anything.'

31

Jojo almost bought a bin for her bathroom; it was blue plastic and had little dolphin shapes cut out of it, but when it came to picking it up and queuing at the cash desk, she was just too disheartened.

She traipsed back to the office and ate a ham and cheese croissant, watching hopelessly as the flakes floated down and stuck to her desk.

When Manoj buzzed with a call her heart nearly jumped out of her jacket – could it be Patricia Evans?

'Olive Liddy on line one.'

'I only have one line.'

'So? It doesn't mean she's not on line one.'

Jojo sighed heavily. 'Put her through.'

'Olive? What can I do for you?' *Want to add another fiver to your bid?*

'*Love and the Veil*? I hope it's not too late. I'd like to make an offer.'

'Have you had a knock on the head, Olive? You already made your bid. I laughed, remember?'

'I want to increase it.'

'To what?'

'Six hundred thousand.'

'Wha –? Hey, what's going on, Olive?' *How did you manage to get another five hundred and fifty thousand approved in three hours?*

'I misread the worth of the book. I got it wrong.'

Then Jojo got it. Olive had been hoping no one else was interested and that she'd pick it up cheap. Some nerve! But so what? Everything was back on! Thank Christ.

'I'll get back to you on that.'

Monday 3.07 p.m.

'Tania? We've had some bids higher than yours.'

'How much higher?'

'You know I can't really say . . .'

'Jojo!'

'Six.'

'OK. Seven.'

'Thanks, I'll get back to you.'

3.09 p.m.

'Olive? I've had another bid. Higher than yours.'

'How much higher?'

'You know I can't really say . . .'

'How much?'

'Seven.'

'Eight, then.'

3.11 p.m.

'Tania? We've had another bid.'

'I need more time. I'm not authorized to go any higher.'

'When will you get back to me?'

'Soon.'

Tuesday 10.11 a.m.

'Jojo, it's Olive. Is the book mine?'

'I'm waiting to hear back from another interested party.'

'I need to know soon.'

'Gotcha.'

10.15 a.m.

'Tania, I'm going to have to hurry you.'

'Sorry, Jojo. We've been trying to get hold of our publisher. I need him to approve more money, but he's sailing around the Caribbean.'

'How soon can you get back to me?'

'I'll try for close of business today.'

4.59 p.m.

'Olive, it's Jojo, can you give me until tomorrow morning?'

'Well, I don't know . . .'

'Please, Olive. We're old friends.'

'OK.'

Wednesday 10.14 a.m.

'Tania?'

'Jojo! Look, um, sorry I didn't get back to you yesterday. I still haven't been able to get hold of him.'

'I'm sorry, Tania, but the other party is really leaning on me.'

'Give me until after lunch. Please, Jojo, we go back a long way.'

2.45 p.m.

'Jojo?'

'Tania?'

'Nine hundred!'

2.47 p.m.

'Olive?'

'Jojo?'

'Nine hundred's the figure to beat.'

'Fuck! I thought it was mine. Well, I'll have to go further up the feeding chain to get more money approved.'

'When can you get back to me?'

'Soon.'

2.55 p.m.

'Jojo, it's Becky. I fell asleep at lunchtime and dreamt all my teeth fell out. What does it mean? Fear of what? Commitment? Death?'

'Fear of all your teeth falling out. I have to go now, Becks.'

Thursday 10.08 a.m.

'Jojo, it's Tania.'

'Still waiting to hear from the others.'

'I need to know, you know. Nine hundred is a huge sum and I know Olive Liddy is the other editor . . .'

'What makes you say that?'

'Word gets around. And she'll never get anything higher authorized. They're hopeless over there.' (Tania had been made redundant from Southern Cross after a bitter falling out. Feelings still ran high.)

'Please, Tania, can you just give me until after lunch?'

'Two-thirty, but then I'm pulling out.'

10.10 a.m.

'Olive, Jojo here.'

'Yes, sorry, look, we're having an emergency meeting this afternoon with the heads of sales, marketing and publicity. I'll call you back as soon as it's over.'

'Can't you have the meeting any sooner? It's just I'm being leant on . . .'

'Not really. Our Marketing Manager is having an ingrowing toenail removed this morning, he's been waiting months for the appointment and he won't be out of surgery until twelve-thirty. Then he's coming straight in. Please, Jojo, like you said yesterday, we're old friends . . .'

'Yes, I know but I need a quick decision. Otherwise I'm going to have to give it to the other party.'

'It's that bitch Tania Teal, isn't it? And you don't want to listen to her, she hasn't the guts to walk away.'

'Look –'

'Three-thirty. I'll get back to you then. It's the best I can do.'

2.29 p.m.

'It's Manoj. I've Tania Teal on the line.'

'It's not even two-thirty!'

'What'll I tell her?'

'Something. Anything. Buy me an hour.'

'Broken leg?'

'Maybe not so serious.'

'*Suspected* broken leg?'

'Go for it.'

3.24 p.m.

'Jojo, you're not going to believe it.'

'Becky, hi, I –'

'I was in a meeting this morning and guess what? One of my teeth fell out. I was just about to speak when a tooth began rattling around in my mouth like a cola cube. Just like my dream!'

'How could a tooth just fall out?'

'It wasn't exactly a tooth, it was a crown, but this could mean I'm psychic.'

'Has the crown been wobbly lately?'

'No. Well, just a little, ha –'

'Becky, I'm sorry, sweets, I've got to go.'

3.31 p.m.

'Jojo, it's Olive. OK.' Deep, deep breath. 'A million.'

3.33 p.m.

'Tania, they've bid a million.'

'A million! How can they authorize that dodo that kind of money? She couldn't edit her way out of a paper bag –'

'Are you in or are you out?'

'In, but I have to try to loosen those purse strings a bit more. By the way, how's your leg?'

Now that she'd got the offer back up to a million, the original pre-empt, Jojo was as high as a kite.

'What happens next?' Manoj asked.

'That's it for today, but they'll be back tomorrow. They both love the book – *and* it's a grudge match, which can only be good news for us.'

'How are you going to celebrate tonight? Yoga?'

'Yoga, my ass. Rampant sex with my boyfriend.' *Fuckkkkk.* Shouldn't have said that. Soaring spirits had made her careless.

Manoj moaned. 'Who is he?'

'Never mind.'

'It's Richie Gant, isn't it?'

'No. He's your boyfriend.'

'He was yours first, but he dumped you and you were heartbroken and kept calling round to his house and begging him to take you back.'

Jojo pulled a brush through her hair. 'How d'I look?'

'Bend over and shake your hair upside down.'

Jojo looked at him coldly. 'You must take me for a total idiot.'

'No! It gives it more volume. It wasn't so I could look down your shirt.

'OK,' he admitted, 'it wasn't *just* so I could look down your shirt.'

7.15 Thursday evening, outside Jojo's block

The first she knew of Mark blowing her off was when she bumped into the flower-delivery boy at the communal front door.

'Where've you been?' he asked. 'I'm just about to go home. I finish at seven, you know.'

'These are for me?' She looked at the flowers. 'Ah, shit.'

'Thanks a bunch!'

Tucking the flowers under her arm, beside the bottle of champagne that it looked like she'd be drinking on her own, she switched on her mobile. There were three messages from Mark; his little girl Sophie's pony had stood on her foot and broken two of her toes. He was incredibly sorry. (First message)

He was beyond sorry. (Second message) Was she ignoring him? (Third call)

She rang him on his mobile.

'Cassie could have taken her,' he explained. 'But she was so upset she asked me to come with her.'

She heard the agony in his voice: his little girl was in pain and she wanted her dad. She sighed; how could she stay angry?

'Saturday? Sunday?' Mark asked.

'Can't you do tomorrow night? I've got my smoking hypnosis thing and want a get-out.'

'Sorry, Jojo, I've got to take those Italian publishers out. But if you don't want to be hypnotized, don't go. You don't need an excuse.'

'You're right. OK, how about Saturday? Tell Sophie to stay away from that damn horse and barring any other broken limbs, you're on.'

At a loose end she rang Becky but both her home and mobile numbers went to voicemail, so she rang Shayna.

'We'll go out,' Shayna said.

'Can you get a babysitter at such short notice?'

'Babysitter? I don't need no babysitter, I got me a Brandon. Oi! Brandon! I'm going out for a few drinks with Jojo.'

'Shall I come to you?'

'Nah! Believe me, you don't want to go in a pub round here. Not unless you fancy getting shot. How about Islington, the King's Head, in an hour's time, yeah?'

'See you then.'

They talked about the auction, about how much Jojo hated Richie Gant, about Brandon's impotence, then, a few drinks in, Jojo made the mistake of spilling to Shayna about the broken date with Mark.

'It's not good, girl.' Shayna shook her head in contempt.

Contempt of *her*, Jojo realized and, laughing, pushed her. 'Don't *look* at me like that.'

'Just telling you what I see. You don't like it, you change it.

You know what you ought to do?' Shayna decreed. Without giving Jojo a chance to reply she said, 'You ought to bring him out to meet us – me and Brandon, Becky and Andy. That's what people *do*, they meet each other's friends.'

'But he's *married*.'

'Yeah, but if he's as serious about you as you say, he probably wants to meet us.'

'You mean you want to meet him. No, Shayna –'

'You're going to have to normal this thing out. Come on Sunday for brunch. I'll get Mum to cook and mind the little horrors. We'll get pissed and bond. One-thirty suit?'

Oh Jesus. 'No, Shayna. My time with him is too precious. I don't want to share him with anyone else.'

'One-thirty.' Shayna set her jaw.

'No.' Jojo fixed her stare on Shayna.

'One-thirty.'

'No.'

'One-thirty.'

'No.'

'One-thirty.'

'No.'

'One-thirty.'

'No.'

'Oh my God!'

'What?'

'It's one of the Wyatts.'

Jojo swivelled to look at the crowds flooding out of the theatre and into the bar and saw a tall, blonde woman.

'It's Magda!' Her favourite. Shayna's too.

Magda spotted them. 'Jojo! You gorgeous girl!' They embraced. 'And Shayna! How lovely to see you.'

She wasn't as nice to Shayna as she was to me, Jojo thought.

'Is Becky here?'

'No, just us,' Shayna mumbled. She sounded apologetic.

'We're going for supper.' Magda gestured at the nimbus of

beauty that surrounded her. Seven or eight perfect men and women. 'Join us,' she placed a beseeching hand on Jojo's arm.

She sounded like she really meant it but Jojo didn't feel right about gatecrashing so she made a lame excuse about an early start the next day.

'If you're sure, but you must promise to ring me and we'll go out. Promise me!'

Then Magda was gone and the room seemed a lot less glittering.

'She was nicer to you.' Shayna said quietly.

'Yeah. Yeah, she was. She called me "gorgeous".'

There was a moment's silence, then they collapsed in on each other, shaking with laughter. 'You know what we are?' Shayna concluded. 'We're pitiful.'

32

Friday morning

Tania came back with a further fifty thousand, which was less than Jojo was expecting. Then Olive counter-bid twenty thousand.

'Why so glum?' Manoj asked Jojo. But he knew. 'You think it won't get over the £1.1 million Richie Gant got for *Fast Cars?*'

'It's not over yet.'

But Tania's next bid was for ten thousand, and Olive's counter-bid was also for ten. Both editors were almost at their ceilings and the bidding stood at £1.09 million.

'You need ten grand more,' Manoj said.

'Twenty. I want to beat him, not just match him.'

Another five from Tania followed, then five from Olive – then three from Tania! It had passed the marker set by Richie Gant. Only just, but so what.

In small increments Jojo managed to inch the money up until both editors were at £1.12 million.

'Twenty grand more,' Manoj observed. 'You can stop now.'

But Jojo was going to have to stop anyway. There was no more money and because the bids were equal, a beauty contest would be held, where Nathan would be wheeled around to both publishers, who'd put on a bit of a show, then Nathan would decide who he liked best.

Manoj made the calls. 'Next Thursday morning,' he said. 'You go to Dalkin Emery at ten and Southern Cross at eleven-thirty.'

Midnight, Friday, Jojo's flat

Her buzzer rang. Mark. He'd dispatched the posse of rowdy Italians into the night, then arrived, uninvited, at Jojo's.

'I wanted to see you. I got rid of the Italians,' he yelled, a little drunkenly, into the intercom. 'I got a cab.'

'What do you want, a medal?'

She was happy to see him, like, a *lot*, but no way was he to get into the habit of just dropping in for a quick bonk whenever he wanted, before heading home to his wife.

She stood at her door and watched him climb the last section of stairs.

'I could've had my other guy here. How lucky is that?'

He arrived at the top and pulled her to him, with all the ardour of the pissed person. 'There'd better not be anyone else.'

'The married man tells me I'd better not have someone else!'

'You're right.' He wrestled his mobile from his pocket. 'This has gone on long enough, I'm going to tell Cassie I love you and –'

She grabbed the phone. 'Give me that, you drunken moron. Seeing as you're here, I've got plans for you.'

Twenty minutes later

Jojo rolled off him; they were both slick with sweat and fighting for breath.

'That was . . . that was . . .' he heaved.

'Atrocious?'

'Yes. You?'

'The worst ever.'

'All fired up after the auction?'

'Yeah,' she grinned, 'all that testosterone.'

'You played a high risk game.'

'But it worked.'

'So tell me, did you set out to beat Richie Gant?'

'*Course* I did.'

She touched the tip of her tongue to his shoulder. Salt on smooth skin. Then she buried her face in his neck and inhaled his scent. Oh, he was delicious.

They jerked awake simultaneously, looked at the clock and stared at each other, wild-eyed and sticky-up-haired with fear.

'Shit!' Jojo said. 'Mark, quick, get up, go home!'

'Fuck!' Pale and clearly hungover, Mark hot-footed it out of the door, still dressing himself. 'I'll ring you later.'

'OK. Good luck.'

Seconds later Jojo heard the main front door slam; he must have body-surfed the five flights. Her stomach was a hard ball of apprehension: this was crunch time. Cassie would know, Mark would tell her, they'd break it to the kids, it would be awful, he'd move out of Putney, he'd move in here, they'd be a couple and she wasn't sure she was ready yet.

The day was endless as she waited to hear from him. She went to yoga, on the premise that it was so nasty it would take her mind off the waiting. Which it did admirably but only for an hour. When she returned home she half-expected to find Mark waiting outside with a suitcase. But nothing. And no messages. Not good. No news is bad news. Mark and Cassie were probably locked in a horrible cycle of tears and recrimination. Her insides shrank at the vision.

She made Becky go shopping with her. They spent the afternoon in Whiteleys, Jojo checking her mobile for messages every fifteen minutes. Nothing. And she hated the powerlessness of not being able to ring him.

He finally called on Saturday evening when Jojo was at Becky and Andy's.

'Is it him?' Becky mouthed, her eyes wide with apprehension.

Jojo nodded brusquely.

'It's him,' Becky whispered to Andy and they sat and held hands, like they were waiting for a diagnosis of cancer.

Jojo got up and went into the hallway. 'So what happened? Are we busted?'

'No.'

She exhaled, doing it properly for the first time that day. But lacing the relief was some disappointment. In her head, he was already living with her and she'd made peace with the idea. Had become quite happy about it, actually.

'So tell me.'

It transpired that Cassie had actually slept right through the night and only noticed that Mark wasn't there when he barged in at five to seven with his over-rehearsed excuse – long-week-late-night-rowdy-Italians- residents'-bar-comfy-sofa-fell-asleep-here's-their-number-if-you-don't-believe-me.

But Cassie did believe him – Jojo decided she was dumber than she'd already thought – and Jojo and Mark spent much of Sunday on a subdued post-mortem. 'That was too close for comfort,' they agreed. 'We've got to make sure it never happens again.'

It happened again, four nights later. Even though the previous time had caused such horrible anxiety, it hadn't been the end of the world; they'd gotten away with it. And they got away with it again.

33

Thursday morning, Dalkin Emery

Jojo stepped out of the lift, then beckoned Nathan to follow.

'Right,' he swallowed, putting a tentative foot out of the lift and onto the hallowed floor of Dalkin Emery. He felt like kissing it.

'Don't be nervous,' Jojo rubbed his back gently. 'They're only publishers – who want to give you shedloads of money and publish your novel. Most authors would kill to be in your shoes.'

She clicked down the corridor and smiled a breezy hello at the receptionist. 'Morning, Shirley.'

'Morning, Jojo.'

'This is Nathan Frey.'

Shirley smiled politely at the pale, dazed-looking man – the reason she'd had to come to work at seven-thirty this morning and spread sand all over the boardroom floor. 'They're in the boardroom. I'll just tell them you're here –'

'I know the way.'

'Yes, so I'll just –'

But she was gone, Nathan trotting meekly after her.

Kicking their heels in the boardroom were all the high-ups of Dalkin Emery: the heads of sales, marketing and publicity and their assistants, as well as the commissioning editor, Tania Teal, and her publisher. *Love and the Veil* was the most important pitch they'd done all year.

'Bloody Jojo, she's always late,' Tania Teal observed, sticking her head out of the door, then whipping it back in again. 'Christ, here she comes!'

A scramble as everyone prepared themselves, then Jojo was at the door, shepherding in Nathan who was trying to smile, dots of perspiration on his upper lip.

Dick Barton-King, Head of Sales, straightened himself and peered through the eye-hole of his burkha. He could see very little, which was a pity: he loved Jojo.

Under the yards of musty fabric, he swam about searching for his hem so he could shake hands. He loathed this burkha. It had been Marketing's idea – of *course*. So why couldn't one of them have worn it? How come they got away with just wearing National Trust tea-towels on their heads?

Nor had he been given one of the toy machine-guns that Tania Teal herself had personally gone out and purchased. It wasn't fair.

Pitches for 'big' books had become more and more elaborate. But never mind a roomful of sand and other Afghani accoutrements, Jojo thought: let's see the colour of their marketing budget.

They took their seats and the team sprang into action with dazzling talk of television advertising, a three-week publicity tour, a hundred thousand print run, guaranteed profiles in the quality newspapers . . .

'The *Observer* would want to interview me?' Nathan sounded delighted.

'Yes,' Juno, Chief Publicist, said. 'I'm sure we could set it up.' Well, maybe they could. *Probably*.

Suggested jacket covers had already been mocked up, as had advertising posters and projected sales figures. Even Jojo, who was used to publishers' jazz, had to admit it was an impressive display.

As for Nathan, he was so overwhelmed that at one stage Jojo was worried that he'd faint.

When it was all over, the Dalkin Emery staff watched them go.

'That seemed to go well,' Tania Teal said quietly, unzipping her boot and tipping a little pyramid of sand out of it.

'Yes,' said Fran Smith, her assistant, looking around with a sigh at the sand she'd have to sweep up.

Jojo assisted Nathan into a taxi and took him to Southern Cross where Olive Liddy and her team did a very different presentation. No sand, no burkhas, no toy machine-guns. Just talk of Booker prizes.

Though they were offering the same advance as Dalkin Emery they had provided for a much smaller publicity budget. They made it sound like a good thing. 'Overkill can ruin a book,' Olive said earnestly. 'Good books don't need to be advertised in shopping malls and tube stations. They speak for themselves.'

When pressed by Olive, Nathan agreed that, no, he didn't want to be lumped in with the likes of John Grisham and Tom Clancy, all over airports, bookshops and the best-seller lists. That building a quality reputation based on good reviews and word-of-mouth recommendations was far more *him*.

When the meeting ended Jojo took Nathan to a nearby pub and tried to provide a balanced view. 'Even books as wonderful as yours can benefit from advertising.'

'It's my book,' Nathan said, a little angrily, his head turned by the idea of winning literary prizes. 'I want to go with Southern Cross.'

Oh here we go, Jojo thought. It's started already.

34

Friday morning

'It's in,' Manoj said, spinning a copy of *Book News* onto her desk. 'Page five.'

Book News, 2 March

RECORD-BREAKING SALE

Love and the Veil, a debut novel set in Afghanistan, has been sold to Olive Liddy at Southern Cross for an alleged £1.12 million, the highest sum ever paid in the UK for a first novel. Described by Ms Liddy as 'the book of the decade', its author Nathan Frey is a former school teacher who lived as a woman in Afghanistan for six months while researching the book. The sale was agented by Jojo Harvey of Lipman Haigh who has enjoyed a recent run of success. She also represents Miranda England, who is number one in this week's mass market chart with her fourth novel. The underbidder, Tania Teal at Dalkin Emery, was said to be 'devastated'.

Devastated just about described it, Jojo thought. She'd sobbed when Jojo rang her the previous afternoon to break the news. It was one of the hardest things about her job, having to let people down, but there can only be one winner.

'Manoj, could you go out and buy a cake?'

'We're celebrating?'

'No, Louisa is coming to visit this afternoon, with baby Stella.'

Manoj was rattled. 'Louisa?' But he rallied gamely. 'Then

perhaps she can tell me where she filed the Miranda England contract. And you say she was efficient?'

Jocelyn Forsyth knocked on her door, 'Heartiest congratulations, my dear.'

'Thank you.'

'Everything sewn up? All the small print, etcetera, etcetera?'

'Nearly. We're just hanging plastic.'

'Hanging plastic?'

Oh no.

'Another of your wonderful law enforcement adages?'

'No. It's a firefighter one.'

His face was eager and enquiring, so she said, 'When the fire is finally out, they have to secure the building, so they hang plastic over the windows.'

'Hanging plastic. *Mar*vellous.'

Next to arrive was Jim Sweetman who shone his glorious smile around the office.

'Congratulations. It should be fun selling the movie rights.'

'Does that mean I get a trip to LA?'

'Depends. How's your golf?'

'My *golf*?'

'Oh yes, you need to be able to play golf to bond with these movie types.'

'See you got lucky, Cagney.'

Jojo looked up. Richie Gant was standing at her office door and she put down her pen. 'What? You mean my £1.12 million deal for Nathan Frey?'

'How lucky was that?'

'Yeah,' Jojo smiled. 'And you know what? The harder I work, the luckier I get.'

His mouth was working like he wanted to say something but

couldn't get it together. He was visibly in the grip of strong emotion.

'Aww,' Jojo tipped her head to one side. 'Who needs a hug?'

She looked at the clock on her phone. 'It's time for the weekly meeting anyway. Let me walk you up there.' She tried to put her hand on his back but he scooted away.

At the meeting, a major fuss was made of Jojo's deal – the 'book of the decade'. The partners were especially thrilled as they would receive a direct cut of the commission, but even the ordinary agents were delighted; all except for Richie Gant.

'How many books of the decade is that now?' he asked. 'Must be at least six.'

This caused unease. Everyone got jealous but most people were smart enough to keep it to themselves.

'That's not very sporting,' Dan Swann protested.

'Whatcha expect?' Jocelyn Forsyth asked, in a strange, strangled voice. 'The chap's a rookie. I say we wank him off and get him out of here.'

'Jerk,' Jojo whispered as the room filled up with stricken silence. 'Jerk, not wank.'

Friday afternoon

From two-thirty onwards, the female employees of Lipman Haigh clustered into Jojo's office – even Lobelia French and Aurora Hall put their hatred of Jojo to one side – bearing bite-sized socks, pink sweatpants, denim pinafores and minia-ture T-shirts emblazoned with glittery princesses.

'Wouldn't you just love them for yourself,' Pam sighed.

'Always.'

Then Louisa appeared around the door and grinned, 'Hiiiiiii.'

'Your hair!' Jojo yelped. Louisa's sharp haircut had grown out so her face was framed and she looked younger and sweeter than Jojo remembered.

'Oi!' Louisa indicated the bundle strapped to her front. 'Never mind my hair. What about this?'

'Show us,' Pam squealed.

'Form an orderly queue,' Jojo ordered. 'Be*hind* me. I bought the cake, I get first go. 'Hello, sweets.' She bent to kiss Louisa. 'Congratulations. Now gimme.'

'Say hello to your auntie Jojo.' Louisa passed Stella over.

'Wow.' Jojo stared down into the tiny face, at her black eyelashes and unfocused blue eyes.

'Isn't she gorgeous?' Louisa said.

'Gorgeous. And she smells fantastic.' Powdery and milky. In fact, Louisa also smelt of powder and milk; she used to operate in a cloud of Dior.

'Can I have a go now?' Pam pleaded.

'Then me,' Olga Fisher insisted.

As everyone cooed over Stella, Manoj distributed cake and gave Louisa slitty glares.

'Louisa,' he said loudly, 'as we have you here, we can't find Miranda England's contract. Any ideas?'

'Hmmm?' Louisa smiled vaguely. 'Miranda What?'

'Miranda England. Remember the most recent contract she signed? Do you know where you filed it?'

Another vague smile. 'No, no idea.'

And even less interest, Jojo realized.

Then in came Mark, and the cluster of women parted to make way for him. 'Congratulations,' he kissed Louisa and looked down. 'I see she has her mother's looks.'

'Would you like to hold her?'

Mark gingerly took Stella and cradled her in the crook of his arm, then smiled at her and said softly, 'Hello, beautiful.'

Ohmigod. The piece of cake which had been on its way to Jojo's mouth, paused, then returned to the paper plate.

'I'm in love,' Mark cooed, stroking Stella's face with his finger and Louisa laughed and said, 'I hate to break this up, but I'd better go.'

'What already?!' Everyone asked in alarm.

'I came on the bus so that I could breast-feed her but if I

don't go now I'll get stuck in the rush-hour traffic and it'll be all hours before I get her home.'

'Stay a bit longer,' Olga Fisher urged.

'I really can't.'

'OK.' Reluctantly they let her go and drifted back to their own offices.

Jojo gathered up all the gifts, walked Louisa to the lift and asked, just so that Louisa would ask her back, 'Are you all right?'

Louisa did another of those beatific smiles and said, 'Jojo, I've never been happier. I am totally blissed out.'

'I'm still seeing Mark.'

'He's a lovely man. See how nice he was to Stella.'

Ah. OK. The connection Jojo wanted wasn't going to happen, not today, anyway. It was as if Louisa wasn't really Louisa at the moment; she was someone else, in thrall to a tiny bundle. Let's face it, the whole time she was in the office the only person she'd really made eye-contact with was Stella, even though Stella could barely see.

She kissed her goodbye. 'Stay in touch and see you in . . . when are you due back? June?'

'Mmm, June. See you then.'

'Well!' Manoj spluttered at Jojo, when she returned. 'Did you see that?'

'What?'

'When Mark Avery held the baby, all the women went, "Ahhhh!" Women hold babies all the time and no one says, "Ahhhh!" What's that about?'

Jojo studied him. 'You tell me?' She was keen to know why the sight of Mark cooing over Stella had shut down her appetite for nice cake.

'It's obvious!'

'Because he looked manly but gentle?'

He rolled his eyes. 'Because he's the boss and they were sucking up to him.'

Four weeks later

'Perhaps you should have a look at this.' Pam handed Jojo a bundle of pages. 'I think it's a manuscript.'

'You *think*?'

'Yeah. It's like emails and stuff.'

'Non-fiction?'

'Not exactly. And the person who wrote it isn't the person who submitted it. The author is called Gemma Hogan, but her friend Susan is the one who sent it in.'

'Sounds way off.'

Pam shrugged. 'I recommend you take a look. I'm not sure but I think it might be great.'

LILY

Even though I made my choice, I shall never forgive myself. This sounds wildly melodramatic, I know, but I mean it simply as a statement of fact. There are many times – to this day – when I wish I had never met him. It's the most dreadful thing I've ever done, and even now, though we're together and have Ema, frequently I find myself in the middle of ordinary stuff, making Ema's bottle or washing my hair or whatever, and realize that I'm still waiting for a catastrophe. Building one's happiness on someone else's misery is no foundation for long-term stability. Anton says I have Catholic guilt. But I wasn't brought up Catholic – apparently I don't have to be.

Journalists. In my short career as an interviewee I'd met two varieties. Those who displayed their 'serious' credentials by dressing like the homeless (a look I inadvertently favoured myself since becoming a mother). Or those who appeared to spend their entire lives attending functions at foreign embassies. The one now stepping over my threshold – Martha Hope Jones from the *Daily Echo* – was a foreign embassy merchant. She wore a red suit with gilt buttons and braided epaulettes on the shoulders, and high shoes the precise red of her suit. I wondered how she had managed that. Perhaps she'd gone to one of those wedding service places who dye the bridesmaids' shoes the exact colour of the bridesmaids' dresses. Not that I would know much about that.

'Welcome to my humble abode,' I said, and almost bit my tongue. I so did not want to draw her attention to how humble my abode actually was: a one-bedroomed ex-council flat, which housed Anton, Ema and me.

When Otalie, my publicist at Dalkin Emery, had set up this interview, I had begged to be permitted to meet Martha in a hotel, a bar, a bus shelter – anywhere but here. But as it was an 'At home' piece, I was left with little choice.

'Delightful,' Martha declared, poking her nose into the kitchen and taking in two clothes-horses laden with garments which were defiantly refusing to dry.

'You weren't supposed to go in there.' I flushed. 'Pretend you didn't see.'

But Martha had reached into her (same red as her shoes) bag, taken out a notebook and scribbled something. I tried reading upside down and thought one of the words looked like 'pigsty'.

I directed her into the living room which Anton – bless him – had tidied. Well, he'd herded forty or fifty of Ema's squashy toys in a corner, then emptied a full can of peach air-freshener into the air in the hope of masking the smell of mildewing laundry.

Martha plonked herself on the sofa, yelped, 'Jesus!' and sprang to her feet again. We both looked at the small piece of Lego which was the cause of Martha's painfully indented buttock.

'Sorry, it's my little girl's . . .'

Martha scribbled something else in the notebook.

'Don't you use a tape recorder?' I asked.

'No, this is much more intimate.' She brandished her pen with a smile. Yes, and she could misquote me till the cows came home.

'Where is your little girl?' She looked around the room.

'At the playground with her dad.' Where they would remain, hogging the swings, until I called them to say the coast was clear. I could not involve them in this.

Martha accepted tea, refused biscuits, then the interview began.

'Well! You've done rather nicely for yourself, dear, haven't you? Mmmm?' Her eyes were a little like blue marbles, rather glassy and avid. 'You and your *Mimi's Remedies*.'

She made it sound as if I had pulled off a confidence trick on the gullible public. Nor did I know how to respond. 'Yes, I have done rather nicely, thank you'? Would that seem arrogant? By the same token, if I shrugged, 'It's not as if I've invented time travel,' would she snap her notebook closed and leave?

'I've read part of your biog, but I'm sure you know that Martha Hope Jones' profiles are quite different from the pieces regular hacks produce. I prefer to start with a clean slate, get to know who Lily actually is and *really* get under her skin.'

She made a burrowing motion with her hand and I nodded warily. I so did not want her under my skin.

'You've not always been a writer, Lily?'

'No. Until two years ago I worked in Public Relations.'

'*Did* you?' Her manifest surprise was insulting even though I knew I didn't look like the archetypal PR person.

Snappy, quick-thinking, image builders, who go to bat for other people, ought to *look* like snappy, quick-thinking, image builders; suits, salon-perfect hair and professional-style maquillage. But even at the height of my modest success my hems mysteriously unravelled and my long blonde hair fell out of its grips and into my coffee at important meetings. (This was the reason that my account manager stopped inviting me to get-to-knows with the clients. He lied to the client, usually saying I was having physiotherapy.)

'What area of PR?' Martha was intrigued. 'One-hit-wonder singers? Soap stars on the slide?'

'Nothing so worthy.' And I was not trying to be funny.

PR's image is one of attempting to get tacky, talentless singers/actors/models into the paper. If only. PR is also about selling powdered milk to penniless Africans, by insisting it's better for their babies than breast milk. It's a PR person in the pay of a tobacco company who informs susceptible governments that having a population of smokers is a good idea because it kills everyone off before they're too old to need pensions and geriatric care. It's a press release written by a talented PR person which convinces a community that it does not matter if their water system is being poisoned by a chemical corporation because the company is also bringing jobs to the area.

Advertising and bribes to politicians can only do so much. When push came to shove and the indefensible required defending, I came to the rescue by producing press releases.

My sympathy with those who were having a huge dump installed outside their town, or a motorway snaking through their back garden, was sincere. As a result my press releases carried conviction; to my shame, I was seriously good at my job and innumerable times I *longed* for a couple of singers with flagging careers.

'So there you are working away in PR.' Martha's pen was doing overtime. 'Where was this?'

'Dublin, initially, then London.'

'What were you doing in Ireland?'

'My mum went to live there when I was twenty and I went with her.'

'And now you're back in the UK. What happened?'

'Cutbacks. I was made redundant.'

My own fault. I had done such an effective job on two huge campaigns that both companies got what they wanted and we no longer had their lucrative retainers. It coincided with a shrinkage in jobs in Irish PR and I was unable to get another. Truth to tell, I was violently relieved. PR work was depressing the hell out of me.

'My mum had moved back to the UK, so I did too. Did some freelancing . . .' I stopped.

'And then you got mugged,' Martha prompted.

'And then I got mugged.'

'Could you bear to tell me a little about that?' Martha asked, pressing her hand on mine, her tone suddenly soap-opera 'caring'.

I nodded. Not that there was ever any doubt. If I held out on the only truly dramatic part of this story, there would be no interview, certainly no two-page colour spread in Britain's fourth highest-selling daily. I told it quickly, leaving out as much as I could and rushed to the finish, the part where the bloke pushed me over and disappeared with my bag.

'Then he left you for dead.' Martha was scratching furiously at her page.

'Um, no. I was conscious, I was well enough to walk home.'

'Yes, but you *could* have been dead,' Martha insisted. 'He wasn't to know.'

'Perhaps.' I shrugged reluctant approval.

'And though gradually your physical wounds faded, the mental scars remained?'

I swallowed. 'I was rather upset.'

'Upset! You must have been devastated. Utterly traumatized! Yes?'

I nodded obediently – and a little wearily.

'Post-traumatic stress disorder set in,' Martha was scribbling faster and faster. 'You couldn't go to work?'

'Well, I was freelancing at the time –'

'You couldn't leave the house –'

'Yes, I cou –'

'You stopped washing? Eating?'

'But I –'

'You simply couldn't see the point in anything.'

A pause. An exhalation. 'Sometimes. But doesn't everyone feel lik –'

'And in this dark, lonely place there came a tiny glimmer of light. A vision and you sat down and wrote *Mimi's Remedies*.'

Another pause, then I gave in. 'Go on then.' She so did not need me here.

'Then an agent took you on, she found you a publisher and hey presto – you're an overnight success!'

'Not exactly. I'd been writing for about five years in my spare time, and I'd actually finished a novel but no one would –'

'How many copies of *Mimi's Remedies* have been sold now?'

'The latest figure is 150,000. At least that's how many are in print.'

'Well, well,' Martha marvelled. 'Almost a quarter of a million.'

'No, it's –'

'Give or take.' Martha's shark smile permitted no argument. 'And you wrote it in a month.'

'Two months.'

'Two?' She seemed disappointed.

'But that's extremely fast! My first novel took me five years, and it's still not published.'

'And you've already got quite a devoted following, I hear. Is it true that some of your fans have formed reading groups in your honour, calling themselves "covens"?'

Well, one group of oddballs in Wiltshire, who had tired of pretending to be Druids, had. Probably hell trying to keep those white robes clean. But I nodded, yes, covens, that was correct.

Suddenly Lady in Red changed tack. 'Although the critics haven't always been kind, have they, Lily?'

She was doing that false sympathy thing again. I preferred being steamrollered.

'Who cares what the critics say?' I said, stoutly. Actually, *I* did. Immensely. I could recite large chunks of the savage reviews I had been getting since *Mimi's Remedies* had begun to haemorrhage from bookshops on word-of-mouth sales. When the book had first come out and no one had expected it to sell more than two thousand copies, one consolation-prize review in the *Irish Times* had damned me with faint praise. But the commercial success had coincided with an outpouring of bile from the broadsheets. The *Independent* had called it –

'Candy floss for the brain,' Martha said.

'Yes,' I said humbly. I could go on. *This debut novel is a preposterous by-product of the current touchy-feely sensibility. A 'fable', it tells of a white witch, the eponymous Mimi, who arrives unexpectedly in a picturesque village and sets up shop providing magic remedies for the townsfolk and their various neuroses.*

'And the *Observer* said it was . . .'

'"Sweet enough to rot the readers' teeth",' I finished for her. I knew. In fact, I could have gone on to recite the entire critique, chapter and verse. 'Please,' I said, 'I only wrote the book to cheer myself up. I couldn't have known that anyone would publish it. If it hadn't been for Anton it would never have been sent to Jojo.'

Martha's pen sped up again.

'And how did you meet your husband, Anton?'

'We're not married yet.' Journalists got so much wrong anyway, but I had to at least try to get the facts straight. I loathed reading interviews full of inaccurate details about me because I worried that people might think I was lying. (I never inhaled. I fought in Vietnam, etc.)

'So how did you meet your *fiancé*, Anton?'

'Partner,' I said, just in case she asked me to produce a ring.

Martha looked at me sharply. 'But you will marry?'

I made vaguely positive noises but in truth it made little difference to me whether or not we did. My parents, by contrast, are great believers in the institution of marriage. They love it so much that they keep on doing it; Mum has been married twice and Dad three times. I have so many half-siblings and step-siblings that a family get-together would resemble one of the later episodes of *Dallas*.

'Where did you meet Anton?' Martha asked again.

How ought I to answer this? 'Through a mutual friend.'

'Would that mutual friend like to be named?' She twinkled.

'Um, no. Thank you.' I don't think so!

'Oh. Are you quite sure?'

'Quite. Thank you.'

Martha was alerted, she knew there was a story, and it was as though I had swallowed ice. I loathed, loathed, *loathed* doing these interviews. I was terrified of being found out and if this level of intrusion into my life continued, I would be.

But she let it go. For the moment, at least.

'And what does Anton do?'

Another tricky question. 'He and his partner, Mikey, run a media production company called Eye-Kon. They made *Last Man Standing* for Sky Digital. A reality game show?' I asked hopefully.

But she had never heard of it. Her and sixty million others.

'And at the moment they're in discussions with the BBC and Channel Five about a ninety-minute feature.' ('Ninety-minute feature' meant made-for-TV movie. 'Ninety-minute feature' sounded a lot better.)

But Martha had no interest in the ups and downs of Anton's career. Well, I had tried my best.

'Righty-ho, I think I've got plenty here.' She closed her notebook, then nipped to the loo. While she was out of the room I fretted over what I had said, what I had not said and whether or not there were clean towels in the bathroom.

I led her to the downstairs front door, past Mad Paddy in the ground-floor flat. I hoped he would not emerge, but of course he did, he missed nothing and craved diversion. But at least he was not aggressive and for this I gave thanks. Indeed he seemed quite jolly because he admired Martha in her crimson gladrags and declared, 'Bedad, I feel a song coming on.'

'"Lady in Red".' Martha shook her head good-naturedly. 'I get this a lot.'

But instead Mad Paddy burst into, 'You'd better watch OUT. You'd better not SHOUT. You'd better not cry, I'm TELLIN' you why –'

Too late I recognized the song and, in my head, sang along. 'SANTA Claus is coming to town.'

'Ignore him,' I smiled gamely and shook her hand. 'Thank you for coming.'

'He knows when you are SLEEPING . . .'

'The picture desk will be in touch about a photo.'

'. . . he knows when you're AWAKE . . .'

'It was a pleasure meeting you,' she smiled grimly.

'. . . he knows if you've been BAD or good . . .'

'Goodbye.'

'SO BE GOOD FOR GOODNESS SAKE.'

*

As soon as she had left, I returned upstairs, took some ragged breaths, then rang Anton on his mobile. 'It's safe to come home now.'

'On my way, sweetheart.'

Ten minutes later he gangled in the door, all legs and elbows. Little Ema was fast asleep, bundled into his chest. Whispering, we lay her down in her cot and closed the bedroom door on her.

In the kitchen Anton took off his coat. Underneath he was wearing the pink cashmere sweater which Dad had sent in case I was invited onto *V Graham Norton*. (Dad did not exactly live in a fantasy world, but he was a regular visitor.) The sweater was much too short and tight for Anton, revealing a good six inches of concave stomach and a line of black hair snaking down from his belly button. Cody had once described Anton as the worst dressed man he had ever met, but I was not so sure. Pink was definitely his colour.

'This is *your* ganzee,' he plucked at the sweater in surprise. 'Sorry, sweetheart, I got dressed in a wild hurry, I thought it was one of my shrunk ones. So tell us, how'dit go with your woman?'

'I'm not sure. Perhaps not badly until she met Mad Paddy.'

'Chr-rrrist! Not again. What happened this time? He didn't ask her out?'

'No, he sang to her. "Santa Claus is Coming to Town".'

'But it's April.'

'She was dressed in red.'

'No beard?'

'No.'

'We'll have to move. Any bikkies left?'

'Heaps.'

'I don't get it.'

'Nor me.' The first big interview I had done had shamed me utterly by reporting to the world that I had offered only tea or coffee, no biscuits. Ever since then, in a belated attempt to make restitution, we bought top-of-the-range biscuits each time a journalist came, but not one of them ate any.

36

About Anton. The important thing to remember is that I am not a seductress. To be honest, I'm the least *fatale* of *femmes*. If there was a competition, I would come so last a new category would have to be invented specially for me.

A potted history of how all this came about: I was brought up in London and, after several stomach-knotting years, my parents ultimately split when I was fourteen. The year I turned twenty Mum married a dull-but-worthy Irishman and moved to live with him in Dublin. Although I was perfectly old enough to live on my own I also went to Dublin and eventually made friends, one of my closest being Gemma. After being a drain on Mum and her beau, Peter, for a year or so, I got it together, got a diploma in Communications, then got a job writing press releases for Mulligan Taney, Ireland's biggest PR firm. But after working there for five years, I lost my job and could not get another one. This roughly coincided with Mum and Peter separating. Mum returned to London and I – like a malign shadow – followed her. Though my heart was not in it I secured some freelancing work writing press releases, but remained too broke for any weekend trips to Dublin to see my old muckers. Meanwhile, shortly after I had returned to London, Gemma met Anton; though Gemma visited me occasionally, Anton was too skint to accompany her.

So I never actually met him until he had left a broken-hearted Gemma in Dublin and come to London, to set up an independent media production company. (He and Mikey had had enough of making dull infomercials on safety in the workplace and wanted to move into television; it was much more likely to happen in London than in Dublin, they reckoned.)

Anton's version of events was that his one-year relationship with Gemma was over; she said they were just taking a break, that he simply did not realize it yet. Weeping softly down the phone she told me, 'I'll give it two months, then he'll see that he still loves me and he'll be back.'

However, she feared that he might be distracted by a London girlie and as I was *in situ*, I was ideally placed to be Gemma's 'man on the ground'. My brief was to befriend Anton, stay tight and if he so much as looked at another girl I was to 'poke him in the eye with a sharp stick' or 'throw acid in the girl's face'.

I promised I would but to my eternal shame I did neither. I loved Gemma, she had trusted me with Anton, her most precious, and I repaid her trust by betraying her.

It was almost as if Gemma had had a presentiment. Half-apologetically she had said in one phone call, 'I know I'm a neurotic, jealous, mad woman and I want you to stick close, but please don't get too fond of him. You're good-looking, you know.'

'If you like women who're thinning on top.' (My hair is so fine the pink of my scalp sometimes shows through. Other women say if they won the lottery they would buy themselves bigger boobs or a bum-lift. I would have a hair-follicle transplant, even though there is a chance it might get infected, as apparently happened to Burt Reynolds.)

'You never know, he might like slapheads. I can just see it, you and he'll be hanging out, roller-blading, having your photo taken at Trafalgar Square, Big Ben, Buckingham Palace . . .' Gemma faltered.

'Carnaby Street,' I supplied. 'We'll go there on a red bus.'

'Yes, exactly, thanks. There you'll be, having a lovely platonic laugh. Then one day you get an eyelash caught in your eye, he helps you get it out, then Whoops! You're standing right next to each other, close enough for a snog and you'll see that it's been a slow burn and you've been in love with each other for ages.'

I promised Gemma that she had no need to worry and in a way I kept my word. There was no slow burn and caught-eyelash stuff. Instead I fell in love with Anton the first time we met. But Gemma had also described him as The One. It must have been something he made a habit of.

But that was all ahead of me and I had no idea that any such thing would happen when, two days after Anton arrived in London, I picked up the phone and dialled his Vauxhall number. I had a duty to undertake but how best to keep an eye on him? I could sit in a car outside his flat and stake him out. Except I did not want to. A preliminary meet-and-greet session over a couple of drinks would be the thing, I decided. Depending on how that went, I could introduce him to other people, who might agree to share the monitoring.

We agreed to meet at seven o'clock one Thursday evening outside Haverstock Hill tube station. I was living in a rented hovel in nearby Gospel Oak – walking distance.

As I ascended the hill to the tube station the air was sparkly clean and smelt of lush grass; the cool relief of autumn had just arrived. Day-glo August glare had given way to clear pewter light; the reek of overheated dustbins had been replaced with the musk of golden leaves and a recent rain shower had washed away the last of the summer dust. I was calm now that it was autumn. I could breathe again. Until I realized that, with my typical lack of organization, I did not know what Anton looked like. All I had to go on was Gemma's description, which was that he was, 'Gorgeous. The ridiest of rides.' But one woman's 'ride' is another woman's 'not even if he was the last man on earth'. Arse, I chided myself, narrowing my eyes at the distant station, hoping there wouldn't be too many good-looking men there. (That thought was evidence that I was gearing up for some form of madness.)

But as my eyes searched, I noticed that someone outside the station was watching me. Instantly I knew it was him. I knew it was *him*.

I did not physically stumble but I felt as if I had. In shock, all my thoughts jolted and rearranged and in an instant every-thing had changed. I know it sounds absurd but I promise it's the truth.

I could have stopped. As early as then I knew I ought to turn back and erase the future, but I continued putting one foot in front of the other, as if an invisible thread led me directly to him. There was clarity and fear and an unignorable sense of the inevitable.

Each breath I took echoed loud and slow as if I was scuba diving and as I got closer, I had to stop looking at him. So I focused on the pavement – discarded tube tickets, stubbed-out cigarettes, crumpled Coke cans – until I was next to him.

His first words to me were, 'I saw you from miles away. Straight away I knew it was you.' He picked up a strand of my hair.

'I knew it was you too.'

While throngs of people hurtled in and out of the station like characters in a speeded-up movie, Anton and I remained motionless as statues, his eyes on mine, his hands on my arms, completing the magic circle.

We went to one of the nearby pretty pubs where he settled me on a bench and inquired, 'Drink?' His soft, melodious accent conjured up skippy sea breezes and misty, heather-drenched air. He was from Donegal in the north-west of Ireland; some time down the line I discovered they all spoke like that there.

'Aqua Libra,' I answered, afraid to order alcohol because the mix was already too incendiary. He leant on the bar counter, chatting with the barman and, in dreadful confusion, I cata-logued what I could see. He was all lanky angles and so thin the bum on his jeans bagged, his shirt was a brightly coloured statement, not quite a full-on Hawaiian, but dangerously close. *A geek*. That was how Cody had once described him . . . But his black hair looked slippery silky, he had a beautiful smile

226

and, really, whatever was going on here had little to do with his appearance.

He returned with the drinks and leant into me, twinkly eyed with pleasure. He was going to say something nice, I just knew it, so I got in fast with something neutral of my own. 'Does your flat in Vauxhall have a microwave?'

'It does indeed,' he said, kindly. 'And a fridge-freezer, a hob, a kettle, a toaster and an extractor fan. And that's just the kitchen.'

Haltingly I asked several more questions, each one more inane than the previous. How did he like London? Was his flat near the tube station? Solemnly, he answered them all.

But the real questions were being asked of myself. I analysed Anton's face, wondering, What is it? What is it about him that has me feeling this way?

I wondered if it was because he seemed to be the most alive person I had ever met. His eyes sparkled and with every smile or laugh or frown the contents of his head were displayed on his expressive face.

Every new thing I noticed affected me – the length of his fingers and the big knuckles so different from mine. The boniness of his wrist caught me with something almost unbearable. I wanted to hold its fragility, so incongruous in this tall, vital man, and weep on it.

But there was one topic which we had not touched on and the longer we chatted the more its absence took on a presence. In the end I lobbed it in, like a conversational hand-grenade. 'How's Gemma?'

I couldn't not ask. She was the catalyst for our meeting and I could not pretend otherwise.

Anton looked at the floor, then up again. 'She's doing OK.' His eyes were apologetic. 'I'm not worth it. I keep telling her.'

I nodded, took another mouthful of my drink, then my head went light and urgent nausea rose in me. On jelly legs I made it to the ladies', clattered the stall door closed behind me and retched and retched, until there was nothing but bile left to sick up.

I emerged, still wobbly, ran cold water over my wrists and asked my reflection, *What the hell's happening?*

Quite simply, falling in love with Anton had made me sick. All I could think of was Gemma. I loved Gemma; Gemma loved Anton.

I walked back over to him and said, 'I must go home now.'

'I know.' He understood.

He saw me to my door and said, 'I'll ring you tomorrow,' then touched the tips of his fingers to mine.

'Bye.' I ran upstairs to the sanctuary of my flat, but once in, I felt no better. I rattled around, sick at heart, my concentration destroyed utterly. Everything on television irritated me, my book held no interest, I needed to talk to someone . . . but who? Almost all of my friends were also Gemma's. Jessie, my sister, was travelling around the world with her boyfriend, Julian; their last postcard had been from Chile.

Perhaps my mum . . . but she was still screening my calls. I suspected she would prefer not to talk to me in case I asked to move in with her again. As for Dad, he didn't believe that God himself would be good enough for me, never mind one of Gemma's seconds. I would get little sympathy from him, either. In desperation I actually considered ringing the Samaritans.

Love at first sight was never meant to be like this – only the most romantic people even believe it exists. Certainly, anyone can fall in *lust*. But at the first look, one knows nothing of a man's capacity to look at other women in restaurants and then deny it. Or to refuse to get into a car if you're the person behind the wheel. Or to promise to pick you up at seven-thirty and instead appear at twenty to ten, reeking of Jack Daniels and Jo Malone scent. (Someone else's.)

But, despite that, I had always been a believer, even though it was almost as infra dig as believing in honest politicians. I fell on any stories of instant love as if they were precious jewels. While working for Mulligan Taney, I had met a man – an important captain of industry, who had the right to hire and fire willy-nilly – who told me how he was almost engaged to one woman when he met the LOHL (love of his life). 'The first time I saw her across the room, I knew.' Those were his exact words.

(Actually, I have no idea how we got on to the subject. At the time we were having a meeting about how best to convince a small community that they had nothing to fear from the carcinogenic toxins the man's company was proposing to pour into their water supply.)

So it had come as a nasty surprise to find, contrary to expectations, that falling in love at first sight was not enjoyable. Instead of my entire life simply clicking into place, rendering me joyously whole, I had been knocked entirely off beam.

Even without Gemma, the situation was confusing. But with Gemma . . .

I lay on my couch, therapy-style, and tried to remember what she had said about Anton: that he was great in bed and had a big willy, but that was par for the course. She had never mentioned that he was the type of man for whom every woman falls. An Irish Warren Beatty who seduced effortlessly all in his path. I had always loathed those men, and loathed how women rolled over and begged for them. I refused to be just another besotted girlie toppling for Anton like a brain-dead domino, it simply wasn't my style. (I hoped.)

So, thoughtfully, deliberately, I set about wrapping my heart in resistance. I would not meet him again. It was quite the best way and, once the decision was made, I felt better. Bereft but better.

I had just about calmed myself enough to start concentrating on the film on television when the phone rang. I regarded it fearfully, as I would a ticking bomb. Was it him? Probably. The machine clicked in and I almost threw up for the second time that evening when Gemma spoke. 'Just calling for a progress report.'

Ignore it, ignore it.

'Please, please ring me the minute you get in, doesn't matter how late. I'm going out of my *mind* here.'

I picked up. How could I not? 'It's me.'

'God, you're home early. Did you meet him? Did he talk about me? What did he say?'

'That you're too good for him.'

'Hah! I'll be the judge of that. When are you meeting up again?'

'I don't know. Gemma, isn't this all a bit daft, me spying on him . . .'

'No, it's not. You must meet him! I need to know what he's up to. Promise me you will.'

Silence.

'Promise?'

'OK. I promise.' I was glad to.

I despised myself.

True to his word, Anton rang me and the first thing he said was, 'When can I see you again?'

My hands became clammy and self-disgust rose. 'I'll call you back,' I croaked, skidding to the bathroom to sick up my breakfast coffee.

When it was all gone, I straightened up slowly and sat on the loo seat, my sweaty forehead balanced on the cool porcelain of the wash basin. Sluggishly I wondered what the right thing was. My promise to Gemma was just a red herring. I wanted to see him, but I was frightened to be alone with him. The best solution would be to dilute his presence with other people.

An old schoolfriend, Nicky, had invited me to dinner with Simon, her husband. Perhaps Anton could come too. With a bit of luck he might even hit it off with them; if he knew more people I would not be obliged to meet him so frequently.

Anton did not display any disappointment when he learned that other people would be present when next we met. Indeed he was the perfect dinner-party guest, praising the house and food and chattering easily on non-controversial topics. I, by contrast, was wooden, jerky and consumed with jealousy. I was unable to eat as I watched Nicky watching Anton. 'It's happening again,' I thought. 'He's effortlessly charming her, she's falling for him like a condemned building.'

The following morning, as early as was polite I phoned Nicky, on a thank-you pretext.

She said, 'Anton, well!'

'Well.'

'Yes, well!'

I skirted the issue with a few more 'Well's and I was preparing to hear that she was in love with Anton and about to leave Simon when she said, 'Bit of an idiot. What does your Gemma see in him?'

'You think he's an idiot?'

'Um, yes . . . he's hyper! He's rather,' she imbued the word with utter contempt, '*enthusiastic*. And that accent, all those "ayes" and "ochs", nothing but an affectation.'

'You don't think he's handsome?'

'If you like them eight-foot tall and dorky.'

Would it be unfair, at this point, to mention that Simon was five-foot seven and often wore cowboy boots with three-inch cuban heels? (With the ends of his too-long jeans pulled over them, in an attempt to hide them.)

'I suppose he's got nice colouring,' Nicky said, to the sound of the bottom of barrels being scraped. 'He's quite dark for an Irishman. I thought they were all sandy and freckled.'

'His mother is Yugoslavian.'

'Ah, that explains the cheekbones.'

'Aren't they heaven?'

'Steady on!' She was alerted to something.

'I wish they were mine.' True, but not perhaps in the way Nicky chose to interpret it. Her brief flare of suspicion went out; not for one moment did she think I would poach someone else's man. That was the thing. No one would ever have believed it of me. Least of all myself.

I tried to stay away from him. Goodness knows I tried. But meeting him had shifted my centre of gravity and any element of choice had been removed. Until then my life had felt as if it had been idling. Suddenly it had picked up speed, as if it was swooping down into a tunnel and I was doing my best to hang on.

We endured almost six weeks, forty anguished days, saying goodbye to each other, opting for loneliness and honour instead of the guilt of togetherness. Sincerely, I meant every farewell but sooner or later the constant craving forced me to pick up the phone and whisper to him to come over.

It seemed like I never slept during that dreadful time. We talked late into many nights, batting the pros and cons back and forth. Anton was much more pragmatic than I was. 'I don't love Gemma.'

'But I do.'

I had had other boyfriends; from the age of seventeen I had been a textbook serial monogamist. Four and a half men over thirteen years. (The half had been Aiden 'Macker' McMahon who had two-timed me for all of our nine-month run.) I had genuinely loved those other men and did all the usual things when each relationship ended – cried in public, drank too much, lost weight and insisted that I would never meet anyone else – but Anton was different.

The first time I slept with him it was almost beyond description. I could feel the emotion flooding from me to him and from him to me, slowing my breathing down, like we were underwater, becoming part of each other. It felt like a lot more than sex, it was almost like a mystic experience.

On three occasions we decided to brazen it out and go to Dublin to tell Gemma and twice I chickened out.

It was impossible. I was prepared to live without Anton rather than destroy Gemma.

'It doesn't matter what you do,' Anton said sadly. 'I'll still never love Gemma.'

'I don't care! Go away.'

But after a few hours of Anton's absence my resolve fell apart and the day eventually came when we got on the plane.

I cannot think about what followed. Not even now. But I will never forget the last thing Gemma said to me. 'What goes around comes around and remember how you met him because that's how you'll lose him.'

37

Back in the present the phone rang. It was a man from the *Daily Echo*'s picture desk, following up on Martha Hope Jones's interview. He wanted to send a courier to collect the photographs of my injuries after I had been 'left for dead'.

'I wasn't left for dead.'

'Dead, injured, whatever. So what about the photos?'

'No. I'm sorry.'

Not long after, the phone rang again. This time it was Martha.

'Lily, we need those pics.'

'But I don't have any.'

'Why not?'

'I just . . . haven't.'

'That puts us in rather a pickle.' Her voice was high and accusatory, then she hung up on me.

Rather shakily, I stared gormlessly at the phone, then exclaimed at Anton, 'What type of saddo takes photos of themselves after they've been mugged?'

Though the area I lived in was less than salubrious, I had never expected to be mugged. Being somewhat of a bleeding-heart liberal, I had sympathy with muggers and insisted that they were driven by desperation. I was certain they would intuit that I was on their side.

However, if I had thought about it, I was perfect muggers' prey. To best deter muggers one must walk tall, exuding confidence and a hint of Tae Kwan Do lessons. Handbags ought to be clamped with rigor mortis immobility between elbow and ribcage and pace must be broken for no obstacle.

By contrast I am more of an ambler. I once overheard my

old boss in Dublin describe me as 'very hello trees, hello flowers'. It was intended as an insult and it fulfilled its brief; I was insulted. I had little interest in greeting trees and flowers but nor did I treat life as a treadmill, on which it was vital to keep fleeing forward in order to avoid being sucked off the back and out of the game.

The night of the mugging I was on my way home from the bus stop. I had been at a meeting with a supermarket chain who were planning a spinach promotion and my job was to write the text of the accompanying giveaway leaflet. You might know the sort of thing: a description of the vitamins and properties of spinach. ('Did you know that spinach has more iron than a pound of raw liver?') A list of famous spinach lovers. (Popeye, of course, and . . . er . . .) And finally, new and exotic ways to prepare it. (Spinach ice cream, anyone?)

*Some*body has to write these leaflets and though it was not work I was proud of, it was less shameful than the position I had held in Dublin.

It was cold and dark and I was keen to get home. Not just to see Anton, who had moved into my hovel six months previously, the day we had returned from the unspeakable visit to Gemma, but because I was three months pregnant and desperate for the loo. Like everything else about Anton and me, the pregnancy had not been planned. We were horribly poor, I was making a small amount of money but as yet Anton was making none, and we had no idea how we would afford a baby. But it did not seem to matter. I had never been so happy. Or so ashamed.

My need for the loo became more urgent so I speeded up, then, to my surprise, my shoulder was wrenched backwards; someone had caught the strap of my bag and had given it a violent tug. Idiotically, as I turned around, I had a smile prepared because I thought it would be someone I knew, who was being a little rougher than appropriate.

But I did not recognize the young man at my shoulder. He was tubby, with a pasty, sweating face.

Simultaneously I registered two things: I was being mugged; by a man who looked as though he had been fashioned from a large vat of raw bread dough.

It was all wrong. He didn't look thin and desperate as muggers ought. (I'm somewhat of a purist.) Nor did he have a knife, or a syringe.

Instead he had a dog. A bandy-legged pitbull, packed tight with menace. The chain was wrapped around Doughboy's pillowy hand and the dog began to strain towards me, growling softly. If the chain was loosed only one or two turns, I would be mauled.

My eyes were locked onto Doughboy's curranty ones and without a word being uttered, I was giving him my bag.

He took it, stuffed it inside his jacket, then – with the air of a grand finale – shoved me to the ground.

That, I thought, would be that, but the worst was to come. As I lay on the damp pavement, the dog walked over me, right across my three-month pregnant stomach. Its dense weight dug deep into me and his horrid, meaty breath warmed my face.

It was over in two or three seconds, but even now when I think about it, I am convulsed with revulsion.

One man and his dog waddled away and, feeling dazed and foolish, I clambered to my feet. As I did so I met Irina marching towards me, the metal of her high heels ringing in the night air: a mugger's worst nightmare. She was my upstairs neighbour and although we sometimes nodded in the hall, we had never really spoken. All I knew about her was that she was tall, good-looking and Russian. She wore so much make-up that Anton and I had spent many happy hours wondering about her. I thought she might be a prostitute but Anton said, 'My money says she's a transvestite.'

She stopped and looked at me inquiringly, as I swayed about the pavement.

'I've just been mugged.'

'Mugged?'

'By a man with a dog.'

'Men vit a dug?'

'He went that way.' But Doughboy had disappeared.

'Vos there money?'

'A few quid. Two or three.'

'So little? Thanks Gud.'

She was not exactly tea and sympathy, but she delivered me safely to Anton. However, nothing he said or did could comfort me. I knew what was about to happen: I was going to miscarry. This was divine retribution. Punishment for my wickedness in stealing Anton from Gemma.

Anton insisted on calling the doctor, who did his best to assure me that the chances of me miscarrying my baby were tiny.

'But I'm a bad person.'

'It doesn't work like that.'

'I deserve to lose this baby.'

'But you're highly unlikely to.'

As the doctor was leaving, another person arrived at our door: Irina, with a handful of make-up samples, to replace my stolen stuff. 'They are latest colours. I vurk on Clinique counter.'

In stereo, Anton and I exclaimed, 'Ah, you work on a *make*-up counter.'

Irina studied us with cool intelligence. 'You thought I vos prostitute?'

'Yes!' Then we mumbled to an appalled halt. Honesty is not always the best policy, but Irina didn't give a damn.

The next morning Anton took me to the local police station (or Pig Pen as we'd called it up until then) to make a report.

We took a seat in the waiting area and watched officers passing in and out. We were hoping to hear them calling each other 'Guv'.

'We've got twenty-four hours to solve this case . . .' Anton murmured.

'. . . we've got the DA's office on our back . . .'

'. . . we must drive at high speed through a street full of empty cardboard boxes . . .'

Then quietly we 'Ne neh!'ed the *Starsky and Hutch* theme music to each other until my name was called. My little crime was so not important, but I was assigned a young officer who valiantly went through the motions. I gave a description of Doughboy and a list of all the things in my handbag which I could remember. As well as my purse, house keys and mobile phone, my bag had contained the usual detritus. Tissues (used), pens (leaking), blusher (crumbling), hairspray (to thicken my hair and obscure my pink scalp) and four, or possibly five, Starbursts.

'Starbursts?' the officer inquired eagerly, thinking – I'm sure of it – DRUGS!

'Ex-Opal Fruits,' Anton explained.

'Ah.' Disappointed. He lay down his pen. 'Why do they keep doing that?'

'What?'

'What was wrong with Marathon? Why did they change it to Snickers? And why has Jif become Cif ?'

'Globalism,' Anton said politely.

'Is that what globalism means?' He sighed and picked up his pen again. 'No wonder they're rioting. OK, you've got to call your bank and cancel your credit card.'

Anton and I remained silent (after all, we had a right to). At that stage we were so skint, there was no need to cancel the card. The issuing bank had already taken the precaution of so doing. Along with my cashpoint card.

Shortly afterwards Irina had a day off and invited me upstairs. Within minutes she was chain-smoking and contentedly telling me how 'unheppy' her life in Moscow had been. 'I hed a men,

I did not luff him. I vos unheppy. I meet another men, he did not luff me, I vos unheppy. Mens!'

She now had an English boyfriend who also made her 'unheppy'. Apparently he was 'wery chealous'.

'Why do you bother if he makes you unhappy?'

'Because he is good at making the sex.' Then she shrugged, 'Love is always unheppy.'

Reading between the lines, the real love of her life were the cosmetics she sold. She was truly passionate about them and her face was her showcase. She was excellent at her job (so she said) and earned more commission than any other sales girl. 'I trust you, I show you.'

She left the room and returned carrying a tartan-patterned shortbread tin. She flipped off the lid to reveal that it was stuffed with cash. Notes. Fifties and twenties and tens – but mostly fifties.

'Commission. I count every night. I kennot sleep without.'

I was alarmed. It was unsafe to have so much cash just lying about. 'You ought to put it in a bank.'

'Benks!' She didn't trust them. 'Look.' She took a book from a shelf and opened it to display twenties stashed between the leaves. 'Gogol. Dostoyevsky.' More money. 'Tolstoy.' And more.

'Have you actually read these books?' I had stopped feeling sick about the money and instead felt intimidated by the calibre of literature. 'Or are they just piggybanks?'

'I hev read all. Do you luff Russian literature?' she asked slyly.

'Um, yes.' I knew so little, but I wanted to be polite.

She smiled. 'You Eenglish, you see the movie of *Lolita* and think you know about Russian literature. Now you must go. It's time for EastEnders.'

'You like EastEnders?'

'I luff. They are so unheppy, so like life. Come again to me. Enytime. If I do not want to see, I vill say.'

If I hadn't known better I would have thought she was being kind.

The doctor was right and I did not miscarry but a few days after the mugging, I began a slide into a terrible place. Little by little my vision darkened until all I saw was the bloodiness of human beings and our woeful flaws. We ruin everything we touch.

Why did I fall in love with Anton? Why did Gemma fall in love with him? Why can't we love the right people? What is so wrong with us that we rush into situations to which we are manifestly unsuited, which will hurt us and others? Why are we given emotions which we cannot control and which move in exact contradiction to what we really want? We are walking conflicts, internal battles on legs and if human beings were cars, we would return them for being faulty.

Why do we have such a finite capacity for pleasure but an infinite one for pain?

We're a cosmic joke, I decided. A cosmic experiment which had gone wrong.

I loathed being alive. The prospect of death was the only thing that made my life worth living. But I was carrying a child so I had to keep going.

It was the trauma of being mugged which had triggered such hopelessness, Anton said; I needed to see the doctor again. I disagreed: it was merely my own wickedness which had reduced me to this wretched state. Anton so did not want to know. He kept repeating, 'You are not wicked. I didn't love Gemma, I love you.'

That was my very point. Why could he not have loved Gemma? Why must it be so complicated?

Anton could not agree with me: if he did so, he would be signing our death warrant.

I managed to complete work on the spinach info-leaflet but

when the agency set me up with more meetings, I did not attend.

I had almost no one to talk to. Since Anton and I had taken the hideous step of going to Dublin and telling Gemma about us, all the Irish girls I knew in London – Gemma's and my mutual friends, the Mick Chicks – had severed contact abruptly. The only friend I had who pre-dated Gemma was my old schoolfriend Nicky. But Nicky had her own worries, trying to get pregnant by Simon who, in addition to being a short-arse, appeared to be firing blanks.

Anton was out at work all day with Mikey: taking TV executives to lunch and hustling for cash, taking literary agents to lunch and hustling for cheap scripts, and taking theatrical agents to lunch and hustling for actors to play the parts in the cheap scripts which he had not yet acquired and which he had no financing for. I got a stomach ache whenever I thought about the duplicity involved – swearing to the script writer that the actress was on board, promising the actress the financing was in place, lying to the TV company that the script and director were secured – but Anton said it was necessary.

'No one wants to be the first to commit. If someone else has, they think it's got to be good.'

Despite Anton and Mikey's spinning it was taking time for even one of their projects to go into production.

'It'll all come together soon,' Anton promised, when he returned home each evening. 'We'll get the right script, the right star, and the financing will fall into our laps. And after that, they'll be queuing up to work with Eye-Kon.'

Meanwhile I spent hour after hour on my own and one day, when the loneliness became too much, I went up the stairs to Irina. She opened the door and over her shoulder I saw a pile of notes on the table. She was counting her money.

'Payday,' she said. 'Come and see.'

'Thanks.' I slid in.

After I'd admired her crisp new notes, I spilled my guts on my hellish state of mind.

Irina listened with interest and when I meandered to a conclusion, she murmured, 'You are wery unheppy,' and looked at me with a new respect.

It was only when I had exhausted all other distractions that I turned on my computer, looking for solace in my book. For almost five years I had been working on a novel which drew on my experiences working in eco-PR in Ireland. Tentatively entitled *Crystal Clear*, it went as follows: chemical company is poisoning the air of a small community, PR girl (a prettier, feistier, thick-haired version of me, of course) sticks her neck out, blows the whistle, tips off the townsfolk and does all the courageous stuff I wish I had actually done in real life.

Over the preceding four years, on the urging of enthusiastic friends, I had sent it to several literary agents, three of whom had read it and suggested changes. But even after I had rewritten and redrafted it to their requirements, they still said that it was 'not right for them at this time'.

Notwithstanding, I had retained a nugget of hope that *Crystal Clear* was not utter dross and continued to tinker with it from time to time. But this particular day I simply could not write about babies born with fingers missing and young, clean-living family men succumbing to lung cancer. However, I did not switch my computer off immediately. I loitered, still desperately seeking something. I typed 'Lily Wright', then 'Anton Carolan' and 'Baby Carolan', then the legend, 'And they all lived happily ever after.'

Those words infused me with such unexpected well-being that I typed them again. After I had done it for the fifth time I straightened up my chair, sat four-square to the desk and held my splayed fingers above the keyboard like a virtuoso pianist about to play the 'Flight of the Bumblebee' and give the performance of her life.

I was going to write a story where everyone lived happily ever after, in a fictional world where good things happened and people were kind. This vision of hope was not just for me. Much more importantly it was for my baby. I could not bring this little human being into the world, burdened with my desolation. This new life needed hope.

So I started. I clattered away at the keyboard writing exactly what I wanted, past caring how sugary or sentimental it was. I had no thought of any other person reading it; this was for me and my baby. When it came to creating my protagonist, Mimi, I indulged myself utterly. She was wise, kind, earthy and magical – a mix of several people: she had my mum's wisdom, Dad's generosity, Dad's second wife Viv's warmth and Heather Graham's hair.

That night when Anton came home from a hard day not making films, he was so relieved to find me bright-eyed and enthusiastic that he happily sat and listened to what I had written. And every night thereafter, I read to him what I had written that day. It took almost eight weeks from start to finish and on the ultimate day, when Mimi had remedied all the woes in the village and had to leave, Anton wiped away a tear, then whooped with joy. 'It's fantastic! I love it. It's going to be a best-seller.'

'You like everything about me, you're not what one might call impartial.'

'I know. But I swear to God, I think it's superb.'

I shrugged. I was already feeling sad because I had finished it.

'Get Irina to read it,' he said. 'She knows about books.'

'She'll savage it.'

'She mightn't.'

So, because I was not yet ready to declare the experience over, I climbed the stairs, knocked on Irina's door and said, 'I've written a book. I was wondering if you would read it and give me your opinion.'

She did none of that leaping about and yelping that most

people do. *You've written a BOOK. How amazing!* She simply nodded, stuck out her hand for the pages and said, 'I vill read.'

'Just one thing, please be honest with me. Don't be nice to spare my feelings.'

She looked at me in astonishment and I turned away, wondering what kind of humiliation I was letting myself in for. And how long I would have to wait for it.

But the following morning, to my surprise, she showed up, cigarette in hand. She gave me the bundle of pages. 'I read it.'

'Well?' My heart thudded and my mouth was cottony.

'I like,' she pronounced. 'A fairy tale where the world is good. Is not true,' a long plume of smoke was exhaled ruminatively, 'but I like.'

'Well, if Irina likes,' Anton said gleefully, 'I really think we're onto something.'

38

I needed an agent, Anton had said. Apparently, I could not send *Mimi's Remedies* directly to publishing houses because they did not look at unsolicited work. He got in touch with one of his contacts ('This game is all about contacts, baby.') – an agent whom he had been trying to buy scripts from at rock bottom prices. With typical enthusiasm, he cross-examined the poor woman as though he was state prosecutor and she the defence's star witness. Her advice was to get a literary agent. 'But not her,' Anton said, 'she only does scripts. Pity. It would have been good synergy.' ('This business is all about synergy.')

So I wrote to the three agents who had read *Crystal Clear*; once again, they felt that *Mimi's Remedies* was 'not right for them at this time' but urged me to contact them with my next book, just like the last time.

Around the time of the third rejection letter I threw a little tantrum and announced I would have no more to do with the business of finding an agent; it was too soul-destroying. Anton responded by buying me a six-pack of mixed doughnuts and a copy of the *National Enquirer* and waited for me to calm down. Then he hoisted me back into the saddle by producing a copy of the *Writers' & Artists' Yearbook*. 'Every literary agent in the British Isles is in here.' He brandished the thick red book gleefully. 'We'll go through each one until we nail an agent for you.'

'No.'

'Yes.'

'No!'

'Yes.' He sounded surprised at my vehemence.

'I'm not doing it. You can if you want.'

'OK, I will, then,' he said, a little sharply.

'I don't want to know about it.'

'Fine!'

Over the following three months or so, he tried to keep the rejections from me but each time the manuscript was returned and landed with a thump on the communal hall floor, I knew. I was like the princess and the pea, I could hear the whack from upstairs. Indeed I suspected I could have heard it from a street away.

'That's my book,' I always said.

'Where?'

'Downstairs in the hall.'

'I didn't hear anything.'

Invariably, I was right. Except for the time when it was the delivery of the new Argos catalogue. And the other time when it was the Thompson White Pages. And that one other time when it was Mad Paddy's Next catalogue. (Which, he admitted to Anton in a hallway man-to-man, he only got in order to look at the ladies in their underwear.)

But every time the thump on the hall floor mat (or rather the place where a hall floor mat would have sat had we owned one) really did signal a rejection of my book, I gave Anton a wounded, passive-aggressive 'I told you so' look and my heart bled a little more. Anton, however, was undaunted and blithely chucked each kiss-off letter in the bin. Of course as soon as he was out of the way I rushed to fish them out again, and tortured myself with every cruel word, until he noticed. After that he took the letters with him and disposed of them at work.

Unlike me, he wasted no time musing over the failings of *Mimi's Remedies*. Ever forward facing, he simply consulted his guide for the next agent, once again wished the manuscript good luck and returned to the post office where he had developed a first-name-term relationship with the staff.

At some stage I stopped hoping and almost managed to disassociate enough to regard all this messing about with Jiffy bags and postage as simply another one of Anton's strange hobbies.

Until the morning he wandered into the kitchen, a letter in his hand and remarked, 'Don't say I never do anything for you.'

'Huh?'

'An agent. You've got yourself an agent.' He gave me the letter.

I scanned it. All the letters seemed to be jumping about the page and I could not make sense of them, until I got to the line that said, 'I would be happy to represent you.'

'Look.' My voice wobbled. 'Look, she says she would be happy to represent me. Happy!' Then I sobbed over the letter until the ink of Jojo's signature ran.

Anton and I went to see her in her office in Soho. It was less than a fortnight before I gave birth to Ema so getting me there was a huge undertaking, like crating and transporting a sick elephant. But I was glad I had gone. Lipman Haigh Literary Agents was a big, busy place that inspired excitement and the best part of all was Jojo Harvey. She was pretty damn fabulous. Full of energy and absolutely stunning, she welcomed us like long-lost friends. Immediately, both Anton and I developed a crush on her.

She said how much she loved *Mimi's Remedies*, how all the people in the office had loved it, what a sweet book it was . . . I glowed – until she stopped and said, 'Here's the deal. I'm going to be honest with you.'

My heart dropped like a stone. I loathe people being honest with me. It's always bad news.

'It's going to be tricky to sell because it feels like a children's book but it's got adult subject matter. So it's hard to categorize and publishers don't like that. They're kinda chicken-shit, a little scared to boldly go.'

She looked at our woebegone expressions and smiled. 'Hey, cheer up. It's definitely got something and I'll be in touch.'

But then came October the fourth and everything changed for ever. Priorities were immediately realigned; everything slipped down the list a place because at Number One, in with a bullet, was Ema.

I had never loved anyone the way I loved her and no one had ever loved me as much as she did; not even my own mother. My voice could stop her crying and her eyes sought my face, even before she could see properly.

Everyone thinks their baby is the most gorgeous who ever lived, but Ema really was a beauty. Like Anton, she was olive-skinned and she emerged from the womb with a head of silky dark hair. There was no trace of fair, blue-eyed me in her at all. 'Are you sure she's yours?' Anton asked solemnly.

The person she looked most like was Anton's mother, Zaga. As a nod to that, although we wanted to call her Emma, we decided to spell it the Yugoslavian way.

She was a big smiler, sometimes she giggled in her sleep and she was the squeeziest creature ever. The creases in her thighs were irresistible. She smelt adorable, she felt adorable, she looked adorable and she sounded adorable.

That was the plus side.

On the minus . . . I could not recover from the shock of being a mother. Simply nothing had prepared me and I wouldn't mind but, unusually for me, I had attended pre-natal and mothering classes in an attempt to be properly geared up. I may as well not have bothered, the impact was uncushionable.

To be entirely responsible for this tiny powerful bundle of life scared me to death and I had never worked so hard or relentlessly. What I found most difficult was that there was no time off. Ever. Anton, at least, had a job in the outside world and got to leave the flat each day but for me, being a parent was twenty-four-seven.

As for the breast-feeding; it looks adorably serene. (Except when women try to do it in public without anyone seeing their boob.) No one had warned me that it hurt, that it was, in fact, agony. And that was even *before* I contracted mastitis, first in one boob, then the other.

At times Ema baffled us – we had fed, changed, burped and cuddled her and still she would not stop crying. At other times we baffled ourselves: we were usually desperate for her to go to sleep but if she slept too long we worried that she might have meningitis, so we had to wake her up.

Our flat, never pristine even under optimum conditions, had become Martha Stewart's worst nightmare. Huge plastic sacks of Pampers were scattered about the bedroom floor, ranks of drying babygros were draped on most surfaces, herds of cuddly toys crouched on the carpet stealthily waiting to trip me up and I had a permanent bruise on my shin because each time I passed through the hall I caught my leg on the brake of the buggy.

Somewhere in amongst the blur of twenty-four-hour days, sleepless nights, cracked nipples and colicky screaming, news managed to get through: Jojo had sold *Mimi's Remedies* to a big publishing house called Dalkin Emery! It was a two-book deal and they had offered an advance of four thousand pounds a book. I was out of my mind with the thrill of having got a publisher; at least I was as soon as I could summon up the energy. And four thousand pounds was an enormous sum of money, but it was not the life-changing amount that we had hoped for. It looked as if we were destined to remain poor, especially as Eye-Kon's gameshow *Last Man Standing* had made almost no profit and most definitely had not generated a stampede of TV executives to shower Anton and Mikey with cash.

A visit to Dalkin Emery to meet my editor Tania Teal followed. She was in her early thirties and brisk but pleasant. She said they would publish *Mimi's Remedies* the following January.

'Not until then?' That was a year away but I felt in no condition to protest because not only did I know nothing about publishing but my boobs were leaking and I was afraid that

Tania could see. I had not even had time to shower before the meeting and had to make do with a scrub down with a handful of nappy wipes, so I felt at a dreadful, unwashed disadvantage.

'January's a good time for debut books,' she said. 'Not much else is being published so your lovely book has a better chance of getting noticed.'

'I see. Thank you.'

For a long, long time, nothing happened. Not for about six months, then, out of the blue, I got a phone call from a man called Lee who wanted to know when he could take my photo for the cover of the book. I panicked, 'I'll call you back,' and hung up the phone, wondering, Who am I? Who do I want people to think I am?

'What?' Anton asked.

'Some bloke is coming to take my picture for the book. I need to do something with my hair! I'm not being funny, Anton, I really need to get the Burt Reynolds-style hair transplant. I should have done it months ago! And new clothes! I need new clothes. And nails, Anton, look at the state of my nails!'

I went out and spent half a day and too much money getting my hair cut and coloured (but didn't get a transplant, Anton talked me out of it), bought three new tops, a new pair of jeans, new boots and some face-stuff which was meant to give me a glow, but just made me look bafflingly shiny and oily in the practice run. And when I rubbed it off, I caught the corner of my lipstick, wiping half of it across my face, which rendered me like a care-in-the-community casualty.

'This is a disaster,' I moaned to Anton. 'And I shouldn't have bought the boots, they won't even be in the shot.'

'Doesn't matter, you'll know they're there, they'll give you confidence. Hold on here, sweetheart, I'm going to get Irina.'

He left and returned a few moments later with Irina in tow.

'You're a whizz with cosmetics,' Anton told her. 'You'll fix Lily up for her photo, make her beautiful, won't you?'

'I kennot verk miracles. But I will do best.'

'Thanks, Irina,' I muttered.

The morning of the shoot, she stopped by before she went to work, exfoliated my face like she was scrubbing a kitchen floor, plucked my eyebrows to non-existence, then covered me with frightening quantities of slap, so bright and thick that Ema stared in dismay.

'It's OK, sweetheart, it's me, Mum,' I coaxed.

But that just prodded her to full-blown tears – who was this Aunt Sally clown with Mum's voice?

Irina, Anton and Ema left. Anton was taking Ema to work with him because the shoot was going to take hours and we had no one else to take care of her.

Then Lee arrived. He was young and slept with lots of fit girls – I knew just by looking at him – and armed with a ton of equipment which Mad Paddy helped him carry up the stairs. I wished he would not, I was afraid he might ask Lee for money, but I got him out the door without too much fuss.

Lee dumped several black cases on the floor and looked around. 'Just us? No make-up artist?'

'Um, no, my friend did my make-up for me but I didn't realize . . .'

'No? Everyone uses professional hair and make-up people. Author piccies are mega important. They go a long way to selling the book.'

'But no . . . I mean, it depends on how good the book is, doesn't it?'

That made him chortle. 'You're a bit green. Think about it – only the good-looking authors get on telly. When an author is a dog, telly researchers won't book her. Sometimes the publishers try to keep her off the publicity trail, they tell the media she's a recluse.'

That couldn't be true. Could it?

'Telling you,' he insisted. 'You, Lily, you're not bad-looking, but you could use some help. That's why I asked about the make-up artist. But I'll air-brush as much as I can, I'll do my best for you.'

'Um, thank you.'

He looked around at my living room, which I had tidied specially, sucked his teeth and laughed ruefully. 'Not exactly a photographer's dream, is it? Not much for me to work with?'

'Er . . .'

'Yeah,' he sighed, 'they wouldn't OK the budget for a studio for you. Tell you what, we'll do a couple of insurance shots here, then we'll take it outside and try something different. We're quite near to Hampstead Heath, aren't we?'

'Yes.' Big mistake. In the words of the fabulous Julia Roberts, big, huge mistake.

It took him almost an hour to set up the equipment – umbrellas and lightboxes and tripods – while I perched on the edge of my couch, trying to use the power of thought to stop my make-up from evaporating. Finally, we were ready to go.

'Look sexy,' he commanded.

'Er . . .'

'Think sex.'

Sex? I had heard of it, I was nearly sure of it.

'C'mon, gimme sex.'

I smiled gamely but I was desperately intimidated by his youth, his lack of gayness and worst of all his dispassionate assessment of my appearance.

'Lift the chin.' Behind his camera he chuckled to himself. 'More chins than the Hong Kong phone book.' Then, 'Relax! You look like you're before a firing squad.'

He kept changing lenses and checking light meters so that the 'couple of insurance shots' took as long as the equipment set-up, then I had to endure the fifteen-minute walk to the heath, hefting a tripod, trying to make conversation with him. I had had very little sleep the night before and talking was not my forte.

'Have you done lots of authors?'

'Oh yeah, shedloads. Christopher Bloind? Miranda England? Now *she* is fabulous. A dream to shoot. You couldn't take a bad shot of her. They flew me to Monte Carlo to do her. First class to Nice, then helicopter.' Of course he had to say this at the exact point where we were trudging over the graffiti-covered railway bridge and he had a good old laugh at the contrast. 'One extreme to the other, right, Lily?'

Out on Hampstead Heath, he looked around, narrowing his eyes, then he lit up. 'OK, let's have you climbing a tree.'

I waited for the laugh. Because he was joking, wasn't he?

Actually no.

He made a 'chair' out of his hands for me to hoist myself up on, then I had to stand on a branch about six feet off the ground and wrap my arm around the trunk. And smile.

'Now look down to me, yeah, wind in your hair, yeah, lick those lips.'

If I had had a double chin, sitting on my own couch, having my photo taken at eye-level, what on earth would I look like now being shot from below? A turkey. A toad. Jabba the fucking Hutt.

'Think sex, look sexy. LOOK SEXY.'

'Louder,' I muttered. 'I don't think they quite heard you in Kazakhstan.'

'Look sexy,' he yelled, clicking away. 'Look sexy, Lily.'

A bunch of schoolboys stopped to mock.

'A little change coming up, Lily, down you come and let's have you swinging off a branch.'

I clambered down and saw that my good boots had got scuffed on the trunk. Tears sprang up in me but I couldn't go for it because Lee was making another 'chair' with his hands so I could swing from a branch like a monkey.

'Eyes to me and a big laugh.' Lee cackled like a maniac to encourage me. 'C'mon, big laugh. Like this. AHAHAHAH-AHAAAAAAAH! You're swinging on a branch, having the time of your life, head back, big, BIG laugh. AHAHAHAH-AHAAAAAAAH!'

My arm-sockets were aching, my hands were raw and slippy, my face was killing me, my new boots were scuffed and obediently, I laughed, laughed, laughed.

'AHAHAHAHAHAAAAAAAH!' he went.

'AHAHAHAHAHAAAAAAAH!' I tried.

'AHAHAHAHAHAAAAAAAH!' the schoolboys went.

Just when I thought it could not get any worse it began to rain lightly. Briefly I thought it was a good thing because surely now we could go home. Not a hope. 'Rain?' Lee scanned the skies. 'Could be good. Wild and romantic. Let's see, what shall we try next?'

I spotted one of the schoolboys sending a text. Some dreadful instinct tipped me off that he was rounding up reinforcements.

'Let's try walking up to the top of the heath,' Lee suggested. 'See what's up there.'

Damp, pissed-off and laden with equipment I followed him up the hill, then I looked back, hoping the schoolboys had not decided to follow us, but they had. Keeping a respectful distance but they were still there and was it my imagination, or were there more of them?

Lee stopped by a park bench. 'We'll do it here.'

Panting and sweaty, I sank onto it. Thank goodness, a sitting-down shot.

'Lily, I need you standing.'

'On the bench?'

'Not quite.'

'Not quite?'

He paused. Something very terrible was coming. 'I want you on the back of it, Lily. Like you're on a tightrope. It'll make a fantastic shot.'

Mute with misery, I simply stood and looked at him.

'Your publishers said they wanted wacky shots.'

I slumped with resignation, I had to do this. I didn't want to get a name as a 'difficult' author.

'I'm not sure I can balance.'

'Give it a try.'

Up I climbed, watched by the schoolboys. I could hear them talking about whether or not they would 'do' me.

I planted one foot on the back of the bench, but that was the easy bit, then to my amazement I got the other on too and suddenly I was balancing on a ridiculously thin piece of wood.

'You're doing great, Lily,' Lee yelped, clicking for all he was worth. 'Eyes to me, think sex.'

There was activity amongst the schoolboys, I suspected they had opened a book on how long it would be before I fell off.

'Lily, lift your leg!' Lee called. 'Balance on just one leg, arms out, like you're flying!'

For just a second I had it. For the briefest time I hung in mid-air like I was floating, then I noticed that there were so many schoolboys on the hill that it was starting to look like an open-air rock concert and I wobbled and tumbled heavily to the ground, twisting my wrist and, worse still, muddying my new jeans.

The rain was coming down heavily now and, my nose two inches from the filthy ground, I was thinking, I am a writer. *Why am I on all fours in the mud?*

Lee came to help me up. 'A few more shots,' he said cheerily. 'We almost had it there.'

'No,' I said and my voice was thin and quavery. 'I think we've done enough.'

All the way back down the hill, I was on the verge of tears of humiliation, disappointment and exhaustion and when I got home I went straight to bed.

39

Then it all went quiet again. At some stage I got sent a print of the jacket, then a copy of the proof copy to look for mistakes, of which there was a disturbingly huge number. During this time I ought to have been working on my second book. I certainly made a few stabs at starting, but I was always so tired. Anton tried to be encouraging but as he was nearly as exhausted as I, he too ran out of steam.

The day came when the finished copies were delivered and I was moved to tears. Bearing in mind that I had once got excited about finding myself in the phone book, to see and hold a novel, with *my* name on the cover, was overwhelming. All those words, words that I'd written *all by myself*, gathered and printed by someone other than me, convulsed me with pride and wonder. Obviously nothing like as intense as having Ema, but a definite second.

The author photo was the first one Lee had taken – of me sitting on my couch, looking straight to camera. I had purplish shadows under my eyes and a double chin that I was pretty sure I did not have in real life. I looked slightly anxious. It was not a good picture but it was a hell of a lot better than me swinging from the branch of a tree going 'AHAHAHAH-AHAAAAAAAH!'

That night I came to bed to find the book tucked in under the duvet, with just the title sticking out; Anton had put it there and I went to sleep cuddling it.

Publication day was the fifth of January and when I woke up that morning (the fourth time since I had gone to bed) I felt like a child on her birthday. Perhaps slightly over-expectant; teetering on that narrow wire where high-octane good spirits could topple over into tantrumy disappointment at a moment's notice.

Anton greeted me with a cup of coffee and, 'Good morning, published author.'

I got dressed and he kept up a commentary of, 'Excuse me, Lily Wright, but what's your profession?'

'Author!'

'Excuse me, ma'am, I'm conducting a survey. Can you tell me what job you do?'

'I'm a writer. A published one.'

'Are you *the* Lily Wright?'

'Lily Wright the author? That's me.'

Then we both bounced giddily on the bed.

Ema picked up on the fizzy atmosphere and gave a long incoherent speech, then slapped her plump knees and shrieked with laughter.

'Enter Ema with news from the front,' Anton said. 'Let's saddle her up, Lily, we're going to visit your other baby.'

I unfolded the buggy for the ceremonial walk to our nearest bookshop, which happened to be in Hampstead.

'We're going to visit Mum's book,' Anton told her.

She was all agog at her dad being home midweek. 'Lalalala-jingjing-urk!'

'Exactly.'

We were on top form. It was a cold sunny morning and we walked with a sense of purpose. I was about to see my first novel on sale, what an experience!

I entered the bookshop with my neck so stretched I felt like a goose and on my face was a happy smile. So where was it?

There were no copies on the display at the front and I swallowed away the pang. Tania had gently explained to me that, although she wished things were different, mine was a 'small' book and therefore would not have big, front-of-shop displays. Nevertheless, I had still hoped . . .

But nor was *Mimi's Remedies* to be found on the New Releases shelf. Or on any Recent Publications tables. Increasing speed a notch, I left Anton and the buggy and moved through the shop, searching and seeking. I moved ever faster, my head swivelling like a periscope and my anxiety swelling as my book failed to appear. Though there were thousands of other books I knew I would instantly see mine in amongst them. If it were there.

When I found myself in the Psychology Department, I stopped abruptly and hurried to find Anton. I met him at the information desk.

'Did you find it?' he asked quickly.

I shook my head.

'Me either. Don't worry, I'll ask your man.' Anton nodded at the saturnine youth staring at the computer and endeavouring to ignore us. After a while Anton cleared his throat and said, 'Sorry to cut in on you there but I'm looking for a book.'

'You've come to the right place,' the youth said flatly, indicating the oceans of books on the shop floor.

'Aye, but the one I'm looking for is called *Mimi's Remedies*.'

A few keys were pressed half-heartedly, then the boy said, 'No.'

'No, what?'

'We're not getting it in.'

'Why not?'

'Store policy.'

'But it's brilliant,' Anton said. 'She –' he pointed at me – 'wrote it.'

I nodded over-brightly, yes, I had indeed written it.

But far from being impressed, the boy repeated, 'We don't stock it,' then looked over Anton's shoulder to the person queuing behind us. The implication was clear: *Piss off*.

We loitered by the desk, opening and closing our mouths like goldfish, too stunned to move obligingly along. This was not how it was supposed to be. I had not expected to be carried shoulder-high through the cheering streets, but nor had I thought it unreasonable to expect to find my book for sale in a bookshop. After all, if not here, where else could I expect to find it? In a hardware store? The dry-cleaner's?

'Ah, excuse me,' Anton said, when the other customer had been dispatched.

The youth acted startled to find us still there.

'Can we talk to the manager?'

'You're talking to him.'

'Oh. Well, how can we change your mind about stocking *Mimi's Remedies*?'

'You can't.'

'But it's a great book,' Anton insisted.

'Talk to your publisher.'

'Oh. OK.'

It was a matter of some pride to me that I waited until I was outside the shop before I wept.

'Fucker,' Anton said, his face red with humiliation, as we tramped angrily towards home. 'Patronizing little *fucker*.' He threw a kick at a bin and hurt his foot. I began to cry again.

'Fucker,' I said.

'Fucker,' Ema piped up from her buggy.

Anton and I turned to each other, our faces briefly alight. Her first real word!

'That's right,' I sang, crouching down to her. 'He's a *fuck*-er.'

'A fucking fucker,' Anton said, angry again. 'We're ringing them publishers the minute we get in.'

'Fucker,' Ema said again.

'You said it, babe.'

It took about twenty minutes to reach home and I was still shaking when I dialled Tania's private line.

'Can I speak to Tania?'

'Who's calling?'

'Lily Wright.'

'And what's it in connection with?'

259

'Oh.' Surprised. 'My book.'

'Which is called?'

'*Mimi's Remedies.*'

'And your name again? Leela Ryan?'

'Lily Wright.'

'Libby White. Hold for one moment.'

Two seconds later Tania came on the line. 'Sorry about my assistant. She's a temp, she hasn't a clue. How are you, love?'

Haltingly, not wanting to seem like I was being critical, I relayed what had happened in the bookshop.

Tania cooed and soothed. 'I'm sorry, Lily, I really am. I love *Mimi's Remedies.* But one hundred thousand new books get published every year. Not all of them can be best-sellers.'

'I wasn't expecting it to be a best-seller.' Well, obviously I'd *hoped* . . .

'To put it into context, your print run is five thousand copies. Someone like John Grisham has an initial print run of about half a million copies. Trust me, Lily, your lovely book is out there, but perhaps not in every store.'

I relayed what she had said to Anton. 'This isn't good enough. What about publicity? What about interviews and signing sessions?'

'There won't be any,' I said, flatly. 'Forget it, Anton, it's not going to happen. Let's just move on.'

But I had not reckoned on Anton's energy.

A week or so later he came home from work, all aglow. 'I've got you a signing.'

'What?'

'You know Miranda England? One of Dalkin Emery's major authors? Well, her new book is out soon and a week on Thursday at 7 p.m., she's doing a signing in the West End and I've persuaded Tania to make it a double – with you! Miranda's huge, the crowds will really turn out for her and when they've got her book signed, then we'll bag them. Captive audience.'

'Oh my God,' I stared at him. 'You are amazing.' But I had

to wonder what other authors did. Those that didn't have an Anton? 'For that, young man, tonight you can have the sex act of your choice.'

Oh, how we laughed.

40

The night of the signing, Anton and I arrived at the bookshop embarrassingly early. In the window was a photo of Miranda almost as big as the one of Chairman Mao in Tiananmen Square plus a display of her books, several thousand strong. There was also a poster of me. A smaller one. Quite a lot smaller. It would not have looked out of place in a passport.

In the shop there were several more Chairman Miranda posters and although it was twenty minutes before kick-off, a queue had already formed. Mostly women, all fidgety with excitement.

A minute before seven o'clock, a silver Merc drew up and Miranda emerged, looking slightly entouragey. She had just been on the BBC evening news and was accompanied by her husband, Jeremy, Otalie the publicity girl and Tania our mutual editor. Tania gave me a kiss and a reassuring squeeze of the hand. Through the open door Miranda spotted the ever-swelling throng. There were probably seventy people – some groups so big they might have come in coach parties.

'Fuck,' she said. 'We'll be here all night.' She turned to Otalie. 'Good cop, bad cop, right?'

What were they talking about?

As soon as we entered, a young man hurtled through the shop at breakneck speed. He skidded to a halt in front of Miranda and introduced himself as Ernest the events manager.

'It's a great honour to meet you.' He actually bowed, touching his forehead to the back of Miranda's hand. 'They're all here for you.' He indicated the fans. 'And what can we get for you? We heard you like timtams, so we had them air-lifted in from Australia.'

Otalie shunted me forward. 'And this is tonight's other author, Lily Wright, who'll be signing copies of her new book, *Mimi's Remedies*.'

'Oh er yes, we'll get them.' The tone of his voice said, 'From where they've been buried in the sealed vault, fifty feet underground, beneath the slabs of nuclear waste.'

As Miranda was ushered through the crowds to start signing, the noise level went up and mini-shrieks rose into the air. Excluded from the magic circle, Anton and I looked at each other and shrugged.

'I see your table,' he said. 'Come and sit down.'

He led me to a small neglected table bearing a little sign saying my name and that of *Mimi's Remedies*. A small pile of books eventually appeared.

While I waited for someone – anyone – to approach me, I watched Miranda and tried to keep my envy from showing on my face. All around her, a veritable army of bookshop staff were ferrying in pile after pile of her books, stacking them up in some prearranged configuration. It looked like an artist's impression of the construction of the pyramids.

Otalie was patrolling the crowd, coralling them into an orderly line and distributing post-its. 'Have your book open on the signing page and have your name written, spelt correctly, on your post-it,' she boomed. 'No backlist titles,' she threatened. 'Miranda will NOT be signing any backlist, only the new book. You, madam,' she descended on a woman who was carrying a bulging plastic bag, 'if there are backlist titles in that bag, please put them away. There isn't time for Miranda to sign them.'

'But they're my daughter's favourite books, she read them when she was recovering from a nervous break –'

'She'll enjoy a signed copy of the new book just as much.' Otalie picked up the new book and put it on top of the woman's armload. I thought Otalie was horrible and although the woman looked startled she did as she was told, just shuffling forward when the queue did.

'No dedications,' Otalie yelled, along the line. 'No birthday wishes, no special requests. Do NOT ask Miranda for anything except your name.'

Despite her reign of terror, a party atmosphere prevailed, and occasionally some of the fans' comments to Miranda floated over to me. '. . . I can't believe I'm meeting you . . .'

'. . . I feel like you're my best friend . . .'

'. . . you know in *Little Black Dress* where she finds her boyfriend wearing her knickers, that happened to me, and they were my best ones too . . .'

'I'm so sorry about my publicity girl,' I heard Miranda say again and again. 'I'd love to chat to you all night, she's such a bitch.'

Ah, good cop, bad cop, now I got it.

As people left Miranda some were wiping away tears, and people further back in the queue were asking, 'What's she like?'

'She's lovely,' they always said, 'she's as lovely as her books.'

And still no one came to see me. 'Step back,' I hissed at Anton. 'You're blocking the view of me and putting people off.'

Quickly he moved away from the table and stood to one side.

And then . . . a man approached me! He walked right up to me, with firmness of purpose. I beamed, so, so happy – my first fan! 'Hello!'

'Yeah,' he frowned. 'I'm looking for the real life crime section.'

I froze, paused in the act of lifting a *Mimi's Remedies* from its pile. *I think he thinks I work here.*

'Real life crime,' he repeated impatiently. 'Where will I find it?'

'Just step outside the door,' I heard Anton mutter.

'Um,' I twisted my neck around the shop. 'I'm not sure. Perhaps if you ask at Information.'

Muttering something about know-nothing fuck-wits, he stomped off.

Over in Miranda's queue, the party atmosphere had gone up several degrees and someone had opened a bottle of champagne. Glasses appeared from nowhere and clinking noises filled the air. But, like split-screen reality, on my wasteland side of the shop a cold wind whistled, a ball of tumbleweed lumbered by, then a funereal bell clanged. Well, that's what it felt like.

Flash bulbs were filling Miranda's airspace with silvery light. One of the coach parties was having a group shot done, two layers of giddy, giggly girls, the front row crouching down like for a team photo.

Then I got noticed! Three of the coach party lot, their heads together, stood right in front of me and studied me like I was an animal in the zoo. 'Who is she?'

One of them read my sign. 'Lily someone. I think she's written a book too.'

I smiled in what I hoped was an inviting fashion but as soon as they realized I was animate they recoiled.

Anton stepped into the breach. 'This is the new author Lily Wright and this is her fabulous new book.'

He distributed *Mimi's Remedies* amongst them to have a look at.

'*An*-ton.' I was mortified.

'What do you think?' The girls inquired of each other, as if I were deaf.

'Nah.' They decided. 'Nah.' Then they moved towards the door squealing, 'I can't believe I just met Miranda England!'

Anton and I exchanged sickly smiles. Over on Miranda's side, they appeared to be doing the conga.

Then an elderly lady approached me. After my previous knockback, I was a little less quick off the mark to press a *Mimi's Remedies* into her hand. And I was right . . .

'Can you point me towards arts and crafts, dear.' There was something funny with her teeth, they appeared to be moving up and down inside her mouth. *Dentures.* Possibly someone else's.

'I'm sorry,' I said. 'I don't work here.'

'What are you doing sitting here then? Confusing people?' It was hard to concentrate on what she was saying because her teeth seemed to have a life of their own, it was like watching a badly dubbed film.

I explained.

'So you're a writer?' *A gottle of geer.* 'That's marvellous.'

'Is it?' I was beginning to doubt it.

'Yes, dear, my granddaughter is a marvellous little scribbler and she wants to get published. Give me your address, I'll send you Hannah's stories, you can tidy them up, give them to your publisher and get them published.'

'Yes, but, they may not –'

I stopped. Like it was happening in slow motion, she was picking up a *Mimi's Remedies* and tearing a large piece off the back cover. I turned to Anton who looked as stricken as I felt. Then Gottle of Geer gave it to me with a pen. 'Full postcode, if you don't mind.'

Anton stepped in. 'Perhaps you'd like to buy Lily's book.'

Gottle pruned up at his impertinence. 'I'm on a pension, young man. Now give me that address and let me find the tapestry books.'

Anton stared bitterly after her. 'Mad old cow. Here, hide the torn one at the bottom of the pile, otherwise they'll make us pay for it. And then let's just go home.'

'No.' I would have stayed there for ever, even if the room had filled with a swarm of killer bees and I somehow found myself covered in honey. Anton had done this for me and I would not be ungrateful.

'Baby, you don't have to stay to make me feel better,' he said. 'I'll just tell Otalie we're leaving.'

Even Anton was all out of optimism. Things must be bad.

Otalie came over. 'Just sign these copies of *Mimi's Remedies* and then you can be off. Once they're signed, the shop can't return them to us.'

I started into the modest pile but Ernest, crawling around on the floor, nuzzling and licking Miranda's shoes, saw me. He clambered to his feet and came racing over. 'Enough! Don't sign any more! We'll never shift them!'

We left them, drinking champagne, Miranda signing piles of books that stretched up like biblical towers into the sky.

41

By the end of January it was all over; a total non-event. Basically nothing happened and after the tensest month of my life I realized that nothing would. I was a published author and aside from a tiny, blink-and-you'd-miss-it review in the *Irish Times* it meant nothing. My life was exactly as it had been and now I had to get used to it.

I tried to cheer myself up by thinking, *I lost all my limbs in a bizarre meat-slicing accident, my sister and her boyfriend have been kidnapped by terrorists in Chechnya (even though they're in Argentina), and my child's head is abnormally, embarrassingly large.*

This is a technique I employ when I am terribly unhappy: momentarily I pretend that a terrible catastrophe has occurred so that I can say, 'Before this terrible thing happened I was outrageously fortunate and never realized it. I would give all I possess to turn the clock back.' The idea is that what was once only boring normality now assumes the lustre of Utopia. Then I remind myself that the catastrophe *did not actually happen*, that I have been nowhere near a meat-slicing machine, and that my life *is* a glorious, disaster-free Utopia. That usually makes me grateful for what I have.

I remained flattened by anti-climax and when my dad rang a few days later, I found it hard to be animated. Not that it mattered, he had enough animation for ten people.

'Lily, love!' he exclaimed. 'Got some good news for you. A friend of Debs, Shirley – you know her, tall skinny bird – read your *Mimi's Remedies* book and thought it was genius. Came over here to the house, going on about it.' His voice dropped low with emphasis. '*Didn't even know you were my daughter*, never made the connection. Her book club is going to read it and when she found out I'm your dad, she went a bit mental, know what I'm saying? She wants signed copies.'

'Well, er, great, Dad. Thank you.' Isolated incident though this was, it cheered me a little.

I did not need to ask why it was he who was brokering this and not Debs: it would have killed Debs to be nice to me – we didn't call her 'Dreadful Debs' for nothing.

'I've six books for you to sign, when can I drop them over?'

'Any time you like, Dad. I'm going nowhere.'

He picked up on my tone. 'Cheer up now, girl,' he said gleefully. 'This is only the beginning.'

I had once read a newspaper article which described the actor Bob Hoskins as 'a testicle on legs' and that struck a chord: Dad was a little like that. He was short, barrel-chested and swaggery, a working-class boy made good. Then bad. Then, eventually, good again.

My mum – a 'beauty' – had married beneath her. Those were her exact (if jokey) words. She had hooked up with Dad because he had said to her, 'Stick with me, doll. We're going places.' Those were *his* exact words, and he was true to his promise. They went from modest Hounslow West to detached Guildford splendour to a two-bedroomed flat over a kebab shop in Kentish Town.

(All this has left me with an aversion to house-moving. If the roof fell in on top of me, I would prefer to do a repair job with black bags and masking tape than move.)

Having an entrepreneurial father sounds like a seriously good idea. They make a lot of money very quickly and move their wife and two daughters into a lead-paned-windowed, five-bedroomed house in Surrey. But what you hear about less often is those risk-takers who go too far, who lever everything including the family home, in the expectation of making yet another killing and exponentially increasing their already huge wealth.

The financial pages display great admiration for those men (and it appears always to be men) who 'make a million, lose a million and make another'. But what if that man is your father?

One day I was going to school in a Bentley, then in a white van, then I wasn't going to that school at all. There was Pony Club, then no ponies, and when the ponies were once again on offer, I did not accept them. I could not trust that they wouldn't be taken away again at a moment's notice.

But I adored my father. He was ever optimistic and nothing kept him down for long.

The day we had had to leave the house in Guildford, he cried like a child, his stubby fingers over his tear-drenched face. 'My beautiful five-bed, three-bath house.'

My little sister Jessie and I had to comfort him. 'It's not so beautiful,' I said.

'And the neighbours hated us,' Jessie chimed in.

'Yeah,' Dad sniffed, accepting a tissue from Jessie. 'Naffing stockbrokers.'

By the time, five minutes later, he got into the van, he had convinced himself that he was better off out of it.

I think it was the constant financial insecurity that drove Mum to eventually divorce him but I know they had once loved each other a lot. Affectionately they used to speak about themselves as a third-person unit: 'Davey'n'Carol'. She called him 'my rough diamond' and he called her 'my posh bird'.

I have never fully come to terms with my parents' divorce. A little pocket of resistance in me is still holding out for a reunion. Mum made Dad leave twice, then took him back before she finally called it a day; even though they divorced eighteen years ago, it still feels temporary.

But when Dad met Viv the chances of my parents reuniting receded out of sight.

Viv was nothing like Mum. Mum was not genuinely posh, she was a doctor's daughter, but compared to Viv she was a member of the landed gentry.

Dad met Viv at a dog track, saw her in secret for months then, when he decided he wanted to marry her, sat Jessie and me down and broke the news.

'She's got a good heart,' he said.

'What do you mean?'

'She's like me.'

'Common, do you mean?' Jessie asked.

'Yeah.'

'Oh goodie.'

Dad was terrified that Jessie and I would hate Viv and who could blame him? Not only was Viv the wicked stepmother but I was sixteen and Jessie fourteen – walking balls of teenage broken-home emotions. We hated even those we loved, so what chance did an interloper like Viv stand?

But Viv was a sweetie: warm, squashy and welcoming.

The first time Dad took Jessie and me to her small, cigarette smoke-filled house, a car engine was oozing oil on the kitchen table and one of her two teenage sons – Baz or Jez – was cleaning under his nails with a long serrated kitchen knife.

'Ooh, we're scared,' Jessie scorned.

Baz – or Jez – gave her a dark brooding look and Jessie pretended to stumble, jogging his arm and plunging the knife into his finger.

'Ow!' Baz or Jez yelped, shaking his hand in pain. 'Christ! You stupid cow.'

Highly entertained, Jessie peeked up from under her too-long fringe and smirked. There was a tense moment when I thought that perhaps he might kill her, then he also began to laugh and after that we were mates. We were their posh, blonde stepsisters and they hovered about us, protective and proud. We, on the other hand, hoped that Baz and Jez were criminals but, to our bitter disappointment, discovered that they were all show. 'So you've never been in prison?' Jessie asked in distress. Baz shook his head.

'Not even a young offenders' place?'

Jez looked like he was going to say yes, then changed his mind and admitted the truth. No, no young offenders' place either.

'Oh *dear*,' I said.

'But we've been in plenty of rumbles,' Jez offered anxiously. 'We have scars.' He was rolling up his sleeve.

'And tattoos,' Baz said.

But Jessie and I tossed our posh blonde heads. Not good enough.

Jessie and I lived with Mum in Kentish Town but spent most weekends in Viv's place. Life with divorced parents was not perfect but certainly not as bad as I had expected. In retrospect that was down to Viv's warmth and my stepbrothers' kindness.

Jessie dealt with the divorce a lot better than I did. Cheerfully she pointed out the many advantages of being from 'a broken home'.

'We can be as naughty as we like and everyone must be kind to us. And think of the gifts! In the right hands, this divorce lark could be very . . . what's the word?'

'Lucrative.'

'Does that mean we get heaps of stuff?'

'Yes.'

'Lucrative, then.'

Mum tried to be grown-up and impartial about Dad's new wife, but most Sunday nights when we returned home she could not help asking, 'How are the Pearly King and Queen?'

'Well. They send their love.'

'Have you had supper?'

'Yes.'

'What? Jellied eels and mash?'

'Fish-fingers and chips.'

Three years after they got married, Dad and Viv had a son, Bobby, the Pearly Prince. Named for Bobby Moore, West Ham's hero.

Jealousy sickened me: Dad would not have any time for me now that he had a son.

I was determined not to visit baby Bobby and held out for sixteen days. Only when Mum told me off did I cave in.

'Grow up, darling. Everyone loves you, but they're quite cross that you haven't been to see your little half-brother. Like it or not, he's your family, and hell, if I can visit him, I'm quite sure you can.'

With bad grace I bought a cuddly hippo and, accompanied by Jessie, caught the train to Dagenham. Jessie geed me up with stories of Bobby's enormous sweetness, none of which I believed. Until I saw him. Tentatively I cradled his miniature body in the crook of my arm, then he *smiled* at me – perhaps it was only wind contorting his face but it so did not matter – and he grabbed my hair with his shrimp fingers. How could anyone be jealous of this little darling?

Shortly after the birth of the Pearly Prince, Mum met Peter and more change was afoot: Mum was going to live in Ireland. This sent me into another tailspin. My family were scattering to the four corners of the earth and I needed to hold on to them.

There was no space for me to live at Dad's; the room that Jessie and I stayed in had been turned into Bobby's. I begged Mum to let Jessie and me come with her to Ireland and although Mum was agreeable, Jessie was not. She liked London and planned to remain there. When she broke the news to me, I responded in my usual fashion by sicking up my supper.

It was preposterous: Jessie was eighteen and I was twenty but I felt as if we were being sent to different orphanages. I cried buckets the day I went to Dublin.

Not just the sadness of leaving Jessie behind but because Peter had a daughter, Susan, who was six months older than me. I expected she would resent my arrival and behave like a perfect bitch – but on the contrary. What exercised her most was whether we were half-sisters or stepsisters and she was pleased to find that as soon as Peter and Mum married we would be stepsisters. 'I know it's different in London,' she said, 'but here, having a stepsister is quite glamorous.'

Susan's best friend was called Gemma Hogan and we defied expectation by becoming a tight little unit. For a number of years my family situation was fine; perhaps a little too like a French film where everyone seems to have slept with everyone else. However we all got along.

But nothing stays the same for ever.

Nine years after marrying Viv, Dad met Debs and for some unfathomable reason, fell for her; perhaps Cupid was playing an April Fool.

Debs had been abandoned by her husband, leaving her with two young children and Dad decided to rescue her. He left lovely Viv with the big heart for loathsome Debs.

Everyone expected that he was simply having a temporary fit of insanity but as soon as his divorce from Viv came through, he married Debs. I had acquired two more step-siblings, Joshua and Hattie. Then Debs fell pregnant and gave birth to a little girl, Poppy. Another half-sibling.

After I met Anton I had to draw a chart to explain it all to him.

Family Tree

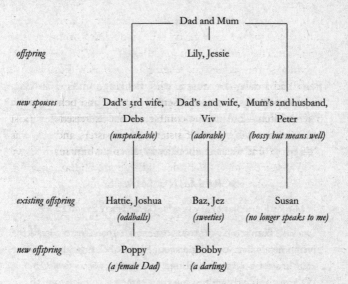

		Dad and Mum	
offspring		Lily, Jessie	
new spouses	Dad's 3rd wife, Debs *(unspeakable)*	Dad's 2nd wife, Viv *(adorable)*	Mum's 2nd husband, Peter *(bossy but means well)*
existing offspring	Hattie, Joshua *(oddballs)*	Baz, Jez *(sweeties)*	Susan *(no longer speaks to me)*
new offspring	Poppy *(a female Dad)*	Bobby *(a darling)*	

42

Then one Monday morning in early February, Otalie phoned. 'There's a fantastic review of *Mimi's Remedies* in this week's *Flash!*'

'What's *Flash!*?' Anton asked. He hadn't left for work yet.

'A kind of celeb magazine.'

'I'll get it!' He was already halfway down the stairs.

SCREAMING MIMI'S

Mimi's Remedies *by Lily Wright. Dalkin Emery 298pp £6.99*

Jonesin'? Bum too big? Tattoo gone septic? Then Doctor Flash! recommends that you sling on your Jimmy Choos, get down to your nearest bookstore and treat yourself to *Mimi's Remedies*. We know you girls are too busy out caning it to have time to read books but this one's worth it, honest guv'nor. Witty, cheery and sweet as Kylie, it'll have you rolling in the aisles.

Best Bit: The married couple at each other's throats – *screamingly* funny. *Mimi's Remedies* puts the FUN back into dysfunctional!

Worst Bit: Finishing it! This book is as yummy as an entire bucket of Miniature Heroes – without any of the guilt. Go girl! *Flash!* Promise: You'll laugh out loud or I'll eat my Philip Tracey.

'They've given you four and a half stilettos,' Anton read, in wonder. 'The maximum number you can get is five. This is a *fantastic* review.'

It was. Even though it had never been my intention to put the fun back into dysfunctional, but never mind.

Then Jojo phoned. 'Great news!' she said. 'Dalkin Emery are reprinting *Mimi's Remedies*.'

'What does that mean?'

'The first print run's sold out and they expect to sell more.'

'But that's good, isn't it?' I stammered.

'Yeah, it's real good.'

I rang Anton and relayed the news. He responded with silence.

'What?' I asked anxiously.

'Is it just me?' he croaked. 'Or is something happening here?'

About a week later Jojo phoned again.

'You're not gonna believe this!'

'I'm not?'

'They're reprinting.'

'I know, you told me.'

'No! They're reprinting *again*. Twenty thousand copies, this time. Your first print run was five, the second, ten. You're selling on word of mouth.'

'But Jojo, why? What's going on?'

'The book has struck a chord. You should see your site on Amazon, your sincerity and lack of cynicism is totally touching people. There's a piece all about it in this week's *Book News*, with a great photo of you, swinging from a tree, laughing fit to bust. I'll have Manoj fax it right over.'

'Lovely! Except . . . you see . . . we don't have a fax.'

'OK. I'll bike it.'

'Um, would you mind just posting it?' They charged me for couriers and photocopying and Anton and I were so skint . . .

'No, I'll bike it. Forget the cost, this one's on us.'

Blimey!

'Read your reviews on Amazon,' Jojo said, ringing off.

I got Anton to help me look up *Mimi's Remedies* on Amazon. There were seventeen reviews and they had all given four or five stars, which was lovely considering that the highest score possible was five stars. I scrolled through phrases like, 'The comfort of childhood ... magical ... enchanting ... transported me to another world ... the recovery of lost innocence ... the absence of cynicism ... hopeful and uplifting ... it made me laugh ...'

I was quite stunned. So much so I thought I might cry with pride and happiness. Who were these lovely people? Would I get to meet them? Suddenly I felt as if I had lots and lots of friends.

Then a nasty thought struck me. 'Anton, this isn't a trick, is it?' I asked carefully. 'It's not someone playing a practical joke on me?'

'No, this is real. And this isn't the norm, Lily,' Anton said. 'Loads of reviews on Amazon are horrible.' He showed me the sites of some other authors who had received a proper slagging from their readers and I recoiled. 'How can people be so nasty?'

'So long as they're not doing it to you, who cares?' Anton said.

Just over another week later, news of the third reprint followed, for the staggering figure of fifty thousand copies. Then Tania Teal phoned me and asked, 'Are you sitting down?'

'No.'

'OK. Get this. You, Lily Wright, author of *Mimi's Remedies* are number four in this week's *Sunday Times* best-seller list.'

'How?'

'Because you sold eighteen thousand, one hundred and twelve copies of *Mimi's Remedies* last week.'

'I did?'

'You did. Congratulations, Lily, you're a star! We're all so proud of you.'

Later that day Dalkin Emery sent flowers. A small mention in the *Daily Mail* described me as a 'phenomenon' and in the following days everyone who phoned asked to speak to the 'phenomenon'. Far from not being stocked by the bookshop in Hampstead, I now had a stand by the front door and a display in their window. They asked me to come and sign copies and Anton urged me to tell them to fuck right off. In fact he asked if he could have the privilege of making the phone call. But, graciously, I decided to forgive them. I wasn't bitter. Joy and happiness abounded.

And then the *Observer* reviewed my book . . .

43

The *Observer*, Sunday 5 March

SWEET AND SOUR

Mimi's Remedies *by Lily Wright. Dalkin Emery 298pp £6.99*

Mimi's Remedies is sweet enough to turn Alison Janssen sour

Reviewing books for a living, I'm the envy of my friends but next time they start complaining about what an easy life I have, I shall give them *Mimi's Remedies* and insist they read it right to the very end. That ought to subdue them.

If I say that *Mimi's Remedies* is the worst book I've ever read, I'm probably exaggerating, but you get the idea. The attached material from the publishers describes it as a 'fable' – messaging ahead not to expect realism, three-dimensional characters and believable dialogue.

And by golly, they're right. It appears to be a cack-handed stab at magic realism without being either magical or realistic. Frankly, the premise was so jejune I spent the first hundred pages waiting for the punchline.

And so will you when you hear what passes for a plot: mysterious, beautiful 'lady' appears out of the blue in a small village which manifests every version of textbook human dysfunction. A sundered father and son, an unfaithful husband, a young frustrated wife – so far, so *Chocolat*. But instead of confectionery, Mimi makes spells and even shares the recipes with us – many of which include the emetic instruction, 'Add a sprinkle of compassion, a tablespoon of love and stir with kindness.'

If this is the remedy, I'll take the problem.

Less than halfway through this – mercifully brief – novel I felt as though I were being flogged to death with liquorice laces or being force-fed candy floss.

The author, one Lily Wright, is an ex-PR girl, so she knows all there is to know about cynical manipulation. And it shows, in every single cloying word. The 'plot' is peppered with coy references to miracles but the only real miracle is how this candy dross ever got published. It is sweet enough to rot the readers' teeth, yet as unpleasant as sucking a lemon.

Mimi's Remedies is lazy, contrived and verges on the unreadable. So the next time you complain about your job, spare a thought for this wretched book reviewer . . .

It was one of the worst things that had ever happened to me. It was a little like the time I had been mugged. After reading it my ears began to hum as though I were about to faint, then I sprinted to the loo and sicked up my breakfast. (Perhaps by now it's clear that I am the feeble type who becomes ill after most upsets.)

Being a bleeding-heart liberal, I was an *Observer* reader and it was particularly painful being attacked by an organ which I respected. If it had been the Torygraph, I could have laughed and said, well what do you expect. Actually, perhaps I might not have laughed because being slagged off in front of *the whole world* is never funny. But I could have called them fascists and thus tried to discount their opinions.

Frequently, I read bad reviews of other people's books, films and plays but I had always assumed they must deserve them. I did not deserve this and this so-called Alison Janssen had just misunderstood me.

Jojo rang to cheer me up. 'It's the price of success. She's just jealous. I betcha she's got some shitty novel that no one's gonna touch, so she's pissed with you cos you got published.'

'Do they do that?' I had always thought of reviewers as noble, detached creatures, disinterested and above petty human concerns.

'Sure. All the time.'

Then Otalie the publicist called. 'Tomorrow's fish and chip paper,' she consoled.

'Thanks.' I put down the phone and began to shiver violently. I had the flu. Except of course I hadn't. Psychosomatic Girl that I am, I just felt as though I had.

Then Dad rang: he had seen the review. Goodness knows how. He's an *Express* man and has no time for what he calls 'the lefty crap' of newspapers like the *Observer*.

He was blustering with fury. 'The muppet. She can't say those things about my girl. You deserve the best, twinkle. I can have a word with Thomas Myles.'

Once upon a time Thomas Myles had been the editor of *some* newspaper but even I knew it had never been the *Observer*. But that was Dad all over.

It felt like the whole world was laughing at me and I was frightened to go out because it felt as though I were walking around naked.

I devoted an obscene amount of time to wondering who this Alison Janssen was and what I had done to make her so nasty. I even thought of hanging around outside the *Observer* to waylay her and demand an explanation. Then I thought of writing to the *Observer* to give my side of the story.

Anton said he knew some 'boys' from Derry who could work her over with iron bars and I was shocked to find that I did not want the boys from Derry to do it. I wanted to do it myself.

But then, in a lapse of self-hatred, I decided that Alison Janssen was right and that I was a talentless moron; I would never again attempt to write a word.

The following Sunday, the *Independent* reviewed me: it was just as savage as the *Observer* piece. Again Otalie rang to offer words of comfort: 'Tomorrow's dog basket lining.'

I took little consolation in this. So now even the dogs would know how abominable my book was.

An interview with the *Daily Leader* followed; it was quite a positive piece except they said that Anton was a chef and that I had not provided biscuits. I was bitterly ashamed of the biscuits bit, but not as ashamed as Dad, who prides himself on his generosity.

The net result was that I was afraid to open a newspaper.

As soon as we heard that *Book News* was coming to interview me, Anton was dispatched to Sainsburys to get the finest biscuits money could buy. But the journalist neither ate any nor mentioned them in the piece. They called Anton 'Tom' and a photo of Anton and me, with our heads tilting towards each other, was captioned 'Lily and her brother Tom'.

Then came word of the 'At Home' with Martha Hope Jones. It was an enormous coup and Otalie was beside herself. 'You've arrived, Lily!'

'Could I perhaps meet her in a café?'

It was proving impossible to prettify our small, dingy flat and trying to sneak the journalists past Mad Paddy was taking its toll on my nerves.

'Lily, it's an "At Home"!'

Anton was once again sent to the shops to buy the best biscuits in the land. The piece had still to run so we were on tenterhooks waiting to see whether Martha would mention them or not.

Amidst the bad reviews the book surprised me by continuing to sell. I thought the readers' group in Wiltshire calling themselves a 'coven' in my honour was a one-off, until a readers' group in Newcastle contacted Dalkin Emery to say that they had done likewise. 'The critics may not love you,' Otalie said. 'But your readers do.'

I got the occasional good review. For example, *Loaded* described the book as 'The most fun you can have with your clothes on.' And the press remained interested. But the odd thing was that the good reviews made little impact on me. I could quote the unkind ones verbatim, but I distrusted the good ones.

44

I opened my eyes and foreboding weighed me down.

Lying beside me Anton said, 'Something awful's happening today, isn't it?'

I sighed. 'We're having Sunday lunch with Dad and Debs at Dettol Hall.'

'Ohh! I thought I was being executed or something. If only . . .

'I mean, your dad's alright but . . .' After another wretched pause Anton picked up the phone and began to speak. 'Debs, I'd love to visit you,' he said. 'But I'm after breaking my leg. Freak accident. I was emptying the washing machine, and *snap*! Just went from under me. That's femurs for you, though. Unreliable johnnies. What's that? You want me to hop over to Dettol Hall on my good leg? Well, I'd love to, Debs, but haven't you heard? About the nuclear warhead they've just exploded over Gospel Oak? No Debs, at least I don't *think* you can clean up nuclear fall-out with Dettol and a soft cloth.'

He clattered the phone down again and lay gloomily on his back. 'Feck,' he observed. 'And it'll take all day to get there.'

Although he could probably have afforded to, Dad had not returned to live in Surrey. After being ejected once I think he feared that there was a bouncer who would refuse him re-entry.

Instead he lived now in Muswell Hill, in a gleaming Edwardian house infused with ferociously artificial smells. Debs shook'n'vacced on a regular basis, was a great fan of the air-freshener and counted antiseptic wipes amongst her close personal chums.

Muswell Hill was not terribly far from Gospel Oak, as the

crow flew. But as the trains went, it was quite a different story.

Anton was in the shower and I was changing Ema's nappy when the phone rang. I let the machine pick up. But after a few seconds, the curiosity overwhelmed me, so I went to the living room and played the message.

It was Otalie. The Martha Hope Jones interview was out; she had not expected it to run on a Sunday. She did not say that it was 'a lovely piece'. This was a bad sign.

'Anton,' I yelped, 'I must go out and buy a paper.'

Anton emerged from the shower. 'What is it?'

'The Martha Hope Jones piece is out.'

'I'll go.' Anton pulled on clothes over his still-wet body and bounded out of the door.

While he was gone, I automatically went about dressing Ema, while I prayed, *Please let it be nice, oh please let it be nice.*

Then Anton was home again, a rolled newspaper under his arm.

'Well?' I asked anxiously.

'I haven't looked.'

We spread the paper on the floor and flicked over the pages with trembling fingers.

And there it was. Spread across two pages, the headline read 'Wright and Wrong'. Which made a change from 'Lily Wrights her way to Success' and 'Wright On!'. What other atrocious puns could they come up with?

At least my photo looked nice; for once I looked intelligent instead of dippy. But underneath Martha's mugshot, her epaulettes up to her ears, was a horrible picture of a black and blue shoulder. The caption said, 'Lily's bruises were similar.' Oh dear.

I began to speed-skim.

Lily Wright is riding high in the best-seller charts with her 'novel' *Mimi's Remedies*. But don't make the mistake of thinking this was laboured over with meticulous care. 'It only took me eight weeks to knock it off,' Lily gloated. 'Most books take five years and even then they don't get published.'

It was like being splashed in the face with iced water.

'I didn't gloat,' I whispered. 'And what does she mean "novel"? It's a novel, not a "novel".'

Lily's book has been described as 'sickly sweet', but not so its creator. Displaying an arrogant disregard for the opinions of others, Lily said, 'I don't care what the critics say.'

My eyes were drawn once more to my photo: I no longer looked intelligent. I looked calculating.

She went on to quote me: 'Welcome to my humble abode.'

Well, one of us had to say it!

She made reference to the laundry drying in the kitchen . . .

Wright cares not a jot for beauty or hygiene in the home.

The square of Lego . . .

When one is invited to sit down, is it foolhardy to expect that one's hostess has removed all sharp objects from the seat?

My single status . . .

Though Wright has a little girl, she has no interest in legitimizing her. And what kind of mother sends her child out to play in sub-zero temperatures?

It was HORRIBLE.

'She makes me sound like Courtney Love,' I said, utterly appalled.

She quoted the worst parts of the *Observer* and *Independent* reviews just in case one or two people might have missed them the first time round. Then told the story of my mugging, putting particular emphasis on my not working or washing myself in its wake. The final paragraph read,

The trauma wrought by her attack still lingers. Though Wright is laughing all the way to the bank, she chooses to remain living in a grubby one-roomed flat that, frankly, looks little better than a squat. Is this all she thinks she deserves? And if so, perhaps she's correct . . .

'Which bank am I laughing all the way to?' I asked. 'Apart from my advance I haven't seen a penny. And which am I? Arrogant? Or beset with low self-esteem? And it's not a one-roomed flat. It's a one-*bed*roomed flat.'

For once Anton was clean out of optimism. There was nothing good to be said about this. Nothing at all.

'Ought we to sue?' I asked him.

'I don't know,' he said thoughtfully. 'It's your word against hers, and a lot of what she's said is just her opinion and people can't be sued for that. But let's talk to Jojo about it.'

'OK.' A fresh wave of iciness hit me. This was a million times worse than the *Observer* piece. That had only been slagging off my book, but this article had savaged me personally.

'Only miserable people are this cruel,' I tried to convince myself. 'She's probably very unhappy.'

'So would I be if I looked like that. What's with the clothes brushes on her shoulders? Do you need to puke?'

I shook my head.

'God, you must be very bad.'

A second read revealed the masses of inaccuracies we had missed on our first horror-stricken burn.

'Anton, you're a brickie, apparently.'

'A brick?'

'A brickie.'

'Where do they get this stuff FROM? And the bitch said nothing about the biscuits – even though they were top-of-the-range ones.'

'I'll ring Jojo.' But her machine picked up.

Anton and I simply looked at one other – we were utterly without the emotional equipment to deal with this. Even Ema was unusually quiet.

We remained in silence until Anton said, 'Right, I've an idea.'

He spread the two horrible pages in the middle of the living-room floor and extended his hand to me. 'Up you get.'

'What?'

He was searching through his CDs. 'Let's see. Sex Pistols? Ah no, this is the one.'

He put on some Flamenco music.

Perplexed, I watched him strutting, stamping and arching his arms above his head, as he danced his way onto the article. In truth he was very good, nearly as good as Joachim Cortes. Ema, relieved that the dreadful atmosphere seemed to have lifted, shrieked and galloped around him. The music sped up and so did Anton, stamping and clapping with great panache until the song ended and he tossed his head back with a flourish. 'Ole!'

'Lay!' Ema yelled, also tossing her head and almost falling over.

The next song began. 'Come on,' Anton said.

I tried one stamp and liked it, so tried another, then really got into it. I concentrated my stamping on Martha's face, until Anton toed my foot aside, 'Give me a go. Right, Ema, your turn.'

Ema galloped on the spot above Martha's picture. 'Good girlie,' Anton encouraged, 'give her a fine pounding there.'

Then Anton retreated several steps and took a running jump, landing with his size elevens on Martha's face.

The three of us stamped and banged until the horrible words and Martha's ugly mug were smeared with print. The grand finale was when Anton held up the page like a matador's blanket and I put my foot through it with a 'Da-dah!'

'Feel better?'

'A little.'

Not terribly, but it was worth a try.

Seconds later Mad Paddy appeared to complain. 'What's all the banging and clattering? A lump of plaster's after falling off the ceiling into me tea!'

'Tea!' Anton scoffed and shut the door on him. 'Long Island Iced Tea, more like.'

'And so what if it is?' Mad Paddy was muffled but indignant on the far side of the door.

'It's probably his bloody fault,' Anton observed. 'If he hadn't sung "Santa Claus is Comin' to Town", that woman wouldn't have been so vicious.'

'I don't know . . .'

'We should move.'

'I'm serious,' he said, when I made no reply. 'We really should think about buying a place.'

'With what? Beads and mirrors? We're just about able to feed and clothe ourselves.'

'The way your career is going, we won't be skint for ever.'

'The way my career is going, I'll be stoned in the street.' I reached for the phone. 'I'm cancelling lunch at Dettol Hall.'

'Why?'

'I'm too ashamed to go out.'

'Fuck them! You've done nothing wrong. Why should you be ashamed?'

'I thought you would jump at the chance to get out of seeing Debs.'

'I would. But it's more important that you hold your head up high. If you go to bits now, Martha Hope Jones will have won.'

'OK,' I said wearily, 'King's Cross, here we come.'

*

The Sunday north London train service was pitifully threadbare
. . . even *before* they cancelled the 11.48. And the 12.07.

Anton, Ema and I sat in the draughty station, waiting for
the next train which hopefully might not be cancelled, and
thought up things we would rather do than visit Debs.

'Stick needles in my eyes.'

'Go to an Andrew Lloyd Webber musical.'

'Lick Margaret Thatcher.'

'Debs isn't a bad person,' I said.

'No,' Anton agreed. 'She's not a person at all. Watch her
today and see how she never blinks. I'm telling you she's an
alien.

'Don't look!' He held his hands in front of my eyes to block
the sight of a woman on the next bench leafing through the
Sunday Echo. My stomach churned wretchedly. Had she seen
the piece about me? How many people throughout Britain
were reading that poison?

Forty-five minutes late we stood on the doorstep of Dettol
Hall. Debs opened the door and regarded us with her round,
blue eyes and, on cue, Ema began to wail.

'You were invited to lunch,' Debs scolded, 'good'
'humouredly'. 'Not supper.'

As always she was kitted out in the pristine pastels of baby
clothes and her little plimsolls were so white my eyes ached.
To look directly at them one would need a piece of cardboard
with a hole in it, of the type used for viewing a solar eclipse.

'Sorry we're late.' I struggled to fold away the buggy as Anton
calmed Ema. 'The trains were up the spout.'

'You and your trains,' Debs said indulgently. She treats
Anton and me as if we are wilfully Bohemian, instead of merely
poor. 'One of you really ought to get a proper job!'

I gave Anton a warning look. No killing the hostess.

'Come through.' Debs led the way down the hall, pointing
each little foot before laying it carefully on the floor.

In the kitchen Dad folded me in his arms as if someone had died. 'My little girl,' he said hoarsely. When he finally let me go, he had tears in his eyes.

'I take it you saw the *Echo*,' I said.

'She's a witch, that woman, an evil witch.'

'That's no way to talk about your wife,' Anton said quietly into my ear.

'Anything I can do for you?' Dad asked me.

'No thanks, I would love just to forget about it. Ema, darling, say hello to Grandad!'

'Look at her little face,' Dad cooed. 'It's a picture.'

Debs prepared drinks and said gaily to Anton, 'Well! I see your lot has been at it again.'

'What's that, Mum?'

Debs frowned slightly at the 'Mum' and continued, 'The IRA. Refusing to give up their weapons.'

We go through this charade whenever the IRA are in the news, and Anton has long given up trying to explain to Debs that, actually, he is not a member of the IRA. Anton is Irish and that is good enough for Debs. Debs's thing is that she disapproves of foreign countries. Except for Provence and the Algarve, she cannot understand why the whole world simply cannot be English.

Then Anton greeted Joshua and Hattie, Debs's eight-year-old son and ten-year-old daughter from her first marriage. 'Ah,' he said expansively, 'the Children of the Corn.'

Debs thinks he calls them that because they are both blond. But *The Children of the Corn* is a Stephen King novel so it's got little to do with the colour of their hair and lots to do with their oddness: they are unnaturally clean and pliant.

'Hi Joshua, hi Hattie.' I crouched down to say hello but they eluded eye contact. However, unlike proper rude children they did not push me over and run away. Instead they stood obediently before me and fixed their sight on an invisible object somewhere behind my head.

Anton says he has faith that they will grow up to be axe-murderers and butcher Debs while she lies sleeping.

Then, like a mini-whirlwind, in came Poppy. She looks oddly like a miniature Dad, but in a wild corkscrew wig. 'Lily,' she yelped. 'Anton. And Ema!' She kissed us all, then grabbed Ema by the hand and ran out of the room with her. She is a total and utter delight and we are all madly in love with her, especially Ema.

When we eventually sat down to it, lunch was rather grim. First came Debs's apologies about the state of the roast beef. 'But unfortunately it was due to be eaten over an hour ago.'

'Sorry,' I muttered.

But that was simply a precursor to the real programme – the gloating over the Martha Hope Jones piece.

'You must be wretched with embarrassment, Lily. I know I would be. *Dying* with it. Afraid to show my face. When one thinks of all those people reading it and judging you, well you must be dreadfully upset.'

'Yes.' I looked at my plate. 'So I'd appreciate it if we didn't discuss it.'

'Of *course*. You must want to forget it ever happened. To have someone write such appalling things and then publish it in a national paper that has a circulation of several million . . . If it were me, I think I should kill myself.'

'I'll save you the bother and do it for you myself,' Anton said cheerfully, 'if you don't shut up right away.'

Debs coloured. 'I beg your pardon. I was being *sympathetic*. After such a dreadful, humiliating, embarrassing –'

'That's enough,' Dad said. He sounded so firm that Debs looked momentarily uncertain, then he made the mistake of licking his butter knife and she pounced, scolding him shrilly.

Over the years Debs had done a *My Fair Lady* on what she regarded as Dad's more objectionable mannerisms: drinking milk straight from the carton, spilling lots of it down his chin and wiping it away with his sleeve. She had even managed to reduce his weight by preparing him special low-fat meals, but it pained me to see how she had literally reduced him.

It was a dreadfully hard day but at four-thirty we were given a surprise early release: Debs was playing a tennis match. She left Dad up to his elbows in sudsy water as she ran off to change. Five minutes later she skipped down the stairs in her flippy white skirt and neat, hairbanded hair.

'Well,' Anton said in admiration. 'You look more like a schoolgirl than a forty-six-year-old alien.'

Debs posed jauntily with her racket over her shoulder, giggled, then frowned, 'A forty-six-year-old *what*?'

'Alien,' Anton said cheerfully.

I wanted to run away.

'Irish word. Means "goddess".'

'Really?' A little uncertainly. 'I see. Well, I should go. Time waits for no man.'

'Or alien!' Anton twinkled.

'Um, yes.'

'Bye. Good luck.'

'And no going out with the girls and getting tiddly afterwards,' Anton chided. 'I know you, you naughty girl.'

She giggled again, then in grim silence ripped Joshua off her leg, flung him towards a corner of the hall, jogged out to her lemon Yaris and drove away.

'Nope,' Anton said conclusively, as we rocked on the homebound train.

'Nope, what?'

'I just can't believe she's ever had sex. She has a brillo pad for a heart. How did little Poppy come about? Let's face it, Mr Muscle is the only man Debs seems interested in.'

'Perhaps she brings a bottle of Dettol into bed with her.'

'Oh stop. I'm having horrific thoughts. God, she's vile.'

'I know,' I said. 'But Dad is mad about her so I feel I ought to try. And in many ways she's terribly good for him.'

'How?'

'She's tempered the excesses of his financial risk-taking.'

'You mean she was astute enough to get the title of Dettol Hall put in her name.'

'At least they'll always have a roof over their heads.'

'True.'

45

'Will you do something for me?' Anton asked.

'Anything,' I said. Foolishly.

'There's a house for sale in Grantham Road. Will you and Ema come to see it with me?'

After a pause I said, 'What's the asking price?'

'Four hundred and seventy-five thousand.'

'Why do you want to view a house that we will never be able to afford, not in a million years?'

'I see it every day on the way to the tube and I'm curious about it. It's like a fairy-tale house, it doesn't belong in London at all.'

'Why are they selling?'

'It belonged to an old man who died. His family don't want it.'

I had a sudden hard place in my stomach. Anton had researched this without telling me.

'It can't hurt to look,' he said.

I so did not agree. But Anton asked so little from me, how could I refuse him?

'This is it,' Anton said, standing before a detached, sturdy redbrick with a pointy Gothic roof. It was like a miniature castle and looked neither too big nor too small. Just right.

Arse.

'Victorian,' Anton said, pushing open a waist-high gate and extending a hand. Ema and I followed him up a short tinder path to a tiled porch with a pitched roof. The heavy blue front door was opened immediately by a young suited and booted bloke. Greg, the estate agent.

I stepped over the threshold into the hall, the door closed behind me and I was infused with calm. The light was quite different in here. The stained-glass fan-window above the front door threw coloured patterns onto the wooden floor and all was peaceful and golden.

'Most of the furniture's gone,' Greg said. 'The old man's family took it. Let's start here, shall we?'

Our feet echoed on the wooden floors as we followed him into a room that stretched the entire depth of the house. At the front was a pretty bay window and at the back, French doors leading to the garden – which looked crammed with old-fashioned, hollyhock-style foliage. A fireplace, patterned with William Morris-style ceramic tiles stood tall by the right wall.

'Original,' Greg said, knocking his knuckles on it.

There was the faintest smell of pipe tobacco and I imagined children wearing button boots, eating toffee apples and playing on a wooden rocking horse.

On the other side of the hall was a cosy little square room, also with a bay window and fireplace.

'This could be your writing room,' Anton said. 'Lily's a writer,' he told Greg.

'Oh?' he said politely. 'Have I heard of you?'

'Lily Wright,' I said shyly.

'Oh,' he repeated, my name clearly meaning nothing to him. 'Er, well done.'

The floorboards by the window creaked and suddenly I remembered reading about an American woman who had wanted to recreate a Victorian house, so had paid for authentically squeaking floorboards. And here they were, already installed.

'I could put my desk here,' I said, stroking the wall. A piece of plaster crumbled into my hand.

'Obviously the house needs a bit of work,' Greg said. 'Ought to be fun pulling it all together.'

'Yes.' And my assent was sincere.

Then the kitchen which was a gloomy hidey-hole. 'We could knock through,' I murmured, not really understanding what it meant, but seizing on the phrase.

I could see it already. My new knocked-through kitchen would be four times its current size and floored with warm terracotta tiles. At all times a heavy ceramic casserole would sit on a pale blue Aga, so should people drop in unexpectedly, I could wander out in my bare feet, welcome them warmly, give them dinner, then press my home-made elderberry wine on them. I would be like Nigella Lawson.

When people had crises, they would appear on my prettily tiled doorstep, knowing they could depend on me for sanctuary. I would bundle them in a mohair blanket, place them on a daybed in the bay window to watch the breeze playing on the branches and supply camomile tea in charmingly mismatched cups and saucers until their *crise* had passed.

Greg led us to the stairs and as I bent down to carry Ema I noticed pinprick holes in the floorboards. Woodworm. How charming. How . . . how . . . authentic. It would be impossible ever to be unhappy in this house.

The three bedrooms were each more delightful than the previous. Visions of iron bedsteads, embroidered quilts, rocking chairs and voile curtains billowing in the gentle breeze entranced me.

I took a brief look at the poky antediluvian bathroom and murmured once again about knocking through.

Then Greg took us downstairs for the property highlight: the charmingly overgrown garden. Along the edges a horseshoe of trees and tangled bushes leant inwards and camouflaged much of the houses and tower blocks of the outside world.

'Blackcurrant bushes. Raspberry vines,' Greg indicated. 'An apple tree. In the summer you'll have fruit.'

I had to clutch Anton.

Near the back fence there was a low, old-fashioned greenhouse growing tomatoes. Beside it was a south-facing garden seat like an old park bench, with white-painted wooden slats and wrought-iron legs.

'Hardly know you were in London,' Greg said.

'Mmmm,' I agreed, quite happy to ignore the screech of a car alarm from a street away.

I saw myself sitting in this garden, writing in a pretty note-book, a basket of freshly picked raspberries by my side. In the sunlight my hair was blonde and ripply, as if my highlights had just been done, and I was draped in a floaty white something from Ghost, or perhaps Marni.

Clearest of all was my vision of Ema playing with other children – her brothers and sisters perhaps? For some reason they all had ringlets and were happily throwing stones at the greenhouse.

I would press flowers. My French windows would have light muslin drapes which shifted in the breeze and I would meander barefoot from garden to house carrying secateurs and an over-arm basket.

It smelt and felt like a half-remembered dream. As familiar as if I had been here before, even though I knew I had not.

I had never been materialistic. For as long as I remembered I had held the opinion that money plays one false: promises the world – perhaps even delivers it briefly – before removing it again.

But suddenly it was clear what an idiot I had been. I ought to have got my foot on the property ladder at the first opportunity. I should have hustled for better pay.

At that moment I wanted the house so badly, I was *avid* with greed. I would have sold my grandmother had she been still alive and had anyone wanted to buy her.

I had never before desired something so intensely. I would die without this house. But there was no need for such melo-drama because it was my house already. I simply needed to find half a million pounds from somewhere.

*

I barely remember the walk home, but when I found myself once again in my poky little flat I rounded on Anton. I felt as though I had had a near-death experience and come face-to-face with the transcendent beauty of the divine, only to be returned to my body because, due to a clerical error, it was not yet my time. It had ruined me for anything else.

'Why did you show it to me? We could never afford it.'

'Listen to me a minute.' Anton was scribbling calculations on a paper bag. 'You've sold almost two hundred thousand copies, so you should get roughly one hundred thousand pounds in royalties.'

'I keep telling you, my first tranche of royalties won't be paid until the end of September and that's nearly five months away. The house will be gone by then.'

He was shaking his head. 'We can borrow against future income.'

'Can we? But Anton, the house is half a million *and* we'd need knocking-through money.'

'Think of the future,' he urged, his eyes shining. 'At some stage Eye-Kon is going to start turning a profit.'

I remained silent because I did not want to seem unsupportive. But until now all Eye-Kon had turned was my stomach when I saw on their balance sheet how much was spent on lunches in Soho buttering people up and how little work it had yielded.

'But much more importantly,' Anton said, 'you have a two-book deal.'

'Yes, but I've written only two chapters of my second one.' And no one at Dalkin Emery had cared until recently. It was only when *Mimi's Remedies* surprised them by selling so many that they even remembered I was signed up for a second book.

'What about *Crystal Clear*?' It was obvious that Anton had been giving this some thought. 'That's finished and it's a great book. Offer that to them.'

It was strange because the very next day, Tania called. She

wanted to see my new book. 'To bring out a hardback to catch the Christmas market.'

I had to make the dreadful admission. 'Tania, there is no new book.'

'Excuse me?'

'What with the baby and the tiredness and everything, I just couldn't manage it. I've only done two chapters.'

'I seeee.' Silence. Then, 'It's just that we thought . . . with it being a two-book deal . . . it's normal to start on the new one as soon as you've finished the old one. But, yes, the baby, the tiredness and you *have* been very busy . . .'

But clearly she wasn't happy. Distressed, I rang Anton.

'Give her *Crystal Clear*,' he reiterated.

'But it's not good enough. I couldn't get an agent with it.'

'It *is* good enough. Those agents were gobshites. It's a great book.'

'You think?'

'I think.'

So I called Tania and explained haltingly, 'I don't know if you will like it, I sent it to lots of agents –'

Tania cut in. 'Are you telling me you've got another book?'

'Yes.'

'Hallelujah. She's got another book,' she yelled. Someone whooped. 'I'll send a bike.'

Later that night, Tania called. 'I love it. Love, love, love it!'

'You've read it? That was fast.'

'I couldn't put it down. It's a different book to *Mimi's Remedies*, *very* different, but still has the Lily Wright magic. Roll on our Christmas best-seller.'

Shortly after that Jojo spoke to me about signing a new contract for my third and fourth books. 'For a much higher advance than the previous one, obviously.'

'See,' Anton said gleefully.

Jojo said we could sign now while my sales were buoyant,

or we could wait until late autumn when, if my new hardback stormed the best-seller lists, my bargaining position would be even stronger.

'But what if my hardback doesn't storm the best-seller lists?'

'That's always a possibility, but it's your call.'

'But what do you think?'

'I think you're in a super-strong bargaining position now but it could be even stronger in November. But Lily, you've gotta know this: there is always a risk, there are no absolutes in this game. I'm sorry, sweets, I know you don't want to, but only you can make the decision.'

Anton talked down Jojo's disclaimer. 'She's not trying to scare you but she has to cover herself. But at the end of the day the decision has to be yours because you're the one who writes the books. You know I'll support you in whatever you decide but it has to be you who makes the final choice.'

I had no clue which was best. I was terrified of making a decision because it might be the wrong one and I trusted the opinions of others more than I trusted my own.

'Anton, what do you think?'

'I don't know why, but I think we should wait.'

'Really? Why don't you want the money immediately?'

He laughed. 'You know me so well. But I'm trying to change the habits of a lifetime. Trying to think long-term, you know. And long-term I think you're likely to get more money if you wait.'

I heard myself say, 'OK, then we'll wait.'

Deciding to wait until November was less of a decision than deciding to sign a new deal now. Certainly fewer immediate consequences ensued from it. But still I felt agonized.

'Oh, poor Lily.' Anton pulled my face to his chest and stroked my hair.

'Careful,' I murmured. 'Don't rub it away, it's too thin as it is.'

'Sorry. Anyway, c'mere, this might put a smile on your little face. You know how I told you our house costs four seven five? They've dropped the asking price! By fifty grand!'

'Why?'

'It's been on the market for nearly four months, they must be getting desperate.'

'Why hasn't it sold before now?'

'Because it was overpriced. But it's not overpriced now, which is why we should get in there. Everyone else will too.'

But I could not commit to borrowing such an enormous sum of money. 'There are too many variables,' I said. 'What if *Crystal Clear* bombs? What if I can't write another book and have to return the advance?'

'*Crystal Clear* won't bomb and we'll get a nanny so that you can devote yourself to writing. We'll even have a bedroom for her in the new house.'

I made a non-committal hmmm.

'What else are we going to do when your royalties arrive?' he asked. 'Buy a one-bed flat in the back-arse of nowhere and live on top of each other for a year or so, just like we're doing here, all of us sleeping in one room? Then when more money comes in, we sell it and buy someplace else so that we end up paying two lots of stamp duty. That's three per cent of the purchase price, it adds up to plenty, it's about fifteen grand on this house alone and we'd never get that back.'

'You've really been thinking about this.'

'At the moment, I can't think of anything else.' He leant into me, conviction in his eyes. 'I think this house is exactly what we need. There's that lovely room that would be perfect for you to write in, we'd have space for a nanny and we'd never have to move again. OK, I agree with you that we don't have the money yet but *it's coming*. But if we wait until all the money is sitting in our bank account, the house will be long gone.' He stopped for breath. 'Lily, you and me, we're crap with money, am I right?'

I agreed. We were hopeless.

'But for once, let's try to get it right. Let's try looking at the bigger picture, Lily, have vision. And let me ask you one thing: do you love this house?'

I nodded. As soon as I had walked in I fell head-over-heels in love and knew it was the one for me.

'I love it too. It's the perfect house – at a *great price*. House prices might have dropped this year but they'll soon take off again. We might never get this chance again. Would it help if we took a second look at it?'

I jumped at the chance, I was longing to see it again.

The calm sense of belonging which had filled me on my first visit was even more profound second time round. Anton was right when he said that it did not belong in London; it was the type of house you might find in a clearing in the woods in an old-fashioned fairy tale. Once I was within its walls I felt safe, somehow touched by enchantment.

Funny how these things happen because the same day that we visited the house, we were notified by Mr Manatee, our landlord, that due to 'unexpected costs' he was increasing our rent. When I saw the new figure I almost died – it had more than doubled. 'That's outrageous! I'm going to speak to Irina about this, and, oh God –' I passed a hand over my eyes – 'and Mad Paddy. If we present a united front, we have a better chance of winning.'

But neither Irina nor Mad Paddy had had their rent increased. Light began to dawn.

'Manatee must have read about you,' Anton said. 'Opportunistic prick. This is extortion.'

'Anton, we can't afford the new rent, it's out of the question.'

Our eyes met, sparking with realization. 'We'll have to move.'

I look for 'signs' everywhere and I reluctantly acknowledged this as one.

Anton seized his chance. 'They're looking for four two five. I say we offer four hundred and see what happens.'

'We haven't got four hundred thousand, we probably haven't got four hundred.'

'Let's just make an offer on the house and busk it. You never know what might happen because this isn't an ordinary chain situation, the vendors –'

Vendors! – he was talking a different language, one that excluded me.

'– the vendors aren't stuck in a chain, they don't need the asking price to buy a new house, they're just waiting for an inheritance windfall. They're a lot more likely to take a lower offer, they must be sick of waiting for all that loot, tied up in Dad's old house that they can't get shot of.'

'Anton! We cannot offer to buy a house when we have no money in place.'

'Of course we can.'

'You're not going to believe it!' Anton cried. 'They've accepted our offer of four hundred grand.'

I felt the colour drain from my face. 'You've offered to buy a house and we've no money! What kind of idiot are you?'

He couldn't stop laughing. He fell onto my neck, giddy with glee. 'We'll get the money.'

'From where?'

'The bank.'

'Do you plan to rob one?'

'I agree with you that we're not standard mortgage application material. What we need is a bank with vision.'

'I want no part in this. I want you to ring that poor Greg and tell him you've been wasting his time.'

That creased him up again. '"Poor Greg" – Lily, he's an *estate* agent.'

'If you don't tell him, I shall!'

'Don't, Lily, please don't ring him, just give me a little time. Trust me.'

'No.'

'Please, Lily, please baby, just trust me.' He pulled me round to him and his love for me was stamped on his face. 'I will never do anything to hurt you. I will spend my life trying to make things beautiful and perfect for you and Ema. Please trust me.'

I shrugged. It was not quite a yes, but it was not a no either. It never was.

He took to making phone calls, the type that necessitated turning away from me whenever I came into the room. When I asked, 'Who was that?' he would tap the side of his nose and wink. The post began to yield up fat letters, which he spirited away to open in private and when I questioned him about them, there was more nose-tapping and mysterious grins. Of course, I could have insisted on disclosure, but manifestly I did not want to know.

I had a bad dream where I was in a huge warehouse packing mountains of my possessions into a sea of ten-foot-high cardboard boxes. A whole box of single shoes, another one filled with broken televisions, then I was trying to squeeze the William Morris fireplace into a box the size of a biscuit tin and a disembodied voice said, 'All fireplaces must be securely stowed.' Then the dream jumped and Ema and I were sitting on the grass strip in the middle of a motorway, with all the boxes and I knew with hollow sick certainty that we had no place to call home.

But when I was awake I thought constantly about the house in a dreamy, love-sick way. In my head I had painted, decorated and furnished all the rooms and I rearranged the furniture constantly, as if it were a doll's house. I had a cream-painted, curvy, antique French bed, with a matching claw-footed armoire, a high-headboarded brass bed with a charmingly squeaky mattress, carved trunks, rose borders, pot-bellied bed-side cabinets, plump bolsters, satin eiderdowns, scatter rugs strewn across my shiny wooden floors . . .

When I thought about living there, different versions of my life opened up. I wanted to have other children, at least two more, but it was a desire I had tamped down firmly because under our current living arrangements it simply was not viable. But it could happen in the new house.

Then Anton came to me and said, 'Lily, light of my life, love of my heart, are you free tomorrow afternoon?'

'Why?' Suspiciously. The light-of-my-life stuff usually preceded a request to collect his dinner jacket from the dry-cleaner's for some media do.

'I've got us an appointment with a bank.'

A beat. 'You haven't?'

'Oh, but I have, *ma petite*, my little pumpkin.'

The following afternoon, we left Ema with Irina and asked her *not* to put the green face mask on her again, we were still picking bits out of her hair. Then kitted out in our most respectable clothes, we arrived at the bank to be greeted by three interchangeable men in sombre suits. I was embarrassed, as though we had got into their offices under false pretences, but Anton was absolutely dazzling. Even I was convinced. He talked about what a star I was, how this was the start of a storming career, how they'd benefit from getting on board now, how we would remain loyal in the future when we were earning millions and owned other homes in New York, Monte Carlo and Letterkenny. (Ancestral seat of the Carolans.) Then, to back up his puff, he produced letters from Jojo and Dalkin Emery's accountants, copies of my sales figures to date and related earnings, a projection of sales of *Crystal Clear* from Dalkin Emery's Head of Sales and an approximate calculation of how much I could expect to earn from that. (A lot, as it happens. I was astonished at their ambition.)

To assuage their anxiety over us having neither a down-payment nor steady income, he passed around a spreadsheet of proposed repayments, with a lump sum due to be paid when I received my first royalty cheque in September and another lump sum when I signed my new contract in November. 'Gentlemen, have no fear that you will get your money back.'

With a final flourish, he produced three copies of *Mimi's Remedies* which I signed for the wives of the sombre-suited men.

'It's in the bag,' he said, as we got the tube home.

The letter bearing the bank's masthead came two days later. My stomach sloshed with nausea as we both tried to tear it open. My eyes skidded along the words, trying to extract their meaning, but Anton was faster than me.

'Shit!'

'What?'

'They wish us luck but they're not making with the readies.'

'That's it then,' I said, devastated yet strangely half-relieved. 'The fuckers.'

But of course, that was not it. Anton, ever the optimist, simply made an appointment with another bank. 'Knock on enough doors, someone will eventually let you in.'

Despite another tour de force from Anton, the second bank also turned us down; he did not even stop to lick his wounds before he had lined up yet another. This time, knowing how likely they were to turn us down, I felt an utter fraud as Anton pitched me. And when they sent their letter of regret, I begged him to stop.

'Just one more,' he insisted. 'You give up too easily.'

I was feeding Ema her breakfast, a protracted, messy experience which usually left the floor, walls and my hair splattered with clods of wet Weetabix, when Anton frisbeed a letter onto the table. 'Have a read of that.' He was grinning like a loon.

'Tell me.' I was afraid to believe, but what else could it be . . .

'The bank said yes, they'll loan us the money. The house is ours.'

This was my cue to launch myself into his arms and be

twirled around the kitchen, both of us laughing our heads off. Instead I became very still, and stared at him, almost in fear.

He was some sort of alchemist, he had to be. How did he continue to conjure up dream solutions out of thin air? He had got me an agent, who had got me a publisher, he had 'found' my second book when I thought I had none, and now he had secured my dream house even though we had no money upfront.

'How do you do it?' I asked, faintly. 'Have you cut a deal with the devil?'

He polished an imaginary medal on his chest, then laughed at himself. 'Lily, take a bow. This is down to you about to bring in a ton of money in September and more when you sign your new deal. Without that, me pestering them wouldn't have cut any ice. They'd have got security to throw me out.'

'Oi!' I wrestled the letter back from Ema, who had been using the back of her spoon to carefully cover it with mushy Weetabix. She squawked in dismay, but was trapped in her high chair and could not do much about it. As I read the typewritten page, joy began a cautious trickle. If the bank had said yes, then everything must be fine. Clearly they thought I would earn enough to pay it all back; this was not just a loan, it was an endorsement of my career.

Then I read a sentence which caused my plucky little trickle of joy to make an emergency stop. I gasped.

So did Ema; her eyes were wide and alarmed, just like mine.

'Anton, it says the loan is "subject to survey". What does that mean?'

'Anton! Whazat *meen*?'

'They want to be sure the house is worth what they're lending us for it, just in case we default and they need to repossess.'

I winced. Talk of repossession froze my innards; it brought back the day we left the big house in Guildford.

'So they do a structural survey to make sure the house is sound.'

'And what if it isn't?'

'Did it look sound to you?'

'Yes, but –'

'Well, then.'

Anton opened the letter. He read it in silence, but something sombre pervaded the room.

'What is it?'

'OK,' he cleared his throat. 'This is the result of the bank's survey.'

'And?'

'They've found dry rot in the front room. Quite bad, they say.'

I belly-flopped with disappointment and tears sprang to my eyes. Our beautiful, beautiful house. What about the raspberry bushes, the daybed in the bay window, me in the floaty dress, carrying the overarm basket? The bohemian dinner parties I would throw to repay Nicky and Simon, Mikey and Ciara, Viv, Baz and Jez and all the other people who had had Anton and me round to their homes and whom I had never invited here because it was far too small?

I heard myself say, 'Well, that's that then.'

'It is not. Lily, don't fold on me, dry rot can be fixed! Piece of piss! They'll still give us a mortgage, but for less. For three hundred and eighty.'

'Where will we find twenty thousand pounds?'

'Catch yourself on, Lily, we don't. We go back to the vendors and drop our offer by twenty grand.'

'But we still need to fix the dry rot! I repeat, where do we find twenty thousand pounds?'

'There's no way a little bit of dry rot will cost twenty grand to fix. A couple of grand, at most.'

'But the bank said –'

'The bank are just covering themselves. What do you think?'

'OK,' I said. 'Do what you have to do.'

To my utter astonishment the vendors accepted the reduced price. How many more signs did I need that this house was meant to be mine? Nevertheless, I got a final-furlong bout of the wobblies: when Anton said, 'Will we buy it?' I heard myself wail, 'No, I'm too frightened.'

'OK.'

'OK?' Surprised, I looked at him.

'OK, you're too frightened. Let's forget it.'

'You don't mean that, you're just trying reverse pyschology.'

He shook his head. 'I'm not. I just want you to be happy.'

I looked at him, with suspicion. I *thought* I believed him. 'Alright then. Talk me into it.'

He hesitated. 'Are you sure about this?'

'Quick, Anton, before I change my mind again, talk me into it.'

'Er, right!' He listed out all the reasons we were meant to buy this house: we had royalty money coming in; my career was on fire and I was bound to get an enormous advance in November; the bank – notoriously cautious – had given us approval; buying this house was better than buying a small place now and having the upheaval of a second move in a year's time; we didn't just want *a* house, we loved this *particular* house, it was very us. And finally, 'If everything goes pear-shaped, we can sell the house and get back more than we paid.'

'What if its value drops instead of increasing and we end up owing heaps of money?'

'A house like that, in that area? – Course it'll go up, it's a no-brainer. We can't lose. Nothing can go wrong.'

PART TWO

GEMMA

I

It was eighty days since Dad had left. Or not even three months which, when I put it like that, didn't sound so bad. Not much was going on when suddenly four BIG things happened, one after the other.

The first thing – at the end of March the clocks went forward. No big deal, I know, but wait, that's not actually the thing, that was just the trigger. Anyway, the clocks went forward and even though I spent most of Sunday changing the time on Mam's cooker, microwave, video, phone, seven clocks, even her watch, the implications didn't hit me until Monday afternoon at work when Andrea put on her coat and said, 'Right, I'm off.' It was still bright so I said, 'It's the middle of the afternoon,' and she replied, 'It's twenty to six.'

Suddenly I got it and nearly choked with terror. The evenings were stretching towards summer; when he'd left it had been the dead of winter. Where had all the time gone?

I had to see him. Nothing to do with Mam; this was about me. Though I rarely left work before seven I was fuelled with such desperate need that not even the combined forces of Frances and Francis could have stopped me.

I jostled my way out of the office, into the car and drove straight over to his work – I wouldn't go to their apartment for a million quid. His car was in the car park, so he hadn't left for the day. I watched anxiously over my steering wheel as the staff trickled out. Funny how they weren't all tubby, I mused. Very few of them actually were and you'd think with all that chocolate lying around . . . Oh Christ, here he comes. With Colette. *Shite*. I'd been hoping to catch him on his own.

He was in his suit and looked much as he'd always looked;

he was as familiar to me as myself, it was too strange not to have seen him in so long.

Colette's hair was still highlighted, it didn't seem like she was letting herself go, now that she'd bagged her man. But on the plus side she didn't look pregnant.

As they neared me they were chatting in a dismayingly chummy manner. I got out of the car and stepped in front of both of them. It was meant to be kind of dramatic but they were walking quite fast and had almost passed me.

'Dad,' I called.

They turned; blank faces.

'Dad?'

'Gemma. Ah, hello.'

'Dad, I haven't heard from you in a while.'

'Ah, sure, you know.' He was uncomfortable. He turned to Colette, 'Will you wait in the car, love?'

'Love' gave me a filthier but swung away towards the Nissan.

'Does she have to be *such* a bitch?' I asked. I couldn't help it. 'What reason does she have to be horrible?'

'She's just insecure.'

'*She's* insecure. What about me? I haven't seen you in nearly three months.'

'Is it that long?' He shifted in a vague, old-man kind of way.

'Yes, Dad.' In a desperate attempt at humour I asked, 'Don't you want custody of me? You could have weekend visitation rights, take me to McDonalds.'

But he just said, 'You're grown up, you're your own person.'

'Don't you even want to see me?'

They say you should never ask a question that you don't know the answer to. Of course he wanted to see me.

But he said, 'It's probably for the best that we don't meet up at the moment.'

'But Dad . . .' Grief rose like a wave and I began to cry. People walking past were looking but I didn't care. The wave became a tsunami. I hadn't seen my father in three months, I was bawling and choking like a peanut had gone down the wrong way – and he wouldn't even touch me. I launched myself at him; he stood like a plank and patted me awkwardly. 'Ah, Gemma, ah don't . . .'

'You don't love me any more.'

'I do, sure of course I do.'

With monumental effort, I forced myself to stop the choking, then cleared my throat, briefly getting it together. 'Dad, please come home. Please.'

'Noel, we have to collect the kids.' Colette.

I swung around to her. 'I thought he told you to wait in the car.'

'Noel, the kids,' she ignored me. 'They'll be wondering where we are.'

'You know what?' I looked at her and pointed at Dad. 'I'm *his* kid and I've been wondering the very same thing.'

Then I added, 'So fuck you.'

She studied me, cool as anything. 'No, fuck you.

'Two minutes,' she said to Dad. 'I'm counting.' She stomped back to the car.

'Classy.'

'How's your mother?' Dad asked.

'Your WIFE,' I shouted the word around the car park. The few people who weren't already looking were now. 'Your WIFE is GREAT. She has a boyfriend. A Swiss fella called Helmut. He has a red Aston Martin with gull-wing doors.'

'Has she, by the hokey? Listen, Gemma, I have to go now. Geri goes mad if we're late.'

Contempt was all that was left to me. I looked at my father. 'You're a coward.'

In the sanctuary of my car the tears started again. All men are cowards.

And this wasn't going to be fixed any time soon; it killed me to admit it but Dad and Colette had started to look permanent. So where did that leave me? What about my life?

Mam was doing her best, she really was trying hard to be brave. She'd found a kind of routine, where she used a string of daytime soaps to get her through each day, like a rope bridge over an abyss. She'd started going to Mass again, she'd even gone to a couple of coffee mornings with Mrs Kelly, but she always came back shaking like jelly. It was still necessary for me to stay with her every night.

So what were the chances of her turning around and saying, 'Gemma, why don't you take this weekend off? Go out on the piss, pick up a couple of men and get them to ride you into the middle of next week. I'll be grand.' No, somehow I couldn't see it.

No one would do this for me. I thought of Owen, the youth I'd picked up the night of Cody's birthday (although I had no memory of it). He'd asked me out twice and the second time I'd said yes, but I couldn't name a day because I didn't know how to get it past Mam.

I'd promised to ring him but so far I hadn't.

2

Second thing – and probably least important of the four – I got a new account at work. The call came the next day – at ten past one, just as I was about to go out to lunch. This was a sign of the way things would continue; some people are super-demanding even when they don't plan to be. The dyed-in-the-wool diva was Lesley Lattimore, an Irish It girl: in other words she went to lots of parties and spent plenty of money, none of it earned by her. Her dad, Larry 'Wads' Lattimore, had made a fortune from dodgy property developing and fleecing Irish tax-payers, but no one seemed to care. Especially not Lesley.

'I want someone to organize my thirtieth birthday party and I heard you did Davinia Westport's wedding.'

I didn't ask if she'd been to Davinia's wedding; I knew she hadn't. She was the daughter of an unconvicted criminal and Davinia was way too posh to touch her. But Wads clearly wanted to buy his only daughter a Davinia-style bash.

'What kind of event were you thinking of?'

'Two hundred plus. A princess theme. Think Gothic Barbie,' she said, so I did and suddenly I *needed* this job. 'When can you come to see me?'

'Today. Now.'

I grabbed some files, which had photos of some of the more imaginative parties I'd done and went along to Lesley's city-centre, river-view duplex. She had the supergroomed hair, the St Tropez tan, the clothes sheeny with newness, the all-over gloss that rich people have, like they've been dipped in lacquer. And of course Lesley had a tiny handbag – confirming my theory that the richer the person, the smaller their handbag. Like, what do they need? Their gold card, the keys to the Audi

TT, a tiny mobile and a Juicy Tube. Me, my handbag is the size of an air-hostess's wheely case, full of work files, make-up, leaking pens, dry-cleaning tickets, half-eaten cereal bars, Sol-padeine, diet Coke, Heat and of course my brick of a phone.

Lesley also had the attitude down pat – it shuttled between brusque and extremely rude, passing all points in between – and that, coupled with her gloss, managed to obscure her less-than-average good looks.

You'd be with her for a while before noticing that she was more than a little bit sharp around the nose and chin area. Indeed if she'd been going for a witch theme instead of a princess one she'd have really looked the part. Funny that Wads hadn't bought her a new chin. However, despite the chip on my shoulder I had to admit we shared a common vision.

'Why should I hire you?' she demanded, and I began to list the number of high-profile events I'd pulled together – weddings, conferences, awards ceremonies – then I hesitated, wobbled and played my ace. 'I have a wand,' I said. 'A silver star, backed by lilac fluff.'

'So have I!' she cried. 'You're hired!'

She ran off and got it, then circled it solemnly over my head and said, 'I grant you the honour of organizing Lesley's birthday party.'

Then she handed it to me and said, 'Say, "I grant you a castle with turrets."'

Reluctantly I took the wand.

'Go on!' she said. 'I grant you a castle with turrets.'

'I grant you a castle with turrets,' I said.

'I grant you a medieval hall.'

'I grant you a medieval hall,' I repeated. I could see this becoming very wearing.

'I grant you a team of jousters.'

'I grant you a team of jousters.'

In between each 'grant' I had to circle the wand over her head and bring it down on each of her shoulders. The mortification was extreme, then she lost interest in the wand and I nearly cried with happiness. Especially as I was meant to be writing down her list of requirements.

And what a list! She wanted a silver empire-line 'gown' (her word) with pointy floor-length sleeves, a white ermine cape, a pointy princess hat and silver shoes (pointy, of course). She wanted pink drinks. She wanted silver chairs with curvy legs. She wanted pink food.

I wrote everything down, nodding, 'Uh-huh, good idea.' I didn't address any hard questions, like could the male guests be persuaded to drink the pink drinks or how the hell was anyone meant to dance to a band of lute minstrels. Now wasn't the time for me to start pulling holes in some of the more impractical parts of her vision. We were still in the warm glow of the honeymoon period and there was plenty of time for screaming matches in the coming weeks – where she'd scream at me and I'd smile mildly – oh, *plenty* of time.

'And when do you want to have it?'

'The thirty-first of May.' Two months away. To do this properly I'd have preferred two *years*, but the Lesleys of this world would never be so obliging.

All the same I went away already buzzing with ideas and everything suddenly seemed a lot *easier*. Bringing in new business always had a good effect – when time was stretching by without me getting the jobs, it was like being deprived of oxygen – but now I was breathing free and clear and it was obvious that this coming Friday night would be perfect for my close encounter with Owen. I could pretend to Mam it was a work do while being able to enjoy a leisurely hangover the following day. I was doing Mam no favours by lying, but I didn't care. After seeing the togetherness of Dad and Colette, I had to try to change things.

By the time I got back to my desk Lesley had left four messages – she'd had some 'great' ideas; the invitations should be delivered personally by a handsome prince; the guests should be given goody bags on arrival – but she didn't want to pay for them. 'Ring Clinique,' she said. 'And Origins and Prescriptives. Tell them we need free stuff.'

Then another message. 'And Decléor and Jo Malone.'

And one more. 'Get Lulu Guinness to design the bags.'

3

Third big thing: my date with Owen.

I rang him and said, 'It's coal scuttle Gemma. How about Friday night?'

I'd already decided that if he couldn't manage that, he could go and fuck himself. However he said, 'What time? Nine?'

I hesitated and he said, 'Ten?'

'No, I was thinking more of eight. It's just that for reasons I can't go into now, I don't get out very often at the moment so I need to wring as much enjoyment as I possibly can from the night.'

'We can make it seven, if that's how it is.'

'No, I won't be finished work in time. Now, where will we meet and please don't say Kehoes. You're a young man about town, you know the hot new places, let's go to them.'

'All of them?'

'Like I said I don't get out very often.'

A thoughtful silence. 'We're only in Dublin, not Manhattan, there aren't that many hot new places.'

'I know, sorry.' I tried to explain. 'I want to go to one of those bars where I'm completely disoriented, especially when I go to the ladies'. I just want to feel I'm living a little, you know?'

'Then how about Crash? There are lots of mirrors and steps. People are always tripping and walking into themselves.'

Perfect. I'd been meaning to check it out for work anyway.

'Eight o'clock, Friday night in Crash. Don't be late,' I warned.

As I stumbled down the mirrored entrance steps of Crash and saw Owen, he wasn't as good-looking as I'd remembered when

he'd been lying on my bedroom floor that horrible morning –
I must have still been wearing beer goggles. Like, he wasn't
bad, just not the criminally young boy-band cutie that I'd
remembered.

But . . . 'I like your shirt,' I said. It was a picture of a Cadillac
driving down a desert highway. Very cool. 'And I like your
hair.' Shiny and sticky-up – obviously he'd put a bit of work
into it.

'Thanks,' he said, paused, then added, 'I put special stuff in,
to make a good impression. Too much information?'

'No.'

'Can I get you a drink?'

'I'll have a glass of white wine now.' I arranged myself on
the couch. 'But every second drink will be a mineral water and
before I came out I had a glass of milk to line my stomach so
I won't be making a show of myself tonight like I did that other
time. Too much information?'

'Er, no.' He went to the bar and the back of his shirt showed
the same desert highway, this time with the Cadillac driving away.

Then the Cadillac was zooming towards me again. 'Your
drink.'

He lifted his glass. 'Cheers. To Gemma's big night out.'

We clinked, sipped, replaced glasses on the table, then an
awkward pause followed. 'So, ah, how's the coal scuttle working
out?' Owen asked.

But it was too late, I'd already pounced. 'Owen, that was an
awkward pause and for reasons I can't go into right now, I
haven't got time to waste on awkward pauses. We've got to
fast-track this thing. There's not enough time to get to know
each other naturally; we must induce it. I know this sounds
mad but could we try to fast-forward through the first three
months or so, and get to the comfortable staying-in-and-
watching-videos stage?'

He was looking at me a little warily but, to my gratification,
said, 'I've seen you without your make-up?'

'Yes, that's the idea. And we don't have sex every night any more.' Then I began to blush: an out-of-control-forest-fire super-blush, as I realized that we hadn't had sex at all. Yet.

'Oh God.' I put my hands over my fiery cheeks. 'I'm sorry.'

I wanted to go home. I wasn't fit to be out and about and I was frightened by my crassness. This wasn't me, what was happening?

'I'm sorry,' I repeated. 'I'm not insane, just a bit . . . under pressure.'

There was a moment when the evening hovered on a knife-edge then Owen looked relieved at my apology and even began to laugh. 'After the last time we met, I know what you're like – you're *wild*.'

I smiled weakly, not exactly happy with being Kooky Girl, but on the other hand if he already thought I was bonkers, I wouldn't have to work so hard at acting normal.

'Let the games begin,' he said. 'Tell me all about you, Gemma.'

Though it had been my idea, I felt embarrassed. 'I'm thirty-two, an only child, I'm an events organizer which is very stressful but I don't always hate it, I live in Clonskeagh . . . what have I forgotten?'

'Car?'

'Toyota MR2. Yes, I thought you'd like that. Now your go.'

'Honda Civic coupe VTi, with all the trimmings, two years old, but in great nick.'

'Good for you. Other info?'

'Leather seats, walnut dash –'

'You're such a boy.' I was pleased. 'I meant details of the rest of your life.'

'I'm twenty-eight, I'm a middle child and Monday to Friday I sell my soul to the Edachi Electronic Corporation.'

'Doing what?'

'Marketing.' A little wearily. 'Trying to make people buy stuff.'

'Do you have lots of disgusting flatmates?'

'No, I live –' giveaway swallow – 'on my own.'

'Right, I'm going to the loo.'

'Good luck.'

When I came back, I was impressed. 'Very cunning how the loos were hidden behind the wash-hand basins and mirrors. It took me ages to find them. You chose well. Now let's move on to relationship history. Two and a half years ago, my best friend stole the love of my life from me, they're still together and have a child, I've never forgiven either of them and I've never met anyone else, you might think I sound bitter, but that's only because I am. And you?'

'Jesus!' He looked a bit shocked at my onslaught. God, I'd done it again – but he answered, 'Er, I was going out with someone. A girl.'

I nodded encouragingly.

'And we broke up.'

'When? How long were you going out?'

'Um . . .'

I nodded again.

'We'd been together nearly two years. We broke up just before –' another giveaway swallow – 'Christmas.'

'Less than four months ago? After two years?'

'I'm fine about it.'

'Don't be silly. Of course you're not.'

And while he insisted he was, I was thinking, But this is excellent! He'll want *nothing* from me.

Over the next three hours and two more disorienting bars I grilled Owen and learned:

1) He did tai chi
2) He had a 'thing' about prawns – he wasn't allergic, he just didn't like them
3) One of his feet was half a size bigger than the other
4) His ideal holiday destination would be Jamaica

5) He thought the original 'Do you love someone enough to give them your last Rolo?' was far more charming and humane than the current one where the boy tries to get the Rolo out of his girlfriend's mouth to give it to the better-looking girl who'd just showed up.

He matched me question for question. 'What are you most afraid of?' he asked.

'Growing old and dying alone,' I said and a little tear escaped. 'No, no.' I waved away his concern. 'It's just the wine. What are *you* most afraid of?'

He thought. 'Being locked in the boot of a ten-year-old Nissan Micra with Uri Geller.'

'Excellent answer! Let's go dancing.'

Hours later, back at his quite-neat-for-a-boy apartment, we wrestled enjoyably in a state of undress on his bed. Of course I thought about Anton, the last man I'd slept with; after him I'd thought I'd never sleep with anyone ever again. Mind you this couldn't have been more different. Not just in emotional intensity but even physically – Anton was lanky and lean and Owen much more compact. All the same, I wasn't complaining. Before taking things any further I caught Owen's wrist and made him look at me, pausing the tiny, delicious bites on my neck, and said urgently, 'Owen, I don't normally hop into bed with someone on the first night.'

'I know.' His hair was wild and he was short of breath. 'It's just that for reasons you can't go into right now, this counts as three months in. Don't worry. Just enjoy it.'

He pulled me to him, pressing his excellent hard-on against me and I did just that.

He awoke as I was climbing into my pants.

'Where are you going?'

'I have to go home.'

He leant and looked at his alarm clock. 'It's half past three, why are you leaving? Jesus, you're not married?'

'No.'

'Have you kids?'

'No.'

'Is it the coal scuttle?'

'No.' A bubble of laughter escaped.

'Wait till the morning. Don't go.'

'Have to. Will you call me a taxi?'

'You're a taxi.'

'Fine, I'll just hail one in the street.'

'You do that.'

'I'll call you.'

'Don't bother.'

Another bubble of laughter escaped. 'Owen, our first row! Now, we're really up to speed.'

4

The fourth thing.

L H Literary Agency
4–8 Wardour Street
London W1P 3AG
31 March

Dear Ms Hogan

(Or can I call you Gemma? – I feel I know you already!) Thank you so much for your pages, forwarded to me by your friend Susan Looby. My reader and I loved them.

Obviously the pages are a long way from being a book and the format would have to be decided on – memoir style, non-fiction or a novel. However, I would be interested in talking to you. Please get in touch and we can discuss it further.

With best wishes
Jojo Harvey

Can you imagine? It was Saturday evening. It had been a lovely day, dozing, drinking Alka Seltzers and thinking about Owen, until I felt well enough to get up and pop over to my flat – which, incidentally, had started to smell funny – to collect my post, water the cat, look longingly at my own bed etc., when I get this. Even before I opened it, my mouth was as dry as the Gobi; every letter with a London postmark has this effect on me because – fool that I am – I hope that it might be Anton telling me it's all been a terrible mistake, Lily is a balding wolf in hippy-chic clothing and that he wants me back. This envelope had a worse than usual effect because it was postmarked London W1 and I happened to know (I had begged Cody to tell me) that Anton's office was around there.

So I open it up and it's on nice, creamy paper but there aren't enough words on it for it to be a proper letter of prostration from Anton. All the same my eyes rush to the bottom and right enough it's not from Anton, it's from someone called Jojo Harvey and who on earth is she? I swallow several times to re-irrigate my mouth and read the letter but instead of being enlightened I'm even more confused. It must be a mistake, I decide. But . . . she'd mentioned Susan. By surname.

I decided to ring Susan. It was mid-morning in Seattle and I woke her up, but she insisted she didn't mind and we were so excited at hearing each other's voices that it took some time to get to the purpose of the call.

'Susan, listen, I'm after getting this letter. I opened it because it was addressed to me, but it's something to do with you.'

'Go on.' She sounded intrigued. 'Who's it from?'

'Someone called Jojo Harvey, from a literary agency in London.'

There followed the longest silence. So long I was the first to speak. 'Susan? Are you still there?'

'Ah . . . yeah.'

'I thought we'd been cut off. Speak to me.'

'Yeah, look. She should have written to me, not you.'

'I'll just send it on to you then.' I was surprised at how defensive she sounded.

After another silence, she spoke quickly, 'Gemma, I've got something to tell you and you're not going to like it, at least not straight away and I'm sorry you had to find out like this.'

They're the worst words in the world – the 'I've got something to tell you' configuration. It's never anything good like, 'You've lost a stone but you don't seem to have noticed and *some*one had to be the one to tell you.' Or, 'An eccentric millionaire has bequeathed you a life-altering sum of money and he just wanted to slip it into your bank account without letting you know, but, as a friend, I felt it was my duty to tell you.' It's always bad news.

My stomach had plunged to the centre of the earth. 'What? Susan, what?'

'You know since I came to Seattle, you've been sending me emails?'

'Yes.'

'And you know that your dad left your mam and you've been making up little stories about them?'

'Yes.'

'Well, look, I just thought they were really funny and I've always thought you'd be a great writer and I know you'd never do anything about it yourself and I didn't really think anything would come of it but,' and suddenly she stopped sounding hunted and said clear as a bell, 'I knew you'd never do it yourself.'

'What wouldn't I do?' But I knew. 'You sent my little stories to this agent woman?'

But this was good, wasn't it? Why did she sound so hunted? Then she said, 'Not just the stories.'

'What else?'

'The emails you've been sending me.'

My memory skittered back over everything I'd sent Susan – Dad leaving Mam, Lily's book coming out, my carry-on with Owen – and the breath left my body. 'Not . . . *all* the emails?'

'Not all, no not all,' she was racing through the words. 'I left out some.'

'*Some?*' Some was nothing like enough.

'I left out all the really bad bits, like how much you hate Lily, and . . .'

'And . . . ?' I was desperate.

'And how much you hated Lily's book.'

'And . . . ?'

'How you feel about Lily.'

'But you already said that. Did you send everything else?'

'Yes.' It was so low it sounded like a crackle of static.

'Oh Susan.'

'I'm sorry, Gemma, honest to God, I thought it was the right thing . . .'

I began to cry. I should have been furious, but I hadn't the strength.

I drove back to Mam's. 'Come on,' she said, handing me a glass of Bailey's. 'We're missing the *Midsomer Murders*.'

'No, I can't.'

I interfaced with my communicator brick, frantic to read back over what I'd sent to Susan and was currently on some stranger's desk in London.

I speed-read through the Sent Items. Ohmigod, ohmigod, ohmigod, it was worse than I remembered. All that private pain about Mam and Dad. Worse still was the mean-spirited stuff that it was OK for my friends to know about, but the thought of anyone else knowing about made me itchy with shame.

5

On Saturday night and all day Sunday, my mobile rang incessantly, as a mortified Susan tried to apologize. I didn't pick up any of her calls; I needed a recovery period.

'I was only trying to help,' she said, several times a message. 'You're a great writer but I knew you'd never do anything about it yourself.'

That's the trouble with Susan. Just because she went to Seattle and followed her bloody dream, she wants everyone else to do it too. In the good old days (last year) she used to sigh, 'We're going nowhere, Gemma,' and I always said, 'I know. Nice, isn't it?' It was a big enough shock when she did something about her own life but to try to kick-start mine in this way was well out of order.

Going to work on Monday I was afraid I might gawk. Every time I thought of the agent woman reading about, say, my first night with Owen or Mam's fake heart attack, I got a hot flush.

And I realized I should have worked over the weekend, instead of treating myself to a hangover – there were several messages on my voicemail including one from Lesley Lattimore saying:

1) She didn't like any of the three dress designers I'd put her in touch with.
2) What free cosmetics had I bagged so far?
3) Where was her turreted castle?

Of course, I'd bagged no cosmetics – it was kind of hard to persuade companies to shell out shedloads of free stuff for an

F-list party that no social pages would touch – and I still hadn't found a turreted castle which was suitable for a party.

Then there were messages from the three dress designers. One called Lesley 'a horrible person'. The second said that Lesley wanted her to make the dress for free in return for publicity. The third called Lesley 'white trash'. *Jayzus.*

I hit the phones in a big, panicky way, putting calls in all over the place – to designers, journalists, cosmetic houses, turreted castles. In the razor-thin sliver of time between me hanging up on one call and beginning another, Cody rang. 'Cody "Kofi Annan" Cooper calling to intercede. Susan says you won't talk to her.'

'No, I won't. This is the worst thing anyone has ever done to me.'

'It is not, you big drama queen. Jesus Christ, you should be gay. Gemma, I'll say one thing to you and I want you to listen carefully: a literary agent is interested in representing you and you *haven't even written a book*. Have you any idea how lucky you are? Thousands of people write books, give up all their free time, break their hearts trying and they still can't get an agent. But one has just landed in your lap.'

I shrugged.

'Did you just shrug?'

'Sometimes you scare me.'

'Girl, it's mutual.'

'What are you talking about?'

'You. The way you never do anything any more.'

'Oi, who's the drama queen now? You *know* how hard I work. My job is so demanding and even if I say so myself, I'm extremely good at it.'

'That's right, you're great at pulling in money for the evil twins so they can buy their farmhouse in Normandy or whatever it is this week. What do you get out of it?'

'I'm on good money and, Cody, don't call them the evil twins, sometimes they listen in on my calls.'

'Set up on your own.'

Everyone in the business, it's their *dream* to set up on their own. But you need money and potential clients and F&F have hung me up with a contract which means I couldn't take any existing clients with me. Besides I'd be afraid that F&F would take a contract out on me.

'Maybe some day . . .'

'In the meantime ring this agent woman. If you've any sense.'

'And what if I get published and the whole world reads about my father deserting my mother?'

'Change the details.'

'*They'll* still know it's them.'

'Look, I don't have the answers. You figure it out.'

I remained silent and Cody said, 'Just one more thing. This agent is also Lily's agent.'

'Lily *Wright*?'

'How many other Lilys do we know?'

'Why did Susan pick her?'

'Because she hadn't a clue how to find an agent. This woman was the only one she knew of, so she asked her dad to ask Lily's mammy who Lily's agent was.'

'God Almighty . . .'

'So ring her.'

'If she wants me badly enough, she'll ring me.'

'She won't. She's very busy and in demand.'

'Whatever.' I wasn't going to ring Jojo Harvey. If this was meant to be it would happen of its own accord.

6

OK, I rang her. I gave it until the following Monday – a full-on, Lesley-Lattimore-filled week – waiting for what was meant to be, to happen and when it didn't, I picked up the phone and rang this Jojo Harvey.

It was Monday morning, I'd spent the weekend criss-crossing Ireland, looking at bloody turreted bloody castles, and I needed *something*.

It took a few moments for Jojo to remember who I was but once she did she said, 'Come in and see me.'

'I live in Ireland, it's not that easy.'

She didn't say she would come to Dublin or that she'd pay my airfare to London. She didn't want me that badly – I suspected she'd only taken my call because she thought I was someone else – and that triggered unexpected anxiety.

However, I refused to make a decision to actually go. Again I took the attitude that if it was meant to be, it would happen of its own accord. But to help fate along I tried to get Francis & Frances to send me, by saying loudly outside their office door, 'God, I hate London, I'm so glad I never have to go there for work. And when you think about it, the opportunities are endless, so many British stars want to get married in Ireland, but the thought of being sent to London to pitch to management agencies just makes my heart sink.'

However – and why was I even surprised? – they double-bluffed me and on Wednesday morning came the news that they were sending Andrea. Evil fucks. Clearly they are honoured guests to the dark side, they probably have frequent flyer cards. And I'd been given my message: this wasn't meant to be.

Fuhgedaboudit.

So I rang Cody who asked, 'How's life in the enclosed order?'

'Not bad. We have nice porridge.'

He clicked and I knew he was flicking his eyes skywards.

'Do you need to go to London for anything in the near future?' I asked.

'No, but I hear you do.'

I gave in. 'I suppose. Will you come with me?'

'If it means you'll go and see this agent woman, then yes. When?'

'Some day next week? Wednesday?'

'Fine, I'll have a migraine that day. Now ring Susan.'

TO: Susan_inseattle@yahoo.com
FROM: Gemma_343@hotmail.com
SUBJECT: Thank you and sorry

I'm going to see Jojo Harvey on Wednesday and thank you, thank you, thank you for making it happen. You're right, I'd never have done it if it had been left to me. I'm so sorry for not taking your calls, I wasn't trying to be mean, I was just a bit freaked. Cody's coming with me, he's going to have a migraine and I'm going to have period pains. I'll ring you when it's not the middle of the night in Seattle.

Lots and lots and lots and lots of love from your grateful pal, Gemma

After the night I snuck out on him, Owen never called, which I found really, really funny. Some people might say I'd 'given him what he wanted' so why would he bother with me again. And I'd have to agree that the first time I sleep with a man is a tricky time – I'm braced for the balance of power to change, for him to become remote and distant, and for me to feel as though I've relinquished something. But with Owen – and I don't know why – I didn't give a flying fuck so, cheery as anything, I called.

'Owen, it's Gemma. Let's go out on Friday night.' Like we'd parted on the fondest terms.

'You've a bit of a nerve.'

'I don't usually,' I admitted. 'It's just the effect you have on me. So how about it?'

'Will you be sneaking off home in the middle of the night?'

'Yes, but I have a reason. Meet me and I'll tell you it.'

Of course he couldn't resist that and eight o'clock on Friday night saw me once again stumbling down the mirrored steps of Crash.

'*Déjà vu*,' I beamed. 'I like your shirt.' A different one but just as cool.

He wasn't smiling but I kept grinning at him until he gave in and cracked his expression-free face. Then, like he was surprised by what he was doing, he stood up, caught me and kissed me. A very nice kiss, which went on longer than either of us had planned and stopped only when someone called, 'Get a room!'

'So what's your excuse for running out on me in the middle of the night?'

'It's a good one. Buy me a drink and I'll tell you.'

I gave it to him chapter and verse, especially how Mam couldn't be left on her own all night or she might fake a heart attack. 'In fairness to her, she's trying very hard to be not so clingy, but we're not out of the woods yet. But now you see that me doing a runner was nothing personal, right?'

'I didn't want you to go.' He managed to sound both sulky and sexy.

And under the circumstances I thought it would be nice to reply, 'And I didn't want to go.'

It was a flirty, touchy-feely night, lots of hand-stroking and meaningful eye-locks and we both got a little bit scuttered. We stayed in Crash until kicking-out time, then on the street we stood very close and he said, 'What now? Somewhere else?'

'Let's go back to your place,' I said, fingering a button on his shirt-front in saucy temptress fashion.

'Are you going to sneak out again in the middle of the night?'

'Yes.'

'Then you can't come back.'

Startled, I looked into his face and saw that he was serious! 'But Owen, that's really stupid.' I'd been looking forward to a ride; I'd got a taste for it now.

'If you can't be bothered to stay for the entire night I don't want you to come at all.'

'But I've told you what's going on! I have to go home to my mother.'

'You're thirty-two,' he cried. 'I could get this sort of grief from a sixteen-year-old.'

'So *get* yourself a sixteen-year-old.'

'OK.'

He turned and walked away from me, very angry and a bit jarred. I stuck my arm up and hailed a taxi.

Shaking with rage, I got in. 'Kilmacud.'

Just before the taxi took off, the door was wrenched open and Owen bundled himself in on top of me. 'I'm coming with you.'

'No, you're not.'

'Yes, I am.'

'My mother will be thrilled to see you. Not.'

'Stop the car!' Though we were barely moving, we screeched to a kerb-side halt but Owen didn't get out. 'Do we have to go to your mother's house? Can't we go to your apartment?'

'I'd still have to sneak home in the middle of the night.'

'OK, I'll settle for that. Her apartment, Clonskeagh,' he told the driver.

'Excuse me? Who said you could come?'

He tried to kiss me and I elbowed him off. But he tried again and he was a very nice kisser so I let him.

Then he slid his palm up my top and caught a nipple between two fingers; an electric shock zipped to my lula and suddenly I was dying for it.

*

339

The following day I was pale and subdued. I'd had a drunken row in the street. I'd committed a sex act in a taxi – at least I'd tried but the driver had asked me not to. And I'd slept with a man who called his nether regions 'Uncle Dick and the twins'. What he'd actually said was, 'Uncle Dick and the twins reporting for duty, sir.'

But you know what, the sex was glorious. Fast and fabulous and sweaty and sexy – and plenty of it.

Between one of the bouts he'd mumbled into my hair, 'Sorry for saying the thing about the sixteen-year-old.'

I'd been angry at the time but to hold a grudge you had to care and I didn't.

'You're a stupid fucker but I forgive you,' I said magnanimously.

'I saw Lorna today.'

Who? Oh, his ex-girlfriend.

'Were you upset?'

'No.'

No, just devastated. And I got what had happened in the street – he hadn't been arguing with me, he was arguing with someone who wasn't there. So what was my excuse?

Sympathetically I stroked his hand until I felt his mickey unfurl and straighten up again, then I turned to him.

'Say it,' I asked.

'Permission to board, skipper.'

He rang me on Sunday afternoon.

'I have tickets for a gig on Tuesday night. Would you like to come?'

'Would I have to stand up?'

'Yes.'

'Then I'll pass. No offence, it's just not me. Bring someone else.'

'OK.' Pause. 'What are you doing now?'

I was working, typing lists for Lesley's bash. 'Nothing,' I said. Something was building in the pit of my stomach.

'Would you like to do something?'

I swallowed. 'Like what?'

'What would you like?'

I knew what I'd like and I'd like it very much.

'An hour,' I said. 'That's all I can spare. Meet me at my flat in twenty minutes. Mam!' I yelled, scooping stuff into my bag. 'I have to go out. Work. I'll be a couple of hours at the most.'

7

On Wednesday morning, by exchanging low meaningful words with desk-boys sporting labour-intensive hair, a suited and booted Cody managed to get us upgraded *and* into a lounge.

'How do you know all those boys?' I asked.

Disdainfully Cody was discarding *Today's Golfer* and *Finance Now*. 'Jesus, would it kill them to have a copy of *Heat*? Oh, just from around.'

As we boarded the plane a male steward noticed Cody and flamed an immediate scarlet. 'Cody?'

'That's my name. At least it is today. But who knows which one of my multiple personalities will be in charge tomorrow?' Cody turned to me. 'Strap yourself in, my dear. Well, would you look at that, I can't seem to buckle my own belt.'

'It's piss easy, you thick, it jus –'

'Excuse me, sir,' Cody shoved away my helping hand and summoned Scarlet Boy. 'Could you help me with this?' He gestured towards his crotch.

'What appears to be the problem?' Poor Scarlet Boy's mortification was manifesting itself in extreme heat.

'I need to be strapped in, if you wouldn't mind . . . whoops, butter fingers . . . that's it, nice and snug. Niiiiiccce and snnnugg.'

'Just from around,' I murmured. 'You get around a lot.'

'Better than living in purdah and taking a vow of misery.'

'I'm not in purdah any more.' Suddenly I was finding this funny. 'And you're a smelly pig.'

'What do you mean you're not in purdah any more?' He looked at me suspiciously, then his eyes went 'ping!' 'It's the bloke in the chemist.'

'No.' I strung it out a little, just to make him suffer. 'It's Owen.'

'Owen the *cutie*?'

On the night of Cody's birthday, Owen had approached him and said, 'Excuse me, is your lady friend spoken for?' As a result Cody thought Owen was delightful.

'Owen the cutie,' I confirmed.

'Have you slept with him?'

I was astonished. 'Of course.'

'You never told me.'

'I haven't had the chance. I haven't exactly seen you, have I?'

'God Almighty. Tell us more.'

'He makes me feel young.' Quickly I forestalled Cody before he started to coo, 'Not always in a good way. Since I've been seeing him I've . . . one –' I counted out on my fingers – 'look aren't my nails a lovely colour? Anyway one, I've had a drunken row with him in the street. Two, felt his mickey in a taxi. Three, snuck out on my mammy on Sunday afternoon just to have sex with him.'

'Just to have sex?' Cody echoed.

'I did it again last night,' I said. 'On the way home from work.'

Owen had called me at the office at about six-thirty and asked, 'What are you doing tonight?'

'I'm going home and you're going to a gig.'

'Not for an hour and a half. Come over.'

Immediately I closed all my files and left. As soon as I rang Owen's bell, the front door opened, he pulled me in and within seconds we were going at it, me pressed against the door, my clothes half off, my legs around his waist.

'What colour are his eyes?' Cody asked, with interest.

'I don't know – *eye* colour. It's not like that. I'm just having a good time and, anyway, Owen's still hung up on his ex-girlfriend.'

'But this is the first person you've slept with since Anton. How does he measure up?'

'That's not fair,' I said. 'I love Anton, it would be like comparing fast food with dinner at the Ivy.' I thought about it some more. 'Mind you . . . I must admit, there are times when a Big Mac is exactly what you want –'

The pilot interrupted. 'We'll be landing at Heathrow in forty-five minutes.'

Owen was instantly forgotten as it hit me what I was heading into in London; the *potential* of it. My mouth went dry as I considered the best possible outcome: if I got published and was successful and I became a human glitter ball . . . But how likely was that?

Instantly sombre I said to Cody, 'Probably nothing will come of all this agent stuff.'

'That's the attitude.'

'No, I'm serious. Probably nothing *will* come of all this.'

'I'm agreeing with you.'

'Oh sorry, I forgot it was you.'

A moment or two of silence.

'Why shouldn't anything happen?' I asked. 'You're so bloody defeatist.'

He sighed and rattled his free *Irish Times*. 'Kettles, pots, etc.'

From the moment we landed in Heathrow ninety minutes later – the pilot was a lying bastard – every blonde woman was Lily, every man over five foot four was Anton.

'It's a city of eight million people,' Cody hissed, when I dug my nails into his arm one time too many. 'We'll never, ever meet them.'

'Sorry,' I whispered. Since Anton and Lily had got together I'd been to London only twice – this was the third time – and being on their territory always reduced me to jelly. While I dreaded bumping into them, I also had a gruesome, voyeuristic desire to see them.

I was shaking when we got out of the tube at Leicester Square and Cody guided us towards Soho – Anton worked somewhere around here but Cody wouldn't tell me which street. 'No stalking!' he chided. 'Remember why you're here.'

You'd want to have seen Jojo Harvey. She was about ten foot tall, pouty and dark-lashed and had auburn wavy hair to her shoulders. If she was in a film, a sax would play mournful, sexy notes whenever she appeared. She was *gorgeous*. But not skinny, you know? There was plenty of her.

Cody said he'd wait in reception so she took me down a corridor and into her office. There were lots of books on her shelves and when I saw *Mimi's poxing Remedies*, I was punched with a bundle of longing and hatred and about sixty other emotions. *I want that for me.*

Jojo waved an untidy sheaf of paper and said, 'Your pages. We laughed so hard, I swear to God.'

'Um, good.'

'All that stuff about going to the chemist. And the dad growing sideburns. It's great!'

'Thanks.'

'So any ideas on format? Fact or fiction?'

'Definitely not fact.' I was horrified.

'Fiction then.'

'But I can't,' I said. 'It's all about my mam and dad.'

'Even that stuff about Helmut? Or the girl – Colette? – dancing around the trouser press in her underpants? Hey, I loved that.'

'Well, no, *that* was made up. But the basic story, the one of my father leaving my mother, that's true.'

'You know, call me unsympathetic –' she swung her feet up on the desk – nice boots, I noticed – 'but it's the oldest story in the book – man leaving wife for younger model.' With a big smile she said, 'Who's going to sue you for stealing their plot-line?'

Easy for her to say.

'You could change the details a bit.'

'How?'

'The father could work in a different industry – although I love all that stuff about the chocolate – the mom could be different.'

'How?'

'Lots of ways. Look at all the moms you know and see how different they all are.'

'Everyone would still know it was my parents.'

'They say everyone's first novel is autobiographical.'

I wanted her to keep saying things, to convince me, to talk me into it, I wanted to keep coming up with objections and for her to keep batting them away. It was nice to be wanted and I was happy to stay there for hours.

But, next thing she was swinging her long legs off her desk, getting to her feet and sticking out her hand. 'Gemma, I'm not going to talk you into something you don't want to do.'

'Oh! Right . . .'

'Sorry we've both had our time wasted.'

That stung. But I suppose she was important and busy. Nevertheless I'd enjoyed being courted and persuaded and I didn't like her so much now.

Then as she walked me back out to Cody, I see this *ride* coming down the corridor towards us, lovely long limbs moving in a lovely suit. Hair as black and shiny as a raven's wing and eyes as blue as ambulance sirens. (A simile I wasn't entirely sure about.)

He nodded a hello at me and said, 'Jojo, will you be long?'

'No, I'll be right back.'

'That's Jim Sweetman,' she said. 'Head of our media section.'

On the tube back out to Heathrow, Cody was disgusted with me and I was super-subdued. An agent, a *literary* agent, had been interested in something I'd written – an event that was rarer, by all accounts, than an eclipse of the sun. Now it was all over. I sighed. And I bet Jojo was having a mad affair with that ridey Jim Sweetman.

It was at me like an itch. I'd wasted a day of precious sick leave – and there was worse to come. At Heathrow I went to the newsagent's to buy magazines to take my mind off myself on the journey home and from six feet away I saw it. From the way my hair follicles prickled, I knew that something very bad had happened. Even before my brain had translated the words in the newspaper into something meaningful, dread had got there first. It was a photo of Lily – on the front page of the *Evening Standard*. Featuring – this is the worst bit – in big, black type, the description, **The Unknown Londoner Who's Been Taking the Literary World by Storm**.

The full story was on page nine. I snatched it up and crackled through the pages until I got to a quarter-page picture of Lily in her sumptuous home (in fairness, you could only see a corner of her couch) with her sumptuous man, talking about her sumptuous best-selling (crappy) book. It pains me to say it, but she looked great, all fragile and ethereal and unbald. Mucho, mucho air-brushing, I suspect.

Anton also looked amazing, far more beautiful than her actually, especially as his hair was his own and not a Burt Reynolds-style weave. I was shocked by the sameness – he looked just like my Anton – and affronted by the differences; his hair had got longer and his shirt was all sharp creases and smooth cotton – a far cry from when his clothes used to look like they'd been through a mangle. (This hadn't added to his charm, I'm not that bad.)

I gazed at the photo and let his laughing eyes look directly into mine. *He's smiling at me.* Stop! You looper! Next I'd be thinking he was communicating with me in code.

Jostled and bumped by other travellers, Cody at my shoulder, I skittered over the story of Lily Wright's rise to bestseller-dominance and I was afraid that I was going to throw up in public.

I rounded on Cody. 'I thought you said she wasn't setting the world on fire.'

'She wasn't.' He was raging that he'd missed a trick. 'Don't take it out on me. It's yourself you should be angry with.' Cody never says sorry; he just shifts the blame. 'Look at the chance you threw away today.'

He nodded at the smiling image in the paper. 'See that? It could have been you.'

I didn't buy the paper – I couldn't – but I thought about Anton all the way home. This was the first time I'd even seen him in over two years but his photo affected me as if we'd split up only last week. And I'd come so close to him today. I might have passed by his very office, I could have been within feet of him. It must mean something.

8

We slipped quietly into the fifth month of Dad's absence. I managed to keep it from myself for a couple of days because I was so depressed about other things, mostly my stillborn writing career.

Jojo was right – a husband leaving a wife for a younger woman really was the oldest story in the book. Even though my novel wasn't going to happen, it all began to unfold in my head, especially since I'd started waking again at five in the morning.

In the book I could have a different job – in fact, I didn't have to have a job at all: I could be a housewife (oh, the happiness!) with maybe a couple of children of my own.

I could give myself two sisters, or maybe a brother and a sister; I played around with various scenarios and in the end I settled for an older sister called Monica. A nice, capable person, who'd lent me her clothes during our teenage years but who now lived a life of constant on-call in a big, four-square house with four square children and she was too far away (Belfast? Birmingham? still hadn't decided) for her to be any kind of practical help.

I also gave myself a baby brother, a charmer called Ben, who had a posse of girls after him. Every time the phone rang he'd rattle instructions to Mam, 'If that's Mia tell her I'm out, if it's Cara again, tell her I'm sorry but she'll get over me – eventually.' Pause for laughter. 'And if it's Jackie I'm on my way. I left ten minutes ago.'

I'd quickly gone off him. The fictional mam wasn't a fan either, which I knew was swimming against the tide; usually mothers are besotted with their selfish, 'charming' sons, pretending to tut-tut as they treat their girlfriends like shite, but secretly delighted, both of them convinced that no woman was good enough for him.

Ben didn't really impact on my plot-line – far too irresponsible and selfish to be of any help to 'our' freshly deserted mammy. I was still left carrying the can and was, to all intents and purposes, an only child.

'My' name is Izzy and I have chin-length corkscrew curls in great condition. Much as I'd have loved it, I couldn't imagine being a housewife so I thought long and hard about Izzy's job. My first choice was a personal shopper but in the interests of realism and popularity – everyone would hate her for having such a jammy job – I decided against it. Instead – and this will probably come as no surprise – she works in PR, and yes, she organizes events.

Izzy also shared a similar romantic history to mine:

1) myriad unrequited teenage crushes
2) a passionate drunken ridiculous thing between the ages of nineteen to twenty-one, which I thought I'd never get over
3) a relationship from twenty-five to twenty-eight with a man everyone thought I should marry – but I just didn't feel 'ready' (in fact every time poor Bryan popped the question I felt like I was choking).

But I didn't give Izzy an Anton, a love of her life who was cruelly snatched from under her nose by her best friend. What if . . . I mean . . . what if Anton read it?

Instead Izzy was having a love/hate flirtation thing with one of her clients. He was called Emmet, a grand sexy name, and he wasn't a film director/farmer because the book was set in Dublin. He ran his own business (still undecided as to exact nature thereof) and Izzy was organizing a sales conference for him. He was a bit narky – but only because he fancied her –

and when she booked all the delegates into the wrong hotel because she was upset about her ice-cream salesman dad leaving her mother, Emmet didn't sack her as would *so* happen in real life. For a while he had a scar on his right cheek, then I got a grip and fixed him. Then for another while, Izzy was beautiful but didn't realize it, but she started to get on my nerves, so I changed her back to being ordinary.

Other modifications: the dad wasn't having an affair with his secretary, that was too much of a cliché. Instead it was with his golf-partner's eldest daughter. And the mammy wasn't quite as incapable as my mother – I suspected that people simply wouldn't believe it.

Some things stayed the same: my car, for instance. And I kept the nice man in the chemist but changed his name to Will.

It was a funny exercise – like being a different version of me, or perhaps knowing what it was like to be someone else. Either way, when I woke into the acid-bright early morning, paralysed with screaming despair, it took my mind off things.

9

TO: Susan_inseattle@yahoo.com
FROM: Gemma 343@hotmail.com
SUBJECT: I've started to write it.

I've been thinking about it so much that I felt I'd burst if I didn't.
I write it in the early mornings and in the evenings. Mam goes to
bed at nine-thirty, sleeping the sleep of the heavily tranquillized
and I'm able to clatter away on the PC. But even while I'm
watching *Buffy* I'm thinking about it and itching for Mam to go
so I can get started.

Is this what it means to be a tormented artist? Answers on a
postcard, please.

Love,
Gemma

Back in the real world, I'd finally found a castle with turrets. It
was in Offaly – a tough drive if you had to go there and back
in a day. I'd also run to ground a dress designer so down on
her luck that she was prepared to take on Lesley and her
unreasonable requests.

I'd hired twenty-eight Louis XIV *chaises* and had arranged
for them to be re-upholstered in silver lamé. I'd rung a model-
ling agency and said, 'I'm looking for a handsome prince,' and
the man on the other end of the phone said, 'Aren't we all,
love?' I was carrying a copy of *Sleeping Beauty* – my source
document – with me at all times.

But still no luck with the goody bags and God knows I'd
tried.

'Remind me again, what am I paying you for?' Lesley asked. (And that was another thing, no money had changed hands yet, despite me asking so many times that I was now too embarrassed to bring it up again.) 'There are plenty of other party planners in Dublin. Maybe I should go to one of them?'

God, I *hated* her. 'I'm working on it.' And I was. I was in the final moments of securing coverage from a glossy magazine and if the cosmetics people were guaranteed publicity, they were a lot more likely to sponsor us.

Even though I say it myself, I'm GREAT at my job. To take this piece-of-shit party and spin it into something approaching C-list takes some doing!

Lesley backed down and extended an olive branch by asking me to meditate with her. I felt I couldn't say no, but maybe I should have, because I fell asleep.

TO: Susan_inseattle@yahoo.com
FROM: Gemma 343@hotmail.com
SUBJECT: I rang Jojo

and told her that I'm going to write the book and she said, 'Well, congratulations, you've got yourself an agent!' Then she asked if it was all OK with Mam and I just said, 'Mmmm.'

I'll jump off that bridge when I come to it.

Love
Gemma

I didn't tell Susan what happened next.

I cleared my throat because I had something important to say. I hovered on the moment for an eternity, then, 'Jojo, I know one of your clients.'

'Yeah?' Not interested.

'Lily. Lily Wright.'

'Oh, Lily's doing great! Really, like, super-great!'

'Yes, well, tell her Gemma Hogan says "hello".'

'Will do. Hey, you know what? I'm jumping guns here but if we sell your book, and I'm so sure we will, at publication time we could do, like, an "Our Friendship" thing for a Sunday supplement. Get you some publicity.'

Time slowed down and my voice echoed in my head. 'You could suggest it to her. But she mightn't want to do it.'

'Sure she will! Lily's a sweetie.'

See, I wasn't sure Susan would approve. She was my friend but she was regarding all this agent stuff as very positive and I have to fess up to coming at it in a more mean-spirited way. I wanted to unsettle Lily with my message: I'm in the same business as you now and I'm on your tail.

Well, come on, she'd stolen the love of my life, she was a millionaire and she was in loads of newspapers. What would you do?

Friday nights with Owen had become a regular thing *and* we usually managed a quick mid-week ride. Owen was great fun and there was no pesky churning-stomach, wobbly-kneed, tongue-tied stuff you get when you're mad about someone. He didn't have two heads, he could hold a conversation, I didn't think about him when I wasn't with him, but I was always glad to hear from him. And he felt the same way about me.

Funnily enough we nearly always had some sort of a row – either he was mean to me or I was mean to him – I'm not saying it was healthy but it was a regular event.

'Guess what?' I said, the next time we met.

'Anton wants you back?'

'No. I'm writing a book.'

'Are you? Am I in it?'

'No.' I laughed.

'Why not?'

'Why should you be?'

'Because I'm your boyfriend.'

I laughed again. 'Are you?'

A pause and he was still smiling but maybe not as much. 'What do you call this? Six weeks of drinks, phone calls, regular contact with Uncle Dick and the twins?'

'You're not my boyfriend, you're my . . . you're my *hobby*.'

'Oh.' The smiley face had disappeared entirely.

'Don't look like that,' I said hastily. 'I'm not your girlfriend, either.'

'News to me.'

'No, no!' I insisted. 'I'm your older-woman experience. Your, er, *lovair*, if you prefer. A rites of passage thing. It's a*l*right,' I reassured him. 'I don't *mind*.'

'So all I am to you is a piece of ass.'

'No,' I protested. 'You're not just a piece of ass – what a great saying – no, I also love Uncle Dick and the twins.'

He got up and left. I didn't blame him but I didn't get up and follow him either. I knew the drill by now – he was always stomping off in a strop and stomping back five minutes later.

I sipped my wine and thought about nice things until – yep – here he was, re-emerging through the door and over to the table.

'You big eejit,' I said. 'Sit down and finish your drink. Crisp?'

'Thanks,' he said gruffly.

'What's up with you?' I asked kindly.

'You don't take me seriously.'

I stared at him in confusion. 'Of course I don't. But you don't take me seriously either.'

'I might be starting to.'

'Don't,' I said. 'That would be awful.'

'Why?'

'One,' I declared, listing on my fingers, 'I think all men are bastards. Two, whenever I start listing things out on my fingers I get distracted by my nail colour, and three, now I've lost my train of thought – see! And three, I think all men are bastards. We haven't a hope. Anyway, you're too young for me. It doesn't work. My father was a younger man and look at what happened.'

'They were married for thirty-five years,' he cried.

'Listen to me,' I said. 'I'm in no state for a relationship. And neither are you. Look at the way we always have a fight, that's because we're both fuck-ups. Only temporarily, but fuck-ups all the same. *And* you're on the rebound.'

'Do you want me to find someone my own age?'

'Not at all. Well, yes, obviously. But not *yet*.'

TO: Susan_inseattle@yahoo.com
FROM: Gemma 343@hotmail.com
SUBJECT: The word is out

Frances comes up and goes, 'I hear you're writing a book.'

Christ, who'd squealed?

'We'll sue, you know,' she sez. 'We'll sue for every penny you've got.'

But they're not called Frances and Francis, of course. Any real people in the book are completely disguised and my fictional pair of bosses are called Gabrielle and Gabriel and known affectionately as Bad Cop and Worse Cop.

I'll keep you posted . . .

Love
Gemma

On Sunday I was doing the weekly shop and dithering before the wall of boxes in the breakfast cereal aisle. My plan had been to wean Mam off her beloved porridge and onto solids like Fruit'n'Fibre but instead I'd fallen in love with porridge: lovely comfort food that was microwaveable and came in *flavours*. I'd just caved in and picked up a carton of banana-flavoured porridge when I noticed a man down by the CocoPops, looking directly at me and smiling warmly.

But he wasn't a comb-over lech, he was In The Zone – you know, the right age and nice-looking. The novelty of it nearly made me laugh out loud; I was being *picked up*. In an Irish supermarket! Howsabout that, San Francisco, I thought proudly. We too can find love amongst the groceries.

But your man looked familiar. Ish . . .

'Gemma?' Christ, he knew me! And I couldn't place him.

'*Gem*ma?' Now he was frowning while still smiling, if such a thing is possible, and I began to panic. That's the trouble with Dublin, it's so small that any attempts at velvet-dark nights of anonymous passion are shot to hell when you come face-to-face with your nameless lover in the merciless strip-lighting of the breakfast cereal aisle. (Mind you, I've only had a couple of one-night-stands and if ever I run into them they completely ignore me, which suits me just fine.)

OhthanksbetoChristitwasonlyJohnnythepharmacist!

'Oh Johnny, I'm really sorry.' Relief made me feel floaty and I abandoned my trolley and porridge to grasp his arm tightly. 'I thought I'd slept with you.'

'No, I'm sure I would've remembered.'

'I didn't recognize you without your white coat.'

'The story of my life.'

A woman picking up a five-kilo sack of Alpen paused in her labours and gave us a look.

Izzy was doing the weekly shop and dithering before the wall of boxes in the breakfast cereal aisle. Her plan had been to wean her mother off her beloved porridge and onto solids like Fruit'n'Fibre but instead Izzy had fallen in love with porridge: lovely comfort food that was microwaveable and came in *flavours*. She'd just caved in and picked up a carton of banana-flavoured porridge when she noticed a man down by the CocoPops, looking directly at her and smiling warmly.

But he wasn't a comb-over lech, he was In The Zone – you know, the right age and nice-looking. The novelty of it nearly made her laugh out loud; she was being *picked up*. In an Irish supermarket! Howsabout that, San Francisco, she thought proudly. We too can find love amongst the groceries.

But your man looked familiar. Ish...

'Izzy?' Christ, he knew her! And she couldn't place him.

'*Izzy*?' Now he was frowning while still smiling, if such a thing is possible, and Izzy began to panic. That's the trouble with Dublin, it's so small that any attempts at velvet-dark nights of anonymous passion are shot to hell when you come face-to-face with your nameless lover in the merciless strip-lighting of the breakfast cereal aisle. (Mind you, she'd only had a couple of one-night-stands and if ever she ran into them they completely ignored her, which suited her just fine.)

OhthanksbetoChristitwasonlyWillthepharmacist!

'Oh Will, I'm really sorry.' Relief made her feel floaty and she abandoned her trolley and porridge to grasp his arm tightly. 'I thought I'd slept with you.'

'No,' he said, holding her gaze. 'I'm sure I would've remembered.'

Suddenly she became aware of the heat of his arm beneath her hand and she stammered.

'I didn't recognize you without your white coat.'

'The story of my life.'

I stopped typing, pushed myself back from the keyboard and stared at it. Oh my God, I thought, I think Izzy fancies Will.

11

After the day in the car park I didn't ring Dad again. I'd been in the habit of calling him at least once a week but I was so hurt I didn't bother any more.

Nevertheless, his absence was ever present and frequent painful reminders jabbed me. Like the night I was flicking through channels and Tommy Cooper appeared on the screen. Not my bag of frogs naturally, but Dad was mad about him. 'Look!' I pointed and my first instinct was to summon Dad to come and watch it, then I closed my mouth, excitement draining away into foolishness, then into grief. Was he watching it with Colette? In their sitting room, whatever it was like.

It was painful even imagining it and immediately I switched my thoughts to my book. Thanks be to Christ for it. It really was the most pleasurable escape, I'd just disappear into it and hours could go by and even though Izzy and her mammy were going through stuff, I knew good times were a-coming. Helmut and the mother were still going strong and had just gone into business together importing La Prairie products into Ireland; they were even thinking of opening a La Prairie spa. Meanwhile things were gorgeous between Izzy and Emmet – he was mad about her, which he showed by being super-narky with her and really nice to everyone else, especially other women.

And while in real life I suspected that Dad and Colette got along very well, in my book I could still comfort myself that their life together was a hellish round of trouser-press dances and pork pie deprivation.

Then one day at work the phone rang and it was Dad. I nearly gawked into the mouthpiece.

'What's up?' I asked. 'Is she pregnant?'

'What? Who? Colette? No.'

'So why are you ringing?'

'I haven't heard from you in a while. Is there a law against ringing my own daughter?'

'Dad, this is the first time you've rung me since you left and that's nearly five months ago.'

'Come on now, Gemma, don't exaggerate.'

'I'm not. It's a fact. You haven't rung me once.'

'Ah, I must have.'

'You haven't.'

'Well, I'm ringing you now. How are you?'

'Fine.'

'And your mother?'

'Fine. I have to go now, I'm busy.'

'Have you?' He was surprised I wasn't all over him but he'd hurt me too much and I was in no humour to make things easy for him. Anyway I was busy, I was on my way to see Owen.

'What do you think will happen?'

Owen and I were lying in his bed in a post-ride rosy glow, fashioning imaginary, happy futures for each other.

'Your book will get published,' Owen said. 'You'll be famous and Lily Every-man-for-myself Wright's publishers will be dying to have you but you won't go to them unless they drop Lily.'

'And Anton will leave Lily and come back to me and revenge will be mine! No offence.' I punched his shoulder to soften the blow. 'Because you'll be married to Lorna and we'll all be friends. We'll hire a *gîte* in the Dordogne and go on our summer holidays together.'

'And I'll always be fond of you.'

'Exactly. And I'll always be fond of you. Maybe you could be godfather to my and Anton's first child. No, actually, scratch that. That's going too far.'

'How will I get Lorna back?'

'How do you think?'

'She'll see you and me together and realize what she's passed up.'

'Precisely! You learn fast, my little one.'

'Thank you, grasshopper.'

I looked at his alarm clock. 'It's ten past eleven, I've a few hours of my curfew left, let's go out for a drink.'

'I've been thinking,' he said.

I passed a hand over my forehead, 'Oh, don't.'

'Why don't I meet your mammy? Maybe I could take you both out for Sunday lunch or something brown-nosey like that. If I bonded with her maybe she'd be OK about you spending more time with me.'

'No way. Every time I said I was working late she'd know I was getting the ride off you.'

I waited for him to do something sulky, but he wasn't dressed, so he couldn't really stomp dramatically off. Anyway, he preferred to stomp off from someplace other than his own apartment. All in good time . . .

Later in Renards, with several speedy drinks under our belts, Owen said, 'Am I coming to this Gothic Barbie party?'

'No.'

'What? Ashamed of me?'

'Yes,' I said, although I wasn't. I just didn't know what got into me sometimes when I was with him. He couldn't come because it was a work do; I wasn't a guest at Lesley's bash, I was a slave.

I shoved my chair back so there was room for him to storm out. 'Off you go.'

Off he went and I sipped my wine and thought nice thoughts, when through the crowds I noticed a man down by the bar, looking directly at me and smiling warmly.

But he wasn't a comb-over lech, he was In The Zone – you know, the right age and nice-looking. The novelty of it nearly made me laugh out loud; I was being *picked up*. In an Irish nightclub!

And he was coming over. She shoots, she scores!

I knew him, though. I just couldn't place him. He was frustratingly familiar, who the hell . . . oh, of *course*, it was Johnny the Scrip. Out and proud. I got a funny warm feeling in my stomach, but that could just have been the wine.

'Who's minding the shop?' I called.

'Who's minding your mammy?'

We wheezed with empathetic mirth.

He nodded at my glass of wine and said, all high-spiritedly, 'Now, Gemma, I'd love to buy you a drink, but should you be drinking while you're on medication?'

'It's notmine, youthick. It's memammies.' I was a little more jarred than I'd realized.

'I know,' he winked. -

'I know you know,' I winked back.

''Scuse *me*.' Owen jostled his way back in, his little face like thunder, jogging Johnny's elbow and slopping his pint.

'I'll leave you to it.' Johnny passed me a your-young-friend-is-a-bit-pissed look and sloped away back to his friends. 'Nice to see you, Gemma.'

'Who the fuck is he?' Owen scowled.

'Just someone I fancy.' Now, what was that all about? There was no need to say that – even if it was true.

And it might be.

Owen gave me a baleful look. 'Gemma, I'm fond of you, but you're more trouble than you're worth.'

'*Me* trouble?' I did a mirthless, 'Hah! And you're the person who's had more comebacks than Frank Sinatra.

'Drunk,' I listed off on my fingers. 'Immature. Unreasonable.' I paused. 'And that's just me. I'm not normally like this.'

I stopped, my eyes suddenly filled with tears. 'I dunno, Owen. Am I going mad here? I don't like who I become when I'm with you.'

'Neither do I.'

'Fuck off.'

'Fuck off yourself,' he said, taking my face in his hands with odd tenderness. He kissed me full on the mouth – he was such a lovely kisser – then he kissed my tears away.

12

The week of Lesley Lattimore's party was seven days of hell. When God created the world, I swear he didn't work as hard as I did that week.

On the first day . . .
Up in the middle of the night to drive to Offaly. Tons to do, starting with a massive external lighting job to turn the whole castle into a twinkling jewel which could be seen from outer space.

Things were going OK until Lesley took a notion that she wanted the outside walls of the castle to be painted pink. So I asked the owner, Mr Evans-Black, and he told me to fuck off. Literally. And he wasn't that kind of man, he was very Anglo-Irish and proper. 'Fuck off, fuck off,' he shrieked. 'Just fuck off, you dirty, Irish philistines and leave my lovely castle alone.' He put his face into his palms and whimpered, 'Is it too late to back out of this?'

I went back and told Lesley it was no go. 'Silver, then,' she said. 'If he won't do pink. Go on, ask him.'

And you know what? I had to. Even though there was a chance it might kill him. I had to because it was my job.

When I returned with the news that silver was equally unacceptable, Lesley said airily, 'Fine, we'll find another castle.'

And it took a very long time and all of my diplomacy to convince her that actually, no, we wouldn't find another castle. Not only was it too late but word had spread . . .

On the second day . . .

Up in the middle of the night to drive to Offaly. Life would have been so much easier if I could have stayed down there but *pas de chance*. Mam wouldn't OK it under any circs.

There was so much to do – the dress, the flowers, the music – the whole deal was very similar to a wedding. Right down to the hysterics. We had the fitting, in situ, of Lesley's pointy-sleeved dress, her pointy shoes and pointy hat. But as she twirled in front of the mirror she placed a finger to her mouth and said thoughtfully, 'Something's missing.'

'You look FABULOUS,' I yelped, feeling the jaws of hell opening. 'Nothing's missing.'

'But there is,' she said, swinging back and forth and behaving all little-girlie. Horrific, it was, especially as she was still watching herself in the mirror and clearly enjoying it. 'I know! I want a hairpiece, a huge fall of ringlets from the crown of my head all the way down my back.'

The designer and I shared a moment of despair, then the designer cleared her throat and dared to mention that the pointy hat would have to be the size of a bucket to stay on top of the 'fall' of ringlets. Lesley took this on board by turning to me and screeching, 'You sort it out! What am I paying you for?'

In my head I said, 'Leave it to me. I'll just fiddle about with the laws of physics. Have a word with that nice Mr Newton, maybe.'

She laughed softly and said, 'You hate me, Gemma, don't you? You think I'm a spoilt little bitch, go on, admit it, I know you do.'

But I just opened my eyes wide and said, 'Lesley, cop on, don't be mad. This is my *job*. If I took this sort of thing personally, I should be in a different business.'

Of course what I really wanted to say was, 'Yes, I hate you, I hate you, I FUCKING HATE YOU! I'm sorry I ever took this fucking job, *no* money is worth it, and you might as well know, no matter how pointy your hat or your sleeves or your shoes are, they'll never be as pointy as your NOSE. You know what we call you? HATCHET-FACE, that's what. Sometimes when you rush towards me, I think someone has flung an axe at me. Oh yes! And even though I'm sometimes jealous that your dad is so good to you, I'd still rather be me than you.'

But I never said it. I'm great. If anyone had badly broken a limb and needed a steel plate to hold it together, they could just have used a piece from the back of my neck, but I'm great.

To add to my stress, I was too busy to do any writing and I was having withdrawal symptoms. It was like when I was giving up smoking. I thought about it all the time and I was narky as anything.

Is this what it means to be a tormented artist?

On the third day . . .
Up in the middle of the night to drive to Offaly. The hairdresser to do Lesley's 'fall' had arrived and I was overseeing the installation of huge drops of pink silk from ceiling to floor when I heard someone boom, 'So this is the woman who's spending all my money.'

I turned around. Christ, it was Wads! And Mrs Wads, who was a too-much-money-meets-too-much-Librium trainwreck.

Wads was fat and smiley – you could tell he prided himself on his bonhomie and his hail-fellow-well-met personal style. He was terrifying: I sensed his conviviality could dissolve in a moment and he'd be telling his 'boys' to take someone to a neglected cellar, tie him to a chair and 'teach him a lesson'.

'Mr Lattimore. A pleasure to meet you,' I lied.

'Tell me now, is there good money in this party organizing lark?' he asked. I'd lay bets that if he met the Queen, he'd ask if there was good money in being a monarch.

I tittered in terror. 'I'm not really the person to ask.'

'Who should I ask, then?'

Oh God.

'That pair? Francis and Frances?' he asked. 'The evil twins? They're the ones who keep all the profit?'

What could I say?

'Yes, Mr Lattimore.'

'Don't bother with that Mister stuff, no need to stand on ceremony with me.'

'If you're sure, er, Wads.'

Mrs Wads's beLibriumed eyes flared briefly into startled life, a piquant little pause followed and Wads eventually spoke. 'The name,' he said with ominous calm, 'is Larry.'

Oh Jayzus, there go my kneecaps.

On the fourth day . . .

Up in the middle of the night to drive to Offaly. The wind machine to move the fabric about had arrived, the furniture was on its way, a new bucket-sized pointy hat was under construction, Andrea and Moses had come down to help me and things were starting to seem less dangerously out-of-control when Lesley had a sudden fit. 'The bedrooms are too ordinary! We have to get them decorated.'

I held her still, looked into her eyes and said through clenched jaws, 'There. Is. No. Time.'

Steadily she eyeballed me back. 'Make. Time. I want those things that go over the bed, like mosquito nets but pretty. In silver.'

I thought of Wads and my kneecaps.

'Phone!' I shrieked at Andrea, dangerously close to losing it. 'Excuse me while I just buy up all the silver lamé in Ireland.'

I had to call every dressmaker I knew: big firms, small firms, even sole operators. It was like the evacuation of Dunkirk.

On the fifth day . . .

Up in the middle of the night to drive to Offaly. The glasses arrived and half of them hadn't survived the journey. Freak stations, trying to get more; they weren't just any glasses, they were pink Italian crystal. But it was the silver lamé mosquito nets that were breaking my heart. Only a few lone operators would take the job at such short notice so I sewed those fuckers myself. I worked through the night. I couldn't go home – I offered to send a car to Mam to bring her to the castle, but in the end, on my assurances that it would never happen again, she said she'd manage one night on her own.

On the sixth day . . .
The day of the party. I'd had no sleep, my fingers were covered in cuts, but I was keeping it together. I was Keeping. It. Together. Ear to the ground, finger on the pulse, that was me. Picking up on any imperfections including the two bullet-headed-thug types bursting out of too-tight suits. Bouncers. God, but they were rough-looking.

I collared Moses. 'That pair. Couldn't we have got bouncers who didn't look quite so psycho?'

'Them? They're Lesley's brothers,' and Moses dashed away to welcome the lute minstrels and give them their tights and curly toed slippers.

And for the rest of the day and night, it was just a succession of people running up to me and saying, 'Gemma, someone's collapsed in the hall.'

'Gemma, have you any condoms?'

'Gemma, Wads wants a cup of tea but Evans-Black has barricaded himself into his room and won't give up the kettle.'

'Gemma, they're booing the lute players. It's getting quite ugly.'

'Gemma, no one's got any drugs.'

'Gemma, Lesley's brothers are beating the shit out of each other.'

'Gemma, Mrs Wads is having sex with someone who isn't Mr Wads.'

'Gemma, the ladies' loos are blocked and Evans-Black won't give up his plunger.'

'Gemma, Evans-Black is after calling the filth.'

And on the seventh day . . .
She lied to her mammy and said she had to go back for the clean-up operation when in fact Andrea and Moses were doing it. Instead she went to Owen's and said, 'I want to have sex with you, but I've no energy. Would you mind if I just lay there and you did all the work?'

'So what's new?'

Which wasn't true; she was quite inventive and energetic in the scratcher with Owen. All the same, he did what she asked, then he made her cheese on toast and she lay on the sofa and watched *Billy Elliot*.

13

Izzy sipped her wine and thought nice thoughts, when through the crowds she noticed a man down by the bar, looking directly at her and smiling warmly.

But he wasn't a comb-over lech, he was In The Zone - you know, the right age and nice-looking. The novelty of it nearly made her laugh out loud; she was being *picked up*. In an Irish nightclub!

And he was coming over. She shoots, she scores!

She knew him, though. She just couldn't place him. He was frustratingly familiar, who the hell . . . oh, of *course*, it was Will the Scrip. Out and proud. She got a funny warm feeling in her stomach, but that could just have been the wine.

'Who's minding the shop?' she called.

'Who's minding your mammy?'

They wheezed with empathetic mirth.

He nodded at her glass of wine and said, all high-spiritedly, 'Now, Izzy, I'd love to buy you a drink, but should you be drinking while you're on medication?'

'It's notmine, youthick. It's memammies.' She was a little more jarred than she'd realized.

'I know,' he winked.

'I know you know,' she winked back.

Izzy *definitely* fancied him. Weird stuff was happening: the book had moved further and further away from where it had begun. The people had changed. The mother, father and 'me' had altered and become people in their own right. That's what they meant by the magic of writing and at times it could be extremely annoying. I had a lovely non-dotcom entrepreneur lined up for Izzy and she persisted with an attraction for the man in the chemist, which I hadn't factored in *at all*. The cheek of her. *Oh my Gott, vot hef I crrreatit?* (My impression of Doctor Frankenstein.)

I must admit that every time I wrote something nice about 'Will' I felt disloyal to Owen. How would he take it that the man in the chemist, and not he, had inspired my romantic hero? But would it matter? By the time the book was finished, Owen and I were bound to be toast. In fact every time we met I felt it could be the final time.

Meanwhile, the more I wrote about him in my book, the more the real Johnny the Scrip was coming into focus, like a Polaroid developing. There was a fine body hiding beneath his white coat. I'd noticed it on Friday night because he'd been wearing clothes. Like, *clothes. Nice* clothes – instead of the white coat which did him no favours.

Did he have a girl, I wondered. I knew he wasn't married because he'd made reference to it at some time, when we were both whinging about our miserable existences. But there was nothing to say that he didn't have a girlfriend – but would he ever get to see her? Probably not, unless she was one of those irritatingly loyal types who was 'standing by him' until his brother was better and this tough time had passed.

The week after Lesley's party I had to collect a prescription (anti-inflammatories, Mam had pulled a muscle in her hand, God only knows how – pressing the remote?) and for the first time ever I was shy about seeing Johnny. As I walked from the car, I felt him looking at me through the shopfront. Naturally I stumbled.

'Hi, Gemma.' He smiled and I smiled. There was just something very nice about him. Such a lovely manner. Mind you, he didn't look like he'd looked in Renards when he'd been sparkly and alive and a little bit bold. Cinderella syndrome: suddenly I understood that he was exhausted. For as long as I'd known him he'd been working twelve-hour days, six days a week and even though he was kind to his clientele, I wasn't seeing him at his best. If only he didn't have to work so hard . . .

I submitted my prescription and asked, 'How's your brother?'

'It'll be ages yet before he's back on his feet. Um, listen, I hope I didn't upset your boyfriend that night in Renards.'

I took a breath. 'He's not my boyfriend.'

'Er . . . right.'

I just didn't have a clue where to begin an explanation of the weirdness that was me and Owen, so jokily I said, 'Yes, I *am* in the habit of kissing men who aren't my boyfriend.'

'Great. I'm in with a chance so.' Did that sound like a man with a girlfriend to you?

'Oh, so you don't want to be my boyfriend?' It was meant to be arch and, you know, *good fun*, but first a red tide roared up his face, then up mine. Mortified and mute, we radiated heat at each other and my armpits were itchy.

'Christ,' I tried to save the day with my scintillating wit, 'we could roast marshmallows on the pair of us.'

He laughed redly, 'We're both a bit long in the tooth to be blushing like this.'

14

Once Lesley Lattimore's life-sapping bash was over, I could focus on my book, which was motoring along beautifully; I reckoned I was over three-quarters of the way through. I had other jobs on – but nothing like as demanding as Lesley's – and the only fly in the ointment, a very big one, was my mother. I suspected she'd never OK my novel being published, even though, as I kept saying to myself, it was the oldest story in the book. *And* the people were no longer anything like us.

I was thinking all kinds of panicky things, like I'd have to publish under a pseudonym and pay some actress to pretend to be me. But then I wouldn't be able to gloat at Lily and show Anton what a great success I was. *I* wanted the honour and the glory. I wanted *Yeah!* to photograph me in my sumptuous home. I wanted people to say, 'Are you *the* Gemma Hogan?'

I went to Susan for advice. 'Just be honest with your mammy,' she said. 'It never hurts to ask.'

Now there she was wrong.

I broached it during an ad-break. 'Mam?'

'Hmmm?'

'I'm thinking of writing a book.'

'What sort of book?'

'A novel.'

'What about? Cromwell?'

'No . . .'

'A Jewish girl in Germany in 1938?'

'Listen . . . ah. Switch off the telly a minute and I'll tell you.'

TO: Susan_inseattle@yahoo.com
FROM: Gemma 343@hotmail.com
SUBJECT: Breaking the news

Dear Susan,

I took your advice and told her. She called me a bitch. I couldn't believe it and nor could she. The worst she ever called anyone was 'Little madam' or 'Rip'. Even Colette hadn't been called a 'bitch'.

But when Mam heard my story-line, her mouth fell further and further open and her eyes became more and more bulgy. Her face had the look of someone who wanted to say plenty but the appalling shock had wiped out their voice, and then finally, in extremis, words were released from a no-go area in her soul.

'Well . . . you little –' big long dramatic pause, while the word was directed along narrow unfamiliar corridors, like backstage at a rock concert, then ushered upwards, upwards, upwards ('go, go, go!') towards the light – 'BITCH!'

It was as if she'd slapped me – and then I realized she actually had. A belt across the face from the palm of her hand. She caught me on the ear with her eternity ring and it really hurt.

'You want the whole world to know how I've been humiliated.'

I tried to explain that it wasn't about her and Dad, at least not any more and that it was the oldest story in the book. But she grabbed the bundle of pages that I'd printed out for her. 'Is this it?' she snarled. (Yes, *snarled*. My mam.) She tried to rip it in two, but it was too thick, so she broke it up into smaller pieces and then *really* went for it. Like, *savaged* it. I swear to God she was growling and I was afraid she was going to start biting it. Eating it, even.

'Now!' she declared, when every page was reduced to shreds and strips of paper were fluttering around the room like a snow-storm. 'No more book!'

And I hadn't the heart to explain about how it's all backed up on the computer.

My ear is still killing me. I really *am* a tormented artist.

Love
Gemma

It badly damaged things between me and Mam. I felt guilty and ashamed – but very resentful. Which made me feel even more ashamed. And still I wouldn't stop writing. If I really loved her, wouldn't I just knock it on the head? But – and you can call me selfish – I felt I'd given up a lot and there was a voice inside me going, *What about me?*

Meanwhile Mam, who had been improving, went back into suspicion overdrive and tried to monitor my every move. Something had to give – and it did.

It was an ordinary workday, I was running around like a blue-arsed fly, getting dressed, and she cornered me. 'What time will you be home tonight?'

'Late. Eleven. I'm having dinner at the new hotel on the quays. The one I want to hold the conference in.'

'Why?'

'*Bee*-cause,' I sighed, pulling up my tights, 'I have to try out the hotel food to see if it's OK for the conference. You can come with me if you don't believe me.'

'I'm not saying I don't believe you, I just don't want you to go.'

'Well that's tough, because I've no choice. I have to do my job.'

'Why?'

'I've a mortgage to pay.'

'Why don't you sell up that old flat and just live here?'

AAAAAAARRRRRGGGGGGGHHHHHHH! My worst fear, by eight million miles.

Something snapped.

'I'll tell you why,' I said, far too loudly. 'What if Dad marries Colette and we have to move out of here? We'll be glad then to have my flat to live in.'

I regretted it immediately. Even her lips went white and I thought she was going to have another fake heart attack. She began fighting for breath and between gasps, said, 'That couldn't happen.'

She heaved and gasped a bit more then, to my great surprise, said, 'It *could* happen. It's been six months and not once has he picked up the phone. He has no interest in me.'

And you know what? The following day, with almost spooky timing, a letter arrived from Dad's solicitor, asking for a meeting to discuss a permanent financial settlement.

I read it, then handed it to Mam, who stared at it for a long, long time before speaking. 'Does this mean he's going to sell my house from under me?'

'I don't know.' I was very nervous but I didn't want to lie. 'Maybe. Or maybe he'll let you have it, if you give up any further claims.'

'To what?'

'His income, his pension.'

'And what am I to live on? Fresh air?'

'I'll look after you.'

'You shouldn't have to.' She stared out of the window and she didn't look quite so bewildered and beaten. 'I ran his home all his life,' she mused. 'I was his cook, cleaning woman, concubine, the mother of his child. Have I no rights?'

'I don't know. We'll have to get a solicitor.' Something I should have done ages ago, but I'd hoped it would never come to this.

Another silence. 'That book of yours? What kind of light did it show your father in?'

'Bad.' Correct answer.

'I'm sorry now I tore it up.'

'How sorry?' Proceed with caution.

'You couldn't write it again, could you?'

TO: Susan_inseattle@yahoo.com
FROM: Gemma 343@hotmail.com
SUBJECT: She said yes!

She says she wants Dad named and shamed, that everyone knows about her situation anyway and that she might even go on *Trisha* and name and shame Dad there too. And guess what? I've finished my book! I thought I had a good bit still to go but it all came together very quickly at the end. I stayed up till six in the morning writing it. OK, the ending is a bit fairy-tale and I might laugh at it in someone else's book but, like everything in life, it's different when it's your own.

Love
Gemma

I rang Dad to find out what his permanent financial settlement comprised. It was as I'd feared: he wanted to sell the house so he'd have money to buy a new one to house Colette and her brats. Mam and I hired a family lawyer, Breda Sweeney, and went to see her.

'Dad wants to sell the house. Can he do that?'

'Not without your consent.'

'Which he won't get,' Mam said.

I expressed pleased surprise because I'd always suspected the law, in these kinds of cases, was skewed against women. This actually seemed quite protective . . .

Not so fast. Breda was still talking. 'But when you've been separated for a year, he can go to court and plead his case.'

'Which is?'

'That he's got two families to support now and that a lot of equity is tied up in the erstwhile family home. What usually happens is that the judge will make an order for the house to be sold and the proceeds to be shared.'

Fear seized me and Mam asked – whispered, kind of – 'Does that mean I'll lose my home?'

'You'll have money to buy a new one. Not necessarily fifty per cent of the proceeds, the judge will decide on that, but you'll have something.'

'But it's my *home*. I've lived there for thirty-five years. What about the garden?' She was moving towards hysteria. She wasn't the only one. House prices in Ireland were so high that even if she got half of the proceeds, I knew Mam would never be able to buy anything remotely similar to live in.

This thing just got worse and worse. Mam was sixty-two, a woman in her twilight years and she was about to be uprooted from the home she'd lived in for over half her life and condemned to live in a starter home halfway to Cork.

'But Dad will have to continue to support her?' I asked.

'Not necessarily. By law Maureen is entitled to be given as much as can be given to maintain her lifestyle without impoverishing him.' Breda made a gesture of impotence. 'There's only so much money to go round.'

'I'm running low on tranquillizers,' Mam said, when we got home. 'I don't want to run out of them. Not now, not with this news. Will you go to the chemist?'

'Oh. OK.' I found I felt funny about going. I hadn't seen Johnny for a couple of weeks, not since our bout of flirting, when I'd tripped on the way in and conducted a conversation of high innuendo.

Why was I reluctant to see him? I asked myself. After all, he was lovely. It was because I knew what I was doing was wrong. Owen – for good or ill – was my boyfriend and it wasn't fair on him to flirt with Johnny. Not unless I was planning to do something about it: like break it off with Owen and boldly go into the chemist looking to have more than my prescription filled. And was I going to do that?

It was one thing to spend a lot of my time with Owen fantasizing out loud about Anton, but Johnny was different. He was real. He was near.

He was interested.

I knew I had an opportunity with him and although it gave me the stomach-churnies (the good ones), I was afraid. I didn't know why, all I knew was that I wasn't afraid with Owen.

JOJO

15

Book News, 10 June

MOVIE RIGHTS SOLD

Movie rights for *Love and the Veil*, the debut novel from Nathan Frey, have been sold to Miramax for a seven-figure sum, rumoured to be $1.5 million. Brent Modigliani at Creative Artists Associates brokered the deal with Jim Sweetman of Lipman Haigh. The novel, which was agented by Jojo Harvey from Lipman Haigh, will be published in spring next year by Southern Cross.

Ms Harvey also represents Lily Wright, author of the huge surprise hit *Mimi's Remedies*, and Eamonn Farrell who's been long-listed for this year's Whitbread.

No mention of Miranda England who'd been in the top ten since January but hey, Jojo wouldn't kvetch. And nothing like some good news to get the old spending instincts into gear. It was lunchtime. Nearly.

'Manoj, I'm going out. I may be some time.'

'Looking at nail colours?'

It was one New York priority Jojo had never lost: the importance of nail-care.

'Nail colours, handbags, who knows? I'm wiiide open.'

But not for long. Out in the sunshiny street, she was hooked by a pale blue leather jacket in Whistles window; such an object of desire, her mouth went dry.

She went inside, found it in her size, held it at arm's length and stroked it like it was an animal. The leather was as thin and supple as skin and it was so beautiful it crimped her insides. It was also expensive, impractical and wouldn't survive more than a season; everyone would laugh at her if she wore it next year – but who *cared*?

Right on the shop floor, she shrugged it on, found a mirror – and abruptly the buzz drained away. It made her chest look as if it had been inflated with a bicycle pump. It was *obscene*. Mark would love it, of course, but where would she wear it with him? Her living room? Her bedroom? Her kitchen?

In her head, she had already bought the jacket, brought it home in its great bag and worn it twice – once to impress the Wyatt sisters. But now she reconsidered. It was way pricey for something that would never be worn outside her flat. She wasn't ruling it out, but she was going to *think about it*. Is this maturity, she wondered. If so, she wasn't crazy about it.

Back in the office, Manoj said, 'Smiler Sweetman was looking for you.'

She looked longingly at her sandwich but Jim would only take a minute. She ran to his office. 'What's up?'

'I've great news. Come in. Sit down.'

'My lunch is waiting. I can hear great news standing up.'

'OK, you stroppy cow. Brent Modigliani at CAA wants to have a "relationship" with us. With Lipman Haigh.'

Brent was the US agent who'd brokered the deal with Miramax.

'Having someone on the ground in LA, fighting our corner, means it's going to be a lot easier to get all our books onto the desks of Hollywood producers. You've got to take some credit for it. *Love and the Veil* got him interested. Opened his eyes to the calibre of work we represent here.'

'You got me, I'm sitting down.'

'He's coming over next week with a colleague. We'll have lunch someplace flash.'

'Who?'

'You, me and them.'

No mention of Richie Gant. Yay! 'You know what? Miranda's work would be PERFECT for Hollywood. Screwball comedies never go out of fashion. And *Mimi's Remedies* is *made* for the screen.'

Jim laughed at her enthusiasm. 'You've gone all Howard Hughes on us lately, but tonight you are coming out for a drink to celebrate.'

She thought about it. Nothing really on. Mark was at Sophie's school play. 'OK.'

'You gave up on the hypnotherapist?'

'No. Well, yeah, I *like* smoking, I'm a smoker. Even though we're a dying breed.'

'Dying, yeah.'

'No zeal like a convert.'

Back at her desk, she ate her sandwich and checked her emails. Just one, from Mark.

TO: Jojo.harvey@LIPMAN HAIGH.co
FROM: Mark.avery@LIPMAN HAIGH.co
SUBJECT: Monday night?

Can I pencil it in? I'm sorry about this weekend. Bloody parents' golden wedding anniversary. Bloody daughter's school play tonight. Have a nice – but not too nice – weekend without me.
M xx

PS Yvooluie

It had snuck up on them but in the past few months she and Mark had been spending more and more time with each other. They spent most Sundays together, Shayna had got them over for her precious brunch and they'd even, on occasion, taken their love to town: they'd gone to Bath for a two-day mini-break over Easter where they'd enjoyed lots of sex between professionally starched sheets and went for meandery strolls through the streets, holding hands, certain they were so far from London, no one would see them. At the end of the two days Mark had had to hurry back to take his family to Austria for a week's skiing, and this suited Jojo just fine. She'd had him full-on for forty-eight hours and now he was being nice to his family so she didn't even have to feel guilty.

'You sure skiing is a good idea?' she had asked. 'Your little guys are kinda accident prone. And don't they have lots of cheese in Austria?'

'That's Switzerland. You Americans, you know nothing about Europe.'

'You are so wrong.' Playfully she'd poked his crotch with the toe of her boot. 'I know about Danish pastries. I know about Swedish massages. I know about Spanish Fly.' She increased the pressure with her boot and began moving it gently back and forth. 'And I know,' she said tantalizingly, '*all* about French kissing.'

'You do?'

'Like, *all* about it.'

In silence they both watched her boot rise, lifted by something rising beneath it. 'Show me,' he asked.

'No. Not until you apologize.'

He apologized.

Since the night with the Italians when Mark had accidently slept through to morning, he now stayed over in Jojo's about once a week. Cassie didn't complain about him not coming home and Jojo was baffled by her passivity. 'What do you *tell* her?'

'That I'm talking to the West Coast or I'm entertaining publishers and that I don't want to disturb her by staggering in at three in the morning when she's got work the next day.'

'She buys it?'

'She seems to. She just asks that I let her know by midnight so she can put the mortice lock on the door.'

'Where does she think you sleep?'

'In a hotel.'

'No way would *I* buy that. No way. If my husband suddenly started staying away nights, when his job hadn't changed, I'd beat the shit out of him with a tyre-iron and wouldn't stop till I'd gotten some answers.'

'Not everyone's like you, Jojo.'

'Yeah.' And she understood that sometimes it's too painful for people to see what's under their noses. That hurt. She didn't want to cause Cassie – anyone – pain.

But what could she do? Stop seeing Mark? Not possible.

TO: Mark.avery@LIPMAN HAIGH.co
FROM: Jojo.harvey@LIPMAN HAIGH.co
SUBJECT: Nice weekend?

Monday night good. Far away but good. But excuse me? Have a nice weekend? How can I have a nice weekend? I will never forgive you for the way you treated me on my birthday.
JJ xx

PS Eoovilyu too

Four weekends previously, on the twelfth of May, Jojo had turned thirty-three. Some time before it, Mark said to her, 'I'm taking you away for your birthday.'

'Yeah?' Hot with pleasure at his thoughtfulness. 'Where?'

He paused. 'London.'

'London? This London?'

Before she had time to tell him to go and fuck himself, he passed her a sheet of paper. 'It's a timetable.'

Jojo's Birthday Weekend

Friday 3.30 p.m.:   Skive off work early. Proceed separately to Brook
                    Street and check into Claridges hotel.

'Claridges! I've always wanted to stay at Claridges!' It figured large in her fantasy, Agatha Christie-style Britain – cream teas and snooty butlers and 'gels' up from the country for the day, taking tea with their eccentric great-aunts, the kind of women who wore the family jewels to do the gardening.

'I know,' he said.

She was so touched that for a moment she half-considered crying, then couldn't be bothered.

Friday 4.00 p.m.:	Try out the facilities of the suite

'Suite! I love you.'

paying particular attention to the bed, then step out onto nearby Bond Street to look for Jojo's birthday gift.

She looked up again. 'Bond Street is *way* expensive.'

'I know.'

She eyed him with admiration. 'What a guy.'

Friday 7.00 p.m.:	Drinks, then dinner in a restaurant where I had to promise to get the chef a book deal, in order to get a reservation this side of Christmas.

***

Saturday morning:	Breakfast in the suite, followed by a swim in the hotel pool, then return to Bond Street to continue the search for Jojo's gift.
Afternoon at leisure:	Perhaps measuring the bounce of the bed.
Saturday 7.00 p.m.:	Cocktails, then dinner in a different but still insanely difficult-to-get-into restaurant.

***

Sunday morning:	Breakfast in the suite, another swim and a final test of the bedsprings.
12 Noon:	Check out and home.

It had been the perfect weekend. When they'd arrived, flowers and champagne were waiting in the room. They'd had sex about sixty times, even in the swimming pool when they'd been the only people there – she hadn't meant to, she thought it was kind of tacky, but at the time he'd worked her up into such a state she was beyond caring.

Patiently he went from shop to shop with her, admired pocketbook after pocketbook, even though she knew they seemed identical to him and paid attention as she pointed out how the stitching was white on one and black on the other and what a difference it made. The only sign that he was cracking slightly was when she couldn't decide between the Prada tote with the shoulder-strap or the identical Prada tote with the slightly shorter hand-straps and he said he'd buy her both.

'Oh, I get it,' she laughed. 'You're worried about the furniture in the suite. We should go back and check it again.'

They had afternoon tea in the Garden Room, they drank the champagne with their room-service lunch on Saturday afternoon and the only hiccup in the two days was when he'd steered her towards the rings in Tiffany.

'Maybe you should pick one,' he said.

'Don't be a dumbass,' she said, suddenly angry at him. The last thing she wanted during this precious time was to be reminded that he was married.

That night in the restaurant, as they looked at their menus he took her hand. She twisted it out of his grasp but again he went for it.

'Mark,' she frowned. 'Anyone could see us.'

'Your point?'

'While we're in London we have to play it safe.'

'Playing it safe is the most dangerous thing a woman like you could do.'

She burst out laughing. '*Moonstruck*? Nicolas Cage says it to Cher? Am I right?'

Mark sighed. 'You were meant to think I made it up. You are the most amazing woman I've ever met. You know everything.'

TO: Jojo.harvey@LIPMAN HAIGH.co
FROM: Mark.avery@LIPMAN HAIGH.co
SUBJECT: Birthday weekend

Didn't you enjoy it?

TO: Mark.avery@LIPMAN HAIGH.co
FROM: Jojo.harvey@LIPMAN HAIGH.co
SUBJECT: Enjoy it?

Yes. Far too much. Nothing will ever be as nice ever again.

16

6.30 Friday evening, the Coach and Horses
Lots of people showed up for the celebratory drink – after all, the company was paying. Richie Gant was sharking around, trying to get a piece of the action, but Jojo and Jim were the focus, seated together like a king and queen, drinking vodkatinis.

'See, it's not so bad,' Jim said. 'I remember when we could always count on you on Friday nights.'

'You're right.' She was flushed and happy. 'I'm having the *best* time. Could be something to do with all this alcohol, but who's complaining? So, how are things with you, Jim? How's Amanda?'

'Jojo, you are so out of touch. Amanda dumped me weeks ago.'

'She did? I'm sorry. Do you have a new girl?'

'Currently auditioning. But no.'

There was a weird little pause and alerted by some sixth sense, Jojo said, 'You didn't ask if I have a boyfriend.'

Then there was another weird little pause and Jim said, 'That's because I know you have.'

Time stopped.

'I know about Mark.'

Her stomach bumped, like she was in an elevator which had stopped unexpectedly. 'He told you?'

'I guessed.'

'Then he told you? When?'

'Today.'

All at once she was completely sober and very angry with Mark. This was a deal-breaker, he wasn't the only one with lots to lose if their relationship became public. It would not play well in the partnership discussions. She thought of how close Jim and Richie Gant were and suddenly felt nauseous.

Mark should have told her! Someone knowing her secrets and her unaware that they knew – it put her *so* on the back foot.

'Don't be too hard on Mark. He needs someone to talk to.'

She couldn't even ring Mark to yell at him. What a pisser.

'Don't worry,' Jim said. 'Your secret's safe with me.'

Jojo didn't know if she should believe him. She didn't know if she should trust him. She was suddenly very paranoid.

'Gotta go.' She gathered up her stuff, made a call and caught a cab to Becky and Andy's.

In the taxi, her anger with Mark suddenly busted out and she thought, I'm not going to suck it up until next time I see him. So she texted, Call me.

Almost immediately he rang back.

'What's the deal with Jim Sweetman?' she asked.

'He already knew.'

'No-he-did-not. You're way off here, Mark. Maybe Jim *thought* he knew but until you tell him he doesn't know for sure. *Capisce*?'

'Jojo, he saw me outside your flat at nine-thirty last Sunday morning.'

'He did? How?'

'He was driving past.'

'Why was he doing that?'

'He lives in West Hampstead. Not so far from you. I was caught red-handed. Believe me, Jojo, try as I might, this was one situation I could not talk my way out of. I would have if I could.'

She kept it zipped. They'd taken so many risks, getting caught at some stage was inevitable. But why did it have to be by someone they worked with?

'Jim can be trusted,' Mark said.

'I sure hope so.' She could still hang him up for something. 'So why didn't you tell me he knew?'

'I did.' He sounded confused. 'I emailed you. As soon as he'd left my office.'

'What time?'

'Four, four-thirty?'

She hadn't checked her emails. In celebratory, Friday mode she'd decided not to bother and had gone straight to the pub. Not like her. A mistake.

'OK.' Mark was clean. He hadn't done anything wrong. 'You're off the hook.'

'Welll! I thought you were going to read me my Miranda rights and allow me my one phone call.'

'Rights? Phone call?' She managed a laugh. 'You'd be lucky.'

'I'm so sorry I can't see you this weekend.'

'It's OK. Mazie Wyatt of the fabulous Wyatt sisters is having her thirtieth-birthday party tomorrow night. It's fancy dress. That'll keep me entertained.'

'Remind me again, which one do you have the crush on?'

'Magda. But –'

'– not in a sexual way,' they chanted together.

'Thanks for letting me know,' Mark said, suddenly very serious.

Huh?

'She's a great author and we'll be sorry to lose her.'

Cassie must have come into the room.

'See you on Monday.'

She filled Becky and Andy in on what had happened.

'Once the people in work start finding out, soon everyone's going to know,' she said.

'But it's not like you're not taking risks anyway,' Andy said. 'You *want* to be caught. Why not just do the decent thing and tell his wife before someone does it for you?'

Jojo took a deep breath. 'I'll tell you why. Because it's the shittiest thing in the world to think about breaking up a marriage. Not just the wife but the pain of his children. How're they going to get over it?'

'I dunno,' Andy said, 'but this sort of thing happens all the time. Well, a lot.'

'This is so not me. It's like starting a war. I can't believe I'm even, like, *con*templating it. How come other people have it so easy? They hate the wife, they say it's her fault for gaining weight or never giving the guy blow jobs. How come it's not like that for me? How come I'm ashamed of myself?'

'So dump him.' Andy was getting bored. He couldn't help it, he was a man.

'I'm not that ashamed. Which makes me even more ashamed.'

'This is all a little post-modern for me.'

'If – when – if – Mark and I go public on this, it's not going to be a rosy fade-out. No matter how it happens, it'll be ugly. Fact.'

'But *is* it going to happen? Yes or no?' Without giving her a chance to answer, Andy continued, 'I'm disappointed in you, Jojo. Most women, they do nothing but talk about things. They talk, talk, talk and never *do*. Look at poor Becky with her job. Sorry, love,' he said in an aside to Becky. 'I know you can't help it. But I'd expected better from you, Jojo. Tell me I've not been wrong. Tell me you're going to put your money where your mouth is. I need something to believe in.'

'City have just sacked their manager,' Becky explained.

'OK,' Jojo swallowed. 'It's going to happen, it's just a question of when. But when I think of myself at Sam's age . . .' She paused, then went on, her voice wobbling, 'When I think of Sophie and Sam being without their dad . . .'

Tears overwhelmed her and she sobbed silently into her chest while Becky and Andy made 'Yikes' faces at each other. Jojo wasn't supposed to cry.

That night in bed, she faced it. She was waiting for a time when the pain of not being with Mark was greater than the pain of breaking up his marriage and leaving his children fatherless. And it hadn't come yet.

She loved Mark but she held back a bit. She'd never – other

than jokingly – told him that she loved him and more than once he'd said, 'You're holding out on me, Jojo.'

Thing was, she didn't want her feelings to overwhelm her to the point where she would do something that conflicted so violently with her moral code.

But Andy was right. She and Mark were taking more risks. Like, *looking* to be caught, for the decision to be taken for them, no?

And what would their life together be like? Where would they live? Would she have to sell her apartment? Yes, and that was OK. She'd have to join a gym, though, the stairs kept her fit. Sorta. They might have to buy a house in the suburbs.

But it didn't frighten her any more. I'm ready for this, she realized. Almost. She and Mark could travel into work together, sleep together every night, wake up together every single morning and all the sneaking around could stop.

And no, she didn't think the thrill of Mark would disappear. People often said that affairs were all about frantic sex and would never survive the transition from snatched meetings to dull domesticity, but when she and Mark were alone, they were dull as *fuck*. Apart from the sex, which was still compelling, they did quiet little things. She cooked him dinner, they read magazines, they did cryptic crosswords, they discussed work. All they needed were the carpet slippers. 'Mark, look at us,' she'd exclaimed, the previous Sunday. 'We're like an old married couple.'

'That can be arranged.'

'Don't!'

She sighed into the darkness. She was going to cause pain to others and shame herself and she was just going to have to tough it out. Lucky she was good at doing stuff she didn't want to, but just because she was good at it, didn't mean she had to like it.

17

Saturday night, the Wyatt family home

Magda opened the heavy wooden front door and yelled at the top of her voice, 'JOJO HARVEY, you gorgeous, GORGEOUS woman. Mazie! Marina! Jojo's here!'

A flurry of blondes gathered around Jojo in her ancient black leggings, fraying red horns and red velcroed tail and showered her with love. Even Mrs Wyatt, 'Magnolia, please,' – who could have passed for another sister – joined in. 'You are SEX on LEGS!'

'What a clever idea, coming as a devil,' Magda said.

Which just goes to show, Jojo thought, that some people deserve to be rich and beautiful. The Wyatt costumes had been hired – or worse yet, probably specially made – and still they raved over her cruddy horns and tail like they were the greatest things they'd ever seen.

Mazie in a white halter-dress was Marilyn Monroe, Marina with several stuffed robins attached to her ice-blue Chanel suit was Tippi Hedren in *The Birds* and Magda was tall and glorious as a *Lord of the Rings* elf-queen. 'Jojo, it's terribly funny, I've never liked my ears. They're so flat and pointy that I wanted to have surgery, but now I'm glad I didn't.'

Magnolia agreed. 'I've always said that if you hold on to something for long enough it comes back into fashion.'

Well-behaved little girls, the offspring of Magda's brother Mikhail, fluttered about. One relieved Jojo of her coat, another took the gift and solemnly told Jojo she'd put it in 'the present room' and one more presented Jojo with a champagne cocktail.

The party was as slick as if a professional had organized it, but Magda had done it all by herself and had thought of everything: a dimly lit chill space; a dining area with buffet table and squashy sofas; and a big room with a sound system and bar, 'the misbehaving room'. Trays of drinks appeared under your nose the nano-second you were over halfway through the one in your hand, you happened upon a chair at the exact moment you decided you wanted to sit down and handsome men gave you admiring glances just when you were curling up with self-consciousness at being the only person there in a home-made costume. *Everyone* had rented proper outfits. In the first five minutes Jojo clocked a gorilla, Gandalf, the Pink Panther, a knight in armour, a damsel in distress, another Gandalf, a nun, Batman, yet another Gandalf and two Marie Antoinettes, both of them men. Even Andy showed up in a Superman costume, and Becky in black skin-tight vinyl and eye-mask was Cat-woman.

Then Jojo saw Shayna and Brandon and exhaled with relief. Shayna, stick-skinny and in a brown faux-crocodile catsuit, had come as a Twiglet and Brandon, with huge, misshapen lumps of styrofoam stuck all over him, was meant to be a piece of popcorn.

'We have some lovely, lovely men for you, Jojo,' Magda said. 'First up is the man who's come as Ali Baba. *Pots* of money and really the nicest chap. You couldn't hope for nicer. There's just one thing and you must promise not to let it put you off.' She clasped Jojo's hand. 'For me, Jojo. Promise?'

Grinning, Jojo promised. She *loved* Magda.

'No one explained to him how to apply fake tan for his Ali Baba look. But he's the sweetest man and as I say, *pots* of money. Come and let me introduce you.'

She pulled Jojo across the room to a man in pink satin harem pants and red cummerbund. 'Jojo, this is Henry. I know you two are just going to love each other.'

Jojo took one look and it took every fibre of her strength not to laugh. Henry's face, beneath his saffron turban, looked like it had been tie-dyed. The badly applied kohl didn't help either.

Magda dervished away and Henry cleared his (tequila sunrise) throat and said, 'I apologize for my streaky face. I was unaware of the correct application of a well-known self-tanning product and this is the result.'

'Hey, how would you know, you're a man.'

'They tell me it'll take a week to fade.'

Jojo nodded sympathetically.

'Which could be rather awkward for work.'

'What do you do?'

'I read the news.'

Another airlock of laughter was threatening to choke her. She clenched her fists.

'The stock market reports, not the full news. But it could still be tricky.'

Jojo wondered how she might escape, but she needn't have worried. Magda Wyatt was several steps ahead of her and reappeared with a pink rabbit. 'Henry, this is Athena, Hermione's youngest sister. I know I can rely on you to take care of her, and Jojo, I'm so sorry to break up your lovely, lovely chat with Henry but I need to whisk you away.'

Once out of Henry's earshot she murmured, 'Was it the fake tan?'

'No –'

'Never mind, we have lots of other lovely men on our books. Now, who shall we say hello to next . . . ?'

There was something about Magda: she invited confidences. 'See, Magda, I already have a boyfriend. But he's married.'

'My God, how thrilling.' But then she saw Jojo's face. 'Not thrilling? Come and sit down.'

Naturally they were right beside a window seat which was so perfectly sized it was as if it had been custom-built for Jojo and Magda. One of the nieces materialized out of nowhere and Magda instructed her to bring a bottle of champagne, which they drank while Jojo spilled her guts about Mark.

'And he's the man for you?' Magda said, when she'd finished.

'I don't know. I think so but how does anyone know for sure?'

'You know how I know if a man is for me? They have terrible shoes. Ones that I'd be embarrassed to be seen in public with. Even if they're fine in every other department, their shoes are always dreadful. And that's how I know.'

'Wish it was that easy.' And this whole thing was gathering momentum, Jojo realized. Looked like she and Mark could no longer contain it. Mark had fessed up to Jim Sweetman. And look at what had happened here – though she was crazy about Magda, she didn't really know her and still she spilled her guts to her.

The following day, Becky and Andy's place

Andy opened the door and stared at her for a moment too long. 'Jojo, you're up. You must have the constitution of an elephant. We're *dying.*'

'I left while I could still walk.' She followed him in. 'Where's Becky?'

'Throwing up, I think.'

'Too much information! OK, you.' She pointed at Andy. 'You're a man.'

'Not today. Once maybe but today I'm ruined. Those bloody Wyatts.'

'It's Mark's birthday next week. What should I give him? What do men like?'

'Unusual sex with dangerous women?'

'He always gets that. Something else, please.'

'Cufflinks?'

'*Nyet.*'

'Handcuffs?'

'*Nyet.*'

'Wallet?'

'*Nyet.*'

'Clothes.'

'*Nyet.* Cassie would see any of the above and she can't be that dumb.'

'I don't know,' Andy said. 'Doesn't she eat cheese sandwiches, even though she knows they give her migraines? A backgammon set?'

'*Nyet.*'

'A book?'

Andy was trying to be funny but Jojo pounced, 'Now you're talking! A first edition of something. He loves Steinbeck. How about a first edition of *The Grapes of Wrath*?'

Becky had crept into the room, grey-faced and subdued. Gingerly she crawled onto the couch and lay flat on her back. 'I just puked.'

'What do you want?' Jojo asked. 'A medal?'

'I'm simply sharing. But if you get him a first edition of something, you won't be able to write anything nice on it because his wife will see.'

'You were listening!' Andy said.

'I can puke and listen at the same time.'

'She wants *my* opinion. As a man. And she can write something on the book if he keeps it in the office.'

'Kids, quit squabbling. I wouldn't write on a first edition, *period.*'

Becky poked Andy with her foot. 'Get me things to take away the pain.'

'Please.'

'Please. Look at me,' she said to Jojo. 'Pyjamas at three in the afternoon, pounding head, churning stomach, nameless fear. Those Wyatt girls really know how to throw a party!'

'It was totally great. Wasn't Marina cute as a button in her little suit?'

'And Mazie in her white dress?'

'And Magnolia in her *Pussy Galore* rig?'

'But Magda . . .' They both cooed in admiration of Magda

and from the kitchen Andy made some prurient noise and Jojo called witheringly, 'Not in a sexual way.'

Andy returned with a fistful of analgesics. 'Apparently, there were five Gandalfs.'

'I think at least one of them was a Dumbledore,' Becky said. 'There were *tons* of men at it. It was a great pulling party, fantastic if you're single.' She inquired of Jojo. 'Well? I know you're not single but the men last night didn't know. So? Any luck?'

'Not bad. I slow-danced with a Gandalf, did my *Saturday Night Fever* with a Mother Superior and got asked out for dinner by an air-freshener.'

'Air-freshener? What kind?'

'One of those pine trees that hang on rear-view mirrors.'

'Him? I thought he was a Christmas tree. Good-looking?'

'I couldn't really see. He had a beaky bit over his face.'

'And I saw you dancing with King Canute,' Andy said.

Jojo shook her head.

'You were. I saw you. Pissed as I was I remember thinking that the pair of you were really going for it.'

'No, I was entangled in his nets. We weren't dancing, that was just the two of us struggling to get free.'

18

Monday morning, opening her post

One was marked personal and Jojo thought she recognized the handwriting. She tore the envelope and tipped out the letter. 'Oh no!'

```
Dear Jojo,
There's no easy way of telling you this but I
have decided not to return to work. I know
I promised you that I would. I meant it when I
said it, but I wasn't prepared for how much I
love Stella and I can't bear the thought of
leaving her every day with a minder. When it
happens to you, you'll know what I'm talking
about.
   I know you're in good hands with Manoj and I
hope we'll stay friends.


With lots of love,


Louisa and Stella
```

She loved Louisa. She was her sidekick, a smarty who always delivered. At least she had been until Childbirth Stole Her Brain. This was not good news. Right away she went to see Mark.

'Louisa isn't coming back.'

'Aaaahhhhh.'

'You knew?'

'I thought she might not. It happens.'

'She swore black was white that she would.'

'I'm sure she meant it at the time.'

'I'm sure she did,' Jojo acknowledged.

'Should we advertise for someone new, or do you want to keep Manoj?'

'Manoj is fine. OK, he's very good,' she admitted reluctantly. 'It's just that Louisa was my friend. She knew about you. Now I've no one to talk to. Guess I could always try Jim Sweetman,' she added.

Mark said nothing. He let the silence endure and Jojo was the one to crack.

'Hey, it's your birthday Friday.' She went for levity. 'Eight o'clock, my bed, for a very special gift.'

A second too long before he spoke. 'I can't.' He sounded pained. 'Cassie's organized something.'

'Oh. What?'

'A night in a country house hotel. Weymouth Manor or something. I'm so sorry.'

Jojo got it together. 'Come on, Mark, she *is* your wife.'

'How about Sunday?'

'Sure.'

Then she went back and broke the news to Manoj that he was going to be made permanent. He was so happy he almost cried. 'You won't regret this,' he wobbled.

'I already am. Pull yourself together. Any messages?'

'Gemma Hogan rang. She was wondering if you've sold her book yet.'

Jojo rolled her eyes. Gemma Hogan was an Irish woman who had sent sheaves of emails to her friend detailing her elderly father leaving her mother. When the bunch of pages arrived on Jojo's desk they weren't in book format but were entertaining and funny enough for her to be semi-interested.

So they met – and it was one of the weirdest meetings Jojo had ever had: every author who came to see her was absolutely wild to be published. But this Gemma was different and the moment Jojo realized she was offering to represent a woman who hadn't written a book and didn't want to be published she drew the meeting to an abrupt conclusion. She'd thought she'd never hear from her again but a few weeks after the meeting Gemma rang to say she was in the process of writing the book – and less than a month later the finished product arrived.

It belonged in the category of books that Jojo called the So-What?s – not special enough to be sold via a headline-grabbing auction; instead Jojo would have to approach each house individually and if they passed, carry on to the next bunch.

The heroine, Izzy, starred in a cookie-cutter love story with a little twist. It had signalled from page one that she would end up with the brooding, cleft-chinned Emmet, a hero straight from central casting; instead she falls for the quietly sexy pharmacist who has been dispensing the mom's happy pills. It was the mom's journey that was much harder to stomach. Sixty-two years of age, so ditsy and dependent that she'd never learned to drive, she was running her own business by page seventy-nine (importing Swiss skincare into Ireland, hand-in-hand with her Swiss toyboy).

It was baloney. In real life, for every abandoned wife who won Businesswoman of the Year, there were thousands of others who understandably never recovered their equilibrium. Which would Cassie be? Jojo wondered. If, *if*, Mark and she ever . . . She sincerely hoped she'd be a Businesswoman of the Year version. Despite its flaws the book was fun and would probably sell. Sure, the critics wouldn't even acknowledge it; books like this – 'women's fluff' – flew beneath the radar. Occasionally, to make an example to the others, they wheeled one out and 'reviewed' it – although the review had been written before they'd actually read the book – and they poured scorn with the ugly superiority of Ku Klux Klan laughing at bound black boys.

Different, of course, if it had been written by a man . . .

Suddenly there would be talk of 'courageous tenderness' and 'fearless exploration and exposition of emotion'. And women who normally made fun of 'women's fiction' would read it with pride in public places.

Now there's a thought . . . What were the chances of convincing Gemma Hogan to pretend to be a man? Not to dress up as one, just to publish under the name Gerry Hogan, perhaps. But there was no way. Like many authors, Gemma was probably in it for the buzz of seeing her picture in *Hello!* and her name in the papers.

When Jojo rang to tell Gemma that she would represent her and her book, Gemma chuckled quietly. 'I'm screaming my head off on the inside, but I'm at work,' she'd said apologetically. 'So you really liked it?'

'I LOVED it.' Well, she had enjoyed it. 'Oh yeah, does it have a name?'

'Of course. Didn't I put it on it? It's called *The Sins of the Father*.'

'Oh no, it's not.'

'Sorry?'

'Not as sorry as I am. Change the name, like, yesterday.'

'But it's representative of the story.'

'This is light, romantic fiction! It needs a light, romantic title. "Sins of the Father" sounds like a clogs and shawl misery-fest: pubescent girls being thrashed with riding crops by half-brothers who want to schtup her. Lame ones.'

'Who's lame? The girl or the brother?'

'I meant the brother. But it could be the girl, in fact it's probably both. How about "Headrush"?'

'But it doesn't mean anything.'

'Gemma, listen to me good. I-can-not-sell-this-book-with-that-title. Get-me-a-new-one.'

After a long pause Gemma said sulkily, '"Runaway Dad".'

'No.'

'I can't think of anything else.'

'OK, we'll use it as a temp. We need a new title but I'll start sending the book out straight away.'

'There's no need to send it to lots of people. I'd like to be with Lily Wright's publisher. Dalkin Emery?'

'Woah.' For a first-timer Gemma was surprisingly knowledgeable about publishers. Then Jojo thought about it – not a bad idea. Dalkin Emery were good with women's fiction: as well as Lily Wright, they'd made a huge success of Miranda England.

'We can try Dalkin Emery but I'll send you to a different editor. It's not a good idea for friends to share editors. You might find it hard to believe now but this could start a huge rivalry . . .' If it wasn't there already and she was beginning to suspect it was. '. . . and ruin your friendship.'

'We're not really friends. We just . . . know each other.'

Nevertheless, Jojo decided against it – the client is *not* always right – and sent it to Aoife Byrne instead.

But Aoife rang her and said, 'Jojo, this *Runaway Dad* book is more Tania Teal's thing. I've passed it on to her.'

The weird thing was that as soon as Jojo hung up, Gemma rang for a progress report and when she heard that Lily's editor was considering her book she said, 'I knew it. I'm meant to be with that editor.'

And although Jojo didn't believe in any of that 'meant to be' crap, she was a little impressed.

For about five minutes. Tania passed. She said it was a sweet book, actually reminiscent of Miranda England's earlier work, but it just wasn't special enough.

Damn, Jojo thought. These so-what books put varnish on her nails but they were a lot of work for little reward.

Who next? Patricia Evans at Pelham. But Patricia had never really forgiven her for not accepting the *Love and the Veil* pre-empt. Sure enough two days after biking over *Runaway Dad* a standard rejection letter arrived on Jojo's desk. She'd have betted that Patricia hadn't even read it. It was now with Claire

Colton at Southern Cross. So even though she had no good news, she rang Gemma. She had a policy of returning calls to all her authors, no matter how unlucrative they were – and giving it to them straight.

'No sale yet, Gemma. We've had a couple more passes. But not to worry, there are plenty of publishers out there.'

'Couldn't we try Lily Wright's editor again?'

'No, we totally can not.'

'OK. I've thought of a new name.'

'Hit me.'

'"Betrayal".'

'Too Danielle Steele. In fact . . . you know, maybe it's not for me to say, but could be you need to, like, *move on*. All the titles you've picked, they're a little . . . well . . . bitter.'

'That's because I am.' She sounded proud.

'OK. Whatever. Let me know when you get the right title.'

19

Brent and Tyler, the two agents from CAA, arrived and lit up reception with a bright sunshiny glow. Brent was blond and Tyler dark-haired, and both of them were buff, tan and oozing easy West Coast charm from every perfect pore. They wore box-fresh chinos and polo shirts and even though they were jet-lagged, their eyes sparkled. They had suspiciously beautiful skin.

Jim Sweetman introduced Jojo as the woman who 'discovered' *Love and the Veil.*

'We've got a lot to thank you for,' Brent cooed super-appreciatively.

'Yeah, we would not be here were it not for you.'

'And we cannot wait to read your other authors. We've heard am-*ayyyzzz*-ing stuff about them.'

'Am-*ayyyzzz*-ing.'

'Truly am-*ayyyzzz*-ing.'

Jojo had to laugh. 'Right back atcha, boys.'

On the way back to her office, she bumped into Mark. 'Check out the Ken dolls from CAA,' she muttered out of the side of her mouth. 'Makes the rest of us look like *Night of the Living Dead.*'

Mark cut his eyes to them. 'Christ! They're the only things in colour in a black and white world.'

'Like the yellow brick road at the start of *Wizard of Oz.*'

'Or the child in the red coat in *Schindler's List.* OK, I'm off to schmooze.'

'Careful. They'll be all over you like a cheap suit.'

*

'More like a rash,' Mark said quietly to her, when they met in the boardroom ten minutes later at a major meet-and-greet session.

Jojo watched all the agents file in. Here came Dan Swann who never seemed to take his mossy green hat off any more – looking to be promoted to a fully fledged Eccentric, Jojo decided. He sat beside her and stared, mesmerized, at the suntanned pair. 'They're like men,' he said faintly. 'Only shinier.'

Then came Jocelyn Forsyth, marching about in his pinstriped suit, being deb'ly, deb'ly Brrritish, calling Brent 'my de-ah fellow' and Tyler 'de-ah, de-ah boy'.

Next came Lobelia French and Aurora Hall who, like always, looked right through her, then the Hon Tarquin Wentworth who shot her a glance of unabashed hatred. Not pleasant, but hey, could she help it if she worked harder and generated more money than they did?

But there was one person they despised even more than her and here he was now – Richie Gant who looked more unsavoury by the day. For a second all four were as one in their contempt of him.

Olga Fisher sat on the other side of her and looked at Brent and Tyler. 'Marvellous skin, haven't they?'

'I wonder what they use?'

'La Mer. I asked them. I have a video on warthogs for you. Not the prettiest of creatures, but interesting. I'll drop it in to that boy.'

'Manoj. He's permanent now. Louisa isn't coming back.'

'If I were mother to that little angel, I don't think I'd return to work either.'

'You wouldn't?' But they called her a ballbreaker.

'No. Authors are as demanding as children but not quite so rewarding. Would you return to work?'

'Of course!'

'You say that now.'

'For sure I would –'

But Mark was calling the meeting to order and Jojo had to shut up.

The meeting wound up at noon and then came the moment of truth: Jojo was having lunch at the Caprice with Jim and the CAA boys but she was way anxious that Jim would spring Richie Gant on them at the last minute. But he didn't and as she said to Jim in the taxi on the way back to work, 'I had the *best* time.' Brent and Tyler were so enthusiastic they made it sound as if movie rights for all her books had already been sold and were currently being cast. They'd encouraged her to let her imagination run wild and tell them who she thought should play each of her author's characters, even which directors she'd prefer. 'I know they're a little over the top,' she sighed happily to Jim. 'But I really feel my books will go to the head of the queue.' She'd had three glasses of champagne and felt a song coming on. 'Top of the HEAP!'

'Well?' Manoj asked. 'Swanning back in at ten to four. I hope it was good.'

'Mucho bonding. Mucho, mucho bonding. They loved me up so much, it was as good as sex. Hey, better than sex.'

'Are you going out to spend money?'

'You betcha. Late night shopping and all. How lucky is that?'

Friday morning, first thing
There was an email from Claire Colton at Southern Cross, saying thanks but no thanks for Gemma Hogan's book. She said what Tania Teal had said and what Jojo thought – it was fun but not special enough.

OK, Jojo thought, taking it on the chin. Who's next? B&B Calder. Thing was, though, she was starting to run out of publishers; they'd all taken over each other so that now there were only six big ones left in London. Several imprints existed within the umbrella of each house but if one editor rejects the manuscript, you can't just readdress it to another editor in a different part of the house; with each publisher you only got one chance so you had to choose your editor very carefully. Who at B&B Calder should she approach? Not Franz 'Editor of the Year' Wilder, that was for damn sure! She could already hear his bitchy laughter when he read a few pages of *Runaway Dad*.

Someone fresh and on the way up would suit this book. Then she got her girl: Harriet J. Evans, young and hot, starting to make her mark with a couple of statement purchases. Why hadn't she thought of her before now? She picked up the phone.

'Email it to me,' Harriet said.

Then she went to show Manoj the fabulous pocketbook she'd bought the previous night. She was demonstrating the secret section where cigarettes could be hidden when Richie Gant passed by Manoj's desk. She felt him before she saw him – a vague feeling of revulsion crawled up the skin of her back. And there he was, with his hair too gelled, his suit too cheap, his neck too spotty.

He paused, cast a scornful eye over her and then, to her surprise, laughed right into her face.

'Laughing at jokes only you can hear?' Then she added kindly, 'You poor fuck.'

But he laughed again and the breath caught in her chest. She watched him amble down the corridor, still chuckling to himself. 'Something's going on,' she said to an alarmed-looking Manoj. 'Find out.'

After loitering for fifteen minutes by the photocopier, Manoj reported back. 'Last night they all went out.'

'Who?'

'Brent, Tyler, Jim and Richie.'

'So why didn't they ask me?'

'They went to a lap-dancing club.'

'So why didn't they ask me?'

'Could've been embarrassing.'

'I wouldn't have been embarrassed.'

'But *they* might have been. Duh.'

A lap-dancing club! Richie Gant, the little *fuck*. He'd done it again: lunch in the Caprice was nothing compared to a night boozing and bonding over naked women. She was burning up, feeling horribly patronized that Brent and Tyler had taken her for lunch when they had a proper good time – the *real* one – planned for later. All the time they'd been simply humouring her.

She wasn't naive, she knew this stuff happened, but she'd thought publishing had a little more class. She remembered how happy she'd been in the taxi and cringed. Jim Sweetman should have told her that they were going out with Richie Gant later, but Jim was the chicken-shit kind of guy who believed that the messenger got shot. He only passed on good news.

Men, she thought, in contempt. Useless fucks with a brain and a penis but not enough blood to run both simultaneously.

Then her anger came to rest on the women who took their clothes off to enable men to bond and take business away from other women. How can men respect working women when they can pay other women to take their clothes off? How can they help but think of all women as toys?

She'd never before felt that as a professional woman she had anything other than Access All Areas. Well, she'd been wrong. She was a great agent, but she could never forge relationships by buying dances for dickbrains. Men could, though, giving them the advantage. The unfairness hit her like a slap in the face. Men and their dicks ran the world – and for a moment she felt the full weight of the imbalance. She was raging and, unusually for her, depressed.

She'd been blue anyway: it was Mark's birthday and she wanted to spend it with him. Instead, some time in the afternoon, Cassie was coming by to whisk him away for a night in a mellow-walled hotel with four-poster beds, seven-course dinners and a Roman-esque pool (she'd looked it up on the net).

20

Friday afternoon

The day didn't get any better. Right after lunch, Harriet J. Evans rang.

'Well?'

'Sorry. No.'

'But you didn't have time to read it!'

'I read enough. Actually I enjoyed it, it made me laugh, but there's just too many others like it. Sorry, Jojo.'

Next!

Paul Whitington at Thor. He was a man, but he was good with commercial fiction – unlike a lot of male editors, he didn't think a sense of humour was something to be ashamed of.

Jojo rang him, bigged up *Runaway Dad* like it was the book of the year and Paul promised to read it over the weekend.

'Manoj! Send a bike!'

Eamonn Farrell, author and piss-head, was her three-thirty. He showed up at five to four, smelling of tobacco, fast food and Paco Rabanne, laced with a suggestion of urine. This was because he was a genius. As one of Jojo's star authors, second only to Nathan Frey, she had to kiss him. It doesn't happen often but sometimes I hate my job, she thought dolefully.

He sat in front of her in clothes that looked like they'd been tied to the back of a car and dragged around town for a couple of hours – another sign of his genius – and complained for a solid forty-five minutes about every other male author on the planet. Then abruptly he stood up and said, 'Right, I'm off to get pissed.'

'I'll walk you to the lift.'

On the way they passed Jim. 'Jojo, will you be long?'

D'ya have a good time last night paying women to take their clothes off? She pushed down her anger.

'No, coming right back.'

'Come and see me.'

'Who's he?' Eamonn asked. 'Jim Sweetman, the film rights bloke? The one who sold Nathan Frey's pile of shite to Hollywood? What's he doing about mine?'

'Your pile of shite? We're working on it.'

'Wha –?'

'Lift's here.' She hustled him and his smelliness in. 'Take care, Eamonn. Missing you already.'

The doors slid shut, taking an astonished Eamonn Farrell away from her. The relief! Her usual author's bedside manner had deserted her today. With a lighter heart she turned to go back – and at the far end of the corridor she saw Mark with a blonde woman. An author? An editor? Every nerve-ending prickled when she realized that it was Cassie.

Who wasn't exactly as she'd remembered her. Taller and slimmer, wearing jeans, a white shirt and a – WHAT? Oh my GOD! It couldn't be. But she looked again – it was! – and her brain squeezed with the unlikeliness of it. *She's wearing my jacket.* She's in her forties, what in the hell is she doing with a leather jacket from Whistles? A style item that'll be toast in three months' time. Something that *I've* balked about buying and I'm only thirty-three.

Mark saw her, his face lit up with alarm and they exchanged a stare that flashed the length of the hallway. Jojo would have spun on her heel and sprinted to the lift except it might have looked a little obvious; she *had* to walk towards them. The corridor was like a runway and there was no escape, no side-doors to pop into and the twenty feet took a long time to cover. Cassie was walking faster than Mark, her voice was loud and she sounded like she was telling him off for something. 'You silly man,' she was saying, then she laughed.

When she reached them, Jojo ducked her head, mumbled, 'Hi,' and slid past but then she heard Cassie say, 'Hello.'

Fuuckkk. 'Hi.'

Both Mark and Jojo attempted to keep moving but Cassie was going nowhere so Mark had to introduce them, which he did with all the enthusiasm of a man en route to the electric chair. 'This is Jojo Harvey. One of our agents.'

'Jojo Harvey.' Cassie took Jojo's hand in both of hers, looked her in the face and said, 'My God, you gorgeous creature.' Her eyes were blue, proper Scandinavian blue and although they were lined, she was very attractive. 'And I'm Cassie, Mark's long-suffering wife.'

Fuuckkk. But Cassie twinkled and Jojo understood that she was joking.

'I've been meaning to write to you, Jojo.'

Fuuckkk. 'You have?'

'You have so many good authors. Aren't you clever?'

How does she know about my authors?

'I loved *Mimi's Remedies,*' Cassie exclaimed. 'It was brilliant, a wee gem.' Exactly what Jojo thought. *Fuuckkk.* 'And I hope you don't mind, but I asked Mark to steal a copy of Miranda England's latest from your office. She's great, isn't she? Pure escapism.' Exactly what Jojo thought. *Fuuckkk.*

'You read a lot.' She sounded robotic but hey, she was in shock. She'd expected broad-in-the-butt chambray skirts with elasticated waists, flat feet in wide loafers and a deathly dull woman with a fondness for tea and gardening.

'I love books,' Cassie sparkled with glee, 'and the only thing better than a book is a *free* book.' Exactly what Jojo thought. *Fuuckkk.*

'Hand. Y. For. You,' she said, in her Dalek monotone, 'Know. Ing. Some. One. In. Pub. Lish. Ing.'

Cassie smiled affectionately at Mark, 'He has his uses.' Then she giggled. Giggled! Like she'd thought of other uses for Mark. She tugged him by the tie, 'Come along, birthday boy.'

As Mark was led away he gave Jojo a beseeching look; he was the colour of freshly poured cement.

'Nice to meet you, Jojo,' Cassie called. She waved her free Miranda England. 'And thanks for this.'

Jojo watched them get into the lift and was suddenly desperate to yell, 'Mark, please don't sleep with her.'

In fact, when was the last time Mark had slept with Cassie? Something she'd never cared about. Jealousy of Mark's wife had never before figured. She'd resented the time that his family drained him of, but this was the first occasion she'd thought of Cassie as a rival. Until now, she had actually felt sorry for her. Sorry and guilty.

He talks to her, he tells her about work. She reads, she's smart. She has great taste in jackets. And men. Fuuckkk. I'm going outside, I need a cigarette.

She got her cigarettes and lighter and on the way to the lift, as she passed Jim Sweetman's office, he shouted, 'Jojo Harvey, in here!'

She pushed his door with her foot, letting it bang against a cabinet and leant heavily against the jamb.

'That Eamonn Farrell smells like a bin lorry!' Then Jim noticed her strange mood. 'Oh-oh. You met Cassie?'

'She was wearing my jacket. I'm going downstairs for a cigarette. I'll come see you in a few.'

The lift smelt of Eamonn. Out in the street she inhaled her first welcome lungful of nicotine and sank against the wall when, with a jolt, she saw Mark and Cassie in a car on the other side of the road. They hadn't left yet. Instinctively she stepped back into the doorway in case they saw her. Mark was in the passenger seat and Cassie was driving. She had a cigarette clamped between her lips and was reversing out of a tight space, her eyes narrowed against the smoke. *She smokes! My kinda woman!*

At a sharp angle she shot out onto the road and almost collided with another car. The driver, an elderly man, beeped her angrily but Cassie took the cigarette out of her mouth and blew him a kiss; Jojo could see her laughing. Then they drove away.

Holy fuck.

She ground her cigarette under her foot, smoked another one, then another, then went upstairs to Jim.

'Whatever you want to talk to me about, can we do it over a drink?'

'When? Now?'

'It's past five. Come on.'

'Where? The Coach and Horses?'

'Anywhere they sell strong liquor.'

21

It wasn't such a complicated proposal that Jim outlined but by the third vodkatini, Jojo was having trouble keeping up to speed.

'. . . crying out to be packaged, instead of the usual studio rounds, Brent thinks if we get a "name" director or actress on board first, the deal is as good as done –'

'Which? *Mimi's Remedies*?'

'No. Miranda's first book.'

'Yeah, 'course.' She giggled softly.

'Jojo, darling, I don't think I have your full attention.'

'No, sorry,' she sighed and swilled her nearly empty drink. 'Time for another.'

'I'll go.'

When he came back, she said jovially, 'Hey, Jim, *you* know Cassie? Tell me about her. And don't LIE to me.'

'Would I do that?'

'Probably. You want everyone to love you, so you only tell people what they want to hear.'

Abruptly the smile left Jim's eyes and his mouth became a hard line.

'Whoops,' Jojo laughed fuzzily. 'He didn't like that.'

He wouldn't look at her. He crouched away and drummed his fingers on the table. 'Wish you still smoked?' She scrambled for her cigarettes and thrust them at him. 'Can I tempt you?'

He turned with sudden speed and looked her full in the face, 'No, Jojo, you can't tempt me.'

She stared hard at him. What the fuck did that mean? 'Oi.' Bumped back to unpleasant sobriety. 'What's up?'

He didn't answer and dropped his eyes. She waited until she was calm before she spoke.

'Jim, I'm sorry. I'm a little loaded and a little sore.'

Now his turn to apologize. But he didn't.

'I've left you a space,' she said.

'For what?'

'To apologize.'

'For what?'

'How about you tell me? For implying I'm trying to sleep my way into a partnership?'

'Oh, is that what you're doing? Funny, I thought you were good enough at your job not to have to do that.'

Great! She'd just made things worse.

'And for making me look like a total idiot in front of Brent and Tyler.'

'You what?'

'A lap-dancing club with Richie Gant while I get to have a boring lunch? Hey, like, *thanks*.'

'Lunch wasn't boring, lunch was great. They loved you, they love your books.'

'A fucking lap-dancing club.'

'Horses for courses. I'm going to do my best for each individual agent because,' he said with heavy emphasis, '*that's my job*.'

Jim wasn't usually so dark, he was Mr Sunshine, Smiler Sweetman, all things to all men. In silence, they drank too fast. Jim was drumming the table again and Jojo drawing in mouthfuls of air with each lungful of nicotine.

Minutes passed. People arrived in the pub, more people left, Jojo lit another cigarette, smoked it and crushed it into the ashtray. Further time elapsed, then she touched Jim's sleeve, 'Look, let's start over.'

He moved his arm away but said, 'OK and let's get a couple of things straight. I don't think you're trying to sleep your way to a partnership, you're a brilliant agent. And you're as important to Brent and Tyler as Richie Gant is, if not more.'

Jim was smiling again but Jojo wasn't convinced. He was

doing that thing that she did – pretend that things are a certain way and most people are dumb enough to go along with it.

'So you want to know about Cassie? OK, I'll give it to you straight.' Another smile. 'She's a doll, a real sweetie.'

'But she seemed very smart when I met her today.'

'Very. Mark likes strong, smart women.'

She didn't like the way he said that, making it sound as though Mark ran a whole string of girlfriends, all of them strong and smart.

'And you said she was wearing your jacket? How on earth did she get it? You didn't leave it in Mark's car or anything mental like that?'

'It wasn't really my jacket. I saw a jacket I liked and Cassie was wearing it. Yes, I know, we've a lot in common.' Without planning to, she asked, 'Does Cassie know about me?'

Jim looked at her, his eyes blank and unreadable. 'I have no idea.'

They'd finished their drinks and they both knew they weren't having any more.

'Can I get you a cab?' Jim asked, way too politely.

'Let me make a quick call.' She got out her mobile. 'Becky, you're home? Can I come over?'

She said to Jim, 'I'm getting a cab to West Hampstead. You live there? I'll drop you off.'

But he wouldn't come with her. He was smiley and polite but unmovable. Feeling worse than she had in the longest time, she arrived at Becky and Andy's, where they poured her wine and let her vent.

'I had the shittiest day. I've just had a bust-up with Jim Sweetman and I think I've ruined our bond which is a major bummer because I might need him to vote for me if Jocelyn Forsyth ever retires and I'm up for partner. But Richie Gant probably bought him a long time ago so it's all moot anyway. But worse than that, far worse, is that I met Cassie Avery and she's a bit of a babe.'

Becky snorted.

'No really. She was warm and fun and her hair was beautiful. She made me feel like Magda Wyatt does. Under different circumstances, I might have got a crush on her.' She turned and yelled at Andy, 'NOT IN A SEXUAL WAY.'

Quietly she returned to Becky. 'She called me a gorgeous creature, kinda like Magda does. And this is the fur-eek-iest thing, she was wearing the blue leather jacket that I nearly bought.'

Becky couldn't mask her shock at that.

'I reckon she knows all about you,' Andy said. 'She's had you followed and was sending you a message with the jacket. Good job you don't have a rabbit.'

'You watch too many low-rent thrillers,' Becky said. 'And you always say the wrong thing. But Jojo, I think she must suspect about you. Sounds like she was putting on a show. I mean come on, the jacket. And you say her hair was nice. Like she'd just had it done?'

'Yes.'

'See?'

'It wasn't like that. I honest-to-God think the jacket was just a coincidence. I mean, it was pure chance that I met her at all. I really don't think she knows about me.'

'I thought she was just a silly woman who ate cheese sand-wiches even though she knew they gave her migraines,' Andy said.

'And me. What a difference a week makes. Last Friday I felt so guilty, I didn't want Mark to ever leave her, this week I want him to, so bad, but I'm afraid he never will.'

'He will. He's not playing games,' Andy said. 'I saw him that day at Shayna's. He looks at you like he wants to eat you.'

'Eat me, yeah. Leave his wife and live with me, I don't think so. You know how he stays nights with me now and how she doesn't question it? I thought it was because she'd decided not to notice. Then I wondered if, like, she *had* noticed but didn't care! That they were living separate lives, staying together for the sake of the children, and all that and maybe she had a guy too. But today they didn't look like they were living separate lives. Do you know what they looked like?'

'What?'

'They looked like a happily married couple.'

'Yikes.'

Up until now she'd been refusing to touch the sides of her life, refusing to think too hard about this affair. Now she was forced to. Was she the same as every other woman who was involved with a married man? Was she a fool? Would Mark never leave his wife?

'I haven't felt this bad since Dominic, when he was meant to be making his mind up, and I'll break up with Mark rather than go through that again.'

'But you love him,' Becky protested.

'It's because I love him that I couldn't take waiting for him to decide between us.'

'No it's not,' Andy said. 'You just want to punish him. You're hurt and you want to scare the shit out of him for having a good-looking wife. But what about your job? If you dump him now, what's that going to do to your promotion chances? You'll have to leave Lipman Haigh and go somewhere else, start all over again.'

She went hot and cold with fear. Until now, she'd been in control but that one short encounter with Cassie had cast her adrift; she felt as powerless as a cork on the waves.

Ages ago Andy had said something about the danger of getting involved with your boss. He'd been right.

'I feel sick. What if he picked me to have a fling with because he thought I'd never ask him to leave her? And why did he make me think she was a frump?'

'But did he?'

Jojo thought. Maybe not. And hadn't he told her at dinner that first night that his wife understood him. He'd even said that sometimes they still slept together. But she felt so shaken and uncertain . . .

She told them the rest of what happened and Becky concluded, 'At least she didn't put the cigarette in his mouth, so that they drove away looking buddy-buddy, like Thelma and Louise.'

'And you're a bit pissed,' Andy said. 'Things always seem worse when you're pissed.'

'They always seem *better* when you're pissed, you moron.'

'Oh right. Sorry.'

22

Saturday morning

Flowers arrived. It had happened once too often and now she hated them.

Shortly afterwards her phone rang. She checked caller-display: Mark's mobile. She picked up and, dispensing with pleasantries, asked, 'Where's Cassie?'

'Oh. In the spa.'

'How was your seven-course dinner?'

'Wha –?'

'And the four-poster bed?'

'The –?'

'And the Romanesque pool. Look, stop sending me flowers.'

'But they're to let you know I love you when I can't be with you.' He sounded hurt.

'I know, yeah, I know, but arranging them, picking up dead petals from the floor and fitting dead bunches in a garbage bag without getting stem-slime on my fingers – you know what? I seem to do fuck all else and I've had it.'

'This is about Cassie.'

'I guess.'

There was the longest silence, then he said in a heavy, resigned voice, 'We've got to talk.'

She was shot through with a thrill of something very nasty.

Then he said, 'This couldn't have gone on for ever,' and her head lifted with shock.

She wasn't ready for this to be over yet. 'Talk to me now, Mark.'

'I can't. Cassie will be back soon. I'll see you tomorrow.'

She hung up. Fuck. Twenty-four hours to get through.

Right away, she rang her mom. Not to discuss this with her, just looking to be reminded of who she was. 'How's everyone?'

'Fine. Little Luka gets more beautiful by the day.'

Luka was the toddler son of her brother Kevin and his wife, Natalie.

'I got the photos. He's a honey.'

'They've enlisted him in a model agency.'

'Good idea.'

'No, it is not. It's bad enough for a man to be good-looking, but to be *told* he's good-looking – oh dear! Luckily your father never had that trouble.'

'I heard that,' Charlie shouted faintly.

'Far better for a man to develop his personality,' her mom said. 'Mind you, your father didn't do that either.'

'I heard that too,' Charlie shouted again.

When she hung up she rang Becky, who arrived an hour later with Andy.

'You must be in agony,' Becky observed.

Jojo shrugged.

'You're being ever so brave.'

'That's me, Becks. Tough. Stronger than the average woman.'

'Yes.' Becky and Andy exchanged a look, acknowledging the bottle of red wine that Jojo was ploughing through, the cigarette smouldering in the ashtray, the other cigarette between her fingers, the video of *Meerkats United* on the telly.

'There's one good thing,' Jojo mused. 'At least I didn't spend all my money on a first edition of *The Grapes of Wrath*. I just got him a first edition of *The Pearl* because *The Grapes of Wrath* was way pricey.'

'Don't give it to him. Resell it on the Internet,' Becky said.

'Give it to him,' Andy said. 'Stay on his right side. Whatever happens, he's still your boss.'

'I'm sure her career is the least of her worries,' Becky chided.

'This is Jojo,' Andy chided back. 'Not you.'

*

The following day Mark arrived at Jojo's at one-fifteen. He tried to embrace her and she stepped away from him. He followed her into the front room where they sat in sombre silence.

'I love my kids,' he said.

'I know.'

'I never wanted to leave them. I told you that right from the start.'

'Always.'

'I've been looking for the right time to leave them. I thought about the end of the school year, but I didn't want to ruin their summer. Then I wanted them to have one last happy-family holiday, so I thought I'd go after we come back from Italy in August, but then they're about to start a new school year, so that's a terrible time.' He hitched and dropped his shoulders. 'Jojo, I've realized there is no right time. There will be no right time. Ever.'

Her heart seemed to stop.

'So let's do it now,' he said. 'Today.'

'Excuse me?'

'Today. I'll tell Cassie today. I'll leave her today.'

'*Today?* Waitaminute, you're way ahead of me. I thought you were breaking up with me.'

'Break *up* with you?' He was a picture of confusion. 'Why would you think that? I love you, Jojo.'

'Because you said we had to talk. And because you never told me Cassie was so, like, attractive.'

'But you'd seen her before. You knew what she looked like.'

'I don't remember her looking like that.'

'Because at the time it didn't matter to you what she looked like.'

She acknowledged that. 'But you get along so well.'

'I also get along well with Jim Sweetman. It doesn't mean I should be married to him.'

She lit a cigarette; the turnabout had been too speedy. She'd thought she was losing him, she'd half come to terms with it and instead things were accelerating in the other direction. He was coming to live with her. Today.

After thinking she'd lost him, she wanted him with an intensity that frightened her. But first there was a question she needed the answer to. 'Mark, did you sleep with her this weekend?'

He laughed. 'No.'

'Why not? You had the four-poster bed, the seven-course dinner . . .'

'None of that matters. I don't love her, at least not in that way, and I love you.'

'When was the last time you slept with her?'

He lowered his eyes, he crinkled his forehead, then he looked up again, 'I honestly have no idea.'

'You don't have to lie to me. You told me at the start that you sometimes had sex.'

'Yes, but since I've been with you, I couldn't be with anyone else.'

She had to believe him.

He got to his feet. 'I'm going to go home now and tell her. I don't know when I'll be back –'

'Wait, wait, no wait. Today is too soon.'

He looked at her curiously. 'When, then?'

She thought about it. When would be the best time to deprive Sam and Sophie of their dad? Next week? Four weeks' time? When? The procrastination couldn't go on for ever, they needed a definite date. 'OK,' she said, finally. 'Have your family holiday in August.'

'Are you sure?'

'I'm sure.'

'OK. The end of August. Now can we go to bed?'

23

Monday morning

'On line one I have Miranda England's husband, Jeremy. Accept or reject?'

'Accept.' Click. 'Hi, Jeremy. To what do I owe –'

'Miranda's pregnant.'

'Congrat –'

'She's had three miscarriages in the past eight months and her gynie says she has to rest completely. No work AT ALL. Which means her next book won't be delivered on time. Tell them at Dalkin Emery.'

'OK –'

'Bye.'

'Wait!'

But he was gone. Straight away she rang back and the answering machine picked up. 'Jeremy, it's Jojo here. We need to talk about this –'

The phone was snatched up. 'There's nothing to say. We're having a baby, she needs to rest, she's not going to write that book until she's good and ready.'

'Jeremy, I can hear that you're upset –'

'They work her into the ground. A book every year and all that promotional stuff. Fucking journalists wanting to know what colour her knickers are. No wonder she keeps losing the babies.'

'I understand, I completely understand. Miranda works very, very hard.'

'And I know she's under contract but they can have the money back. Some things are more important.'

Jojo closed her eyes. He wasn't saying that two years ago before she'd got Miranda a six-figure advance. Biggest mistake an agent could make: getting the author so much money, she no longer needed to work.

'When is the baby due?'

'Next January. And you needn't think she'll get straight back to writing once she's had it, so tell them at Dalkin Emery they can whistle for their book. And not to bother ringing us trying to get us to change our mind. We won't and Miranda can't have any stress.'

He hung up again and this time Jojo didn't bother calling back. She'd got the message loud and clear. What now? She'd better ring Tania Teal and try telling her her cash-cow author had gone on strike. This would so not play well.

Tania wasn't in yet so she left a very detailed message with Tania's assistant.

Ten minutes later Tania was on. 'I heard Miranda's wonderful news. I tried to ring her but it went to voicemail.'

And would continue to, if Jeremy had anything to do with it.

'Jojo, Miranda's pregnancy is great news, but I have a sales director breathing down my neck. What are the chances of Miranda finishing this book in time?'

Jojo weighed her words. 'There's always a chance Miranda and Jeremy will change their mind, but – honestly? I'd say forget it. They really want this baby and sounds to me like they're going to totally do what the doctor tells them. To publish next May, she should really have delivered the book by now and she's only halfway through writing it.'

'But if she recommences writing as soon as she's had the baby? If she gets the manuscript to us by next March we'll do a rush job. We can copy-edit, proof-read and turn any manuscript around in five weeks max. Then three weeks at the printers and we'll be ready to go.'

Jojo would remember that timescale the next time publishers had a go at her about an author delivering late.

'There's no way anyone can write with a newborn in the house,' Jojo said. 'Tania, this is not going to happen.'

Tania went silent, then, almost experimentally, 'She *is* under contract.'

'She doesn't care. Jeremy says you can have the money back.'

Tania fell silent, and Jojo knew what she was thinking: if Miranda needed the money she'd write the book; perhaps they should never have given her that big advance. But she had the grace not to say it. Instead she sighed, said, 'Poor Miranda, she can do without this sort of grief. Give her my best, Jojo. Flowers are on the way, of course.'

TO: <u>Jojo.harvey@LIPMAN HAIGH.co</u>
FROM: <u>Mark.avery@LIPMAN HAIGH.co</u>
SUBJECT: Meet me for lunch

I've something to tell you.

TO: <u>Mark.avery@LIPMAN HAIGH.co</u>
FROM: <u>Jojo.harvey@LIPMAN HAIGH.co</u>
SUBJECT: Re: Meet me for lunch

Tell me now. Especially if it's bad.

TO: <u>Jojo.harvey@LIPMAN HAIGH.co</u>
FROM: <u>Mark.avery@LIPMAN HAIGH.co</u>
SUBJECT: Re: Meet me for lunch

Not bad, but confidential. Antonio's in Old Compton Street at 12.30

TO: <u>Mark.avery@LIPMAN HAIGH.co</u>
FROM: <u>Jojo.harvey@LIPMAN HAIGH.co</u>
SUBJECT: Re: Meet me for lunch

ANTONIO'S??! Last time I was in that dump, I was working as a bargirl and Becky got poisoned. This'd better be good.

Mark was already there when she arrived, a thick white cup of watery cappuccino in front of him.

'Nice place,' Jojo laughed, swinging through the corridor of tightly placed Formica tables and almost dislodging lunches with her hips. 'Not.'

'But no one will see us here.'

'You could say the same about a room at the Ritz.' She squashed into the too-small booth. 'What's up?'

'Jocelyn Forsyth is retiring.'

Her breath caught. 'Yay! When?'

'November. It'll be announced when he's told his clients but I thought you'd like to know asap.'

'Thank you.' She was suddenly excited and bright-eyed. 'Sometimes it can be very handy sleeping with the Managing Partner. So Lipman Haigh will be taking on a new partner, right?'

'Right.'

'Who's it going to be?'

He laughed regretfully. 'I don't have that much power, Jojo. That's up to all the partners to decide.'

'So I'd better be real nice to all the partners.'

'Starting with me.' He slid his thigh between hers. 'Shall we order?'

'I dunno. Eating in here is a form of extreme sport.'

He nudged his thigh in a bit further. 'A little more,' she said quietly.

'Wha –? Oh, right.' Instantly his pupils turned almost black. Romantic novelists came in for a lot of stick but Jojo had to hand it to them about the dilating pupils.

Mark slid his leg along an extra couple of inches and she shifted down slightly in her seat, letting her legs fall open until his knee had made contact.

'Bingo,' she said quietly. 'I could get to like it in here.'

'Jojo. Jesus Christ,' he said with low intent. He gripped her hand and stared at her mouth, then at her nipples which were straining through her bra, her shirt and her close-fitting jacket.

He began to move his knee against her and she caught his hand in her mouth then, all of a sudden, she was sitting up straight and dropping his hand like it burned; someone she recognized was coming in. She actually felt it before her brain made the connection – it was Richie Gant. And he was with – of *all* people – Olga Fisher!

High-speed, four-way eye-contact was made, like a complicated knife-throwing trick and everyone froze, locked in a bond of mutual mortification.

Fuck, Jojo thought, feeling strangely dislocated, *I thought Olga was mine.*

'Surprisingly good lasagne in here,' Olga said, smoothly. 'But perhaps we should have Chinese instead.'

They backed out of the door and Jojo and Mark looked at each other.

'How many people know about Jocelyn retiring?' Jojo asked idly.

'It was only meant to be me, but clearly the silly old fool has been telling everyone.'

'I thought,' and her throat tried to close on her saying it, 'I thought Olga was on my side. What's she doing with Skanky Boy?'

'Maybe they're having an affair.'

She laughed, although it wasn't remotely funny. And then it *was* kind of funny. Refined Olga having sex with the poster boy for acne, what a thought.

'It's OK,' she grinned. 'You, Dan Swann and Jocelyn are dead certs.'

'And Jim.'

'I don't think so.'

'I think so. Really,' he insisted. 'He thinks you're great. And so do the boys in Edinburgh.'

'They do? You know, perhaps I should take a trip to Edinburgh. See how Nicholas and Cam are doing.'

'Great idea. And I'm long overdue a visit, maybe I should come with you.'

Fully cheered up, she said, 'Now, where were we?'

When she returned, Tania Teal had left a message on her voicemail. 'We've just had a sales meeting about the Miranda situation. We were wondering if there's any way round this.' She was trying to sound cheery but her voice kept cracking with anxiety.

Jojo rang her back and Tania launched into the plans they had come up with. 'We could provide a secretary to go to Miranda's home and take dictation from her. Miranda needn't even get out of bed. She could stay lying down –'

'But that will still be stressful for her.'

'But –'

'The hard part is not sitting upright, it's being creative.'

'But –'

'You can publish sometime later next year.'

'But we'll have missed the big summer sales. We were hoping for a huge increase –'

'Tania,' Jojo said, warningly.

'Sorry,' she said quickly. 'Sorry, sorry.'

TO: Jojo.harvey@LIPMAN HAIGH.co
FROM: Mark.avery@LIPMAN HAIGH.co
SUBJECT: I've been thinking . . .

Maybe we should wait until after the partnership appointment in November before we become official. I don't want 'us' to damage your trajectory.
M xxx

Jojo stared at her screen in dismay. Was Mark bailing on her? November was a long, long way away; so long that it might never happen. Was he getting cold feet?

The possibility scared her so much, she was actually surprised. She went to his office and walked in. 'What's going on?'

'With what?'

'We agreed on August, now you want to change it to November. If you're trying to bail on me, forget it. I'll just laugh in your face.'

Mark raised his eyebrows in polite inquiry. 'Some of the partners – Jocelyn Forsyth, Nicholas in Scotland – are family men.' He was calm, cold even, but Jojo knew him well enough to realize he was angry. When he was incensed he kind of looked too big for his suit. 'They won't be impressed by our home-wrecking. In fact, I don't think any of the partners will appreciate it. I don't want to run the risk of you losing any votes.'

She had to admit that this was something which had flitted across her own mind.

'I made the decision – suggestion – with your career and only that in mind.'

She nodded, a little intimidated by his clipped tones. 'But Jim already knows,' she said. 'Olga has probably guessed. And I bet Richie Gant has told all of them he saw us together.'

'Maybe, but an affair is different from my having left my wife and set up shop with you.'

She thought about it: he was right. It would be better to wait. And November was only a short while after August. It was just that . . .

'I'm usually the one who keeps deferring our big day,' she admitted.

'I had noticed,' he said, drily.

'You've been very patient.'

'I would wait for you for ever.' Then he added, 'Although obviously I would prefer not to have to.'

'November it is. When? The day of the decision?'

'Why not wait until it's official and published in *Book News*? No point spoiling the ship and all that.'

'You're doing it again.'

434

'What?'

'Scaring me.'

'There's nothing to be afraid of.'

'Except fear itself.'

'And wardrobe monsters.'

'And giant rocks that fall out of the sky and land on your head.'

'Exactly.'

Tuesday morning

The first piece of post she opened was a letter from Paul Whitington, turning down Gemma's book. That only left Knoxton House and after that it would be time to move on to the independents. At this late stage in the game, she acknowledged there was a good chance she wasn't going to sell it, and if she did, only for a tiny advance – maybe a thousand quid.

'Choose your next editor carefully, Ms Harvey,' Manoj said. 'It may be your last.'

She decided on Nadine Steidl and forced herself to sound enthusiastic. 'I've got a wee gem for you.' She was using Cassie's phrase, she liked it.

But Cassie's phrase wasn't enough to convince Nadine and on Thursday morning, she came back to Jojo with a no.

Thursday afternoon

'Tania Teal on line one for you. Accept or reject?'

'I'd rather stick a rusty compass in my eye.'

'I didn't ask you that. Accept or reject?'

'OK. Accept.'

Click, then Tania's anxiety was pouring down the phone line. 'Jojo, because of Miranda, next summer's schedule is in bad shape.'

Again with the pregnant author!

'We need a popular women's fiction book to fill Miranda's May slot and we have nothing.'

'But you've got so many authors.'

'I've looked at what we have and every book coming out next year is tied in to time-specific promotions or won't be ready for May.'

So what do you want me to do, Jojo wondered. Write the fucking thing myself?

'I was thinking of that Irish thing you sent me,' Tania said. 'That would do. Have you managed to sell it?'

She meant Gemma Hogan's book: the one Jojo couldn't even give away.

But she wasn't telling Tania that! 'You might just have got lucky,' she said. 'It's still available but only just. I've got two houses about to bite –'

'How much?' Tania interrupted. 'Ten grand?'

'Er –'

'Twenty? Thirty, then.'

Jojo said nothing. Why should she? Tania was doing the bidding for her.

'Thirty-five?'

Jojo made her pitch. 'A hundred for two.'

Tania whispered, 'Christ.' Then in a proper voice asked, 'Is there a second book?'

'Sure.' She didn't know for certain, but there probably was.

'Sixty for one,' Tania said. 'And that's it, Jojo. I don't want another author, I've too many as it is. I just need a stop-gap.'

It wasn't perfect. A two-book deal was always better because it meant the house was commited to the long-term future of the author.

But still a deal was better than no deal. Sixty grand was better than a thousand. And who knows, if the book did well, she could get Gemma a second deal for a lot more.

'OK. *Runaway Dad* is yours.'

She could actually feel Tania wince. 'That name will have to go.'

Then Jojo rang Gemma, who was thrilled she'd been sold to Lily Wright's editor.

'Thank you for trying again for me. I knew you could convince her.'

Authors, Jojo thought. Buncha know-nothings. Then Jojo told Gemma about the money.

'*Sixty* grand. Sixty *grand*. Oh, my good Christ. Great. Fabulous. Fantastico!'

Fantastico indeed. No need to tell Gemma she was the literary equivalent of a band-aid, because this might work out very nicely.

LILY

24

Book News, 5 August

RECENT ACQUISITIONS

Tania Teal from Dalkin Emery has bought *Chasing Rainbows*, the debut novel from Irish writer Gemma Hogan. Agented by Jojo Harvey from Lipman Haigh, the book sold for a reported £60,000. Described as a cross between Miranda England and Bridie O'Connor, it will be published next May as a paperback original.

I was skimming through *Book News*, looking for any excuse not to write, when the words 'Gemma' and 'Hogan' leapt off the page, waited until they had my full attention, then punched me in the stomach. Gripping the page too hard, I read the piece properly, then reread it while little waves of shock broke over my head. *Gemma. Book. My agent. My editor. Lots of money.*

Fear in my heart, I stared at the black letters until my eyes went blurry. There could be many Irish Gemma Hogans, it was not such an unusual name, but already I knew: this was my Gemma. She had often talked about writing a book and her having *my* agent and *my* editor was too much of a coincidence. But how on earth had she swung it? It was difficult enough to get a book published, never mind to bag the agent and publisher of one's choice. She must have become a practitioner of the black arts. I sank my face into my hands; this was a message, like the horse's head in the bed in *The Godfather*.

I am gifted at intuition, at premonitions even, and I knew the game was up. Although I had feared some form of retribution, so much time had passed that I had begun to hope that Gemma had moved on with her life and perhaps even quietly forgiven me. But I had been mistaken: all this time she had been planning revenge. I was not sure exactly how she was going to ruin my life, I could not have given precise details there and then, but I knew this was the start of an unravelling.

In an instant I saw my entire life falling away from me. Gemma hated me. She would tell the whole world what I had done to her and would turn everyone against me.

And the money! Sixty thousand! As compared to the paltry little four thousand advance I had got. Her book must be stunningly good. My career was finished, she would blow me out of the water with her sixty-grand masterpiece.

I picked up the phone, blew the dust off it through trembling lips and rang Anton.

'Gemma's written a book.'

'Gemma Hogan?'

'It gets worse. Guess who her agent is? Jojo. And guess who her editor is? Tania.'

'No, that can't be right.'

'It is, I promise. It's in *Book News*.'

Silence. Then, 'Christ, she's sending us a warning shot across the bows. It's like the horse's head in *The Godfather*.'

'That's just what I thought.'

'Ring Jojo, find out what it's about. But it's got to be about us, right?'

'Yes, and the worst bit of all.' I could hardly utter the words, so great was my jealousy. 'She got a huge advance.'

'How much?'

'You won't believe –'

'How much?'

'Sixty thousand.'

Anton became quiet for a long, long time, then I heard a little whimper.

'What?' I almost shouted.

'I picked the wrong girl!'

'Oh, ha bloody ha,' I said crossly.

I phoned Jojo. Though my head was racing with the need to know, I managed the polite 'Howareyou?' thing, then striving for casual but actually sounding half-strangled, I said, 'Er, I read in *Book News* that you have a new author called Gemma Hogan. I was just wondering –'

'Yeah, it's the one you know,' Jojo said.

Arse. Arse, arse, arse, arse, ARSE. 'Are you sure? Living in Dublin, working in PR, Liza Minnelli hair?'

'That's the one.'

I wondered if I might weep.

'Yeah,' Jojo said. 'She said to say hey to you. Ages ago. I'm sorry I forgot.'

'She . . . . she had a message for me?'

'She just asked me to say hello.'

Dread swamped me. Any hope that this was a bizarre coincidence dissolved. Gemma had planned this. It was deliberate and targeted.

'Jojo, can I ask . . . do you mind, is it breaking client confidentiality . . . what's her book about?'

'Her dad leaving her mom.'

'And a best friend stealing someone's boyfriend?'

'No, just the dad leaving the mom. It's fun! I'll get a copy to you, soon as they're proofed.'

'Thanks,' I whispered, and hung up.

Jojo was lying to me. Gemma must have already got to her and inducted her to the dark side.

Ema has run away with a marauding gang of chartered accountants, I thought. *Anton has a touch of dry rot in his left leg and I lost my mother in a card game.*

I forced myself to concentrate hard on the horridness of this scenario. I furrowed my brow and really *tried.* For a brief moment I caught a glimpse of how vile it would be to share a home with a man with dry rot. Then I did the mental equivalent of elbowing myself and saying, 'Silly! None of those things are true!'

This exercise usually makes me grateful for my lot.

Not today, though.

25

Anton rang back, 'Have they turned up yet?'

No need to ask who 'they' were: the builders. Our obsession, our fixation, the centre of our lives.

Despite the best efforts of most of the banks in Britain, we had bought our beautiful redbrick dream house and had moved in at the end of June. Spirits had been sky-high. I was so happy I thought I might die and for an entire week did nothing but look at cast-iron beds on the Internet.

Before we had even moved in, we had a building firm lined up to repair our dry rot as a prelude to 'knocking things through'. We had not even fully unpacked when a small army of Irish labourers, all bearing an uncanny resemblance to Mad Paddy, descended upon us.

The Mad Paddys wielded their claw hammers and set to work with zeal, behaving as though they were on a demolition job – they ripped the plaster from the walls, then the bricks, then pretty much removed the entire front of the house; the only thing that kept it from toppling over into the front garden was a mesh of scaffolding.

For almost a week they slashed and destroyed and just at the point when they were meant to start reassembling our ruined house, they discovered the dry rot was a lot worse than originally thought. Those in the know, who have had a lot of construction done, tell me this is what usually happens. However, on account of Anton, Ema and I being the Crap Family, for whom nothing ever works, who are always led inexorably to the restaurant table with the wobbly leg, I took it personally.

And the cost of the job? In light of the new discoveries, the original quote doubled overnight. Again, this was text-book and again I took it personally.

Muttering something about needing new window lintels – whatever on earth they were – and not being able to do anything until they arrived, the boys – again, in time-honoured tradition, so I am told – disappeared. Once more, I took it personally.

For two full weeks we saw nothing of them. Gone, but not, however, forgotten. Anton, Ema, Zulema – I will get to Zulema – and I, were existing in squalor. Boot-shaped cement marks marched across the beautiful old wooden floors, I kept stumbling across tabloid newspapers in the oddest of places (beneath Ema's pillow, anyone?) and sugar crunched underfoot; people complain about builders drinking too much tea – it was not the tea I objected to but the wretched accompanying sugar.

Nightly, I expected someone to shin up the scaffolding, slip in through one of the many holes in the wall and burgle us. Although they would have been bitterly disappointed as the only thing we had worth stealing was Ema.

Builders' tools were strewn about the house and one of them, a foot-long wrench, had become the unlikely object of Ema's affections. She had become so attached to it, she now insisted on sleeping with it. Other children become fixated with velveteen rabbits or small blankets; mine had fallen in love with a builder's wrench as long as her soft, squeezy arm. (She had named it Jessie after my sister Jessie who had come home in June for a short visit from Argentina, where she was now permanently located with her boyfriend, Julian. Ema had been quite dazzled by her.)

But worse than all the other plagues put together was the omnipresent dust ... Beneath our fingernails, between our bedsheets, behind our eyelids – it was not unlike living in a sandstorm. Every time I put on face-cream I exfoliated instead and I had given up cleaning the house because it was so staggeringly pointless.

It was wretchedness beyond description, especially for me

because I 'worked' from 'home', but when I begged Anton to do something, he insisted the men would return when the lintels had arrived from wherever lintels come from.

I still had no idea what lintels were. It did not matter. They were still managing to break my heart.

One dusty morning, before Anton left for work, he was eating muesli. Suddenly he hurled down his spoon and exclaimed, 'I keep thinking it's dust!'

He foraged with his fingers in the bowl and retrieved something. 'Look at that!' He extended it to me. 'It's a piece of dust.'

'It's oatmeal.'

'It's fucking dust.'

I pretended to study it more closely. 'You're right, it's dust.' Perhaps now he would ring them.

He put a call in to Macko, the foreman, and the news was horrifying; the lintels had arrived from LintelLand but the Mad Paddys had started another job. They would finish us off when they got the chance.

We blustered and stomped and complained in the strongest possible terms. They *have* to come. Look at the *state* of the place. We can't *live* like this.

That was more than a week ago, and since then Anton and I had to take it in turns to be the grown-up, to ring them and insist in our firmest voices that they return to the job and finish it within the week, but they just laughed at us. This was not mere paranoia, I knew they laughed at us because I *heard* them.

Eventually Anton secured a promise. 'They'll be here next Monday. On their mothers' lives, they'll be here with the lintels on Monday.'

It was now Thursday. Three days later.

'No, Anton, no sign of them yet.'

'It's your turn to ring them.'

'Excuse me, I think not. I rang them first thing this morning.' We rang them four or five times daily.

'You didn't, Zulema did.'

447

'Because I bribed her to.'

'What was it, this time?'

I hesitated. 'My toner.'

'The toner I bought you? The Jo Malone stuff?'

'Yes,' I said. 'I'm sorry, don't be cross. I did love it, I do. But I loathe ringing them so much and she's quite good at it. They don't laugh at her.'

'This has gone too far,' Anton said, with sudden grim resolve. 'I'm going to get us some legal advice.'

'No!' I exclaimed. 'Then they'll *never* come back!' One of the things I heard over and over was that if you even mention taking legal action against them, it was game over. 'Please, Anton. That's the last thing we should do. Let's just keep grovelling.'

'OK, I'll ring them,' he said.

Then I remembered we had agreed to grant him an exemption because he had got a filling in his tooth the day before.

Over the past week, regarding ringing the builders, Anton and I had developed a complicated system of obligations, exemptions and rewards. Because my job paid more than Anton's he had to make two phone calls for every one of mine. But the chore could be sold, bartered or passed to another person if you could persuade them to do it; twice since Monday I had bribed Zulema with cosmetics. Anton had tried to get Ema to do it. Also illness could mean an exemption; Anton's filling guaranteed him a free go. Likewise, I was looking forward very much to having my period.

I heard a key in the front door; Zulema and Ema were home from their walk.

'I forgot about your tooth exemption,' I said to Anton. 'Please don't worry. I'll ring them.'

With this magnanimous offer, I rang off.

I would make Zulema do it.

OK, Zulema: Zulema was our au pair. She was part of our brave new world – new house, me writing my next book, etc.

She was a tall, good-looking, strong-willed Latina who had arrived three weeks ago from Venezuela.

I was terrified of her. So was Anton. Even Ema's perpetual grin dimmed a little in her presence.

Her arrival in our lives had originally been planned to coincide with the end of the building work. We had hoped to welcome her into a beautiful dry-rot-free home and when it became evident that the house would still be a wreck on her arrival date, I phoned to put her off. But she was as inflexible as a missile on a pre-ordained, computerized course. 'I am comeeng.'

'Yes, but Zulema, the place is quite literally a building site –'

'I am comeeng.'

Anton and I ran about like headless chickens, preparing the bedroom at the back of the house – the only bedroom with intact walls – for her. We gave her our cast-iron bed and our best duvet cover and it actually looked very pretty, far nicer than ours or Ema's room. But Zulema took one look at the scaffolding-clad house and its all-pervasive dust and announced, 'You leeve like animals. I weell not stay here.'

With terrifying speed she found a boyfriend – someone called Bloggers (Why? I have no idea.) who had a nice flat in Cricklewood – and moved in with him. 'Do you think she'd let us come too?' Anton had asked.

Zulema was very helpful. Dreadfully helpful. All day long she policed Ema so that I was entirely free to write but I missed Ema and I loathed the very concept of having an au pair. The exploitatively tiny sum we paid her made me squirm with shame – even though we gave considerably more than the going rate, as I discovered at Tumble Tots when I tried discussing my guilt with Nicky. (Nicky and Simon had had their much longed for baby three months after I had Ema.) She said, 'Simon and I pay our au pair half of what you pay yours *and* she's bloody glad to get it. Think about it, this Zulema is learning English, she's working – legally – in London, you're doing her a favour!'

Because Zulema lived elsewhere, we did not have a built-in babysitter, but I so did not care. I was horribly relieved at not having to share the house with her. How could I ever relax? Sharing one's home with a stranger is always difficult even if the person is adorable. Which Zulema was not. Hard-working, undoubtedly. Responsible, I grant you. Honest, apart from using my Gloomaway shower gel. (Which I *needed*. It was the only thing that could persuade me to wash in that grimy old bathroom.) But she was not much fun. Not even slightly. Every time I saw her in all her grim, beetle-browed beauty, my heart sank.

'Zulema,' I called.

She pushed open my study door. She looked displeased. 'I feed Ema.'

'Yes, um, thank you.' Ema appeared between Zulema's legs, winked at me – conspiratorially? But she was only twenty-two months . . . much too young to wink conspiratorially? – then clattered away. 'Zulema, would you mind ringing Macko again. This time, *beg* him to come?'

'What weell you geeve mee?'

'Er, cash? Twenty pounds?' I should not have been offering her money, we were so short of it ourselves . . .

'I like Super-line Corrector from Prescriptives.'

I looked at her beseechingly. My beloved night-cream. And it was only new. But what choice did I have?

'OK.' At this rate I would have no skin-care left at all.

She returned within seconds.

'He say he ees comeeng.'

'Do you think he meant it?'

She shrugged and stared at me. What did she care? 'I weell take Super-line Corrector.'

'You do that.'

Zulema thumped upstairs to spirit away my night-cream from my dressing table and I resumed staring at my desk. Perhaps they would come this time. Just for a moment I let myself hope and my spirits inched upwards. Then my copy of *Book News* caught my eye and I was reminded of Gemma's huge book deal – I had forgotten briefly – and my spirits lowered themselves back to base. Cripes, what a day.

Gloomily, I opened the rest of my post, hoping it would not contain anything too insane; now that I was a 'successful' 'writer' I averaged one mad missive a day.

I received letters from people who were looking for money; letters from people who said that writing about witchcraft was the devil's work and that I would be punished (these were written in green ink); letters from people who had 'lived a very interesting life' and who were willing to sell me the details (the usual terms offered were a fifty-fifty split of profits); letters from people inviting me to spend the weekend with them ('I don't have much, but I am happy to sleep on the floor and you can have my bed. Local sights include the clock tower which is an exact, if smaller, version of Big Ben and only six months ago a Marks and Spencer opened – there's posh!'); letters from people sending their manuscripts and asking me to ensure they got published.

Every day was different. Yesterday it had been a letter from a girl called Hilary whom I had been at school with in Kentish Town. She was one of a trio of bitches, who had made my life hell. It was just after the move from Guildford when I had been wretched with unhappiness and fear that Mum was going to leave Dad. Hilary and her two fat friends had decided I was 'a stuck-up cow' and got everyone to call me, 'Her Majesty'. Whenever I opened my mouth in class Hilary led a chorus of, 'Ooh, la-di-*dah*.'

In her letter there was no mention of any of that, however. She congratulated me on the success of *Mimi's Remedies* and said she would 'love us to get together'.

'Yeah, now that you're famous,' Anton had scorned, speaking out of one side of his mouth because of his filling. 'Tell her to go and fuck herself. Or if you like I'll do it for you.'

'Let's just ignore it,' I said, chucking the letter in the bin and thinking: How peculiar people are. Did Hilary really think we would meet? Had she no shame?

I decided to ring Nicky about it; Nicky had also been bullied by Hilary. Then I decided *not* to ring Nicky. She and Simon kept having Anton and me over for dinner and I was acutely embarrassed that although we now had a house, we still could not repay their hospitality.

I turned back to my post.

Today it was a letter from a woman called Beth who had sent me her manuscript a month earlier, asking me to forward it to my editor, which I had done. However, Tania must not have liked it enough to publish it because this was an angry couple of pages, letting me know what a selfish person I was. Thanks a bunch, Beth said. So nice of me to destroy her chance of being published, especially when I had everything. She had thought I was a good person but, boy, had she been wrong. She would never buy another of my books again for as long as she lived and she would tell everyone she knew what a piece of work I was.

I knew Beth's career setbacks were not my fault but, never-theless, the attack upset me and made me tremble a little. The delights of the post at an end, it was time to – aaagghh! – do some writing.

My new book was about a man and a woman who had been childhood chums and had met again as adults on Friends Reunited. Almost thirty years earlier, when they had both been five years old, together they had witnessed a murder. At the time they had not understood what they had seen, but their reunion had unlocked and recontextualized long-dormant memories. They were both married to other people but as they began to explore what they thought might have happened, they became closer to each other. As a result their marriages were suffering. It was not what I wanted to write, it made me unhappy, but it was still what my fingers persisted in typing.

I frowned at my screen to show that I meant business, and off I went. I did my best. I typed words, yes, they were definitely words – but were they any good?

I yawned. Sleepiness settled on me like a blanket and I found it hard to concentrate. I had had very interrupted sleep the night before. And the night before. And the night before that . . .

Most nights Ema woke two or three times and even though, in theory, Anton and I shared the getting-up, in practice I did most of it. Partly my own fault – I had to check for myself that she was OK; and partly her fault – in the middle of the night she preferred me to Anton.

I would make myself a cup of coffee. Just as soon as Zulema went out for the afternoon; I simply could not bear to have to stand in the 'kitchen' and make 'conversation' with her while I waited for the kettle to boil. Alert for noises of her departure, I waited. I longed to put my head down and have a short nap but, inevitably, Zulema would catch me and she thought I was pitiful enough as it was.

Then I heard her frogmarching Ema back out. I hurried to the kitchen, made my coffee, then resumed 'work'.

When my word-counter told me I had done five hundred words, I stopped. But in my heart I knew that about four hundred and seventy of the five hundred were rubbish. If only this book would not persist in being a sad one.

Looking for advice – or at least distraction – I rang Miranda. Yes, Miranda England, *that* Miranda. When we had met at my catastrophic first signing, I had thought she was as faraway and remote as the stars. But we had run into each other at a couple of subsequent publishing events – the Dalkin Emery sales conference and the author party – and she had been a lot warmer. Anton said she was only being nice because I was a success now, and perhaps there was some truth in that. But she was different to the person I had first thought she was, and when I discovered she had been having a terrible time trying to have a baby, it humanized her for me.

She had finally managed to get pregnant and had taken time off from writing to avoid having a miscarriage, but she was still available to listen to my writing woes.

'I'm stuck,' I said, and explained my dilemma.

'When in doubt,' she advised, 'put in a sex scene.' But I could not write a sex scene. Dad might read it.

All at once, I became aware of the noise of a lorry chugging outside. At that moment the doorbell rang and voices sounded from the front step. Male voices. Shouty, tarry, cement-coated male voices. I thought I overheard the word 'cunt'. Could it be . . . ?

I glanced through my little window. They had arrived! Macko and his team had finally arrived to fix my house!

'Miranda, I must go! Thank you.'

It had been worth losing my toner and night-cream. I could have kissed Zulema. Had I not been afraid of being turned into a pillar of salt.

I opened the front door and let the Mad Paddys stomp in. Because they all looked the same, I was never sure exactly how many there were but today there appeared to be four. The pick-up that chugged on the spot outside contained big, thick pieces of wood – the elusive lintels! Shouting and trying to order each other about, the Mad Paddys carried them upstairs, dislodging lumps from the walls and sizeable chips from the coving. (Original, irreplaceable, but at the time I was happy enough to overlook it.)

I rang Anton. 'They're here! With the lintels! They're removing the old ones as we speak! Leaving enormous holes in the walls!'

Silence. More silence.

'Anton? Did you hear me?'

'Oh, I heard you alright. I'm just so happy I might puke.'

For the rest of the day I sat in my study trying to write while a team of builders swarmed over my house shouting, banging and calling each other 'cunts'. I sighed happily. All was well with the world.

When Anton came home from work he looked around furtively and mouthed, 'Is she still here?' He meant Zulema.

'She's left for the day but the boys are still here!'

'Jayzus.' He was impressed. On the rare days they came, they tended to slope off at about four.

'I have a suggestion,' I said. 'But you're not going to like it.'

He eyed me warily.

'Because they're here in person, let's have a word with them,' I said. 'It will have more impact than doing it over the phone. We need to praise them for the good work they've done.' I had read this in some article on how to manage staff. 'Then we have to, you know, *scare* them into finishing off the work. Kind of like good cop, bad cop. How about it?'

'So long as I can be the good cop.'

'No.'

'Arse.'

'Come on.' I led him into our front room, where the lads were sitting on the new lintels, drinking tea, ankle-deep in sugar granules.

'Macko, Bonzo, Tommo, Spazzo.' I nodded at each one politely. (I was *fairly* sure these were their names.) 'Thank you for coming back, and removing the old lintels. Those lintels are well and truly, er . . . removed. If you replace the new lintels as efficiently as you removed the old ones, we will be very happy.'

Then I dug Anton in the back and urged him forward. 'As you know, lads, you were meant to be finished more than three weeks ago,' he said sternly, then seemed to lose his nerve. He clutched his head and said, 'Please, lads, we're going mad here. There's a small child involved. Er, thank you.'

We took our leave, and as soon as we had closed the door, the room exploded with guffaws. I swung the door open again; Macko was wiping his eyes and saying, 'Poor cunts.'

We backed out once more. Anton and I presented wary looks to each other and I was the first to speak. 'Well,' I said. 'I think that went rather well.'

Anton and I were in bed. It was only eight o'clock but we were in the back bedroom, the only room in the house with intact walls. We had moved the television in three weeks earlier and since then we pretty much lived in there. Because there was nothing for us to sit on, we were in bed.

I was flicking through the Jo Malone catalogue, wishing I could climb through the glossy pages and live in it; it was a serene, fragrant, dust-free world. Anton was watching a sitcom because he was putting together a deal with Chloe Drew, the young, hot lead, and Ema was marching about purposefully in her vest and pants combo and favourite pink wellies that she even slept in. Her round, squeezy thighs could have been made of latex.

'Ema, you look like the circus strongman,' Anton flicked his eyes from the TV. 'All you're missing is the handlebar moustache.'

Ema had a selection of her favourite things – Jessie, her beloved wrench; a curly dog, which Viv, Baz and Jez had given her, also called 'Jessie' and an old moccasin of Anton's, which *also* answered to the name 'Jessie' – which she was moving from one part of the room to the other, lining them up according to some vision only she was privy to. 'Dinky,' she said.

Her hair grew strangely with two long pieces framing her face, but shorter at the back and on top. She looked like a mod – even at times like Paul Weller – but was the most adorable creature. I could have watched her for ever.

I waited until Anton's programme had finished before showing him the piece in *Book News* about Gemma. I watched him reading it, studying his face, trying to gauge his response.

'What do you think?' I asked. 'And please don't be all optimistic and say it means nothing.'

'OK,' he said. 'It's a bit freaky. How did she manage to get both your agent and your editor?'

If Anton, optimist of the century, thought it a bit freaky, it must be catastrophic.

'The book isn't about us, Jojo said.'

'Well, that's good. Better than a poke in the eye with a sharp stick.'

'But Gemma told Jojo to say hello to me. The whole thing . . . I know it's illogical but I feel this awful . . . *dread*. Like something terrible is going to happen.'

'What sort of something terrible?'

'I don't know. Just a feeling I have, that she's going to destroy everything for us, for you and me.'

'You and me? She can't touch us.'

'Tell me that you will always love me and never leave me.'

He looked at me with the utmost seriousness. 'But you know that.'

'So say it.'

'Lily, I will always love you and never leave you.'

I nodded. Good. That should help.

'Would it make you feel any bit more secure if we got married?' Anton asked.

I winced. Getting married would fast-track any dormant disasters.

'I'll take that as a no, then. Better take the twenty-grand ring back to Tiffany's in that case.'

Ema shoved her wrench at me; it clanged off my teeth. 'Lily, kiss.'

I gave the wrench a big smacker.

Entirely unprovoked, Ema had started calling Anton and me by our first names. This had alarmed us terribly, we did not want people thinking we were liberal Islington types. To lead by example, we had taken to calling each other Mum and Dad.

'Now bring your wrench and get a kiss from Dad.'

'Anton,' she corrected me, with a frown.

'Dad,' I said.

'Anton.'

After Anton had kissed the wrench, he said, 'I have a present for you.'

'Not a twenty-grand ring from Tiffany's, I hope.'

He fished his arm under the bed on his side and produced a Jo Malone bag. It was a replacement of the toner I had given Zulema.

'Anton! We're skint!'

'Not for ever. When me and Mikey pull off this deal, we'll be loaded. And there's your royalty dosh coming at the end of September.'

'OK,' I was already mollified. 'My pores thank you. But why are you giving me a present?'

'We have to live a little. And I'm hoping you'll have sex with me.'

'You don't have to give me presents to get me to have sex with you.' I smiled.

He smiled back.

'Just ring the builders for my next three turns,' I said. 'And I'll do anything you want.'

'Deal.'

26

Another week passed. And another. Macko and the boys continued to appear spasmodically and unexpectedly – enough to keep us balanced precariously on a knife-edge of hope – but not so often that anything meaningful was achieved. They had removed the old lintels, but done very little about installing the new ones.

Having holes in the bedroom wall is fine in July and August – agreeable even – but not when it is almost September and the weather is heading towards autumn.

Every morning, I felt as though I was holding my breath until one of them arrived and Anton rang me about twenty times a day to see if anyone had showed.

I bartered away most of my phone obligations – I was having *a lot* of sex with Anton, and Zulema had just about cleared me out – so I did not get to hear most of the builders' inventive excuses, but according to Anton they were good; Spazzo broke his wrist, Macko's uncle died, Bonzo's uncle died, Tommo's van was stolen, then *his* uncle died.

'What is this?' Anton raged. 'Dead Uncle Week?'

Then, just when we managed to get a couple of days without anyone's uncle dying, it rained; the new lintels could not go in while it was raining. For four unprecedented weeks the weather had been glorious but as soon as we needed it to be dry, it rained.

I was being dragged, dragged up from the bottom of the sea. With effort I broke the surface of sleep. Woken by the sound of Ema crying, the fourth time tonight. It had been a bad night, even by Ema's standards.

'I'll go,' Anton said.

'Thanks.' I tumbled back into a coma. Then someone was shaking my shoulder and I was a dead weight, trying to hoist myself to consciousness. It was Anton. 'She's sick. She's puked on herself.'

'Change her clothes and bedclothes.'

It felt only two seconds later when I was again pulled up from the bottom of the ocean. 'I'm sorry, baby, she wants you.'

I must wake up, I must wake up, I must wake up.

I forced myself from my bed, one of the hardest things I have ever done and went to Ema. Her face was bright red, her room smelt of sick and she was still grinning like a loon.

'Lily!' She was thrilled to see me, even though it was only fifty minutes since the last time.

I lifted her to me; she was so hot. She rarely got ill. She was a hardy little creature who, when she fell over and sustained the kind of bumps that had other children shrieking the house down, just rubbed her wounded limb and got up. In fact she was so hardy that there were times when she mocked other children who had hurt themselves and were crying: she laughed at them, then screwed her knuckles in her eyes and went, 'Boo hoo, hoo,' mimicking their wails. (I had tried to stop her from doing this because it went down extraordinarily badly with the other mothers.)

'Let's take your temperature.'

Her armpit temperature was 98.1, ear 98.3, oral, 98.5, rectal – 'Sorry, darling' – 98.6. In every orifice, no matter what way you looked at it, she was OK.

I checked for a rash, then lifted her neck to see if it was stiff. 'Oi,' she said. That worried me, so I did it a few more times, until she began to laugh.

'You're fine,' I told her. 'Go back to sleep. I have to write a book tomorrow.'

She placed her hand over her eyes and sang, 'I see you.'

'Darling, it's quarter past four in the morning, visibility is terrible.'

I sat down in the rocking chair, hoping to lull her back to sleep when, to my enormous astonishment, a head appeared at the bedroom window. A man who looked to be in his early forties. It was a moment before I realized he was a burglar. I had always thought burgling was a young man's game. Evidently, he had climbed up the scaffolding. We looked at each other through the window, frozen in surprise.

'Don't bother,' I said. 'We have nothing.'

He did not move.

'Our Venezuelan au pair refused to live in,' I called, holding Ema tight to me. 'She would prefer to stay in Cricklewood with a man she barely knows. A man called Bloggers. I had some expensive skin-care but she's cleaned me out. It's all in Cricklewood now.'

I let that information settle and when I looked again, the burglar had gone as silently as he had arrived. Then I went back to my bedroom, woke Anton and told him what had happened.

'This is fucking ridiculous,' he said. 'I'll talk to Macko in the morning.'

True to his word, first thing, Anton got on the phone with jauntiness born of terrible rage.

'Morning, Macko. Any chance of seeing you and your colleagues today? No? Why's that then? A death in the family? Don't tell me who, let me guess. Your dog? Your fourteenth cousin, once removed? Oh, your father? That must be, ooh, the third time this month your old man has passed over. Another bout of death, eh? He really should try a course of cod liver oil.'

Anton fell silent, listened, listened some more, then muttered something and hung up. 'Shit!'

'What?'

'Macko's father really has died. He was crying. They'll never come back now.'

I was in despair. I could not blame Gemma for this, but I decided I would anyway.

*

Later that morning, I had reason to think once more of Gemma: Tania Teal biked over a completed copy of *Crystal Clear*. It was a beauty, an impressively weighty hardback with a cover similar to *Mimi's Remedies*. That cover had been a slightly blurry oil-painting of a pretty, witchy woman against a background of duck-egg blue. This was a slightly blurry oil-painting of a pretty, witchy woman against a lavender background. It actually looked like the *same* slightly blurry oil-painting until I compared it with *Mimi's Remedies* and saw there were tons of differences. The *Mimi's Remedies* woman had blue eyes. The *Crystal Clear* lady had green eyes. The *Mimi's Remedies* woman wore button boots. The *Crystal Clear* woman wore kitten heels. *Tons* of differences.

It would go on sale in two months' time, on the twenty-fifth of October, but from tomorrow would be on sale in the airports. 'Good luck, little book,' I said and kissed it, trying to protect it from whatever black magic Gemma had spun.

If I had not died of exhaustion by tonight, I would bring it to Irina's.

Irina's circumstances had changed. She had met a Ukrainian 'businessman' called Vassily who had plucked her from grim old Gospel Oak and installed her in a serviced apartment in St John's Wood. He was bonkers about her. She still worked part-time but that was only out of love of Clinique, not because she needed the money. 'I think of having to live without the free semples and I think I might die.' (She had struck her breast dramatically, then flipped a compact to examine her lipline.)

I had already visited her in her new home: a large, three-bedroomed apartment in a purpose-built block boasting a service entrance. Green leaves clustered at the second-floor windows and even though this was the home of a Russian kept-woman who was being bankrolled by a Ukrainian gangster, it felt terribly respectable. A little bit more gold than I would choose, but all in all, it was very nice. I especially admired the lack of dust.

27

We sent flowers to Macko's dad's funeral and he must have forgiven us because the following Monday four of the builders appeared. They had an unfamiliar air of purpose about them and it looked like the lintels might finally be installed when Bonzo veered around too quickly and accidentally stuck a scaffolding pipe through the stained-glass fanlight over the front door, shattering it as if he was splintering light.

I had endured these neanderthals discussing my au pair's nipples, spending far too much time in my bathroom with the *Sun*, and teaching Ema how to swear in Irish, all without a word of complaint. But the fanlight was old, beautiful and irreplaceable. It was too much for me. Everything, all the waiting and disappointment and terror that the house would never be finished, tumbled in on top of me and, in full view of Bonzo, Macko and Tommo, I cried my heart out.

Weeks of exhaustion, money worries, trying to write a book that did not want to be written and dread of what Gemma would do to my family, all washed out through my eyes.

Tommo, the most soft-hearted of all of them said, awkwardly, 'Ah, now.'

But as punishment for criticizing him, even obliquely, Bonzo stalked out. Then he stalked back in again and angrily summoned his colleagues, who trooped sheepishly after him. Two days later, they had not yet returned and I hit rock bottom. Every time something went wrong I thought of Gemma. I feared she had magical powers. Bad ones. She was Darth Vader to my Luke Skywalker and Voldemort to my Harry Potter and – illogically – I felt she was orchestrating the demise of every good thing in my life. I tried telling Anton, but he – quite sensibly – said it was nothing to do with Gemma.

'Even *I* feel homicidal,' he said. 'The Dalai fucking Lama himself would lose his equilibrium in this house.'

We talked about getting another crew in to finish the job but we had no money and would not have until I got my royalty cheque at the end of September, a month away.

Anton was too depressed to have sex and I had given Zulema every cosmetic I owned except for my Jo Malone flight bag, so I had no choice but to ring Macko and ask for Bonzo to return.

'You've hurt him,' Macko said. *As I was hurt*, his tone said, *when your live-in lover mocked the death of my only father.*

'I'm sorry,' I said. 'I didn't mean to hurt him.'

'He's sensitive.'

'I really am sorry.'

'I'll talk to him and see what I can do.'

The phone rang. It was Tania Teal. But her voice was stretched thin and she was speaking very quickly.

'Yes, Lily, news, good news really. Decided to redo the jacket for *Crystal Clear*. Old one, very pretty, but too similar to *Mimi's Remedies*. Done a new one, biking it over to you for approval.'

'Oh. I see.'

'Good really. Don't want confusion with *Mimi's Remedies*.'

'Are you OK, Tania?'

'Fine,' she said. 'Yes, fine, fine. But need fast appro. Must get to printer today. Can't miss our pub date. Bike on its way now. Ring me if it's not there in half an hour, I'll send another.'

Within half an hour the new cover arrived. It was brown and blurry, very serious-looking. The polar opposite of the current jacket, but actually far more appropriate for the book. I liked it. I rang Tania who was still talking a mile a minute.

'You like it? Good, great. Obviously the airport editions have the lavender cover but when the book comes out in the real world, it'll have this new one.'

'And you're sure you're OK?'

'Yes, fine, fine.'

Something's going on.

It was quite the Dalkin Emery day because then Otalie, my publicity person, rang.

'Great news! *Elevenses* want you on!'

Elevenses was a cheesy daytime television show; despite its name, it was on from ten-thirty to midday and was presented by two women who allegedly hated each other but treated each other with disturbing sweetness. It got massive viewership.

'I know *Crystal Clear* isn't out yet, but it's national television, too good a chance to pass up!'

'When do they want me?'

'Friday.'

The day after tomorrow. I spasmed with fear. I was a mess. Again I thought of Gemma; if she were to go on *Elevenses*, she would look stunning. Gemma had sharp suits, glossy (thick) hair and high heels, she always looked groomed. At the best of times I was a mess and these were not the best of times.

'Lovely!' I said, hung up and rang Anton.

'I have to go on *Elevenses* on Friday!' I was almost shrieking. 'National fucking television! And I hate myself. I have no clothes, I still haven't got my Burt Reynolds-style weave and I hate myself.'

'You already said that. Let's go shopping.'

'Anton! I need you to be practical. I need you to HELP ME!'

'Meet me under Selfridges clock in an hour –'

'We can't go to Selfridges. WE HAVE NO MONEY.'

'We have credit cards.'

'WHAT ABOUT EMA?'

'I'll ring Zulema on her mobile and ask her to stay late.'

'SHE'LL BLEED YOU DRY!'

'So be it.'

He was so calm that it began to affect me.

'Selfridges,' he repeated. 'One hour, we'll kit you out.'

'Anton.' I managed to hook some air and drag it down into me. 'Seriously, we have no money.'

'Seriously, we have two credit cards. Which are not up to their limits. I don't know about you, but I'm never comfortable with a credit card that isn't at its limit. I get that nagging feeling, like I've left the gas on . . .'

He was already waiting when I showed up, my face like thunder. I reached him and kept walking. 'Come on. I need black trousers and some type of top. As cheap as possible.'

'No.' He stopped and made me stop too. 'No. We're going to have fun with this. You deserve it.'

'Let's go to the ground floor. The clothes there are reasonably priced.'

'No. We're going to the unreasonably priced second floor. That's where the good stuff is.'

I took a breath. Another one, then I surrendered to him. I felt myself do it, like it was an actual physical sensation. He was taking charge so I did not have to feel guilty. Responsibility lifted, leaving me giddy, almost airborne.

'Remember, Lily, we're not here for a long time, we're here for a good time.'

'OK. Lead on.'

On the second floor, Anton began pulling clothes from rails and loading up his arms. He chose things I had not even noticed and although some were unwearable, some surprised me with their desirability. This was a metaphor for my life with Anton: he expanded my vision, made me look at life, and clothes – and myself – in a new way.

In no time he had bagged an assistant, who picked up on his mood; between the two of them they drowned me in beautiful clothes.

He urged me to try tons of things: short leather skirts,

'Because you have the legs, Lily.' Sexy black Lycra dresses, with panels cut out, 'Because you have the skin, Lily.'

I tried out several identities – I was an angular rock-chick, a soignée French film star, a Prada-clad librarian. My black fear had dissipated and I was laughing and having fun. This was Anton at his very best; a man of big gestures, extravagance and vision.

Since we had first got together, he had regularly bought me presents – things I would not buy for myself because they were so indulgent. Like my Jo Malone flight bag, which I had read about in a magazine and longed for like a six-year-old girl longs for a pink bike. I rarely went on flights, I did not *need* a perfect little bag of goodies but Anton, with his incredible attention to detail noticed that I *wanted* it. And although I berated him for spending money we did not have, I loved it so much I slept with it. It was the one thing I had not – and would not – give to Zulema.

He fully indulged this you-may-not-need-it-but-do-you-want-it sensibility as he ferried clothes to and from the changing room. I was forbidden from knowing the price of anything and he said, 'I will only close this changing-room door if you promise not to look at the tags.'

After over an hour of trying beautiful things, I made my decision: a pair of black trousers with a breathtaking cut and a strange torn top which revealed my shoulders. Anton also persuaded me to buy one of the short leather skirts and a clingy, cashmere dress.

'Can I wear the trousers and top now?' I asked.

Compared to these beautiful duds, the clothes I had come in were elderly and saggy. Having endured months of dust and squalor I discovered I was *longing* for shiny new things.

'You can do whatever you like.'

Anton went to the cash desk to pay and from the wistful looks on the girls' faces, they were thinking he was a flash fuck and I was a spoilt bitch. If only they knew that both Anton and I were praying for the card not to be declined.

But the card was not declined and the dress, the skirt and my nasty old clothes were wrapped in tissue. As we moved away from the cash desk, Anton said, 'Now for the shoes.'

'What shoes? You're pushing your luck.'

'No need to push it, the luck is with us.'

That was how it was with Anton. If you got him on a good day, life with him was supercharged. I went along, happy to be compliant; it took him moments to find the perfect shoes – boots, actually. I tried them on and they seemed to nuzzle my feet, whispering reassurance.

Anton watched me and his face was set. 'They're yours.'

'They're Jimmy Choos! I don't even want to know what they cost!'

'You're a best-selling author. You deserve Jimmy Choo boots.'

'OK.' I could not contain a – mildly hysterical – giggle. 'Why the hell not?'

'Do you want to wear them right now?'

'Yes. And what shall I do about my hair?'

'Blanaid's got you an appointment tomorrow morning in some new groovy Soho place.' Blanaid was his and Mikey's assistant. 'She says all the models go there. She hasn't booked you for a follicle transplant,' he said quickly. 'I don't think they do that. But they'll blow-dry it the way you like it.'

'With volume,' I said anxiously.

'Yes, with volume, that's what I told her to say.'

'And what about my nails? I can't paint them myself, I get varnish all over my fingers.'

'I can ask Blanaid to get you a manicure. Or I can paint them myself.'

'You, Anton Carolan?'

'Aye. In my youth I used to paint model soldiers with some degree of precision. At the time I was accused of being a geek, but I knew it'd come in handy some day. I also painted my van with the Furry Freak brothers. I'd broken my leg and couldn't get around on my bike so I took up painting instead. I'll do your nails.'

'Fabulous!'

The purchase of the boots went through without any drama – it was that kind of day – then we left. On the ground floor, as we cut through the cosmetic department, we were assailed by a perky girl who asked if I would like a make-over. I hurried on; I could see daylight. I was terrified of those women, although they usually blanked me.

'Lily,' Anton called, 'do you want a make-over?'

Frantically I shook my head and mouthed, 'NO!'

'Come back,' he coaxed. 'Let's see what she –' he looked at her badge – 'what Ruby has to say.'

Although I did not want to, I found myself sitting on the low-backed high stool having a cotton ball wiped over my face, while passers-by sniggered at me.

'You have good skin,' Ruby said.

'She does, doesn't she?' Anton beamed. 'That's mostly down to me. I buy stuff for her.'

'What brand do you usually use?' Ruby asked me.

'Jo Malone,' Anton answered, 'Prescriptives and Clinique. Although I don't buy her the Clinique stuff, she gets it free from her mate Irina.'

'I'm going to apply a light base,' Ruby said.

'Good,' I said. Any base, light or heavy, was good. Sitting in the middle of Selfridges with a naked face was too bloody. Sod's law said I would meet someone I knew. *Gemma* flashed into my head, even though Gemma lived in Dublin.

Ruby did her stuff, while Anton asked questions. 'What's that pink gear?' 'How do you get the eyeliner to go on so thin?' And when she was finished I looked like me, only far, far nicer.

'You're beautiful, Babe,' Anton told me, then to Ruby, 'She's going to be on *Elevenses* on Friday morning. She'll probably wear this top. Have you anything to make her shoulders shiny?'

Ruby produced an iridescent compact and a big fat make-up brush and buffed up my shoulders.

'We'll have to take that,' Anton said. 'And the pink gear and the thin eyeliner, so Lily can do it herself at home.' To me he said, 'It's an investment.'

I gave him a look. This was not an investment but, caught up in the mood, I did not care.

'Anything else you'd like?' he asked.

'Perhaps the base,' I said, in a little voice. 'And I liked the lipstain.'

'Both of them, so,' Anton told Ruby. 'And sure, fire in the mascara while you're at it. After all her work,' Anton murmured to me, as Ruby crouched down to retrieve products from drawers, 'it would have been criminal not to buy something.'

Before she sealed the bag, Ruby threw in several free samples.

'That's fantastic,' Anton said. 'That's so nice of you.'

'Oh.' Ruby seemed surprised by the extent of his gratitude. 'Have a few more.' She grabbed another handful and chucked them into the bag and I smiled to myself.

Anton was without guile and I loved how people loved him. He flirted non-stop, but never in a sleazy way.

Then Ruby handed over the glossy bag and we left the store.

I was high: high from shopping, high from looking good, high at my shiny dust-free newness.

'I don't want to go home.'

'That's good because you're not going home. Zulema is on duty. We're going out, you and me.'

He took me to a private members' club in Soho, where he seemed to know everyone. But we sat in a secluded corner, in a padded-leather booth and everyone stayed away. Anton did not ask me what I wanted to drink; there was never any doubt that we would have champagne. I sat in my shiny new clothes and shiny new face and forgot, for a while, our destroyed house, sugar-coated floors and ever-present Gemma-generated dread.

I felt glamorous, beautiful and madly in love.

The groovy hairdresser in Soho volumized my hair beautifully, Anton did a wonderful job on my nails and my new clothes and boots were perfect.

I only discovered at the last minute that the reason I was on *Elevenses* was because they were doing a feature on mugging. They had zero interest in me or my books, they just wanted to know how bad my mugging had been.

'Were you hospitalized?' one of the 'sympathetic' interviewers asked in an exaggerated 'caring' tone.

'No.'

'No? Oh dear.' She was so disappointed that I told her how I had feared I might miscarry, and that cheered her up.

Afterwards I had phone messages from Viv, Baz and Jez saying how proud they were of me, and from Debs saying, 'I know you're short of money, but surely you didn't have to wear rags.' A reference to my fabulous new top. 'Hahaha,' she tinkled.

28

September saw both advances and reverses in our fortunes.

Anton and Mikey had spent much of the summer pulling together a big, glitzy deal – a hot edgy script, finance from three dependable sources and commitments from young, hot actress Chloe Drew and up-and-coming director Sureta Pavel. This was the deal that would make Eye-Kon; it was all gelling satisfactorily and contracts were ready to be signed when the script attracted sudden Hollywood interest. Before you could say 'knife' the script was withdrawn and the whole deal collapsed like a house of cards. It plunged Anton into a black depression.

Witnessing his despair was truly frightening because his default state was irrepressible optimism. But too many deals had gone wrong for him to bounce back this time. He talked about what a failure he was, how he had let me and Ema down, and he began making noises about seeking out an alternative career. 'Bar-tending, perhaps,' he said, prone in bed. 'Or bee-keeping.'

On the plus side, something about his dark, brooding despair affected the builders. Without us even having to chivvy them, they quietly installed three out of four of the new lintels and even began to replaster the main bedroom.

For a whole week Anton stayed away from work. 'I've no stomach for it,' he said. 'It's so hard to get good material, this was our big chance. I feel it'll never come right for us.'

He spent a lot of time with Ema. He had somehow managed to shake Zulema for the week. I suspected – but did not ask – that he had had to pay her to stay away.

*

Anton stood at the door of my study and watched me typing. Several emotions fought on his face. 'You work so hard,' he said, then called, 'Ema, where are you?'

Ema marched in, wearing a red and blue horizontal-striped all-in-one vest and shorts. Anton watched her tenderly.

'You look like a Hungarian weightlifter,' he said, then after further scrutiny, '*circa* 1953.'

I knew then he was getting better.

However, he never fully returned to his old self. He made countless references to how hard I worked, to the fact that any money coming in was generated by me and that if it wasn't for me, we would have nothing.

It frightened me because even though at that precise time, all of our income was being produced by me, I had not considered that situation to be a permanent one. In fact, I was poised constantly for Anton, with all his ideas and energy, to suddenly start generating enough money to keep us safe. I did not enjoy the feeling that everything – from our home to our food – depended on me.

On the last day of September, my first royalty cheque for *Mimi's Remedies* arrived. It was for such a ridiculously large sum – one hundred and fifty thousand pounds – that it seemed like a joke cheque. I wept with pride. From the dusty shelf I took down a *Mimi's Remedies*, gazed at all the little words and marvelled at how they had resulted in this money, which was guaranteeing our home ... The whole thing was a miracle, from the book's unhappy genesis to unlikely success.

Anton took a photo of me holding the cheque, like a pools' winner – then I kissed it goodbye because almost all of it was committed elsewhere. To the bank, the builders, the credit card people ...

'Only you and I could get a cheque for a hundred and fifty grand and two days later be left with almost nothing!' I said to Anton.

'But we've spent it on good stuff,' he said. 'Look at us –

responsible adults. We've paid the first instalment on the house to the bank, now they won't repossess.'

I winced. I was the wrong person to appreciate repossession jokes.

'Sorry.' He noticed. 'Youthful high spirits.'

'And our next instalment is due –'

'On the thirtieth of November, when you've signed your new contract with Dalkin Emery.' He paused and I felt one of his declines coming on. Not today. Not when we had reason to be cheerful! 'I hate that all the burden is on you,' he said, miserably.

'Don't,' I begged. 'At least don't hate it today. Take a day off.'

'I'm depressed!'

Miranda England was on the phone.

'Hormones,' I said. 'It happens when you're pregnant.'

'It's not hormones. It's fucking Amazon. I just went online – I don't know why I do this to myself – and my latest book is only averaging three and a half stars. The previous one has five. And the reviews from readers are so fucking mean!'

'Oh dear,' I said, ineffectually. 'They really can be horrible.'

'You've nothing to worry about,' she said gloomily. 'I looked up *Mimi's Remedies*. They love you. Nearly every review gives it five stars. They'd give it six if they could.'

I should not have done it.

After she hung up, I went to Amazon and looked up *Mimi's Remedies* and spent some happy minutes scrolling through page after page of glowing five-star praise for *Mimi's Remedies*.

But pride comes before a fall because then – and this is where I should have stopped – I wondered if anyone had written anything about *Crystal Clear*. Although it was not due out until the end of October, early copies had gone on sale in the airports.

I typed in 'Crystal Clear' and was excited to discover that there were reviews already! Only three, but a start.

Then I saw the header from the first review and felt a little sick. 'Piss Poor' it said. 'Piss Poor from a reader in Darlington.'

Of the star rating, she had given me one out of five. At least she had given me one, I thought, clutching at straws. Then I began to read.

The only reason I gave this book one star is because it's not possible to give none.

Oh.

I pissed myself laughing at Mimi's Remedies, but there is not one good laugh in this bag of shite. I bought it in the airport on the way to a week in the sun and I wish I'd saved my money and bought myself an extra Sex on the Beach instead.

Oh dear. Oh God. With a thumping heart, I rushed onto the next one, hoping it would be nicer. It was a two-star score.

Back on the SSRIs from a reader in Norfolk.

I had been depressed and not left the house for almost six months when I read Mimi's Remedies. It cheered me up so much I was able to go back to Weight Watchers. Imagine my delight when I discovered that Lily Wright had a new book out. I asked my neighbour to bring me one from the airport when she was visiting her mum in Jersey. I hoped I would feel well enough to start looking for a part-time job after reading it. But have you read it? It's so depressing. It has set me back terribly. I have given two stars because even though I did not enjoy this book at all, I regard myself as a nice person.

The next one was also a two-star.

Extremely disappointed from an avid reader in the north-west.

*

I very much enjoyed Mimi's Remedies *even though it is not what I would normally read. (I am a great fan of Joanne Harris, Sebastian Faulks and Louis de Bernieres.) I must admit I was looking forward to reading Lily Wright's new book, as I felt she showed a good deal of promise in* Mimi's Remedies. *When I saw it in the airport (en route to an art appreciation weekend in Florence), I bought it. However, my hopes were stillborn.* Crystal Clear *is not a good book and I'm at a loss as to what to compare it to. It is almost (although obviously not quite!) as bad as chick-lit. It deserves only one star but I have decided to give it two simply for not being chick-lit!*

'An-TON,' I yelped. 'ANTONNNN!'

Skidding – almost surfing – on sugar, he arrived at speed and I showed him the reviews.

'What if everyone hates *Crystal Clear*?' I said. 'What if no one buys it? Dalkin Emery won't give me a new contract and we'll be buggered. It's not like my new book is any good!'

'Easy, now,' he said. '*Mimi's Remedies* got bad reviews too.'

'But only from smelly old reviewers. Not from real people, not from readers!'

Now I understood why Tania had been so high-pitched and peculiar about the cover change. They were worried that readers would expect a second *Mimi's Remedies* – as the three here had obviously done. Flooded with fear, my mouth tasted metallic.

This hellish mess could not be Gemma's doing – unless she had written all three reviews herself – but I decided to blame her anyway.

'*Crystal Clear* has to do fantastically well,' I gabbled at Anton, 'because if it doesn't, Dalkin Emery won't give me a new contract. And without a new contract, we won't have enough money to pay the next instalment on this house.'

Losing this house! My scalp crawled with terror. I could not imagine anything worse.

Calmly, Anton began to intone, '*Crystal Clear* is a great book. Dalkin Emery are doing a massive campaign for it. It will be a great success. Dalkin Emery have talked about it being a

Christmas number one. In a month's time Jojo will go to them and they will offer you a new contract with a huge advance. Everything will be fine. Everything *is* fine.'

PART THREE

Jojo

Since the day Olga and Richie busted Jojo and Mark having lunch in Antonio's, Jojo was anxious about everyone at work knowing. But apart from Skanky Boy frequently calling her 'Hojo', then denying it, no one else treated her differently.

In fact, without her even asking, both Dan Swann and Jocelyn Forsyth assured Jojo that when the time came in November to decide on the new partner, she'd be getting their vote. Considering Mark was already in the bag, she only needed one more and wondered who she should lobby. Jim Sweetman? Why bother even trying? Things had been gnarly between them for months, since the day Cassie Avery came into the office. *And* he'd gotten into bed with Richie Gant a long time ago. But the smart girl didn't hold grudges and Jojo saw nothing wrong with being nice to Jim. But not too nice because it was tacky to look needy, right?

Olga Fisher? Despite having busted her having lunch with Richie Gant, Jojo decided there was nothing to lose fighting back there either. So she bought her a video on the mating habits of Emperor Penguins and skipped any remarks about female solidarity. Olga was not one of those women.

And Nicholas and Cam in Edinburgh? Obviously, she'd met them lots but they'd never really bonded. They didn't come to London often and when they did they stayed just long enough to let everyone know how much they hated the place. 'Why,' they always groused, 'can't these bloody meetings take place in Edinburgh?'

They were a tricky pair. Nicholas was a fierce, beardy forty-something and Cam a super-pale Celt with pastel blue eyes, mid-brown hair and a fine line in bitchy comments.

Jojo tried corralling them one Friday after a meeting. 'Hey, Nicholas, I –'

'I hate this London place,' Nicholas moaned. 'Full of traffic –'

'– and English people,' he and Cam chanted together.

'C'mon, Cam, let's get the flock out of here.'

'Yes, but –' Jojo said, anxious to talk to them.

Nicholas turned a furious glare on her and Cam fixed her with his baby blues. 'We have a *flight* to catch.'

'Hey, sorry, I . . . Yeah, safe trip.'

Before their next visit to the London office, Jojo emailed them to suggest a lunch – nothing doing. Unless there were compelling reasons not to, Nicholas said, they liked to catch the three-thirty shuttle back to Edinburgh. Obviously Jojo didn't count as a compelling reason.

Damn, she thought. This pair were as hard to nail down as mercury and she could see only one other option. A little extreme, maybe, but it looked like the only way to have a proper conversation would be to go visit them.

Hey, not such a problem. She'd heard Edinburgh was beautiful and maybe Mark could also discover a reason to visit . . .

But it was hard to get a window. Cam went on holiday for three whole weeks in September, then Jojo had to attend the Frankfurt book fair, then Nicholas disappeared for a fortnight. They finally agreed to a meeting at the end of October, less than four weeks before Jocelyn left. Jojo was not happy about leaving it so late, but could be late was good. She'd be in their minds at the time of the vote.

She flew with Mark to Edinburgh obscenely early one Friday morning; she was seeing the guys in the a.m., Mark was meeting with them in the afternoon, then . . . weekend at leisure in a nice hotel. Yay!

On the plane she asked Mark, 'Any advice?'

'Whatever you do, don't patronize them. They're a little . . . shall we say . . . *touchy* about their satellite status. Especially because they do an astonishing amount of business. Scotland seems to have a disproportionate number of saleable writers. Think R-E-S-P-E-C-T.'

'Gotcha.'

Mark went to check into the hotel and Jojo got a cab to Lipman Haigh's Edinburgh HQ which was in a four-storeyed, grey-stone house in an ancient-looking crescent. Jojo loved it. Nicholas and Cam greeted her with polite, though not effusive, welcomes. But she was beaming. She was really happy to be here; it was all so *old*.

She was introduced to the seven other members of staff and showed around the offices, the mini-boardroom, even the kitchenette. 'This is where Nicholas and I microwave our lunchtime pot noodles.'

'Aye,' Nicholas growled, 'or our lean cuisines.'

Jojo didn't know if she should laugh. Safer not to, she thought.

Back in Nicholas's office, he said, 'But you've not come all this way just to admire our premises. What can we do for you, Jojo?'

Pretending this was just a social call felt dishonest; she was happier at the idea of it all being upfront.

'Guys, you've got something I want.'

'Och, I'm a happily married man,' Nicholas said.

'And I'm a pillow biter,' said Cam.

'Damn!' Jojo clicked her fingers. 'Foiled!'

'Anyhow,' Nicholas drawled, 'a little bird tells us that you're humping our Managing Partner.'

Jojo coloured. She hadn't expected this. Did this mean that all the partners knew? 'What little bird? Let me guess.'

'That spotty youngster, Richie Gant.'

She shrugged, keen to hide her anger. 'What can I say?'

'And the very same Mark Avery's coming in to see us later,' Nicholas turned to Cam and feigned surprise. 'Isn't that a coincidence, Cameron? Both of them here in Edinburgh on the same day?'

'Aye, Nicholas, a coincidence is right.'

'But they'd have come up on different flights, of course.'

'Of course,' Cam said and turned to Jojo, 'Did you?'

She forced a laugh. 'OK, you busted me.' Jeez, this pair were *tough*.

'Relax, doll,' Nicholas purred. 'Have your dirty weekend away. Where are you staying? Somewhere *gorr*geous? The Bal*morrr*al?'

Jojo inclined her head. Damn. She wished now she'd booked them into some grungy B&B with twin beds and a bathroom down the hall. It looked like she'd fitted this meeting in around her sexy mini-break and these guys were way touchy as it was.

'We don't like Richie Gant,' Nicholas said, languidly. 'Do we, Cam?'

'No,' Cam agreed, almost dreamily, 'he's heinous.'

'Might I suggest *o*dious.'

'At*rro*cious.'

'*Monnn*strous.'

'He's been to see you, right?'

'Oh aye. Months ago, soon as old Jock announced he was off.'

You had to hand it to the little fuck, Jojo thought. He doesn't miss a trick.

Keep smiling, she told herself. There was nothing else she could do. And try not to be patronizing, however you did that. Think R-E-S-P-E-C-T.

'So you know why I'm here?' She produced her presentation, which went through her list of authors, using pie-charts, graphs and venn-diagrams to show what excellent long-term prospects they were.

'Not now,' Nicholas waved it away. 'Leave it with us. We'll have a read of it when there's nothing good on telly.'

'Now we have you to ourselves, we want to know something about you.'

Jojo sighed theatrically. 'You want me to prove I'm a real red-head. The number of times . . .'

That made them laugh. Luckily.

'Tell us about you being a policewoman. Did you ever have sex in uniform? With a male colleague?'

'Oh Caaam,' Nicholas berated. 'You can't ask the girl that.'

'Sure he can!'

'So did you?'

''Fraid not. I'm sorry, Cam. But I did have sex with a firefighter – he was my first real boyfriend – and sometimes he was in uniform, well kinda, as much as he could be. And sometimes I wore his helmet.'

'Tell me more!'

'But I want to know about chasing the bad guys,' Nicholas said.

'I can multi-task.'

It wasn't quite what she'd expected from the meeting but if this was what it took to get her a partnership, then this was what she'd do. So she told them about the man who pulled a gun on his neighbour for having his TV on too loud, about finding a suicide victim hanging in a closet and about her dad's corrupt phase when he used to come home with household appliances that he insisted he'd paid for. She worked hard at making her stories dramatic and scary, and when it was time for Nicholas and Cam to leave for their lunch meeting, Nicholas said, 'Jojo, you're a tonic!'

'I know we joshed you a bit but we do appreciate you coming to see us,' Cam said. 'You're a good sport, not like that cry-baby Aurora Hall.'

'She's been too?'

'Her and that other Sloane, Lobelia French, and the chinless wonder, they've all been. We were wondering what was taking you so long. We thought we might have off*ain*ded you.' They leant into each other and shared yet another in-joke chuckle.

She stood up, extended her hand, said, 'Thank you for your time,' and turned to go.

Nicholas and Cam looked at each other – startled. 'No presents?'

Shit, Jojo thought. Richie Gant probably brought bottles of booze, cigars . . . dancing girls. And the Sloanes would have been able to bring ancient bottles of wine from Dad's cellar. She should have thought of this.

'No gifts,' she said sorrowfully. 'I didn't think of it.'

'We like gifts.'

'I'm sorry.'

'But we respect you for coming empty-handed.'

'You do? So am I in?' She grinned.

'We'll have to look at the records of all the candidates – *Goad*, how tedious – but we like you. Don't we?' He turned to Cam.

'Oh aye, we like you well enough.'

'I'm not heinous?'

'No. Or odious, atrocious or monstrous. In fact you're quite aro*maa*tic.'

'And pictur*esque*.'

'Ex*aac*tly. An area of outstanding natural beauty. Have a lovely, *saixy* weekend with the lovely, *saixy* Mark Avery.'

On Sunday night, when Jo touched down at Heathrow, she was happy. All in all, after a ropey start, her meeting with the Edinburgh partners could not have gone better.

* * *

Monday morning, early November

TO: Jojo.harvey@LIPMAN HAIGH.co
FROM: Mark.avery@LIPMAN HAIGH.co
SUBJECT: News. Possibly bad

Jocelyn's changed his leaving date to January. He started with Lipman Haigh in January thirty-seven years ago and, ever the traditionalist, he wants a nice round sum.

TO: Mark.avery@LIPMAN HAIGH.co
FROM: Jojo.harvey@LIPMAN HAIGH.co
SUBJECT: Thirty-seven isn't a nice round sum

!

J xxx

Brits, Jojo thought. Mad as cut snakes.

TO: Jojo.harvey@LIPMAN HAIGH.co
FROM: Mark.avery@LIPMAN HAIGH.co
SUBJECT: News. Possibly bad

This means the partnership decision won't be until January either.

Jojo stared at her screen. 'Shit.' She'd been totally geared for
the end of November. Her life, while it hadn't exactly been on
hold, had been way, way focused.

Monday night, Jojo's flat
'What do we do now?' Mark asked.
   'About what?'
   'About us.'
   Jojo lapsed into thought. 'We said we'd wait until after the
partnership decision. Nothing has changed. We just push it
back a couple of months.'
   'What's the point in waiting? Everyone in work knows
anyway, thanks to Richie Bigmouth.'
   'I thought we were on the same page here.'
   'I'm tired of waiting and everyone knows.'
   'But like you said in the summer, everyone knowing we're
having an affair isn't as bad as you leaving your wife and setting
up home with me. C'mon,' she cajoled Mark. 'There's not that
much longer to wait.'

But he wouldn't be persuaded. He was pissed off with her and didn't even try to hide it.

'You were the one who wanted to wait until after the partnership decision!' she said.

'But now that everyone knows, it's kind of moot. I'm going home.'

She heard the door close behind him. Oi, she thought. This didn't feel so good. And there was something else on her mind . . .

Wednesday morning

Jojo switched on her computer. She was anxious. The new best-seller list appeared at nine o'clock, every Wednesday morning and she was a little spooked about how Lily Wright's new hardback was doing. After the runaway success of *Mimi's Remedies*, everyone had blithely expected it to fly and in some of Dalkin Emery's more upbeat marketing meetings there had been talk of a Christmas number one. But, initially at least, Jojo had had slight, niggly doubts; *Crystal Clear* was a very different book to *Mimi's Remedies*. (Actually, it was excellent; an intelligent, compassionate slice of social commentary. But extreme realism, as opposed to *Mimi's Remedies*, which was *uber*-escapism.)

Tania had got Lily to send *Crystal Clear* to her without Jojo having seen it and by the time they'd involved Jojo it was a done deal – a little bit naughty of Tania. If Jojo *had* seen it she might have advised against publishing it, she might have suggested it would be better for Lily to take a year out and write another book. But she wasn't given the chance.

And it had to be said, Tania raved about *Crystal Clear* – and Tania knew her stuff. More importantly, she'd secured a massive advertising and marketing budget; clearly all of Dalkin Emery were on board. In May, just after Tania had accepted the book, Jojo had attended a preliminary marketing meeting and they were all so wildly gung-ho that even she was genuinely convinced. They were spending shedloads, everyone – booksellers, readers – loved Lily and *Crystal Clear* was a great book. This would work.

But there had been late-in-the-day wobbles. In August two supermarket chains halved their orders after their buyers read a proof copy and discovered how different *Crystal Clear* was to *Mimi's Remedies*. Then Dalkin Emery lost their nerve with the jacket – which was very similar to *Mimi's Remedies* – yanked it and replaced it with a more serious one.

Publication date had been the twenty-fifth of October. Early, but unscientific, reports from shop floors indicated that sales were slow but this list was the acid test.

Jojo scrolled down through the top ten: nothing. The top twenty: nothing. There was Eamonn Farrell, at 44, and Marjorie Franks, one of her thriller writers, holding steady at 61. But where was Lily? On she scrolled, down, down, down. I must have missed it, she thought – and then she spotted it, buried deep at number 168. In its first week on sale it had sold a pitiful 347 copies. Shit. *Crystal Clear* had been expected to debut in the top ten but it looked like it was sticking to the shelves.

'*Mimi's Remedies* was a slow starter,' Manoj reminded her.

'*Mimi's Remedies* didn't have a two hundred k campaign behind it.'

Right away, she got onto Patrick Pilkington-Smythe, Dalkin Emery's Head of Marketing, pushing for a bigger spend. 'We need more print ads, especially in Sunday papers, coming up to Christmas. And the cover price needs to come down.'

'Steady. Let's not do our headless-chicken act just yet,' Patrick drawled. 'Early days. Lot of big books out at the moment.' OK, maybe he had a point. From September onwards there was always a glut of hardbacks, published just in time to be considered for the Booker. Not to mention biographies from every F-list celeb in the country hoping to be bought as Christmas gifts. 'It'll pick up nearer to Christmas.'

Jojo's gameplan had been to open negotiations for Lily's new contract the week after *Crystal Clear* came out – like, *today*

– when, if everything had gone as it should, Lily's star would be at its zenith. Jojo had hoped she could do the negotiations in her sleep; that all she would have to agree with Dalkin Emery was whether they'd like to give Lily an obscene amount of money, or simply a disgusting quantity. Now she wasn't so sure.

On the plus side, Lily was about to start a three-week promotional tour. Perhaps that would kick-start sales.

She rang Tania Teal. Making sure she sounded upbeat and confident, she sang, 'Time to talk turkey. Lily Wright's new deal. We're ready for our close-up.'

'Close-up of what?'

Shit. Jojo kept it steady. 'Of her new contract.'

'Rii-iight. I see. You said she was working on something new? It would probably be best if I took a look at it. Like, before we settle on a figure.'

This was not the enthusiastic response Jojo had hoped for. Was this the same woman who had bugged her day and night last May, to sign a new deal?

But staying cheery, she said, 'Seven chapters of Lily Wright's FABULOUS new book being biked over to you right now. Get your cheque book ready!'

Wednesday evening

She met Becky after work for a quick pizza.

Once they were settled Jojo said, 'Guess what? My period's late.'

Becky became very still. 'How late?'

'Three days. I know it's nothing, but I'm always way regular. And I feel weird.'

'How?'

'Sort of . . . dizzy. And I sort of don't want to smoke.'

'Christ. Oh my God.' Becky bit her knuckles. 'Have you done a test?'

'This morning. Negative. But it's early, like, too early?'

490

'Could it have happened?'

'Mmmm, we use condoms but . . . accidents happen. And we did it right in the middle of the month. Easy to remember exactly when, when you're seeing a married man.'

'Less of the violins,' Becky said. 'Andy and I haven't had sex at all in the past month.'

'Are you two OK?'

'Never better. You just wait until you and Mark stop having sex, then you'll *really* be together. How d'you think Mark will take it?' Becky chose her words carefully. 'Is there a chance he might not be happy?'

Jojo considered. 'Sure.' She half-laughed. 'But he might be psyched. But what about me? Am I happy?'

'Are you?'

'It's not the right time to have a baby.'

'But it's never the right time – for anyone, not just you. By the time it's the right time, it's often too late.'

'You're right. A baby isn't the end of the world. It's just . . . I feel so bad for Cassie and the kids. This will make things far worse.'

'Maybe this is no accident,' Becky suggested. 'Perhaps he's trapping you. Or perhaps you're trapping yourself.' She sighed. 'Lucky you, I'd love to get up the duff but we can't afford to have a baby yet.'

'If I become a partner my income is actually going to drop over the next three years.'

'You what?'

'Partners have to invest money. Now that Jocelyn is leaving – if he EVER does – he's taking his moolah with him. The new partner will have to replace it.'

'How much?'

'Fifty grand.'

'*Fifty* grand? Where are you going to get that sort of money?'

'I'm not. So how they do it is they deduct it from future earnings and pay me fifty grand less over the next three years.'

Thursday evening, Becky and Andy's
Andy answered the door. 'Well?'

'Test is still negative. But . . .'

Andy shook his head, ruefully. 'My advice? Don't tell him. Just go away and quietly have a termination.'

'No way,' Jojo scorned. 'This is his problem too.'

'Oh-ho!' Andy clapped his hands together. 'This will separate the men from the boys.'

'Get over yourself.' But Jojo couldn't help wondering if Mark would run for the hills? Try to insist she had an abortion and hot-foot it back to the haven of his marriage? 'I'm going to tell him. And you know what? If he tries to dick me around, I'll laugh in his face.'

Friday evening, Jojo's flat
'Guess what?' Jojo said.

Mark looked at her, did a once-over and something changed in his eyes, as if he'd retreated. 'You're pregnant.'

She paused, startled. 'Damn, you're good. Well, my period is five days late, but the test is negative.'

'Doesn't mean a thing. Same with Cassie. Test kept showing up negative but she was pregnant alright.'

They stared at each other, taking in that statement, then both dissolved into horrified giggles.

'Fuck!' Jojo breathed. 'Well, we all know what happens next. This is the part where everything falls apart for me. You bail on me *and* you fix it so I get sacked.'

'Then you find out Cassie is also pregnant, slightly ahead of you and we're having a big party to renew our wedding vows.'

'I only find out when I get sent the invite by mistake.'

This was familiar stuff and it made them laugh.

'You should know this: my dad will go apeshit and want to kill you. He'll call on you late some night with my three brothers and a shotgun.'

'I'd better make an honest woman of you, in that case.'

Then the news seemed to hit him and he lapsed into silence. He wiped his hand across his mouth once, then again. 'Um, this kind of focuses the mind.'

'*Are* you going to run out on me?'

His hand froze and he looked up at her, horrified. 'No.'

'Correct answer.'

'But this is big stuff, Jojo. Big, unplanned stuff.'

'Duh! I had noticed.'

'I reckon I always assumed this would happen *sometime*. Us. Babies.' He paused and added dismally, 'But not this soon.'

'How bad do you feel?'

'Quite honestly, Jojo,' he met her eyes and she could tell he was wavering between fobbing her off and producing an answer that came from some very honest, deep-buried part of him, 'quite honestly, I would have preferred us to have some time together on our own, before children came along. Starting our life together already sharing it with someone else, I suppose I . . .' he sought the right word '. . . I resent it.' He sighed heavily. 'You know how much I love my kids. And I'll love ours too. But after the months of hole-and-corner stuff, I wanted us to have some –' he half-laughed at himself – 'uncomplicated time together.' He furrowed his brow. 'How did this *happen*?'

Jojo eyed him. 'The man agent went to bed with the lady agent and stuck his –'

'No, I mean, we've been careful, haven't we?'

'Accidents happen.'

He acknowledged that. 'Yes, I suppose they do. But this is not a good time, financially. I'll have to take care of Cassie and the kids. But you and I will have to get a place. We can't stay in your apartment for ever, especially with a baby. Then if you stop working, we lose your income.'

'But why would I stop working? I'm pregnant – if I even am – not ill. You're afraid I'm going to turn into Louisa.'

'Not just Louisa. I've seen it again and again: women who have babies, their priorities change. This isn't a judgement call, just an observation. It's their prerogative.'

'I'm different.'

He shrugged, not agreeing.

'Mark! I am.'

He laughed at her fury, then she laughed too and they said simultaneously, 'That's what they all say.'

'I have to tell Cassie right now. It can't be put off any longer.'

Jojo's insides crumpled with shame. 'Me being pregnant is going to make it far worse for her.'

'I know. But it's not fair to her not to tell her.'

'You're right but couldja wait until I get a positive result and we know for sure?'

Mark looked irritated, then he became sorrowful and took her hand. 'Jojo, listen to me, I want to tell you something very important. Cassie will have to be told some time. Fact.'

'I know.' But she mumbled it.

'You've met Cassie. You saw she's an intelligent woman with a lot of self-respect, not the type who likes being the last to know. I honestly think she would prefer to be told than to be made a fool of.'

'You do?'

'But I'll tell you now, it's not going to be pleasant. It will be very *un*pleasant, but then it'll be done. *I've* made peace with it and she's my wife. You're a courageous person, Jojo, and you're going to have to be brave for this. It's not magically going to take care of itself.'

'What if she met someone else and she was the one to leave you. I'd like that.'

He sighed. 'OK, pray for Cassie to meet someone else.' Then his tone changed. 'Or else stop stringing me along.'

Something plummeted in her. 'I'm not stringing you along.'

'Aren't you, Jojo? Because that's what it's starting to feel like. Listen to me, the partnership decision is in eight weeks' time. Then I am leaving my wife and coming to live with you. If that's not what you want, you'd better tell me.'

She felt panicky. 'I do want it. But this is hard for me. I hate dissing Cassie and stealing her husband. These are not the values I was brought up with.'

'They're not the values I was brought up with either. You're not the only one it's hard for, but I'm doing it because I love you. And I'm beginning to feel we're not on the same page.'

Some instinct was telling her she was suddenly in very dangerous territory. She was a hair's-breadth away from losing him.

'Mark, you were the one who said we should wait until after the partnership decision. I don't recall being any too thrilled about that.'

'Not straight away. But once you got over your suspicion that I was stalling, then you were keen. Slightly too keen, in my opinion.'

That was the trouble with Mark. He was way smart.

She had a choice to make here: jump, or get off the bridge. OK, she would jump.

'Wait until I know for sure that the test is positive, then we'll tell her. OK?'

He stared at her with his dark eyes and said, slowly, 'You're on notice but OK.'

'"On notice"? Don't speak to me like that. I'm not a fucking publisher who's late paying royalties.'

But he didn't apologize. He left without saying anything.

That night she lay awake thinking. Mark, smartie that he was, was right to question her dragging her feet. She was so busted: she'd never wanted to give the signal for Mark to leave Cassie. She'd hoped that some outside event would take care of things – her favourite scenario being Cassie meeting someone else. But Mark was wrong to think she was flaking on him; her core commitment was rock steady. Sometimes she wondered what it was about him. OK, he hit the big three – smart, funny and sexy – but it was bigger and far more ephemeral than that. You can look at the reasons why you love someone, you can even list them – his confidence, his smarts, his bulky physicality, the fact that he never bored her – but there's always something missing, the x factor, the magic ingredient. And Mark had the magic ingredient, whatever it was, in spades.

He was her favourite person and everything that she did, she felt – at least subconsciously – that it hadn't really happened until she'd told him about it. After a couple of days away from him, she began to ache, almost physically. He *knew* her. Their connection was full-on honest and two people could not be better matched.

She could see them together years into the future, Mr and Mrs Senior, cryptic crossword ninjas, still wild about each other, still best buddies.

Today Mark had articulated her resistance and his anger had forced her past some sort of barrier. He was going to leave Cassie and that was OK. A saying came to mind: *The only way out is through.* Her only other option was to risk losing Mark and, frankly, that was no option.

She was ready. Or as ready as she'd ever be. But she felt for Cassie . . .

She thought about what Becky had said: that maybe this pregnancy was no accident. Maybe she'd let it happen to take the decision for her. The funny thing was, though, she wasn't fully sure she *was* pregnant, everyone else believed it more than she did. But she'd started to believe it a little and she kinda liked the idea. Her and Mark and a baby, it'd be fun. Life would be different, but only a little, and in a good way. She had to fess up that she hadn't been broody. She didn't really *get* the hunger that came over people, to have a baby, no matter what. But because this was part of a package, because it was Mark's baby, that was different.

She put her hand on her stomach, because that was what

you did, right? See, she was a natural at this mom stuff. What would their baby be like? Dark, fair, red-headed? Strong-willed, she decided. No matter which of them it favoured. In fact, right now, their DNA were probably duking it out, looking to be on top.

Lily

'*Caitriona had been gravid with dread for so long and now her fear was made flesh in the fourth baby affected. She did not need any further proof. She knew. She had known for a very long time. This level of cancer was unusually high and something was causing it . . .*'

They were not listening. I was in a bookshop in Sheffield, on my killer three-week promotional tour for *Crystal Clear* and the eighty or so women crammed into the room were inspecting their nails, counting the carpet tiles, planning tomorrow night's supper – anything to while away the boring time until I had finished reading.

I took a quick look at my audience; the cluster of women in their white robes; the trio who had been asked to move to the back of the shop because their tall pointy hats were blocking the view; the gang of friends in the front row all bearing home-made wands, a riot of glitter and fluff. Of course, there were also many ordinary women in the room; however, the over-the-top ones tended to catch the eye.

It had been the same all week: at every reading lots of people had made a big effort to look like something out of *Mimi's Remedies*. But at the risk of sounding ungrateful, I wished they would not. It made me think, What have I created? (And it diverted attention from *Crystal Clear*, the book I was very much hoping they would buy.)

Another bout of restless shifting reached me, perched on my high stool, and I decided to cut the last page of the reading: I had done so on every other night also. I was simply too aghast at their manifest boredom to prolong their agony.

'*Caitriona picked up the phone. This call was long overdue . . .*'

I let a little pause build up, to let them know I had finished,

498

then said, 'Thank you,' and quietly lay down the book on the lectern. Polite applause ensued and when it had died away I asked, 'Does anyone have any questions?'

One woman leapt to her feet. *Don't ask it*, I begged. *Please don't ask it.* But of course she asked it. It had been the first question at every reading on every night of the tour.

'Will you be writing another *Mimi's Remedies*?'

The approval of the room was almost tangible. Everyone nodded. *I was going to ask that*, hung in the air, like a whisper. *Good question. Yes, very good question.*

'No,' I said.

'Awwww,' the room went, as one. Their tone was not mere disappointment, but hurt, almost anger. The front-row line of home-made wands waggled in agitation and the three 'witches' at the back removed their pointy hats and held them to their chests, as if showing respect for the dead.

Desperately, I tried to explain how *Mimi's Remedies* had been a one-off, written as a response to being mugged.

'But couldn't you try getting mugged again?' another woman asked. Joking, of course. I think.

'Hahahah,' I said, my smile stapled to my face. 'Any other questions?' I touched the copy of *Crystal Clear* beside me, just to remind them why we were here, but nothing doing. The ensuing questions were all, without exception, *Mimi's Remedies*-related.

'Is Mimi based on you?'

'Is Mimi's town a real place?'

'Did you do any training as a white witch before you wrote the book?'

I tried to answer graciously but I was starting to hate Mimi and it was leaking out in my answers. Then came the signing and the line snaked gratifyingly towards the back of the shop. But instead of picking up lovely hardback copies of *Crystal Clear*, everyone fetched from their handbags copies of *Mimi's Remedies* which were so battered they looked as if they had been fought over by marauding gangs of cocker spaniels. I felt slightly sick.

However, I could not help but be humbled by the warmth of every single person who came to the table.

'Thank you for writing *Mimi's Remedies* . . .'

'I loved this book . . .'

'It saved my life . . .'

'I've read it at least ten times . . .'

'I've given a copy to all my friends . . .'

'It's better than anti-depressants . . .'

'Better than chocolate . . .'

'I couldn't wait to meet you . . .'

I was presented with wands, home-made fudge, spells written on little scraps of paper and an invitation to a Druidic marriage. Most people asked to have their photo taken with me, like they had that day with Miranda England so long ago.

If my career had not depended on *Crystal Clear* selling well, I could have enjoyed their kindness and savoured that I had created something which had touched so many lives. But the fact was, my career *did* depend on *Crystal Clear* selling well and of the eighty or so people who had come to the reading, only two had bought copies. The previous night in Newcastle, only three copies had sold, the night before in Leeds only one had gone, the same number in Manchester, and in Birmingham at the start of the week, not a single copy had been shifted. This was not good. And nor was the news from the best-seller list.

On the walk back to the hotel I turned on my mobile and prayed with every fibre of my being for a message from Jojo. Saying that Dalkin Emery wanted to offer me half a million pounds for my next book, I thought, indulging in a sudden desperate flight of fancy. Or anything, anything at all. She had sent Tania the seven chapters of my new book over a week ago now, surely she must have some news? But the horrible electronic voice intoned *You Have No New Messages* so I rang Anton who was at home with Ema. 'Heard anything?'

'Jojo rang – she didn't want to ring you at your reading – but she has nothing to report. Tania didn't get back to her this afternoon and she thought it was better not to badger her.'

I swallowed hard. Today was Friday. That was it until Monday. A whole weekend to endure, wondering what our future was.

The extent of Anton's and my miscalculation appalled me. Clearly we should have signed the contract with Dalkin Emery back in May when it was offered to us. But at the time things were going so wonderfully that it was unthinkable that a few short months down the line, my new book would be selling badly enough to signal the end of my writing career.

In retrospect I could see that Dalkin Emery had begun their retreat from me as long ago as August. Tania's hissy fit over the cover was triggered, I subsequently discovered, by some of the major trade buyers getting the wobbles when they discovered *Crystal Clear* was as different from *Mimi's Remedies* as carrots are from Adolf Hitler's moustache.

Nobody ever said anything. I was never told officially that orders were being reduced and that Dalkin Emery had lost faith in me, but I intuited it from the forced cheer in their greetings and the wary expressions in their eyes. However, this reality was so bloody that I kept pushing my hope to the forefront. If I did not acknowledge how dreadful the situation was, then perhaps it was not.

The bottom line was this: if Dalkin Emery decided not to renew my contract, not only was my career in publishing over, but Anton, Ema and I would probably lose our home; the loan to buy our house had been given on the condition that we paid the bank a lump sum of a hundred grand when I got my new deal with Dalkin Emery. We had no other sources of income. All we had was my next royalty cheque, which wasn't due until March, almost five months away. The bottom line was: no new deal equalled no money to pay the lump sum equalled no house.

I went back to my lonely hotel room and had a large gin and

tonic and a bag of cashews from the minibar. I was exhausted – it had been a tough week of early starts, countless bookshop visits and so many local radio and press interviews they had all blurred into one – but terror had me in its grip and prevented me from sleeping.

To cheer myself up I thought, *Anton has left me for the head waiter at the Fleet Tandoori, I have gangrene of the foot and everyone is complaining about the smell, and some soothsayers in Tibet have decided that Ema is the next Dalai Lama and she's going to be taken from me, to a Himalayan eyrie, where she will sit cross-legged in orange robes and say wise, incomprehensible soundbites.*

I lay on my bed, drinking gin and savouring my misfortune.

How awful . . . especially the smelly gangrenous foot. And the wise, incomprehensible soundbites.

I waited until I felt really dreadful, then did the mental equivalent of jumping out of a cupboard and shouting, 'Gotcha!'

Yes, I thought, a slight but definite uplift in my gloom, this reverse psychology thing definitely works. Then I noticed I had drunk three gins and that the mood improvement was probably thanks to them.

Jojo

Wednesday morning

When Jojo's period arrived, ten days late, she was actually a little embarrassed; she wasn't usually a drama queen. Because the test had continued to be negative, she'd never fully believed she was pregnant, so she didn't feel like she'd lost a baby. But she was vaguely interested in what had caused the delay: anxiety about Mark leaving Cassie? Waiting too long for the vote on the new partner? Work stress? And, yeah, there was *lots* to be stressed about.

On Lily Wright's second week on sale, there had been an improvement, but nothing like enough. She 'shot' from 168 to 94, selling a paltry 1743 copies. Considering there wasn't a railway station in the land that wasn't plastered with ads for *Crystal Clear*, this wasn't good.

Dalkin Emery were way rattled. They'd printed a hundred thousand hardbacks – an initial run, so they'd thought at the time, the first of many – but now were already calculating the hit their Profit & Loss was going to take.

On the third week, Lily got as far as number 42 in the chart but celebrations were premature, because on her fourth week, she slipped back to 59.

Jojo continued to push Dalkin Emery for more ads and further discounting. Patrick Pilkington-Smythe obliged and that was scary. The rule was that agents pushed and marketing men resisted. To be on the same page meant things were bad.

Then *Book News* ran a snide little piece on the situation and although Dalkin Emery insisted that it was still too soon to call and that sales would pick up nearer to Christmas, Jojo knew that privately they were not optimistic.

What was really wrecking her head was that Dalkin Emery were dicking her around on Lily's new contract. They weren't saying they *wouldn't* re-sign her but Tania kept stalling, saying that she needed the higher-ups in Dalkin Emery to read Lily's new book, before they could make any decision. Jojo had thought that showing Tania the new book was a mere formality but now she knew Dalkin Emery's game: they were hedging their bets, watching to see how *Crystal Clear* performed, before deciding if Lily Wright was still a viable investment.

Poor Lily had dragged her sorry ass around the country, doing one gnarly reading after another. Daily, either she or Anton phoned, their voices small and scared, as they asked, 'Is there any news? Any word on the new deal?'

They were horrified that Dalkin Emery were taking so long but the situation was too delicate for Jojo to force.

Several times she reassured them, 'Tania has promised me a decision by the end of the week.' But the end of the week would come and a phone call from Tania Teal wouldn't and somehow over four weeks had passed, without an offer coming through.

Jojo felt very, very badly for Lily. No one liked watching a much-hyped book bomb but in this case there were serious consequences for Lily's career. Advising Lily to wait for a new deal had been a gamble. Now it was clear she'd miscalculated the odds: after a disaster the size of *Crystal Clear*, chances were that Dalkin Emery wouldn't sign her for any more books. And nor would any other publisher.

Tuesday afternoon, end of November
'Tania Teal on line one.'

'Accept!'

This was the call, Jojo knew. The one that would condemn or save Lily Wright.

'Tania, hey.'

'Sorry, Jojo, it's no go on Lily Wright.'

'Slow down a minute –'

'We're not going to renew her contract.'

'Tania, you cannot be serious. Have you read her new book, do you know how great it is –'

'Jojo, I'm going to say what everyone is thinking. *Mimi's Remedies* was a one-off, a one-hit wonder. Readers' loyalties are not to Lily Wright the author but to *Mimi's Remedies*, the book. *Crystal Clear* is the biggest disaster we've ever had.'

'OK, the hardback sales are slow but you know what this means?' Jojo forced herself to sound wildly cheerful. 'The paperback will go through the roof! Just like *Mimi's Remedies* did! I guess it was too soon to publish Lily in hardback. Writers have to build a fanbase before hardbacks are a dead cert. Coupla books' time, that's when her hardbacks will really fly.'

Tania said nothing. She was not a fool. And too many people had shouted at her; she would not be swayed.

'I think the book Lily is working on now is great,' Jojo insisted.

'If Lily Wright wants to write another *Mimi's Remedies*, I'd be happy to publish it,' Tania said. 'Otherwise, it's no go. I'm sorry, Jojo, I really am.'

Despite her frustration, Jojo understood. Tania was probably getting it in the neck from everyone at Dalkin Emery. She had accepted a book, bigged it up to the entire company as the publication of the year and it had exploded in her face. Her career trajectory had been knocked sideways by the disaster. No wonder she was being careful.

'Lily Wright is one of the hottest authors around,' Jojo said. 'If you don't want to publish her any longer, there are plenty of others who will.'

'I understand, and good luck with it all.'

'Your loss,' Jojo said, clattered the phone back and sat in gloomy contemplation. One of the hottest authors around, indeed. If things continued the way they were going, Lily Wright would have to start wearing a bell around her neck.

She buried her face in her hands. Rats. Now she had to tell Lily and she would prefer to shoot herself in the head. With a sigh, she lifted the phone again. Better to get it over with.

'Lily, I've heard from Dalkin Emery about the new contract.' Very quickly, before Lily had time to get any false hope, she said, 'I'm so sorry but it's bad news.'

'How bad?'

'They don't want to buy the new book.'

'I can write another.'

'Unless it's another *Mimi's Remedies*, they don't want to renew the contract. I'm so, so sorry,' Jojo said, and meant it.

After a period of silence, Lily said quietly, 'It's OK. Please, Jojo, it's really OK.'

That was Lily all over: too sweet to start yelling and blaming.

'I feel lousy that I didn't get you to sign with them last May.' *When they still wanted you.*

'Don't feel bad. No one forced me to wait,' Lily said. 'It was my choice. Mine and Anton's. Just one thing? Is there any hope that *Crystal Clear* might still resuscitate at this stage?'

'There are still some ads to run.'

'Perhaps if *Crystal Clear* rallies at the last minute, they'll change their mind. Or someone else might want to publish me.'

'Attagirl. That's the spirit.'

Then Jojo hung up, wiped out. Passing on bad news was as much a part of the job as delivering good stuff, but she was feeling more shitty than she had in a long, long time. Poor Lily.

And, on a selfish note, this wasn't such a great time for Jojo to fuck up. She didn't often make mistakes and hated when she did. But with the partnership decision coming up, this miasma of high-profile failure was not welcome. She was still in line to generate more income than any other agent this year but the gloss was gone from her crown a little.

The following morning

Jojo called up the best-seller list, trying to type with crossed fingers, praying for a last-minute reprieve. Miracles did happen – although only a sap would have expected it here.

She scrolled down, down, down, down . . . then stopped.

'Well?' Manoj asked, his fingers crossed too.

Jojo sighed. 'Like a stone off a cliff.'

Her phone rang and she knew who it would be: Patrick Pilkington-Smythe. 'We're calling a halt on Lily Wright's ads. We've been throwing good money after bad.'

'Pulling the plug? Too bad. That last pre-Christmas push could've made all the difference.'

He gave a bark of incredulous laughter. 'Never say die, do you, Jojo?'

'Calling it like I see it.'

Patrick said nothing. He'd been in this game a lot longer than Jojo had. Pretending things were alright didn't mean they were. The crater-sized hole in his marketing budget was witness to that.

Deeply subdued, Jojo hung up. She didn't believe it either.

Gemma

You know, writing a book isn't as easy as it looks. First, my editor (I love saying that: 'my editor') made me rewrite loads of it, making Izzy 'warmer' and Emmet 'more human and less of a Mills & Boon caricature' – the cheek of her. Sorry, I mean, the cheek of 'my editor'. Then when I'd done that to 'my editor's' satisfaction – and it took ages, all of August and most of September – some copy-editor (not 'my editor') went through it and came back with eight million queries: What was a 'yoke'? Was Marmoset a real restaurant? Had I got permission to quote from 'Papa Was a Rolling Stone'? And to change it to Papa Was a Faithless Fuck?

Then I had to proof-read it, scrutinizing each individual word to make sure it was spelt correctly, until the little black letters started linking arms and dancing jigs in front of my blurring eyes.

Mind you, with the advance they'd given me I wasn't complaining; I'd nearly collapsed and died when Jojo told me: sixty grand. *Sixty grand.* Sterling. I'd have happily sold the book for four pee because being published was reward itself; instead they wanted to give me one-and-a-half times my annual salary and, to add whatever the opposite of insult is to the opposite of injury, it was tax free. (In Ireland income from 'artistic endeavour' isn't taxable.)

My imagination, fevered at the best of times, went wild entirely at the thought of all that loot: I'd give up my job and travel around the world for a year. I'd replace my heartbreaking car. I'd go to Milan and buy up all of Prada.

Until I returned to earth and saw that this windfall was a result of my mother's misfortune. She was going to have to move house early in the new year; the advance money could make the difference between a hell-hole and a hovel.

Also I owed Susan big and when I asked her what she'd like she admitted she'd gone a bit mad buying furniture and stuff for her apartment in Seattle and would appreciate one of her store cards being paid off. (On account of Susan's dad being a stingy yoke, she had no control with money.) 'Pick a card,' she'd said. 'Any card.'

So I picked her Jennifer Convertibles one and promised to wipe out the two grand debt.

Promised but not done because as yet, by the end of November, I hadn't actually seen any of the advance. It had been divided up into a third on signature – but they'd spent forever tinkering with the contract and I'd only signed it a month ago – a third on 'delivery' then a third on publication. I thought I'd 'delivered' at the end of June when they'd bought the book, but they saw it differently. I hadn't 'delivered' until they had a manuscript they were happy with and this had taken until two weeks ago.

We'd finally agreed on a name. No one had liked my suggestion of 'Sugar Daddy'. Or 'Mars Attack'. 'Shockolat' was a runner for a while, then someone at Dalkin Emery suggested 'Chasing Rainbows' and suddenly everyone was happy. Except me, I thought it sounded a bit *nice*.

The day the cover arrived was a great one, though. A soft-focus watercolour, in blues and yellows, it was a smudgy image of a girl looking like she'd lost her purse. But it had my name on it. My name!

'Mam, look!'

Even she got excited. She was nothing like as pitiful and bewildered as she'd been in the first post-Dad months. Dad's desire for a permanent financial settlement had changed her – it made her angry, no bad thing.

The dreaded phone call about Colette being up the pole still hadn't come from Dad. But in the summer he'd sent us a letter confirming that the minute the year's separation was up, he'd be applying to the courts to sell the house. From then on, it was like we were living on borrowed time. And something else was different – from the day he'd left, Mam and I had regarded his absence as temporary, like our lives had just hit the pause button. But after we got this letter, I had to negotiate some changes; we couldn't go on as we were.

It wasn't easy – Mam produced rivers of tears and a selection of illnesses both fake and real – but then she seemed to come to terms with my need for space and by the end of the summer I got to sleep in my own flat three or four nights out of every seven. I saw her a lot more than most thirty-something women see their mothers, but it still felt like glorious freedom.

She studied the blurry girl on my book cover. 'Is she meant to be you?'

'No, only figuratively.'

'Only I was going to say her hair is the wrong colour. And she looks a bit all-at-sea.'

'Like her father has just left her mother?'

'Like she thinks she's left the gas on or can't remember the right word for something. Mummifying, say. She's thinking to herself, it's what they did to Egyptian kings when they died, before they put them in the pyramids. It begins with M, it's on the tip of my tongue, oh, what *is* it?'

I looked again. Mam was right. That was exactly what she looked like.

'You'll have to show it to Owen,' she said slyly.

She knew about Owen: in fact she'd met him. And oddly enough, considering her suspicion of anything that interfered with my time with her – like my job – she approved of him. I told her not to bother because he wouldn't be around for long. Our string of encounters – I wasn't going to call me and Owen a relationship, that would be overstating the case – continued to have a ramshackle, rickety feel, like we could have a bust-up at any minute and never see each other again. And yet, we carried on, bickering enthusiastically, past the summer and into the autumn. And now here we were in November and we were still an item – an item that would be in the damaged-goods section were it for sale, but all the same.

'Owen.' I shrugged dismissively.

'Don't play it down for me,' she said. 'He's a younger man, he'll break your heart, but you're going to marry him.'

'Marry him. Are you insane?'

We made wary eye-contact, then Mam said, 'Please don't ask questions like that as – what's that they say? – a punch in the mouth often offends.'

I smiled at her. Sometimes I had hope, I really did.

'I keep telling you,' I said. 'Owen is a temporary measure, a bodge boyfriend, something that'll do until the professionals get here.'

But Mam was adamant he was my Mr Right. 'You're yourself with him.'

Yes, but I was the wrong self with him: not the nice Gemma. All the same. He:

a) was very good in bed
b) er . . . um, was a good dancer
c) ah . . .

'I didn't get to my age without learning a thing or two about romance,' Mam went on.

I didn't say anything. It would have been too cruel.

'You girls talk about finding The One, but The One comes in all shapes and sizes. Often you don't realize that that's who you've met. I know a woman who met her The One when she was on a ship, following a man out to Australia. On the journey out she palled up with a lovely chap but she was so fixated on the man in Australia that she didn't realize the chap on the ship was her The One. She tried to get the first fellow to marry her, then came to her senses. Luckily the second chap was still interested. And I know another girl who . . .'

I tuned her out. Marry Owen? I didn't think so. How could I marry Owen when I was going to get back with Anton? Something that Owen knew all about and approved of. (He'd get back with Lorna, I'd get back with Anton, we'd all go on holidays to the Dordogne together. We often discussed it.)

On Mam went, getting almost animated, which was good because it meant I didn't have to talk to her and I could have a little think. I felt slightly uncomfortable because there was someone besides Owen I wanted to show the book jacket to: Johnny the Scrip. It only seemed fair because he knew all about the book; he'd been so encouraging about it, when I used to be a regular visitor.

I didn't see him so much any more and not just because Mam no longer needed so many tablets. No, around the time the flirting with Johnny was starting to blossom into something more meaningful, I'd had a little think. Fair-to-middling insane, as I was, I'd experienced a window of sanity and realized that Owen was my boyfriend. Despite our ups and downs, despite the fact that I'd never expected we'd last, for as long as it continued I was going to treat him right – like I was a grown-up or an unselfish person, or something.

Johnny must have been having similar thought processes because the next time I went to him after having had my little think, he asked, 'How's your non-boyfriend?'

I coloured. 'OK.'

'Still seeing him?'

'Yes.'

'Ah.' The word, as they say, spoke volumes.

He didn't say that he wasn't going to step on someone else's toes, but it was clear that that was what he meant. He had more respect for himself. So by silent mutual agreement, we both retreated. Besides, the thing that had united us – our isolation from the rest of the world – was no longer a factor. I'd gone and got a life for myself and though I knew it was mad, I felt like I'd abandoned him.

Sometimes when I was out on the piss with Owen I'd see him and he'd smile but wouldn't come over. Once I thought I saw him with a girl. Well, he was with a lot of people but he was standing closer to her than any of the others. She was nice-looking, with a really cool, choppy haircut and I will admit to feeling jealous but that might have been because of her fabulous layers as much as anything. However, the next time I saw him he wasn't with her, so maybe I imagined the vibe.

Mostly, I was very good: *I respected our decision.* Once when I'd had a demanding week with Mam's prescriptions requiring several visits I even went to another chemist.

But occasionally I still made an excuse to see him – come on, I'm not Gandhi. He was like a tub of strawberry cheesecake Häagen Dazs – off-limits but it didn't mean that I didn't sometimes get overtaken by an emotional version of the hunger I get when I'm premenstrual. The same kind of Unstoppable Force feelings that had me wrenching open the freezer door and eating the entire tub, compelled me to manufacture an excuse to see Johnny, drive over to his chemist and buy a jar of zinc tablets (say). But I always came away dissatisfied. He was polite, chatty even, but there was no longer any frisson – and that was because he was a decent man with a healthy dose of self-respect. But I suppose no one's perfect.

'Mam.' I interrupted her story about someone else who'd missed her The One when he'd been right under her nose, dancing around in his pelt. 'Do you need anything from the chemist?'

She thought about it. 'No.'

'Should you think about getting your anti-depressant dose increased?'

'Actually, I was thinking I might try coming down a couple of milligrams.'

'Oh. OK.'

Fuck it, I'd go anyway.

Echinacea, I decided. That was a reasonable thing to buy, especially at this time of year. At the chemist Johnny greeted me with a smile. Mind you, he did that to everyone, even the old men with all-over-body psoriasis.

'Name your poison,' he said.

'Echinacea.'

'Coming down with a cold?'

'Er, no. Just precautionary.'

'Sensible thinking. Well, we have quite a choice.'

Shite.

He went into details about dosage, liquid or capsule, with or without vitamin C, until I was sorry I hadn't asked for something more straightforward.

'Busy at the moment?' I asked, trying to get him to turn around and talk to me.

'Oh yes. The six weeks coming up to Christmas is the worst time.'

'Me too. How's your brother doing?'

'Recovering nicely. Or should I say, recovering unpleasantly. He's doing a lot of physiotherapy on his banjoed leg and he's not enjoying it.'

I made a couple of 'ah, well' style noises, then went, 'Oh!' like I'd just remembered something and pulled the cover from my bag. 'I thought you might like to see it.'

'What's this? The cover of your book!' He lit up. He looked genuinely happy for me. 'Congratulations!'

He studied the cover for ages, while I studied him. You know, he really was very nice-looking, his intelligent eyes, his lovely shiny hair. Mind you, it would be a disgrace if his hair *wasn't* shiny with him having access to all those hair products . . .

'It's really good,' he said finally. 'It's only smudgy lines but they've managed to make her look bereft. Very effective. I'm looking forward to reading it.'

I got a twinge of something peculiar, which I didn't understand at the time.

'But the title?' he questioned. 'I thought we'd agreed on "Shockolat"?'

'Shockolat' had been his suggestion.

'I loved "Shockolat",' I said, 'But the marketing people didn't.'

'Well, we don't always get what we want.'

Was I imagining it, or was there a deeper meaning to what he'd just said? And the way he'd looked at me while he'd said it? Had I just experienced a leakage of the old frisson?

I suspected I had, then the guilts kicked in and, flustered, I took my leave.

'Your echinacea,' he called after me.

Back in August, after Dalkin Emery's publicity department sent a page from *Book News* which mentioned my book deal (I wondered if Lily had seen it) I paid for it to be sent every week, just in case there was anything else about me. Although I went through each issue in minute detail I found nothing, but some time in November I came across a mention about Lily. It was part of a piece about how Christmas books weren't selling well.

Retailers are reporting 'extremely lacklustre' sales of Lily Wright's *Crystal Clear*. Wright, author of publishing sensation, *Mimi's Remedies*, was expected to storm the hardback charts this Christmas but has not even made it into the top ten. The title, originally priced at £18.99, has been discounted widely, retailing for £11.99 in Waterstones and appearing as low as £8.99 in some outlets. Dick Barton-King, Dalkin Emery's Head of Sales, was quoted, 'We always knew *Crystal Clear* was a gift-purchase, not a self-purchase. We expect strong sales in the two weeks before Christmas.'

Around the same time I saw a review of *Crystal Clear* in the paper – I read reviews now. It said that *Mimi's Remedies* had been delightful but this was a hectoring, charmless book which would disappoint her present fans and wouldn't win her any new ones. How awful for her.

OK, I admit it, I was glad.

*　*　*

One day in December when I got home from work, there was a small box sitting on the kitchen table. 'I shook it,' Mam said, all excitement. 'I think it's books. Open it. Here.' She handed me a pair of scissors.

I split the seal and found six copies of *Chasing Rainbows* inside, looking just like real books. My knees went watery and weak and I had to sit down to read the accompanying note. 'These are only proof copies. That means they're full of spelling mistakes, and the covers aren't embossed yet. They're really just for reviewers.'

'But it's a book,' Mam whispered. 'You wrote it. It's got your name on it.'

'Yeah.' Seeing my book looking like a book made me feel very strange – and not in a good way. As I flicked through it, I got the inside trembles and suddenly understood the twinge I'd had in the chemist; there was page after page about the loveliness of 'Will', i.e. Johnny, and I marvelled at the size of my stupidity. When I'd been writing the book I'd been so worried about getting it past Mam that it had barely occurred to me that other people might get upset by it. Especially Owen. I'd never seriously considered that he'd still be around when I'd finished it – after all he kept 'storming off' and we did nothing but squabble. But the book was finished, Owen was still here and my romantic hero was based on another man. Owen was super-sensitive to slights; he knew that I spent – or at least used to spend – a lot of time at the chemist.

Even while I'd been making all the changes and corrections, I'd just thought of it as an academic exercise, not something that would eventually be in the public domain and available for all to pick up and read. How could I have been so thick?

And what about Johnny? He was bound to recognize himself; he was going to know I fancied him. Or had fancied him. He probably knew anyway, but still, how mortifying . . .

These were real people and they were going to be hurt. Perhaps I could nip this in the bud. How? I had no clue what to do with Owen. With Johnny, maybe I could give him a copy of the book now and joke about the contents. But I suspected that would make things worse; best to just leave it alone.

Squeezed by fear, I wondered if there was any way now I could stop this whole thing. Then I opened another item of post: an envelope – containing a cheque. An enormous cheque, the first money I'd seen from Dalkin Emery.

I stared at it: thirty-six grand in sterling. Shit. They'd sent both the signature and delivery money together, minus Jojo's ten per cent.

It looked like there was no going back.

I decided that the best way to handle Owen was to keep him from reading the book for as long as possible; he never read anything anyway. That calmed me, I felt more in control. The mistake I made was, when I went to the loo, I didn't bring my mobile with me.

I heard it ring and let it go to message service. But the next thing the ringing stops and I hear Mam going, 'Which button do I press? Hello. Owen, love, how are you? Great news today. She's after getting the first copies of the book. Of course you can have one, they sent her six. *And* she's after getting a pile of money but I think that's a secret.'

I rushed out, just to see her disconnect.

'Owen rang for you on this yoke,' she said, blithely unaware of my panic. 'He's coming over to see the book.'

I stared at her in desperation. She never answered my mobile, why did she have to do it today?

Maybe Owen wouldn't come. He was very unreliable.

But just this once, Owen arrived in super-quick time and

burst into the house, all excited. 'This is so cool.' He ran his fingers over my name. 'Nice cover.'

'Doesn't the girl on it look like she can't remember the right word for something?' Mam prompted.

Owen studied it. 'It looks more like she has a puncture and doesn't have a jack. Like she's trying to flag down a passing car to help her.'

Why did everything have to come back to cars with him?

He handed me the book in his hand. 'Will you sign it for me?'

'These are only proof copies. They're full of mistakes.'

'That makes it even more special.'

OK. I was not going to get out of this. It wasn't going to happen.

I scribbled 'To Owen, with love from Gemma' then handed it back, and said nervously, 'Just don't forget it's fiction. It's made up, it's not real.'

'Bottle of stout, Owen?' Mam tempted. She'd started getting in bottles of Murphys for him.

'Yes, stay and have a drink, Owen.'

'No thanks, Mrs Hogan, I'm going to go home to read this.'

Off he went and I wondered if I'd ever hear from him again.

The weird thing was that Owen, who was super-touchy and took offence even on those times when I genuinely didn't intend any, didn't get upset when he read *Chasing Rainbows*.

He rang the following day. 'I'm taking you for dinner on Friday night to celebrate. At the Four Seasons.'

I loved the Four Seasons more than life itself. (He hated it, said all the luxe furnishings made him feel like he couldn't breathe.) This was a good sign.

'Have you read it already? Did you like it?'

'We'll discuss it over dinner.' But it was clear that he did.

'Well?'

'I thought it was great. I mean, there was more kissing than

I like in a book and not as many dead bodies, but still, it was a laugh. And I bet you based hunky Emmet on me. I should get a credit – "Inspired by Owen Deegan."'

I laughed weakly. I couldn't believe I was getting away with it.

'Am I the bloke in the chemist? Is he based on me too?'

'Here.' I handed him a gift-wrapped parcel. 'I bought you a Ferrari. A toy one,' I added, lest he combust with excitement.

He unwrapped it, declared himself delighted, 'A red one!' And whizzed it up and down a bit, going, 'NEEEEEEE-AAARRNNN!' Until it hit an American businessman on his hand-tooled shoe and the maître d' asked him to stop, then he returned to the table and said, 'I've been thinking . . .'

Those dread words. 'I've spoken to you before about this,' I said wearily.

'To celebrate your advance we should go on holiday, you and me. There's this place I read about, a resort in Antigua. They do loads of watersports and here's the best bit – it's all free. Even the drink, and it's premium brand liquor, not some manky local stuff that would send you schizo. We should go, Gemma, it'll be good for us, good for our, like, relationship.'

'You mean you want to learn to windsurf while you're banjoed out of your head on free Pina Coladas.' No way was I paying for me and Owen to go anywhere. I needed every penny for Mam's move. I wasn't going to start spending money on myself. I knew what I was like. If I started, I'd never stop.

'My girlfriend got a publishing deal and all she got me was this lousy toy car,' Owen said, then we sat in sulky silence. At least he did, I just sat in ordinary silence.

'It's a great achievement getting a book published,' he eventually said. 'You should mark it and you've got the money to do it. You should do something nice for *you*. I know you worry about your mother, but life must go on.'

I could never decide if he was a selfish brat or just giving me tough love.

'Alright, get the brochure, but we're only going for a week.'

Owen was *thrilled*. 'Congratulations,' he said. 'You're finally starting to behave like a normal person.'

This was a milestone. I was going to go on holidays. I was going to leave my mother to fend for herself for a week: I was getting better. My life was getting better.

'And if we manage to survive a week together without killing each other, I think we should get married,' Owen said.

'Grand.' I knew there was no chance.

'I've just asked you to marry me.'

'Thanks.'

'I've never asked anyone to marry me before. To be honest, I expected more enthusiasm than "Grand" and "Thanks".'

'Real life isn't like the movies.'

'Oh. So anyway, is the bloke in the chemist based on me?'

'No.' I couldn't lie.

'So who is he?'

'Owen,' I said, with superiority, 'I'm a lot older than you. I've had several boyfriends and in a way they all inspired the character of Will.'

'Don't patronize me. You're not that much older than me and I bet I've had as many lovairs as you have.'

This segued into a competition over how many people each of us had slept with and neatly diffused the Johnny the Scrip situation. We ended up having a messy squabble, when it transpired that I'd slept with more people than he had, but all the same . . .

Lily

FIRST NATIONAL BANK
23A Edgeware Square, London SW1 1RR

5 December

Dear Mr Carolan and Ms Wright,

Re: 37 Grantham Road, London NW3

I refer you to clause 7(b) subclause (ii) of the agreement drawn up between The First National Bank and Mr Carolan and Ms Wright on 18 June of this year. The clause states that a payment of £100,000 (one hundred thousand pounds sterling) is payable by Mr Carolan and Ms Wright to the bank no later than the thirtieth of November. As of the fifth of December such payment has not been received (and a telephone conversation with Mr Carolan has confirmed that the payment will not be received in the foreseeable future). I am left with no choice but to refer you to clause 18(a) which states, 'In the event of non-payment of any of the scheduled monies, the property is immediately forfeit.'

Therefore the property at 37 Grantham Road must be vacated by the nineteenth of December, two weeks from this date, and all keys for the property must be posted by first-class mail to the above address.

Yours sincerely,

Breen Mitchell
Special Loan Executive

It was like the end of the world.

It all happened so quickly. When Jojo rang with the terrible,

terrible news that Dalkin Emery were not going to give me a new contract, I did what I usually do under pressure: I sicked up my lunch. Then, formalities out of the way, Anton and I reviewed our limited options. The biggest worry looming over us was that we were unable to make our second lump-sum payment to the bank. But we squared our shoulders and decided that, instead of hiding behind the sofa and gibbering, we would behave like responsible adults and be honest with the bank. So Anton rang Breen, the 'Loan Arranger', and explained that although we had no money right now, a royalty cheque for *Mimi's Remedies* was due at the end of March. If they could give us until then?

Breen thanked us for the call and said it would be best if we came in for a proper chat – but before we had agreed on a time, we received the letter, saying we had broken the terms of the loan, that in view of our circumstances there was no hope that our payments could get back on track and they were foreclosing. We had to vacate the house by the nineteenth of December and post the keys to them.

Shortly before Christmas, our worst-case scenario had come to pass.

Anton responded with, 'They can't do that' bluster and swore to me, 'We won't lose our home, baby.' But I knew he was mistaken. A house being repossessed by the bank? I had seen it happen before and knew that it could – and very probably would – happen again.

Of course we rang the bank and did all we could in an attempt to convince them to give us until March, when everything could hopefully be salvaged. I pleaded, Anton implored, we even considered (briefly) putting Ema on the line to sing 'Twinkle twinkle little star'.

But Breen and his colleagues were immovable and there was not one thing we could do; we had nothing to offer. Finally, we faced it: it was not going to happen. So, wearily, we asked for a grace period until after Christmas – and they refused. For the first time in this whole horrible nightmare we became indignant, but still they would not budge. They reminded us that under the terms of the contract they were under no obligation to give us *any* notice but had offered two weeks as a sop to the season of goodwill. Some time in this hellish period, Zulema gave notice with immediate effect. She had got another job, with a family in Highgate, who had given her her own self-contained flat and a car. It was not a good time for her to leave, but I acknowledged we could no longer afford to keep her.

By then, with all the toing and froing with the bank, we had already wasted one of our two weeks of notice. It was twelve days before Christmas and we had a week to find somewhere to live. We could have moved into Dettol Hall but Anton said – and I agreed – that living with Debs would be too much for us. 'We'd be better off in a Salvation Army doss-house.'

So Anton bought the *Standard* and racked up several flats to view. Before I even saw the first one, I hated them all.

I know the letting agents thought Anton and I slightly weird. Anton, habitually so charming and likeable, was absent. The person looking out from behind his eyes was not the Anton I knew. His skin looked like that of a corpse and, with a shock, I noticed greying strands in his shiny black hair. He suddenly looked a lot older.

As for me, I found it hard to maintain proper eye-contact because my eyes kept scudding from side to side, doing that constantly-moving-fish thing, that happens to extremely stressed people. But the agents could not know that, they must have simply thought I was a dodgy prospect.

I was so oppressed by the time constraint that I could almost hear clocks ticking, rushing us towards the dreadful moment when we were obliged to vacate our house. As a result, I could barely look at each flat; I wanted to run from room to room, in order to do it as quickly as possible, so that I could get on to the next place.

Our plan was to get taxis between the different flats, but if a yellow light did not appear after three seconds, I forced Anton to walk – very, very quickly. Anxiety was burning me up, filling me with so much nervous energy, that I could not pause.

From flat to flat we went and I had entirely forgotten the previous one as soon as we arrived at the new one. The circuits in my head were moving at such speed, they could not contain the information.

After three days of viewing, we were obliged to make a decision and I opted for the last flat we had seen because it was the only one I could remember. It was in Camden, not far from our current home, and was new and characterless, with white boxy rooms. We signed a lease for three months. We had to pay cash because we were in such a hurry to move in. Also, because our bank references would not have passed muster.

And then we were on our knees, on a dusty floor, working through the night, packing an infinite number of boxes. It was like the nightmares I had had while we were agonizing about buying the house last May. Then it was the final morning, the removal van had arrived and a team of young Kiwi blokes in red shorts were loading it up. I leant against a wall and wondered, Is this really happening? Any of it? Especially the red shorts?

Then the house was completely empty and there was no further reason to stay.

'C'mon, Lily,' Anton said gently.

'OK.'

But leaving my dream house buckled me. As I waited just a second too long to shut the front door behind me for the last time, I actually felt something change irrevocably within me. I was saying goodbye not just to four walls (three and a half, in any case – the builders had still not finished the small bedroom, not that it mattered any more) but to a life that Anton and I would never now get to live.

If it had been just me, I am not sure I would ever have unpacked in the new place. I would have located my duvet and a pillow and lived quite comfortably in the forest of cardboard boxes. However, because of Ema, it was necessary to get some things immediately functional. Her cot had to be assembled and kitchenware unpacked. The TV, of course, was something she insisted upon. As was the sofa, to facilitate comfortable viewing.

By eight o'clock that night, most of the essentials were in place, Anton had even cooked dinner and the speed of the transition was too much for me. This was our home now. This bleak little place was filled with our belongings and this was us, acting out a domestic tableau here. But how? Perplexed, I looked at Anton and asked, 'How did things go so horribly wrong?'

I stared around at the smooth white walls, it was like being inside a cube. I loathed it.

Anton grabbed me by the wrist, trying to get my attention. 'At least we have each other.'

I was still surveying the bleak white walls. 'What?'

He looked at me in despair. 'I said, at least we have each other.'

Gemma

Christmas day, with just me and Mam, was horrendous. I only survived it by drinking nearly a litre and a half of Bailey's. It would have been a pretty cheerless occasion anyway, but when I'd told Mam a few days beforehand that Owen and I were going on holiday at the end of January, she went pale with shock. She tried to hide her distress, she even said, 'God knows, love, you could do with a break,' but her attempts to be brave made me feel worse.

All through Christmas day, like a broken record, she kept saying, 'This is our last Christmas in this house.'

Last Christmas? It could be our last *month*. January was looming, when Dad would be applying for the court order. How quickly would it happen? How soon would the house be put on the market? Breda, our solicitor, said it could take months, but knowing my luck, we'd probably be due to move the day I was going on holiday.

Anyway, you'll never guess what happened next . . .

No, go on. Try. OK, brace yourself.

On the eighth of January, a year to the day since he left, Dad came home. Just like that. I don't think he was even aware it was the anniversary of his leaving, it was just another weird turn in the weirdness that was the whole episode. His return was as low key as his departure: he simply showed up at the front door with three shopping bags full of his stuff and asked Mam – at least he had the decency to ask – if he could come back.

Mam responded by pulling herself up to her full height and

saying, 'Your floozie thrown you out then, has she? Well, you'd better make it up with her because there's no welcome for you here.'

Ah no, only joking. I wasn't there at the time, so I don't know exactly *how* quickly Mam hustled him into the house and set about cooking for him, but I'd put money on it being very, *very* fast.

He was back and the status quo was restored before I could blink. By the time I came home from work that evening, he was settled in his chair, doing the crossword, Mam was in the kitchen cooking up a storm and I had a moment when I genuinely wondered if I'd just dreamt the entire past year.

I ignored a nervous-smiling Dad and cornered Mam at the chopping board. 'Why did you let him back straight away? You could at least have made him suffer for a *while*.'

'He's my husband,' she said, going all weird and devout and unreachable. 'I made my wedding vows before God and man.'

Ah, vows. Them yokes; they'd made martyrs and eejits of generations of women. But what can you do? There's no reasoning with that sort of lunacy.

I wanted to ask her to reconsider – it was never too late to tell him to go and fuck himself. Self-respect could be hers. But what was the point? She was too old, too determined not to change. If it hadn't happened at any stage over the past year, it was unlikely to happen now. I wanted her to strike a blow for women everywhere, but sometimes people can be very annoying and refuse to do the right thing – preferring to do what they *want* to do.

And from a selfish point of view, his return was my get-out-of-jail card. Life could get back to normal.

'Why did he come home?'

I'd figured a Christmas trapped with Colette's two little monsters had done for him. (I had no proof those children were monsters, maybe I was doing them a terrible injustice.)

'Because he loves me and doesn't love Her any more.'

'Any explanation for why he spent the last year living with a thirty-six-year-old?'

'Something to do with facing turning sixty and his brother dying.'

Right. Late-onset mid-life crisis – nothing we hadn't figured out for ourselves.

'And you forgive him?'

'He's my husband. I took my marriage vows in a *church*.' She said it in such a non-negotiable way, my hand itched for a stray hammer to beat some sense into her.

Thank God I'm an atheist, is what I say.

If something like this happened to me, I didn't think the relationship would ever recover and I doubted I'd ever be able to forgive. As it was, I didn't think I'd ever be able to stop despising Dad. I suppose it was Mam's denial which made it possible for her. Thinking of herself as a dutiful wife, instead of a woman with feelings and rights, meant that Dad was able to slot right back into the life that she'd kept warm for him. It infuriated me beyond belief.

'How do you know he's not going to turn around in a month's time and do it again?'

'He won't. He's got whatever it was, out of his system.'

'But he's going to see your one Colette every day at work.'

'No, he's not.' The way she said it got me interested – she sounded kind of triumphant. 'He's taking early retirement. Do you think I'd let him go into that place where she is every day? No way, hose-ay, whatever that means. I told him to sack her or to leave himself. And I'd prefer it if she lost her job, but this will do instead.'

Suddenly I had a great idea. 'Come on,' I urged, 'let's drive over to their work and laugh at her.'

Briefly a light lit Mam's eyes, then she said, 'You go. I've to get your father's tea on.' Then she said half-heartedly, 'We have to forgive her.'

Pah! Too much was made of forgiveness. There was no way I was ever going to forgive Colette and I had no problem with that. A little bit of hatred never hurt anyone. Look at how I'd hated Lily for *years* and it had never done me any harm.

Speaking of hatred, there was something I had to tell Dad.

'I'm getting a book published.'

He expressed great delight – as much to do with the fact that I was talking to him, probably – and when I showed him the proof copy, he declared, 'That cover is marvellous. She's locked out of her house, is she?' He rubbed his finger over my name. 'Would you look at that: Gemma Hogan, my little girl. *Chasing Rainbows*, now that's a marvellous title. What's it about?'

'You leaving Mam and taking up with a girl only four years older than me.'

He was deeply shocked and looked, open-mouthed, at Mam to see if I was having him on.

'It's no joke,' I said.

'It's not.' Mam looked extremely uncomfortable.

'Jesus, Mary and Joseph,' he sounded panicked, 'I'd better read the fecker.' Six pages in he looked up, ashen-faced, 'We'll have to put a stop to this immediately. Im*med*iately. This can't get out.'

'Too late, Dad. I'm under contract.'

'We'll see a solicitor.'

'And I've spent loads of the advance.'

'I'll give you the money.'

'I don't want your money. I want my book to be published.'

'But look at it.' He smacked the pages with the back of his hand. 'All that personal stuff. And I wouldn't mind but plenty of it isn't even true! If this comes out I'm going to be very embarrassed!'

'Good,' I said, putting my face too close to his. 'It's called living with the consequences of your actions.'

'Gemma!' Mam summoned me into the kitchen. 'He's said he's sorry,' she said. 'And he means it. He was going through a crisis, in a way he couldn't help what he did. You're being very hard on him, in fact you can be very hard on everyone. Do you know what? I think you have anger issues.'

'What would you know about anger issues?'

'I watch *Doctor Phil*.'

'Oh, right. Anyway, I don't have anger issues, I just like people to be punished when they do wrong.'

'Vengeance issues, then.'

'Yes!' I agreed. 'I do. I'm sort of an emotional vigilante. I am Gemma the . . . what am I . . . ? Destroyer? Not really, more's the pity. Punisher? Gemma the Punisher? Not such a great ring to it. Avenger! I am Gemma the Avenger.'

I darted around the kitchen, holding my fingers like a gun and singing *The Avengers* theme music.

'Don't make it sound like a good thing,' Mam said. 'Because it's not.'

'And that's not *The Avengers*'s music,' Dad yelled from the next room. 'That's *The Professionals* you're singing.'

I stood in the doorway, held up an imaginary handbag and scorned, 'Wooooooooooooh! Get him!'

That very night, I removed all my belongings from my parents' and officially moved back into my own flat. I'd wondered if I'd become institutionalized at Mam's or if my new freedom might feel like when you finish exams and for ages you feel guilty for not studying, even though you no longer need to. But no, I wasn't a bit afraid of resuming my old life.

I rang Owen to report the good news. 'We can see each other all the time now, if we want. Come over now, let's try out our new life for size.'

Half a *Coronation Street* later he arrived.

'I need to talk to you,' he said.

'Why?'

'Guess what?' He was smiling, but in a strange way.

'What?'

'Lorna rang me.' Lorna was his twenty-four-year-old ex and the prickly feeling on my scalp told me what was coming next. 'She wants us to get back together.'

'She does?'

'It happened exactly like you said it would: she saw us together on Saturday when we were in town shopping and she realized what she was missing. You're brilliant!'

'That's me.' My voice went annoyingly wobbly.

'Christ, you don't mind, do you?'

'Of course I don't mind,' I choked, overwhelmed by ridiculous tears. 'I'm really happy for you. We always knew it was going nowhere.' But it had gone nowhere for nearly nine months.

He was silent and when I looked up from my crying jag I saw why: he was crying too. 'I'll never forget you,' he said, wiping fat tears away from his face.

'Oh stop being so melodramatic.'

'OK.' As if by magic, the tears disappeared and, really, he couldn't hide his happiness and how keen he was to get going.

'What about our holiday?'

He looked blank.

'In Antigua. Windsurfing while banjoed out of your head on free Pina Coladas? We're meant to be going in three weeks.'

'Right, sorry, wasn't thinking. You go. Bring your mammy. I can see her up on the windsurfer, she'll be great.'

Just before he got into his car, he yelled, in frothy high spirits, 'We'll all go out soon, me and Lorna and you and Anton. We'll plan the route for our holiday in the Dordogne!'

'And don't forget to call your first child after me,' I managed.

'Consider it done. Even if he's a boy.'

Then he gunned the car away, beeping and waving like he was in a wedding cavalcade.

Jojo

January

Jojo returned to London, full of hope for the new year. She'd had a happy holiday in New York with her family but knew that her next year's Christmas would be different. Not in NYC. More likely to be sharing space with accident-prone Sophie and dipso Sam, in Mark's and her new home, wherever that might be.

On her first day back, Manoj came in and dumped a box on her desk. 'Proof copies of Gemma Hogan's *Chasing Rainbows*.'

Dalkin Emery believed in recycling; the jacket was an old Kathleen Perry one, which Jojo had rejected almost a year ago for being too drippy and which had resurfaced in the autumn in a new guise – as *Chasing Rainbows*'s jacket. It was a pastel watercolour of a woman and even though it was just vague, blurry lines, every time Jojo saw it, it looked to her like the woman badly needed to use the bathroom but was miles from one.

It was a cute little package, though. She gathered up ten copies and took them to Jim Sweetman, to send to his movie contacts. 'Do your magic.'

The partnership vote was due on Monday, the twenty-third of January – three weeks away. The first week passed without incident. Then the second week. The countdown for week three was underway – Monday, Tuesday, Wednesday was gone – then on Thursday morning the email arrived.

TO: Jojo.harvey@LIPMAN HAIGH.co
FROM: Mark.avery@LIPMAN HAIGH.co
SUBJECT: News. Possibly bad

I need to talk to you. My office asap?
M xxx

What now?

Mark was sitting behind his desk, looking super-serious. 'I wanted to tell you in advance of tomorrow's meeting, Richie Gant has come up with something.'

'What?' Instantly Jojo was nervous as fuck. Skanky Boy was full of surprises, none of them nice.

'He's made friends with some of the marketing people from Lawson Global.'

'Who?'

'A multi-national. They own soft drinks, cosmetics, sportswear ... and it looks like they're interested in paying for mentions in some of Lipman Haigh's authors' books.'

She opened her mouth, she could barely speak. 'You mean, corporate sponsorship?'

'Not actual sponsorship of a title, not like *Coca-Cola's Horse Whisperer*, just mentions of a particular brand in the text.'

'Corporate sponsorship,' Jojo repeated. 'Exactly what you and I discussed, like, a year ago. We thought it sucked. I still think it sucks.'

'With the right fit, it doesn't have to be offensive.'

She gave him a long, perplexed look. 'This isn't happening. Mark, you're way off here. You told me it was a cruddy idea.'

'Jojo, it's business, possibly very lucrative.'

He let this hang and the implication was clear. Leaving Cassie and setting up a second home with Jojo was going to cost them.

Whatever. Angrily, she said, 'When I floated the idea, why come you didn't tell me to go for it?'

'Because we were just joking and it was obvious you despised it. If you really thought it a good idea, you wouldn't have needed encouragement, you'd have gone ahead and done it.'

Maybe that was true but, if anything, it fanned her rage. 'So what happened? Gant came to you with the concept and you told him, good job, fella, go for it?'

'No. The first I knew about it was this morning. He's already made the contacts and pulled together some proposals.'

'Bet none of them are for my authors,' she said bitterly. 'So how come Gant came up with the same idea as me?'

'Possibly because the two of you think alike?'

Jojo shuddered. 'I'm nothing like that . . . greasy creep. And you know what, Mark? I'm disappointed in you.'

He became very calm. Scary calm. 'I'm running a business. It's my job to explore the idea of bringing in more money. I have principles but being too high-minded doesn't work in a commercial arena. And yes, I did think it was a crass idea but I reserve the right to change my mind. Especially when it's presented as a fait accompli.'

'Gotcha,' Jojo said. 'Loud and clear.'

She powered out and he made no attempt to follow her, then she stood on the street and smoked with so much fury a passing man said, 'What did that poor cigarette ever do to you?'

How had Richie Gant made those contacts, Jojo brooded. If *she* worked for a multi-national and that slimy little fuck showed up for an appointment, she'd get security to throw him out. In fact, when he lay on the street afterwards, she'd kick him in the kidneys. They really hurt. And the balls, obviously. And the head – but then her boots would be covered in the oily stuff he put in his hair . . . Eewww.

Greater than her anger with Richie was anger for herself. She shouldn't have listened to Mark, she should have capitalized on her idea. But this wasn't just about hurt pride, it could have profound practical implications: the partnership decision was next Monday, less than a week away. You had to hand it to the guy, she thought, sucking down another three-second drag – he'd picked the perfect moment, throwing this proposal in so the partners would be making their decision whipped into a frenzy at the thought of all those corporate millions.

But there was the small consolation that she still thought it was a gross idea. And in her heart of hearts, she hoped that instead of being blinded with greed, the partners might agree with her.

Friday morning meeting
Everyone already knew about Richie's new corporate connections, so at least Jojo didn't have to endure everyone going 'Ooohhh' approvingly, like he'd just pulled a cruddy old silk hanky out of a cruddy old silk hat.

But it wasn't over yet. Ever the showman, Richie gave possible scenarios. He stretched out an arm and said, 'Olga!'

'You, madam,' Jojo said, not quietly enough.

He turned to her, 'Jojo, don't you worry. I'll do my best with your authors. See if we can't earn them a little sponsorship money.'

'No need,' Jojo said crisply. 'My authors earn enough from *writing books*.'

'Up to them,' Richie shrugged, 'if they want to turn down free money. Just seems like a funny thing to advise them, that's all. Glad you're not *my* agent!'

'Not as glad as I am, dog-breath.' Although she only said 'dog-breath' in her own head. Ever the professional.

Richie turned his attention back to Olga. 'Let's take Annelise Palmer.' One of Olga's biggest earners, a writer of racy bonkbusters. 'She'd be a good match with one of the expensive champagnes in Lawson Global's portfolio. If Annelise was game – and I know that old bird, I bet she would,' he chuckled with such audience confidence that Jojo had to sit on her hands in case they hit him without her say-so, 'that could net her up to a million quid. You'd get your ten per cent and if we ask nicely they'll throw in a couple of crates of champers just for you.'

Jojo nearly imploded with impotence. Suck it up – a million quid for an author kinda overshadowed a video on the mating habits of Emperor Penguins.

'Have they actually proposed this?' Mark challenged. 'Have they actually mentioned this kind of money for individual authors?'

'Mentioned? You mean *promised*. For real,' Richie nodded seriously. 'Believe me, this is going to happen.'

The entire room went into shock. Even the ever-restless molecules of air seemed to pause their perpetual circling. A million smackers just for mentioning champagne!

Jojo watched everyone's expression change – they were looking at Richie like he was an alchemist. And they were already spending the loot. A new Merc. A holiday home in Umbria. A retirement spent on the QE2. Enough cash to leave your wife and set up a comfortable, worry-free home with your girlfriend. Even Aurora French and Lobelia Hall, people who hated Gant and who would never see much, if any, of this promised money were at it. Shoes and handbags lit up Aurora's eyes and the gleam of a week in Vegas playing the high-roller's tables was in Lobelia's. Jojo had to do something.

'So Olga could ring them right now,' she said, 'and tell them that Annelise is on for it, and to bike us over the million big ones in used fivers.' She pulled her handbag onto the table, produced her mobile phone and held it out for Olga. 'Let's make that call.'

Once again the room froze into stillness. All that moved were optic muscles as everyone played eye-tennis between Richie and Jojo. The seconds ticked for too long, Jojo's hand beneath the phone became slick with sweat, then Richie caved. 'Obviously this is only an example. Like, *obviously*.'

'Oh,' Jojo feigned breathy surprise, 'it's only an *example*. Don't make that call just yet.' She folded the sweaty phone away and winked at Olga. 'Could be embarrassing.'

As people watched their dreams waver and dissolve, suddenly they were staring at Richie like he was a trickster.

But the sting in the tail was the announcement that the following day three of the Lawson Global guys were going with Richie, Jim Sweetman and Mark to a luxury country hotel to play golf and bond. Jojo tried to hide her disbelief. Mark had not told her about this and also, when did that shit-head Gant learn to play golf?

'How come I'm not invited?'

'Why should you be?'

'I brought in more money than any other agent last year and I'm on course to do it again this year.'

'Can you play golf?' Richie asked.

'Sure I can.' Like, how hard could it be? Especially if she pretended every golf ball was his head.

'Shame,' Richie wall-eyed her. 'It's already booked and there are no more places.'

'So no women? Isn't that a little sexist? There are laws against that sort of thing.'

'What law says a bunch of guys can't get together to play golf? And who's saying there won't be any women?'

He let that sink in and Jojo said, 'Oh, I'd forgotten about your fondness for lap-dancers.'

'I hadn't,' he grinned and rage filled her up. 'Jim likes them too and Mark is bound to love the –'

'Excuse me,' Mark interrupted.

Dan Swann roused himself from his customary reverie and began to murmur quietly, 'Fight, fight, fight!'

Mark took control. 'OK, that's enough. And Richie, don't be ridiculous, there won't be any lap-dancers. At least there'd better not be.'

Jojo thought that that actually made things worse. Everyone was thinking, Mark Avery's girlfriend doesn't want him near lap-dancers. These were her colleagues and they were looking at her like she was a nagging wife. The boundaries were way too blurred.

After the meeting closed she went to Mark's office, closed the door behind her and said, 'You never told me you were going away to play golf with these guys.'

'You're right, I didn't.'

'Why not?'

'You're not the boss of me.'

It was like a staple gun to the heart. 'Mark! What's happening? Why are you being so horrible?'

'Why are *you* being so horrible?' He was far too calm and at times like this she remembered, *really* remembered why she'd fallen for him in the first place: his strength of character, his ability to see the big picture . . .

'I'm not being horrible, Mark.'

He shrugged. 'And I'm just doing my job.' He was still not engaging.

'Even when it conflicts with me?'

'I don't see it that way. You may not believe me, but everything I do, I'm doing for us.'

Thanks to Slimeball Gant things with Mark were starting to get messy; she would not allow it. She made a big, almost superhuman effort to get over herself.

'I believe you.'

* * *

Saturday morning, Jojo's flat

Before Mark left for his golf weekend, Jojo said, 'You're not to tell those Lawson guys what I'm like in bed.'

'Why would I do that?'

'I know what guys are like, telling sexist jokes and discussing women.'

'How?'

'Because I'm one of them.'

He put his hand on her waist, then slid it upwards. 'Oh, I don't think so.'

He took his hand away and she replaced it.

'Jojo, we don't have time for this.'

'Yes, we do.'

'I'll be late.'

'Good.'

Twenty minutes later

'I really have to go now, Jojo.'

'Go.' She smiled from the bed. 'I have no further need of you. Bye, honey. Have a horrible time.'

'I will.'

That afternoon

Jojo was in Russell & Bromley with Becky when her phone rang. Caller display showed it was Mark. 'Mark!' she exclaimed. 'Just the man I want to speak to. What's the difference between a bonus and a penis? I'll tell you – your wife will blow your bonus! Ba-boom!'

'Jojo –'

'What do you do when your dishwasher breaks down? Hit her! Ba-boom!'

'Jojo –'

'Which one do you give the job to? The one with the biggest tits! Ba-boom!'

Sunday afternoon, Jojo's flat

Mark came straight from the hotel to her.

'Hey, baby.' She gathered him in her arms like he'd just come home from war. 'It's OK, you're OK now.'

She followed him into her living room and asked, 'How bad was it?'

He smiled. 'Bad. I had to smoke a cigar and you know how you have to cut a bit off the end?' Jojo didn't.

'Well one of the Lawson blokes kept making circumcision jokes about it.'

'Eeeww. Worst moment of the entire weekend?'

Mark thought about it. 'When one of the Lawson blokes described another man as, "He's the one guy who if he fell into a pool of tits would come out sucking his thumb."'

'Eeeww,' Jojo repeated.

Then Mark admitted, 'I told them your dishwasher joke. I think they liked it.'

'Happy to help. How was Gant?'

Mark just shrugged.

'Help me out here?' Jojo burst out. 'Just tell me how anyone could like him. Like, what am I missing?'

Mark thought about it. 'He's good with people, he intuits what they like and then homes in on it.'

'He doesn't do it with me.'

'He doesn't need you to like him.'

'He will when I'm a fucking partner and he isn't.'

Her words hung in the air and when Jojo spoke, the anxiety that had dogged her all weekend, and made her buy an impractical, ridiculously expensive clutch bag, broke through. 'Can we talk about tomorrow? Do you think I'll get it?'

'You deserve it.'

'But do you think I'll get it?'

'Tarquin Wentworth, Aurora French and Lobelia Hall have all been there longer than you. If we go on longevity, Tarquin should get it.'

She hit him. 'C'mon, stop being Mr Let's-Look-at-the-Facts, we all know it's between me and Richie Gant.'

'OK, it's between you and him.'

'Yeah, and *let's* look at the facts. I'm a great agent, I make more money than anyone else including Gant *and* I've done everything I can to blacken his reputation. Can I do more than that? I don't think so.'

She believed in thinking positive. But she woke up in the middle of the night, thinking not so positive. Mark had gone home and she was glad; she didn't want him to see her like this.

She was imagining what it would be like if she wasn't made partner tomorrow. Apart from the shock and humiliation, Richie Gant would be her new boss, well, one of them. And he would not be a gracious winner. She'd have to leave Lipman Haigh and start all over again for someone else. Prove herself, build alliances, generate income. It would set her back at least two years. The panic was starting to spiral within her, moving up and up to block her throat.

She got it together. Richie Gant was good – and sneaky. But his corporate sponsorship project was all talk. No one was in any immediate danger of making any money from it. She was a better agent. Fact. She generated more income. Her authors were excellent long-term prospects. How could she not get it?

Lily

Anton was home from work. He shot into the room and said, 'Look at what I got sent today.' I had not seen him so animated in a very long time.

He brandished a book and when I saw that it was Gemma's book, *Chasing Rainbows*, I lunged and grabbed it, desperate to read it. Nausea set up a familiar churning.

'How did you get this?'

'Proof copy. Jim Sweetman, the media fella over at Lipman Haigh, sent it to me. And the good news,' Anton said, all aglow, 'is that it's not about us.'

'And the bad news?'

'There is no bad news.'

But no one ever says, 'The good news is . . .' if there is no bad news.

'What's it like?' I asked. 'Is it good?'

'Nah.' But excitement was hopping from him, zigzagging like colour through the air.

Surprised, I accused, 'You like it.'

'I don't.'

'You do.'

'I don't.'

I held my breath because I knew there was a 'but' coming.

'But,' he said, 'I'd like to option it.'

I was stunned into silence.

All I could think was that he had not optioned my book. Either of them.

It was five weeks since we had moved out of our house, but it felt a lot longer. We had passed a bleak Christmas in our cubey flat – the bleakness made worse by Jessie and Julian being expected home from Argentina but delivering a last-minute cancellation.

Despite several invitations for New Year's Eve – everyone from Mikey and Ciara to Viv, Baz and Jez to Nicky and Simon – we spent the night alone and toasted each other with the champagne Dalkin Emery had given me in those long ago days when *Mimi's Remedies* had been storming the charts and they still liked me. Our toast was to 'next year', in the hope that it would be better than the year just gone. Then January had dawned but – what can I say? – it was January. The best anyone can do is breathe in, breathe out and wait for it to pass.

Crystal Clear did not, as I had prayed for, rally at the last minute. My confidence and creativity were in shreds and since October I had done no writing. What was the point when no one would publish it? It was too cold to go out and I spent my days with Ema, watching *Dora the Explorer* and *Jerry Springer*.

Losing our home had been catastrophic but I was under no illusions that there was still a lot further to fall. Anton and I were unravelling. I was watching it happen from a distance, like it was happening to another couple.

We no longer had anything to say to each other; our disappointment was too huge a presence. I bitterly resented Anton's recklessness with money. I was obsessed with the house we had lost and felt it was all his fault. He had persuaded me to buy it – I kept remembering my many and varied objections – and if we had never bought it, we could not have lost it. The loss was excruciating and I felt unable to forgive him. For some reason I kept thinking of the day he had taken me shopping in Selfridges; we had not had a penny and what did we do? Go further into debt. At the time, I saw it as a glorious *carpe diem*, now it signalled idiotic irresponsibility. The type of irresponsibility that urged us to buy a house which we could only lose.

And, although Anton did not articulate it, I knew *he* blamed *me* for not writing another hit book. Briefly, we had been on the crest of the wave and it was difficult to adjust to all that excitement and hope being whipped away.

We barely spoke and when we did, it was simply to snap childcare instruction at each other.

It felt like a long, long time since I had drawn a proper breath. Every inhalation was a shallow panicked little effort which brought no relief and I never slept more than four hours a night. Anton kept promising me that life would improve. And he seemed to think it just had.

'Chloe Drew would be perfect for the lead!' he enthused.

'But Eye-Kon have no money to option the book.'

'The BBC are interested in a co-production. They'll put up the money if Chloe is on board.'

I leant towards him quizzically. He had already spoken to the BBC? He was putting a deal together? 'Have you actually spoken to Chloe about this?'

'Yep. She's game.'

Oh my goodness.

'Gemma will never let you option it. After what we did to her, you haven't a hope.'

But he had a hope. I could see it in his eyes. Already he was persuading her and using whatever means necessary. I knew that Anton, for all his shabby, laid-back charm, was ambitious but the extent of it impacted like a blow to the chest.

Because our lives had collapsed so spectacularly before Christmas, he needed this desperately. It had been a long time since he had successfully pulled a deal together. He had gone back to making his dreaded infomercials to bring in some money, but this was where his heart lay.

'Lily, this will be the saving of us!' He was a ball of fervour. 'It's got fantastic commercial potential. Everyone could make a pile of money from it. Life would get back on track for us.'

Anton needed this for his pride. And he needed to feel something good could happen to us. But to secure the rights to her book, how far would he go with Gemma? Because of the fierceness of his desperation, I was hit with a powerful conviction that it could be quite some way. Her last words to me flashed into my head: *remember how you met him because that's how you'll lose him.*

'Don't get involved in this,' I urged, low and desperate. 'Please, Anton, nothing good will come of it.'

'But Lily!' He insisted. 'What an opportunity! It's exactly what we need.'

'It's Gemma!'

'It's business.'

'Please, Anton.' But the light would not go out in his eyes and I could have wept.

How the world turns.

During the past three and a half years, Gemma had been a constant source of worry. But since I had read about her book, my ephemeral dread had solidified and taken real shape. For months now I had been braced for some form of consequence. But I could not have guessed it would manifest itself in this shape; that she would hold the key to Anton salvaging his career, his pride and his sense of hope.

And she could not have timed her rearrival in Anton's life any better if she had tried: he and I were so shaky . . .

How shaky? I had to ask myself, as terror darkened my vision. How shaky? What would happen if Gemma launched a bid for him . . . ?

It was then that I discovered I no longer had faith in me and Anton. I had once thought that, as a unit, we were indestructible. Now we seemed small and fragile and perched on the rim of a catastrophe. I didn't know the precise nature of it, or exactly how it was going to come about, but with hideous certitude, I reached a calm still place right at the centre of me and saw my future set in stone: Anton and I were going to split up.

Jojo

Probably the most important morning of Jojo's entire career. On her way to her office, she passed the boardroom – behind the closed door, they were all in there, even Nicholas and Cam. *Vote for me.* She tried to send voodoo thought waves. Then she laughed at herself: she didn't need voodoo thought waves. She was a good enough agent.

All the same she was very jumpy. She accused Manoj of banging her coffee cup too loudly on her desk and when her phone rang her heart almost pushed out through her ribcage.

'We'll know by lunchtime,' Manoj soothed.

'Right.'

But just after ten, someone appeared in her doorway. Mark! But it was far too soon. Could be they were on a break . . .

'Hi . . .'

In silence, Mark closed the door behind him, leant against it, then looked her in the eye. Immediately she knew. But couldn't believe it. She heard herself say, 'They gave it to Richie Gant?'

A nod.

She still couldn't believe it and for a moment felt she might burst from her body. This wasn't happening. It was just another worst-case-scenario imagining. But Mark was still standing there, looking at her with concern and although she felt like she was dreaming, she knew it was real.

Mark crossed and tried to hug her but she moved out of his arms. 'Don't blow my low.'

She stood by the window and stared at nothing. It was over. The vote had happened and she hadn't got it. But it was too soon. They'd only been in that room for an hour. So long had been spent waiting for this that she wasn't ready for it to have happened yet. A bubble of panic rose. *This isn't real.*

She was trying to think logically but her processes were hit hard. 'Is it because of you and me, do you think?'

'I don't know.'

Mark looked grey and exhausted and Jojo had a momentary insight into how horrible this was for him. 'Who voted for me? As well as you?'

'Jocelyn and Dan.'

'I lost three-four. Close, but no cigar, right?' She forced a wry smile. 'I just can't believe Nicholas and Cam didn't vote for me. I really thought they would.'

Another powerless shrug from Mark.

'I so don't get it. I've great authors who're going to have long careers. Short-term *and* long-term I'm a better bet. What d'you think happened? Seeing as I bring in more money than Gant.'

'Only just.'

'Excuse me?'

'That came out wrong. What I mean is they looked at this year's income and you and Richie are neck and neck.'

'No, we are so not. I'm ahead, by lots. How can we be neck and neck?'

Mark looked like he wanted to die and she was sorry for taking it out on him. He couldn't control the other partners, they made their own decisions. But she needed to know. 'Tell me.'

'I feel so bad for you.' His eyes glistened with unshed tears. 'You deserve it and it means so much to you. But the way they look at it is, if Richie pulls off even one corporate deal, that puts him way ahead of the game.'

'But he's delivered zilch. He's talking the talk and they fell for it. It's a crass, crap idea and I bet no one will go for it. Writers still have some self-respect.'

Mark shrugged and they stood in silence, miserable and separate.

Then Jojo got it and surprise, more than anything, made her blurt, 'It's because I'm a woman!' She'd heard about this but never thought it would happen to her. 'It's the glass ceiling!'

Right up to this minute, she wasn't even sure she'd believed in the existence of glass ceilings. If she'd thought about it at all she'd suspected it was something lame-duck female employees used to salve their pride when their more deserving male colleagues got promoted over them. She'd never felt part of a sisterhood: it was up to each woman to do it for herself. She'd always thought she was as good as men and that she'd be treated on her own merits. But guess what? She was wrong.

'This has got nothing to do with you being a woman.'

'The bottom line,' Jojo said slowly, 'is they made him partner because he might pull off a deal with one of his golf-course cronies.'

'No, they made him partner because they think long term he'll bring in more money.'

'And how's he going to do that? By playing golf with other men. Stop peeing in my ear and telling me it's raining. This is a case of glass ceiling.'

'It isn't.'

'It is.'

'It isn't.'

'Whatever.'

'It isn't.'

'I hear you. Hey, we'll talk about it later.' She wanted him out of her office. She needed to think.

'What are you going to do?'

'What do you think? Whack Gant?' She pointed towards her desk. 'I've got a job to do.'

He looked relieved. 'I'll see you later.' He tried to hug her again and she slipped away from him. 'Jojo, don't punish me.'

'I'm not.' But she didn't want anyone touching her. She didn't want anything. She was on auto-pilot until she figured out what to do.

Ten minutes later

Richie Gant stood in her doorway, waited until he had her attention, then sniggered, 'They're oversexed, they're overpaid and they're OVER.'

He moved off, leaving Jojo with a heart racing with anger.

Manoj came in. 'What's going on?'

'Richie Gant is the new partner, not me.'

'But –'

'Exactly.'

'It's not fair! You're far better than him.'

'Exactly. But, hey, no one died, right?'

'*Jojo*.' He sounded surprised, almost disappointed. 'Are you just going to take this lying down?'

'Manoj, I'm going to tell you something I've told very few people.'

'Because you like me?'

'Because you're the only person in my office. The reason I left the force and came to London?'

Manoj nodded encouragingly.

'Because my brother killed someone. He was a policeman – still is. Needed overtime money so went out cruising to arrest someone. Happens a lot in October when they're trying to make the overtime pay for Christmas. Anyhow, he finds a dealer who, in the course of arrest, pulls a gun on him. My brother loses it. Pulls his own gun and kills the guy. And yeah, maybe he had to, get them before they get you, like they say, but you know what? I so did not want to do a job where I might kill someone. Very next day I gave notice, came to England three weeks later. Worked in a bar, worked as a reader and when I became an agent I was happy because no matter what happened, I wasn't going to kill someone. Nothing – negotiations, whatever – mattered to me *that* much because, bottom line, it wasn't life and death.'

Manoj nodded.

'So Richie Gant has been made partner when it should have been me, it's all wrong, but no one got hurt, no one died, right?'

'Right.'

In silence she twisted it over in her head. 'But all the FUCKING same!'

'Quite.'

'I should have got that promotion. I'm a better agent and I deserve it.'

'Too right. You can't just take this.'

Jojo considered. 'Yeah. I'm going to see Mark.'

Instantly, Manoj's head was full of images of Jojo on her knees in front of Mark giving him an on-duty blow-job. Jojo put her face very close to Manoj's and hissed, 'I don't do that sort of thing.'

Manoj swallowed and watched her departing back. How did she know?

Mark's office

She didn't mean to bounce his door against the wall. She wasn't looking to be dramatic, but hey, these things happen. He looked up, startled.

'Mark, I'm going to sue.'

He looked even more startled, 'Who?'

'Lipman Haigh.'

'For what?'

'For what? A broken ankle? A dented fender?' She widened her eyes. 'Sex discrimination, what else?'

Mark went the colour of dust. Suddenly he looked ten years older. 'Don't, Jojo. Richie got it fair and square. It's just going to look like sour grapes.'

Slightly perplexed, she focused on him. 'This is my career. I don't care what it *looks* like.'

'Jojo –'

But she was gone.

Back in her office, she hit the phones. She rang Becky but the only solicitor she knew was the one who helped her and Andy buy their flat and – because of the last-minute shenanigans involved – whom they hated. 'Ring Shayna. Brandon will know someone. Or else ring Magda, she knows everyone in the whole world.'

There was no need to ring Magda because Brandon knew someone. 'Eileen Prendergast, the best there is. She's like you: nice but scarily good at her job. When do you want to see her?'

'Now.' Jojo was surprised. 'When else?'

'You *do* mean business. Eileen's booked up weeks in advance but let me see what I can do.'

He rang back three minutes later. 'You owe me big. She's cancelled a lunch. Come over now.'

'See you in twenty.' She grabbed her bag and told Manoj, 'If Mark is looking for me, tell him I've gone to see the employment lawyer, but don't tell anyone else.'

Monday lunchtime

Walking into the glass tower in the City, Jojo had a moment. Her circumstances zipped by her head like something tangible and she actually felt dizzy. How did it ever come to this? And so quickly? This time yesterday she'd been looking forward with tentative confidence to celebrating her partnership. And now it had turned one-eighty and she was *suing*.

Brandon met her in reception and took her to meet Eileen, who was tall, beautiful and had more than a touch of Liv Tyler about her.

He made introductions, left, then Jojo sat down and launched into the details of Richie Gant. 'I bring in more money than him. But they picked him because he can play golf, bond with corporate guys and try to shake them down for sponsorship. As a woman I can't do that.'

Eileen listened, making notes in a pad, interrupting occasionally to ask questions.

'There isn't a pattern of you being passed over in favour of him or another man?'

Jojo shook her head.

'So this is a one-off, which will make it harder to prove.'

'I'm not sticking around, waiting for it to happen again!'

Eileen smiled. 'Fair enough. Now, things you should know: even if you win, the tribunal doesn't have the power to order an appointment. In other words, no matter what the decision of the tribunal, you won't make partner.'

'So why am I doing this?'

'If you win, you get awarded compensation and your reputation recovers.'

Jojo made a face. 'Better than a kick in the head, I guess.'

'Some other things. This is a tribunal, not a trial. It's meant to be accessible, in other words, there's meant to be no need for legal representation, but in practice, most people do. But because of that, they don't award costs. So Jojo, even if you win, you could be looking at a bill for ten thousand, twenty thousand, even more. Any compensation you receive could be wiped out by legal costs. And that's if you win.'

'What are the chances of that?'

Eileen thought about it. 'Fifty-fifty. Even if you win, it may be difficult for you to continue working there. And if you lose, you'll find it impossible. And probably very difficult to find employment in another agency – you might have acquired a reputation for being difficult.'

'For what? Doing the right thing?'

'I know, but unfortunately some women use this process in a vexatious way. For example, if they've been having a relationship with a male colleague and it ends messily, sometimes they cry "sexual discrimination" to cause trouble . . . what? What is it?'

'Yeah, look.' Jojo took a breath. 'I've been having, *am* having, a relationship with, as you say, one of my colleagues. The Managing Partner. But we haven't broken up, we're very together. Is this a problem?'

Eileen considered. 'You promise me the relationship is on-going? That he hasn't just dumped you and you're doing this for revenge?'

'I promise.'

'And you're ready for it to be in the public domain?'

'Excuse me?'

'These hearings are held in public and they're haunted by members of the press looking for a juicy story. I've a feeling yours might count as one of them.'

'People from the newspapers?'

'Yes.'

'But do I have to tell this tribunal about Mark?'

'You won't be able to keep it secret.' Eileen was stern. 'All relevant details must be submitted. And if you don't volunteer it, it could be used against you.'

Jojo thought about it. It was tacky but it was all going to come out soon anyway. 'OK. So have I got this straight? I have a fifty-fifty chance of winning. My legal representation – you, yeah? – will cost me thousands but if I win I'll get compensation which should cover it. If I lose I'll have to eat it – but hey, I won't lose because I have right on my side!'

Eileen couldn't help smiling but had to add, 'The tribunal may not agree with you. They may decide that Richie was simply the better agent, that he deserved the appointment –'

'They won't. They picked him because the slimy fuck can play golf. The sole reason. So let's do it. What happens now?'

'The first thing we do is serve your employers with notice. Let them know they're being sued.'

'When can we do that?'

'Asap.'

'Yay!'

But in the taxi back to work, Jojo's positive mood dwindled. She'd just embarked on a long, scary ordeal. Eileen had said she had a fifty-fifty chance of winning; Jojo had thought the odds would be better than that, but Eileen was an expert . . .

What if she lost? She went cold with fear that she might. Just because *she* knew Richie didn't deserve the promotion didn't mean it would be clear to a tribunal. Justice didn't always get done; she'd been in the police, if anyone knew that, she did.

She had a sudden powerful desire to halt it. It would be easy to stop right now, before notice had been served on Lipman Haigh. What was the point of suing them? Even if she won, Richie Gant wouldn't be removed and she wouldn't be installed in his place. Like, the worst had already happened; she could not undo the decision of the partners. Nothing would fix that. Did she want to run the risk of being humiliated again, this time in public?

But she wasn't giving up. She refused to let Gant waltz away with it. It didn't mean she was happy, though. The next three months or however long the process took were going to be tough, tough, tough. Lucky she was too.

Back at work
'Mark's been looking for you,' Manoj said.

'I know.' He'd left two messages on her mobile, saying he needed to talk to her, and when she checked her emails, one from Mark asked her to come and see him as soon as she got back. So she did.

'I don't believe it,' he said. 'You went to see an employment lawyer?'

'Yes.'

'And?'

She swallowed, not looking forward to telling him, 'I'm suing Lipman Haigh for gender discrimination. Notice will be served by the end of the week.'

He looked like she'd slapped him. 'I don't believe it.'

'But Mark . . . That partnership was mine. It was wrong that he got it.'

He looked at her and despair was stamped on his face.

'Please don't look at me like that,' she begged, 'I'm not your enemy.'

'Get real, Jojo. You're suing my company.'

'It's not *your* company –'

'I'm the managing partner. What's all this going to do to you and me? Jojo, I'm asking you, for *us*, to stop this.'

'Mark, don't. It's OK for you, you're a partner, you're a *managing* partner. Please, Mark, I need you to be supportive.'

'This will destroy us and you don't care.'

'I do! And it won't destroy anything! I still want you to tell Cassie tonight. Tell her, then come over to me.'

He rubbed his eyes. 'OK.'

'It'll all be OK, I promise.'

But later she got a text from him. Not even a voice message. *Can't do tonight. M xxx*

OK, so that's how it was.

Ten minutes later

The phone rang and she seized it. But it was only Anton Carolan, partner of Lily Wright.

'Gemma Hogan's book? *Chasing Rainbows*? I need to talk to someone about it but I can't get hold of Jim Sweetman. I read the proof and we at Eye-Kon think it would make a fantastic made-for-TV feature. We've already had a verbal commitment from Chloe Drew for the part of Izzy.'

'Yeah?' Why bother getting excited? Chloe Drew was hot but Eye-Kon hadn't a bean.

'I've been speaking with Gervase Jones, Head of Drama at the BBC, and he's keen too.'

But if the BBC were interested in a co-production . . . Trying to inject some animation into her voice, she said, 'OK, I'll let Gemma know right away.'

That evening, deep in dark depression she went home. She didn't want to see anyone. What a shit day for her career and now it looked like Mark was backing out on her. Double whammy.

What if she and Mark split up over this? What if Lipman Haigh suspended her for the duration of the suit? And it was too late to undo stuff. If she called off the suit, she'd blame Mark for trying to hold her back. And hey, if she backed down surely Mark would be disappointed in her. The feisty girl he fell in love with wouldn't keep schtum just to keep the peace. He *wanted* her to sue, he just didn't realize it! Yeah right, she wasn't convincing even herself.

She admitted it – she was angry with him; if he loved her enough, he'd support her decision to sue. But it was his company, she could see how he felt she was attacking him. It was a mess! If only she'd been made partner, they'd be blissfully celebrating their first official night together. Well, maybe not blissful, what with their guilt and everything . . .

This was what happened when you got involved with someone you worked with. Then again, they'd never have fallen in love if they hadn't worked together.

But what was going to happen? How could she keep working at Lipman Haigh? Where else could she go? Her stock had gone down, other firms mightn't be as keen to employ her if she wasn't good enough to be a partner at Lipman Haigh. The only other option was to set up on her own and that was too expensive and scary to be viable.

All evening her thoughts swirled round and round and eventually she fell asleep on the couch, aided by exhaustion and most of a bottle of Merlot. At ten-fifteen, the phone rang, waking her.

'Yeah?' she said sleepily.

Mark's voice said, 'Howdy, partner.'

'Excuse me?'

'Howdy, partner.'

She was confused. Was Mark trying to be funny?

'I've just come out of an emergency meeting with the other partners of Lipman Haigh,' Mark yelled, 'and they want to offer you a partnership.' He sounded giddy and high.

She scrambled to sit up properly. 'They changed their mind? Me? Instead of Gant?'

'No, as well as.'

'How? I thought there could only be seven partners.'

'If every partner is in agreement, the terms of the partnership can be altered – and they're all willing to do that because they want to bring you on board! This is a big, big deal, Jojo, they don't want to share the profits any more than they have to, but they were willing to do it because they love you.'

And they didn't want the negative publicity of a lawsuit, but no need to rub their noses in it.

'Can I come over?'

'Sure. Hurry.'

The following morning

A mass email was sent to everyone in Lipman Haigh, breaking the news. Official confirmation would appear in Friday's *Book News*.

'Happy now?' Mark asked.

'Mmmm.'

'So tonight's the night with Cassie.'

'Let's wait until Friday,' Jojo said. 'Just so's it's all nice and official.'

He gave her a look.

'This isn't a trick.'

'OK.'

In her office she was going through stuff with Manoj when a shadow fell on them. She could smell the hair oil: Richie Gant.

He grinned nastily at her. 'See you got your boyfriend to make you a partner.'

'Get out of my office,' Jojo said serenely.

'So why didn't he vote for you in the first place?'

'Just get out.'

'He didn't vote for you. He voted for me.'

She felt herself flash white with shock but kept it steady. She eyed his skinny frame and said, 'I've got at least twenty pounds on you. I could snap your arm like a twig. Don't make me hurt you. Now get out.'

He backed away, still grinning, and when he'd disappeared from sight, she began to shake. One thing she'd learned: the *SkankMeister* didn't lie. If he said Mark didn't vote for her, then Mark didn't vote for her. But how could she find out? Who could she ask? Because at this stage she trusted no one.

'Could you really snap his arm like a twig?' Manoj asked.

'I don't know.' Her lips felt annoyingly mumbly. 'But I wouldn't mind the chance to find out.'

'Ignore him. He's pissed off because he's not the one and only. He's just trying to cause trouble with you and Mark.'

Maybe. It was possible. But there was only one thing for it.

'I'm going to see Mark.' And for once, Manoj didn't have an image of Jojo on her knees, fellating Mark. No way was it going to happen. Not today.

Mark's office

He looked up, as she came in.

'Mark, tell me the truth because I'll find out anyway. Did you vote for me?'

A too-long silence. Then, 'No.'

She stood stock-still for the longest time. Yet again, she felt like she was dreaming. She was getting kinda tired of these out-of-body experiences.

She pulled up a chair in front of his desk. 'Why not? And this'd better be good.'

'Actually it is.' He sounded so sure of himself that Jojo was surprised – and super-relieved. This was going to be OK, this was going to be alright. This was *Mark*.

'Do the sums, Jojo,' Mark said. 'Me leaving Cassie and you and me setting up a home together is going to cost shedloads. Richie said that if he wasn't made partner he'd leave, taking his money-spinning idea with him. Plus, if you were made partner, your – *our* – income would go *down* for three years. And after you had the pregnancy scare, it made me realize that you might be planning to give up work anyway. It sounds a bit made-for-TV, but I did it for us. And there's more. Everyone knows we're together and they're watching for signs of favourit-ism. If I wanted to retain the respect of my partners, I *couldn't* vote for you – not when it made perfect financial sense to vote for Richie.'

Mute with frustration she stared at him. Everything he said added up – at least on paper. All she could manage was, 'Why didn't you talk to me about it?'

'Because I know you, Jojo. I knew you'd choose the job over me. Us.'

She couldn't keep her anger from busting out. 'You wrecked my chance of being a partner so we'd have the money to be together.'

He eyed her shrewdly. 'Put it another way. You'd risk wreck-ing the chances of us being together just so you could be a partner.'

It took her a long time to answer. 'I didn't realize it was a choice.'

She left, sunk deep in a crisis of the soul. Was Mark right? Was she too ambitious? But that description was never applied to men – in the same way it was impossible for a woman to be too thin, it was impossible for a man to be too ambitious. A man would never have to choose between his ambition and his emotional life.

Rising up in her again was something she wanted not to see – Mark had had no right to take that decision for her.

But she loved Mark. Like, she *loved* Mark. Something her dad used to say came to mind: Which would you rather be – right or happy? And like Mark had said, she was a partner now. She'd got what she wanted. Everything was fine, all she had to do now was wait for her feelings to catch up with the facts.

* * *

Dan Swann's office

She needed to talk to someone and she trusted Dan, he was too mad to be treacherous.

'Delighted you're a partner,' he told her.

'Thanks, and I appreciate you and Jocelyn standing by me.'

'And Jim.'

'Jim? Sweetman? Jim Sweetman voted for me?' That dream-like feeling again. This was getting so old.

'Er, yes.'

'Why?'

Dan looked startled. How the hell did he know? 'Because he thinks you're good?'

'OK, Dan, like, thanks. I have to go.'

She went directly to Jim's office.

'Jim, why did you vote for me?'

'And hello to you too.'

'Sorry. Hello.' She sat down. 'So why did you vote for me?'

'Because I thought you were the best person for the job.'

'Not the *SkankMeister*?'

'I have a lot of respect for Richie, he's a very good agent, just not as good as you. His corporate sponsorship stuff swung it with the others, but I thought – think – books are the wrong medium, they just aren't sexy enough. I might be wrong, but I don't think those promised millions will ever materialize.'

'I see. Well, thanks.' She got up to go, then sat down again. 'Jim, we used to be buddies. Then after the night in the Coach

560

and Horses when you said I couldn't tempt you, things went kinda weird. What was going on?'

Déjà vu – she'd had this conversation before. When? Then she remembered: it had been with Mark – it was the trigger for him declaring his love for her. Oh, Christ . . .

Jim looked embarrassed, shifted in his chair then laughed uncomfortably. 'OK, I might as well tell you. I had a bit of a thing for you. Face it, Jojo Harvey, you're more than a little fabulous.'

Shit, she thought. Shit, shit.

'But I'm over it now. For the past three months I've been seeing a very nice woman.'

Shit, she thought. Shit, shit. Hey, she was only human.

'She's great. I'm very –' he sought the right word – '*fond* of her.'

'Great, happy for you.'

Back in Jojo's office

Something clicked and suddenly she was left with no choice. Worth trying anyway . . .

She said to Manoj, 'I need you working late every night for the rest of this week.'

'On what?'

'It's a secret.' She leant in close to him. 'And if you tell anyone, I will kill you.'

'Fair enough.' He swallowed and she felt a little bad; she shouldn't go round scaring him but it was so *easy*.

'I want phone numbers for all my authors.'

'Why?'

'What did I just tell you?'

Gemma

After Owen dumped me, to my great surprise, I was devastated. Even though I knew it was silly, I cried all the way driving to work the next day, I cried *at* work and I cried at home that evening. Then I got up the following day and repeated the pattern exactly. It was like being fifteen all over again.

It was very different when Anton had dumped me – that made me bitter and warped, it had changed me. But I didn't call Owen a bastard and I didn't fantasize about getting him back. I had no intention of even trying. Instead of generating bile his departure had opened up a big boxful of sad.

I rang Cody and he took me for a drink and some serious hand-holding.

'I never took it seriously, but what if Owen is The One?'

Cody snorted.

'The One comes in all shapes and sizes! Often you don't realize that that's who you've met. There's a woman who met her The One when she was on a ship to Australia, but she was stalking some other bloke in Australia and when she got there he was riding rings around himself and then she realized the man on the ship was her The One . . .'

'What woman? Who is this?'

'Someone Mam knows.'

'Dear God, she's taking romantic advice from Maureen Hogan. Like taking flying lessons from Osama Bin Laden.'

'Now I've no one to have my fantasies about Anton with.'

'Excuse me?'

'We'd make up stories, where Owen would get back with Lorna and I'd get back with Anton. And now Owen's back

562

with Lorna and I've . . . I've . . .' Big long pause, as I tried to get past a wave of tears. 'NO ONE.'

'You spent your time with your boyfriend fantasizing – out loud, I take it? – about getting back together with your previous boyfriend. He-llo.'

'It's not how it sounds. We were comforting each other.' I was weeping so much I was making the sucky sounds Hannibal Lecter does, but not voluntarily. 'I was so fond of Owen and now I miss him so much . . .' A fresh consignment of tears pushed up through my eyes and toppled down my face. *This isn't right . . .*

Cody watched me in fascination. 'God Almighty. But all you did was fight.'

'I know. I *know* this doesn't make any sense.'

'When did you last cry like this?'

I tried to remember. When Dad had left? I'd barely shed a tear. When Anton left? No, not then either, not like this. I'd just closed up and hated everyone. I'd been too tight with anxiety to cry, and that tightness had never really left me.

'Dunno. Never, maybe. Oh God, Cody, am I having a nervy breaker?'

Anyone else would have said, 'Shush, shush, don't be silly, you're just a bit upset.' But not Cody. Sounding serious, he said, 'Something's happening, that's for sure. Delayed something or other. Transference, that sort of thing.'

'I suppose it's better to let it all out.' I gulped.

'Yaays,' he said doubtfully. 'But try not to do it in public.'

'Thanks, Cody.' Another bout of sucky-noised convulsions gripped me. When I could speak again, I said, 'You've been very supportive, for you.'

I cried when I tried to cancel the holiday to Antigua and cried even more when they wouldn't give me my money back. 'Your boyfriend going back to his old girlfriend isn't covered by the terms of your insurance policy,' the woman in the travel agent told me.

'There's always some bloody loophole,' I said and broke down.

'Why don't you go anyway?'

'I couldn't. I'm in no condition to get on a plane.'

Because the woman felt sorry for me, she broke the rules and said I didn't have to lose the money but could book something for the same value when I was 'feeling better'. 'And I know you think that will be never.' She beat me to it. 'But you'd be surprised.'

I was a liability. I cried at everything. I did it *deliberately*. I rented soppy videos that you'd have to have a heart of stone not to cry at. On nights out I collared people and force-fed them my tragedy. At my work Christmas party (we had to have our work Christmas party in January because as party planners we were too busy in December organizing everyone else's) I was the girl who got scuttered and had to be taken home weeping incoherently. I suppose there has to be one.

Even work was breaking my heart. I was working on a very unusual event – Max O'Neill, a young man, only twenty-eight, was terminally ill and had hired me to plan his memorial service. Initially I'd been touched and flattered that he'd picked me. (Although F&F hadn't been. Frances had grumbled, 'It's not like we're going to get much repeat business from him.') Every time I saw him and we made videos in which he told his friends not to grieve for him, or when we planned the drinks for the 'party', I came away a wreck.

And in the middle of all this lachrimosity I descended on Johnny. After a particularly wrenching session with Max, I'd been driving past the chemist and on a wild whim, called in, looking for comfort, emotional ice cream. After we'd exchanged New Year felicitations, he asked, 'What can I get you?'

I hadn't given this any thought. 'Oh, ah . . . a glucose lollipop. And – what's this? Surgical gauze? OK, I'll take a packet.'

'Are you sure about that, Gemma?'

'No, no, I'm not. Just the lollipop.'

Even after I'd tried to pay (He wouldn't let me, 'For God's sake, it's only a lollipop.') I still wouldn't leave.

'How are things?' he asked.

'Great,' I said miserably. 'Dad's back. How's your brother?'

'Very good, he'll be back at work soon and my life will be my own again. Your book should be out soon, shouldn't it?'

'May. And it goes on sale in airport duty-frees sooner than that. Some time in March.'

'You must be very excited.'

'Mmmm.'

'I'm looking forward to reading it.'

'I'll try to get you a free copy.' My worry about him reading about himself had diminished, washed away by sadness.

Eventually he asked – and it wasn't like I hadn't been fishing for him to – 'And, er, how's your non-boyfriend?'

'Oh, that's all over. He went back to his old girlfriend. It was very amicable.'

My eyes filled with tears, not the shame of full-blown crying, but enough for Johnny to hand me a tissue. Well, he had a shopful of them.

Later, in the comfort of my own home, I realized that the kindness of the tissue gesture was what prompted the ensuing insanity. I dabbed my eyes and heard myself say, 'You know, maybe we should go out for a drink some time, you and me.'

I cocked my head to listen. *Did I really say that?*

Then I saw his face. You'd want to have seen it. He looked really insulted.

'Oh God, I'm sorry,' I said, hurrying away. 'I'm very sorry.'

I got into the car, clutching my free lollipop. Dad was back and I was worse mad now than I ever was.

Little did I know that life was about to change in a major way.

It began with a phone call from Jojo.

'Like, totally great news,' she said. 'I've had a call from a production company called Eye-Kon. They're interested in optioning *Chasing Rainbows* for a made-for-TV feature. They're crazy for it but they've no money. But they're talking about a co-production with the BBC. Anton says –'

'*Anton?*'

'Yeah, Anton Carolan. Hey, he's Irish, you probably know him.'

'I know him.'

Pause. 'I was only kidding. But you know Lily, so of course you know him.'

'I knew him before Lily did.' But I didn't really try to score points. I was way too stunned: Anton wanted something I had. *I had something that Anton wanted.* Even in my most elaborate fantasies, I'd never imagined this situation. I thought back to three and a half years previously when I'd been almost suicidal without Anton. When I wanted him so badly and I was totally and utterly powerless. How insane life is. Breathlessly, I urged, 'Jojo, tell me more.'

'I've told you all I know. They've no money but the BBC has. So you're interested, in theory?'

'Of *course* I'm interested!'

'I'll tell them. These things take time, don't hold your breath, I'll keep you in the loop.'

'But –'

She was gone and I sat staring at the phone, too astonished to carry on with my day. Anton! Out of the blue! Wanting my book!

Jojo had said his company was called Eye-Kon so immediately I looked it up on the net and *could not* believe what I was reading: they were in deep shit. There was a recent article from a trade magazine, saying that Eye-Kon had made no decent programmes or any money in over a year and if they didn't get it together soon, they'd have to shut up shop. It sounded like *Chasing Rainbows* was a last resort for them, an all or nothing. I could have been wrong, but what if I wasn't? How much would

Anton want it? For the first time in a long time I wondered about him and Lily. Lily can't be much fun at the moment, I thought, what with her new book having tanked. Maybe Anton had had it with her, maybe he was ready to jump ship.

What should I do, I wondered. Should I let this option thing go through the official channels or should I contact him directly? After all, we were old friends . . .

For the next two days I thought of nothing else; in fact I was so caught up in it I almost forgot to cry.

Then Jojo rang again. 'Gemma. Can you talk? I've got a proposal for you.'

'Another one? Go ahead.'

'I have decided,' she sounded excited, 'to set up on my own and I'd like to take you with me.'

The lucky cow. I'd love to do that, set up my own agency. But I enjoyed my facial features in their current configuration.

'So whatcha say? Are you in or out?'

It was a total no-brainer. This was the woman who'd got me sixty grand. Why wouldn't I stay with her? 'Count me in. What other authors are coming with you?'

'Miranda England, Nathan Frey, Eamonn Farrell . . .'

'Lily Wright?'

'I haven't spoken to her yet, but yeah, I hope so.'

'Even though her latest book didn't do very well.' *Catastrophically.* There had been yet *another* piece in the latest *Book News* about it bombing and Dalkin Emery taking a huge hit on it. She was out of contract with Dalkin Emery and the article indicated she'd be lucky to ever get another deal.

'It got great reviews,' Jojo said.

It did? Well, I hadn't seen any of them.

Jojo

Friday morning

Jojo checked that the announcement of her partnership was in *Book News*, then she went to Mark's office and handed him a letter. He looked at it. 'What's this?'

'My notice. I'm leaving.'

Mark looked weary beyond weary. 'Jojo, for God's sake . . . You're a partner, isn't that what you wanted?'

'Only because my boyfriend pulled strings.'

'If your boyfriend had done the right thing in the first place by voting for you, he wouldn't have had to pull strings. I'm so sorry.'

'You did what you thought was right.'

'Don't do this,' he beseeched. Horrified, she realized he might cry. 'You need a job.'

'I have a job.'

'Working for whom?'

'Myself. I'm setting up on my own.'

Mark made a jaded sound, halfway between a laugh and a sigh.

'I have to, Mark. I can't stay here. Me working alongside Gant when I didn't get my partnership through the normal channels? It would never work. And no way am I going to work for another agency and watch the same shit happen again.'

He laughed in a beaten way, then asked, 'Jojo, what about us? You and me? Are you setting up on your own in a personal capacity as well as a professional one?'

Funny, she hadn't really decided what to do, not until that moment. She looked at him, at his beloved face, so familiar and handsome to her, she thought about their affection and fondness for each other, their friendship, their hope for their future, the children they'd have together, the companionship and intellectual stimulation they'd always shared and would share as they got older.

'Yes,' she said. 'It's over, Mark.'

He nodded, like it was what he'd expected to hear.

Then for the first – and last – time she did something she never did on work time: she hugged him. She pressed herself against the length of him, in the hope that she could remember how he felt, how he smelt, the hard heat of his body. She held him fiercely, trying to stamp him for ever on her memory. Then she walked away.

* * *

Clearing out her desk Jojo wondered where were the cardboard boxes that always materialized when people in movies left their jobs at short notice. Not that she had much, she wasn't a pot-plant kind of person, they were so *needy* . . .

The hallways of Lipman Haigh whispered with speculation: Jojo was emptying her desk, what was going down?

Her phone rang and absently she picked it up. Miranda England.

'Jojo, I've been thinking . . .'

Jojo went cold.

'In your new company you don't have a foreign rights department, do you?'

'Not yet. But I will.'

'And you don't have a media department yet?'

'But I will.'

'Jojo, now that I'm not writing a book a year, I need the income from my overseas sales. Germany pays me almost as much as the UK. And the movie options bring in plenty too.'

'Miranda, who got to you? Richie Gant?'

'Nobody did!'

'What did he offer?'

'Nothing!'

'A lower commission rate? Is that it? Nine per cent? Eight? Seven?'

Miranda paused and admitted unhappily, 'Eight. And he's right about the media and foreign rights department.'

Manoj was dancing in front of her, holding up a page which said, 'Gemma Hogan holding. Urgent!'

'Miranda, I'll offer you seven per cent and I'll have media and foreign rights departments up and running in three months.'

'I'll think about it.'

Gemma

I was driving back from a meeting when my mobile rang. I answered and a man's voice said, 'Speak to Gemma Hogan?'

'Speaking.'

'Richie Gant here, of Lipman Haigh literary agents.'

Jojo's company. 'Hello.'

'Gemma, I love your book.'

'Thank you.' Why was he ringing me?

'You've probably not heard but your agent Jojo Harvey has decided to leave Lipman Haigh and go it alone.'

'I've heard.'

'Oh. Well, yeah. Thing is Jojo is a great agent but to go it alone? Us partners here are worried about her clients.'

'Really?'

'On her own she'll have no foreign rights department. No media department. I reckon *Chasing Rainbows* would make a great little movie but no way will Jojo be able to do this for you in her new set-up.'

'Yes, but . . .'

'I'm saying, why not stay with Lipman Haigh? There are several excellent agents here and I myself would be happy to represent you. And I'm one of the partners.'

I told him I'd think about it and right away I rang Jojo. She was on the phone so I told her assistant it was urgent. She rang back immediately.

'Jojo, someone called Richie Gant has just rung me, saying you've no foreign rights and he wants to represent me. What's going on?'

'You as well? I've barely handed in my notice and already

he's trying to steal all my clients.' Her voice went a little shrill. 'It's like *Jerry* fucking *Maguire* round here today.'

In her previous call she'd made founding a new agency sound like a great thing, but now I heard her panic. For some reason she *had* to leave and she was scrabbling around for clients, in order to help her set up.

In one shocking moment it all became clear to me and I couldn't believe the opportunity that had just landed in my lap: Jojo needed clients – what if I said I'd only go with her, if she didn't take Lily? I was worth a lot more to Jojo than Lily was: Lily's writing career was in freefall, whereas mine was only beginning.

Without an agent, Lily's career would be toast; I could make it happen. *And* Anton needed to option my book – how much would he be prepared to sacrifice in order to save his career? Anton was fiercely ambitious, at least he had been three and a half years ago.

In my wildest fantasies about getting revenge on Lily, I hadn't come up with anything like this – this was bigger, better and above all, real.

A fresh wave swept over me. Where did it all go so right? Suddenly and astonishingly, I'd just been handed the chance to flip my life over, to wipe out years of humiliation, so that I was the one on top. I saw the power I had and it made me dizzy. I wondered if Lily saw it too.

I had to go to London. It was time to meet Anton.

Lily

Gemma was out to get me. Until this point I will admit to being paranoid with regard to her, my guilt rendered me so. But I was not imagining this.

Anton was pushing ahead with his great plan to option her book. They had not yet forged personal contact, but that was only a matter of time, and then everything would end. However, she was not content merely with that, as I discovered on Friday afternoon when Miranda England rang.

'Lily,' she said. 'I've been thinking about this Jojo situation. Aren't you worried about her not having a foreign rights or a media department? That slimy Gant bloke just called –'

'What Jojo situation?'

Miranda squawked. 'Don't tell me you haven't heard? Jojo is leaving! Setting up on her own!'

I had heard no such thing.

'She's contacting all her authors, to take them with her.'

Did this mean that she did not want to take me? Panic tightened my chest like a vice.

'Who else is going?' I asked.

'Eamonn Farrell, Marjorie Franks, that weirdo Nathan Frey . . .' So many authors had been contacted, but not me. I was not stupid. I knew this meant something. Then Miranda said the words I had been waiting for. '. . . that new author, Gemma Hogan.'

Sweat erupted onto my forehead. Now I knew exactly why Jojo had not phoned me. Manifestly, Gemma had said that she would not go with her if Jojo kept me on as a client. If I did not have an agent, the tiny little ember that remained of my writing career would be extinguished. No other agent would take me on; without Jojo I was finished.

Gemma

I caught the 6.35 a.m. from Dublin and went straight from Heathrow into Lipman Haigh. I wore my new black suit. By Donna Karan. No, Prada. Either way it made me look tiny-waisted and chic. I'd got it in the sales for an astonishingly reasonable sum.

'Jojo – you and your new company? I'm on board.'

'Great, you won't regret it!'

But before I grasped her outstretched hand and sealed the deal, I said, 'There's just one thing.'

'Yeah?'

'Lily Wright.'

'Lily Wright?'

'I don't want you to bring her with us.'

Jojo looked concerned. 'Lily Wright couldn't get arrested right now. If I leave her at Lipman Haigh it's unlikely anyone else would want to represent her. It would mean an end to her publishing career.'

I shrugged. 'Those are my terms.'

Jojo considered me for a while. I saw respect in her eyes. Slowly she nodded. 'OK. No Lily.'

'Great.' I pumped her hand. 'Pleasure doing business with you.'

In the lift I clenched my fists. Success was within my grasp. Soon vengeance would be mine. Mine, I tell you! Mine! Mine!

Eye-Kon's office was only three streets away but en route I passed a shoe shop and bought two pairs of boots in the sale so by the time I arrived for my appointment with Anton I was twenty minutes late. Who cared? I swung in, brazenly displaying my shopping bags.

Meeting Anton for the first time in three and a half years

was weird. He looked exactly the same: same dancing eyes, same through-a-hedge-backwards chic. And same charisma, of course – lots of it. Some things never change.

'How's it going, you mad woman?' He grinned. 'Come in, sit down. Drink? Take a seat. You're looking fantastic.'

The last time I'd seen him, I'd been sick with love for him. The Begging Incident[1] came briefly to mind and I magicked it away. Back then Anton had had all the power. But not now. Due to some mad quirk of fate, due to life being, for once, *fair*, I held his future in my hands.

He smiled at me, a wide, winning smile. 'Sell us your book, Gemma. Go on, it's great. We'll make an excellent movie out of it. I promise we won't let you down.'

'Is that so?' I asked coolly. 'Anton, I've done a little research. Eye-Kon is screwed. You really need this book.'

That knocked some of the skittishness out of him. 'Maybe.'

'No maybe about it. And the good news is, Anton, you can have it. Without it costing you a penny.'

'I can?'

'Under certain conditions.'

'And they are?'

I waited a moment, building dramatic tension. 'How's Lily?' I asked. 'How are you two getting on?'

To my surprise – I hadn't expected him to admit it so quickly, things must be AWFUL – he hung his head.

'Not great.'

'Not great? Good. That'll make leaving her easier for you.'

I expected a flurry of what-are-you-talking-abouts and don't-be-mads. But he just nodded and said quietly, 'OK.'

---

1. A rite-of-passage incident, which marks the end of all relationships, where the dumpee begs the dumper to sleep with her one last time and he, concerned that he may not already have caused enough humiliation, refuses. Sometimes he has met someone new and he will invoke her name, saying, 'I could never do that to Anne/Mags/Deirdre (insert as appropriate).'

'OK?' I queried. '*OK?* That simple? You can't love her very much if you're prepared to put your career before her.'

'I don't. I don't love her at all. I never did. It was all a mistake. I was lonely when I first came to London and I mistook friendship for love. Then she got pregnant and how could I leave? But then I read your book and it's so *you*. It reminded me of what a great girl you are and the laughs we used to have. Seeing you here today, in your lovely Prada suit, I've no doubt in my mind that it was you I loved all along.' He stood by the window and stared out at the porridge-coloured London sky. 'I've known for a long time that being with Lily was a mistake. Ever since she got the Burt Reynolds-style hair-weave to cover her bald patch.' He sighed heavily. 'I should have left then, but the follicles became infected and she had to go on a course of antibiotics which upset her stomach. It would have been criminal to walk out . . .'

I paused. No, it was no good. The fantasy wasn't working any more. There was no way I'd be able to go to London and proposition Jojo and Anton, in an attempt to destroy Lily. I was almost disappointed with myself – some Avenger I made. It was one thing to want to drive over to Colette's work and make fun of her in the company car park after Dad had left her. But this kind of revenge-style fantasy – would any real person be able to do it?

Maybe if you were really, really peculiar you could. Maybe if you lived your life like it was a *Dynasty* script. But vengeance issues or no vengeance issues, I wasn't that kind of person. Had I ever been? Or had I simply forgiven Lily?

Even if I was able to force myself to negotiate with Jojo or Anton, they'd either laugh or tell me to fuck off.

And what kind of pitiful creature would be happy to bag a bloke by kick-starting his career? It would be like buying someone.

Jojo was still on the other end of my mobile, waiting for my answer.

I said, 'Jojo, don't worry, I'm sticking with you. There's just one thing, seeing as you mentioned *Jerry Maguire* . . .'

I turned on my car radio, looking for rap. Eminem, that would do. I turned it up deafeningly loud and yelled, 'Jojo, for the laugh, would you shout, "Show me the money."'

She hesitated, clearly in no mood, 'Aw, what the hell. SHOW ME THE MONEY.'

'Congratulations,' I said, giving my ear a rub. 'You're still my agent.'

Jojo

'Jim,' Jojo asked. 'Your new relationship. Is it serious?'

He looked surprised, suspicious even. 'Yes, yes, I suppose it is.'

'No chance you might change your mind about me?'

Carefully he said, 'I don't want to give offence . . .'

'I'll take that as a no?'

'Er, yes.'

'Excellent!'

'Why?'

'I'd like to offer you a job.'

'Wha-at?'

'Yeah, as my media person, and I don't want any pesky crush of yours ruining things. Now what do you think the chances are of getting Olga to come and run our foreign rights department?'

'Jojo, I – look! No –'

'Think about it,' she said. 'Equal shares. We'll make a ton.'

She got up to leave and he yelled after her, 'Jojo, I want to talk to you about something else.'

'What?'

'I don't know if you're still interested, but Gemma Hogan's book? *Chasing Rainbows*? Eye-Kon were pulling a deal together with the BBC and Chloe Drew?'

'Sure I'm interested. Gemma's still my author.'

'Heard at lunch that Chloe's had a major coke and alcohol meltdown and gone into rehab. I've made a few calls to confirm.'

'Say it ain't so.'

'Sorry, Jojo.'

'The deal is off?'

'The deal is *so* off. Chloe was the clincher, without her the BBC won't make with the readies. But no one wants to work with a drunk, even an ex-drunk. The insurers won't touch her.'

Lily

The funny thing was that less than an hour after Miranda England rang, Jojo called, explained that she was setting up on her own and asked me to stay as her client. When I took my courage in my hands and asked why she had not called me before now she explained that her other authors were all mid-contract. 'I needed to know if they were coming, so I could do the necessary untangling.'

I, by contrast, was wonderfully simple; I had no contract for Jojo to worry about. 'But if you decide to write another book,' she said, 'you bring it to me and let's see what we can do.'

Later that same day Anton found out that Chloe Drew had had some sort of breakdown – the rumours said it was alcohol-related. She had been pivotal to *Chasing Rainbows*; without her the BBC were not interested and the deal was not going to happen.

I should have been happy. Anton and I were safe now, were we not?

Unfortunately, no: Anton's brush with Gemma, or at least her book, had revealed the full extent of the rot in Anton's and my relationship.

And the fact that, once again, another of Anton's business ventures had collapsed, convinced me that my life with him would always be a financial roller coaster. I could not live that way. I owed it to Ema to seek stability.

That evening, I went to see Irina in her beautiful new apartment. At first we talked make-up and skin-care but in a conversational hiatus I threw out an experimental line: 'Anton and I are going to split up.'

Most people would yelp, 'What? You and Anton? You're bonkers about each other! You're just going through a bad patch!'

But Irina simply exhaled a thoughtful plume of smoke and shrugged, 'Thet is the nature of love.'

Her phenomenal pessimism led by example and encouraged my own pessimism to walk tall through every aspect of my life. She provided precisely the right environment to enable me to see the full extent of the wreckage. There was no chance that any ersatz optimism might pop up cheerily and scoot my hopelessness back into hiding – not in Irina's home. She would not stand for it. I heard myself say, 'I have to find somewhere for Ema and me to live.'

'I hev two spare bedrooms. You can stay vit me. Vassily is not in London werry often. Thanks Gud. All he wants to do is make the sex.' She seemed to hear herself and slightly changed tack. 'But when you meet him you will like.'

It was a beautiful apartment and I was tempted. But my imagination conjured up images of Ema and me caught in some Russian Mafia turf-war, of both of us tied to kitchen chairs with duct tape as big-moustachioed, stone-washed-leather-jacket-wearing men called Leonid and Boris, threatened us with knives to encourage us to reveal the whereabouts of the man/money/briefcase.

She read my mind. 'Vassily is legit.'

'Is he?' I was sure she had implied his activities were illegal.

'He is criminal.' She sounded bored. 'Of course he is criminal. But not Mafia.'

Well, that was all right then!

And what were my other options? Dettol Hall? Far more likely to have a negative impact on Ema than being duct-taped to a kitchen chair. Even a DSS hotel would be better than Dettol Hall.

So, from the moment Irina made her offer, the die was cast.

Jojo

On Friday evening, Manoj helped Jojo carry her cardboard boxes down to the taxi.

'I can't believe you're leaving,' he quavered.

'Don't be such a girl,' she said. 'I'll send for you. Soon as I'm up and running.'

The high of her dramatic resignation was wearing off. It had all happened so quickly – on Tuesday she had started calling her authors to see if a solo career was viable. It was now only Friday.

All week she had surfed on the idea of bucking the system. She would be the one who would transcend the sexist pecking order. It had fired her up, made her believe what she was doing was right. But when she looked at Manoj's wobbling chin, she lapsed back into the dream state that had been such a feature of this week and wondered, What have I done?

She had walked out of Lipman Haigh and she would not be going back. The realization was like a ten-pound sack of sand falling on her from a height.

No going back. To her well-paid position as partner. Or to Mark.

And she was the one who had made it happen.

The cab ride home was like a bad dream. What was she doing – *had already done* – to herself?

Her mobile rang. She checked caller display – Mark – and let it roll over to message service. Once in her flat, she dumped the cardboard boxes and noticed that her machine was flashing with messages. Already?

The first was from Jim Sweetman. 'Jojo, I'm flattered by your offer, but I'm staying with Lipman Haigh.' Damn, she thought. Then – So what? She'd get another media person, and Olga was still on board. OK, Olga had not actually said yes when Jojo had made her pitch. She had simply sat wearing an expression of utter astonishment. But she had *not said no* and right now Jojo decided that that was as good as a yes.

The second message was from Mark. 'You're good, I'll say that for you, you nearly had me convinced there. But there's no need for any of this, Jojo. I've already torn up your resignation letter, just come in on Monday, same as ever and we'll get everything back on track. You're a *partner* now, Jojo. And as for you and me, you're the most important person in my life, the most important person I've ever met, we *have* to work this out, Jojo, we *have* to, because the alternative is unthinkable –'

At that point the message time ran out, but the next message was also from Mark, carrying on like he hadn't been interrupted, '– this can all be fixed right now. You and me, Jojo, we can make it all alright. We can make anything alright. You can have your old job back, or the partnership or anything you want. Just say what you want and you can have it . . .'

In all there were six messages from him.

She went to stay with Becky and Andy for the weekend.

'Because you want to be with people who love you,' Andy said sympathetically, as he opened the door.

'No, because I just bet Mark will call round to my apartment in the middle of the night and lean on the buzzer until I let him in.'

'Have a glass of wine, put your feet up and forget about it all for a while,' Becky soothed.

'I can't.' Right on cue her mobile rang. She looked at caller display. Not Mark, not this time. She hit 'talk'.

'Hey you, Nathan Frey! Yeah, I did call earlier. I was, like, wondering if you'd had a call from Richie Gant, offering, like, *the earth*.'

Jojo took the call into the hall, where she paced back and forth, talking up a storm. Then she came back and collapsed onto the couch. 'That was Nathan Frey. Looks like Gant's got to all my authors. All the big ones, anyhow. Gonna spend my weekend doing damage limitation, trying to get them back on side.'

Her phone shrilled into life again and she dove on it, checked caller display, then said, super-jovially, 'Mr Eamonn Farrell, how the devil are you?'

Out to the hall again, her anxiously pacing feet at odds with her upbeat tones. Then she was back. 'Jesus H! This is a nightmare! Gant is offering such super-low percentages that he'll barely make any money. He's just doing this out of spite.'

Her phone burst into life again.

'Ignore it,' Becky urged.

'I can't.' But when she checked caller display, she clattered the phone back onto the table, as if it burned. 'Mark again.'

The phone rang and rang, sounding louder and more insistent with each unanswered peal. The three of them regarded it fearfully, then the ringing stopped and the air hummed with merciful silence.

'Turn it off now,' Becky begged.

'Sweets, I'm sorry, I can't. I'm still waiting to hear from . . .' she counted on her fingers. '. . . *eight* authors. I put calls in to all my major ones when I found out what Gant was up to. He's freaked them out with how crap I'm going to be on my own. I've got to be available to reassure them.'

The phone chirruped once, twice.

'A message from Mark,' Jojo said.

'Are you going to listen to it?'

'I don't need to. He's just going to say that he loves me and we can work this out.'

'And you're not going to?' Becky asked. 'Work it out, I mean?'

Jojo shook her head curtly, then leapt as her mobile rang again.

She studied the number, then handed it to Andy. 'Answer it?'

'Mark again?'

'Not his number, but I've a feeling . . .'

Gingerly, Andy answered. 'Ah, Mark.'

'Sneaky,' Jojo told Becky. 'Must've used a phone box.'

Andy spoke for a short while then hung up.

'Mark,' he said. 'Standing outside your flat. He's been buzzing for the last half-hour. Says he's going to stay there until you let him in. All night if he has to.'

'He's gonna have quite a wait.' She sounded upbeat but she felt shitty. She didn't want him to be like this.

All weekend and through into the following week, her phone was on fire, but with the wrong sort of calls. Her resignation had – understandably – generated great furore in publishing circles; she had resigned the day her partnership was announced – WHY? Theories abounded. She'd discovered that Richie Gant was the illegitimate son she'd had when she was twelve and given up for adoption (from an editor who specialized in sagas). She'd been having a lesbian affair with Olga Fisher who had taken up with Richie Gant instead (from someone who worked at Virago). She'd been having an affair with Mark Avery, who hadn't voted for her, then dumped her (from the vast majority of London publishing).

But far worse than the people exercising their naked curiosity were the calls from her authors. On Tuesday afternoon, there was a call from Miranda England. She was making it official – she was going to Richie Gant. It hit Jojo like a blow from a baseball bat.

On Wednesday, Marjorie Franks signed to Richie. On Thursday, Kathleen Perry, Iggy Gibson, Norah Rossetti and Paula Wheeler jumped ship and on Friday a trio of thriller-writers went, all of them steady-sellers.

Every time an author walked, the chances of her making it as a solo agent shrank further.

Becky said over and over, 'Why don't you go back? You could just go back into your job as a partner. A *partner*, Jojo.'

'I will not collude in that patriarchal system.' Jojo had learned the word 'patriarchy' from Shayna. She liked it. She produced it whenever someone tried to persuade her to return to work. 'Now that I know what I know, it would be too soul-destroying.'

But it was way, way tempting.

And all the time, she was bombarded with messages from Mark; day and night, he emailed, texted, wrote letters, sent flowers and a box of goodies from Jo Malone, he rang on her home phone and mobile and he loitered outside her apartment. Two drunken nights he had leant on her buzzer, each time for over three hours. He stood in the street and yelled stuff at her window. Her neighbours complained and threatened to call the cops if he did it again. She could have called the cops herself but the idea affected her like lemon juice on an oyster. She couldn't do that to him, it was too fucking sad.

But far worse than Mark behaving insanely was when he was being smart – when he left messages reiterating that a position of partner was still waiting for her in Lipman Haigh and that a life with him was available any time she wanted. Jesus H, it was enticing.

His buzz-phrase was, 'Just say what you want, Jojo, and you can have it.'

But she could not have the one thing she wanted, and that was to rewrite the past: she wanted Mark to have voted for her and not for Richie Gant.

It was weird – she knew she was angry with him even if it didn't feel that way and although she missed him like a limb, there was no way back. Whatever had happened – and she still wasn't sure exactly what – had contaminated them beyond fixing. It was so over.

The amazing thing was that, despite him almost stalking her, she never spoke to him or even saw him. And yeah, that made it easier to stick to her guns. She suspected that if they saw each other, she would crumble. Things, right now, were so scary and bad that walking back into the cocoon of her old life, where she was loved and secure, would be just too hard to resist.

Monday morning

Her second Monday as a self-employed agent. She felt confident and hopeful, like she was turning a corner.

The phone rang. It was Nathan Frey's wife, to say that Nathan's new agent was Richie Gant.

Fuccckkk.

She had only one big author left: Eamonn Farrell.

She decided to ring Olga Fisher. Over a week had passed and she had heard nothing about when she was coming to work for her.

'Hey, Olga. Have you given notice? When're you coming to work for me?'

'Don't be so impertinent. Of course I've not given my notice.'

'Hey, you might have told me,' Jojo said hotly. 'I thought you were coming to work for me.'

'But, but my dear girl, the very idea is so patently ridiculous . . . why on earth would I . . . Oh!' On that note of exasperation, Olga ended the call.

On Tuesday, only two smaller authors walked.

But Wednesday was Meltdown Day.

When she switched on her computer, waiting was an email from Eamonn Farrell, saying he had found new representation. She leant her forehead against the screen. That was it, her last big author gone.

Then the phone rang: Mark. He left a frantic, pleading message for her every morning around this time. But today he sounded different. Like, *sane.*

'Jojo,' he said, 'I'm going to stop bothering you now. I'm sorry we didn't manage to work it out, I've never been sorrier about anything. We were one inch away from perfection, we were almost there, but I know when I'm beaten. Good luck with everything. I mean that.'

Then he clicked off and she almost felt the molecules of her phone relaxing after its recent spate of very demanding work.

This wasn't some dumbass trick of Mark's to get her to change her mind. She knew his MO; he had given this his all, it hadn't delivered the desired results, so he was quitting. Game over.

This was what she had wanted. She had never intended to go back to him.

But, like an out-of-body experience, she saw herself, sitting in her apartment on a bleak Wednesday morning in February, with her best friend gone and her career in ruins.

At that Jojo cried so hard and for so long she barely recognized herself in the mirror. When she stuck her face in a sink of cold water to calm the red swelling she found herself considering just staying there and letting herself drown. For the first time in her thirty-three years she could understand the urge to take her own life.

For about half a second.

Then she got it together. Colleagues? Who needs 'em? Authors? Hey, plenty more where they come from. And another Mark? Plenty of them too, if she could be arsed.

Lily

For over a week I lived with the certainty that Anton and I were finished. I held it within me, a hideous knowledge, like being aware of a murder weapon under my bed – unsettled constantly by it, but unable to take the first step.

My conviction that we were out of time was given extra weight because I had been here before; not in my own life but with Mum and Dad. I knew the worst *did* happen and it happened every day. Anton and I thought we were special, somehow immune from love's travails but, in truth, we were nothing out of the ordinary, just another pair of souls who could not hold it steady when the going got tough.

Nevertheless, I was deeply surprised by Anton's reaction when I said that I was leaving. I had thought that he was of the same mind as me: that we both knew it was over but were simply going about our business until the appropriate time came. In the weeks since the move, we had been so silent with each other that I genuinely believed we were finished in all but name. I was sure that he would let me go quietly, acknowledging sadly that it was a shame it had not worked out, but that under the circumstances it was a miracle we had stayed together as long as we had, etc.

But he went wild.

When Ema had gone to bed that night, I picked up the remote and, without preamble, turned off the TV.

He looked at me in surprise. 'What?'

'Irina has said Ema and I can stay with her for a while. I think we should go sooner rather than later. Tomorrow?'

I was ready to deliver my little piece about how he could see

Ema whenever he liked but I never got to say it because he lost it.

'What are you talking about?' He gripped my wrist so hard that it hurt. 'Lily?' he questioned. 'Lily? What?'

'I'm going,' I said, faintly. 'I thought you knew.'

'No.' He looked utterly horrified.

He implored. Pleaded. Took my keys from my bag and stood with his back to the door even though I was not actually planning to leave there and then.

'Lily, please,' he choked. 'I beg ... *implore* you to think about it.'

'But Anton, I've done nothing but think about it.'

'At least sleep on it?'

'Sleep? I haven't had a proper night's sleep in months.'

He rubbed his hand over his mouth and muttered some imprecation; I caught the words 'please' and 'God'.

'What did you think was going to happen to us?' I asked.

'I thought things would get better. I thought they were getting better.'

'But we never speak to each other any longer.'

'Because we've lost our home, a terrible thing has happened. But I thought we were regrouping!'

'We're not regrouping. We will never regroup. We should not have been together ever, it was wrong from the beginning and it was always going to end horribly. We always *knew* this.'

'I didn't.'

'You persist with looking on the bright side but the reality is that we are disastrous together,' I reminded him. 'Look at the mess we've made of our lives. We had a lot going for us and we've screwed it all up.' I said 'we' but what I really meant was, '*I* had a lot going for me and *you* screwed it up.' I did not need to say it; he was no fool, he would have already grasped that.

'We were unlucky,' he insisted.

'We were arrogant and grandiose and foolish.' (*You* were.)

'Because we tried to buy a house with money that everyone

thought would pony up? What's grandiose about that? Common sense combined with bad luck is what it sounds like.'

'Reckless and risky is what it sounds like to me.'

He leant heavily against the door. 'It's because of your history, your dad losing the family home. It had a terrible effect on you.'

I said nothing. It was probably the truth.

'You're angry with me,' he said.

'Absolutely not,' I said. 'I hope that eventually we will be friends. But Anton, we're bad for each other.'

He looked at me, his face stricken and I dropped my eyes. 'What about Ema?' he asked. 'Us breaking up can't be good for her.'

'I'm doing this *for* Ema.' Suddenly I was furious. 'Ema is my number-one priority. I don't want her brought up like I was. I want security for her.'

'You're angry with me,' Anton repeated. 'Very angry.'

'I'm not! But keep on insisting that I am and I probably will be.'

'I don't blame you for being angry. I could shoot myself for getting it all so wrong.'

I decided to ignore this. It did not matter what he said, he would not change my mind. Anton and I were finished completely and I actually felt it was necessary for us to part, that we would both be dogged by bad luck, until we had righted the wrong we had committed when I first stole him from Gemma.

When I told him that, he exploded, 'You're just being superstitious. It doesn't work like that.'

'We were never meant to be together, I always knew it would end in disaster.'

'Lily, but Lily . . .'

'It doesn't matter what you say or do,' I said. 'I'm going. I have to.'

He lapsed into beaten silence, then asked, 'If you're really going to do this, can I ask one thing?'

'What?' I asked warily. Surely he would not be crass enough to ask for some form of sex as a farewell gift?

'Ema? I don't want her to see this. Could someone take care of her while you're . . .' he paused, then choked on the word, 'packing?'

He began to cry silent tears and I watched him in wonderment. *How had this come as such a shock to him?*

'Of course. I'll ask Irina to take her.'

Then I went to bed. This was proving a lot tougher than I had expected and the sooner it was over the better. I heard him come to bed and in the darkness he lay his head on my back and whispered, 'Please Lily,' but I lay rigid as a crab, until he moved away again.

In the morning, I rang Irina who came, nodded at Anton with something akin to sympathy and took Ema with her. Then I tried to persuade Anton to go out. I did not like him being there, hanging around, looking sick, following me from room to room, watching my actions like he was watching a snuff video. I was not enjoying any of it and his manifest misery made me feel worse. He watched me pack three bags, refusing to pass anything, saying, 'I want no hand nor part in this.' But when I struggled to get a holdall from the top of the wardrobe, he muttered, 'For God's sake, don't kill yourself,' and swung it down for me.

'Perhaps it would be better if you weren't there when I actually go,' I suggested.

But no way. He kept trying to talk me out of it, right up to the last minute. Even as I was getting into the taxi, he said, 'Lily, this is only temporary.'

'This is not temporary.' I held his eyes. I had to let him know this. 'Please get used to it, Anton, because this is for ever.'

Then the car drove away, taking me to my new life, and I know this sounds horribly cruel but, for the first time since I had met him, I felt clean.

* * *

For far too long now, I had coexisted with wretched guilt about Gemma. Freedom from it brought delicious relief and almost from the second I left Anton, life began to improve: I got work immediately – via an agency, doing freelance copywriting from home – and this was the sign I needed.

Irina's apartment was big and quiet. I worked in the morning when Ema was in playgroup and in the evening when she was asleep. If I needed to work in the afternoon, I had no shortage of babysitters: Dad and Poppy were regular visitors and Ema and Irina got on beautifully. I think Ema's quarter Slavic side responded to the Slav in Irina and Irina regarded Ema's round little face as the perfect showcase for the latest Clinique products. I tried to stop Irina but I was not capable of impassioned pleas. Or impassioned anythings.

I liked my new life. It was peaceful, devoid of drama and very little happened. I never saw any neighbours in the silent landings; no one else even seemed to live in the building.

Even the nondescript weather conspired to numb me. Colourless skies and mild, still air guaranteed an absence of response from me. When we went on walks to nearby Regent's Park, I felt nothing.

There was no hope of me doing anything creative. After the succession of knockbacks, I had nothing to write and I was quite content doing press releases and leaflets. I had no grand plans, no vision for the future, all I wanted was to get through the day. I enjoyed my life's smallness. Until recently everything had been done on a grand scale – novels and book deals and houses – and I was happy that it had all been reduced to bite-sized pieces.

Anton had been right about one thing: I was angry with him for being so flaky with money. But since I had left him, it was as if my anger was happening to someone else; I knew it was there, I knew it affected me, but I could not feel it. All I could feel was gladness at being in charge of my own destiny.

Not that every day was easy. There were some dreadful moments, like when Katya, a Russian friend of Irina's, came to visit, bearing a beautiful brown-eyed baby boy, only six months old. He was called Woychek and he even looked like Ema. This plunged me into an awareness of all the other children that Anton and I would never have. The brothers and sisters that Ema already had in a parallel universe but that we would never meet. That started something terrible within me but before the grief had me fully in its grip, Katya said of Ema, 'This child has werry beautiful skeen,' and my attention was diverted. Had Irina been putting stuff on Ema? Again? The pore-minimizer? She was obsessed with it and pressed it, with evangelical zeal, on everyone. Yes, Irina admitted surlily, she had given Ema a 'barely there' layer of pore-minimizer. When pressed further she also confessed that she had used some glow gloop and in my irritation I forgot to be sad.

One day clicked over into the next and all of them were interchangeable and without character. Not once did I contemplate the future, except in terms of Ema. Constantly I watched her, alert for signs of dysfunction. She did not wet her bed at night but that was because she had not yet been fully nappy-trained. Sometimes when she heard Irina's key in the door she would widen her eyes and gasp, 'Anton?' But other than that it was business as usual.

She had always been a hardy little creature, and perhaps her physical robustness was also an indication of emotional resilience. I had to admit she certainly did not seem shaken by her ruptured life. But I fretted that she was 'internalizing' and everything would emerge at age thirteen when she would become a shop-lifting, glue-sniffing termagant.

My one comfort was that I had made what I thought was the best choice for her and I knew that being a mother means experiencing almost constant guilt.

Even though she was living separately from him, she saw Anton frequently. Most days he took her to the park after work, and she stayed overnight with him on Saturdays. After the first few visits where his eyes were bleak with heartbreak, I could not bear to see him and asked Irina if she could oversee him picking up Ema and again when he returned her home. To my extreme gratitude, Irina agreed. This arrangement worked well, until one evening, perhaps three weeks after I had left him, when Irina was in the bathroom at precisely the wrong time and I had to open the door to readmit Ema.

'Lily.' Anton looked shocked to see me. As I was shocked to see him. He had always been thin but during the weeks since I had seen him, he had become haggard. Not that I was in imminent danger of gracing a fashion shoot myself. (If it had not been for Irina's lavish generosity with her pore-minimizer, I would have needed a head transplant.)

Ema scooted past me into the apartment and seconds later I heard the opening notes of *The Jungle Book*.

'I wasn't expecting to see you . . .' Anton said. 'Look . . .' He fumbled in his leather jacket and produced a letter. It was so crumpled and battered it looked as if it had been in his pocket for weeks. Regularly, he had been bringing my post but I knew this letter was different. 'This is from me. I wanted to give it to you by hand, to make sure you got it. You won't want to read it now, but you might want to some time.'

'Fine,' I said stiffly, unsure what to do. I wanted to read it but instinct was warning me not to. Horribly shaken by seeing him, I said goodbye, closed the door on him, then went into my bedroom, put the letter in a drawer and waited to forget about it.

I was standing at my second-floor window, still feeling my heart beating in every part of my body, when I saw Anton leave the building. When Irina was on duty, I never permitted myself even a sneaky glance but today the routine was ruined and I remained watching him. He walked along the pavement, a few yards from the front entrance door, then paused and his shoulders began moving up and down, as if he were laughing.

I stared, wounded to the quick, and thought, what the hell is he laughing at? Meeting him face-to-face had upset me terribly but he thought it was funny? Then with a heave of dreadful insight I understood that he wasn't laughing, he was crying. Crying with his whole body. I stepped back in horror and at that moment I thought the grief would kill me.

It took me the rest of the evening and a quarter of a bottle of dog-rough vodka to regain my equilibrium. But then I was fine. I understood that inevitably this would be painful. Anton and I had been in love, we had had a child together and we had been each other's best friend from the moment we had met. The ending of something so precious could only be bloody. But at some stage in the future the pain would stop and Anton and I would be friends. I just had to be patient.

I knew that one day my life would be utterly different; full of feelings and friends and laughter and colour and with an almost entirely new cast to the one currently peopling it. I was wholly certain that some day there would be another man and more children and a different job and a proper home. I had no idea how I got from the small bare life I was now living to the full, colourful one I envisioned. All I knew was that it would happen. But right now it was a long way away, happening to a different Lily and I was in no rush for it.

So complete was my passivity that I could not even feel guilty about Irina's staggering generosity with her home and with caretaking Ema. Under normal circumstances, I would be a squirming mess, fashioning plans to leave as soon as we could and feeling like a wretched freeloader each time I switched on a light. Sometimes I had to borrow money from her – my copywriting paid spasmodically – and I even had no shame about that. Invariably, she handed it over without comment, except for once when I came in from yet another feeling-free walk in the park and said, 'Irina, the cashpoint wouldn't give me any money. Can you loan me some until I next get paid?'

She replied, 'Why do you hev no money? You got a big cheque last week.'

'I had to pay you back, then I bought Ema a tricycle, all the other little girls have tricycles, then I had to get her hair cut into a Dora the Explorer bob, all the other little girls have Dora the Explorer bobs . . .'

'And now you do not hev enough to feed her,' Irina said. Slyly, she added, 'You hate Anton for being bed vit money but you are werry bed too.'

'I never said I wasn't. I can't help it, it was the way I was brought up. And it just goes to show what a mismatch Anton and I were.'

She sighed and indicated a biscuit tin. 'Help yourself.' Then she handed me a postcard. 'Mail for you.'

I looked at it in surprise: a picture of three grizzly bears, standing in a stream, against a backdrop of pine trees and the great outdoors. It looked as if it had been sent from Canada. The biggest bear had a huge salmon between his jaws, the medium-sized bear was scooping a fish from the water and the smallest bear held a flipping fish in its paws. I turned it over and the caption read, 'Grizzly bears at a weir'. But someone – a person with Anton's handwriting – had crossed out the official caption and handwritten, 'Anton, Lily and Ema enjoy a fish supper.' To my enormous surprise I heard myself laugh.

He had also scribbled, 'Thinking of you both. All my love, A'.

It was utterly imbued with the spirit of Anton; funny and clever and mad, and I thought joyfully, this is the start of the happy memories. I am finally getting to the point where I can look back at my time with him without feeling wretched.

I felt happy all day long.

A few short days later the post yielded up a postcard of Burt Reynolds, looking very matinee idol and luxuriant of moustache. Anton had written: 'I saw this and thought of you.' Again I laughed and felt hopeful about the future.

I was starting to look forward to the postcards and soon another one arrived, this time of a vase bearing Chinese-style line-drawings of people and cups and stuff. The caption read, 'Ming vase depicting tea ceremony', but Anton had crossed it out and written, 'Anton, Lily and Ema, *circa* 1544, enjoying a cup of tea after a hard day's shopping.' When I looked again, it even seemed like there were shopping bags beside the figures.

I turned to Irina and said, 'I've been thinking. When Anton comes for Ema today, I think I can deal with it.'

'Very well.'

That evening when I opened the door to him, Anton did not even seem surprised. He simply exclaimed, 'Lily!' As if he was thrilled to see me.

He looked a lot better than he had at our previous encounter, not remotely as drawn and gaunt. His aura of shine and vitality had returned; clearly he was on the mend, we both were.

'Where's Irina today? What's up with her?' he asked.

'Nothing. Just … you know … I'm ready, it's time … Anton, thank you for the postcards, they're so funny, they made me laugh.'

'Great. And I'm glad I've met you because I wanted to give you this.'

He handed me an envelope which triggered a guilty memory of the unread letter in my underwear drawer. 'What's this?'

'Dosh,' he said. 'Lots of it. Now that I'm back making infomercials, the money is rolling in.'

'Is it really?' This was the final sign I needed that we were better off apart.

'Buy yourself and Ema something nice. I read in the paper that Origins has a new perfume out – and don't forget to get yourself something too!'

The twinkle was back in his eyes and I felt a huge rush of affection towards him that almost translated into me lunging at him in a hug. I restrained myself this time but wouldn't have to for much longer. Soon we could embrace as friends.

Gemma

I thought I would never get over Owen, I had no interest in it, I was quite happy being totally miserable. So it came as a bit of a rude awakening when I came to one morning to find myself feeling really fine. Actually, it took a while to identify the emotion because it was so unfamiliar.

Suddenly I saw the Owen thing differently: it was time for him to return to his own planet, Planet Younger Man, where Lorna was waiting to welcome him home.

And I was prepared to acknowledge how interesting the timing was; he'd broken it off with me the very day Dad had returned home. It was like he'd been sent to me for as long as I'd needed him. I don't usually believe in a kindly God (I don't usually bother believing in any sort of God) but it made me wonder. I stopped focusing on how much I missed him, instead I felt grateful I'd gotten a go of him for as long as I had.

OK, I was still a bit watery and wobbly but I couldn't believe the change in me – it was like having one of those twenty-four-hour 'flu's. When you're in the throes, you feel like you're in it for the long haul, then you wake up the next day, unbelievably back to normal.

To discuss my perplexing condition, I asked Cody to meet me for a drink and, to his credit, he agreed.

'I promise I won't start crying.' But I'd said that the last time too.

'We'll go somewhere suburban just to be on the safe side,' he said, and one hour later, in an anonymous pub in Blackrock, I confessed my new-found peace of mind.

'And your problem?'

'I'm worried that I'm very shallow,' I said. 'To get over him so quickly. Last week, even two days ago, I was still devastated and now I feel OK. I miss him, but I don't feel like my heart is breaking.'

'You did a year's worth of crying. Anyway it wasn't just him you were upset about. I spoke to Eugene about you.'

'Eugene who?'

'Furlong.' One of Ireland's most famous psychiatrists, often on telly. 'He says your reaction was disproportionate because you were grieving for your dad.'

'But my dad was back.'

'Exactly. It was safe to do so.'

'That makes no sense.'

Cody shrugged. 'I agree. Load of nonsense. I prefer the theory that you're just really shallow.'

I never got to work with Anton on making a film of *Chasing Rainbows*. Something happened with the actress and the deal fell apart. I was disappointed – but only because I thought it would have helped the book to do well and would be a right laugh, especially going on set and wearing a revealing dress and fake tan to the premiere – not because I was disappointed that I wouldn't get up close and personal with Anton. Then I emerged from the little dip and discovered that actually I felt oddly relieved.

Lily

It was still dark outside when I emerged from sleep and reached for Anton; I discovered he was not there and for a moment, before I remembered all that had happened, I was *surprised*.

The next night I awoke again and this time his absence caused me to weep. Since I had left him I had slept very well, considerably better than when I had been with him. I could not understand why this was happening now, when we were so close to the end of the process that we were almost ready to be friends. Before I had even left him, I had already made my peace with our situation. Grief had not incapacitated me and it did not occur to me to question why I was coping so well. I was simply grateful to have been spared.

So why, two months after I had left him, did I feel sadder than ever?

The following morning when the post came, Irina handed me an official-looking envelope and I asked, 'Anything else for me?'

'No.'

'Nothing?'

'No.'

'Like a postcard?'

'I said no.'

A thought jumped into my head: *I need to go away for a little while.*

A visit to Mum in Warwickshire was long overdue – it had been a long time, too long, since I had given her a scare about living with her.

I was worried about the income I would lose by not working but when I opened the official-looking envelope, I found it contained a huge royalty cheque for *Mimi's Remedies*. The royalty cheque – the money that could have saved our home, had we received it last December.

Tears sprang to my eyes. How different would our lives be? But I dried my wet eyes and admitted that, knowing us, not very. In January, we had been due to start regular monthly payments and regular income had never been our strong point.

It was terribly odd getting the cheque, it belonged to such a different part of my life that it was like a message from a long-dead galaxy. Nevertheless, it was the 'sign' I needed; it meant I could take a break from work, so I rang Mum and gave her the good news.

'How long do you plan to stay?' she asked. Anxiously?

'Ages,' I said. 'Months. Before you start to hyperventilate, about a week. OK?'

'OK.'

I went to pack and, a couple of strata down in my underwear drawer, I ran into the battered letter from Anton. It lay in a bra cup, and I watched it, almost expecting it to move. I itched to open it. Instead I picked it up by a corner and chucked it in the wastepaper basket; something I should have done weeks ago.

Then I loaded up the car (Irina had let me borrow her new Audi – another gift from Vassily), mostly with cuddly toys.

It was a clean spring morning and it felt good speeding along the motorway, as if I was leaving danger behind me in London. Less than two hours after we had left we were turning off the motorway. 'We're almost there!' Then, 'Whoops!' as my carefree twists and turns brought us up right behind a lorry laden with columns of concrete bollards, rumbling along at about fifteen miles an hour. The road was too narrow and bendy to overtake, but, 'We're in the country now, Ema. No need to rush.' Ema agreed and we launched into the four millionth verse of 'The Wheels on the Bus.'

Bellowing, 'Swish, swish, swish!' we crawled along behind the lorry when suddenly – and it was rather like watching a film

– it bumped over a hump in the road and the bollards had broken free of their chains and were flying loose, like so many concrete skittles. Raining down on us, bouncing off the road, flying right at me; there was not even time to be surprised. One glanced off our windscreen and, as if by magic, the glass had morphed into an opaque shield that sagged inwards. Some hit the roof of the car and it buckled down on us, I could not see in front of me, my foot was on the brake but we were still moving. At some stage we had stopped singing and I knew, with crystal clarity, that we were about to die. I was about to perish with my child on an A-road in Warwickshire. *I'm not ready* . . .

In the child mirror my eyes met Ema's and she looked puzzled but not alarmed. *She's my child and I have failed to protect her.*

The skid went on for ever. It seemed that years had passed: Ema had started school, gone through adolescence and had her first pregnancy scare before I became aware we were even slowing down. It was like being in a dream, where you want to run but your legs refuse to work; the brake was pressed to the floor but would not respond.

Finally, eventually, we reached a halt. I sat for a moment, barely believing the stillness, then turned to Ema. She extended her hand. There was something in it. 'Glass,' she said.

I got out of the car and my legs were so light I seemed to be floating. I retrieved Ema from her babyseat and she too seemed to be weightless. Her Dora the Explorer hair was studded with hundreds of little nuggets of glass – the back window had caved in on her head, but the strange thing was that she did not appear to be injured. Neither was I. Nothing was painful and neither of us bore any sign of blood.

The driver of the lorry was a gibbering wreck. 'Oh my God,' he kept saying. 'Oh my God. I thought I'd killed you, I thought I'd killed you.'

He whipped out a mobile and made a call – sending for help,

I thought passively – and I stood, holding Ema and looking at the battered car and bollards everywhere, strewn back along the road. I felt an urgent need to sit down, so I lowered myself on my not-there legs onto the grass verge and pulled Ema to me. As we sat by the side of the road I suddenly understood that the reason I was without a scratch was not because I had been ridiculously lucky but because I was, in fact, dead. I pinched my arm. I thought I felt something but could not be sure. So I pinched Ema and she looked at me in surprise.

'Sorry.'

'Oh, Lily,' she said. 'Play nice.'

It was quite a cold day – I could see it when I breathed out – but I felt perfectly comfortable: dizzy, like the air was thin, but very serene. I gathered Ema into me and, cheeks touching, stillness descended on us as though we were posing for a photo. In the distance I heard the sound of sirens, then an ambulance had arrived and men were jumping out and coming towards us.

This is it, I thought. This is the part where I watch them strap my lifeless body onto a stretcher and find I am floating fifteen feet above the scene. What I could not figure out was whether or not Ema was dead too.

A slender torch was shone into my eyes, a blood-pressure meter was strapped to my arm and people asked me stupid questions. What day was it? What was the Prime Minister's name? Who won Pop Idol? The ambulance man, a middle-aged reassuring type, looked at the crumpled car and winced. 'You were bloody lucky.'

'Really?' This was my chance. 'Are you telling me we're not dead?'

'You're not dead,' he said matter-of-factly, 'but you're in shock. Don't do anything rash.'

'Like what?'

'I don't know. Like anything rash.'

'OK.'

*

We were taken to hospital, pronounced to be in health as perfect as it was remarkable, then Mum came to ferry us to her home: an idyllic little cottage in an idyllic little village on the edge of a farming community. Mum's garden bordered a field containing three stolid sheep and a baby lamb skipping about like a happy half-wit.

Ema, a city girl, was dazzled by her first real-life sheep.

'Bad dog,' she shouted at them. 'BAD dog!'

Then she began to bark – a wholly convincing rendition – and the sheep gathered at the gate to look at her, their woolly heads together, their expressions tender.

'Come inside,' Mum said to me, 'you've had a dreadful shock, you need to lie down.'

I was reluctant to leave Ema or to even take my eyes off her, after I had so nearly lost her.

But Mum said, 'She'll be quite safe here,' and somehow I believed her. Moments later she had installed me in a wooden-beamed, rose-patterned room, and I was sinking into a soft bed with smooth, cotton sheets. Everything smelt clean and nice and safe.

'I have to sort out Irina's car,' I said. 'And I have to contact Anton. And I have to ensure that nothing terrible happens to Ema ever again. But first I have to go to sleep.'

And then it was morning and I opened my eyes to find Mum and Ema in the room, Ema grinning her melon grin.

The first thing I said was, 'We didn't die yesterday.'

Mum gave me a 'Not in front of Ema' look and asked, 'How did you sleep?'

'Wonderfully. I went to the bathroom in the middle of the night but I didn't walk into the doorjamb and damage my optic nerve, ensuring double vision for the rest of my life.'

'Your father is on his way from London, he has to see for himself that you've been saved from the jaws of death. But we're not going to get back together,' she added quickly. She always had to say that to me whenever she and Dad met. 'And I rang Anton.'

'Don't let him visit.'

'Why not?'

'Because I don't want to do anything rash.'

She looked sad. 'It's a terrible shame about you and Anton.'

'Yes,' I acknowledged. 'But at least I never caught him wearing a red basque and black stockings, masturbating in front of my dressing-table mirror.'

'What on earth,' she frowned, 'are you talking about?'

I frowned back. 'Nothing. I'm simply saying how good it is that that never happened. It would make things considerably more difficult between us because each time I saw him I might want to laugh.'

'And what was that about not walking into the doorjamb?'

'Just that I am happy that it didn't happen.'

A shadow crossed her face and she pulled Ema to her protectively and said, 'Let's make pancakes, shall we?'

They disappeared into the kitchen and I dressed slowly and sat in the sunny window seat humming to myself until the wheels of a twenty-year-old Jag crunched on the gravel outside announcing Dad's and Poppy's arrival from London.

Mum watched Dad getting out of the car and rolled her eyes. 'Just as I expected, he's in tears. He has such an obnoxious streak of sentimentality. It's terribly unattractive.'

She opened the front door and Ema was so excited to see Poppy that she began to choke. Hand-in-hand they ran off together to break things and Dad gathered me in his arms, so tightly that I also began to choke.

'My little girl,' he said, his voice thick with tears. 'I haven't been right since I heard. You were so lucky.'

'I know.' I managed to break free and take a breath. 'When you think about it, all my life I've been lucky.'

He looked slightly puzzled but because of my brush with death he was obliged to humour me.

'Think about it,' I said. 'Of all the times I drank from a can of Coke on a summer's day, and not once was I stung by a wasp which had crawled in. Never did I go into anaphylactic shock so that my tongue swelled up like a rugby ball. Isn't it wonderful?'

Mum looked at Dad. 'She keeps saying things like that. Why, Lily?'

'Simply making conversation.'

We lapsed into awkward silence, all the better to hear the happy shouts of Ema and Poppy tormenting the sheep. ('Bad dog. NASTY dog.') Mum looked in the direction of the racket, then snapped her head back and pounced. 'What are you thinking now?'

'Nothing! Just how happy I am that all my toenails grow in the right direction. Having ingrown toenails must be bloody. And the operation to remove them sounds dreadful.'

Mum and Dad gave each other a look. ('Dirty dog. HAIRY dog.')

'You ought to see a doctor,' Mum said.

I ought not. I was simply in the grip of one of those bouts of gratitude which sometimes assail me post-disaster. I tried to explain. 'Yesterday, there were so many ways Ema and I could have died. We could have been hit by a bollard, I could have driven the car into a ditch because I couldn't see where we were going or we could have ploughed into the back of the lorry. Being saved in so many different ways has made me think about all the terrible things that could happen but actually don't. Even though not everything is going well for me at the moment, I feel lucky.'

Their faces were blank and I ploughed on. 'Last night I dreamt that I was carrying Ema through a wasteland, and huge rocks were falling from the sky, landing just behind us, and cracks in the earth were opening up just after we'd stepped over them. But Ema and I were untouched, and a path to safety generated itself and came up to meet my foot, precisely when I needed it.'

I finished. Their faces had remained set in blankness.

Finally Dad spoke. 'Perhaps you have concussion, love.' He turned on Mum, 'Look at what we've done to her. This is our fault.'

He was full of grandiose talk of taking me to Harley Street, nothing but the best, but Mum slapped him down. 'Please don't talk such nonsense.'

'Thanks, Mum.' At least one of them understood.

Then Mum added, 'The local chap will do fine.'

I tried to hide it but could not. It was like when I had been mugged, except the entire opposite, if you know what I mean. Back then all I saw were the terrible things that could happen to human beings. This time all I saw were the bad things that *did not* happen.

The world is a safe place, I thought. And life is a low-risk activity.

The following day Dad returned reluctantly to London – Debs needed him urgently, to open a jar of jam or something – and it was just Ema, Mum and me. The weather was glorious and so was my mood. I thought I might burst with the joy of not having tinnitus. Or leprosy.

With shining eyes I said to Mum, 'Isn't it wonderful to not have gout?'

She snapped, 'Right, that's it!' lifted the phone and requested a home visit.

Dr Lott, a young, curly haired man, appeared in my rose-covered bedroom, less than an hour later. 'What appears to be the problem?'

Mum answered for me. 'Her relationship has failed, so has her career, yet she feels very happy. Don't you?'

I assented. Yes, that was all true.

Dr Lott frowned. 'That is worrying.

'Worrying,' he went on, 'but not actually a sign of illness.'

'I was almost killed,' I said.

608

He looked at Mum. Raised his eyebrows questioningly.

'No, not by her.' I explained about the accident.

'Ah,' he said. 'This makes perfect sense. Your body is so surprised at still being alive that you're experiencing a massive rush of adrenalin. This explains your elation. Don't worry, it should soon pass.'

'I should be feeling depressed again shortly?'

'Yes, yes,' he reassured. 'Possibly even worse than usual. You may experience what's called an adrenalin crash.'

'Well, that's a relief,' Mum said. 'Thank you, Doctor, I'll see you out.'

She walked him to his Saab and their voices floated in through the window.

'Are you sure you can't prescribe something for her?' I heard Mum ask.

'Like what?'

Mum sounded puzzled. 'Something like the opposite to anti-depressants?'

'There's nothing wrong with her.'

'But she's quite unbearable. And I'm worried about what all this positivity is doing to her little girl.'

'The one who was shouting at the sheep? She doesn't seem traumatized. And, frankly, her mother being upbeat and positive after such a shock is the best thing for her.'

I felt like clenching my fist in a victory salute. Worry about Ema was a constant stone in my shoe; I was overjoyed to discover that – entirely by accident – I was doing the best for her.

'Don't worry,' Dr Lott promised Mum. 'Lily's elation will pass soon.'

'And while we're waiting?'

'She's a writer, isn't she? Why don't you try persuading her to write about all of this. At least if she's writing about it, she won't be talking.'

He had barely finished his sentence when I had reached for

a pen and notebook and watched my hand write, 'Grace woke up and discovered that once again a plane had not landed on her during the night.' It was a good opening sentence, I thought.

And so was the paragraph which followed, where Grace had a shower and did not scald herself, had a bowl of muesli and did not choke to death on a nut, put on the kettle and did not get electrocuted, thrust her hand into a drawer and did not sever a vein on a knife, left the house and did not skid on a stray apple core into the path of a speeding car. On the way to work, her bus does not crash, she avoids contracting ear cancer from her mobile phone and nothing heavy falls out of the sky to land on her work-station – all before nine o'clock in the morning! I already knew my title. *A Charmed Life*.

* * *

It took me less than five weeks. During this time Ema and I stayed at Mum's and for fifteen hours a day I sat at Mum's home computer and clattered at the keyboard, my fingers unable to keep up with the flow of words from my brain.

When it became clear I was in the grip of something big, Mum assumed care of Ema.

On the days she had to go to work (a part-time post selling National Trust aprons at the local stately home) she simply took Ema with her. And when she was not at work, she and Ema wandered the fields together, picking wild spring flowers and becoming (in her words) 'women who run with the sheep'. Leaving me free to transfer my story from my head to the computer.

My heroine was a woman called Grace – not very subtle, I know, but it was better than calling her Lucky – and she was the star of a complicated six-way love story set against a background of all the terrible things that do not happen to us.

That first night I read what I had written to Mum and Ema.

'Darling, it's adorable,' Mum said.

'Dirty,' Ema agreed. 'Filthy.'

'It's absolutely wonderful. So cheery.'

'But you're my mum,' I said. 'I need someone impartial.'

'I wouldn't lie to you, darling. I'm not that kind of mother.' Blithely, she added, 'When I insisted you saw the doctor I hope you didn't think I was being unkind, I was simply concerned about you.'

'I understand.'

'By the way, Anton rang again, he desperately wants to see Ema.'

'No. He can't come. I can't see him. I've had medical advice. I might do something rash.'

'You can't deny him the right to see his child, especially after she almost died. Lily, please do try to be less selfish.'

Never mind Anton, I had to think of Ema. Although she was handling this latest trauma with her characteristic aplomb, regular contact with her dad was vital for her well-being.

''K,' I mumbled, surly as a teenager.

Mum left the room and returned some time later. 'He's coming tomorrow morning. He asked me to thank you.'

'Mum, when Anton comes today, you'll have to greet him and hand Ema over, because I can't.'

'Why on earth not?'

'Because,' I repeated, 'I've had medical advice. I might do something rash.'

'What manner of rash?'

'Just . . . rash. I need this . . . adrenalin rush, phase, whatever it is, to pass, then I can see him again.'

She was displeased, more so when I drew the curtains in the study, in case the sight of Anton caused a bout of rash behaviour. I immersed myself in Grace's complicated love life and lucky escapes and waited for the time to pass.

Hours later Mum walked in. I pulled the earplugs from my ears (inserted in case the sound of Anton's voice triggered an onslaught of rashness) and asked, 'Is he gone?'

'Yes.'

'How was he?'

'Fine. Thrilled to see Ema and *she* was beside herself. *Such* a daddy's girl.'

'Did he ask about me?'

'Of course.'

'What did he say?'

'He said, "How is Lily?"'

'That's all?'

'I believe so.'

'And then what did you talk about?'

'Well, nothing, really. We were playing with Ema. We were mocking the sheep.'

'And when he was leaving, did he say anything about me?'

Mum thought about it. 'No,' she said finally. 'He didn't.'

'Charming,' I muttered at the screen.

'Why do you care? You left him.'

'I don't care. I just can't believe how rude he was.'

'Rude?' Mum asked. 'From the woman who sat in the study with the curtains drawn and her ears stuffed with silicone. Rude, darling?'

His second visit did not disturb like the first: he had come to see his daughter and had every right to do so. As Mum said, I should have been glad that my child had such a devoted father. Thereafter, he came from London every five or six days and on each visit I remained cloistered. Although once – even through the earplugs – I heard him laughing and it was like bumping a once-broken limb; I was shocked at how much it was still capable of pain.

One night I was lifting Ema into bed and she whispered into my neck, so quietly I barely heard it, 'Anton smells nice.' It did not mean anything, Ema was not big on coherent sentences and she could just as easily have said, 'Anton licks trees,' or

'Anton drinks petrol,' but it generated a longing so intense and familiar, I wanted to howl.

I was obliged to resuscitate the mantra which had helped me through the early days of the split: Anton and I had been in love, we had had a child together, we had been soul-mates from the moment we had met. The end of something so precious could only be bloody and perhaps the break would always remain capable of hurt.

I thought of those halcyon days just before I left London, when I had thought Anton and I were one encounter away from being friends. I had been astonishingly deluded: we were nowhere near it.

Daily, I continued to write, the words pouring from me, and every night, before we put Ema to bed, I read that day's work and Mum raved about it. Ema too offered comments. ('Jiggy.' 'Seedy.' 'Farty.') I did not experience the 'adrenalin crash' that Dr Lott predicted but over the five weeks, the more I wrote the more my sense of salvation dwindled. By the start of May, when I finished the book, I was almost back to normal. (Although perhaps still a little more buoyant than I had been before the accident.)

I knew that *A Charmed Life* was a dead cert; people would love it. This was not arrogance; I also knew the reviews would be savage. But perhaps I had learned a little about publishing by then. I had seen how people had reacted to *Mimi's Remedies* and intuited that this would generate a similar response. The story and setting of *A Charmed Life* were nothing like those of *Mimi's Remedies*, but the *feel* was. For a start, it was terribly unrealistic. If I wanted to be nice about it (and why not?) I could say it felt magical.

It was time to return to London and Mum was sad but tried to hide it. 'It's not me,' she said. 'The sheep will be devastated. They seem to have adopted Ema as some sort of goddess.'

'We'll come and visit.'

'Do, please. And send Anton my best. Will you see him in London? Has the fear of doing something rash passed?'

I didn't know. Perhaps.

'Can I give you some advice, darling?'

'No, Mum, please don't.'

But she was on a roll. 'I know Anton is unreliable with money but better to be with a spendthrift than a skinflint.'

'How would you know? Who was a skinflint?'

'Peter.' Her second husband. Susan's father. 'He doled out money like he was pulling teeth.' I had not known that. Or had I? Perhaps I had suspected it, but after all the insecurity with Dad, I had assumed that Mum enjoyed it.

'At least being with your dad was fun,' she said, moodily.

'So much fun that you divorced him.'

'Oh darling, I am sorry. But he bored me to *sobs* with all those wretched money-making schemes. However, after living with a man who calculated how long loo rolls ought to last, I've reached the conclusion that it's better to spend one day as a spendthrift than a thousand years as a skinflint.' Then anxiety bruised her face. 'But that doesn't mean your dad and I are going to get back together. Please don't get the wrong idea.'

Ema and I returned to London.

I had felt so abject about writing off Irina's lovely car, that I bought her a new one – well, I had all those lovely *Mimi's Remedies* royalties just sitting in my bank. Irina, however, was far from impressed by my flashness. 'You did not hev to. The insurance people will buy me a new car.'

I shrugged, 'When – if – you get the insurance cheque, you can pay me back.'

'You are foolish with money,' she said, coldly. 'You make me engry.'

However, despite my buying her a new car, she forgave me enough to let Ema and me resume living with her until we got a place of our own.

As soon as I walked into my bedroom I noticed that the wastepaper basket had not been emptied in all the time I had been away – clearly Irina had been respecting my privacy. *Shit*. The letter from Anton was still there, a corner poking out. I looked at it, wondering what to do, then quickly picked it up and shoved it back in my underwear drawer, unsettled that it was still clinging to me.

Before I gave *A Charmed Life* to Jojo, I decided to try it on someone who would not humour me; the obvious choice was Irina, who read it in an afternoon. She gave me back the pages, her face impassive. 'I do not like,' she said.

'Good, good,' I encouraged.

'So much hope in it. But other people, they will like very much.'

'Yes,' I said happily. 'That's what I thought.'

Gemma

All of a sudden, it was spring and life was good. Dad was at home with Mam, my book was coming out soon – already it was out in the airports but it was too soon to know how it was selling – and now that I didn't need to bail Mam out, I had enough dosh to pay off my credit card, sell my car and buy one that men didn't feel the need to assault.

Maybe, eventually, I could do like Jojo and set up on my own. But because of my writing career, I decided to do nothing for the moment.

The only fly in the ointment of my life was that I was still mortified about my carry-on with Johnny the Scrip and avoided driving past his chemist. But show me someone whose life is entirely cringe-free and I'll show you a dead person.

In April, a few short weeks before my book came out in the real world, I finally went on my holiday to Antigua. Andrea was coming in place of Owen. Then Cody said he'd like to come and so would Trevor and Jennifer and maybe Sylvie and Niall, and Susan said she'd come from Seattle, and suddenly there were eight of us. Looking at it that way, a week no longer seemed enough, so we changed the booking to a fortnight.

Even before we left Dublin, there was great excitement. In the airport bookshop, seven of us clustered around the small display of *Chasing Rainbows* and said loudly, 'I hear this is a great book,' and 'I'd buy this book if I was going on my holidays.' Then when a woman bought one, Cody collared her and told her I was the author and even though she clearly suspected we were taking the piss she let me sign her copy and didn't object to me shedding a tear or Cody videoing the event.

Then when we arrived at our resort, a woman lying by the

pool – a different woman to the one at Dublin airport – was reading *Chasing Rainbows*. And six hundred and forty-seven were reading *Mimi's Remedies*, but never mind. I will admit to getting a little pang every time I saw it but nothing I couldn't handle.

We met Susan who'd flown in a day earlier from Seattle and for the next two weeks, we had an absolute blast. The sun shone, we all got on with each other, there was always someone to play with, but the place was big enough if we needed (that awful word) 'space'. There was a spa, three restaurants, excellent watersports and all the premium brand liquor we could drink. I had loads of facials, went snorkelling, read six books and tried learning to windsurf, but they told me to come back when I wasn't banjoed out of my head on free Pina Coladas. We met millions of other people and Susan, Trevor and Jennifer all got the ride. Most nights we danced until sun-up at the crappy disco but – this was the best bit – we didn't have the fear the following day. (That's premium brand liquor for you.)

The holiday was a turning point for me. I think I'd forgotten how to be happy but I rediscovered it there. On our last night, sitting at the beach-front bar, listening to the suck and roar of the waves, cooled by fragrant little breezes, I understood that I was free from the bitterness I'd carried for so long towards Lily and Anton. And I no longer wanted to drive over to gloat at Colette. I actually felt for her; with two children, life can't have been easy, and she must have had *really* atrocious luck with men – miles worse than mine – if she thought my dad was a catch. (All due respect, lovely man, yadda yadda, but I *mean*.) I even felt forgiveness towards my dad. I breathed in well-being, breathed out calm and felt benign goodwill to all.

I looked at the people sitting around me – Andrea, Cody, Susan, Sylvie, Jennifer, Trevor, Niall and some bloke from Birmingham whose name escapes me but who was there because he was getting the ride off Jennifer, and thought, this is all I need: good friends, to love and be loved. I have health, a well-paid job, a book coming out, a hopeful future and people who love me. I am whole and complete.

I tried explaining to Cody how light and free I felt.

'Course you do,' he said. 'You're banjoed out of your head on free Pina Coladas.' (It had become the holiday catchphrase.) 'You've given up on men,' he said. 'You can't do that.'

I tried to explain that I hadn't given up, merely reshuffled my priorities, but I didn't do a very good job of it, probably on account of being banjoed out of my head on free Pina Coladas. But it didn't matter. Happiness means not having to be understood.

Jojo

Jojo woke up – thought the two thoughts she had every morning – and knew that today was the day that something had to change.

In the first two weeks after she had left Lipman Haigh, life was busy. The phone rang all the time – authors telling her they were jumping ship to go to Richie Gant, Mark begging her to come back, publishing people desperate to know what the story was – then, like the flick of a switch, everything suddenly went very quiet. It was almost like a conspiracy. The silence was deafening and time – very slowly – began to pass.

Jojo discovered that sitting in her living room, trying to run a literary agency with almost no authors, sucked. The final shake-down showed she had lost twenty-one of her twenty-nine authors to Richie Gant and only the small – unlucrative – ones had stayed.

No money was coming in – like, *nothing* – and it freaked her right out.

Since age fifteen, she had never not had a job; being without an income felt like flying a trapeze without a safety net.

For thirteen straight weeks, every single morning, it was the second thing she thought of when she woke up. All through February, all through March, all through April. Now it was the start of May and nothing had changed.

She needed new authors but no one knew about her and, funnily enough, Lipman Haigh weren't forwarding on any manuscripts which had been mailed personally to her.

A profile in *The Times*, swung by Magda Wyatt, had started a trickle of books coming her way. They were mostly atrocious, but it meant she was still a player. However, so far, none had resulted in a sale.

The days, stuck in her apartment, waiting while nothing happened, seemed way too long. Publishers didn't take her out for lunch in fancy restaurants so much any more and she had a policy of deliberately swerving big industry do's where she was likely to run into Mark. However, it was hard to avoid them all because she had to let publishers know she was still alive.

But she did her best to stay away because Mark was still the first thing she thought of every morning. Even now, more than three months since she had seen him, there were times when the pain made it difficult for her to breathe.

But today was the day that something had to give.

There was no money left; she had sold her small holding of stocks, cashed in a pension scheme and had run her overdraft and cards to the hilt. She had used everything up, she had a mortgage to pay and whatever else happened, she was not going to lose her apartment.

She had two options, neither of them attractive – she could remortgage her apartment or return to work at a big agency. It was going to be hard (like, *impossible*) to remortgage her apartment without a steady job. So really, she had one option left, but saying she had two made it seem better.

One part of her told her she was lying down and giving up by going back into the system which had fucked her over the last time. But another part of her said that the important thing was to survive. She had tried very hard with this but the smart girl knows when to stop digging.

She had to eat. And buy handbags.

Since the news got out that she had left Lipman Haigh, there had been job offers from just about every other literary agency in town, all of which she had politely rebuffed. Indeed, she had said that she might be offering *them* a job in the not too distant future.

And OK, maybe she'd been a little over-confident. But if her authors had stayed with her, it would have all worked out. Anyhow, no point being sore. She had a mental list of who would be least unbearable to work for; she would start at the top and work down.

Feeling a little weird, a little sad, she picked up the phone and rang her number one agency, Curtis Brown. The person she needed to speak to wasn't available so she left a message, then rang Becky to tell her what she was doing.

'Oh Jojo! Going back into that patriarchal system is very bad for the soul,' Becky parroted.

'I'm broke. And what do I need with a soul? I never use it. If I had to choose between my soul and a handbag, I'd pick the handbag.'

'If you're sure . . .'

When the phone rang she thought it would be someone from Curtis Brown returning her call, but it wasn't.

'Jojo, it's Lily. Lily Wright. I have a manuscript for you. I think, I mean, how can anyone ever be sure, but I think you're going to love it. Like it, in any case.'

'You think? Well, let's take a look!' Jojo had no hope for this. Lily, a totally great person, was a literary untouchable. After the train-wreck of *Crystal Clear*, she would never be published again.

'I live quite nearby,' Lily said. 'In St John's Wood. I could drop it over to you now. Ema and I would enjoy the walk.'

'Sure! Why not!' OK, so she was humouring her, but it was better than telling her not to bother, right?

Lily and Ema came, Lily had a cup of tea, Ema broke the handle off a mug and hung it from the inside of her ear like an earring, then they left again.

Some time in the afternoon the woman from Curtis Brown rang back and gave Jojo an appointment for later in the week. And, slooooowly, the day passed. She spoke to Becky several times, watched TV all afternoon even though she had a strict no-daytime-TV rule, went to yoga, came home, made dinner, watched more TV and, at about eleven-thirty, decided it was time for bed. Looking for something to read to ease her into sleep, her glance bounced off Lily Wright's bundle of pages. Might as well take a look.

Twenty minutes later
Jojo was sitting straight-backed in bed, her hands gripping the pages so tightly that they buckled. She was only a short way into the book, but she *knew*. This was IT! The manuscript she had been waiting for, the book which would reignite her career. It was *Mimi's Remedies* mark two, only better. She would sell it for a *fortune*.

She glanced at her clock. Midnight. Was it too late to ring Lily now? Probably. Damn!

How early did Lily get up? Early. Yeah, she had a little girl, it would be early.

6.30 the following morning
Was this *too* early? Could be. She forced herself to wait an hour, then picked up the phone.

Lily

I am not a fool. Even before Ema broke the handle off her mug and wore it as an earring, I knew Jojo was not entirely overjoyed to see me. I did not blame her. The debacle of *Crystal Clear* had not reflected well on any of us.

But she accepted my new manuscript and promised to read it 'soon'. Then I returned to Irina's and waited for Jojo's call. It came at 7.35 the following morning.

'Jesus H,' she shrieked, so loud that Irina heard it in the next room. 'We've got a live one here. Name your price! We don't have to offer Dalkin Emery a first look. They didn't keep the faith last Christmas. We could go to Thor. They'd kill to have this, and they're doing really well at the moment. Or how about . . .'

I already had a plan. I was not sure I would ever write another book; something terrible seems to have to happen to me before I can produce anything worthwhile, and frankly, I would rather be happy. But this was my chance for a downpayment on a secure future.

'Sell it,' I instructed Jojo, 'to the highest bidder.'

'You got it! I'm on my way to the local copy shop, then I'm gonna make the calls, order the bikes, then sit back and watch them throw money at us.'

Gemma

When I came back from being banjoed out of my head on Pina Coladas it was nearly a week before I saw my parents – just like the good old days. When I did finally get it together to call over, Mam said, 'This came for you.'

She handed me an envelope that had several addresses crossed out then written over. It had originally been sent to Dalkin Emery and they'd forwarded it on to Lipman Haigh, who'd sent it to my parents. It had a Mick stamp on it.

'It might be a fan letter,' Dad said.

I didn't bother replying. My epiphany in Antigua had mostly survived the transition back to real life, but not how I felt about Dad.

I opened the letter.

```
Dear Gemma,
I just wanted to let you know how much I
enjoyed Chasing Rainbows. (I got it in the
airport on my way to Fuertaventura.)
Congratulations on a great read. I was happy
that Will and Izzy finally got it together
after all their trials and tribulations. I
didn't think it was going to happen,
especially when that other man was knocking
around. I was concerned that Izzy was on the
rebound but now I'm convinced - they make a
lovely couple.
Love,
Johnny
```

    PS Come and see me. I have some new surgical
    gauze in that you might find interesting.

Johnny. Johnny the Scrip. I didn't know any other Johnny. And he'd signed it 'Love'.

It was like someone had drilled down and filled up every part of me with relief. He'd read the book. He didn't hate me. He'd forgiven me for treating him like a stop-gap.

I hadn't realized the weight of the mortification I'd been carrying.

He wanted to see me . . .

How did I feel about that? I felt that I'd call in on my way home, that's how I felt! I understood something: I was finally ready. For the past year – more – I'd been way too mad to pursue anything with Johnny and I think I'd wanted to wait until I was myself again before trying to embark on anything with him. I reckon it was why I'd stayed with Owen – being with him kept me from pushing for anything with Johnny. He'd acted as a kind of emotional bouncer.

Not that I felt too bad about using Owen; I had fulfilled a similar role for him.

Then I noticed the date on Johnny's letter and I was shocked. It was the nineteenth of March – six weeks earlier. It had spent all that time passing from publisher to agent to parents. Suddenly it seemed imperative to leave.

'What is it? A fan letter?' Dad asked.

'Look, I'm off.'

'But you've only just got here.'

'I'll come back.'

I drove as fast as I'd driven that first night long ago when I was on a mission to secure drugs to stop my mammy going totally doolally. I parked outside, pushed open the door, and there he was, in his white coat, bending solicitously over some old lady's hand, admiring her ringworm or something. My heart swelled with good stuff.

Then he looked up and I got the fear: it wasn't him. It was very like him but *it wasn't him*. For a mad moment I feared bodysnatchers, then I realized this must be Hopalong, the famed brother.

I stretched to have a look behind the melamine divider, hoping to see Johnny back there, filling a jar with pills or whatever he did, but Hopalong intercepted me. 'Can I help you?'

'I'm looking for Johnny.'

'He's not here.'

Something about the way he said it gave me a bad feeling. 'He hasn't, by any chance, emigrated to Australia?' It would be just my luck. And he'd probably meet his The One on the boat . . .

'Um, no. Well, he didn't mention it yesterday evening if he has.'

'OK.'

'Can I give him a message?'

'No, thanks. I'll call back.'

The following day I called again but, to my great dismay, Hopalong was still manning the decks. And likewise the next.

'You're sure he hasn't gone to Australia?'

'No, but if you want to see him, why don't you come in the daytime?'

'Because I have to work in the daytime. He used to work evenings.'

'Not any more. He only does one evening a week now.'

I waited patiently. Hopalong continued rearranging the packets of Hacks.

'And what evening is that?'

'Hmmm?'

'AND WHAT EVENING IS THAT?'

'Oh! Sorry. Thursday.'

'Thursday? Tomorrow is Thursday? You're sure about that?'

'Yes. Well, *nearly* sure.'

I was clambering into my car when he called after me, 'Don't forget, we close at eight now.'

'Eight o'clock? Not ten? Why?'

'Because we just do.'

Lily

Jojo set the auction date for *A Charmed Life* a week hence but, as she predicted, there were a flurry of pre-emptives. Pelham Press offered a million for three books. 'No,' I said. 'There won't be a second or third book. This is a one-off special.'

Knoxton House offered eight hundred for two. I repeated that this book was a stand-alone event. The weekend intervened, then on Monday morning, Southern Cross offered five hundred for one.

'Take it,' I told Jojo.

'No,' she said. 'I can get you more.'

Three days later, on Thursday afternoon, she sold it to B&B Halder for six hundred and fifty thousand. Giddy and giggly, she said, 'We have to celebrate. Come on, meet me for a drink. Don't worry, I won't keep you late, I've got a do this evening.'

We agreed on six o'clock in a wine bar in Maida Vale. When I arrived, Jojo was already there, with a bottle of champagne.

After a couple of glasses she asked me – as I had known she would – 'Why were you so insistent that you would only sign for one book? I could have got you *millions*.'

I shook my head. 'I'm not going to write another book. I plan to go back full-time to copywriting. It's steady money, I quite enjoy it and no one humiliates my efforts in the Sunday newspapers.'

'You know what they say?'

'A hazelnut in every bite?'

'How to make God laugh? Tell him your plans.'

'OK,' I conceded. 'None of us know what's going to happen. But if I have anything to do with it, I won't write another.'

'What will you do with your advance money?' Jojo asked. 'Invest it?'

That made me laugh. 'Whatever I invest in is bound to go immediately to the wall. I would prefer to keep it in a biscuit tin under my bed, that feels safest, but I'll be very boring and buy somewhere to live.'

And this time, I would do it properly.

Some time later, Jojo looked at her watch. 'Seven-thirty. Gotta go. Meeting my cousin Becky. She's coming with me to the Dalkin Emery author party tonight.'

'The Dalkin Emery author party?' I put my head to one side. 'Wasn't I one of them once? Well, I wasn't invited to the party.'

'Guess what?' She leant in to me, laughing. 'Neither was I, until about five minutes ago. They biked me over an invite yesterday. Thanks to you and your fabulous new book, I'm back in the game.'

'How fickle of them. How rude. And you're going to go? I'd tell them to get lost!'

'I've got to go,' she said, lapsing into an unexpected dark mood.

I said nothing, but I, like everyone else, had heard the rumours. Something to do with an affair with her boss and her having to leave because he had broken up with her or some such.

Then her cousin arrived and they left.

Gemma

All day Thursday I was a bit flaky at work – excitement, see? About finally seeing Johnny that evening, see? But every fecking thing conspired against it because I had to work until six-thirty, then I had to collect Dad from the day hospital. He'd had a minor operation (something to do with his prostate, I *so* did not want to know) and because he'd had an anaesthetic, he wasn't allowed to drive himself home. But he took forever to leave, saying goodbye to the nurses as if he'd been there for six months and not six hours, and by the time we left the hospital it was seven forty-five. Johnny's chemist closed at eight, so I took an executive decision.

'Dad, before I drop you home, I've to go to the pharmacy.'

'What do you need?'

'Plasters.'

'But you haven't cut yourself.'

'Tissues, then.'

'Have you a cold?'

'Alright, Hedex,' I said irritably.

'Have you a headache?'

'I do now.'

I parked outside and he clipped off his seatbelt. Anxiously, I said, 'Dad, stay in the car. You're not a well man.'

Not a chance. He'd got wind something was up. 'I need to buy something myself.'

'What?'

'Er . . .' he scanned the window for ads '. . . Oil of Evening Primrose.'

Clutching his groin, he followed me in.

Lily

After Jojo and her cousin left the wine bar, I walked home, put Ema to bed, then braced myself. It was time to read Anton's letter.

I had no choice. I knew it would not go away.

I lay down on the sofa and slid out three crumpled handwritten pages.

My dearest Lily,

When are you reading this? Six months after we've broken up? A year? No matter how long it is, thank you for doing so. There is only one thing I want to say in this letter and that is to let you know how very sorry I am for all the unhappiness I've caused you but, being me, I'll probably take several pages to do so.

At the moment, you're repelled by our time together, keen to put distance between it and you, and convinced that it was all a big, fat mistake from start to finish.

When we first met, the choice you had to make – between Gemma and me – was a terrible one. I tried to understand, I thought I understood, but at the time I was just one big, insanely happy eejit, so bowled over at our 'rightness', that I didn't really get it. In retrospect, I don't think I ever fully understood the depth of your guilt and the fear that you'd be punished. In my defence, I tried, but the happiness at our being together kept rushing in and sweeping it away.

I don't know if you can ever be convinced that our being together was right. But would you please try, don't ruin the rest of your life by dragging around a big sack of shame with you. Would it help if you looked at Ema? She's such a sparky little soul, she makes the world a better place, and we made her, you and me. Some good has come out of us.

I would also like to apologize about losing you and Ema your home. Words are ridiculously inadequate at conveying the extent of my shame.

Looking back at my enthusiasm for buying the house, it looks to me now like I bullied you, which I am sick about. But can I explain how my head was working at the time? Buying the house was a risk, but as risks go, it seemed as safe as it got. All the signs were good that the money would pony up – Jojo thought so, Dalkin Emery thought so, even the bank thought so.

I was afraid that if we didn't buy a home for the three of us that we'd fritter away all your hard-earned royalties and end up with a load of crap (cars, stereos, Barbie merchandise) but no security (you know what we're like). It was a stab at behaving like a responsible adult. Buying beyond our means seemed like the smart thing to do – instead of buying a smaller place for a year, then moving again and paying two lots of stamp duty, it seemed smarter to leapfrog over the intermediate process. Like the fool I was, I thought I had vision. But none of that matters now. I didn't listen to your fears, it all fell apart and I hate listening to my pathetic attempts to justify myself.

I thought I was an optimist, you said I was a fool; you were right and if I had the chance to do it all again, I would do absolutely everything differently.

With your homelife as a child, it was extra-important to offer you security and all I gave you was mayhem.

I regret the mistakes I made, I bitterly regret the unhappiness I caused you but I will never regret our time together. When I'm eighty and looking back on my life, I'll know that there was at least one good pure thing in it. From that first time we met outside that tube station, I felt like the luckiest bastard on the planet and that feeling never went away. Every single day that we were together I couldn't believe my luck – most people don't have in a lifetime what we had in three and a half years and I will

*always be grateful for that. You will go on and meet someone
else and I'll just be a chapter in your tale, but for me, you were,
you are and you always will be, the whole story.*

Yours always,
Anton

I put down the letter and stared at the ceiling. Stared and stared.

I had known this was coming. I had known for weeks, since before I had gone to Mum's. It had been *why* I had gone.

When I had left Anton I thought I had already made my peace with it. Then, around the time the postcards started coming, I discovered I had made peace with absolutely nothing. I had been as numb as an arm that has been slept on for a week and when I began to feel again, I fled to Mum's, in a fruitless attempt to outrun the inevitable.

Even then I had known that I would have to make this choice. My love for Anton had crept stealthily back; banished for a while by my heartbreak over the house, it had returned in force, clamouring for me to address it.

And how should I do it?

I had no idea.

At least now I understood what had been going on inside me: I had been very angry with Anton – losing houses was a touchy subject for me. But, and I did not know why – time? distance? – I no longer blamed him. I had thought I could never forgive, but I had.

Even before I had read his letter, I understood what he had been trying to do with the house: he had taken a risk, but as risks go, it had been quite an unrisky one. He had been unlucky.

And what about me? I had been there too, I could have stepped in. Instead I had been complicit and passive, clinging to the position where I could blame if I needed to.

Anton was undeniably careless with money. But I was not any better. Let she who is without debt write the first cheque.

But was understanding where we had gone wrong any guarantee that things would not go pear-shaped again? If it were just Anton and me, we could afford to take risks with our feelings, to try again, knowing that if it, once more, did not work out, we would survive. But we had a child, who had already been through far too much in her short little life. We owed it to Ema to make our next move very carefully. A thought shot into my head: surely it would be better if her parents were together? But perhaps I was just talking myself into this, because I loved him.

And what about Gemma? Could I ever get beyond what I had done to her? If I could have had a choice, I would never have caused her a second's pain. But I had visited untold misery on her. It had happened, I could never undo it, not even if Anton and I remained apart for ever.

I sighed long and wearily, still looking up at the ceiling, hoping to see answers there.

Happiness was a rare thing and you have to take your chances where you find them. I wanted to do the right thing – but how do we ever know? There are no guarantees.

I could rationalize until I was blue in the face but I had no idea what was right or wrong.

I decided to make a list, as if the biggest decision of one's life could be made by writing out bullet-points on the white margin of the TV guide. Well, it was as good as any other way . . .

- Ema would be better off if her parents were together.
- I felt able to get past my guilt with Gemma.
- I had forgiven Anton for the house and we would be more sensible with our finances in the future.
- He was my most favourite person in the whole world. By a million miles. (Apart from Ema.)

Hmmm . . .

Well, I thought, it couldn't hurt to *talk* to Anton. So, invoking the forces of the universe, I made a decision. I would ring him – right now and just this once – and if I did not get him, I would take it as a sign that we were not meant to be. Carefully I picked up the phone, hoping to convey to it how important its next mission was. I wondered where Anton was right now, what the plan for us was. Then I pressed the numbers, put the phone to my ear, heard it begin to ring and prayed.

Jojo

At the Dalkin Emery author party, Jocelyn Forsyth was loitering by the door, bored out of his skull. He'd been finding his retirement difficult – still hankering after the action. But perhaps asking for an invitation to this party had been a mistake. So far, it had disappointed terribly. The place was overrun with Young Turks. No fillies to speak of. Then, just coming in, he saw something that filled his heart with gladness. 'Jojo Harvey! We'd given you up for dead.'

She was looking particularly luscious and accompanied by a creature almost as delightful, whom she introduced as her cousin Becky.

'Well done, you, on your wonderful news with Lily "Lazarus" Wright. Her career pronounced dead on the slab how many times now? Always a gamble setting up on one's own.' He leant closer. 'That was a beastly business with young Gant. Delighted it's all working out for you. Of course, if anyone could do it, it would be you.'

Jojo shook back her hair and beamed. 'Thanks, Jocelyn,' then moved away. She didn't have time to stand around chatting, she was on a mission. Of sorts.

Becky at her side, she moved through the crowded space, accepting plaudits and praise. Her senses were on red-alert, her nerves were stretched like cat-gut and she did a lot of hair-tossing and over-animated laughing. Even when she was only talking to Becky, the show went on, until Becky hissed, 'Stoppit, you look like you're on coke.'

Jojo hissed back, 'But what if he's here? I've got to look happy!'

'Jojo, maybe you're not ready for this.'

'I'm gonna have to meet him some time. I can't be sneaking around scared of bumping into him. It's time.'

But after twenty more minutes of being on show, she admitted to Becky, 'I don't think he's here. Let's get some chicken satays and leave.'

Gemma

Shadowed by Dad, limping like he had had his bollocks removed, I hurried into the chemist. I was nearly *sick* with anxiety. There was a man behind the counter, he was wearing the regulation-issue white coat, he had the right size body, but I couldn't see his face.

If he turns around and I'm looking at Hopalong, then I'm giving up, I thought. Me and Johnny the Scrip are just not going to happen.

Then, with excruciating slowness, the man turned and – *oh, thank you, God* – it was Johnny!

'Gemma!' His face lit up, then he looked inquiringly over my shoulder.

'Oh, that's my dad,' I said. 'Just ignore him.'

'Right.'

I stepped closer. 'I got your letter,' I said shyly. 'Thank you. Did you really like the book?'

'Yes. Particularly the love story between Izzy and Will.'

'You did?' I'd gone the colour of a fire engine.

'It was nice the way they got it together in the end. He seemed like a nice bloke.' He flicked a slightly perplexed look behind me, at Dad. *Selfish old fucker. Why did he have to come in?*

'Oh, Will *is* a nice bloke,' I tried to focus on the job in hand, which was securing the heart or at least the interest of Johnny. 'He's great.'

'So's Izzy.'

Behind me, I heard Dad exclaim, 'Christ Almighty, you're Will! Out of the book!' He hobbled forward. 'I'm Declan Nolan, the father that does the runner –'

I stopped him; this was getting way too pally. 'And I'm Izzy.'

'Good girl.'

'As in Will and Izzy.'

He finally got it. 'I'll, ah, leave you to it.' He stepped towards the door and I turned back to Johnny. I had a sudden dreadful vision of us stuck like this for all eternity: the melamine counter splitting us right down the middle, me asking for stupid medical things I didn't need and him selling them to me, kindness in his eyes. This was the moment of truth. Something had to be said to move things beyond this point.

'Gemma,' he said.

'Yes?' I was holding my breath.

'I was thinking.'

'Yes?'

'Something you said ages ago.'

'Yes?'

'About going out for a drink.'

'Yes?'

'Well, isn't it about time . . . ?'

Yesssssssss!!!!!

Some time later, back in the car, Dad said, 'I can't believe that. You drove over to a man and laid your cards on the table. What's the world coming to?'

'Come on, Dad, what's the big deal? It's not like I asked him to leave his wife of thirty-five years, is it?' *Did I really say that?* We looked at each other, watching warily.

Eventually Dad spoke. 'I think we might have to go for family counselling or something. What do you think?'

'Dad, don't be ridiculous, we're Irish.'

'But this sort of bad feeling can't go on.'

I thought about it. 'It'll pass. Just give me time.'

'Time heals everything, doesn't it?'

I thought about it. 'No'. Then I conceded, 'But most things.'

Jojo

And then, halfway through flicking her hair over her shoulder and into Kathleen Perry's drink, Jojo saw him – at the far wall and wearing a dark suit; he was watching her. Their eyes connected and it hit her like a punch in the stomach. It was just like (those dilating-pupil novelists again) they were the only two people in the room.

Her heart was pumping hard, the hand around her glass was instantly sweaty and everything felt super-real. He mouthed something at her: 'Wait.' Then, 'Please.' Then he turned his shoulder and began pushing through the people, moving in her direction.

'He's coming over,' Becky hissed. 'Run!'

'No.' This had to be done. There could only be one first time for them to meet again, it might as well be now.

He disappeared from view and then reappeared, hacking his way through a nearby thicket of Young Turks. Becky melted into the background.

And there he was, right in front of her.

'Jojo?' It sounded like an inquiry, as if he was checking she was real.

'Mark.' Even saying his name felt like a relief.

'You look –' he sought a good enough word – 'great.'

'That's me,' she quipped. He lit up with delight and for a moment it was like old times. Until Jojo asked, 'How're Cassie and the kids?'

Warily he answered, 'OK.'

'You and Cassie are still together?'

He hesitated. 'She found out about, you know, us.'

'Shit. How?'

'After you left it was obvious that something was wrong.' He half-laughed. 'I went to pieces.'

She hadn't exactly been, like, on cloud nine herself. 'Had she known?'

'She'd guessed there was somebody. She didn't know it was you.'

'I'm sorry. I'm sorry to hurt her.'

'She says – I mean, who knows? – but she says it was a relief to finally find out. She says pretending not to notice that I was never there was doing her in. For the past few months we've been trying to patch things up.'

'Having a big party to renew your wedding vows?'

He managed a smile. 'No. But going for counselling. We're doing our best,' he stopped. 'But I still think about you all the time.'

She'd been moving closer, reeled in by him. Straightening her shoulders, she shifted away – too scared of catching even a hint of how he smelt, that would be the undoing of her.

'Could we meet some time?' he asked. 'Just for a drink?'

'You know we couldn't.'

Suddenly he blurted, 'Even now, every day, I can't believe I got it so wrong. I was so selfish, thinking about us instead of you. If I could have that hour in that meeting again –'

'Stop. I've been thinking about it too. It wasn't just the partnership thing. The guilt and stuff about Cassie and your kids – when it came down to it, I think I couldn't do it. Close, but no cigar. And you know what? I don't buy much into psychotherapy stuff, but I guess you couldn't go through with it either. That's why you stitched me up.'

'No,' he protested. 'No way.'

'Way,' she said firmly.

'Absolutely not.'

'Whatever. Just a theory.' She wouldn't persist with this. It didn't matter enough.

People were looking at them, their intimacy all too obvious.

'Mark, I have to go now.'

'Do you? But –'

She pushed her way through the crowds, knowing everyone, smiling, smiling, smiling her way to the door.

Once outside, she walked at speed, Becky skipping in her wake, trying to keep up. When they were at a safe distance, she abruptly stopped in a doorway and jack-knifed over, clutching her stomach, her hair streaming towards the ground.

'Are you going to throw up?' Becky whispered, circling her hand on her back.

'No,' she answered, thickly. 'But it hurts.'

They stood for several minutes, Jojo making funny whimpery noises that Becky found unendurable, then Jojo straightened up, tossed her hair back and said, 'Kleenex.'

Becky found one in her bag and passed it over. 'You could get back with him, you know.'

'That will never happen. It is so over.'

'How can it be? You miss him terribly.'

'So what? I'll get over him, hey, I'm nearly there already. And if I want, I'll meet someone else sometime. I mean, look at me – I run my own business, I've got all my own teeth and hair, I can fix bikes –'

'You look like Jessica Rabbit.'

'I'm a cryptic crossword ninja.'

'You do a brilliant Donald Duck impersonation.'

'Exactly. I'm *fabulous*.'

Lily

Anton's phone rang once. It rang twice. My heart was pounding, my hands were slippery, I was mouthing, 'Please God.' It rang three times. Four times. Five times. Six times.

Shit . . .

On the seventh ring, there was a click, a burst of pub-like chatter and laughter, then someone – Anton – said, 'Lily?'

Joy rendered me light-headed. (Though I must admit, I had called him on his mobile. I had not taken any chances.) And before I had uttered a word he had known it was me! Another sign! (Or else he had caller display.)

'Anton? Can I see you?'

'When? Now?'

'Yes. Where are you?'

'Wardour Street.'

'Meet me at St John's Wood tube station.'

'I'll leave now. I'll be with you in fifteen, twenty minutes at the latest.'

Infused with wild energy, I ran to the mirror and pulled a brush through my hair. I rummaged through my make-up bag but I didn't need any, I already looked transformed. Nevertheless, I quickly rubbed on blusher and lipgloss, because it couldn't hurt. And mascara. And some weird brow-bone highlighter stuff that Irina had forced upon me. Then I made myself stop – I was starting to obsess – and went to ask Irina to watch Ema. 'I'm popping out for a while.'

She asked, 'Why?'

'I'm going to do something rash.'

'Vit Anton? Good. But you kennot go looking like that. You

need pore-minimizer.' She reached for her crate of cosmetics but I fled.

I had to leave the apartment. Although Anton would not yet have arrived at the station, I had far too much nervous energy to be contained within walls.

Dusk was falling, the light was navy blue and at the speed I was walking, it took me less than five minutes to walk to the station.

The vision of my future I had had when I was in the numb stage of grieving for Anton returned with force; I had been convinced that a new life was waiting for me, full of feelings and laughter and colour and with an entirely new cast of people to its current one. I had not stopped believing in that vision, but some of the cast were the same. Anton was still the leading man, he had made the part his own.

I rounded the corner to do the last stretch and, through the gloom, fixed my eyes on the station entrance, the magical portal that would deliver him to me.

Then I noticed that a rangy figure outside the station was watching me. Although it was too dark to see properly and very soon for Anton to have arrived already from central London, I knew instantly that it was him. I knew it was *him*.

I did not physically stumble but I felt as if I had. It was like seeing him for the first time.

My footsteps slowed; I knew what was going to happen. Once I was beside him, that would be it. There would be no talking; we would be fixed, fused, forever.

I could have stopped. I could have turned back and erased the future, but I continued putting one foot in front of the other, as if an invisible thread led me directly to him.

Each breath I took echoed loud and slow as if I was scuba diving and as I got closer, I had to stop looking at him. So I focused on the pavement – a Fortnum and Mason carrier bag, a champagne cork, posh rubbish, after all this was St John's Wood – until I was next to him.

His first words to me were, 'I saw you from miles away.' He picked up a strand of my hair.

I moved closer to his height, his beauty, his Anton-ness and into the light of his presence. 'I saw you too.'

While people hurried in and out of the station like characters in a speeded-up movie, Anton and I remained motionless as statues, his eyes on mine, his hands on my arms, completing the magic circle. And I said what I had always known, 'As soon as I saw you I knew it was you.'

Epilogue

Almost nine months to the day that Owen broke it off with me, he and Lorna had a little girl and called her – wait for it! – Agnes Lana May. Nothing that could remotely be construed as 'Gemma'. They didn't ask me to be her godmother. Currently, there are no plans to go to the Dordogne together.

My book came out in the middle of May and it bombed. They blamed the cover, the title and the atrocious reviews. The general tone was, '. . . escapist pap. The abandoned wife undergoes a serious make-over, picks up a much younger man and within six months she's running her own business. This makes a mockery of the situation of real women who've been abandoned after years of loyal service. Naturally, the husband returns at the end of the book, worn out from demands for sex from his mistress and finds his wife won't have him . . .'

It was horrifically humiliating. The only nice reviews were in crappy magazines that print a lot of 'I stole my daughter's husband' type stories. One of them called it Revenge Literature and clearly this was something they approved of.

But even that wasn't enough to sell any books and I must admit I didn't help: just before the book came out, Dad asked me not to do publicity where I told the real story behind the book, and something must have softened in me because I took pity on him and agreed. (It didn't make me very popular with Dalkin Emery's publicity department. They'd all kinds of things lined up where me and Mam would go on daytime telly and trash Dad. But Mam had backed out of it as soon as Dad came home.)

There won't be a second book; I have no imagination and nothing bad has happened to me – apart from my first book getting horrible reviews and not being able to write a second book, but that's all a little post-modern. The fact is my life is too nice and there are worse complaints.

At the moment I limit my artistic endeavours to making up stories for abandoned women about their runaway boyfriends. I'm very good at it and, within my circle, I have quite a reputation. It'll do me. I still have most of the advance money (they didn't make me give it back even though the book sold almost nothing) and maybe one day in the misty future I'll set up on my own. Not as easy as it sounds, we're not all Jojo Harvey, who now has fabulous coloured-glass offices in Soho and four people working for her, including her old assistant Manoj. Not only am I a cringing coward by comparison but I'm under contract not to take any clients with me.

Lily's career goes from strength to strength. She wrote a new book called *A Charmed Life*, which was like another *Mimi's Remedies* and sold in its millions. Then *Crystal Clear*, the book that nearly broke Dalkin Emery, surprised everyone by getting short-listed for the Orange Prize and *that* also sold in its millions. Apparently she's writing something new, they're all very excited.

I actually met Anton and Lily at a publishing do, shortly after *Chasing Rainbows* came out and my publishers were still talking to me. I was moving through the throng, trying to find the ladies' and suddenly me and Lily ended up standing before each other.

'Gemma?' Lily croaked. She looked absolutely terrified.

And after all the fantasies I'd entertained over the years – splashing a glass of red wine in her face, zapping her with death stares, shouting out to the roomful of her peers about what an evil bitch she was – I watched myself take her hand, hold it and say with a certain amount of sincerity, 'I enjoyed *Mimi's Remedies*, and so did my mother.'

'Thank you, thank you so much, Gemma. And I loved *Chasing Rainbows*.' She did her sweet-girl smile, then Anton appeared and that was fine too. We made a few moments of innocuous chitchat, and as they left Anton tried to hold Lily's hand, but she wouldn't and I heard her say, 'Have some consideration.' Meaning, I think, for me.

And yes, I felt sad then. That sort of gesture was Lily all over; she was very mindful of other people's feelings. It was a pity we couldn't be friends because (apart from that one boyfriend-stealing incident) she was a lovely person. I'd been so fond of her.

But onwards and upwards.

When Mam met Johnny the Scrip for the first time, she took in his broad shoulders, his air of kindness and the twinkle in his eye that is a permanent feature now that he's no longer working around the clock, and she leant over to me and murmured, 'Looks like the professionals have arrived.'

She likes him. Shite.

But even that wasn't enough to put me off him.

Colette wasn't on her own for long. She met someone else – a friend of a friend of Trevor's brother's brother-in-law – and because of Dublin being so small, I found out. From what I gather the new bloke is a much better bet than Dad. (At least he doesn't wear a vest.)

As for Mam and Dad . . . well, he does the crossword and plays golf, she buys clothes and makes him guess the price, they watch murder-mysteries and go for drives. Apart from the fact that I've had a book published and we have access to all the surgical gauze we can eat, you'd swear he'd never been away . . .